THE GOLDEN COMPASS

THE GRAPHIC NOVEL

PHILIP PULLMAN

THE GOLDEN COMPASS

THE GRAPHIC NOVEL

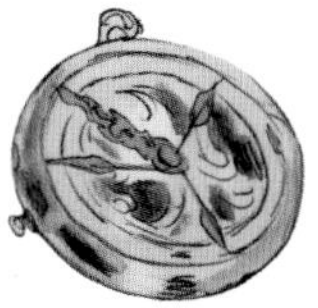

Adapted by Stéphane Melchior, art by Clément Oubrerie
Coloring by Clément Oubrerie with Philippe Bruno
Translated by Annie Eaton

ALFRED A. KNOPF  NEW YORK

THIS IS A BORZOI BOOK PUBLISHED BY ALFRED A. KNOPF

Visit us on the Web! randomhousekids.com

Educators and librarians, for a variety of teaching tools, visit us at RHTeachersLibrarians.com

Library of Congress Cataloging-in-Publication Data is available upon request.
ISBN 978-0-553-53516-7 (trade) — ISBN 978-0-553-53517-4 (pbk.) —
ISBN 978-0-553-53518-1 (lib. bdg.) — ISBN 978-0-553-53519-8 (ebook)

MANUFACTURED IN CHINA
September 2017
10 9 8 7 6 5 4 3 2 1

First American Edition

PART I

OXFORD

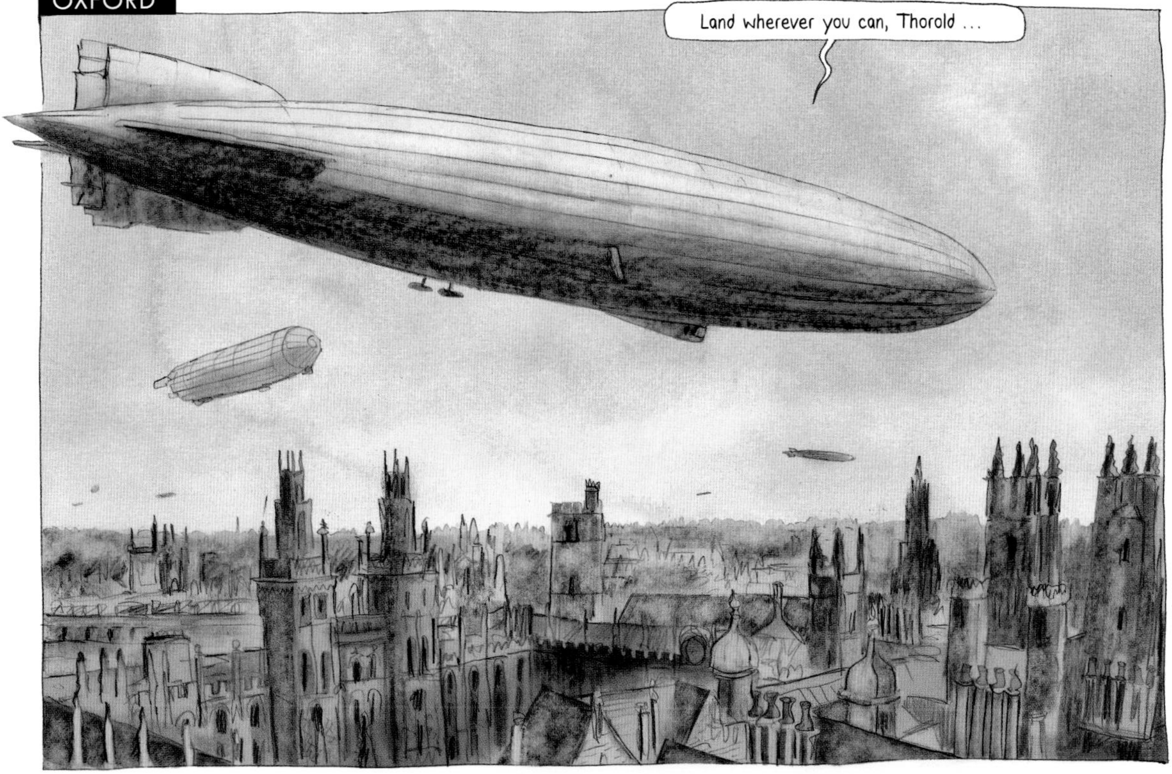
OXFORD
Land wherever you can, Thorold ...

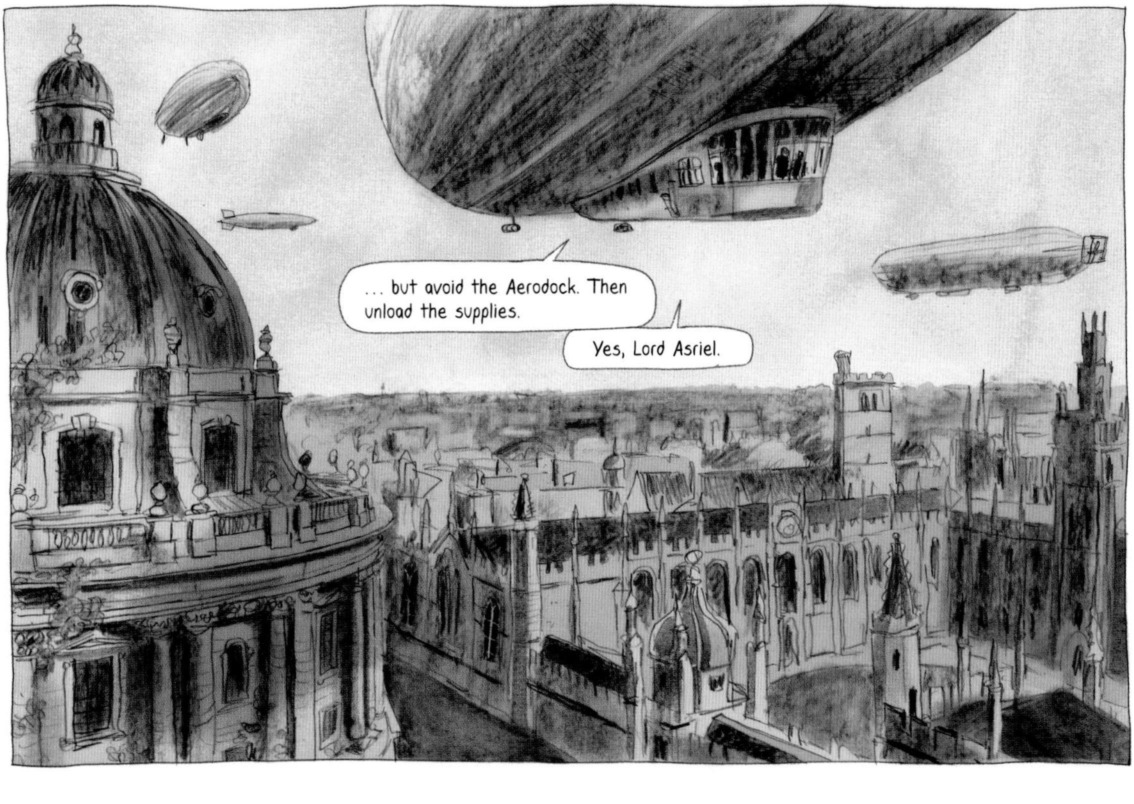
... but avoid the Aerodock. Then unload the supplies.
Yes, Lord Asriel.

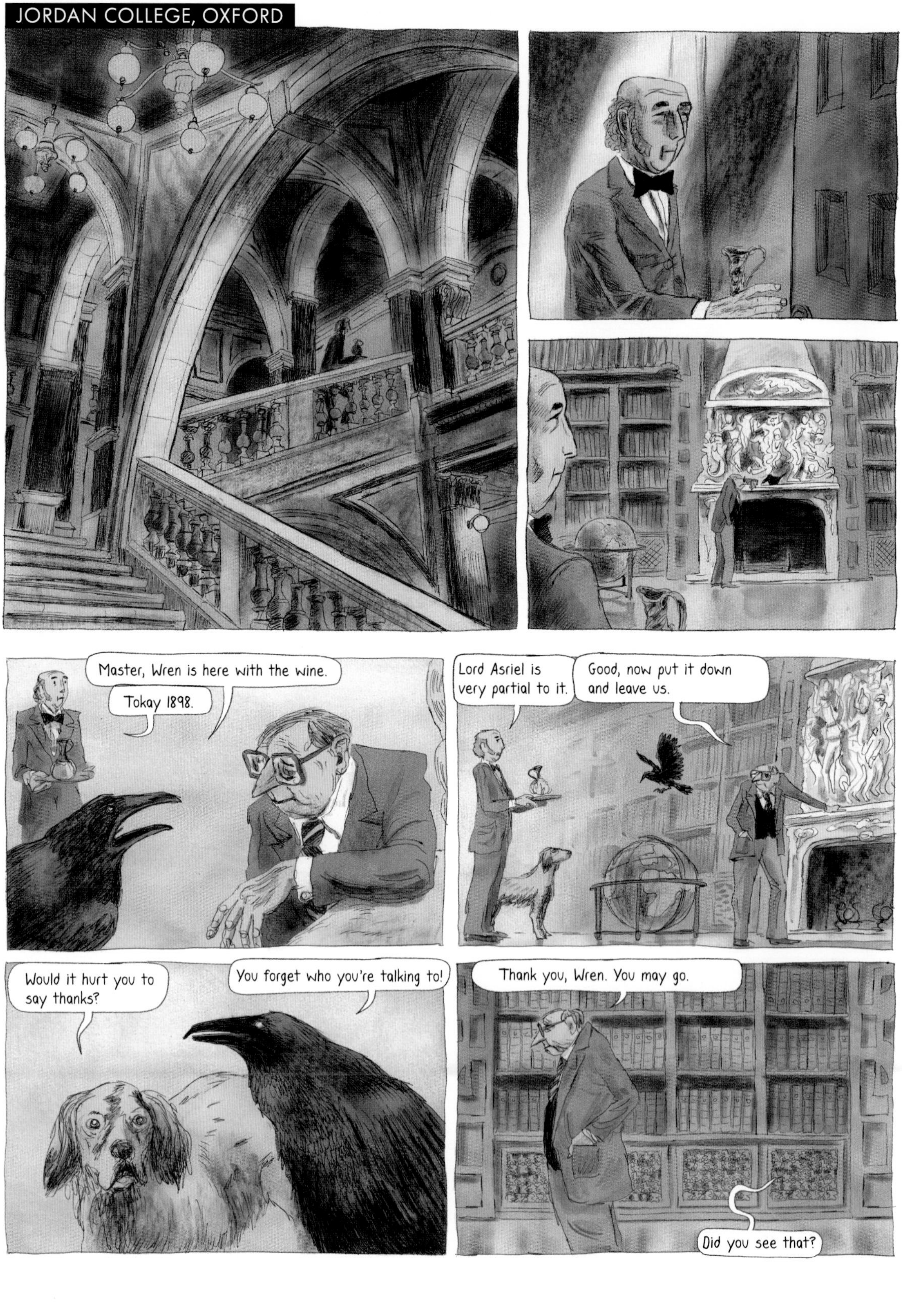
JORDAN COLLEGE, OXFORD
Master, Wren is here with the wine.
Tokay 1898.
Lord Asriel is very partial to it.
Good, now put it down and leave us.
Would it hurt you to say thanks?
You forget who you're talking to!
Thank you, Wren. You may go.
Did you see that?

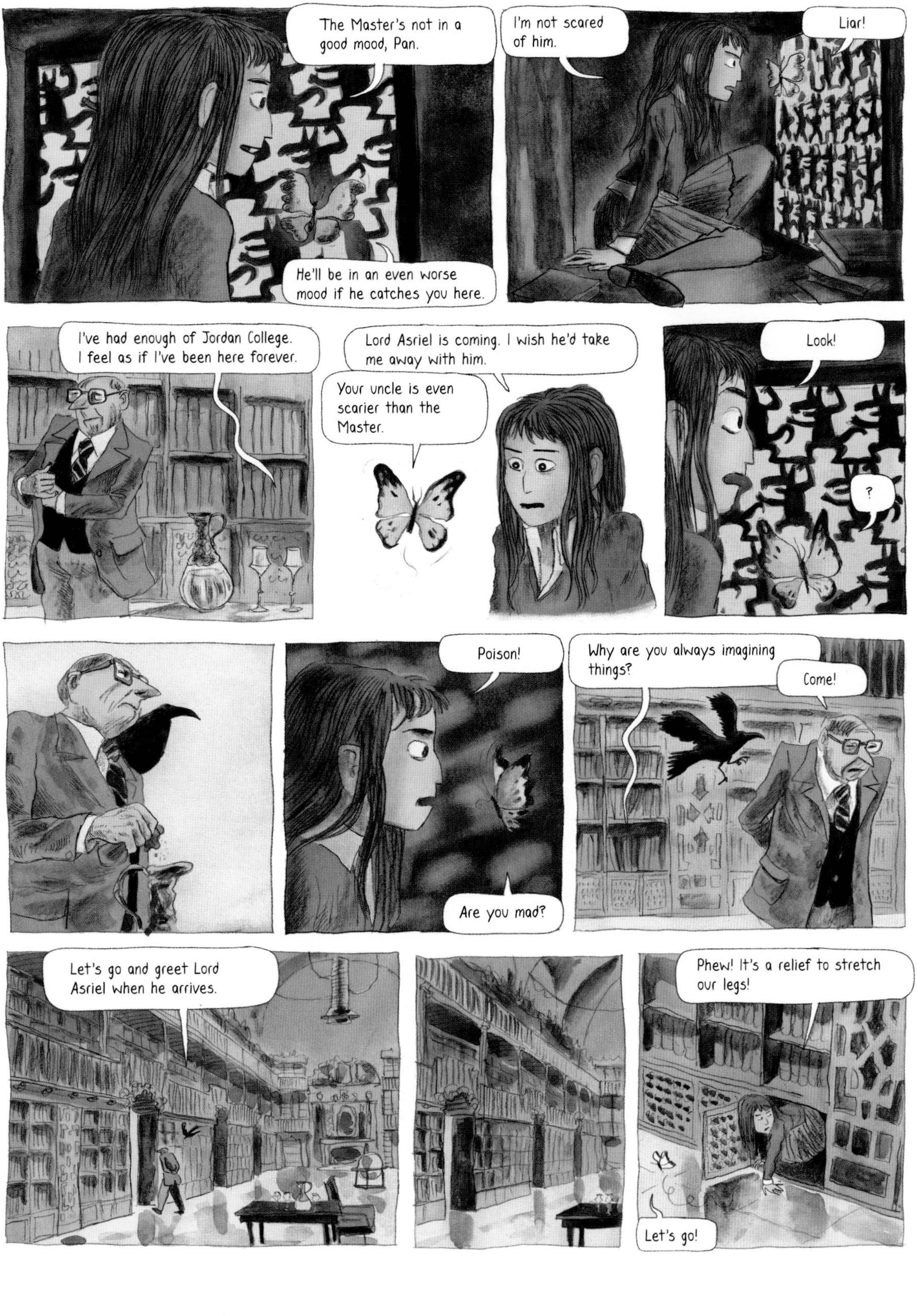

The Master's not in a good mood, Pan.
He'll be in an even worse mood if he catches you here.
I'm not scared of him.
Liar!
I've had enough of Jordan College. I feel as if I've been here forever.
Lord Asriel is coming. I wish he'd take me away with him.
Your uncle is even scarier than the Master.
Look!
?
Poison!
Are you mad?
Why are you always imagining things?
Come!
Let's go and greet Lord Asriel when he arrives.
Phew! It's a relief to stretch our legs!
Let's go!

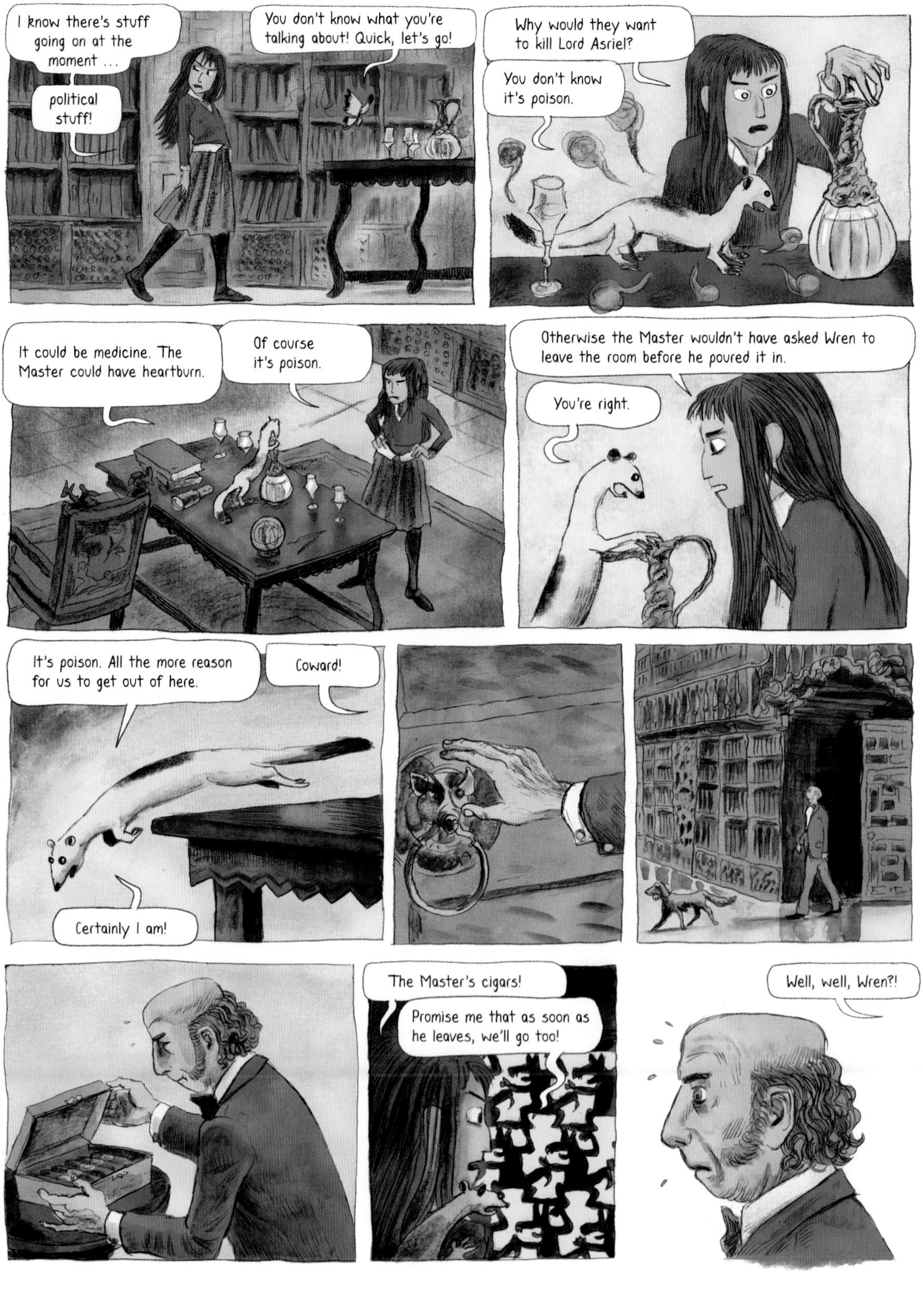
I know there's stuff going on at the moment ...
political stuff!
You don't know what you're talking about! Quick, let's go!
Why would they want to kill Lord Asriel?
You don't know it's poison.
It could be medicine. The Master could have heartburn.
Of course it's poison.
Otherwise the Master wouldn't have asked Wren to leave the room before he poured it in.
You're right.
It's poison. All the more reason for us to get out of here.
Coward!
Certainly I am!
The Master's cigars!
Promise me that as soon as he leaves, we'll go too!
Well, well, Wren?!

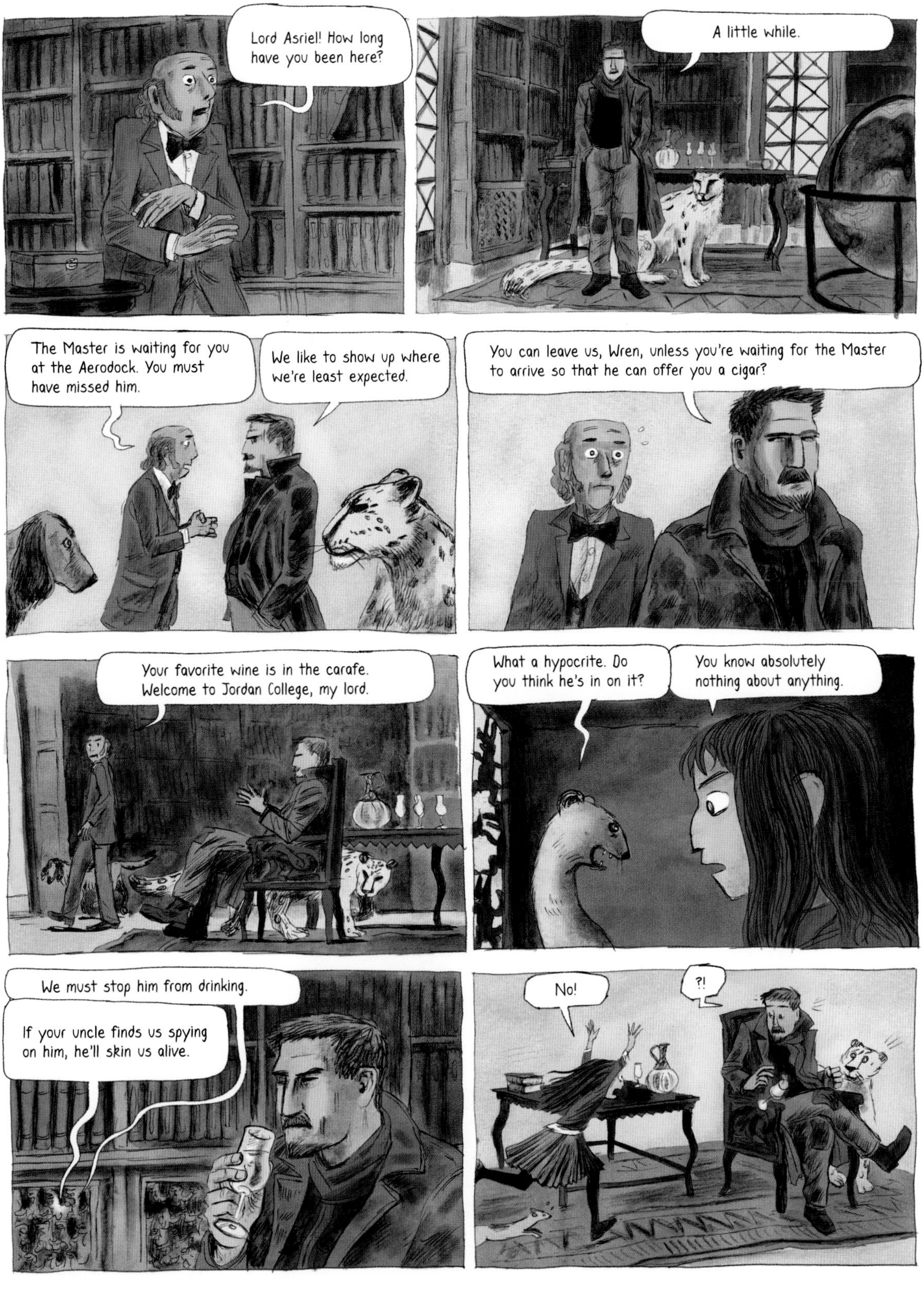

Lord Asriel! How long have you been here?
A little while.
The Master is waiting for you at the Aerodock. You must have missed him.
We like to show up where we're least expected.
You can leave us, Wren, unless you're waiting for the Master to arrive so that he can offer you a cigar?
Your favorite wine is in the carafe. Welcome to Jordan College, my lord.
What a hypocrite. Do you think he's in on it?
You know absolutely nothing about anything.
We must stop him from drinking.
If your uncle finds us spying on him, he'll skin us alive.
No!
?!

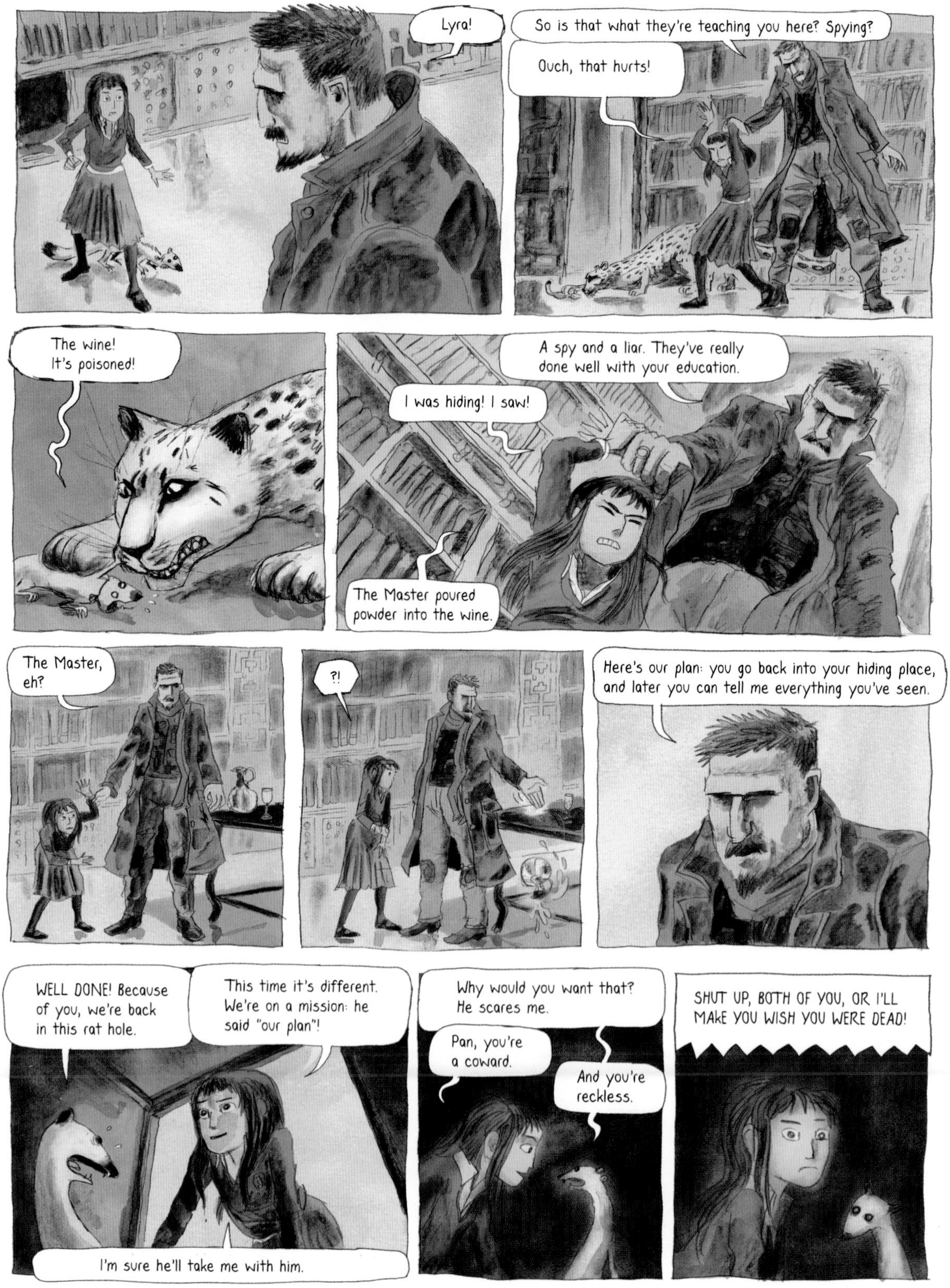
Lyra!
So is that what they're teaching you here? Spying?
Ouch, that hurts!
The wine! It's poisoned!
A spy and a liar. They've really done well with your education.
I was hiding! I saw!
The Master poured powder into the wine.
The Master, eh?
?!
Here's our plan: you go back into your hiding place, and later you can tell me everything you've seen.
WELL DONE! Because of you, we're back in this rat hole.
This time it's different. We're on a mission: he said "our plan"!
I'm sure he'll take me with him.
Why would you want that? He scares me.
Pan, you're a coward.
And you're reckless.
SHUT UP, BOTH OF YOU, OR I'LL MAKE YOU WISH YOU WERE DEAD!

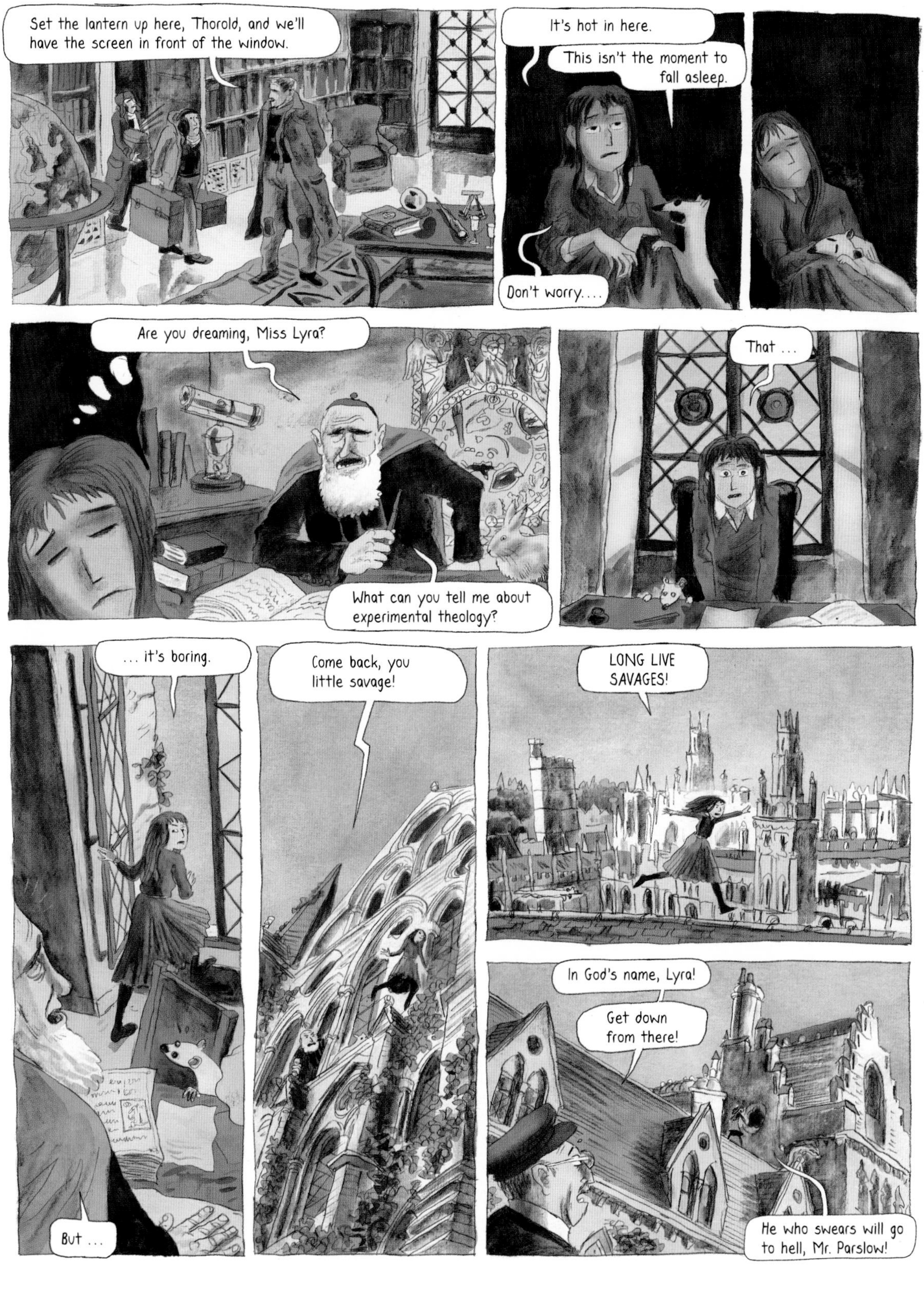
Set the lantern up here, Thorold, and we'll have the screen in front of the window.
It's hot in here.
This isn't the moment to fall asleep.
Don't worry....
Are you dreaming, Miss Lyra?
What can you tell me about experimental theology?
That ...
... it's boring.
But ...
Come back, you little savage!
LONG LIVE SAVAGES!
In God's name, Lyra!
Get down from there!
He who swears will go to hell, Mr. Parslow!

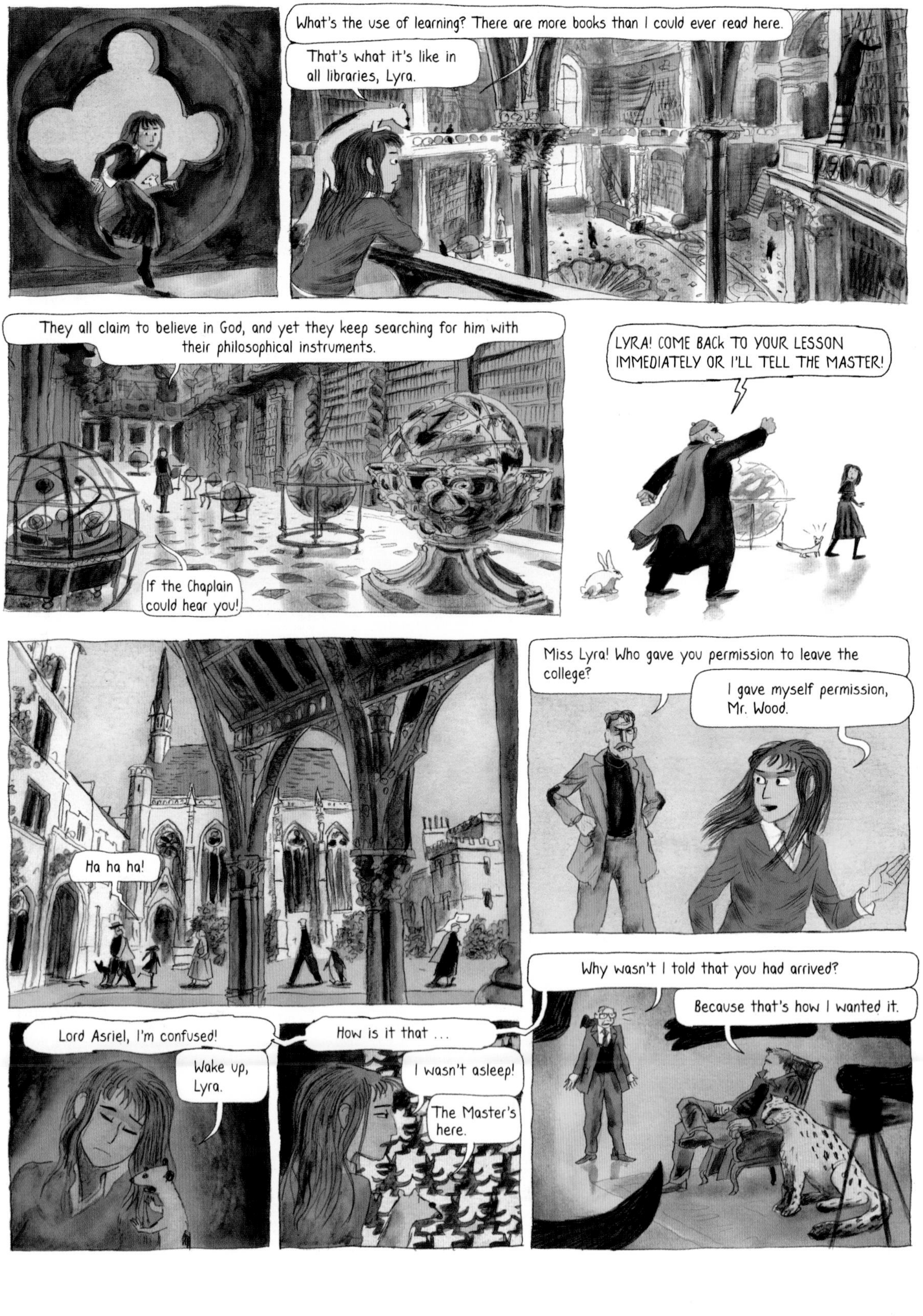
What's the use of learning? There are more books than I could ever read here.
That's what it's like in all libraries, Lyra.
They all claim to believe in God, and yet they keep searching for him with their philosophical instruments.
If the Chaplain could hear you!
LYRA! COME BACK TO YOUR LESSON IMMEDIATELY OR I'LL TELL THE MASTER!
Ha ha ha!
Miss Lyra! Who gave you permission to leave the college?
I gave myself permission, Mr. Wood.
Lord Asriel, I'm confused!
Wake up, Lyra.
How is it that . . .
I wasn't asleep!
The Master's here.
Why wasn't I told that you had arrived?
Because that's how I wanted it.

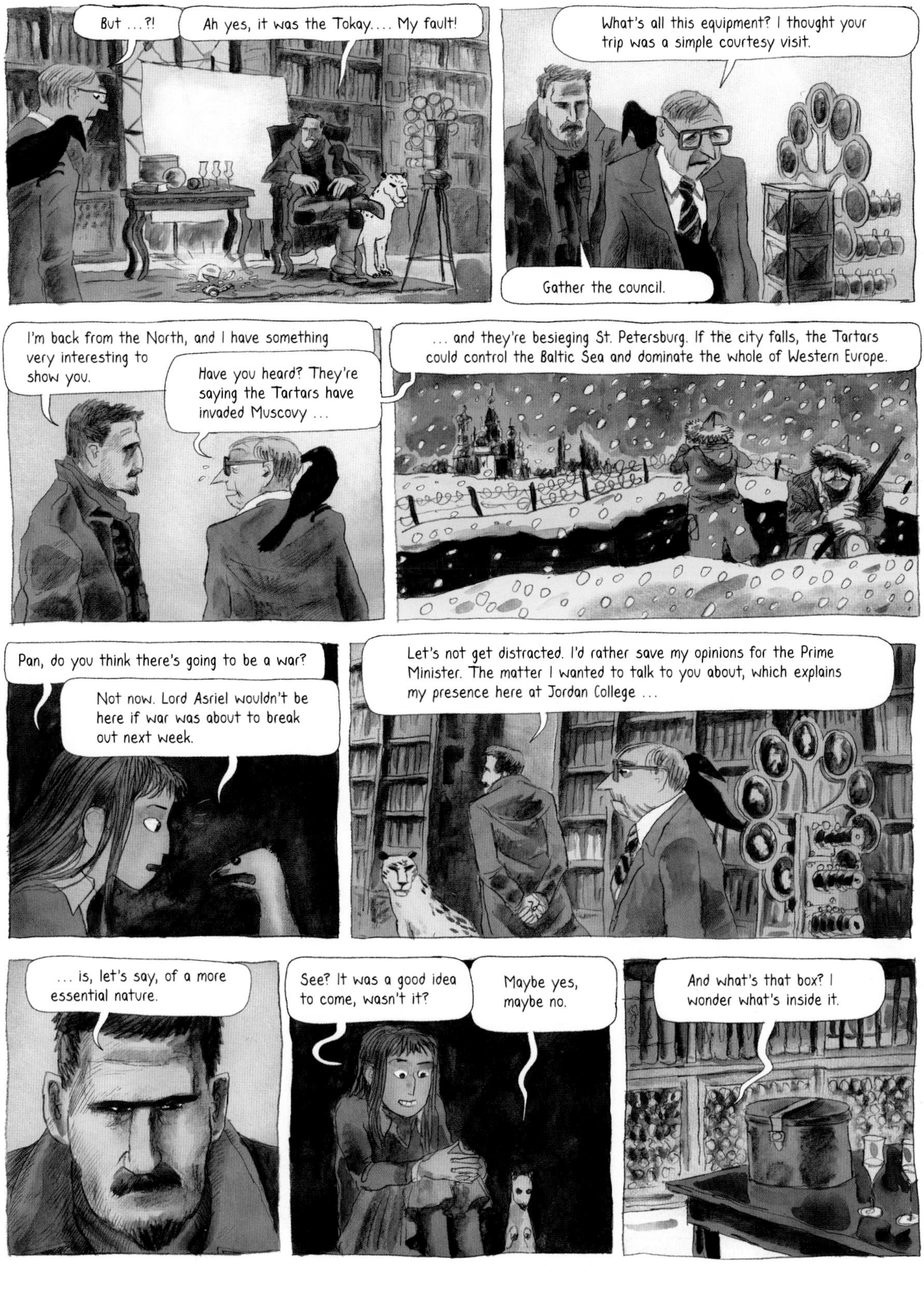
But ...?!
Ah yes, it was the Tokay.... My fault!
What's all this equipment? I thought your trip was a simple courtesy visit.
Gather the council.
I'm back from the North, and I have something very interesting to show you.
Have you heard? They're saying the Tartars have invaded Muscovy ...
... and they're besieging St. Petersburg. If the city falls, the Tartars could control the Baltic Sea and dominate the whole of Western Europe.
Pan, do you think there's going to be a war?
Not now. Lord Asriel wouldn't be here if war was about to break out next week.
Let's not get distracted. I'd rather save my opinions for the Prime Minister. The matter I wanted to talk to you about, which explains my presence here at Jordan College ...
... is, let's say, of a more essential nature.
See? It was a good idea to come, wasn't it?
Maybe yes, maybe no.
And what's that box? I wonder what's inside it.

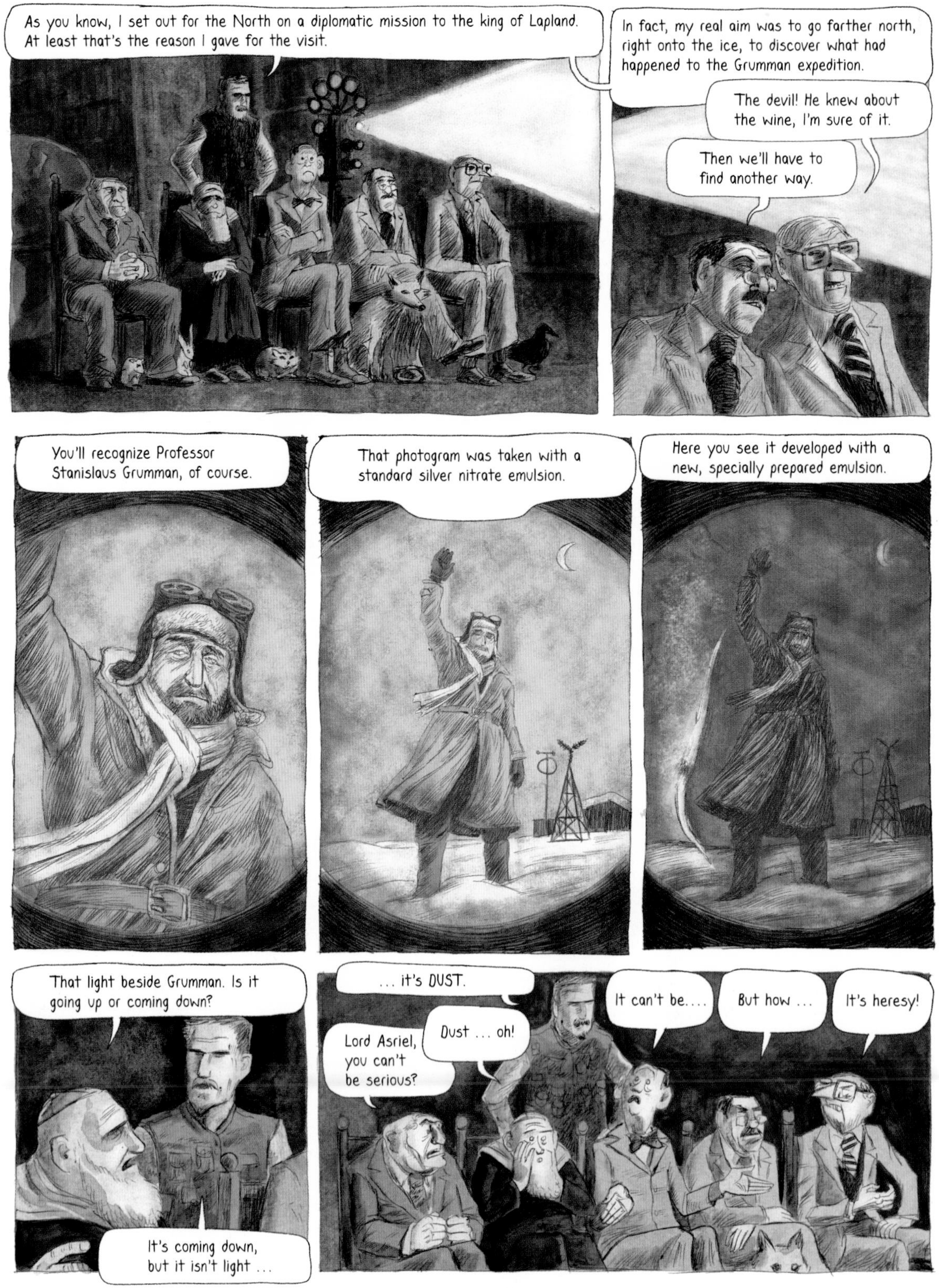
As you know, I set out for the North on a diplomatic mission to the king of Lapland. At least that's the reason I gave for the visit.
In fact, my real aim was to go farther north, right onto the ice, to discover what had happened to the Grumman expedition.
The devil! He knew about the wine, I'm sure of it.
Then we'll have to find another way.
You'll recognize Professor Stanislaus Grumman, of course.
That photogram was taken with a standard silver nitrate emulsion.
Here you see it developed with a new, specially prepared emulsion.
That light beside Grumman. Is it going up or coming down?
It's coming down, but it isn't light . . .
. . . it's DUST.
Lord Asriel, you can't be serious?
Dust . . . oh!
It can't be. . . .
But how . . .
It's heresy!

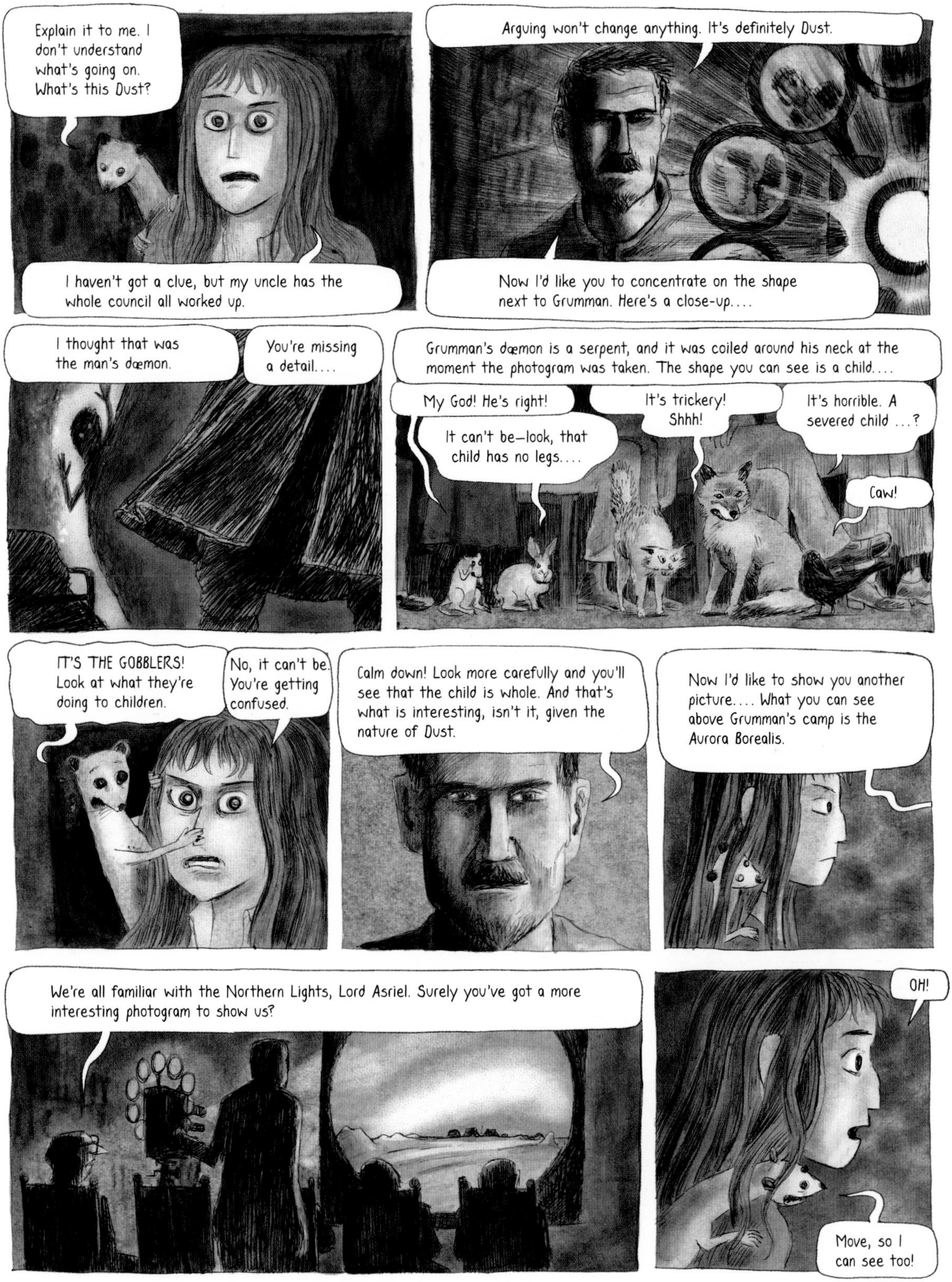
Explain it to me. I don't understand what's going on. What's this Dust?
I haven't got a clue, but my uncle has the whole council all worked up.
Arguing won't change anything. It's definitely Dust.
Now I'd like you to concentrate on the shape next to Grumman. Here's a close-up....
I thought that was the man's dæmon.
You're missing a detail....
Grumman's dæmon is a serpent, and it was coiled around his neck at the moment the photogram was taken. The shape you can see is a child....
My God! He's right!
It can't be—look, that child has no legs....
It's trickery! Shhh!
It's horrible. A severed child ...?
Caw!
IT'S THE GOBBLERS! Look at what they're doing to children.
No, it can't be. You're getting confused.
Calm down! Look more carefully and you'll see that the child is whole. And that's what is interesting, isn't it, given the nature of Dust.
Now I'd like to show you another picture.... What you can see above Grumman's camp is the Aurora Borealis.
We're all familiar with the Northern Lights, Lord Asriel. Surely you've got a more interesting photogram to show us?
OH!
Move, so I can see too!

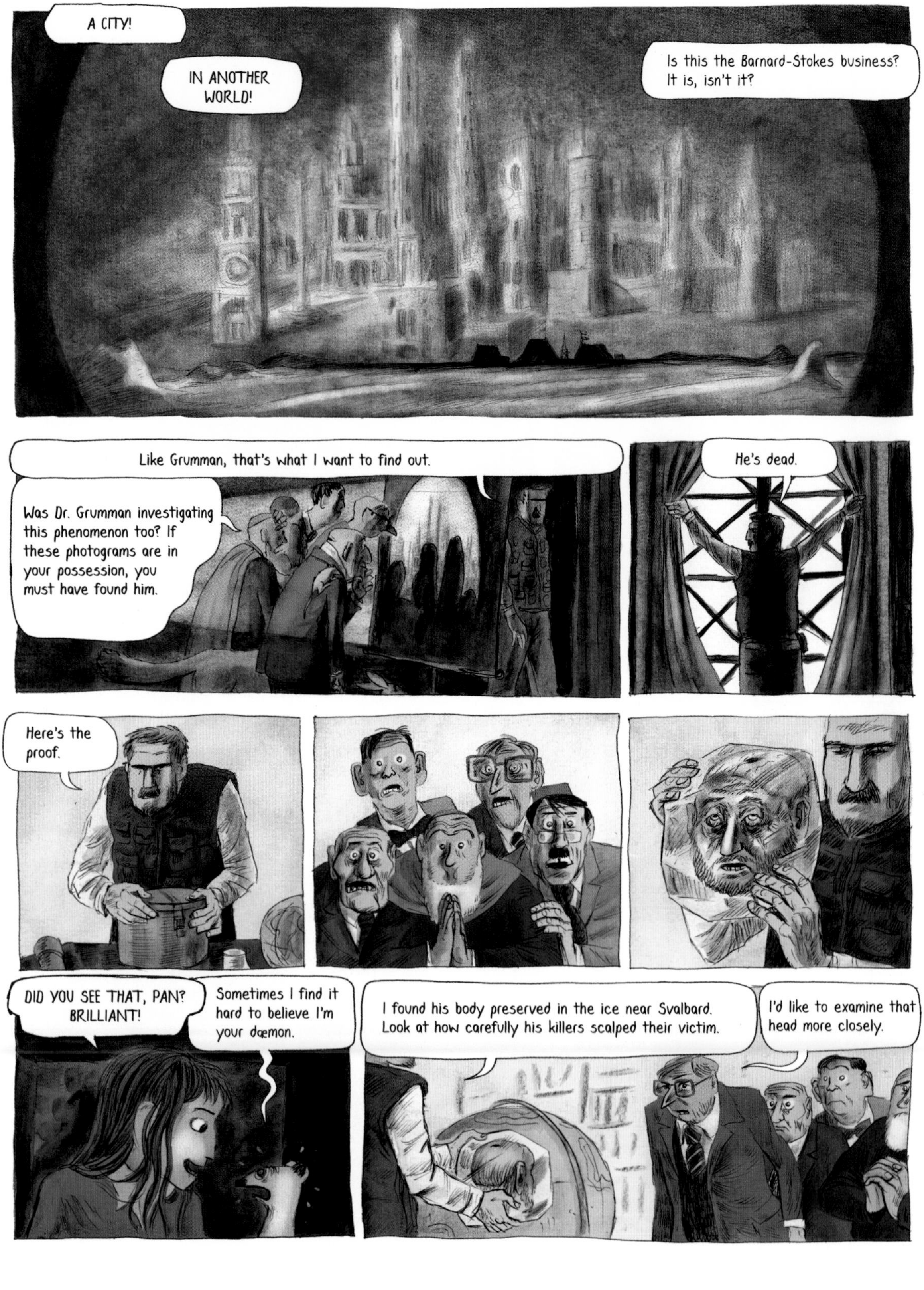
A CITY!
IN ANOTHER WORLD!
Is this the Barnard-Stokes business? It is, isn't it?
Like Grumman, that's what I want to find out.
Was Dr. Grumman investigating this phenomenon too? If these photograms are in your possession, you must have found him.
He's dead.
Here's the proof.
DID YOU SEE THAT, PAN? BRILLIANT!
Sometimes I find it hard to believe I'm your dæmon.
I found his body preserved in the ice near Svalbard. Look at how carefully his killers scalped their victim.
I'd like to examine that head more closely.

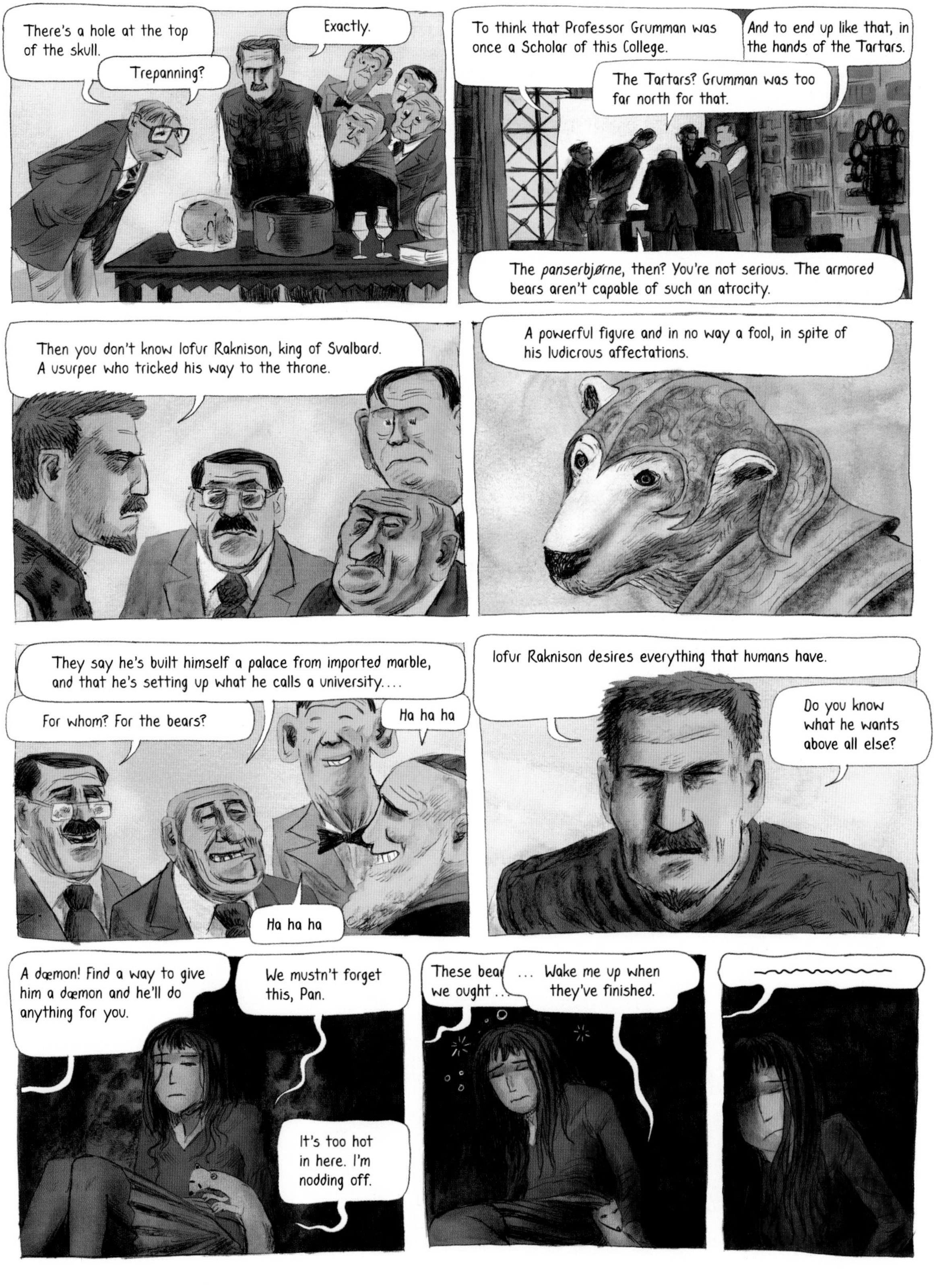
There's a hole at the top of the skull.
Trepanning?
Exactly.
To think that Professor Grumman was once a Scholar of this College.
And to end up like that, in the hands of the Tartars.
The Tartars? Grumman was too far north for that.
The *panserbjørne*, then? You're not serious. The armored bears aren't capable of such an atrocity.
Then you don't know Iofur Raknison, king of Svalbard. A usurper who tricked his way to the throne.
A powerful figure and in no way a fool, in spite of his ludicrous affectations.
They say he's built himself a palace from imported marble, and that he's setting up what he calls a university....
For whom? For the bears?
Ha ha ha
Ha ha ha
Iofur Raknison desires everything that humans have.
Do you know what he wants above all else?
A dæmon! Find a way to give him a dæmon and he'll do anything for you.
We mustn't forget this, Pan.
It's too hot in here. I'm nodding off.
These bea
we ought ...
... Wake me up when they've finished.

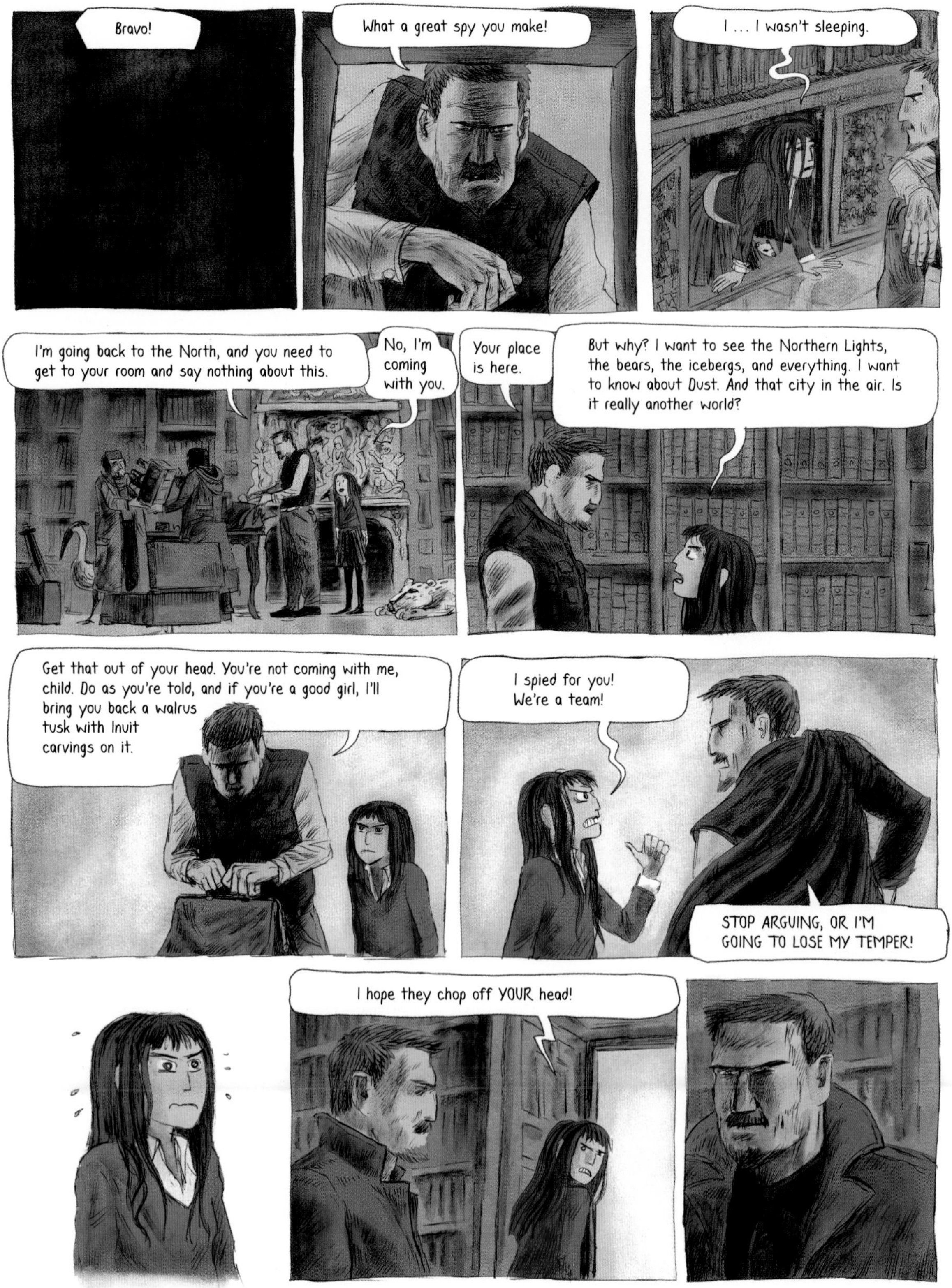
Bravo!
What a great spy you make!
I . . . I wasn't sleeping.
I'm going back to the North, and you need to get to your room and say nothing about this.
No, I'm coming with you.
Your place is here.
But why? I want to see the Northern Lights, the bears, the icebergs, and everything. I want to know about Dust. And that city in the air. Is it really another world?
Get that out of your head. You're not coming with me, child. Do as you're told, and if you're a good girl, I'll bring you back a walrus tusk with Inuit carvings on it.
I spied for you! We're a team!
STOP ARGUING, OR I'M GOING TO LOSE MY TEMPER!
I hope they chop off YOUR head!

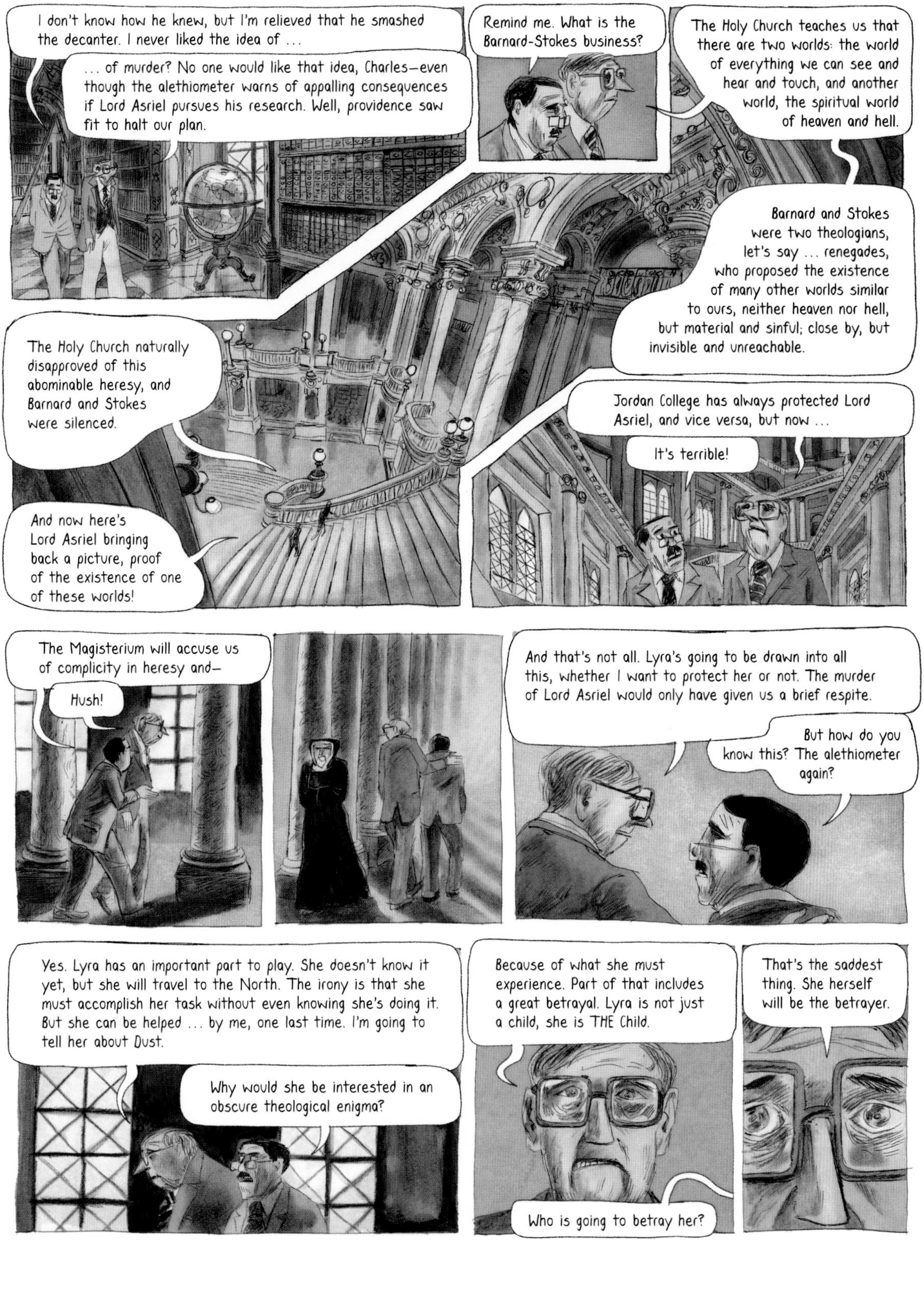
I don't know how he knew, but I'm relieved that he smashed the decanter. I never liked the idea of ...
... of murder? No one would like that idea, Charles—even though the alethiometer warns of appalling consequences if Lord Asriel pursues his research. Well, providence saw fit to halt our plan.
Remind me. What is the Barnard-Stokes business?
The Holy Church teaches us that there are two worlds: the world of everything we can see and hear and touch, and another world, the spiritual world of heaven and hell.
Barnard and Stokes were two theologians, let's say ... renegades, who proposed the existence of many other worlds similar to ours, neither heaven nor hell, but material and sinful; close by, but invisible and unreachable.
The Holy Church naturally disapproved of this abominable heresy, and Barnard and Stokes were silenced.
And now here's Lord Asriel bringing back a picture, proof of the existence of one of these worlds!
Jordan College has always protected Lord Asriel, and vice versa, but now ...
It's terrible!
The Magisterium will accuse us of complicity in heresy and—
Hush!
And that's not all. Lyra's going to be drawn into all this, whether I want to protect her or not. The murder of Lord Asriel would only have given us a brief respite.
But how do you know this? The alethiometer again?
Yes. Lyra has an important part to play. She doesn't know it yet, but she will travel to the North. The irony is that she must accomplish her task without even knowing she's doing it. But she can be helped ... by me, one last time. I'm going to tell her about Dust.
Why would she be interested in an obscure theological enigma?
Because of what she must experience. Part of that includes a great betrayal. Lyra is not just a child, she is THE Child.
Who is going to betray her?
That's the saddest thing. She herself will be the betrayer.

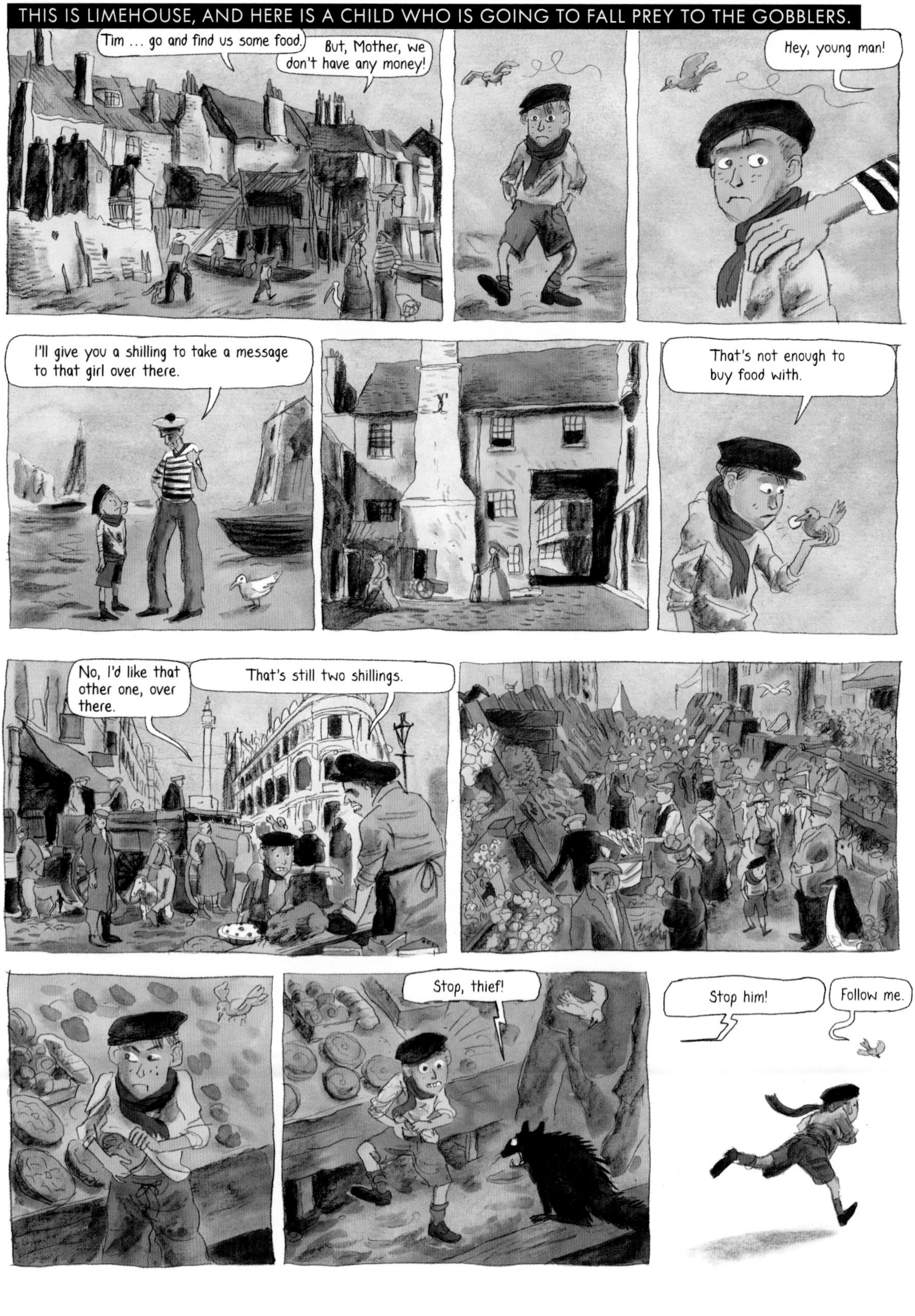
THIS IS LIMEHOUSE, AND HERE IS A CHILD WHO IS GOING TO FALL PREY TO THE GOBBLERS.
Tim ... go and find us some food.
But, Mother, we don't have any money!
Hey, young man!
I'll give you a shilling to take a message to that girl over there.
That's not enough to buy food with.
No, I'd like that other one, over there.
That's still two shillings.
Stop, thief!
Stop him!
Follow me.

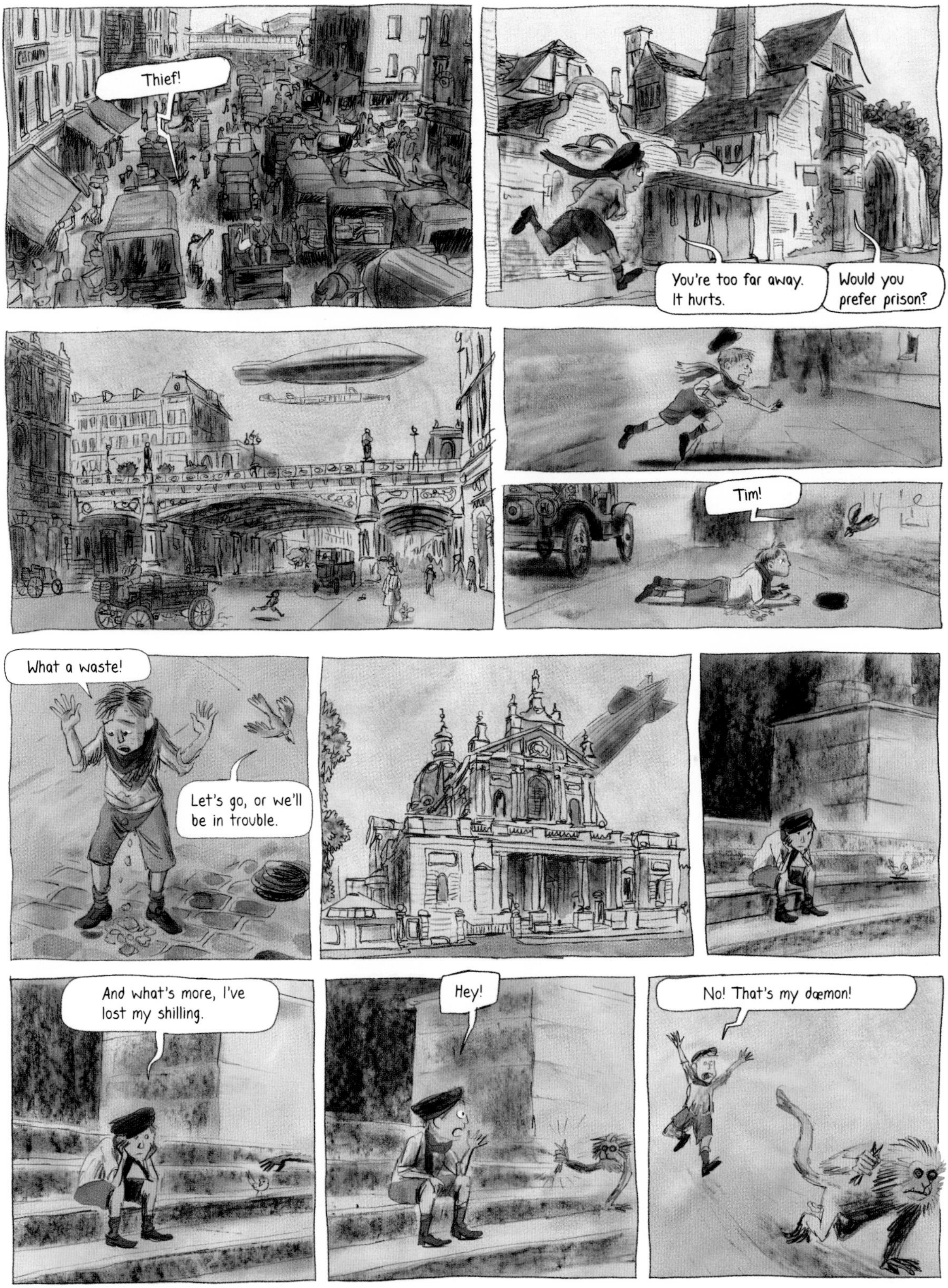
Thief!
You're too far away. It hurts.
Would you prefer prison?
Tim!
What a waste!
Let's go, or we'll be in trouble.
And what's more, I've lost my shilling.
Hey!
No! That's my dæmon!

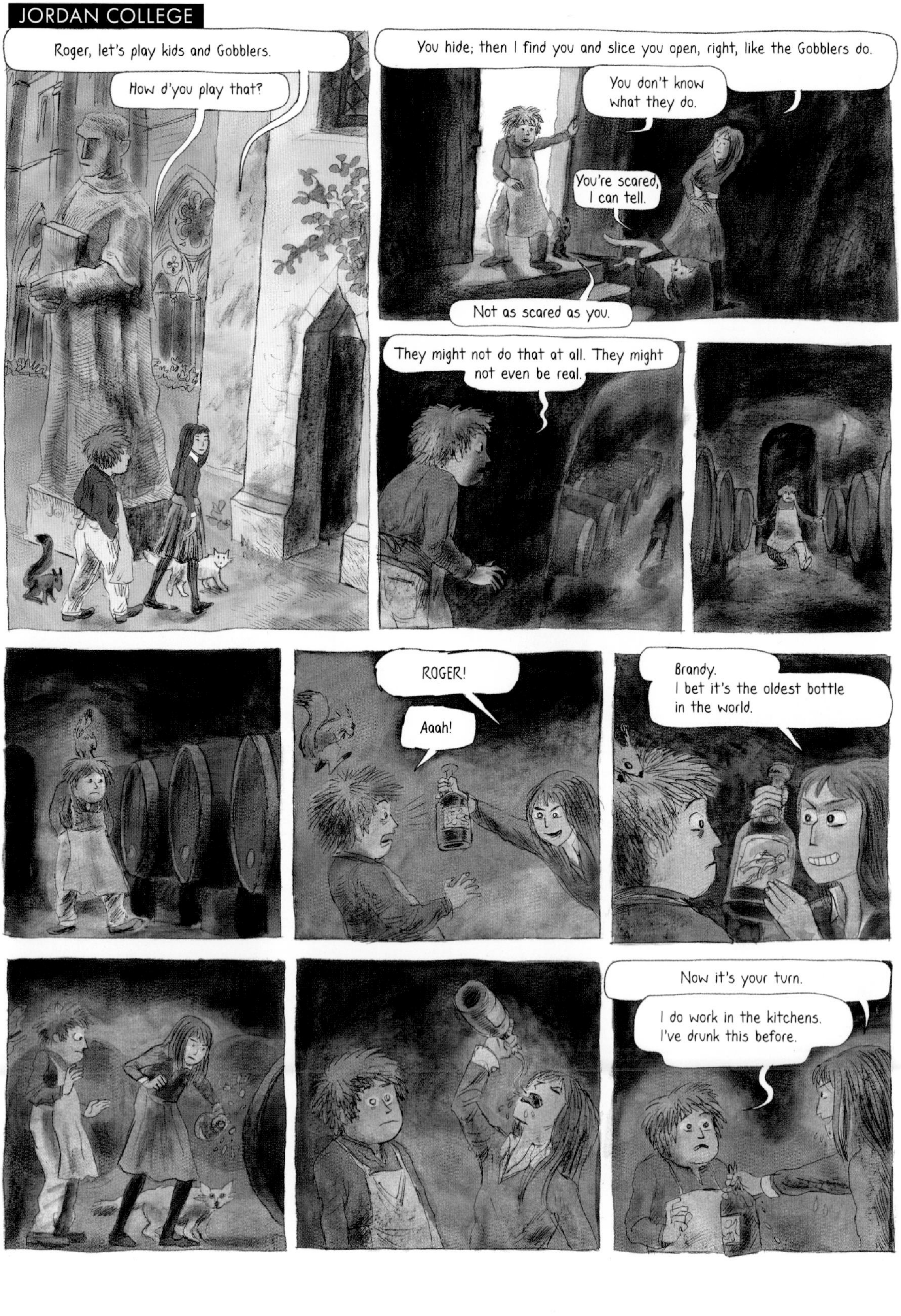
JORDAN COLLEGE
Roger, let's play kids and Gobblers.
How d'you play that?
You hide; then I find you and slice you open, right, like the Gobblers do.
You don't know what they do.
You're scared, I can tell.
Not as scared as you.
They might not do that at all. They might not even be real.
ROGER!
Aaah!
Brandy. I bet it's the oldest bottle in the world.
Now it's your turn.
I do work in the kitchens. I've drunk this before.

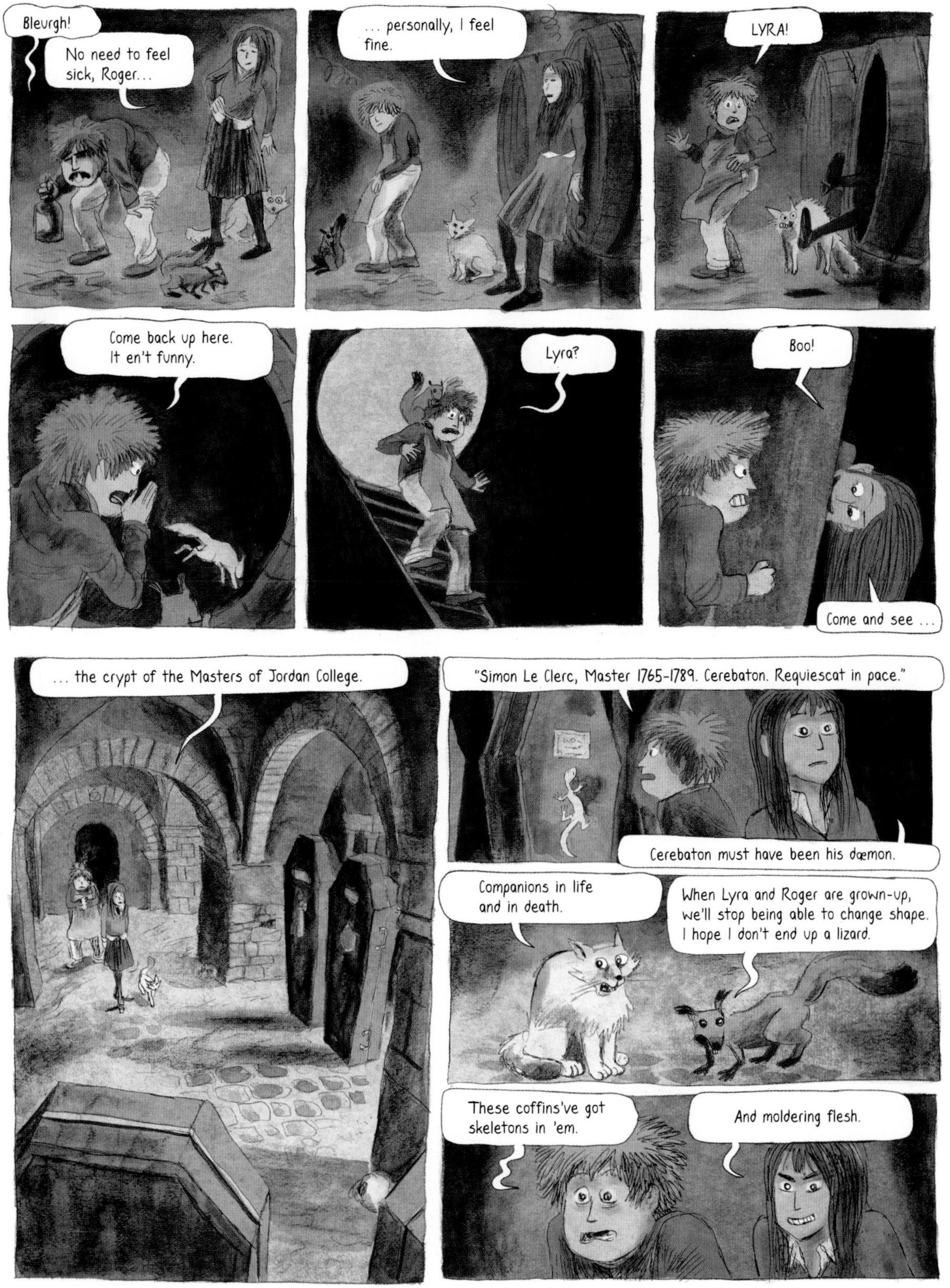

Bleurgh!
No need to feel sick, Roger...
... personally, I feel fine.
LYRA!
Come back up here. It en't funny.
Lyra?
Boo!
Come and see ...
... the crypt of the Masters of Jordan College.
"Simon Le Clerc, Master 1765-1789. Cerebaton. Requiescat in pace."
Cerebaton must have been his dæmon.
Companions in life and in death.
When Lyra and Roger are grown-up, we'll stop being able to change shape. I hope I don't end up a lizard.
These coffins've got skeletons in 'em.
And moldering flesh.

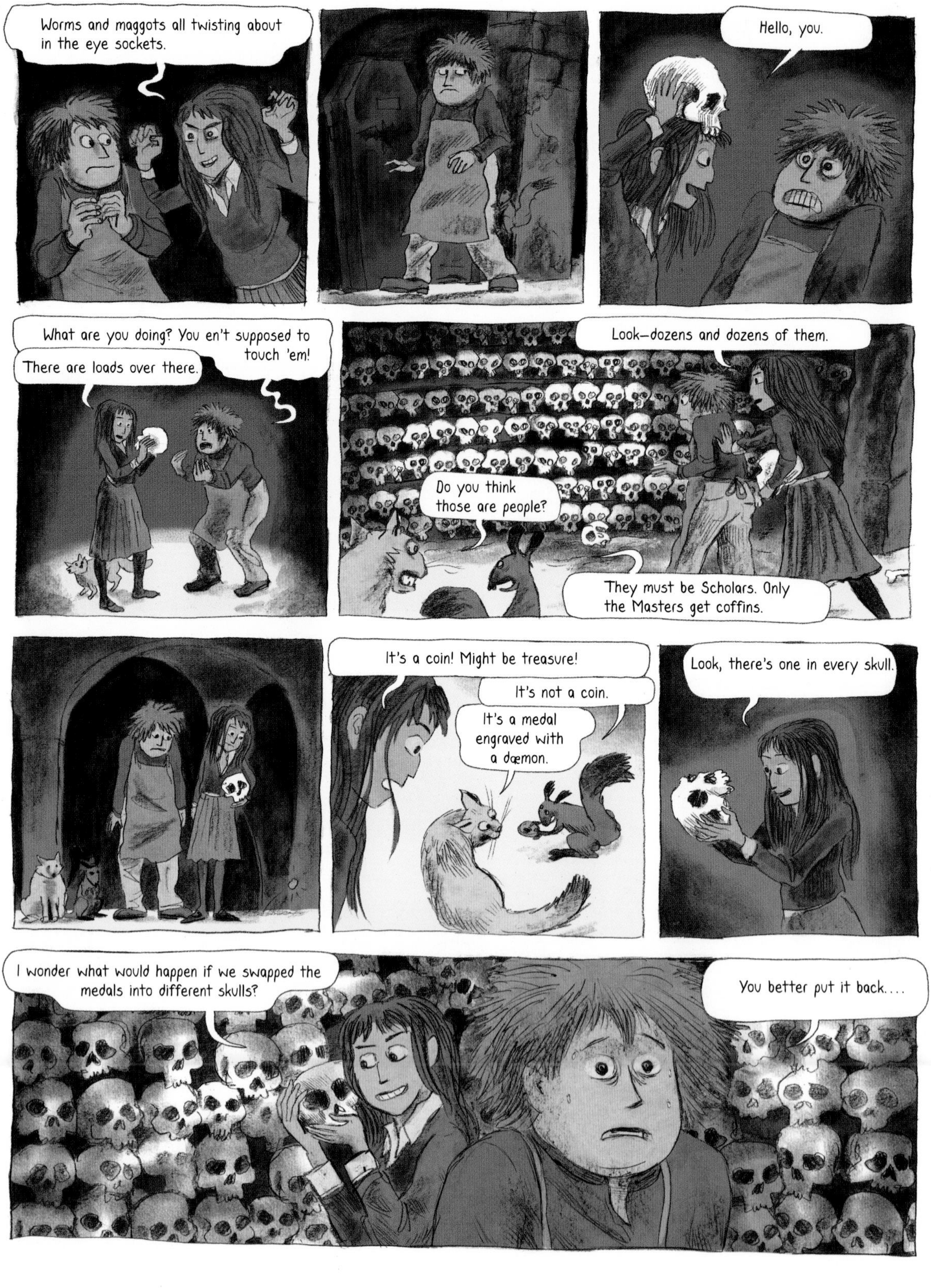

Worms and maggots all twisting about in the eye sockets.
Hello, you.
What are you doing? You en't supposed to touch 'em!
There are loads over there.
Look—dozens and dozens of them.
Do you think those are people?
They must be Scholars. Only the Masters get coffins.
It's a coin! Might be treasure!
It's not a coin.
It's a medal engraved with a dæmon.
Look, there's one in every skull.
I wonder what would happen if we swapped the medals into different skulls?
You better put it back....

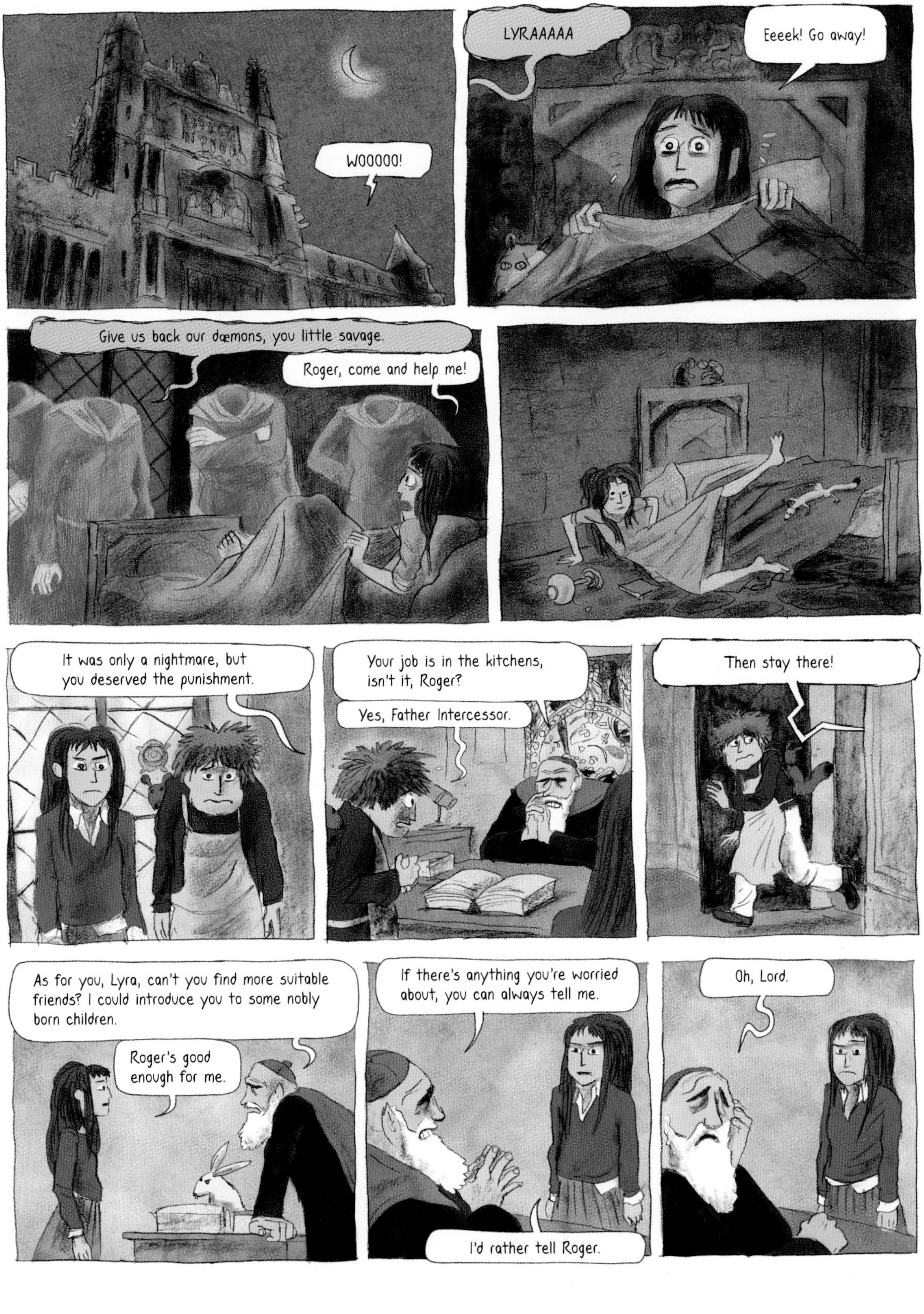
WOOOOO!
LYRAAAAA
Eeeek! Go away!
Give us back our dæmons, you little savage.
Roger, come and help me!
It was only a nightmare, but you deserved the punishment.
Your job is in the kitchens, isn't it, Roger?
Yes, Father Intercessor.
Then stay there!
As for you, Lyra, can't you find more suitable friends? I could introduce you to some nobly born children.
Roger's good enough for me.
If there's anything you're worried about, you can always tell me.
I'd rather tell Roger.
Oh, Lord.

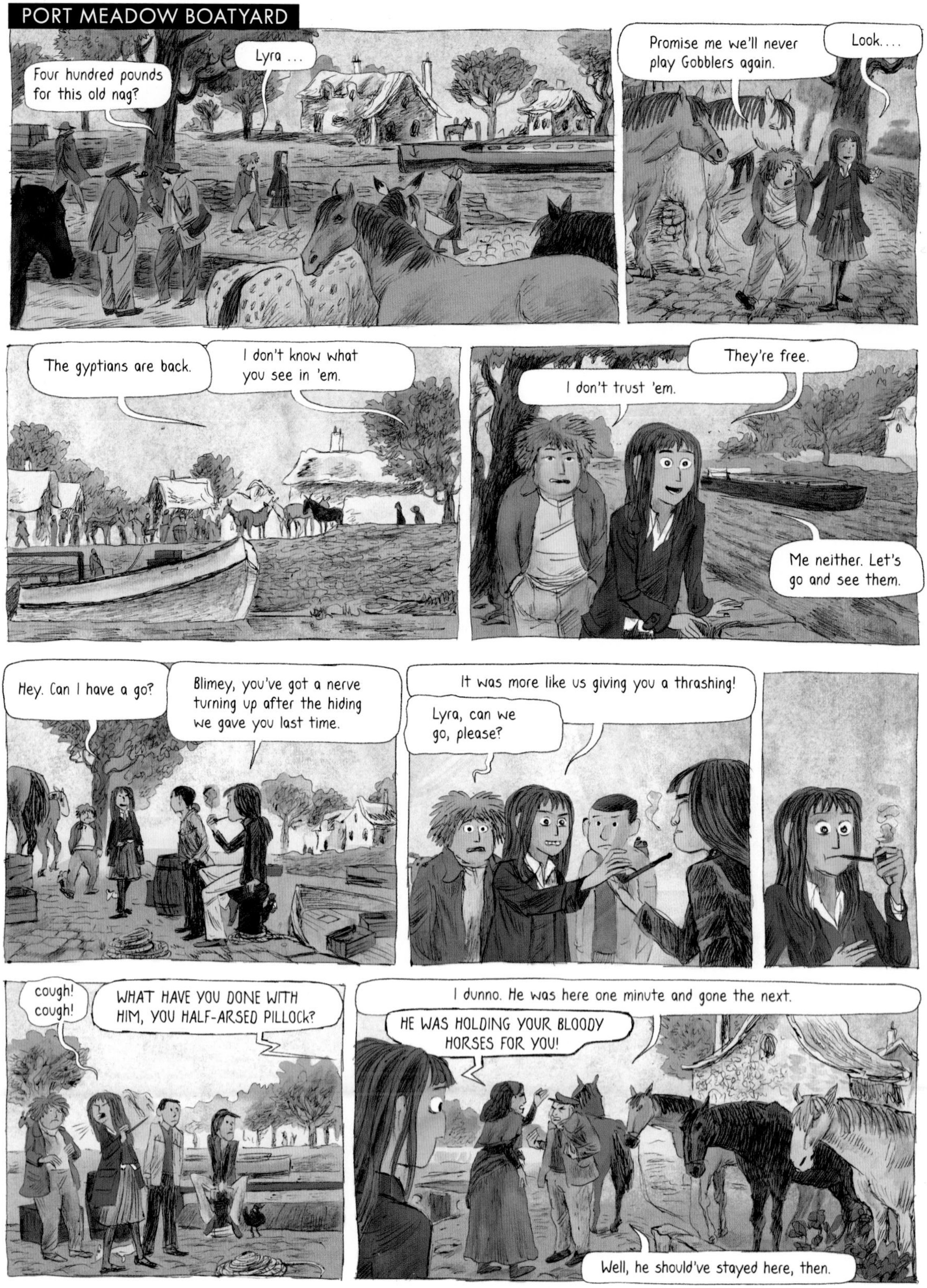
PORT MEADOW BOATYARD
Four hundred pounds for this old nag?
Lyra . . .
Promise me we'll never play Gobblers again.
Look. . . .
The gyptians are back.
I don't know what you see in 'em.
They're free.
I don't trust 'em.
Me neither. Let's go and see them.
Hey. Can I have a go?
Blimey, you've got a nerve turning up after the hiding we gave you last time.
It was more like us giving you a thrashing!
Lyra, can we go, please?
cough! cough!
WHAT HAVE YOU DONE WITH HIM, YOU HALF-ARSED PILLOCK?
I dunno. He was here one minute and gone the next.
HE WAS HOLDING YOUR BLOODY HORSES FOR YOU!
Well, he should've stayed here, then.

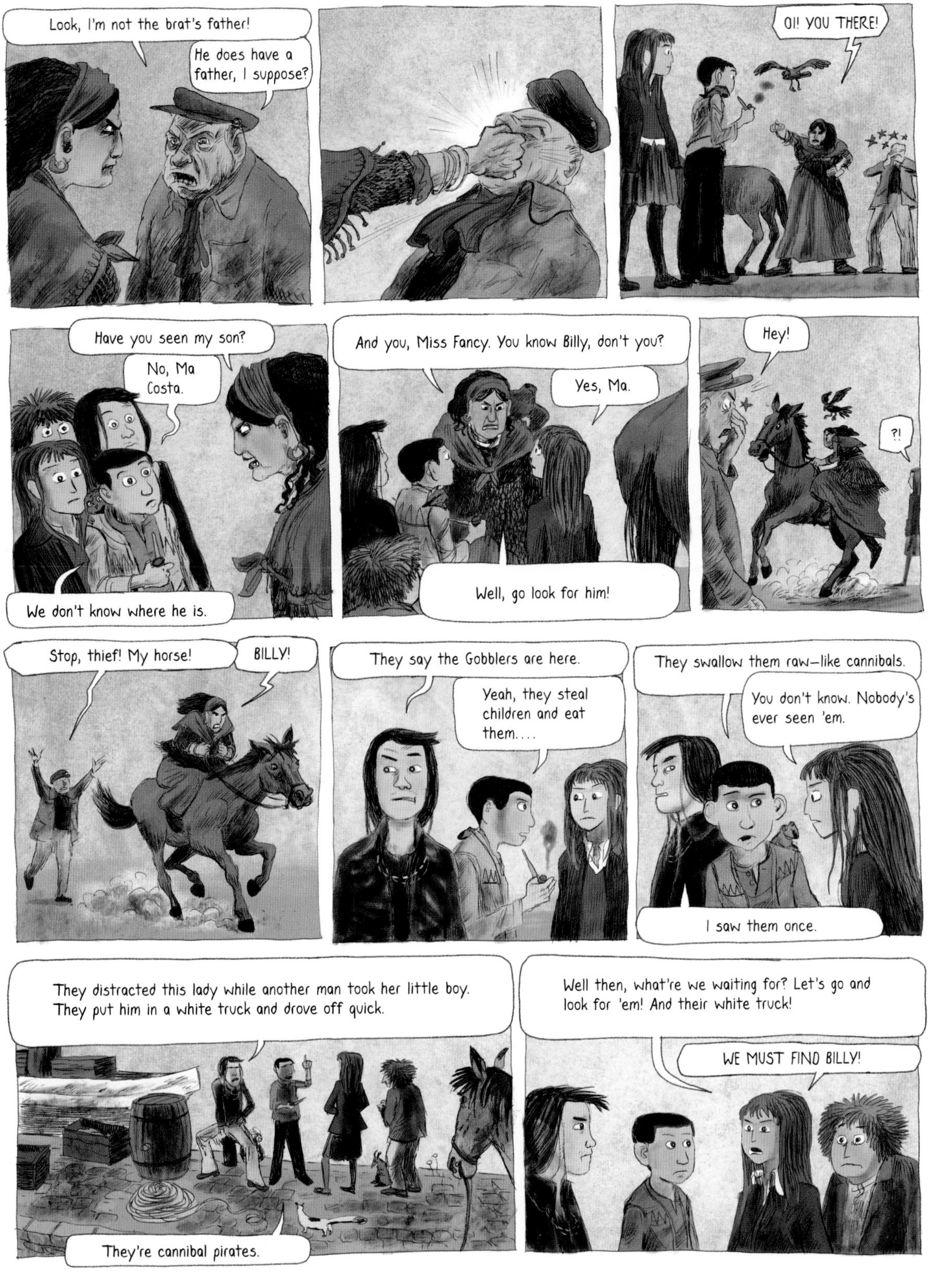
Look, I'm not the brat's father!
He does have a father, I suppose?
OI! YOU THERE!
Have you seen my son?
No, Ma Costa.
We don't know where he is.
And you, Miss Fancy. You know Billy, don't you?
Yes, Ma.
Well, go look for him!
Hey!
?!
Stop, thief! My horse!
BILLY!
They say the Gobblers are here.
Yeah, they steal children and eat them....
They swallow them raw—like cannibals.
You don't know. Nobody's ever seen 'em.
I saw them once.
They distracted this lady while another man took her little boy. They put him in a white truck and drove off quick.
They're cannibal pirates.
Well then, what're we waiting for? Let's go and look for 'em! And their white truck!
WE MUST FIND BILLY!

BILLY!
BILLY!
BILLY!
BILLY!
BILLY!
BILLY!
BILLY!
BILLY!
BILLY?!
Er ...
Lyra?
Lyra?
Oh well ...
let's go home.
When did Roger get home? You should know that—you were together, weren't you?
He's not here?
I'm going back to look for him.
Oh no, you're not. You're not allowed to go out again tonight. Master's orders.
NO, LET GO OF ME!
YOU DON'T UNDERSTAND! ROGER!

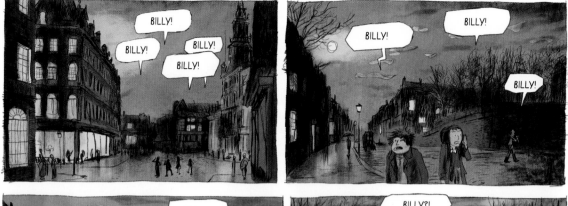

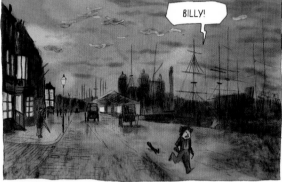

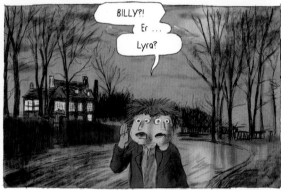

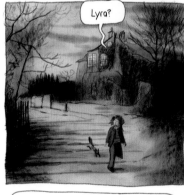

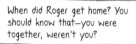

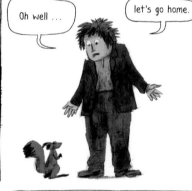

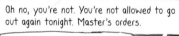

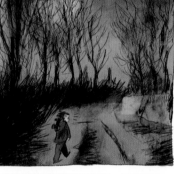

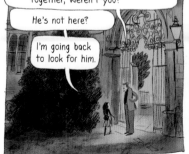

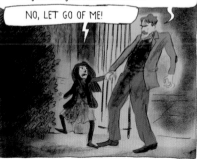

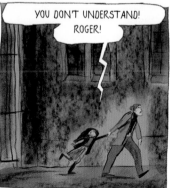

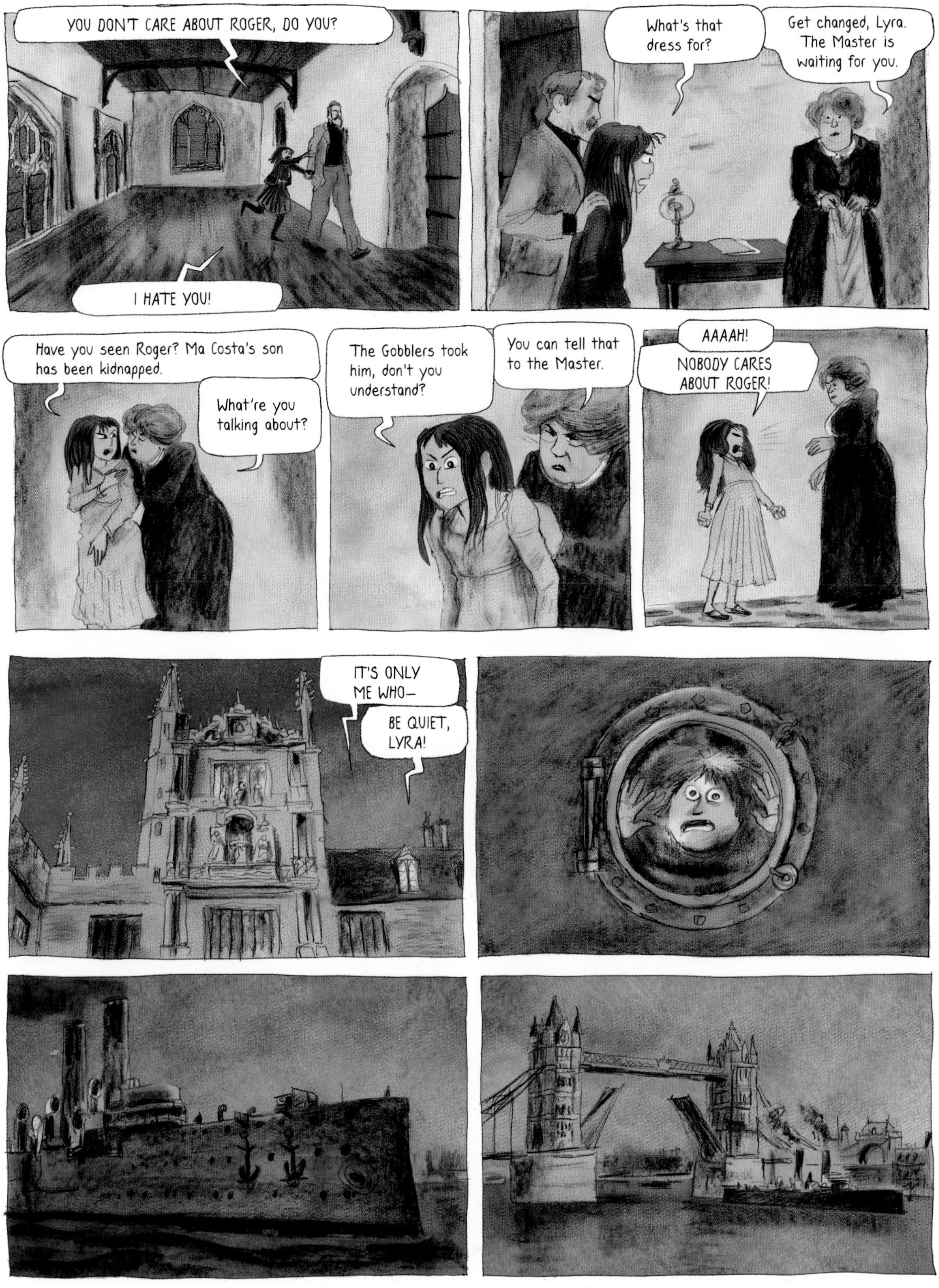
YOU DON'T CARE ABOUT ROGER, DO YOU?
I HATE YOU!
What's that dress for?
Get changed, Lyra. The Master is waiting for you.
Have you seen Roger? Ma Costa's son has been kidnapped.
What're you talking about?
The Gobblers took him, don't you understand?
You can tell that to the Master.
AAAAH!
NOBODY CARES ABOUT ROGER!
IT'S ONLY ME WHO—
BE QUIET, LYRA!

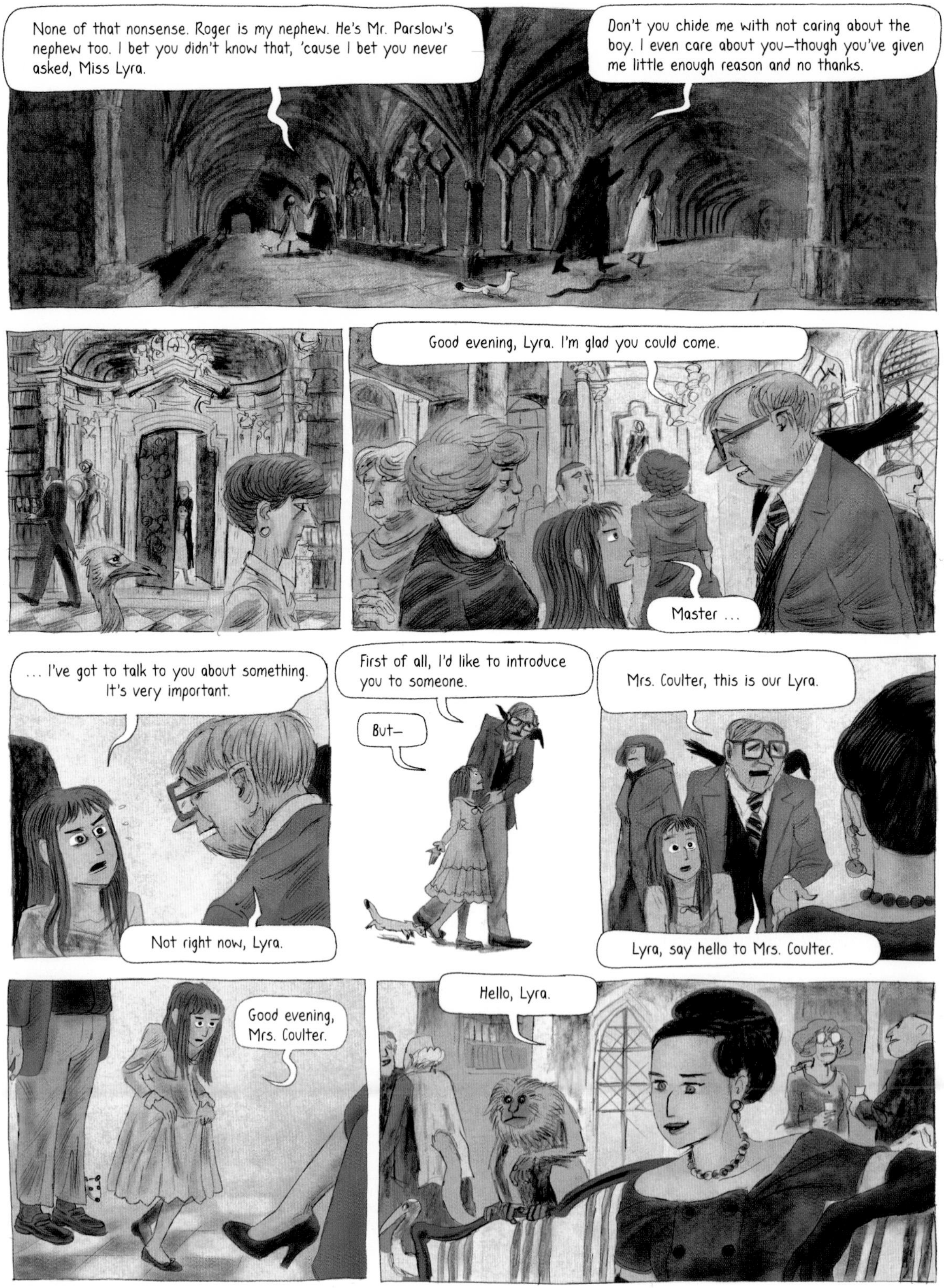
None of that nonsense. Roger is my nephew. He's Mr. Parslow's nephew too. I bet you didn't know that, 'cause I bet you never asked, Miss Lyra.
Don't you chide me with not caring about the boy. I even care about you—though you've given me little enough reason and no thanks.
Good evening, Lyra. I'm glad you could come.
Master ...
... I've got to talk to you about something. It's very important.
Not right now, Lyra.
First of all, I'd like to introduce you to someone.
But—
Mrs. Coulter, this is our Lyra.
Lyra, say hello to Mrs. Coulter.
Good evening, Mrs. Coulter.
Hello, Lyra.

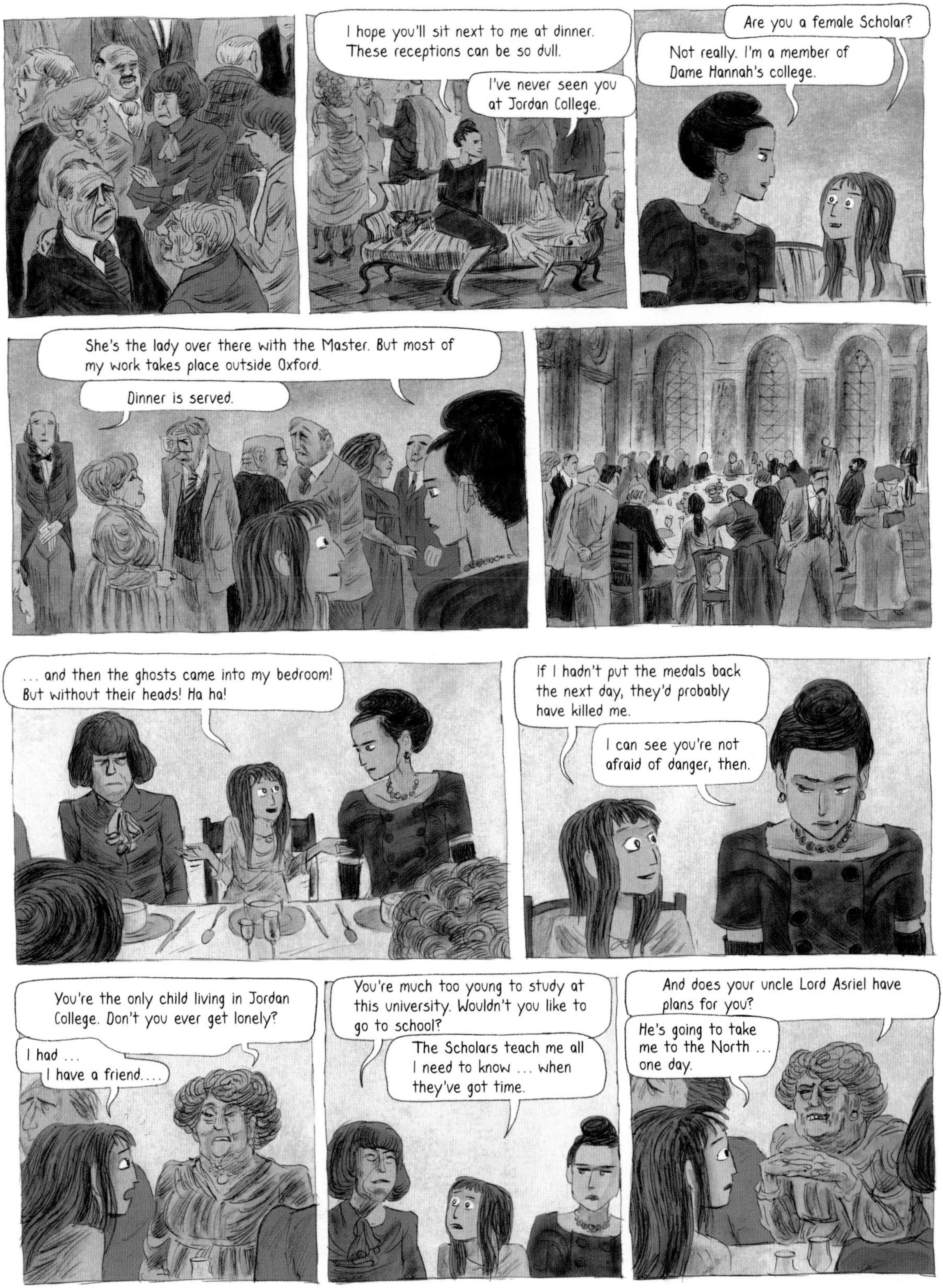
I hope you'll sit next to me at dinner. These receptions can be so dull.
I've never seen you at Jordan College.
Are you a female Scholar?
Not really. I'm a member of Dame Hannah's college.
She's the lady over there with the Master. But most of my work takes place outside Oxford.
Dinner is served.
. . . and then the ghosts came into my bedroom! But without their heads! Ha ha!
If I hadn't put the medals back the next day, they'd probably have killed me.
I can see you're not afraid of danger, then.
You're the only child living in Jordan College. Don't you ever get lonely?
I had . . . I have a friend. . . .
You're much too young to study at this university. Wouldn't you like to go to school?
The Scholars teach me all I need to know . . . when they've got time.
And does your uncle Lord Asriel have plans for you?
He's going to take me to the North . . . one day.

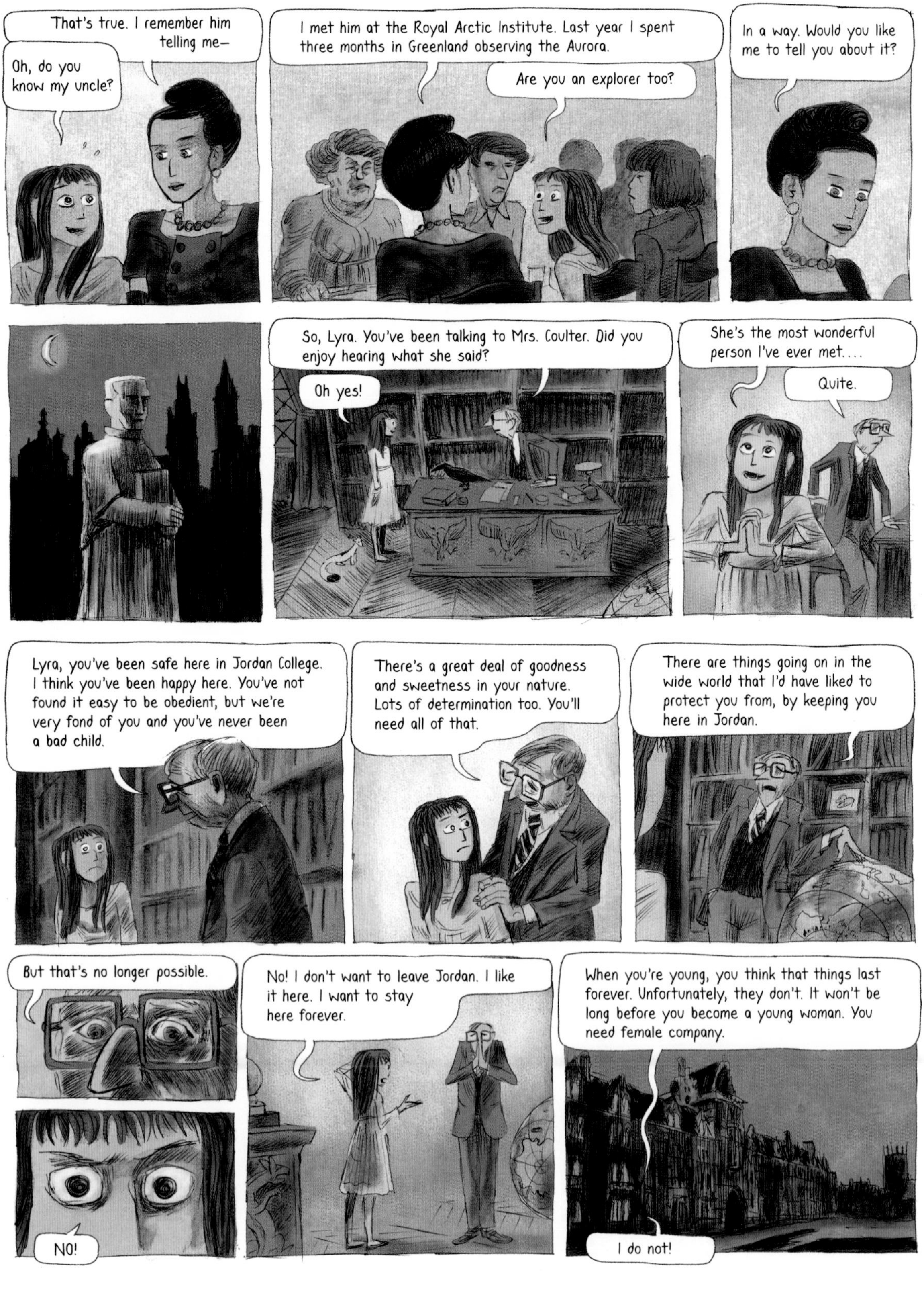
That's true. I remember him telling me—
Oh, do you know my uncle?
I met him at the Royal Arctic Institute. Last year I spent three months in Greenland observing the Aurora.
Are you an explorer too?
In a way. Would you like me to tell you about it?
So, Lyra. You've been talking to Mrs. Coulter. Did you enjoy hearing what she said?
Oh yes!
She's the most wonderful person I've ever met....
Quite.
Lyra, you've been safe here in Jordan College. I think you've been happy here. You've not found it easy to be obedient, but we're very fond of you and you've never been a bad child.
There's a great deal of goodness and sweetness in your nature. Lots of determination too. You'll need all of that.
There are things going on in the wide world that I'd have liked to protect you from, by keeping you here in Jordan.
But that's no longer possible.
NO!
No! I don't want to leave Jordan. I like it here. I want to stay here forever.
When you're young, you think that things last forever. Unfortunately, they don't. It won't be long before you become a young woman. You need female company.
I do not!

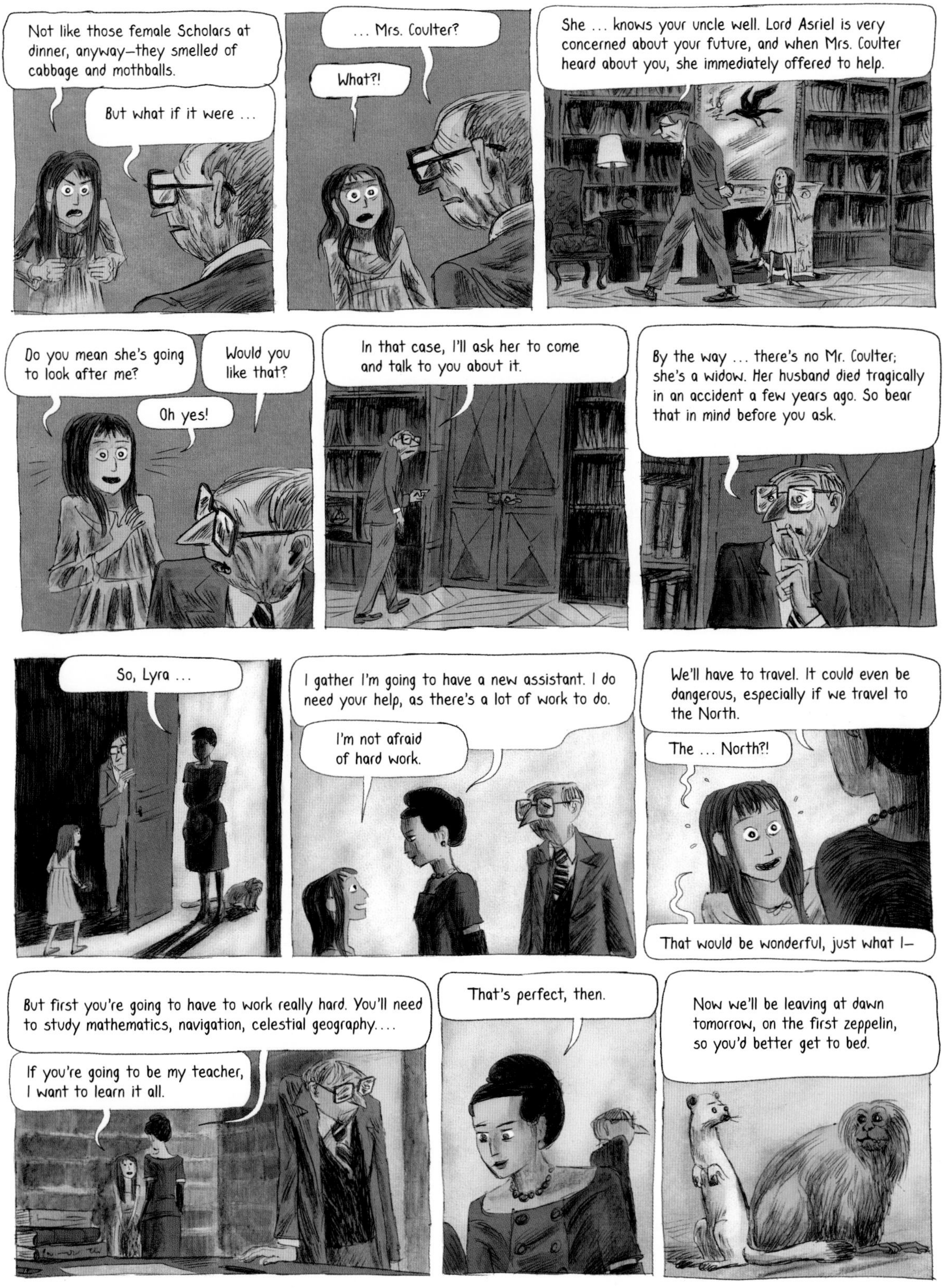
Not like those female Scholars at dinner, anyway—they smelled of cabbage and mothballs.
But what if it were . . .
. . . Mrs. Coulter?
What?!
She . . . knows your uncle well. Lord Asriel is very concerned about your future, and when Mrs. Coulter heard about you, she immediately offered to help.
Do you mean she's going to look after me?
Would you like that?
Oh yes!
In that case, I'll ask her to come and talk to you about it.
By the way . . . there's no Mr. Coulter; she's a widow. Her husband died tragically in an accident a few years ago. So bear that in mind before you ask.
So, Lyra . . .
I gather I'm going to have a new assistant. I do need your help, as there's a lot of work to do.
I'm not afraid of hard work.
We'll have to travel. It could even be dangerous, especially if we travel to the North.
The . . . North?!
That would be wonderful, just what I—
But first you're going to have to work really hard. You'll need to study mathematics, navigation, celestial geography. . . .
If you're going to be my teacher, I want to learn it all.
That's perfect, then.
Now we'll be leaving at dawn tomorrow, on the first zeppelin, so you'd better get to bed.

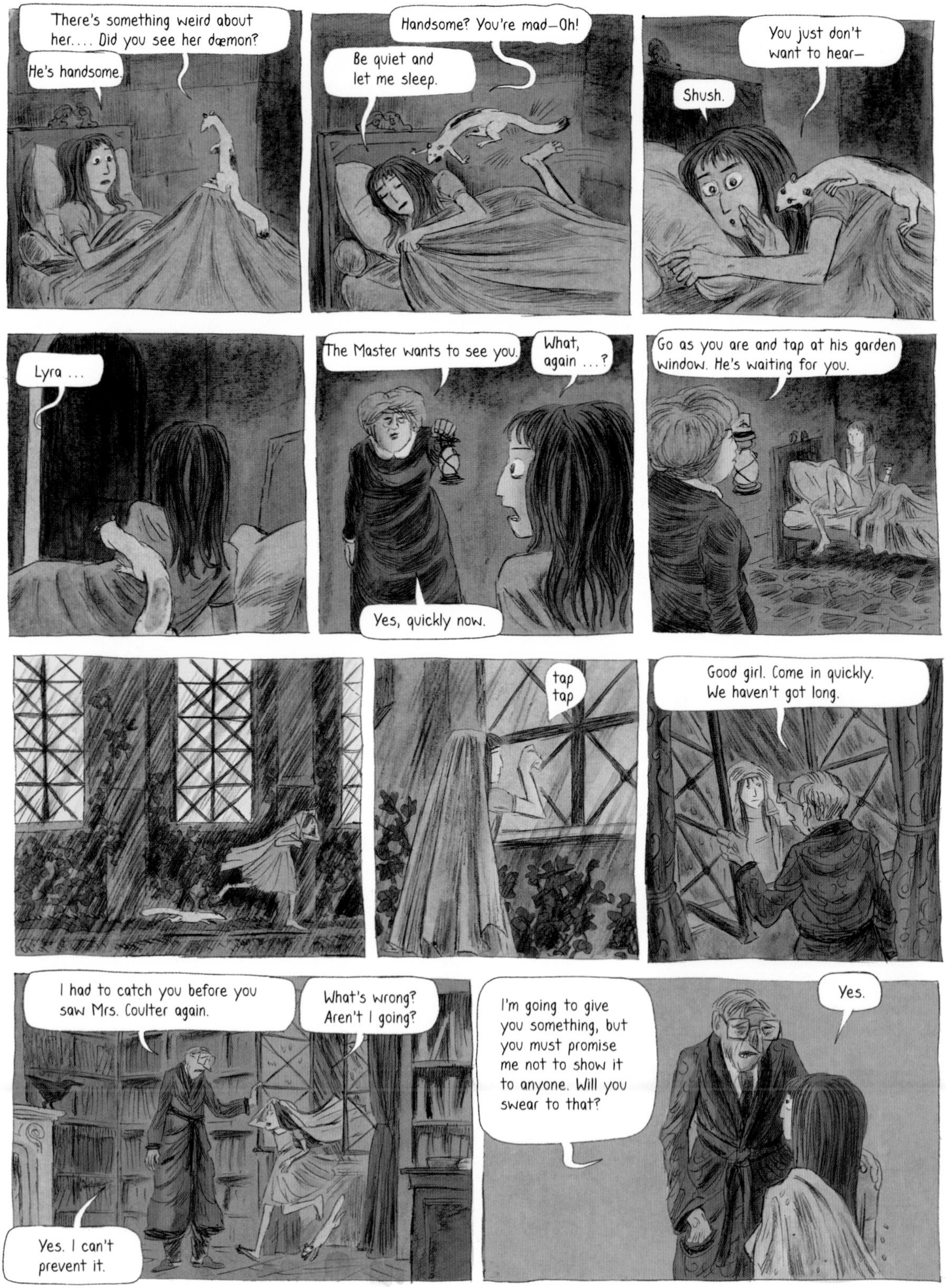
There's something weird about her.... Did you see her dæmon?
He's handsome.
Handsome? You're mad—Oh!
Be quiet and let me sleep.
You just don't want to hear—
Shush.
Lyra ...
The Master wants to see you.
What, again ...?
Yes, quickly now.
Go as you are and tap at his garden window. He's waiting for you.
tap tap
Good girl. Come in quickly. We haven't got long.
I had to catch you before you saw Mrs. Coulter again.
What's wrong? Aren't I going?
Yes. I can't prevent it.
I'm going to give you something, but you must promise me not to show it to anyone. Will you swear to that?
Yes.

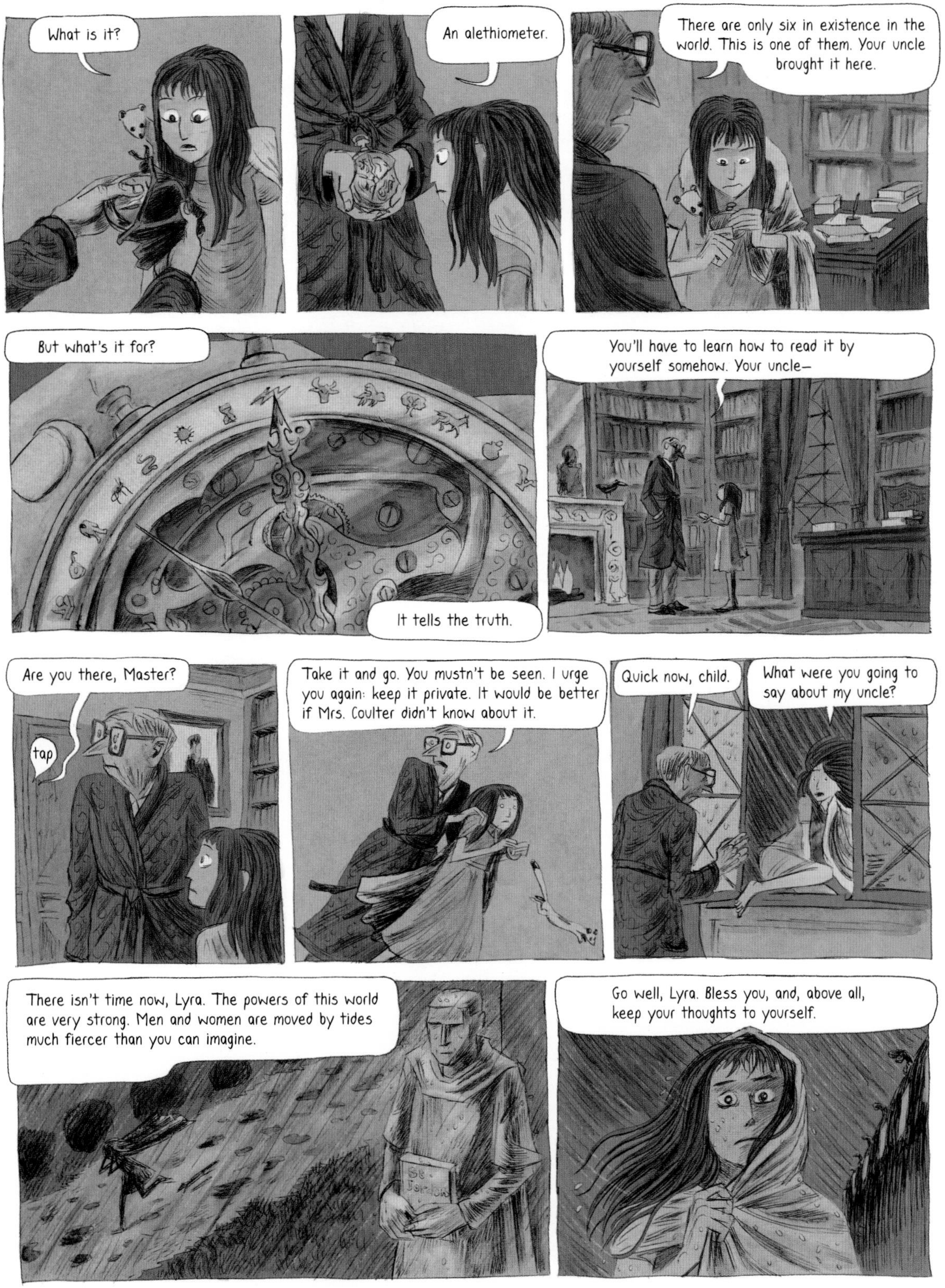
What is it?
An alethiometer.
There are only six in existence in the world. This is one of them. Your uncle brought it here.
But what's it for?
It tells the truth.
You'll have to learn how to read it by yourself somehow. Your uncle—
Are you there, Master?
tap
Take it and go. You mustn't be seen. I urge you again: keep it private. It would be better if Mrs. Coulter didn't know about it.
Quick now, child.
What were you going to say about my uncle?
There isn't time now, Lyra. The powers of this world are very strong. Men and women are moved by tides much fiercer than you can imagine.
Go well, Lyra. Bless you, and, above all, keep your thoughts to yourself.

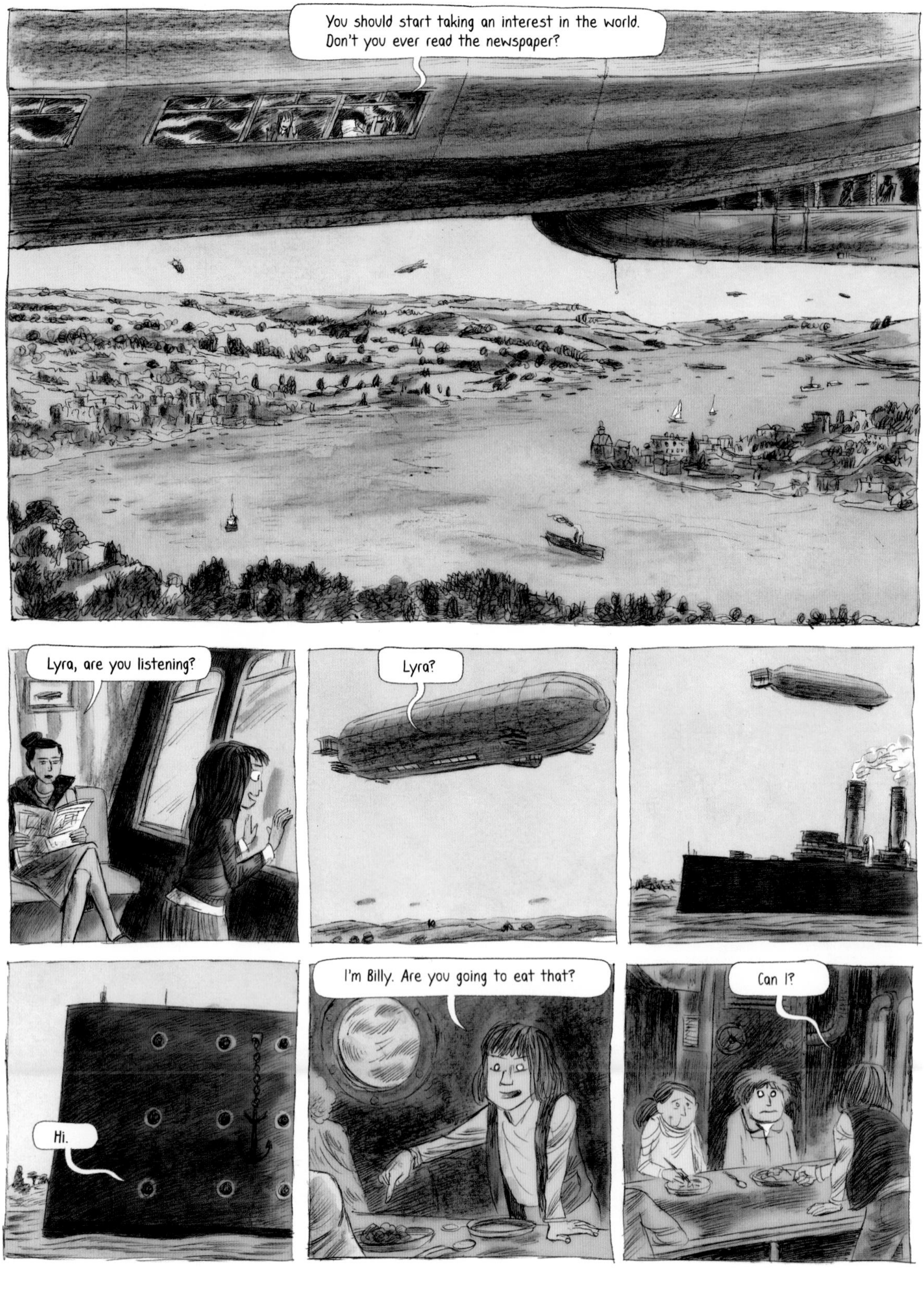
You should start taking an interest in the world. Don't you ever read the newspaper?
Lyra, are you listening?
Lyra?
Hi.
I'm Billy. Are you going to eat that?
Can I?

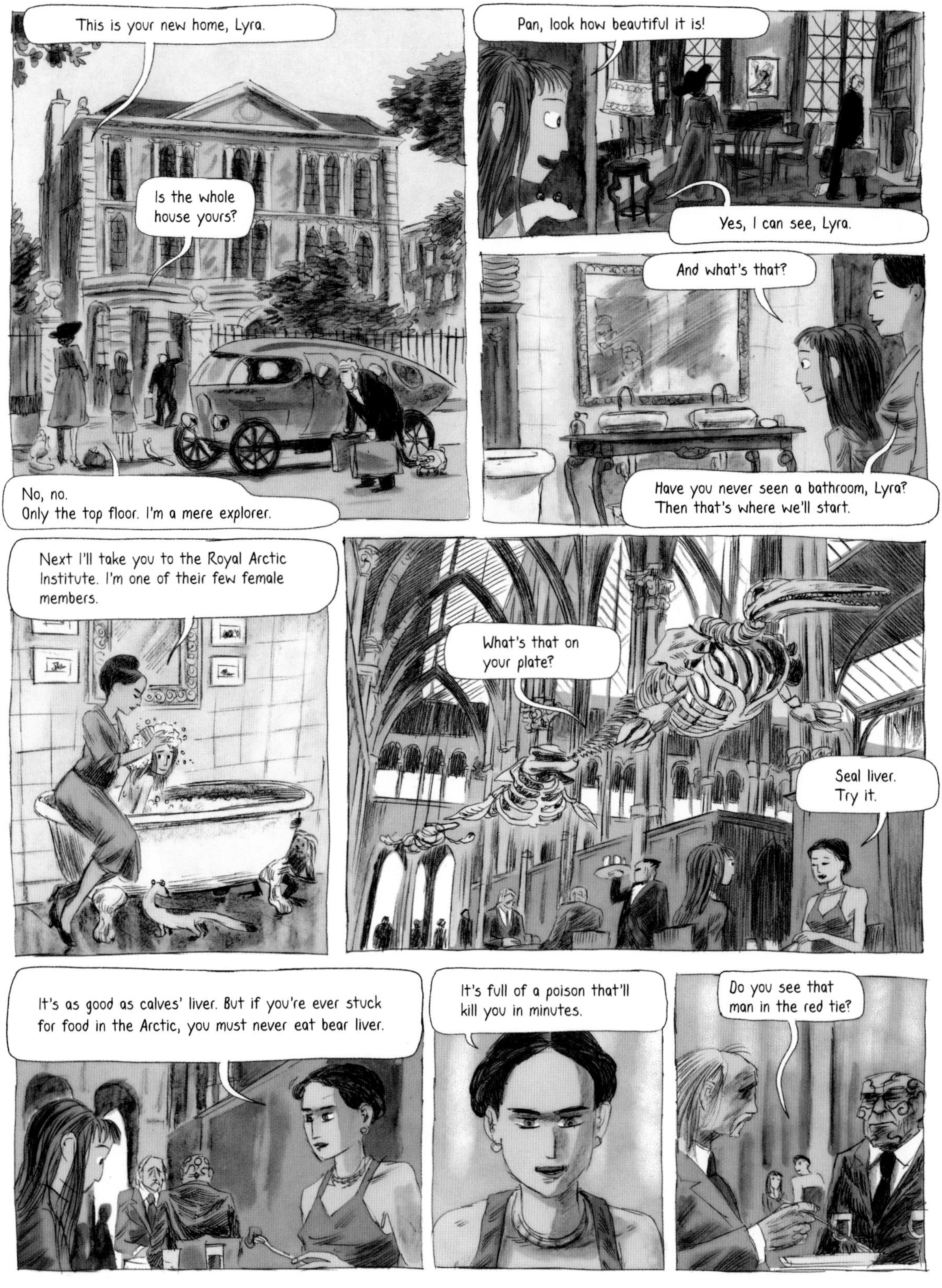
This is your new home, Lyra.
Is the whole house yours?
No, no.
Only the top floor. I'm a mere explorer.
Pan, look how beautiful it is!
Yes, I can see, Lyra.
And what's that?
Have you never seen a bathroom, Lyra? Then that's where we'll start.
Next I'll take you to the Royal Arctic Institute. I'm one of their few female members.
What's that on your plate?
Seal liver. Try it.
It's as good as calves' liver. But if you're ever stuck for food in the Arctic, you must never eat bear liver.
It's full of a poison that'll kill you in minutes.
Do you see that man in the red tie?

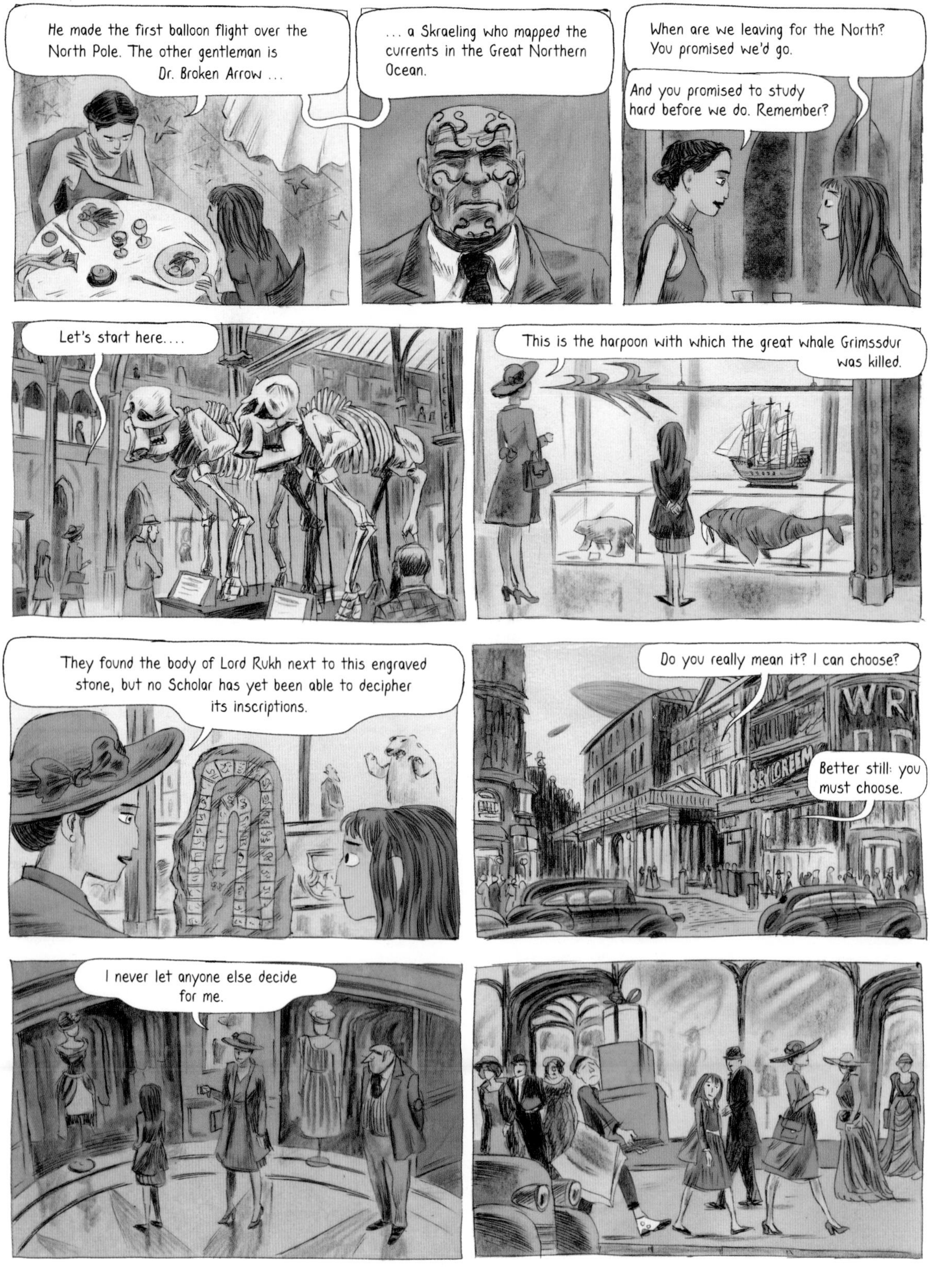
He made the first balloon flight over the North Pole. The other gentleman is Dr. Broken Arrow ...
... a Skraeling who mapped the currents in the Great Northern Ocean.
When are we leaving for the North? You promised we'd go.
And you promised to study hard before we do. Remember?
Let's start here....
This is the harpoon with which the great whale Grimssdur was killed.
They found the body of Lord Rukh next to this engraved stone, but no Scholar has yet been able to decipher its inscriptions.
Do you really mean it? I can choose?
Better still: you must choose.
I never let anyone else decide for me.

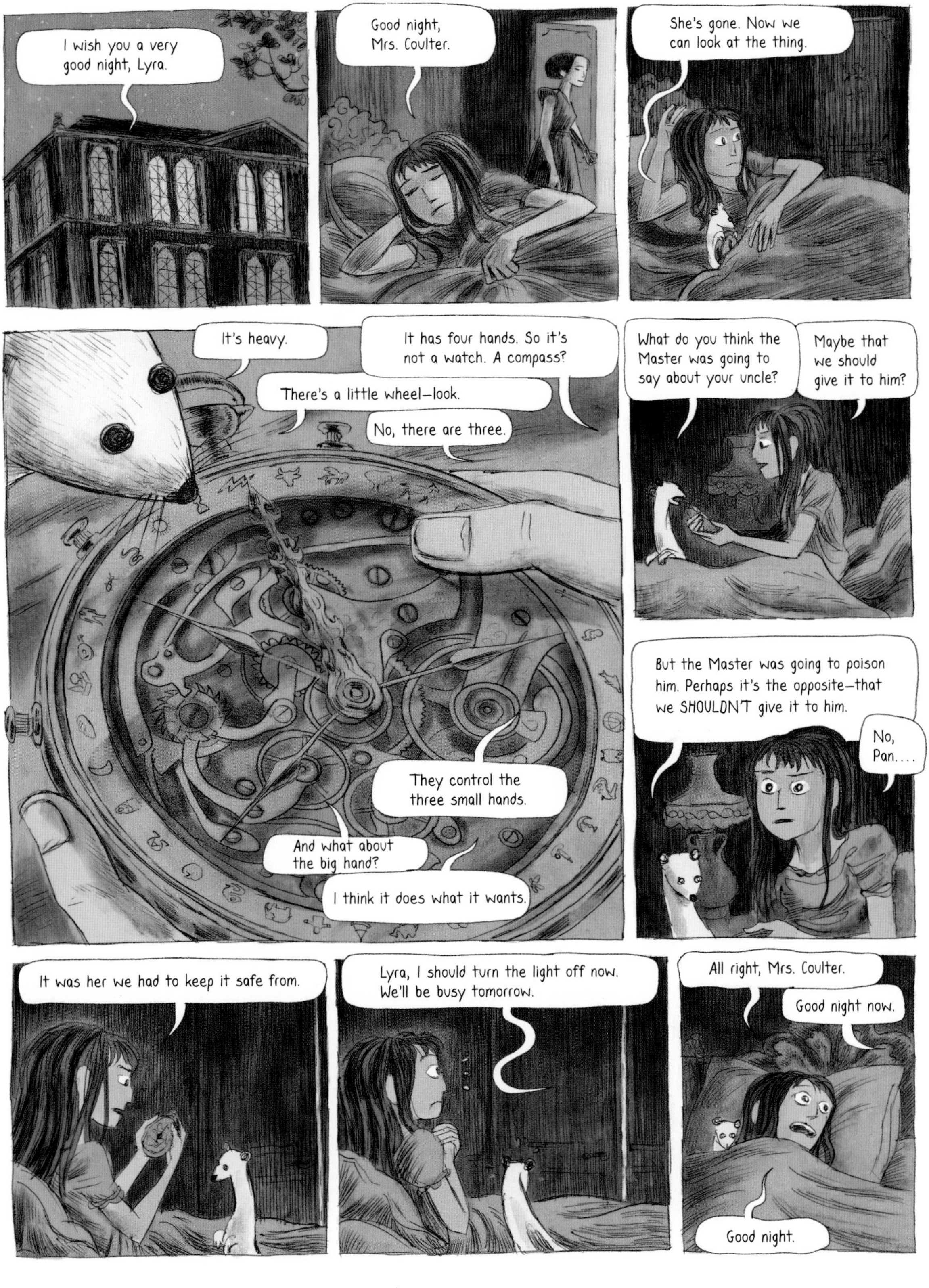
I wish you a very good night, Lyra.
Good night, Mrs. Coulter.
She's gone. Now we can look at the thing.
It's heavy.
It has four hands. So it's not a watch. A compass?
There's a little wheel—look.
No, there are three.
They control the three small hands.
And what about the big hand?
I think it does what it wants.
What do you think the Master was going to say about your uncle?
Maybe that we should give it to him?
But the Master was going to poison him. Perhaps it's the opposite—that we SHOULDN'T give it to him.
No, Pan....
It was her we had to keep it safe from.
Lyra, I should turn the light off now. We'll be busy tomorrow.
All right, Mrs. Coulter.
Good night now.
Good night.

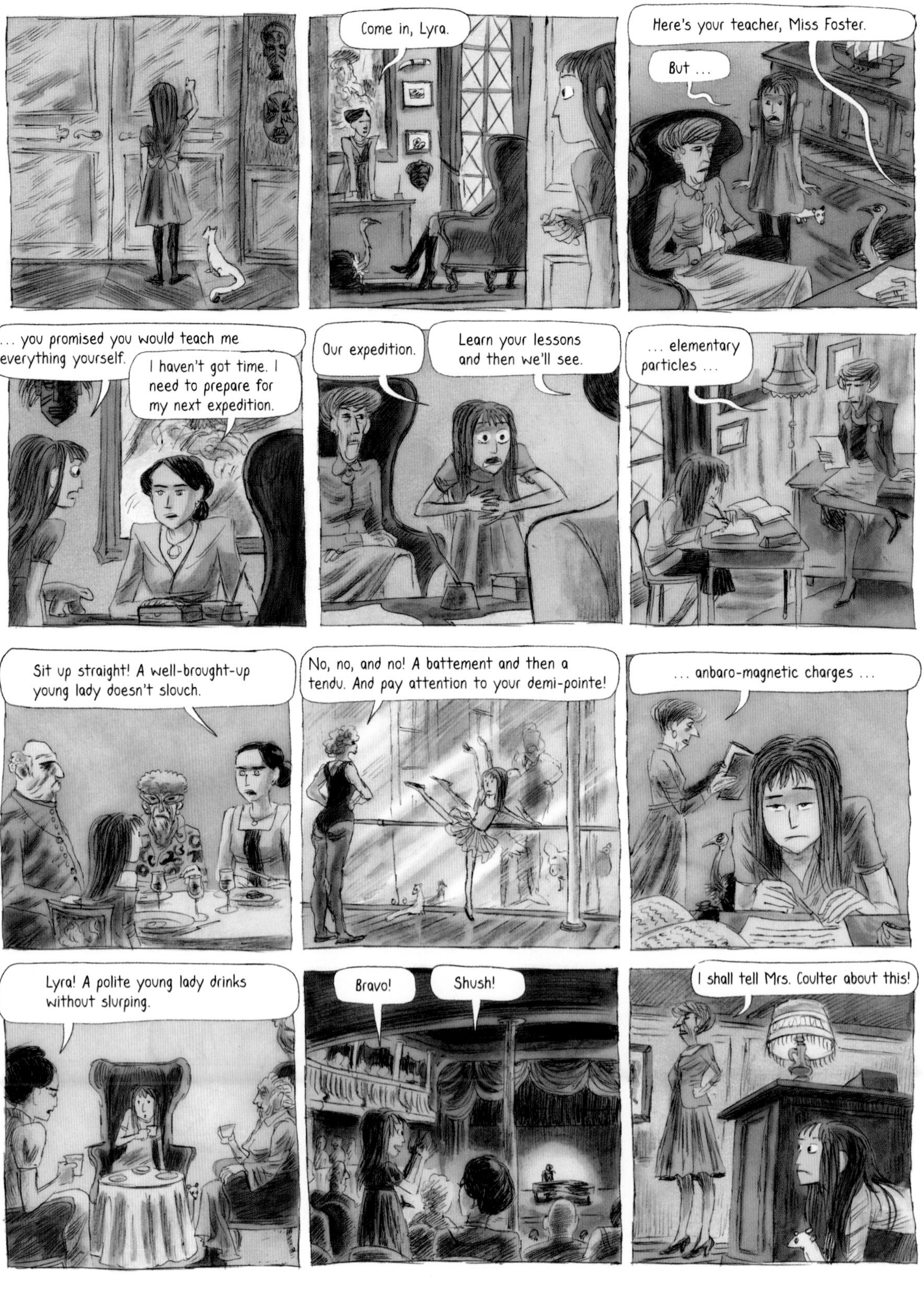
Come in, Lyra.
Here's your teacher, Miss Foster.
But ...
... you promised you would teach me everything yourself.
I haven't got time. I need to prepare for my next expedition.
Our expedition.
Learn your lessons and then we'll see.
... elementary particles ...
Sit up straight! A well-brought-up young lady doesn't slouch.
No, no, and no! A battement and then a tendu. And pay attention to your demi-pointe!
... anbaro-magnetic charges ...
Lyra! A polite young lady drinks without slurping.
Bravo!
Shush!
I shall tell Mrs. Coulter about this!

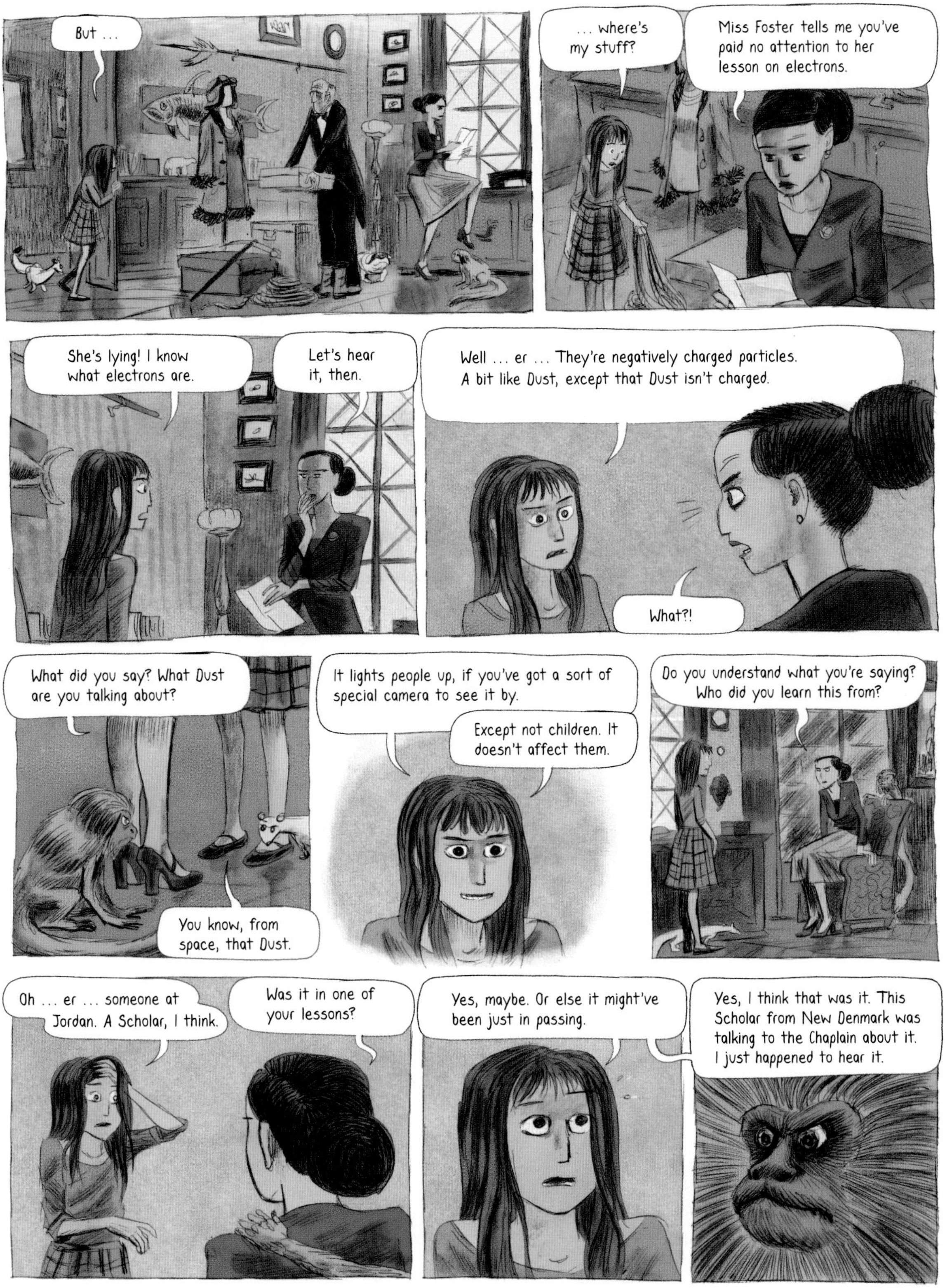

But ...
... where's my stuff?
Miss Foster tells me you've paid no attention to her lesson on electrons.
She's lying! I know what electrons are.
Let's hear it, then.
Well ... er ... They're negatively charged particles. A bit like Dust, except that Dust isn't charged.
What?!
What did you say? What Dust are you talking about?
You know, from space, that Dust.
It lights people up, if you've got a sort of special camera to see it by.
Except not children. It doesn't affect them.
Do you understand what you're saying? Who did you learn this from?
Oh ... er ... someone at Jordan. A Scholar, I think.
Was it in one of your lessons?
Yes, maybe. Or else it might've been just in passing.
Yes, I think that was it. This Scholar from New Denmark was talking to the Chaplain about it. I just happened to hear it.

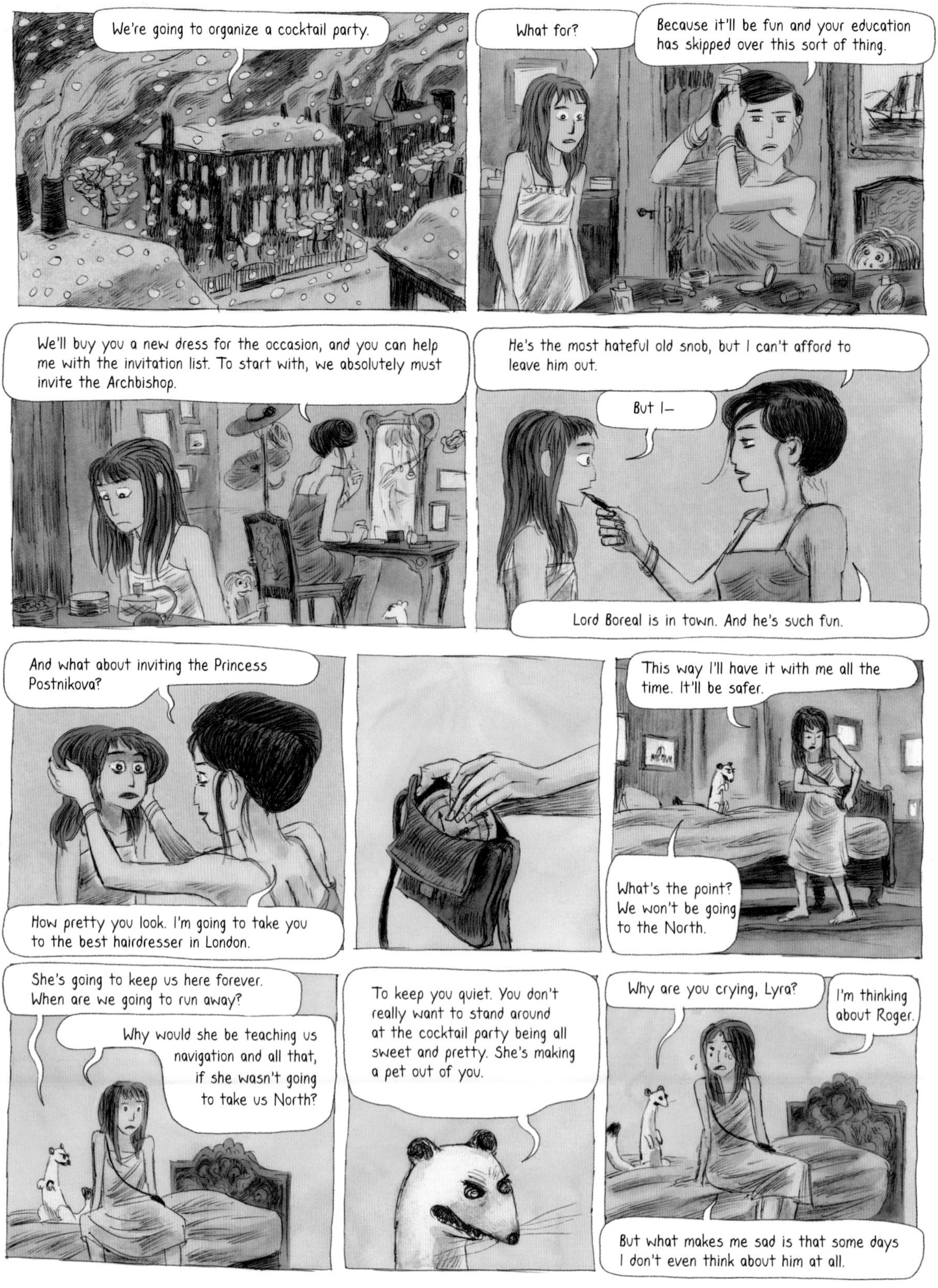
We're going to organize a cocktail party.
What for?
Because it'll be fun and your education has skipped over this sort of thing.
We'll buy you a new dress for the occasion, and you can help me with the invitation list. To start with, we absolutely must invite the Archbishop.
He's the most hateful old snob, but I can't afford to leave him out.
But I—
Lord Boreal is in town. And he's such fun.
And what about inviting the Princess Postnikova?
How pretty you look. I'm going to take you to the best hairdresser in London.
This way I'll have it with me all the time. It'll be safer.
What's the point? We won't be going to the North.
She's going to keep us here forever. When are we going to run away?
Why would she be teaching us navigation and all that, if she wasn't going to take us North?
To keep you quiet. You don't really want to stand around at the cocktail party being all sweet and pretty. She's making a pet out of you.
Why are you crying, Lyra?
I'm thinking about Roger.
But what makes me sad is that some days I don't even think about him at all.

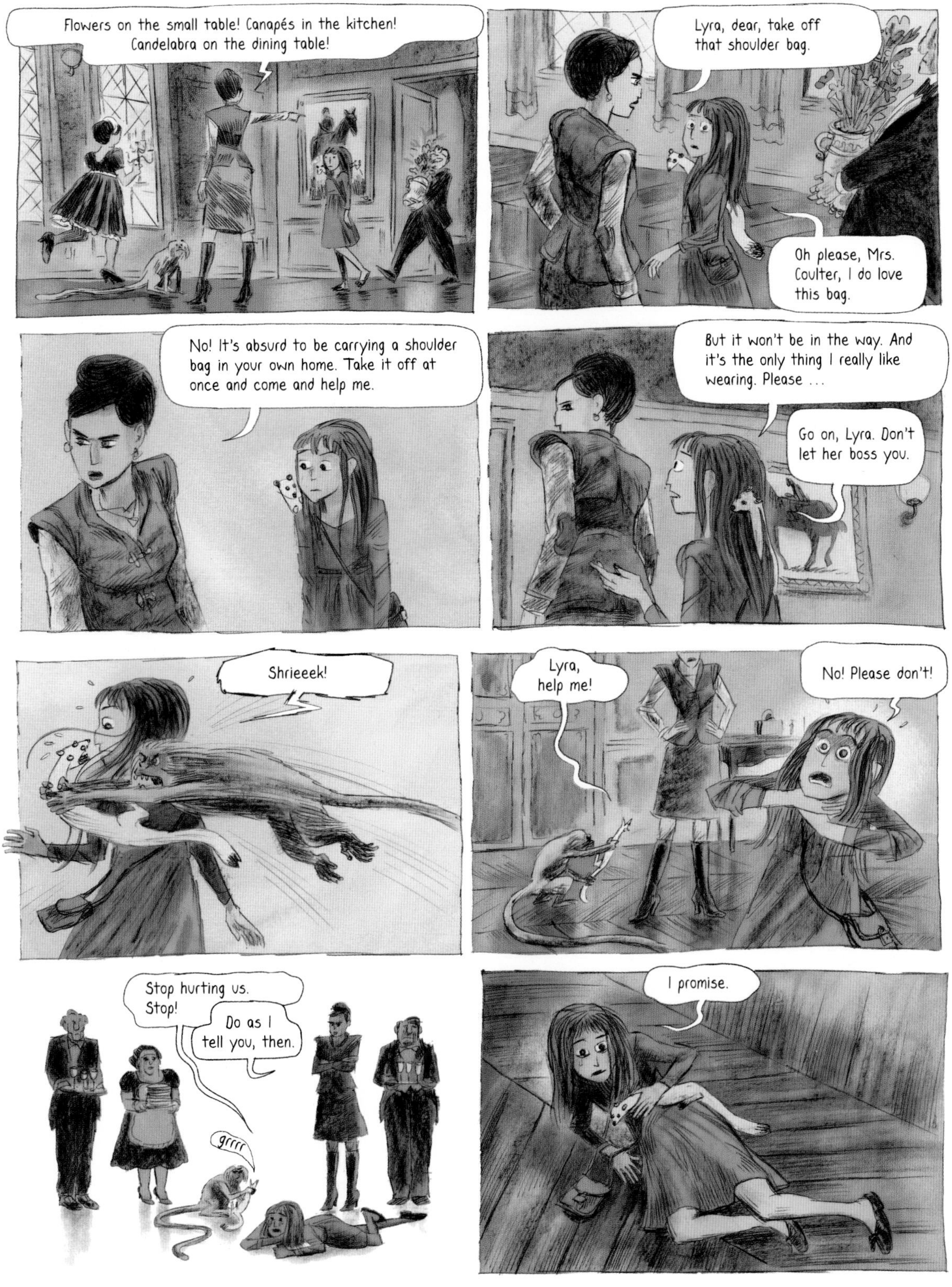
Flowers on the small table! Canapés in the kitchen! Candelabra on the dining table!
Lyra, dear, take off that shoulder bag.
Oh please, Mrs. Coulter, I do love this bag.
No! It's absurd to be carrying a shoulder bag in your own home. Take it off at once and come and help me.
But it won't be in the way. And it's the only thing I really like wearing. Please . . .
Go on, Lyra. Don't let her boss you.
Shrieeek!
Lyra, help me!
No! Please don't!
Stop hurting us. Stop!
Do as I tell you, then.
grrrr
I promise.

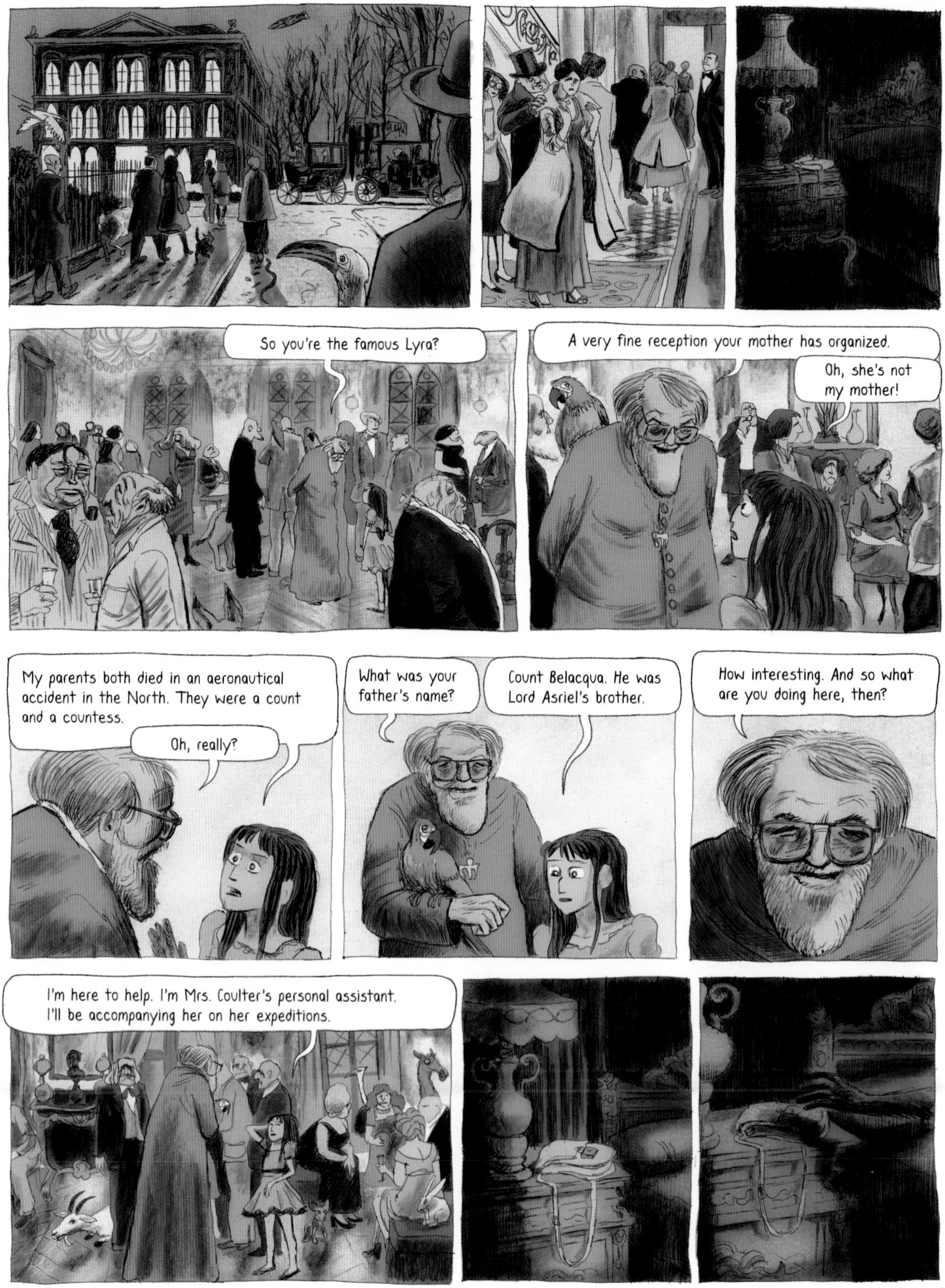
So you're the famous Lyra?
A very fine reception your mother has organized.
Oh, she's not my mother!
My parents both died in an aeronautical accident in the North. They were a count and a countess.
Oh, really?
What was your father's name?
Count Belacqua. He was Lord Asriel's brother.
How interesting. And so what are you doing here, then?
I'm here to help. I'm Mrs. Coulter's personal assistant. I'll be accompanying her on her expeditions.

... Dust ...

... attracted by human beings ...

... by adults but not children ...

The General Oblation Board is entirely her own project.

But you, little lady...

... you don't need to be frightened of the General Oblation Board, do you?

Oh, I'm never scared. Not of gyptians who sell children like slaves to the Turks of the Bosphorus. Or of the werewolf at Godstow Priory ...

... not even of the Gobblers.

The Gobblers?

Yes, that's what the tabloids call the General Oblation Board. From the initials, you see.

Why "Oblation," though?

It's an old story. Back in the Middle Ages, parents gave their children to the Church to become monks or nuns. The unfortunate brats were known as "oblates," which means a sacrifice, an offering, something of that sort.

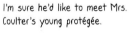

I see. Mrs. Coulter took up the idea again when she became interested in Dust.

More than an idea— it's a passion.

They say the children don't suffer, though.

Why don't you go and have a chat with Lord Boreal?

I'm sure he'd like to meet Mrs. Coulter's young protégée.

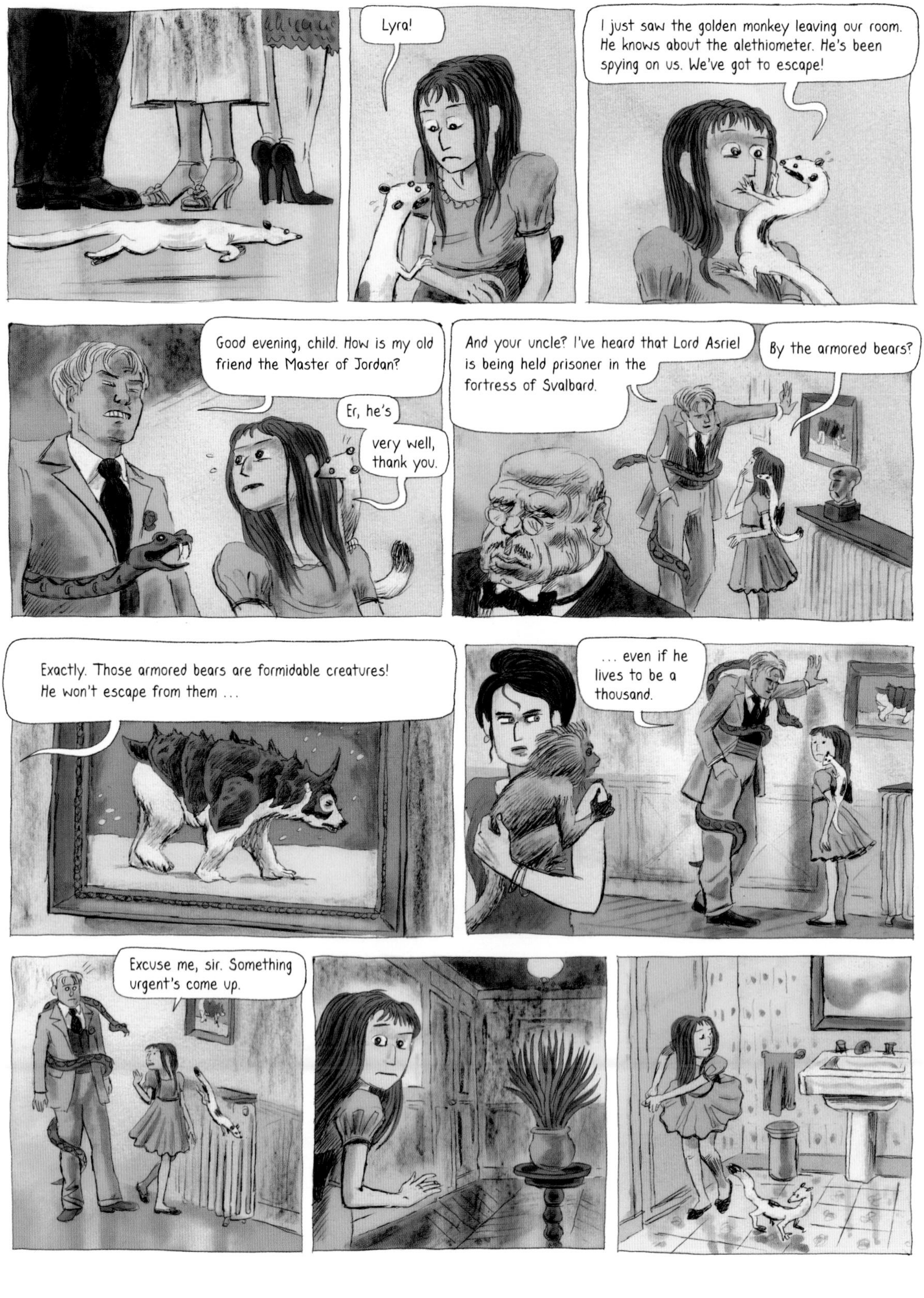
Lyra!
I just saw the golden monkey leaving our room. He knows about the alethiometer. He's been spying on us. We've got to escape!
Good evening, child. How is my old friend the Master of Jordan?
Er, he's
very well, thank you.
And your uncle? I've heard that Lord Asriel is being held prisoner in the fortress of Svalbard.
By the armored bears?
Exactly. Those armored bears are formidable creatures! He won't escape from them ...
... even if he lives to be a thousand.
Excuse me, sir. Something urgent's come up.

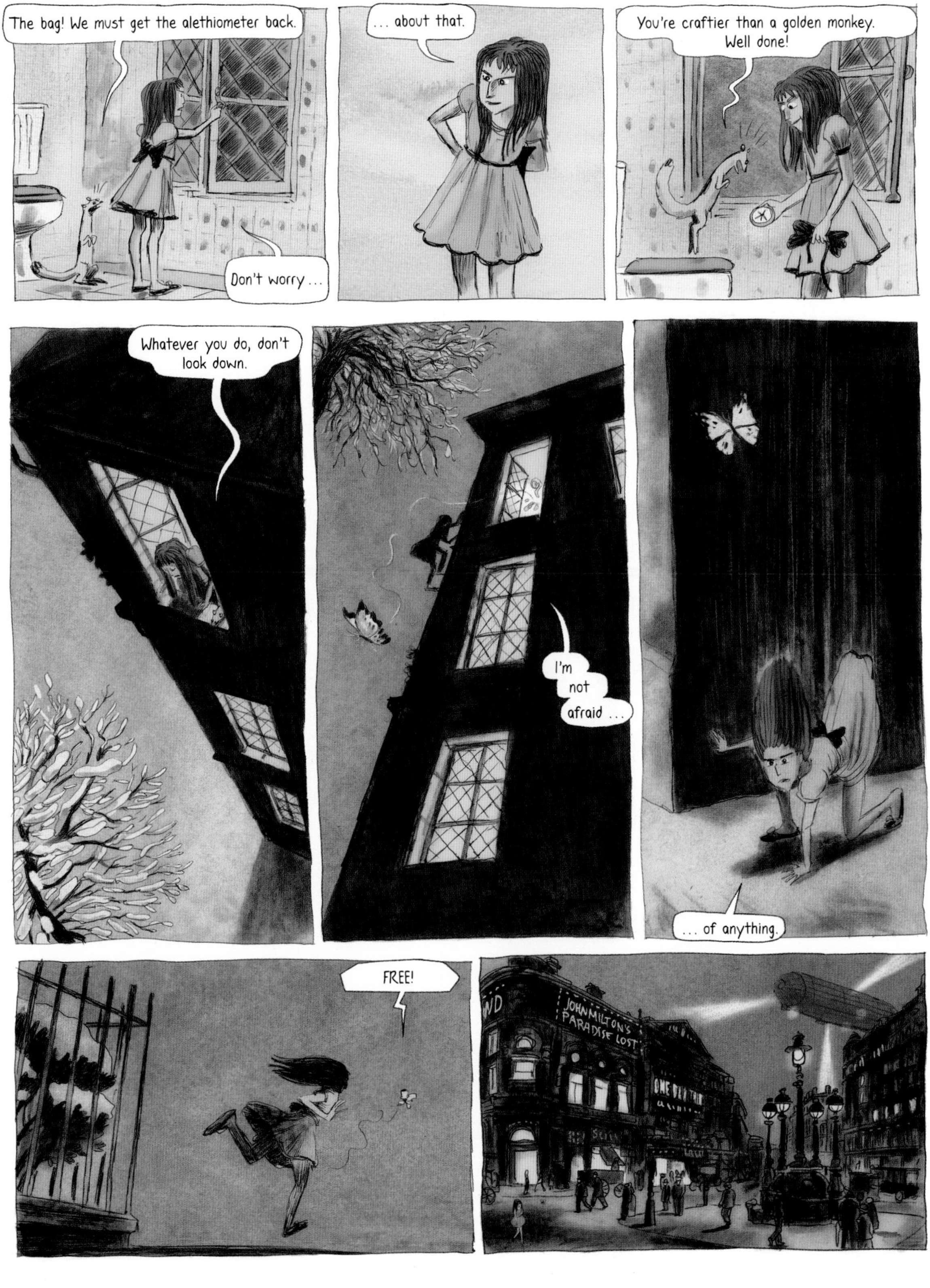
The bag! We must get the alethiometer back.
Don't worry ...
... about that.
You're craftier than a golden monkey. Well done!
Whatever you do, don't look down.
I'm not afraid ...
... of anything.
FREE!
JOHN MILTON'S PARADISE LOST

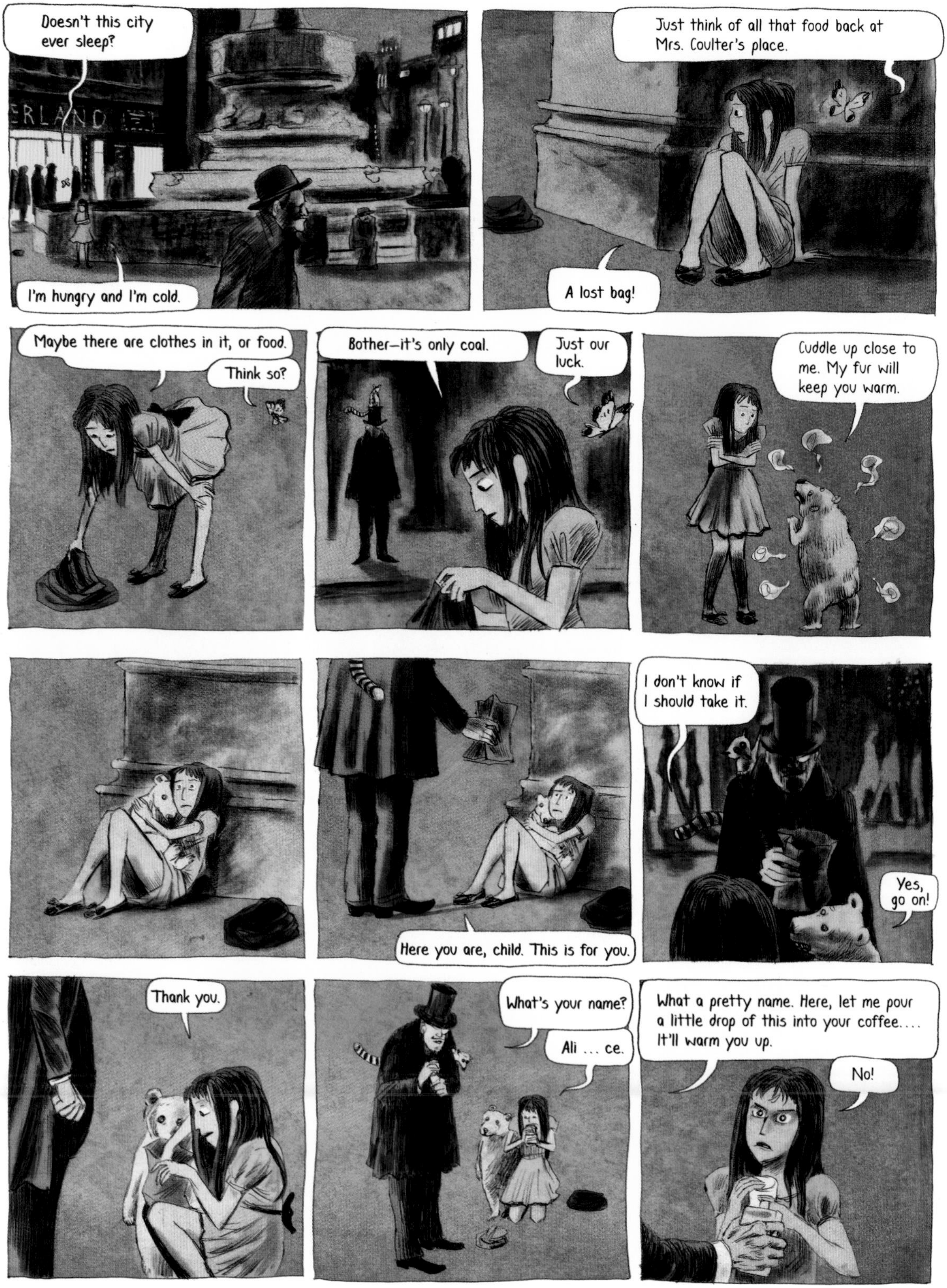

Doesn't this city ever sleep?
I'm hungry and I'm cold.
Just think of all that food back at Mrs. Coulter's place.
A lost bag!
Maybe there are clothes in it, or food.
Think so?
Bother—it's only coal.
Just our luck.
Cuddle up close to me. My fur will keep you warm.
Here you are, child. This is for you.
I don't know if I should take it.
Yes, go on!
Thank you.
What's your name?
Ali ... ce.
What a pretty name. Here, let me pour a little drop of this into your coffee.... It'll warm you up.
No!

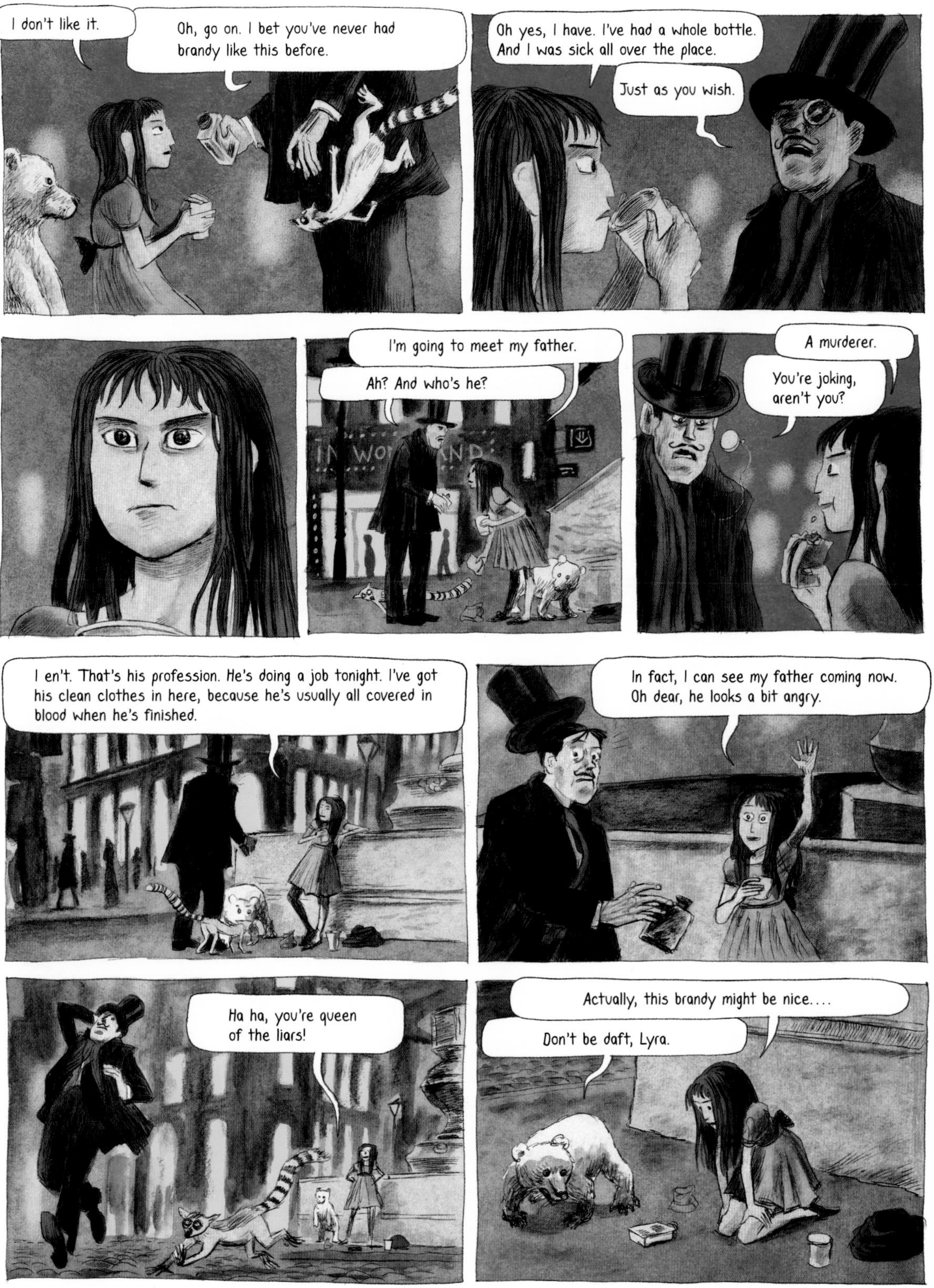

I don't like it.
Oh, go on. I bet you've never had brandy like this before.
Oh yes, I have. I've had a whole bottle. And I was sick all over the place.
Just as you wish.
I'm going to meet my father.
Ah? And who's he?
A murderer.
You're joking, aren't you?
I en't. That's his profession. He's doing a job tonight. I've got his clean clothes in here, because he's usually all covered in blood when he's finished.
In fact, I can see my father coming now. Oh dear, he looks a bit angry.
Ha ha, you're queen of the liars!
Actually, this brandy might be nice....
Don't be daft, Lyra.

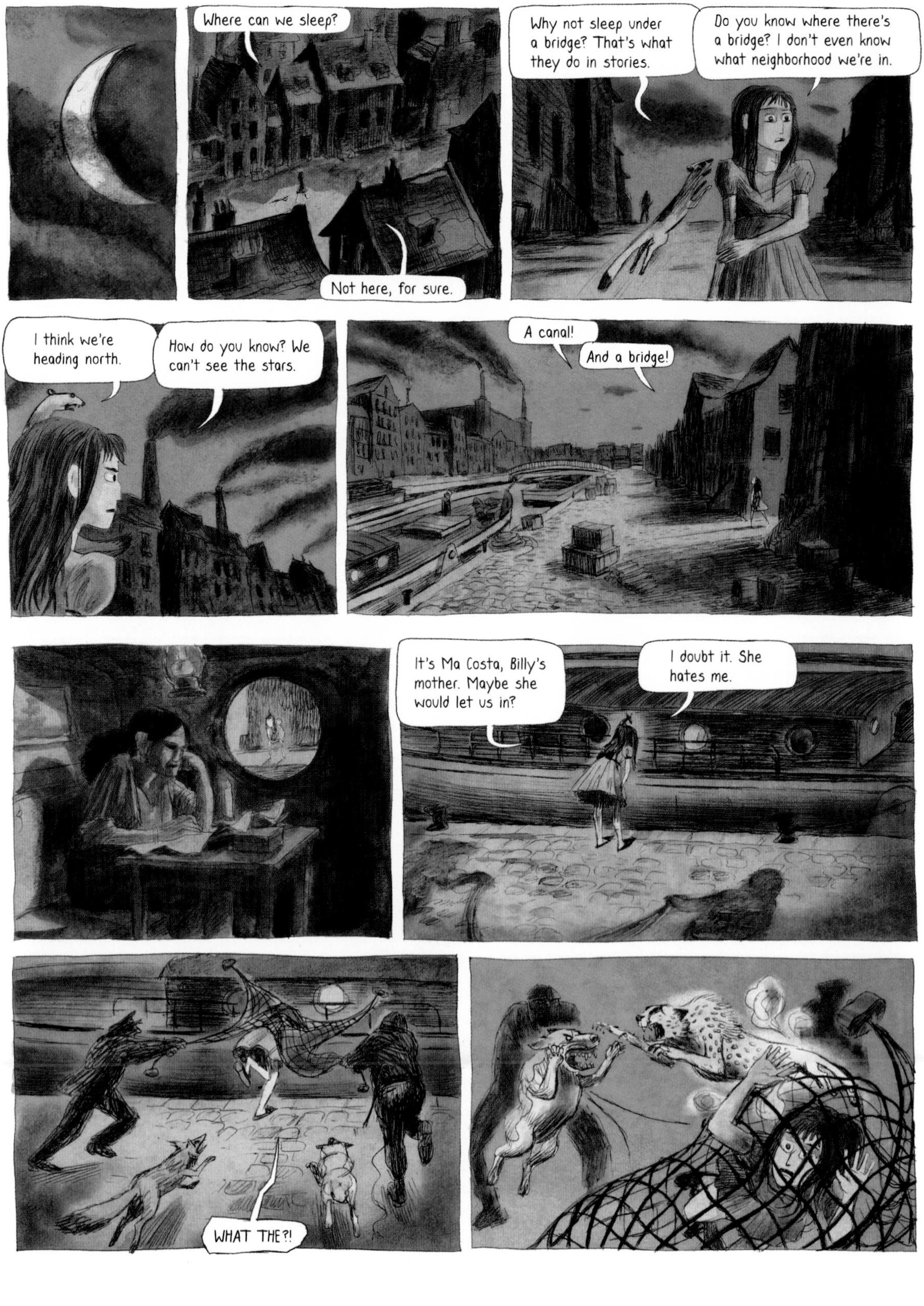
Where can we sleep?
Not here, for sure.
Why not sleep under a bridge? That's what they do in stories.
Do you know where there's a bridge? I don't even know what neighborhood we're in.
I think we're heading north.
How do you know? We can't see the stars.
A canal!
And a bridge!
It's Ma Costa, Billy's mother. Maybe she would let us in?
I doubt it. She hates me.
WHAT THE?!

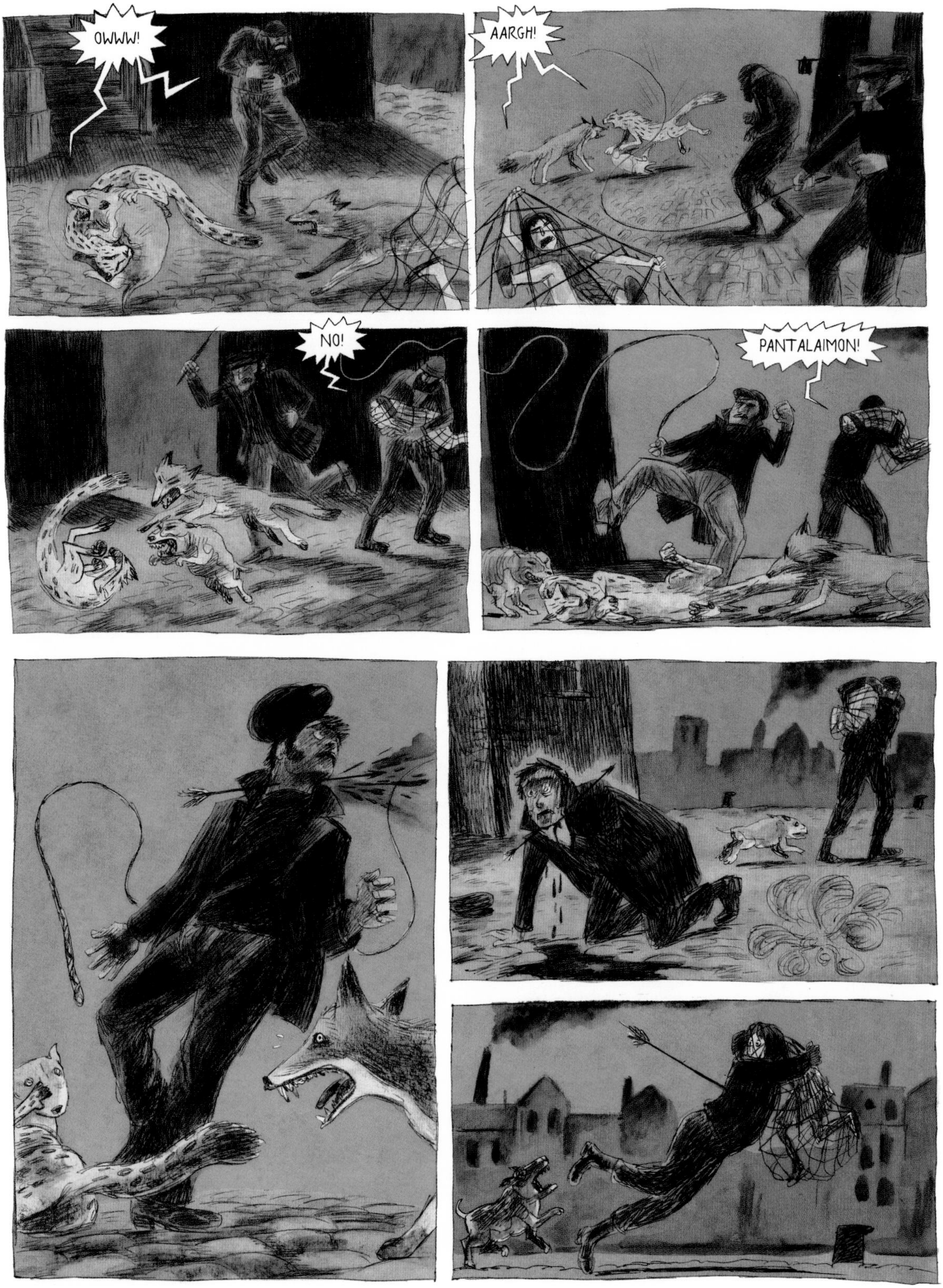
OWWW!
AARGH!
NO!
PANTALAIMON!

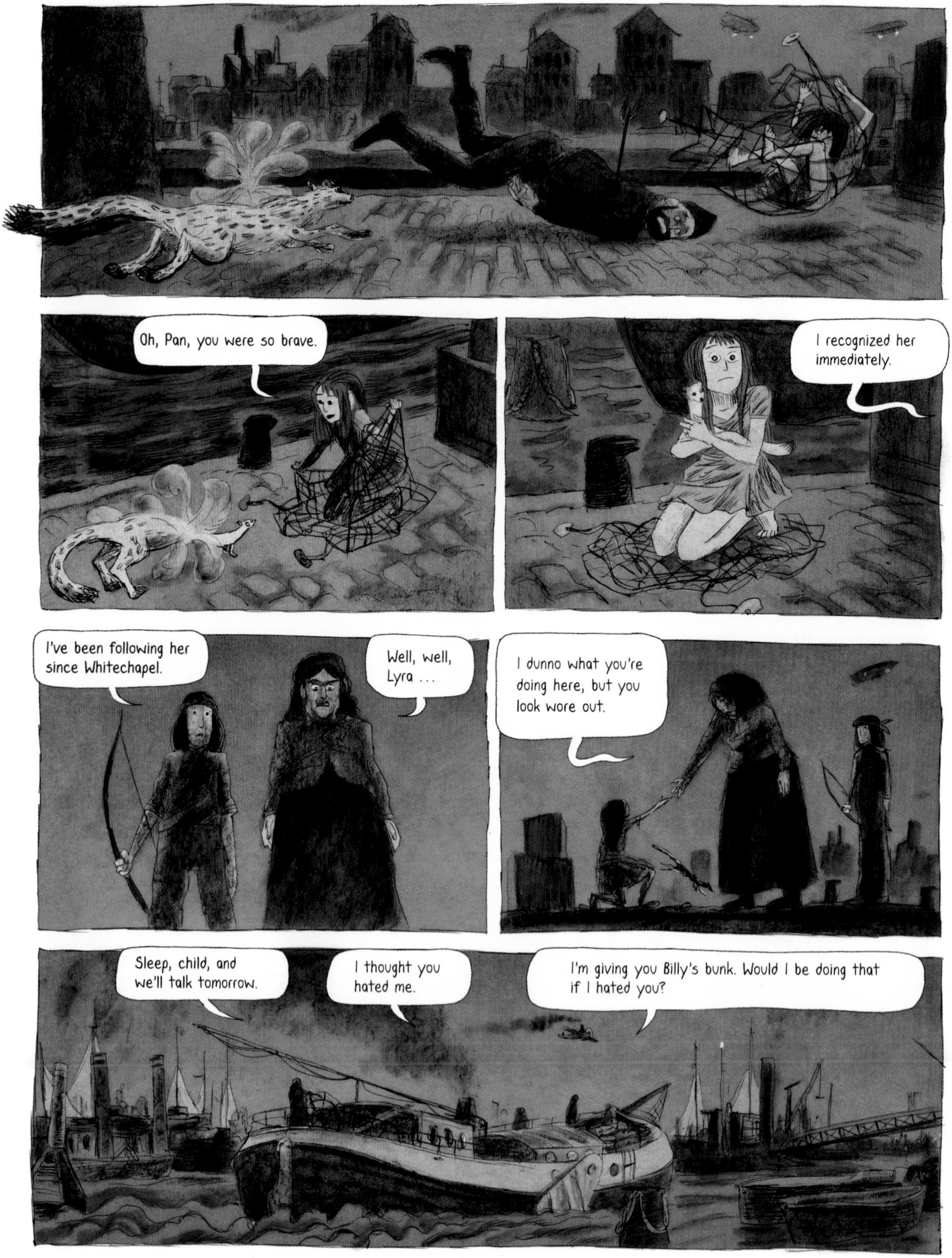
Oh, Pan, you were so brave.
I recognized her immediately.
I've been following her since Whitechapel.
Well, well, Lyra . . .
I dunno what you're doing here, but you look wore out.
Sleep, child, and we'll talk tomorrow.
I thought you hated me.
I'm giving you Billy's bunk. Would I be doing that if I hated you?

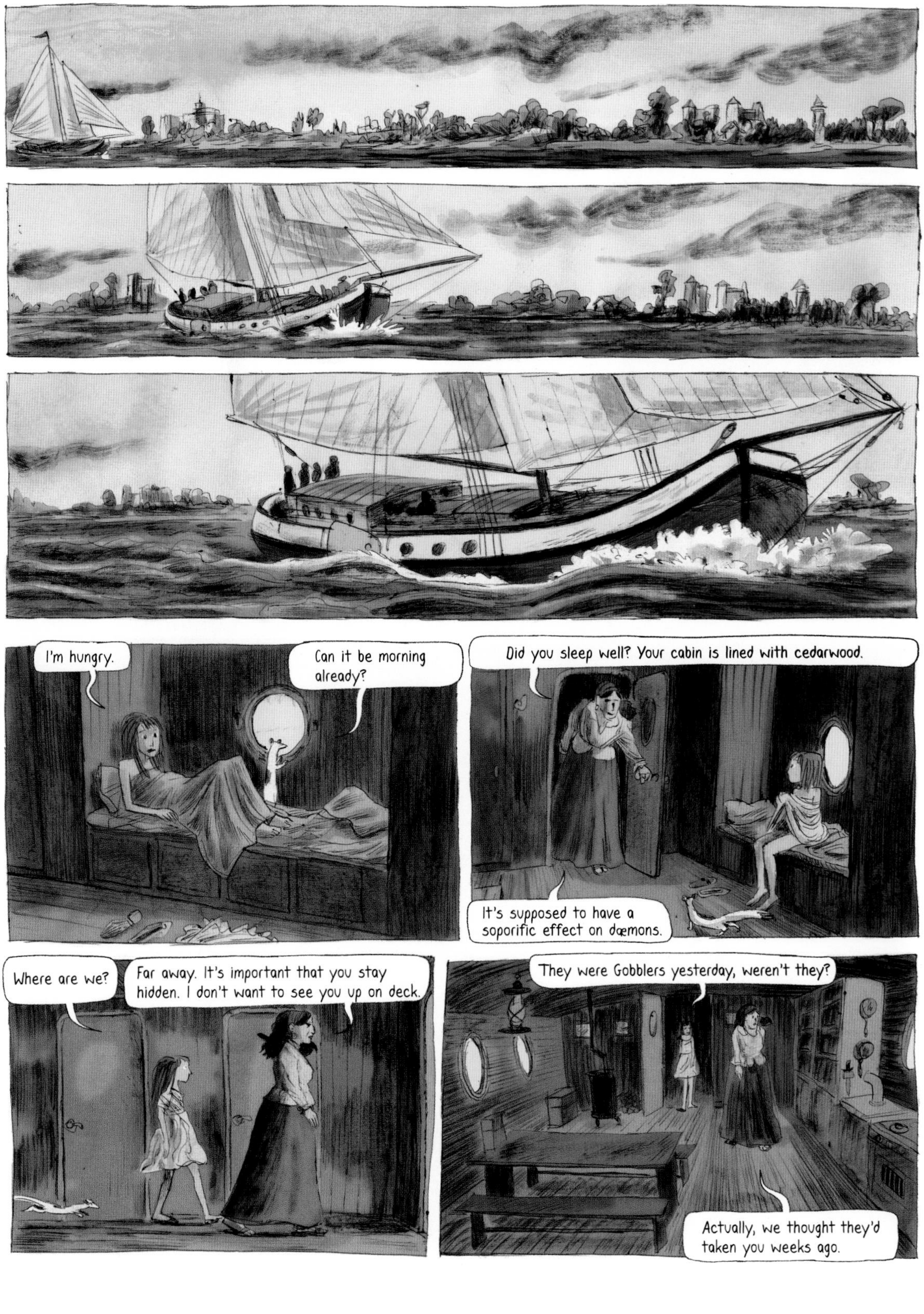
I'm hungry.
Can it be morning already?
Did you sleep well? Your cabin is lined with cedarwood.
It's supposed to have a soporific effect on dæmons.
Where are we?
Far away. It's important that you stay hidden. I don't want to see you up on deck.
They were Gobblers yesterday, weren't they?
Actually, we thought they'd taken you weeks ago.

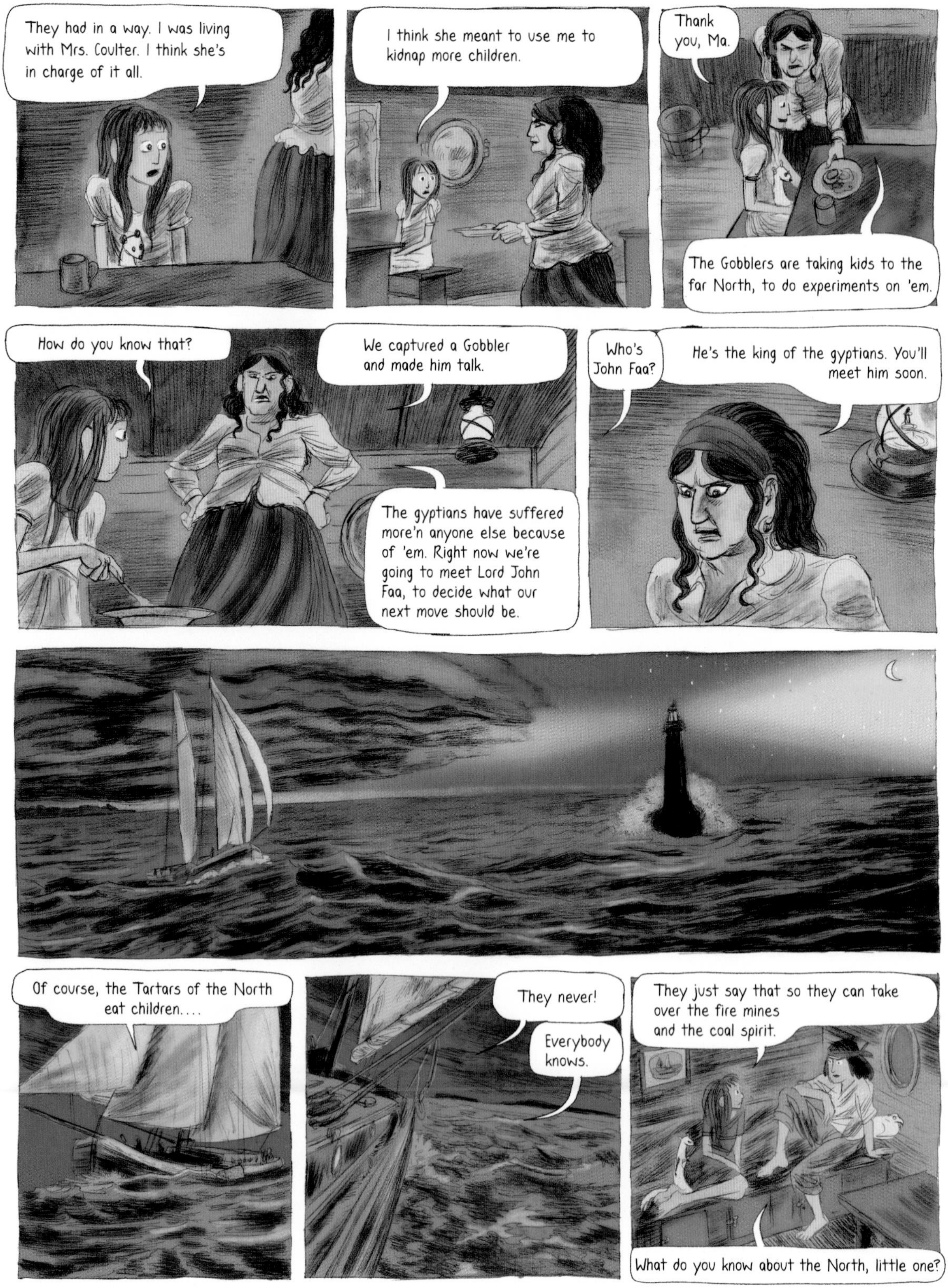
They had in a way. I was living with Mrs. Coulter. I think she's in charge of it all.
I think she meant to use me to kidnap more children.
Thank you, Ma.
The Gobblers are taking kids to the far North, to do experiments on 'em.
How do you know that?
We captured a Gobbler and made him talk.
The gyptians have suffered more'n anyone else because of 'em. Right now we're going to meet Lord John Faa, to decide what our next move should be.
Who's John Faa?
He's the king of the gyptians. You'll meet him soon.
Of course, the Tartars of the North eat children....
They never!
Everybody knows.
They just say that so they can take over the fire mines and the coal spirit.
What do you know about the North, little one?

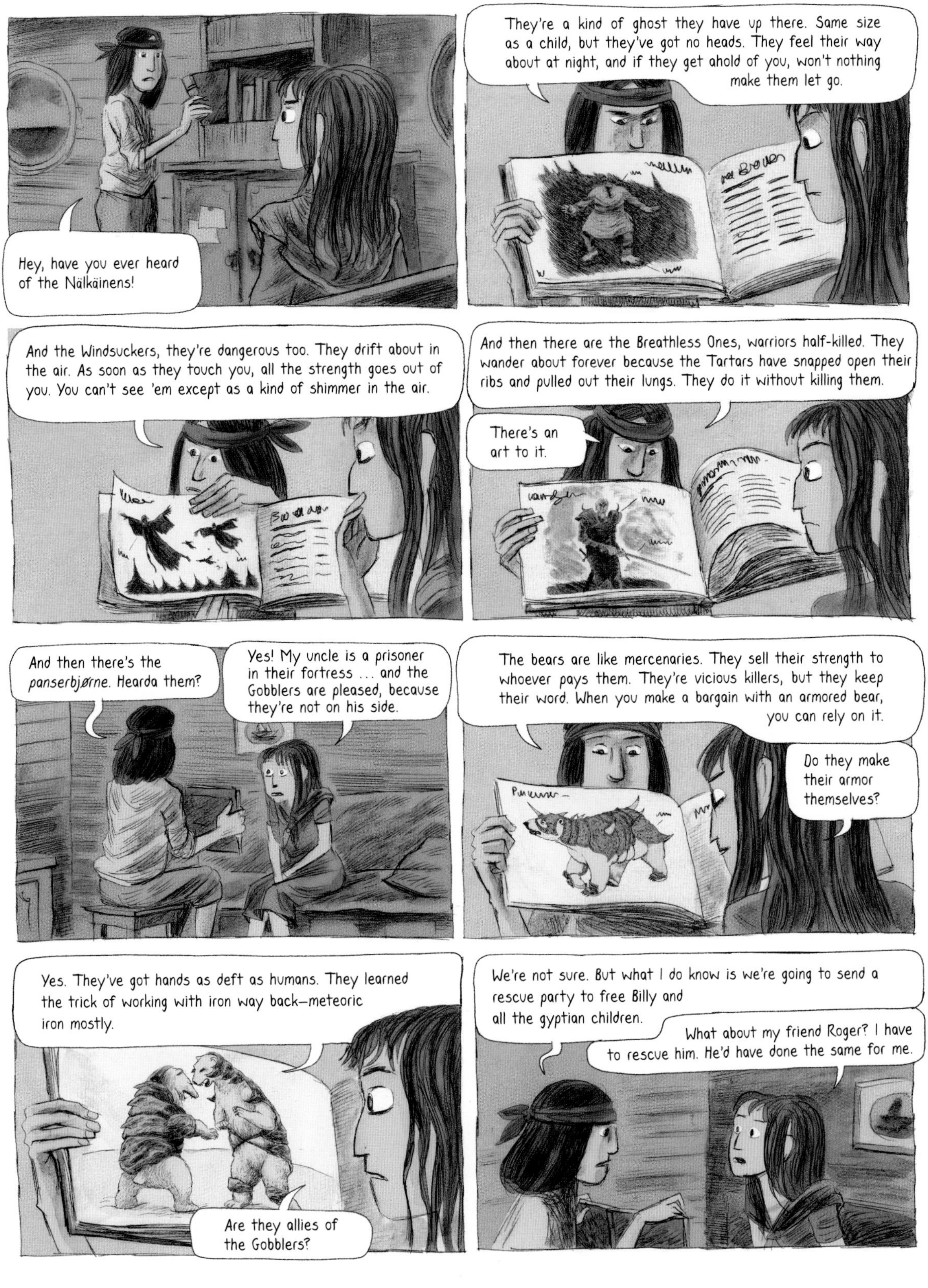
Hey, have you ever heard of the Nälkäinens!
They're a kind of ghost they have up there. Same size as a child, but they've got no heads. They feel their way about at night, and if they get ahold of you, won't nothing make them let go.
And the Windsuckers, they're dangerous too. They drift about in the air. As soon as they touch you, all the strength goes out of you. You can't see 'em except as a kind of shimmer in the air.
And then there are the Breathless Ones, warriors half-killed. They wander about forever because the Tartars have snapped open their ribs and pulled out their lungs. They do it without killing them.
There's an art to it.
And then there's the *panserbjørne*. Hearda them?
Yes! My uncle is a prisoner in their fortress ... and the Gobblers are pleased, because they're not on his side.
The bears are like mercenaries. They sell their strength to whoever pays them. They're vicious killers, but they keep their word. When you make a bargain with an armored bear, you can rely on it.
Do they make their armor themselves?
Yes. They've got hands as deft as humans. They learned the trick of working with iron way back—meteoric iron mostly.
Are they allies of the Gobblers?
We're not sure. But what I do know is we're going to send a rescue party to free Billy and all the gyptian children.
What about my friend Roger? I have to rescue him. He'd have done the same for me.

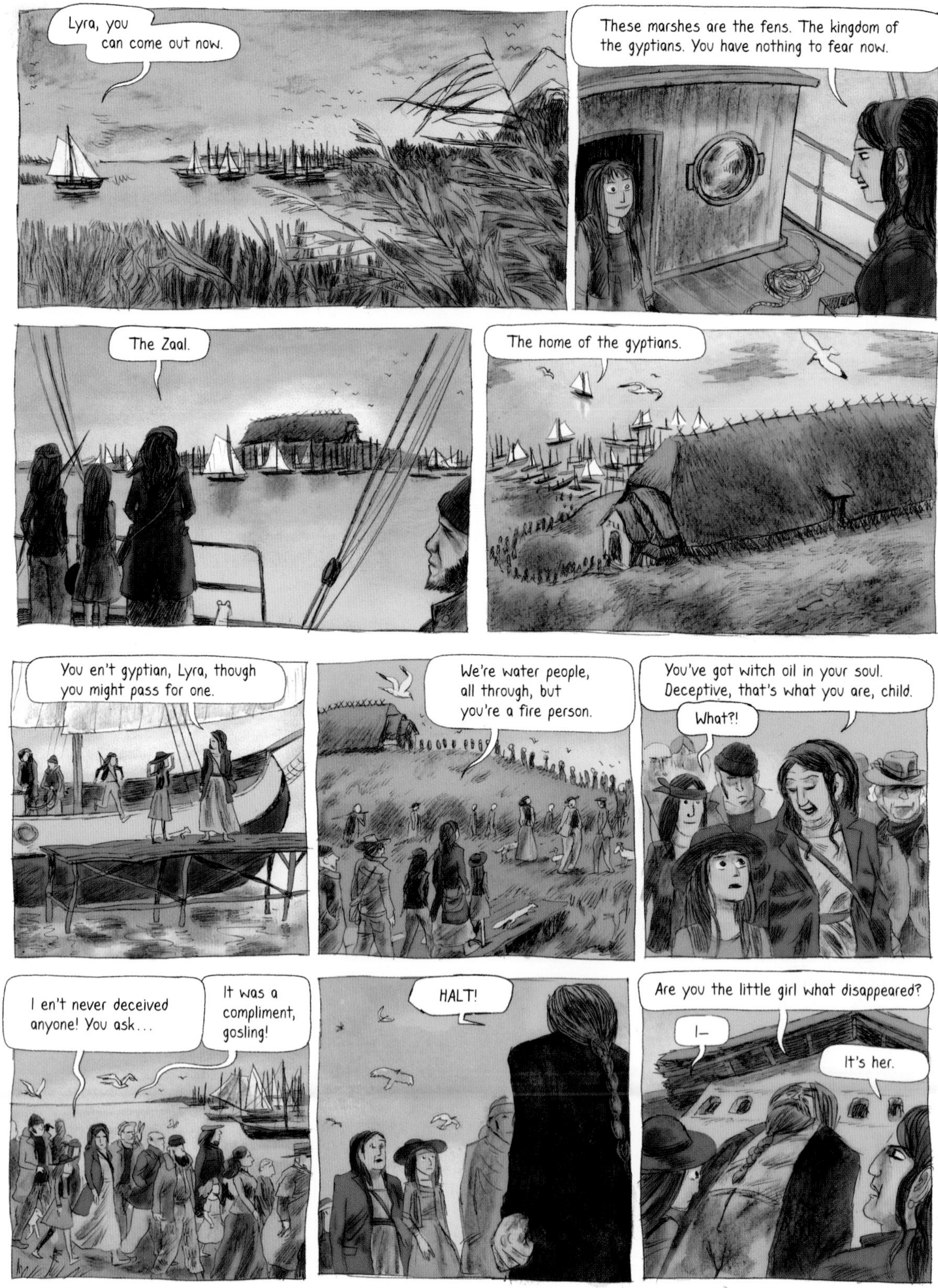
Lyra, you can come out now.
These marshes are the fens. The kingdom of the gyptians. You have nothing to fear now.
The Zaal.
The home of the gyptians.
You en't gyptian, Lyra, though you might pass for one.
We're water people, all through, but you're a fire person.
You've got witch oil in your soul. Deceptive, that's what you are, child.
What?!
I en't never deceived anyone! You ask...
It was a compliment, gosling!
HALT!
Are you the little girl what disappeared?
I—
It's her.

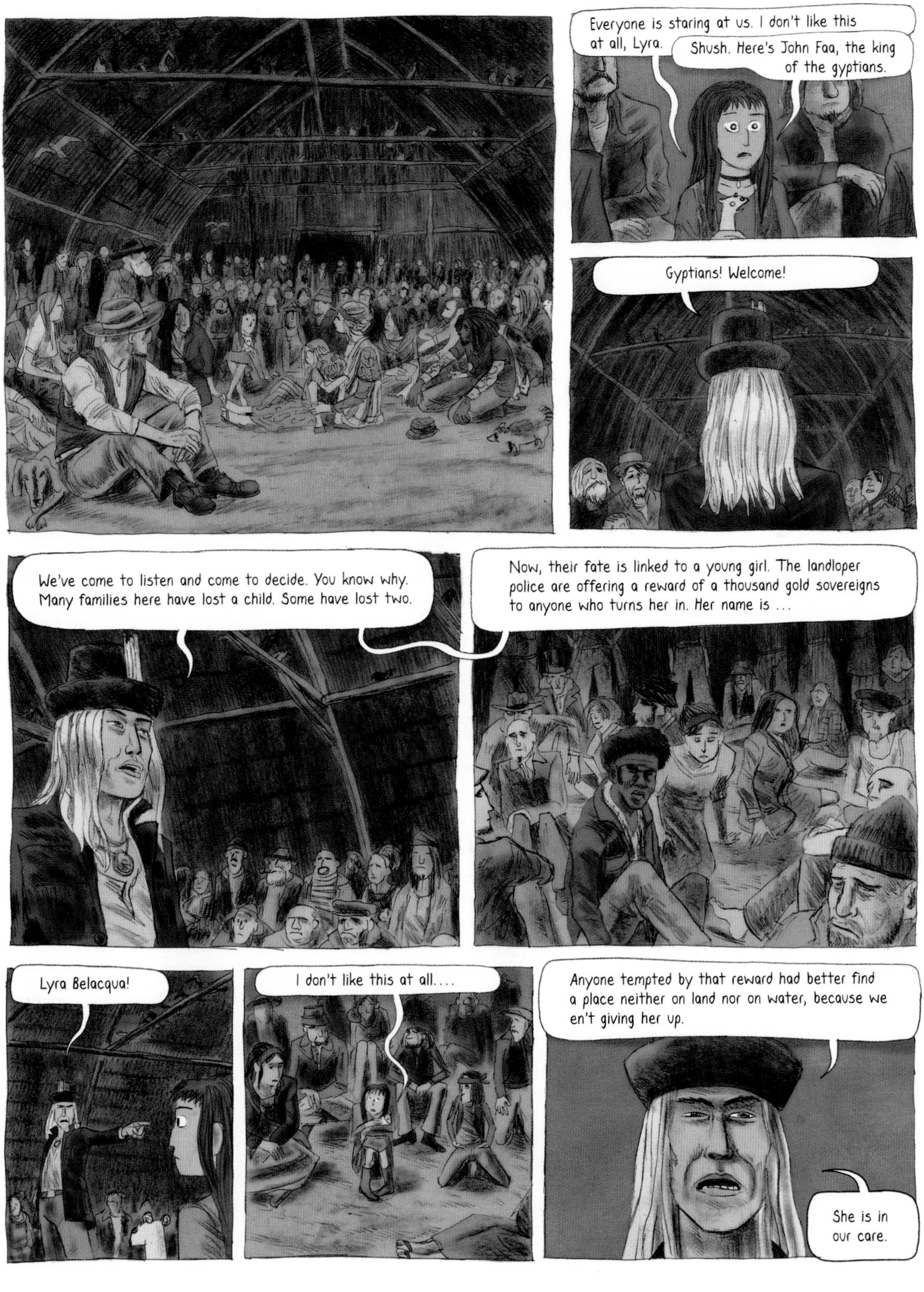
Everyone is staring at us. I don't like this at all, Lyra.
Shush. Here's John Faa, the king of the gyptians.
Gyptians! Welcome!
We've come to listen and come to decide. You know why. Many families here have lost a child. Some have lost two.
Now, their fate is linked to a young girl. The landloper police are offering a reward of a thousand gold sovereigns to anyone who turns her in. Her name is ...
Lyra Belacqua!
I don't like this at all....
Anyone tempted by that reward had better find a place neither on land nor on water, because we en't giving her up.
She is in our care.

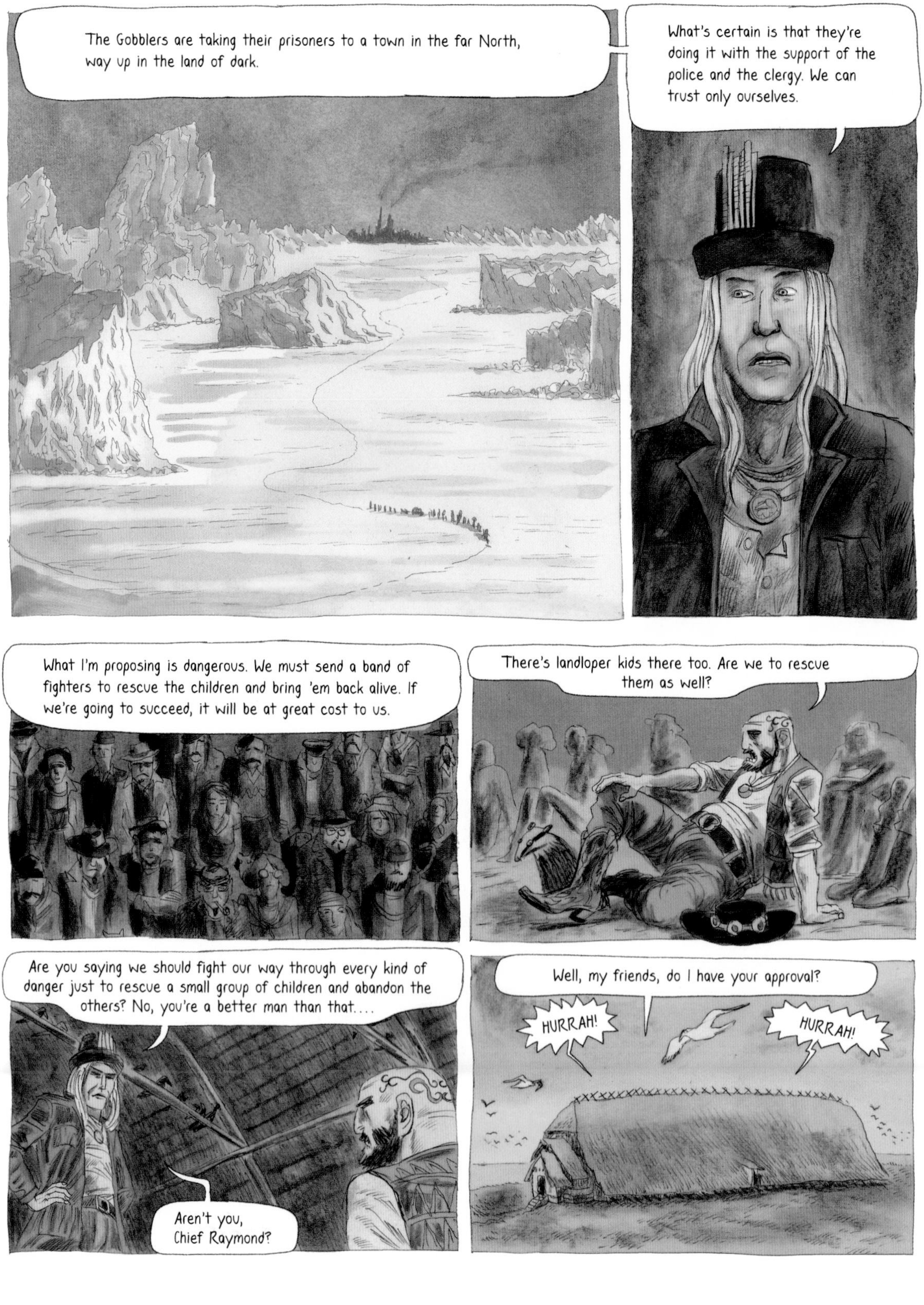

The Gobblers are taking their prisoners to a town in the far North, way up in the land of dark.
What's certain is that they're doing it with the support of the police and the clergy. We can trust only ourselves.
What I'm proposing is dangerous. We must send a band of fighters to rescue the children and bring 'em back alive. If we're going to succeed, it will be at great cost to us.
There's landloper kids there too. Are we to rescue them as well?
Are you saying we should fight our way through every kind of danger just to rescue a small group of children and abandon the others? No, you're a better man than that....
Aren't you, Chief Raymond?
Well, my friends, do I have your approval?
HURRAH!
HURRAH!

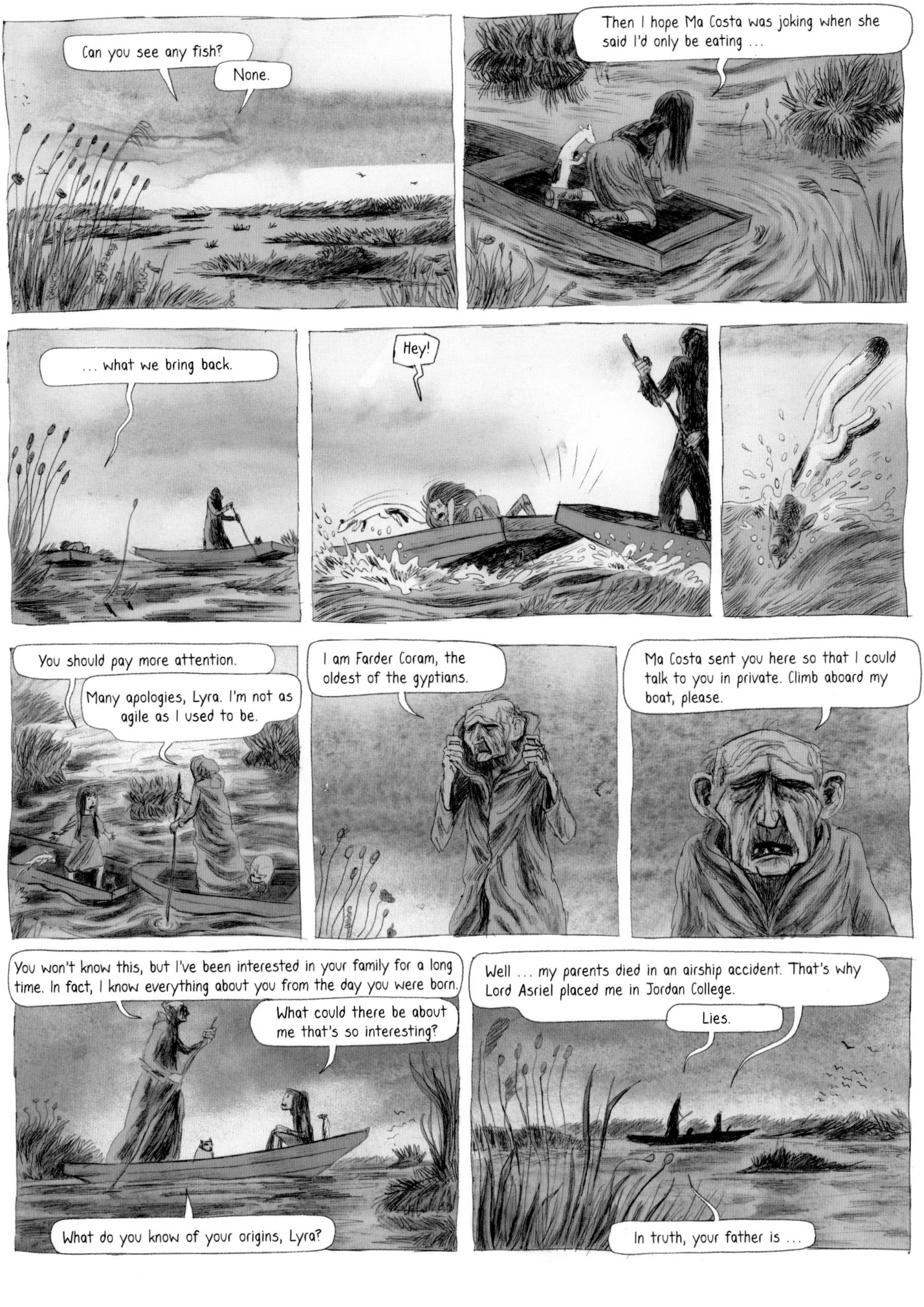

Can you see any fish?
None.
Then I hope Ma Costa was joking when she said I'd only be eating …
… what we bring back.
Hey!
You should pay more attention.
Many apologies, Lyra. I'm not as agile as I used to be.
I am Farder Coram, the oldest of the gyptians.
Ma Costa sent you here so that I could talk to you in private. Climb aboard my boat, please.
You won't know this, but I've been interested in your family for a long time. In fact, I know everything about you from the day you were born.
What could there be about me that's so interesting?
What do you know of your origins, Lyra?
Well … my parents died in an airship accident. That's why Lord Asriel placed me in Jordan College.
Lies.
In truth, your father is …

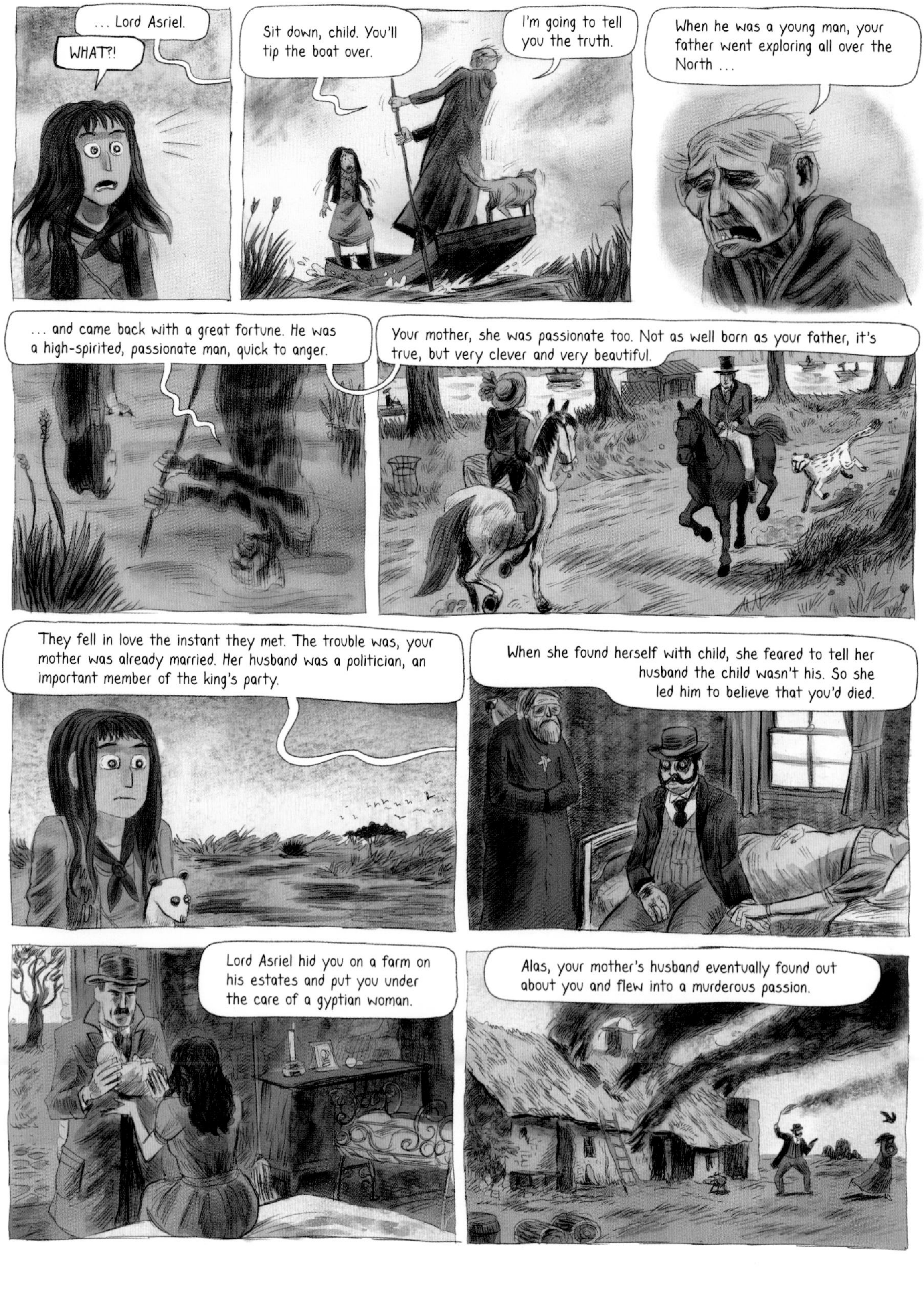
... Lord Asriel.
WHAT?!
Sit down, child. You'll tip the boat over.
I'm going to tell you the truth.
When he was a young man, your father went exploring all over the North ...
... and came back with a great fortune. He was a high-spirited, passionate man, quick to anger.
Your mother, she was passionate too. Not as well born as your father, it's true, but very clever and very beautiful.
They fell in love the instant they met. The trouble was, your mother was already married. Her husband was a politician, an important member of the king's party.
When she found herself with child, she feared to tell her husband the child wasn't his. So she led him to believe that you'd died.
Lord Asriel hid you on a farm on his estates and put you under the care of a gyptian woman.
Alas, your mother's husband eventually found out about you and flew into a murderous passion.

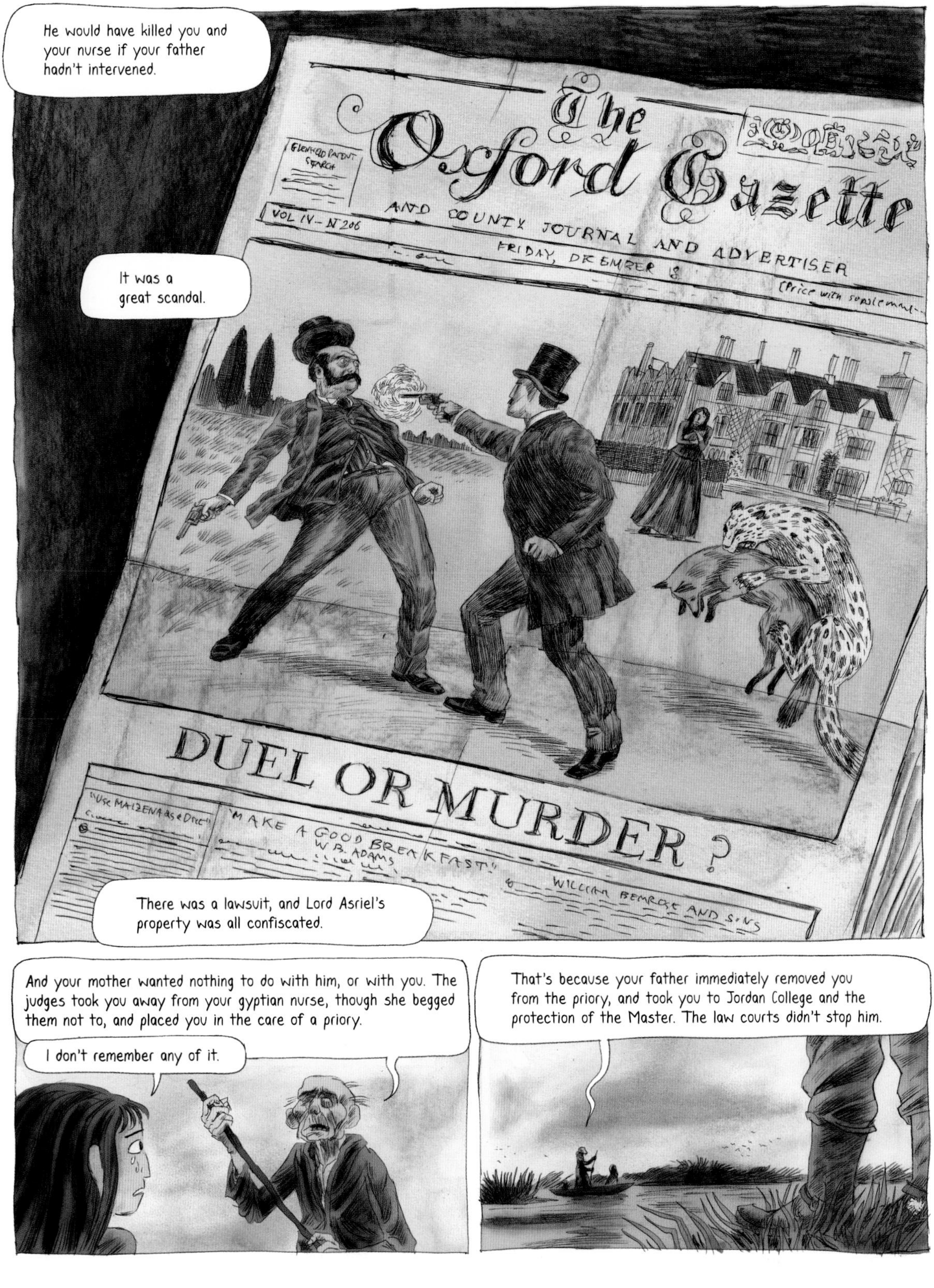
He would have killed you and your nurse if your father hadn't intervened.
The Oxford Gazette
AND COUNTY JOURNAL AND ADVERTISER
VOL IV – Nº 206
FRIDAY, DECEMBER 8
It was a great scandal.
DUEL OR MURDER?
"MAKE A GOOD BREAKFAST!"
W. B. ADAMS
WILLIAM BEMROSE AND SONS
There was a lawsuit, and Lord Asriel's property was all confiscated.
And your mother wanted nothing to do with him, or with you. The judges took you away from your gyptian nurse, though she begged them not to, and placed you in the care of a priory.
I don't remember any of it.
That's because your father immediately removed you from the priory, and took you to Jordan College and the protection of the Master. The law courts didn't stop him.

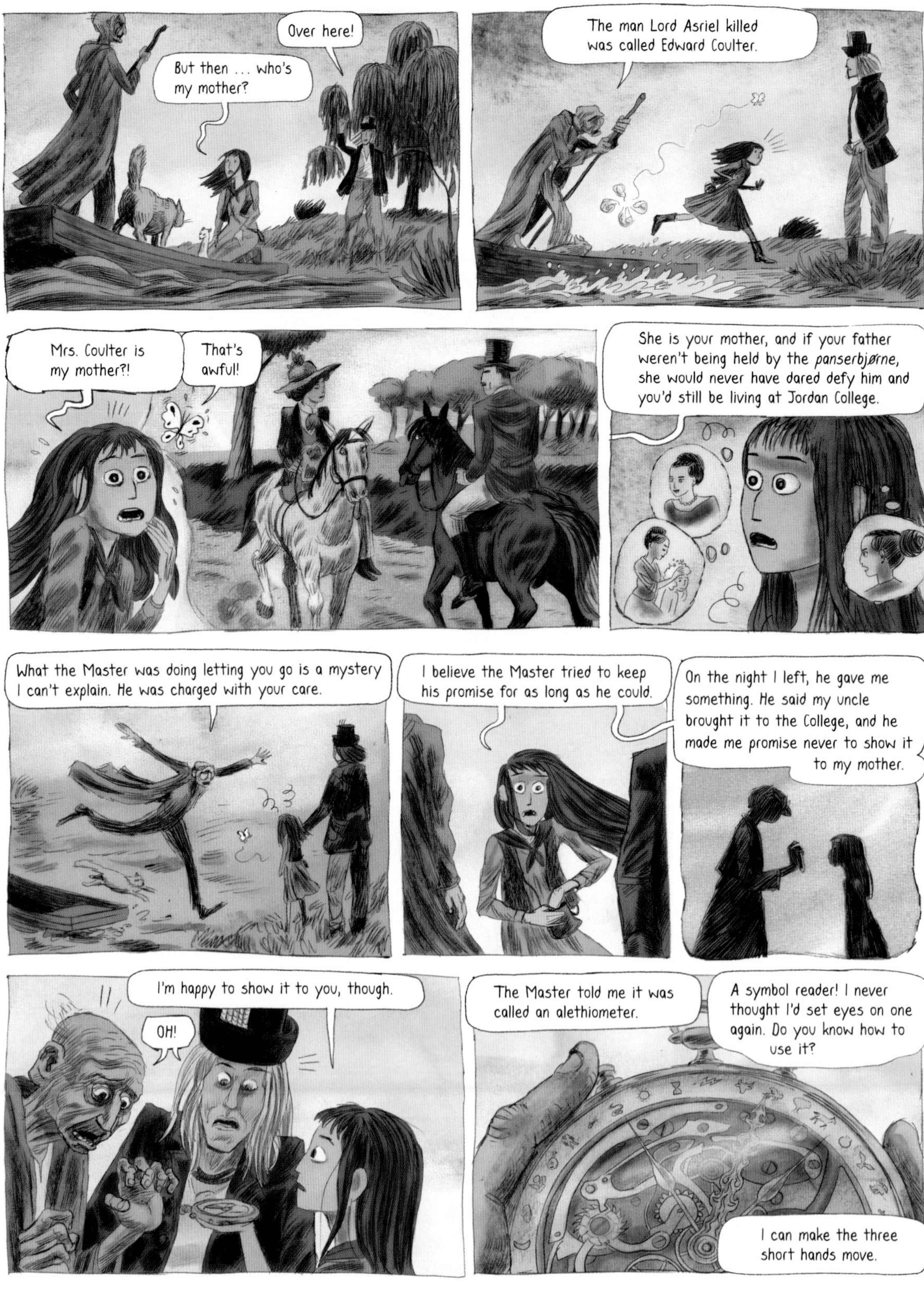
But then ... who's my mother?
Over here!
The man Lord Asriel killed was called Edward Coulter.
Mrs. Coulter is my mother?!
That's awful!
She is your mother, and if your father weren't being held by the *panserbjørne*, she would never have dared defy him and you'd still be living at Jordan College.
What the Master was doing letting you go is a mystery I can't explain. He was charged with your care.
I believe the Master tried to keep his promise for as long as he could.
On the night I left, he gave me something. He said my uncle brought it to the College, and he made me promise never to show it to my mother.
I'm happy to show it to you, though.
OH!
The Master told me it was called an alethiometer.
A symbol reader! I never thought I'd set eyes on one again. Do you know how to use it?
I can make the three short hands move.

But I can't do anything with the long one. Except sometimes, if I concentrate very hard, I can make that hand go this way or that, just by thinking it.

Look. All these pictures around the rim are symbols. Take the anchor, there. Its first meaning is hope, for hope holds you fast like an anchor so you don't give way.

But it also means steadfastness, and prevention, as well as the sea, of course.... In fact, for each symbol there's a never-ending series of meanings!

Do you know them all?

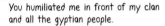

I know some. There's a book that explains them all. I've seen it, and I know where it is, but—

JOHN FAA!

You humiliated me in front of my clan and all the gyptian people.

For that, I'm going to kill you!

Many people have tried, Chief Raymond.

Aaagh!

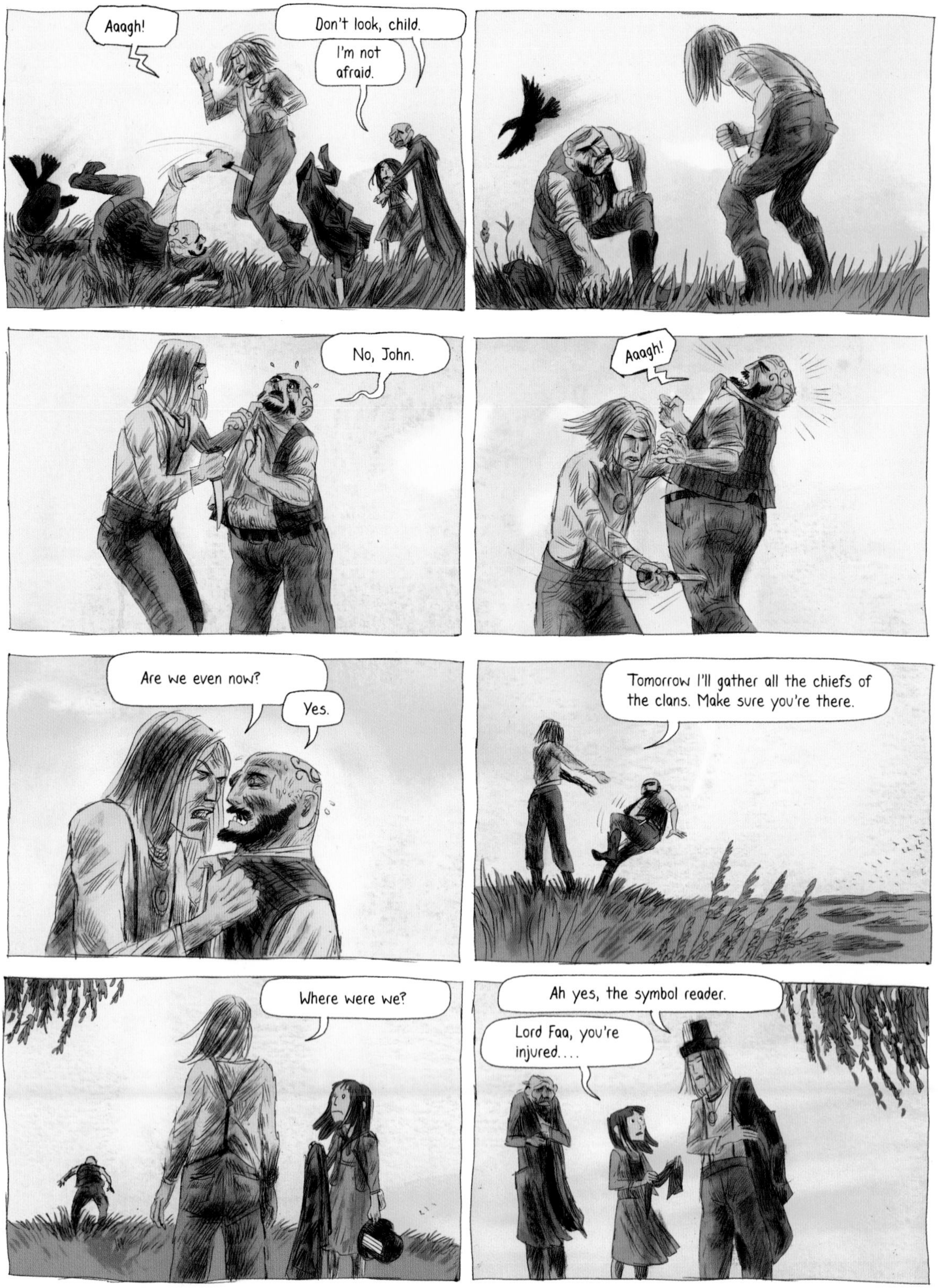
Aaagh!
Don't look, child.
I'm not afraid.
No, John.
Aaagh!
Are we even now?
Yes.
Tomorrow I'll gather all the chiefs of the clans. Make sure you're there.
Where were we?
Ah yes, the symbol reader.
Lord Faa, you're injured. . . .

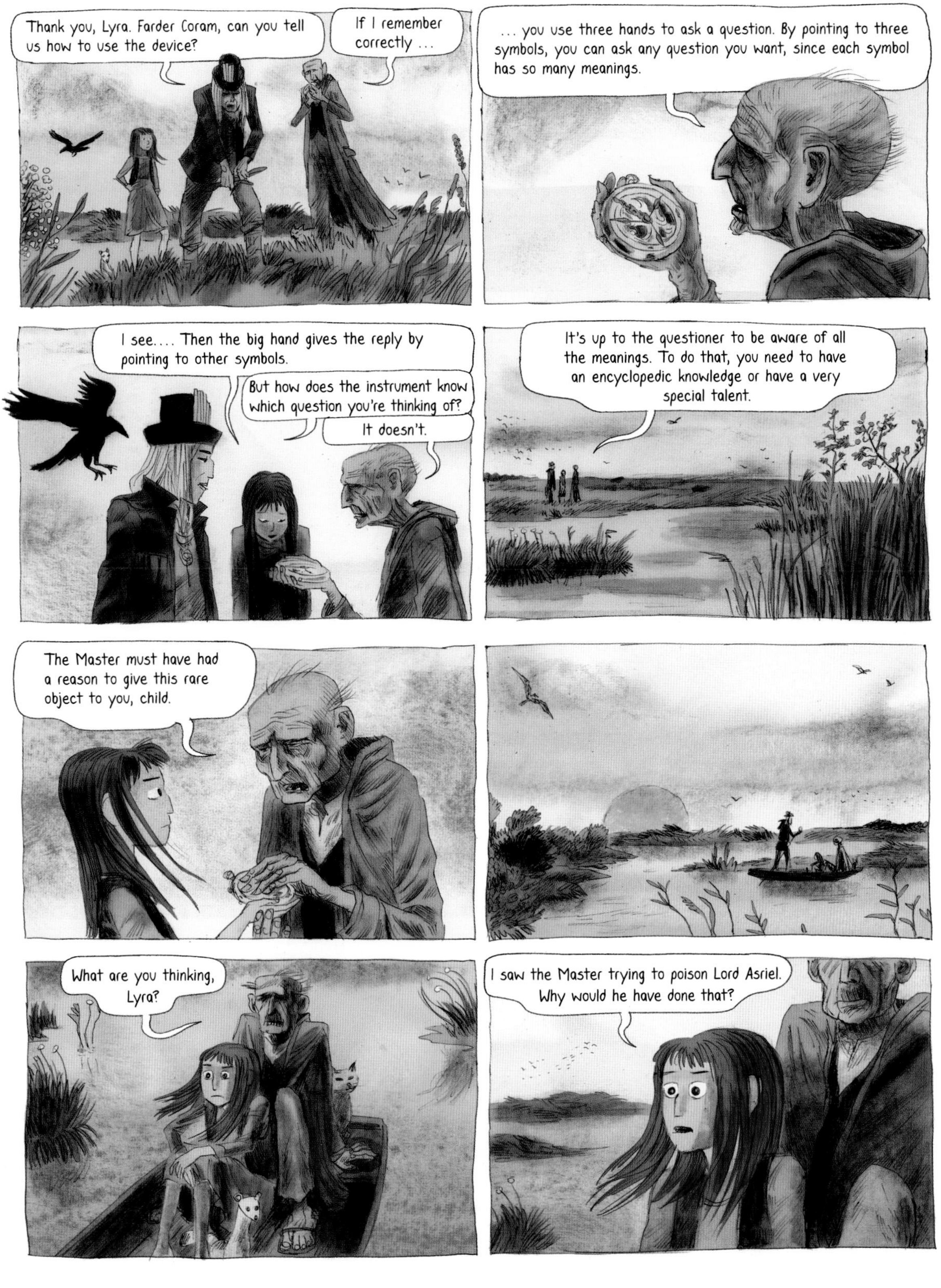
Thank you, Lyra. Farder Coram, can you tell us how to use the device?
If I remember correctly . . .
. . . you use three hands to ask a question. By pointing to three symbols, you can ask any question you want, since each symbol has so many meanings.
I see. . . . Then the big hand gives the reply by pointing to other symbols.
But how does the instrument know which question you're thinking of?
It doesn't.
It's up to the questioner to be aware of all the meanings. To do that, you need to have an encyclopedic knowledge or have a very special talent.
The Master must have had a reason to give this rare object to you, child.
What are you thinking, Lyra?
I saw the Master trying to poison Lord Asriel. Why would he have done that?

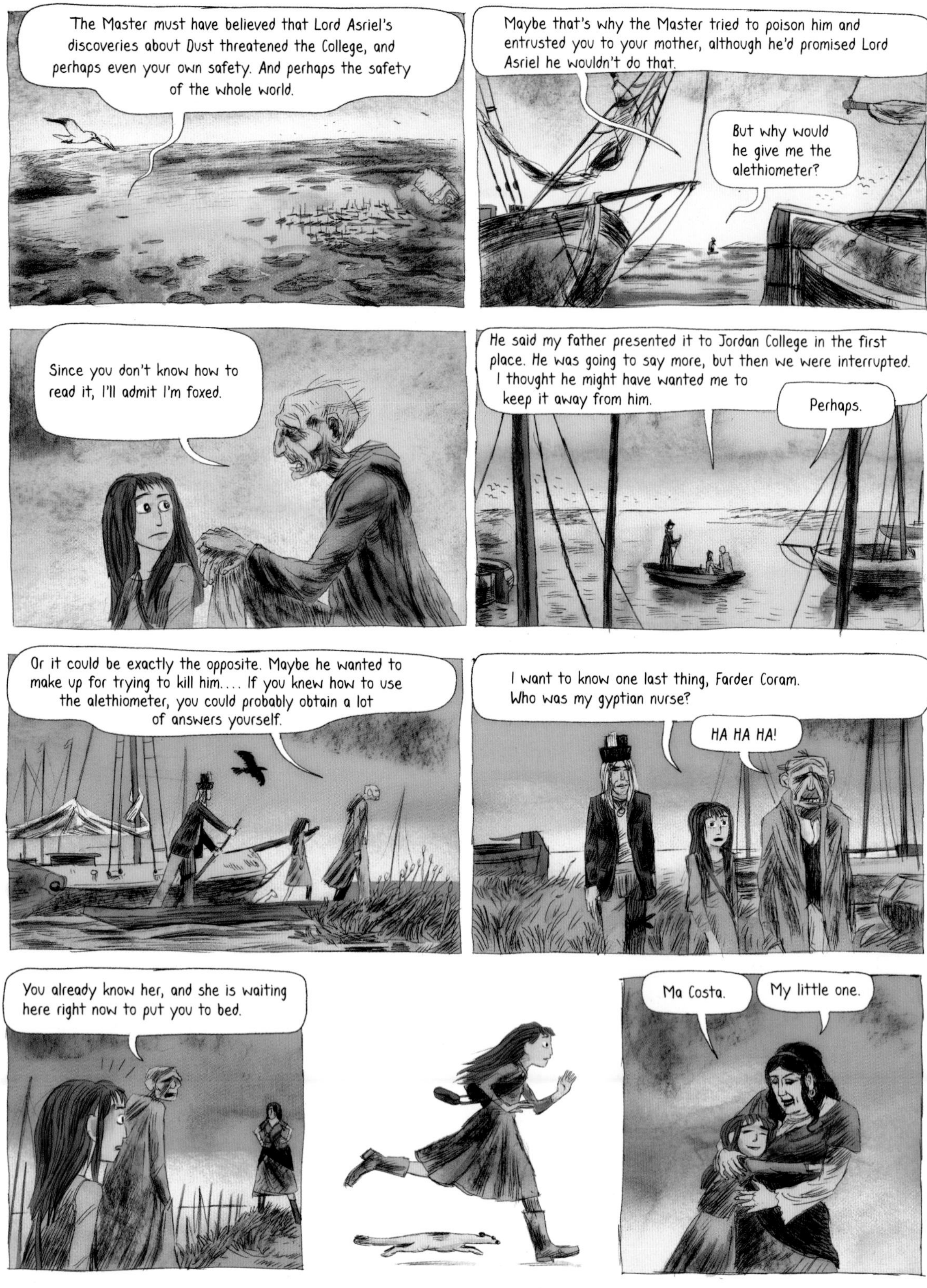
The Master must have believed that Lord Asriel's discoveries about Dust threatened the College, and perhaps even your own safety. And perhaps the safety of the whole world.
Maybe that's why the Master tried to poison him and entrusted you to your mother, although he'd promised Lord Asriel he wouldn't do that.
But why would he give me the alethiometer?
Since you don't know how to read it, I'll admit I'm foxed.
He said my father presented it to Jordan College in the first place. He was going to say more, but then we were interrupted. I thought he might have wanted me to keep it away from him.
Perhaps.
Or it could be exactly the opposite. Maybe he wanted to make up for trying to kill him.... If you knew how to use the alethiometer, you could probably obtain a lot of answers yourself.
I want to know one last thing, Farder Coram. Who was my gyptian nurse?
HA HA HA!
You already know her, and she is waiting here right now to put you to bed.
Ma Costa.
My little one.

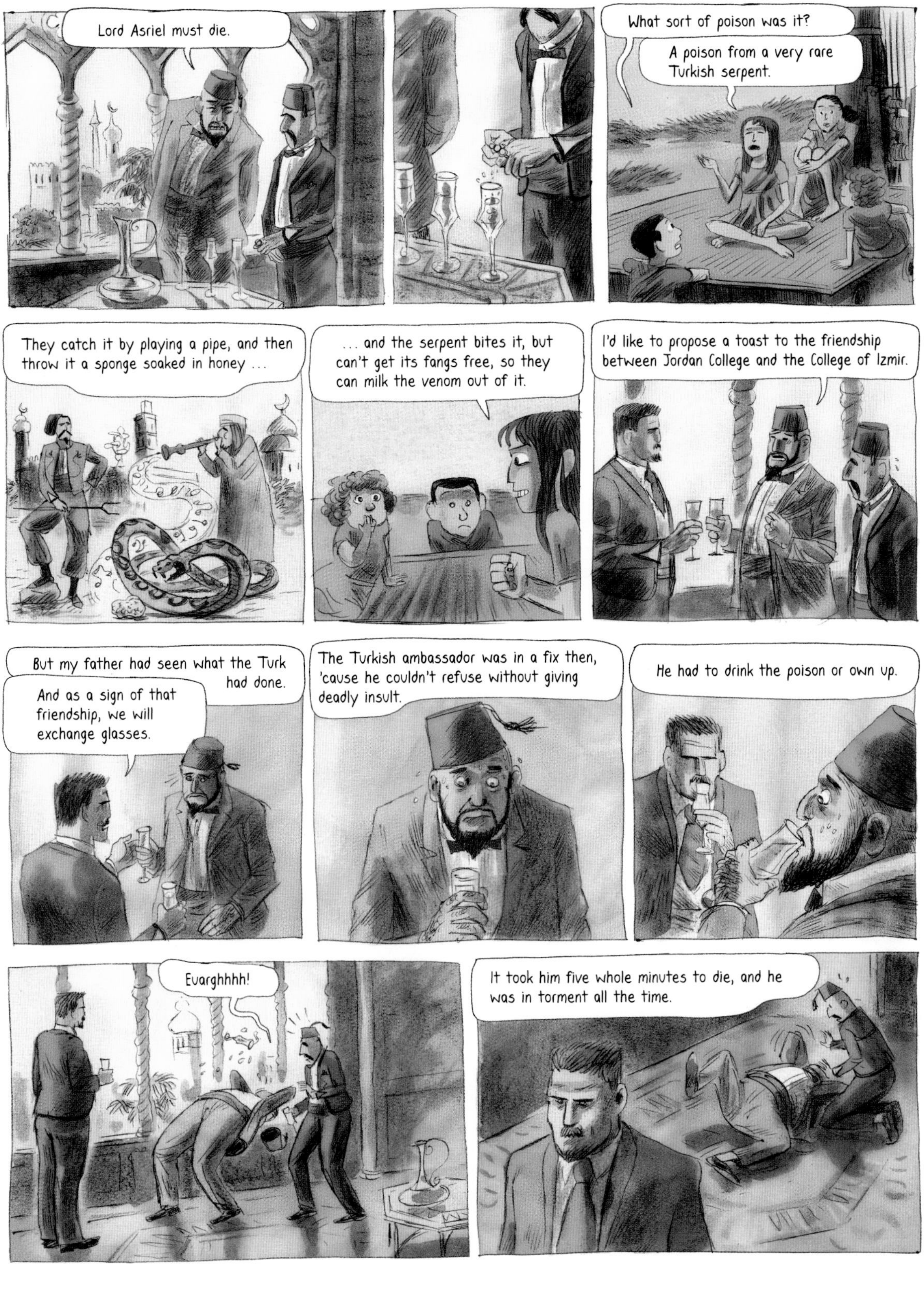
Lord Asriel must die.
What sort of poison was it?
A poison from a very rare Turkish serpent.
They catch it by playing a pipe, and then throw it a sponge soaked in honey ...
... and the serpent bites it, but can't get its fangs free, so they can milk the venom out of it.
I'd like to propose a toast to the friendship between Jordan College and the College of Izmir.
But my father had seen what the Turk had done.
And as a sign of that friendship, we will exchange glasses.
The Turkish ambassador was in a fix then, 'cause he couldn't refuse without giving deadly insult.
He had to drink the poison or own up.
Evarghhhh!
It took him five whole minutes to die, and he was in torment all the time.

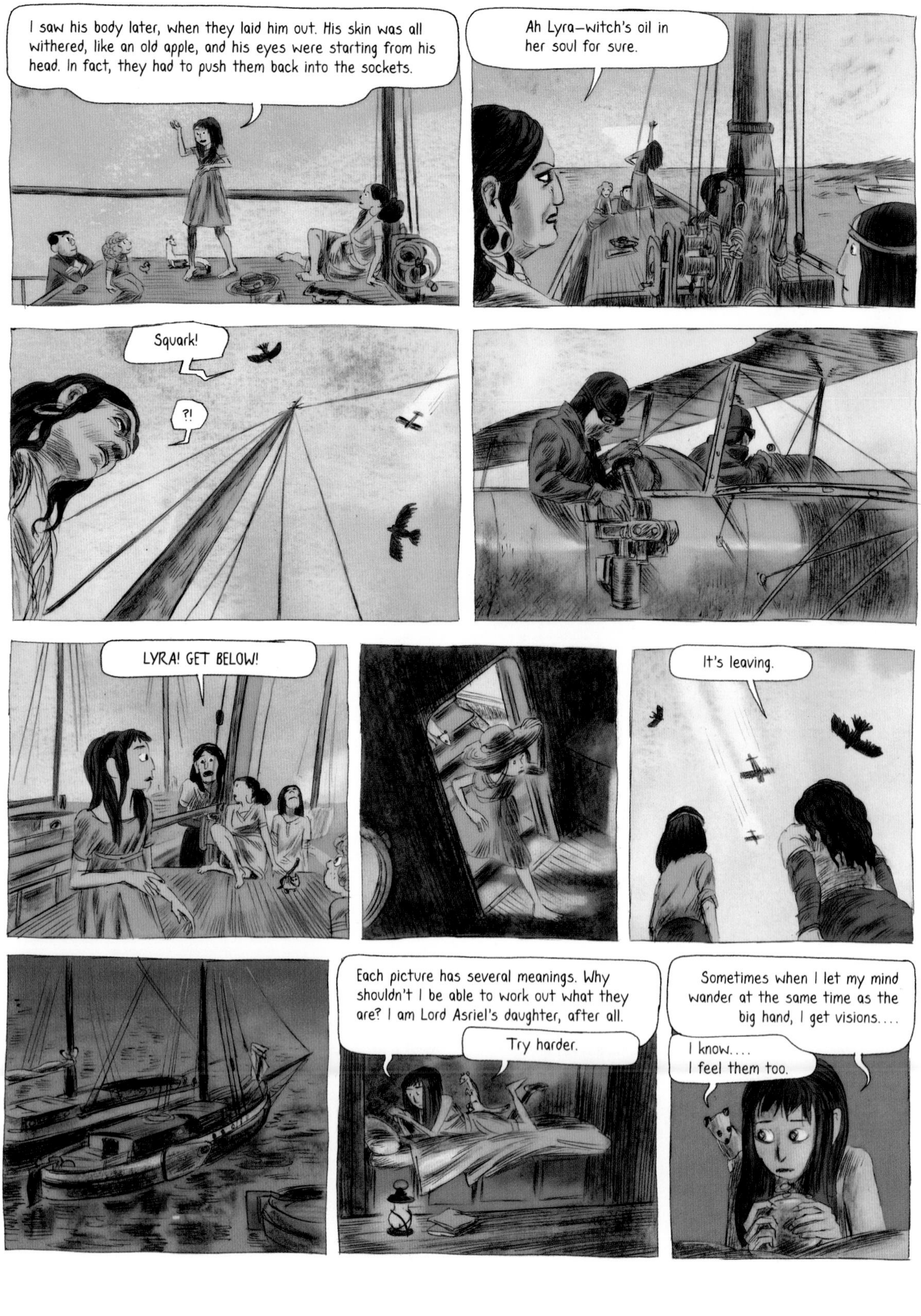
I saw his body later, when they laid him out. His skin was all withered, like an old apple, and his eyes were starting from his head. In fact, they had to push them back into the sockets.
Ah Lyra—witch's oil in her soul for sure.
Squark!
?!
LYRA! GET BELOW!
It's leaving.
Each picture has several meanings. Why shouldn't I be able to work out what they are? I am Lord Asriel's daughter, after all.
Try harder.
Sometimes when I let my mind wander at the same time as the big hand, I get visions....
I know....
I feel them too.

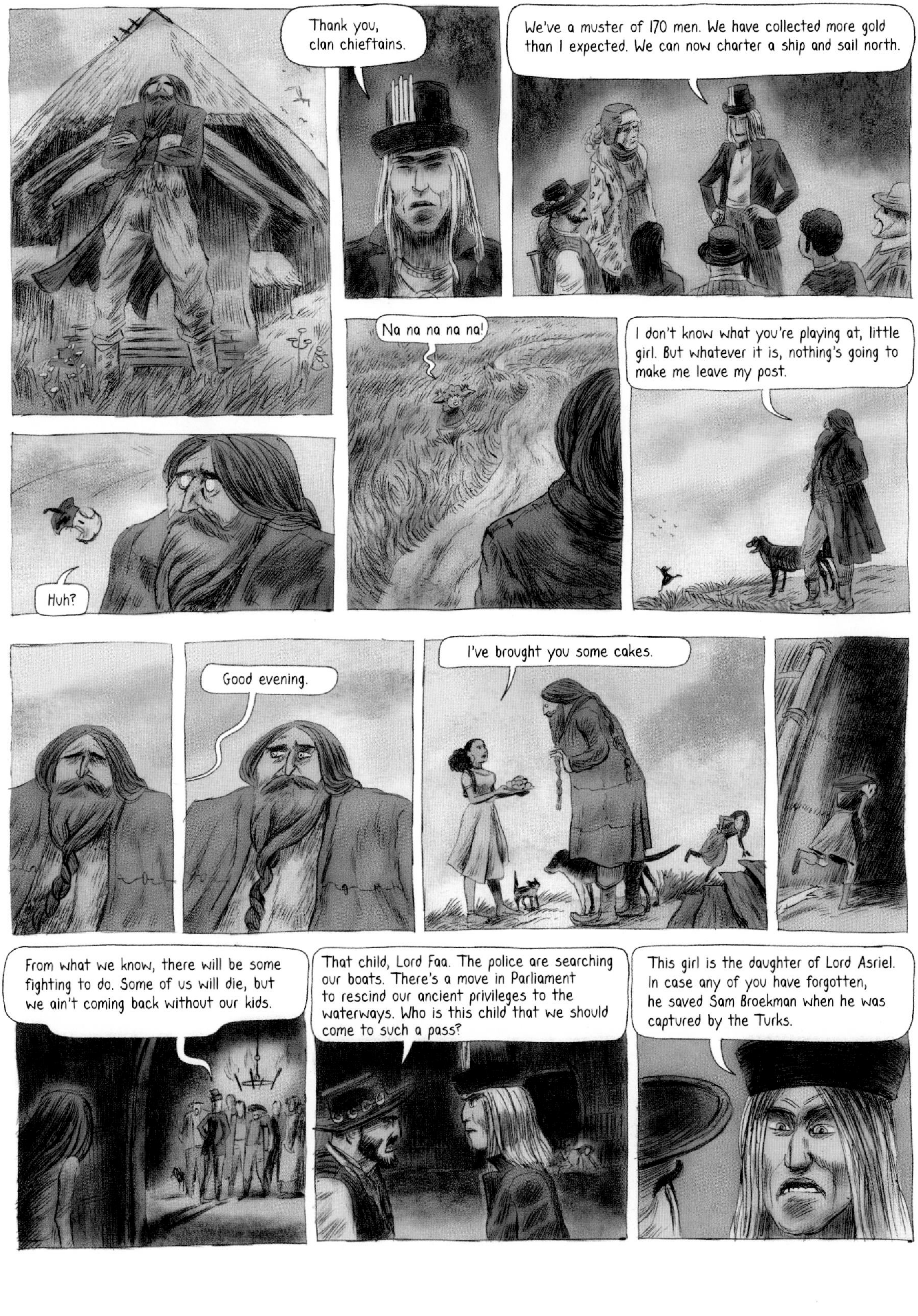
Thank you, clan chieftains.
We've a muster of 170 men. We have collected more gold than I expected. We can now charter a ship and sail north.
Na na na na na!
I don't know what you're playing at, little girl. But whatever it is, nothing's going to make me leave my post.
Huh?
Good evening.
I've brought you some cakes.
From what we know, there will be some fighting to do. Some of us will die, but we ain't coming back without our kids.
That child, Lord Faa. The police are searching our boats. There's a move in Parliament to rescind our ancient privileges to the waterways. Who is this child that we should come to such a pass?
This girl is the daughter of Lord Asriel. In case any of you have forgotten, he saved Sam Broekman when he was captured by the Turks.

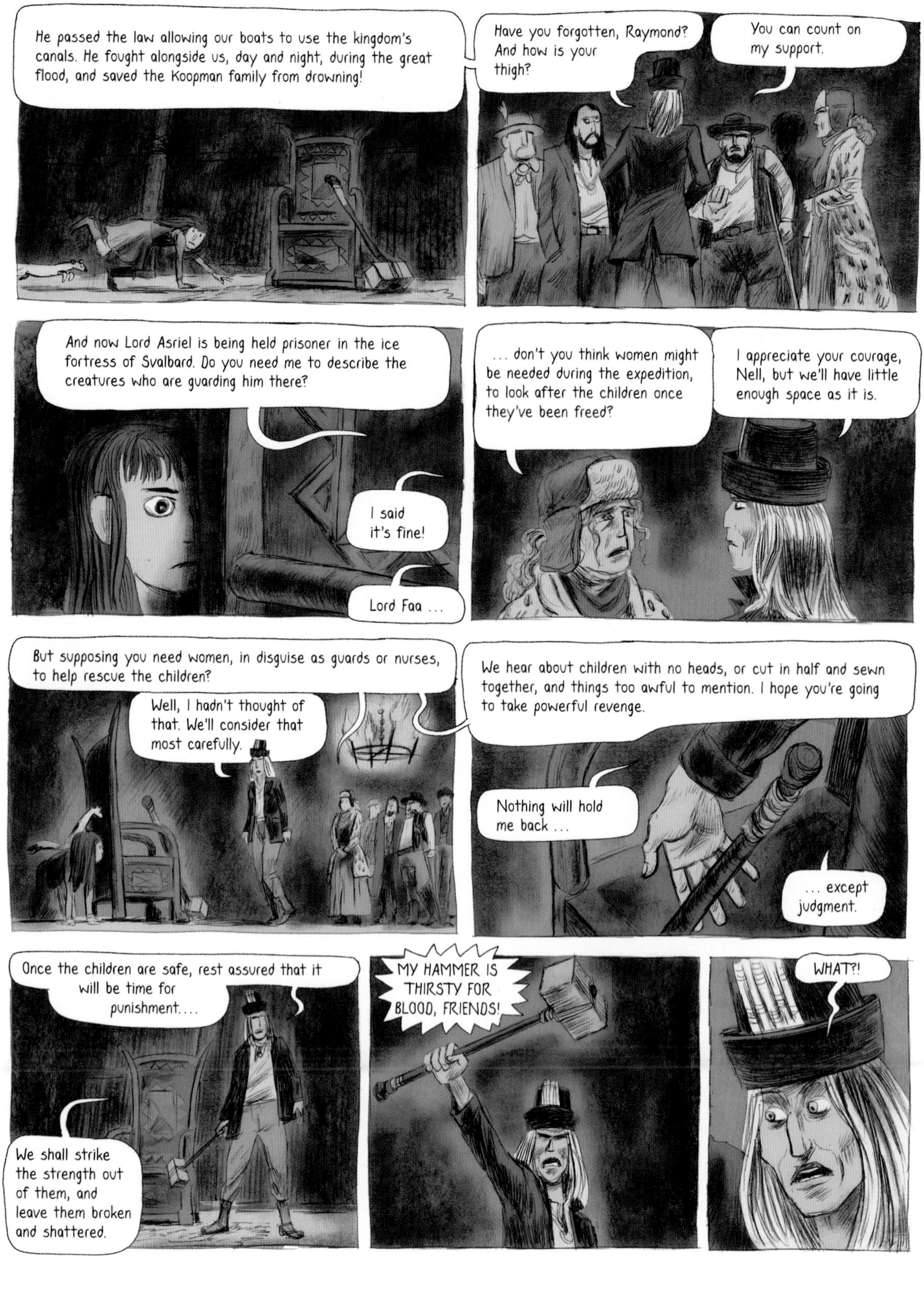
He passed the law allowing our boats to use the kingdom's canals. He fought alongside us, day and night, during the great flood, and saved the Koopman family from drowning!
Have you forgotten, Raymond? And how is your thigh?
You can count on my support.
And now Lord Asriel is being held prisoner in the ice fortress of Svalbard. Do you need me to describe the creatures who are guarding him there?
I said it's fine!
Lord Faa ...
... don't you think women might be needed during the expedition, to look after the children once they've been freed?
I appreciate your courage, Nell, but we'll have little enough space as it is.
But supposing you need women, in disguise as guards or nurses, to help rescue the children?
Well, I hadn't thought of that. We'll consider that most carefully.
We hear about children with no heads, or cut in half and sewn together, and things too awful to mention. I hope you're going to take powerful revenge.
Nothing will hold me back ...
... except judgment.
Once the children are safe, rest assured that it will be time for punishment....
We shall strike the strength out of them, and leave them broken and shattered.
MY HAMMER IS THIRSTY FOR BLOOD, FRIENDS!
WHAT?!

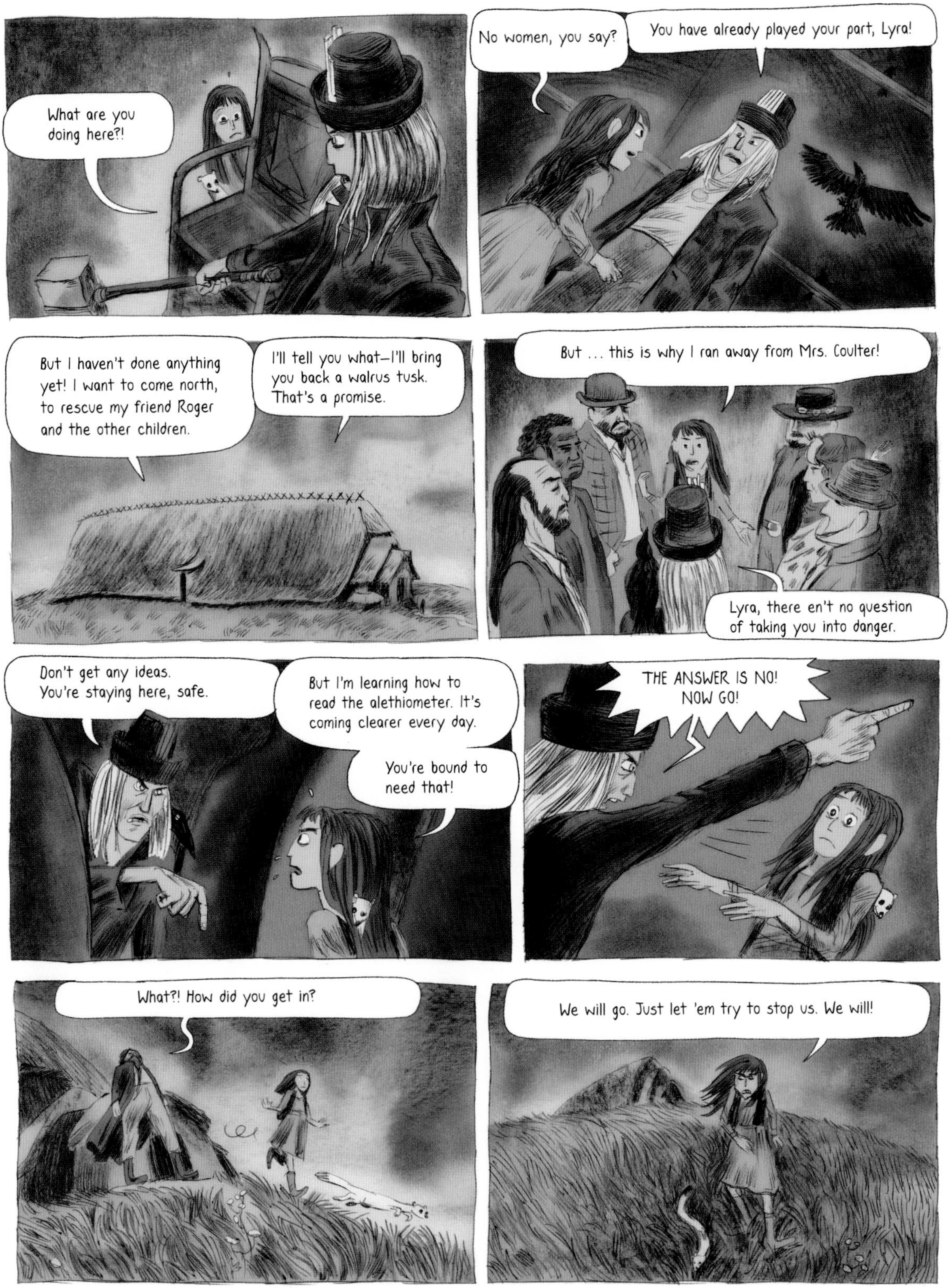
What are you doing here?!
No women, you say?
You have already played your part, Lyra!
But I haven't done anything yet! I want to come north, to rescue my friend Roger and the other children.
I'll tell you what—I'll bring you back a walrus tusk. That's a promise.
But ... this is why I ran away from Mrs. Coulter!
Lyra, there en't no question of taking you into danger.
Don't get any ideas. You're staying here, safe.
But I'm learning how to read the alethiometer. It's coming clearer every day.
You're bound to need that!
THE ANSWER IS NO! NOW GO!
What?! How did you get in?
We will go. Just let 'em try to stop us. We will!

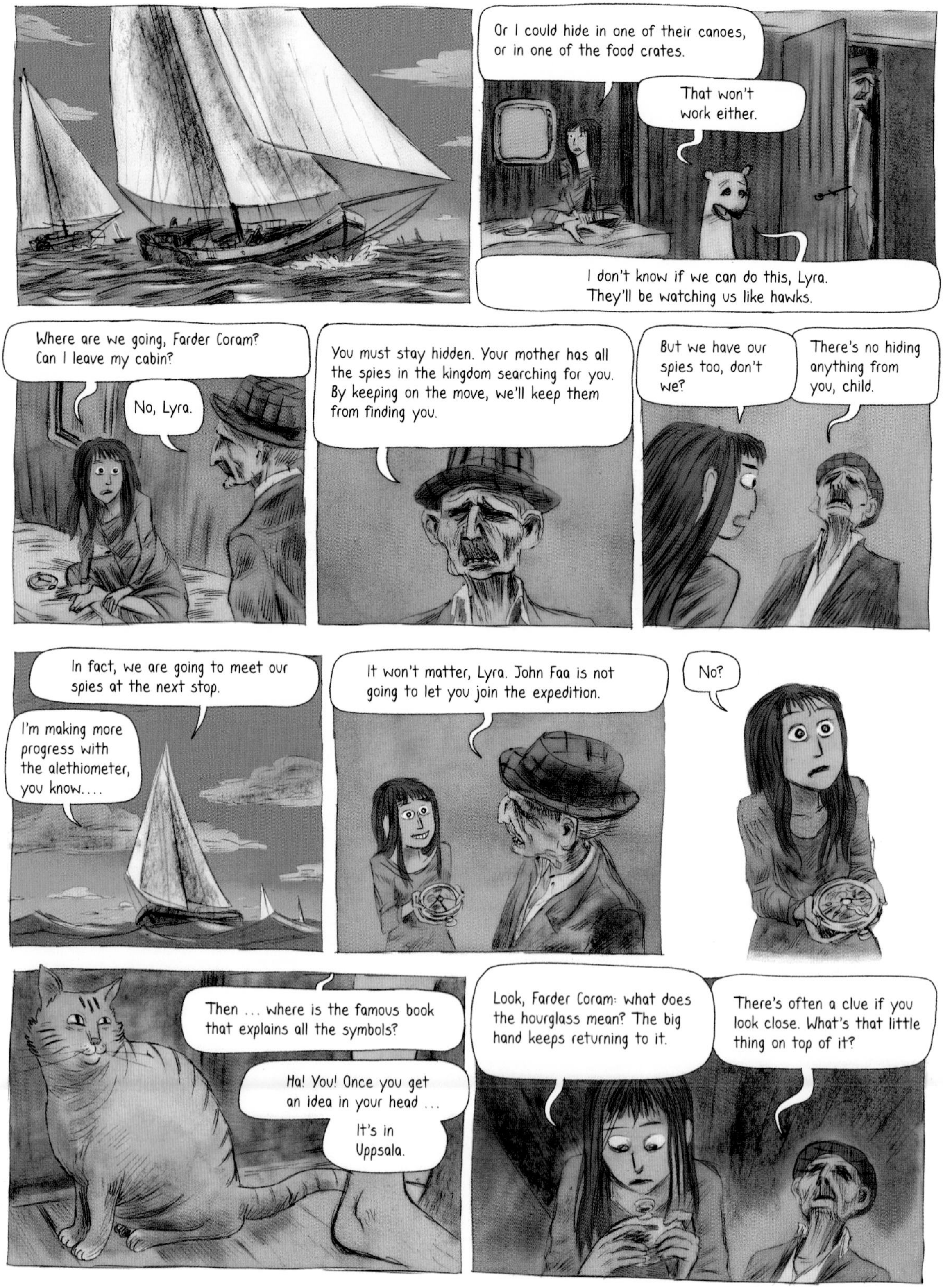
Or I could hide in one of their canoes, or in one of the food crates.
That won't work either.
I don't know if we can do this, Lyra. They'll be watching us like hawks.
Where are we going, Farder Coram? Can I leave my cabin?
No, Lyra.
You must stay hidden. Your mother has all the spies in the kingdom searching for you. By keeping on the move, we'll keep them from finding you.
But we have our spies too, don't we?
There's no hiding anything from you, child.
In fact, we are going to meet our spies at the next stop.
I'm making more progress with the alethiometer, you know. . . .
It won't matter, Lyra. John Faa is not going to let you join the expedition.
No?
Then . . . where is the famous book that explains all the symbols?
Ha! You! Once you get an idea in your head . . .
It's in Uppsala.
Look, Farder Coram: what does the hourglass mean? The big hand keeps returning to it.
There's often a clue if you look close. What's that little thing on top of it?

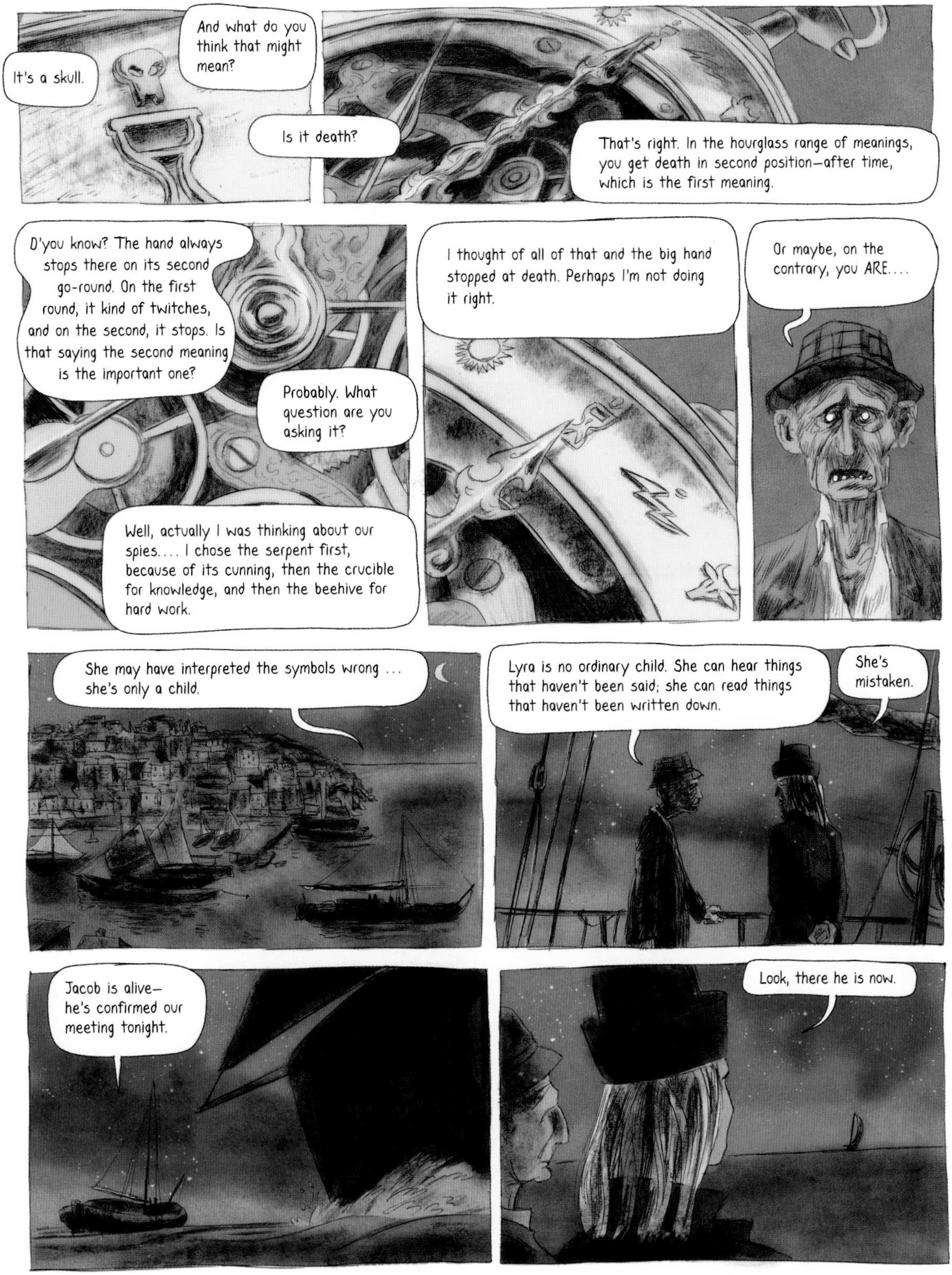
It's a skull.
And what do you think that might mean?
Is it death?
That's right. In the hourglass range of meanings, you get death in second position—after time, which is the first meaning.
D'you know? The hand always stops there on its second go-round. On the first round, it kind of twitches, and on the second, it stops. Is that saying the second meaning is the important one?
Probably. What question are you asking it?
Well, actually I was thinking about our spies.... I chose the serpent first, because of its cunning, then the crucible for knowledge, and then the beehive for hard work.
I thought of all of that and the big hand stopped at death. Perhaps I'm not doing it right.
Or maybe, on the contrary, you ARE....
She may have interpreted the symbols wrong ... she's only a child.
Lyra is no ordinary child. She can hear things that haven't been said; she can read things that haven't been written down.
She's mistaken.
Jacob is alive—he's confirmed our meeting tonight.
Look, there he is now.

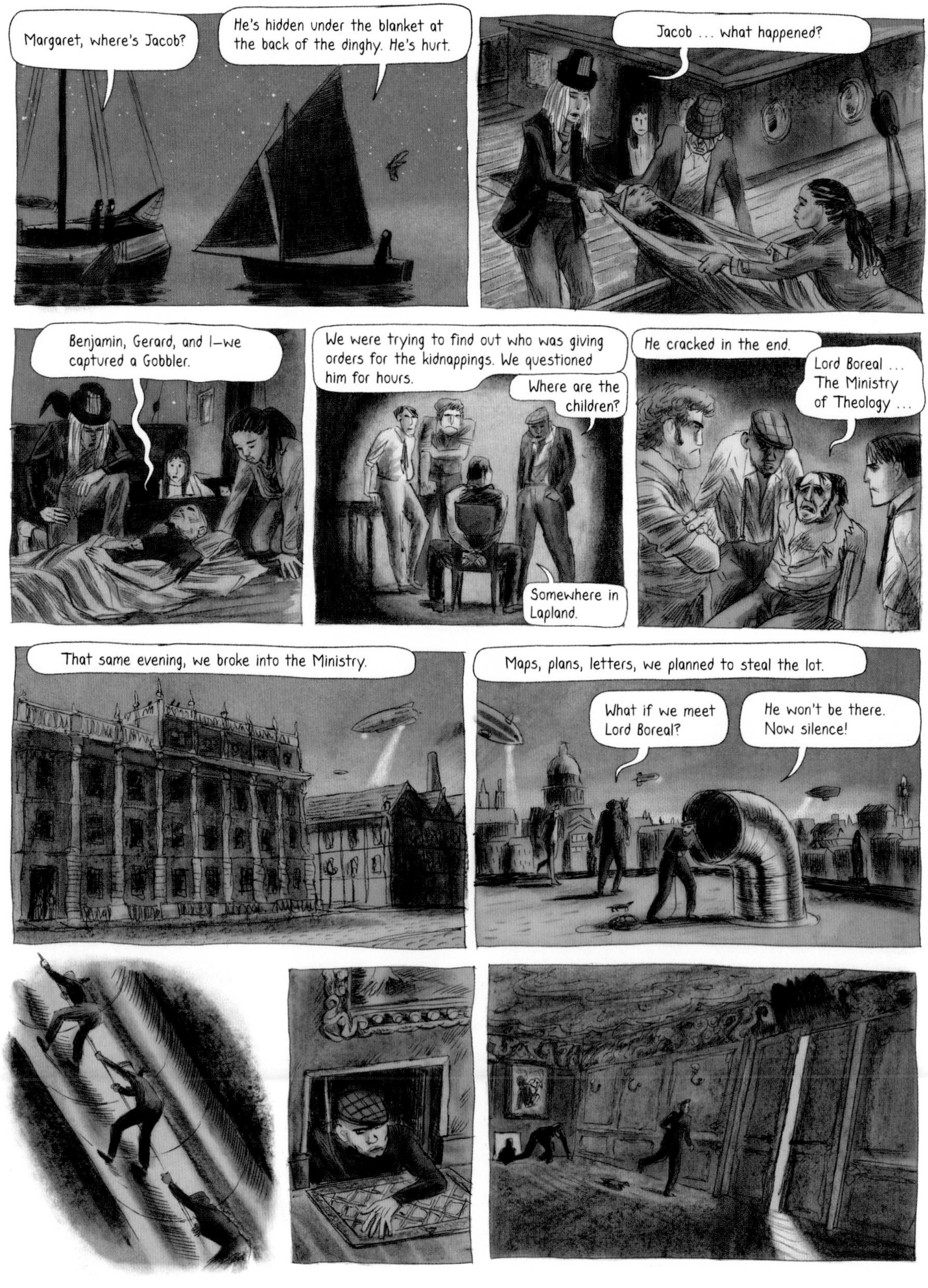
Margaret, where's Jacob?
He's hidden under the blanket at the back of the dinghy. He's hurt.
Jacob ... what happened?
Benjamin, Gerard, and I—we captured a Gobbler.
We were trying to find out who was giving orders for the kidnappings. We questioned him for hours.
Where are the children?
Somewhere in Lapland.
He cracked in the end.
Lord Boreal ... The Ministry of Theology ...
That same evening, we broke into the Ministry.
Maps, plans, letters, we planned to steal the lot.
What if we meet Lord Boreal?
He won't be there. Now silence!

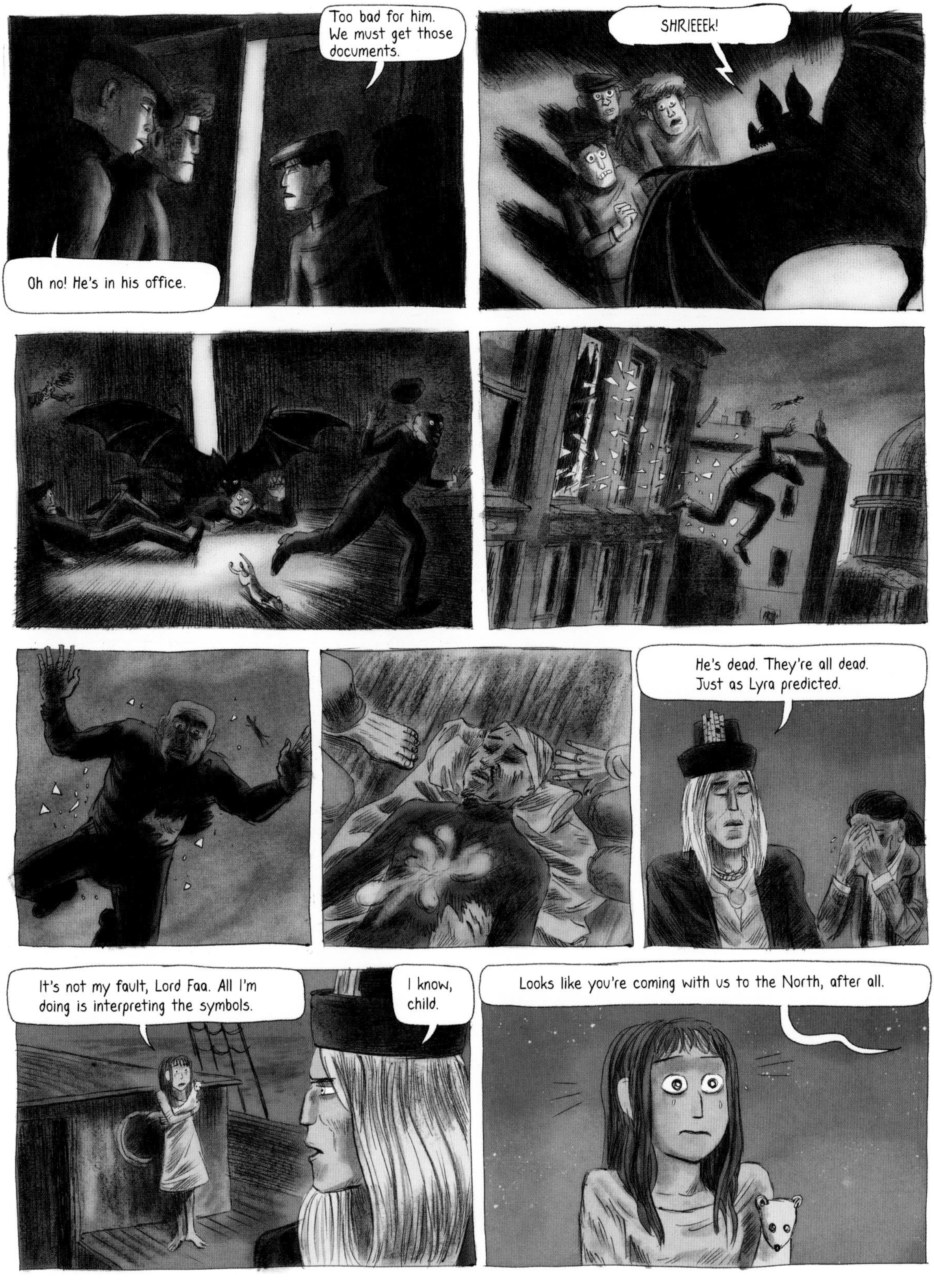
Too bad for him. We must get those documents.
Oh no! He's in his office.
SHRIEEEk!
He's dead. They're all dead. Just as Lyra predicted.
It's not my fault, Lord Faa. All I'm doing is interpreting the symbols.
I know, child.
Looks like you're coming with us to the North, after all.

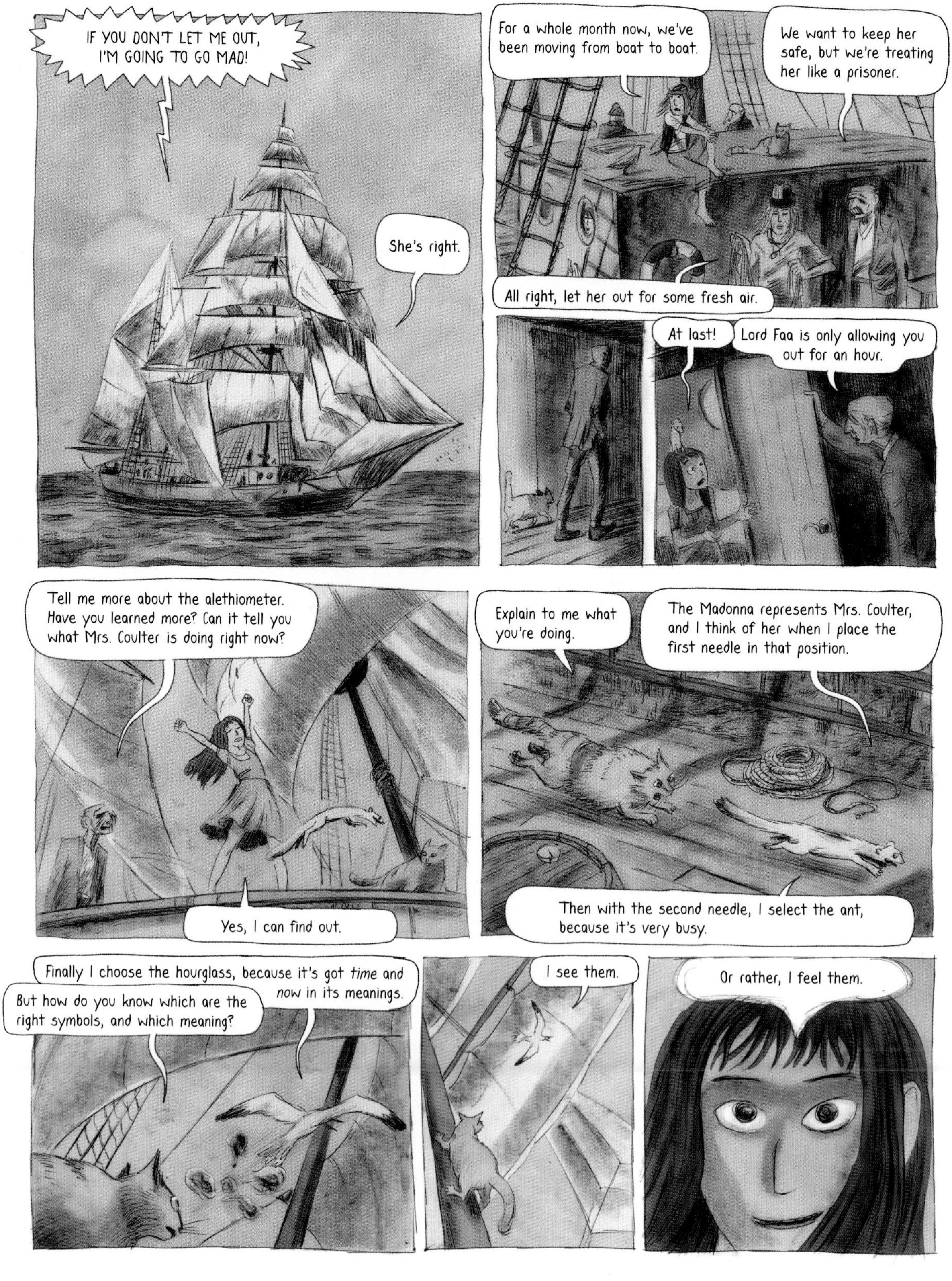
IF YOU DON'T LET ME OUT, I'M GOING TO GO MAD!
She's right.
For a whole month now, we've been moving from boat to boat.
We want to keep her safe, but we're treating her like a prisoner.
All right, let her out for some fresh air.
At last!
Lord Faa is only allowing you out for an hour.
Tell me more about the alethiometer. Have you learned more? Can it tell you what Mrs. Coulter is doing right now?
Yes, I can find out.
Explain to me what you're doing.
The Madonna represents Mrs. Coulter, and I think of her when I place the first needle in that position.
Then with the second needle, I select the ant, because it's very busy.
Finally I choose the hourglass, because it's got *time* and *now* in its meanings.
But how do you know which are the right symbols, and which meaning?
I see them.
Or rather, I feel them.

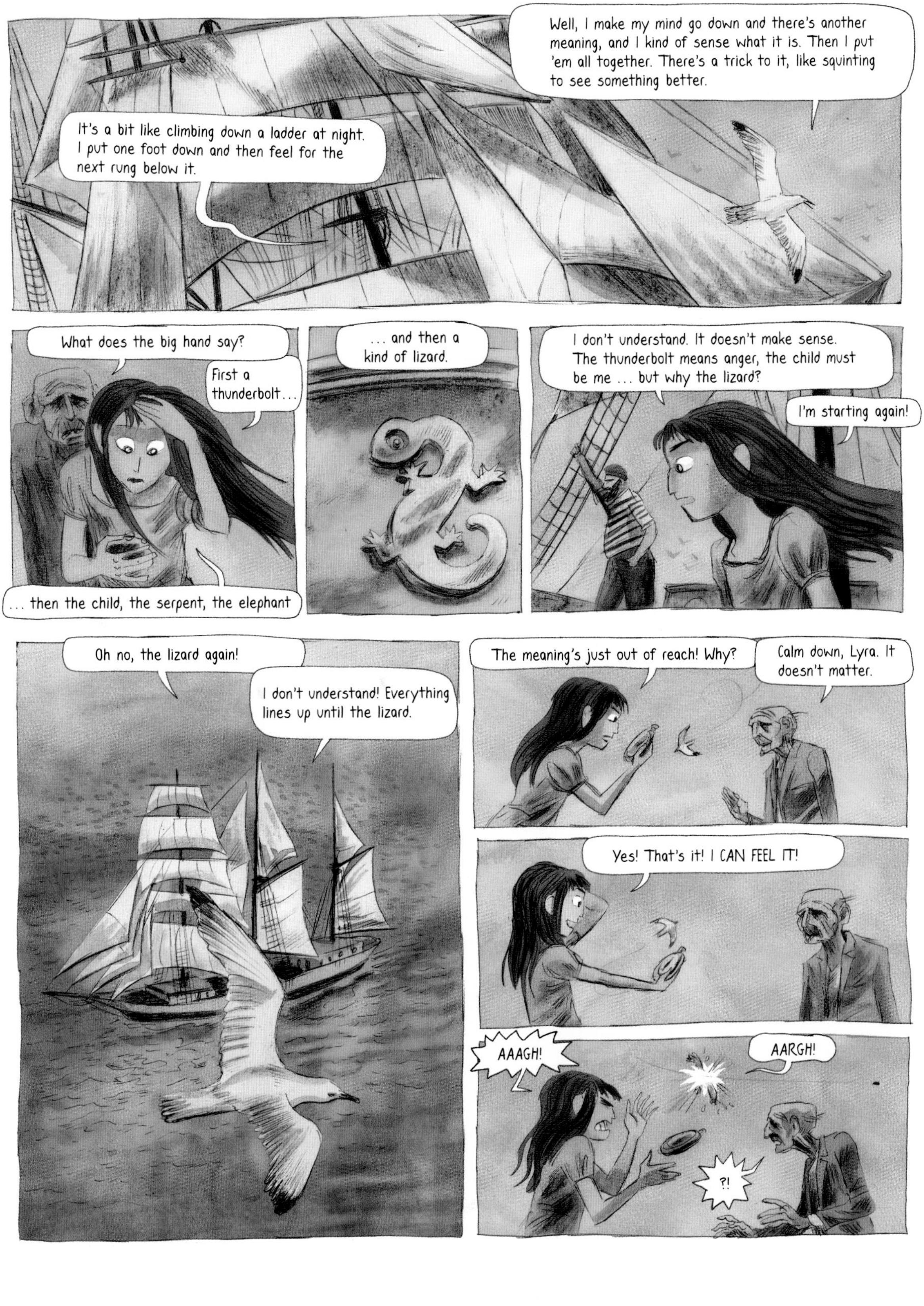
Well, I make my mind go down and there's another meaning, and I kind of sense what it is. Then I put 'em all together. There's a trick to it, like squinting to see something better.
It's a bit like climbing down a ladder at night. I put one foot down and then feel for the next rung below it.
What does the big hand say?
First a thunderbolt . . .
. . . then the child, the serpent, the elephant
. . . and then a kind of lizard.
I don't understand. It doesn't make sense. The thunderbolt means anger, the child must be me . . . but why the lizard?
I'm starting again!
Oh no, the lizard again!
I don't understand! Everything lines up until the lizard.
The meaning's just out of reach! Why?
Calm down, Lyra. It doesn't matter.
Yes! That's it! I CAN FEEL IT!
AAAGH!
AARGH!
?!

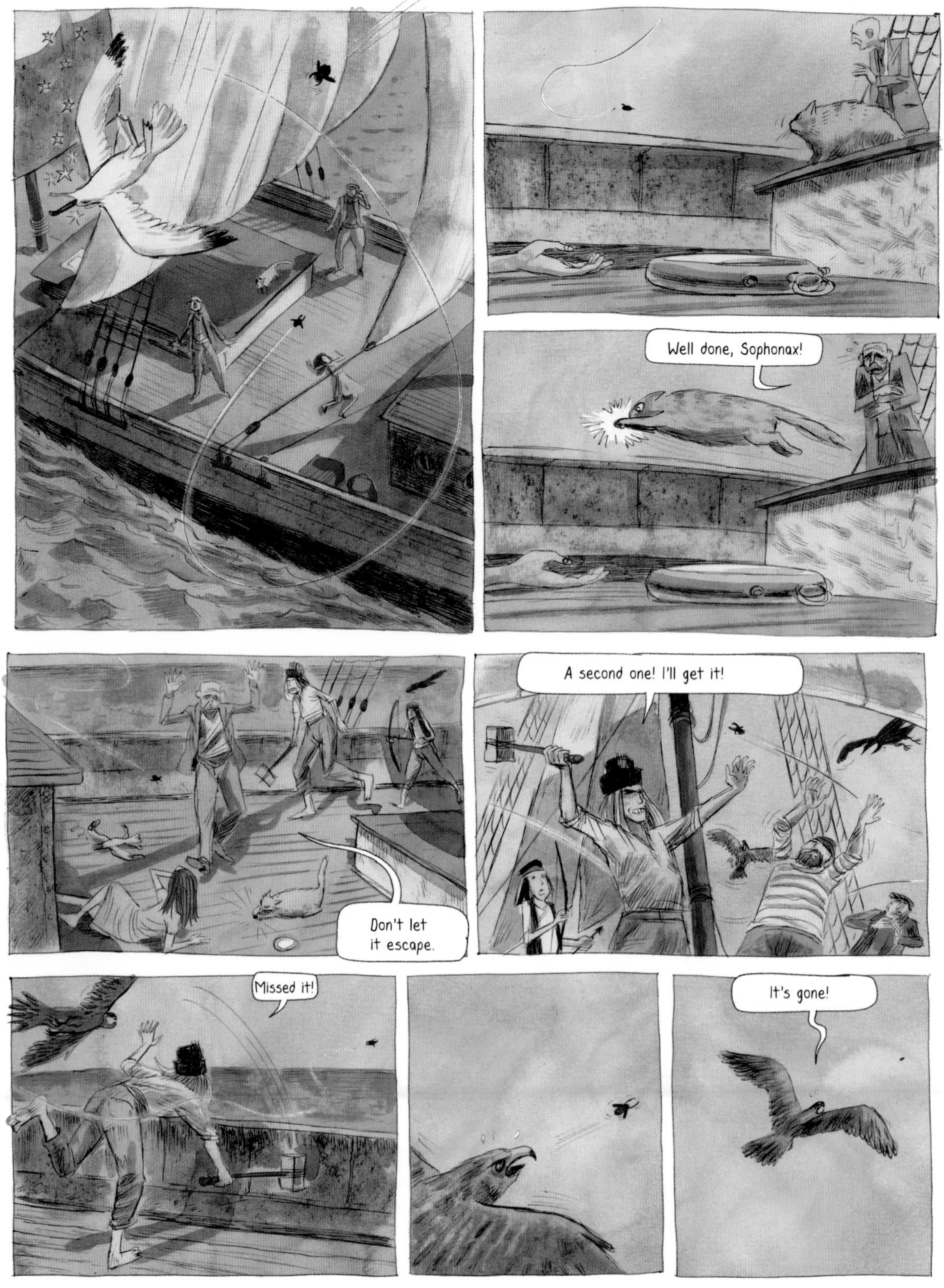
Well done, Sophonax!
Don't let it escape.
A second one! I'll get it!
Missed it!
It's gone!

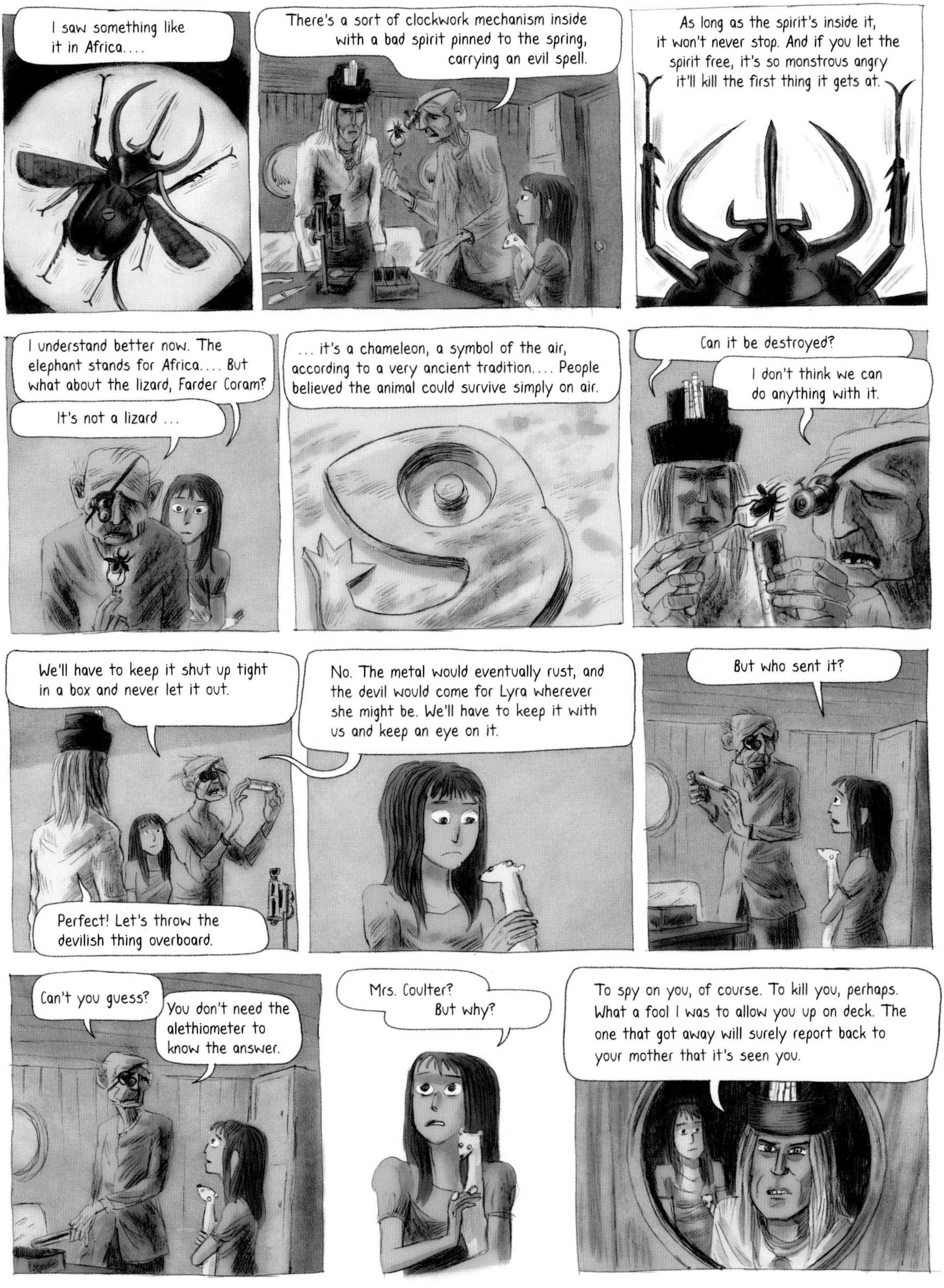
I saw something like it in Africa. . . .
There's a sort of clockwork mechanism inside with a bad spirit pinned to the spring, carrying an evil spell.
As long as the spirit's inside it, it won't never stop. And if you let the spirit free, it's so monstrous angry it'll kill the first thing it gets at.
I understand better now. The elephant stands for Africa. . . . But what about the lizard, Farder Coram?
It's not a lizard . . .
. . . it's a chameleon, a symbol of the air, according to a very ancient tradition. . . . People believed the animal could survive simply on air.
Can it be destroyed?
I don't think we can do anything with it.
We'll have to keep it shut up tight in a box and never let it out.
Perfect! Let's throw the devilish thing overboard.
No. The metal would eventually rust, and the devil would come for Lyra wherever she might be. We'll have to keep it with us and keep an eye on it.
But who sent it?
Can't you guess?
You don't need the alethiometer to know the answer.
Mrs. Coulter?
But why?
To spy on you, of course. To kill you, perhaps. What a fool I was to allow you up on deck. The one that got away will surely report back to your mother that it's seen you.

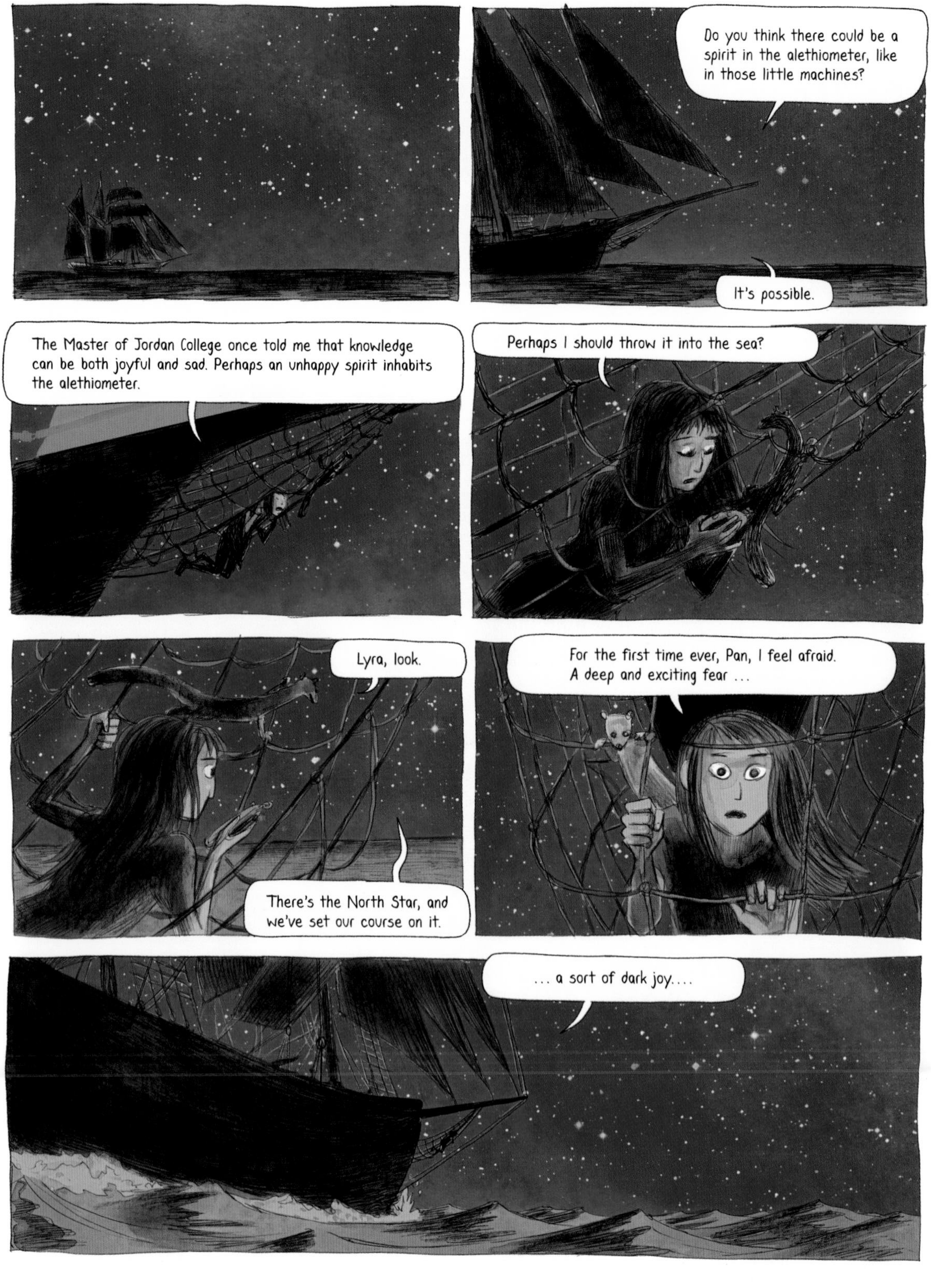
Do you think there could be a spirit in the alethiometer, like in those little machines?
It's possible.
The Master of Jordan College once told me that knowledge can be both joyful and sad. Perhaps an unhappy spirit inhabits the alethiometer.
Perhaps I should throw it into the sea?
Lyra, look.
There's the North Star, and we've set our course on it.
For the first time ever, Pan, I feel afraid. A deep and exciting fear . . .
. . . a sort of dark joy. . . .

PART II

BOLVANGAR

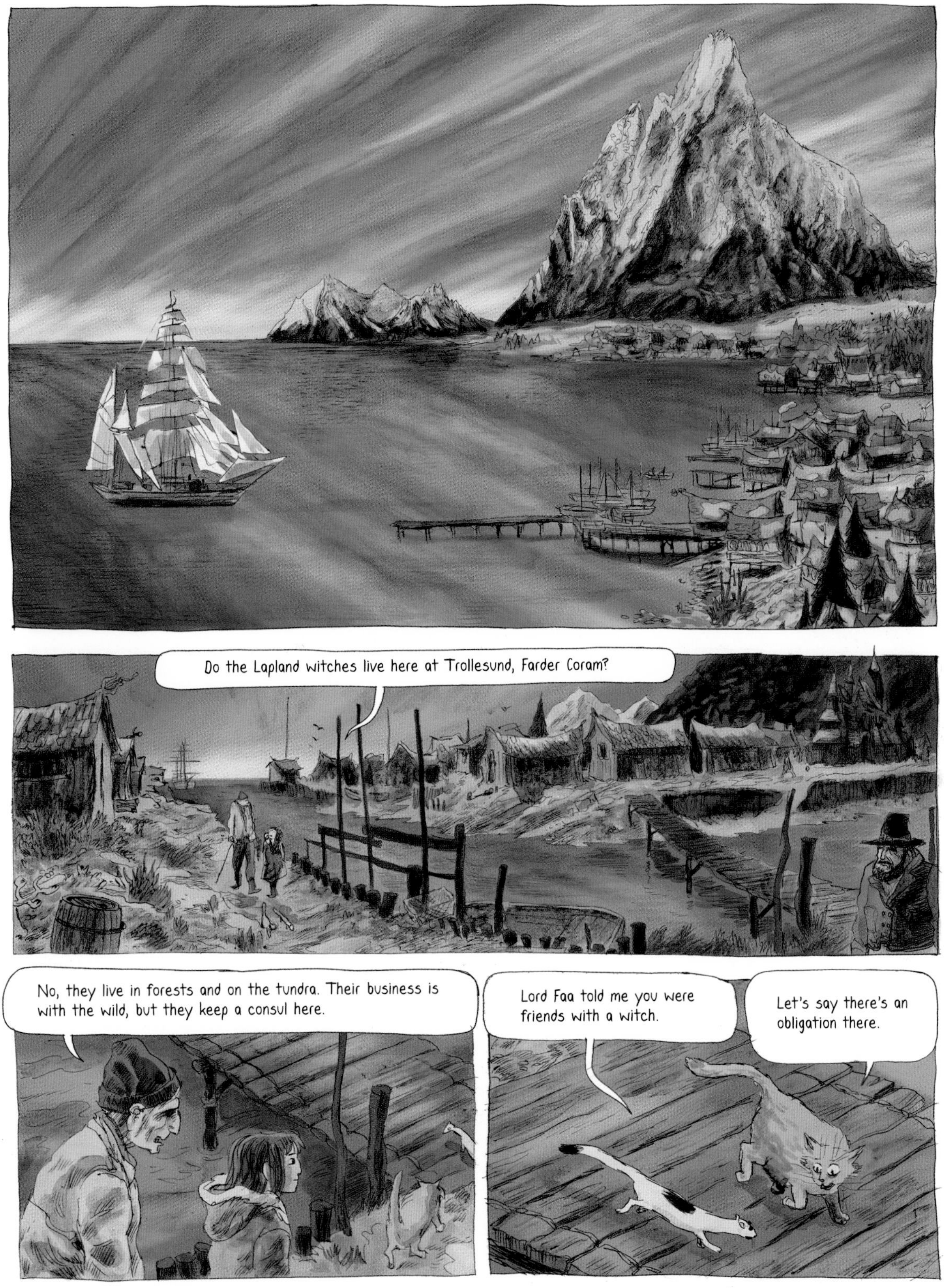
Do the Lapland witches live here at Trollesund, Farder Coram?
No, they live in forests and on the tundra. Their business is with the wild, but they keep a consul here.
Lord Faa told me you were friends with a witch.
Let's say there's an obligation there.

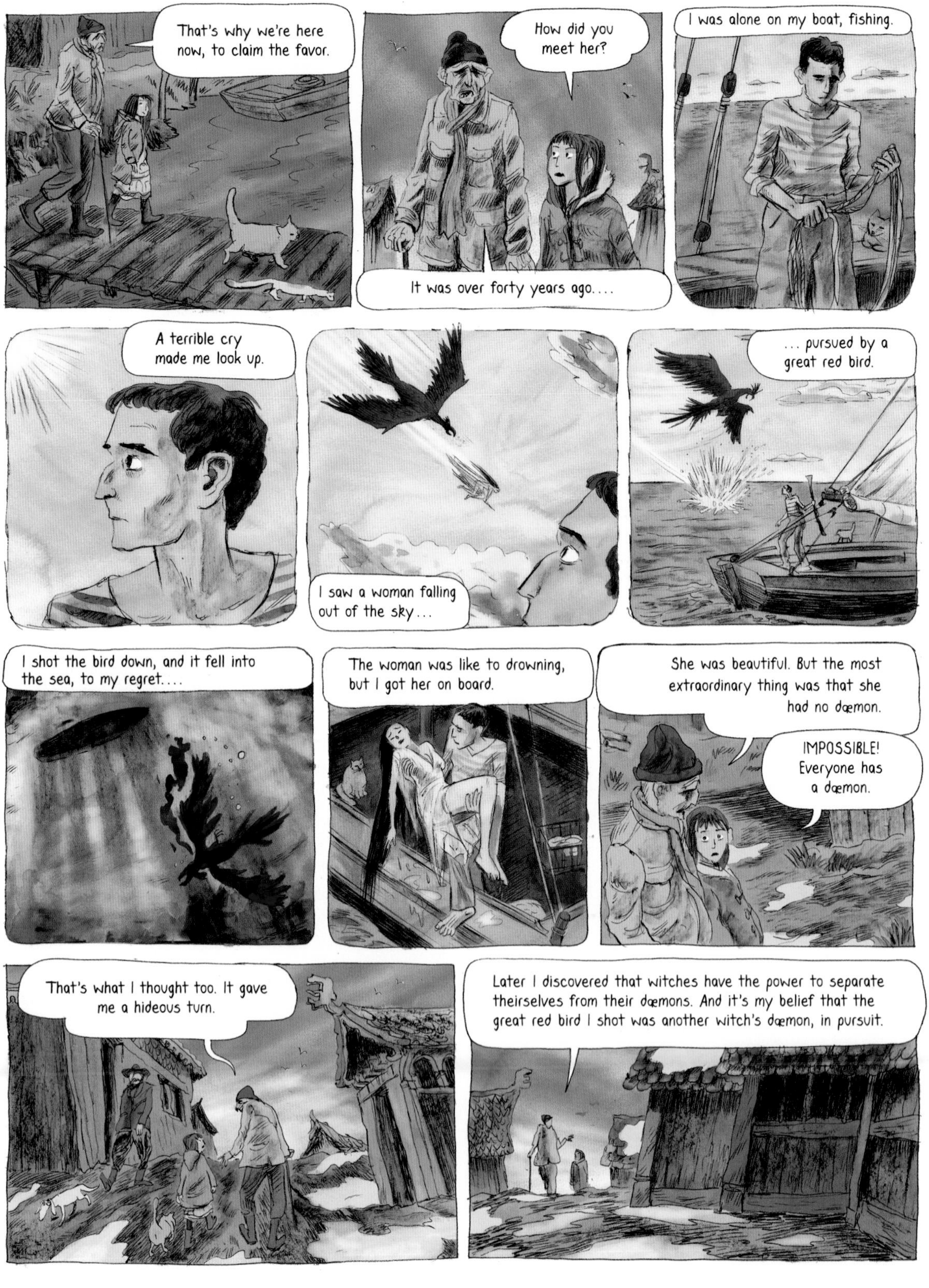
That's why we're here now, to claim the favor.
How did you meet her?
It was over forty years ago....
I was alone on my boat, fishing.
A terrible cry made me look up.
I saw a woman falling out of the sky...
... pursued by a great red bird.
I shot the bird down, and it fell into the sea, to my regret....
The woman was like to drowning, but I got her on board.
She was beautiful. But the most extraordinary thing was that she had no dæmon.
IMPOSSIBLE! Everyone has a dæmon.
That's what I thought too. It gave me a hideous turn.
Later I discovered that witches have the power to separate theirselves from their dæmons. And it's my belief that the great red bird I shot was another witch's dæmon, in pursuit.

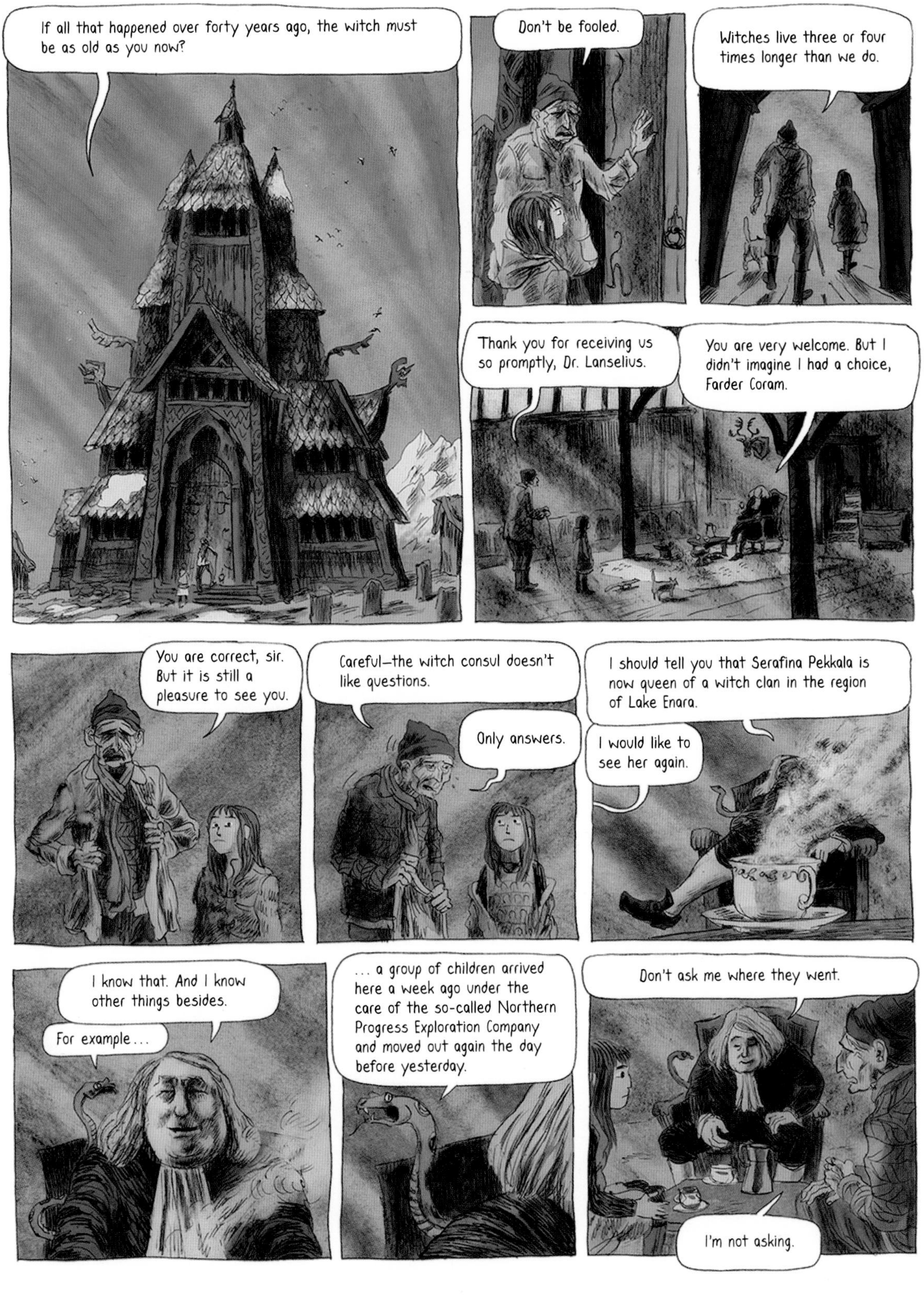

If all that happened over forty years ago, the witch must be as old as you now?
Don't be fooled.
Witches live three or four times longer than we do.
Thank you for receiving us so promptly, Dr. Lanselius.
You are very welcome. But I didn't imagine I had a choice, Farder Coram.
You are correct, sir. But it is still a pleasure to see you.
Careful—the witch consul doesn't like questions.
Only answers.
I should tell you that Serafina Pekkala is now queen of a witch clan in the region of Lake Enara.
I would like to see her again.
I know that. And I know other things besides.
For example . . .
. . . a group of children arrived here a week ago under the care of the so-called Northern Progress Exploration Company and moved out again the day before yesterday.
Don't ask me where they went.
I'm not asking.

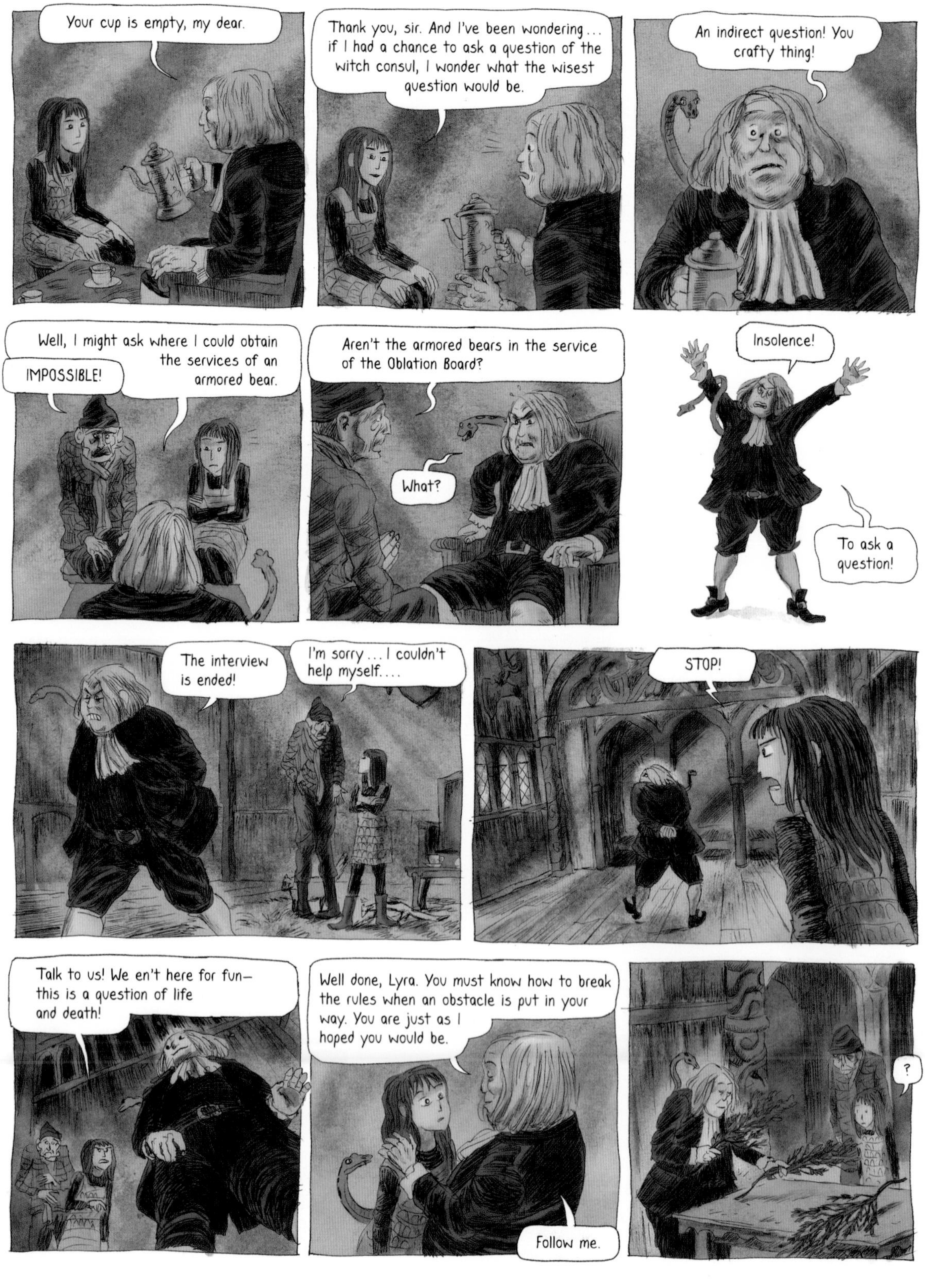
Your cup is empty, my dear.
Thank you, sir. And I've been wondering . . . if I had a chance to ask a question of the witch consul, I wonder what the wisest question would be.
An indirect question! You crafty thing!
Well, I might ask where I could obtain the services of an armored bear.
IMPOSSIBLE!
Aren't the armored bears in the service of the Oblation Board?
What?
Insolence!
To ask a question!
The interview is ended!
I'm sorry . . . I couldn't help myself. . . .
STOP!
Talk to us! We en't here for fun— this is a question of life and death!
Well done, Lyra. You must know how to break the rules when an obstacle is put in your way. You are just as I hoped you would be.
Follow me.
?

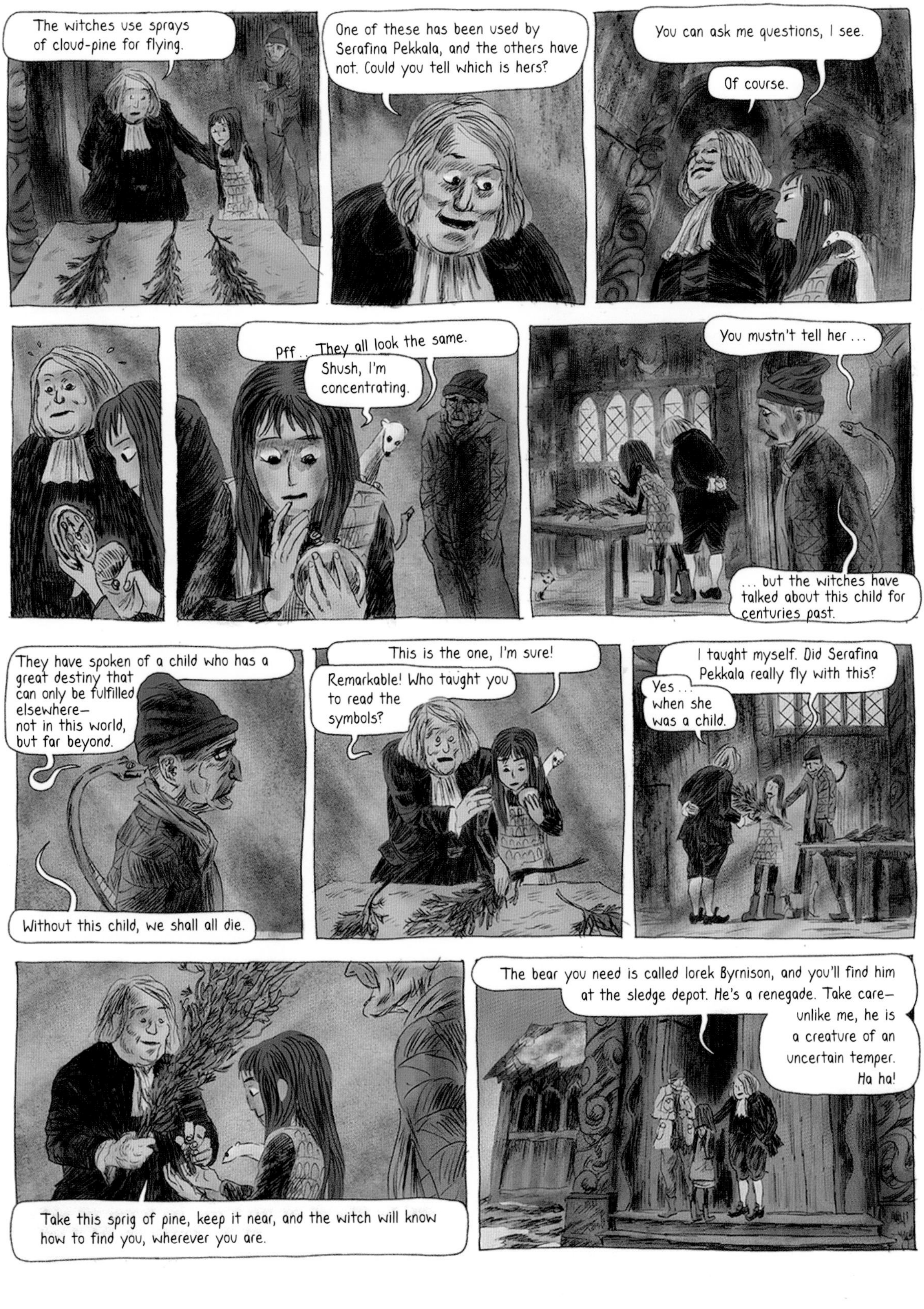

The witches use sprays of cloud-pine for flying.
One of these has been used by Serafina Pekkala, and the others have not. Could you tell which is hers?
You can ask me questions, I see.
Of course.
Pff... They all look the same.
Shush, I'm concentrating.
You mustn't tell her...
... but the witches have talked about this child for centuries past.
They have spoken of a child who has a great destiny that can only be fulfilled elsewhere— not in this world, but far beyond.
Without this child, we shall all die.
This is the one, I'm sure!
Remarkable! Who taught you to read the symbols?
I taught myself. Did Serafina Pekkala really fly with this?
Yes... when she was a child.
Take this sprig of pine, keep it near, and the witch will know how to find you, wherever you are.
The bear you need is called Iorek Byrnison, and you'll find him at the sledge depot. He's a renegade. Take care— unlike me, he is a creature of an uncertain temper. Ha ha!

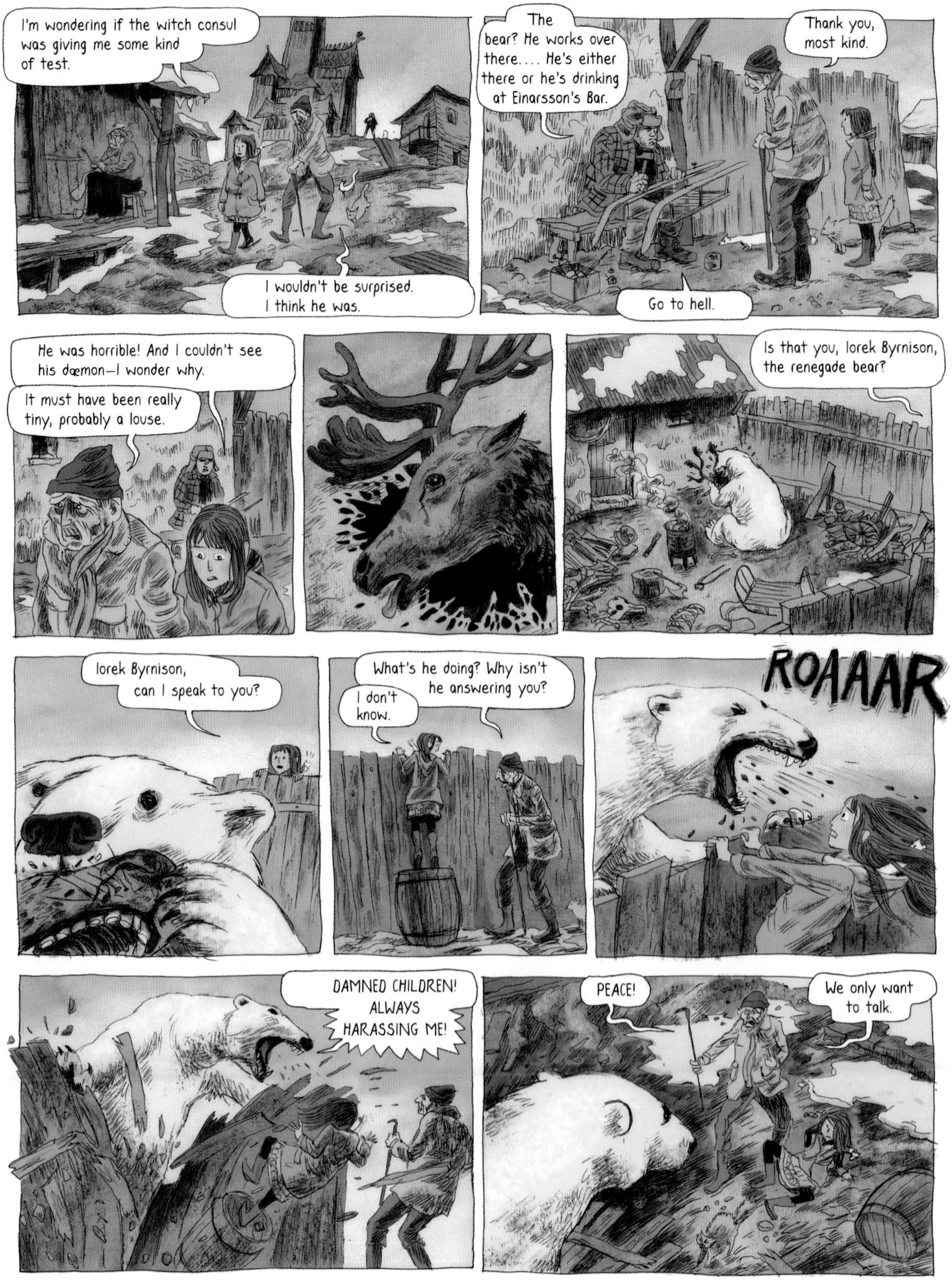

I'm wondering if the witch consul was giving me some kind of test.
I wouldn't be surprised. I think he was.
The bear? He works over there.... He's either there or he's drinking at Einarsson's Bar.
Thank you, most kind.
Go to hell.
He was horrible! And I couldn't see his dæmon—I wonder why.
It must have been really tiny, probably a louse.
Is that you, Iorek Byrnison, the renegade bear?
Iorek Byrnison, can I speak to you?
What's he doing? Why isn't he answering you?
I don't know.
ROAAAR
DAMNED CHILDREN! ALWAYS HARASSING ME!
PEACE!
We only want to talk.

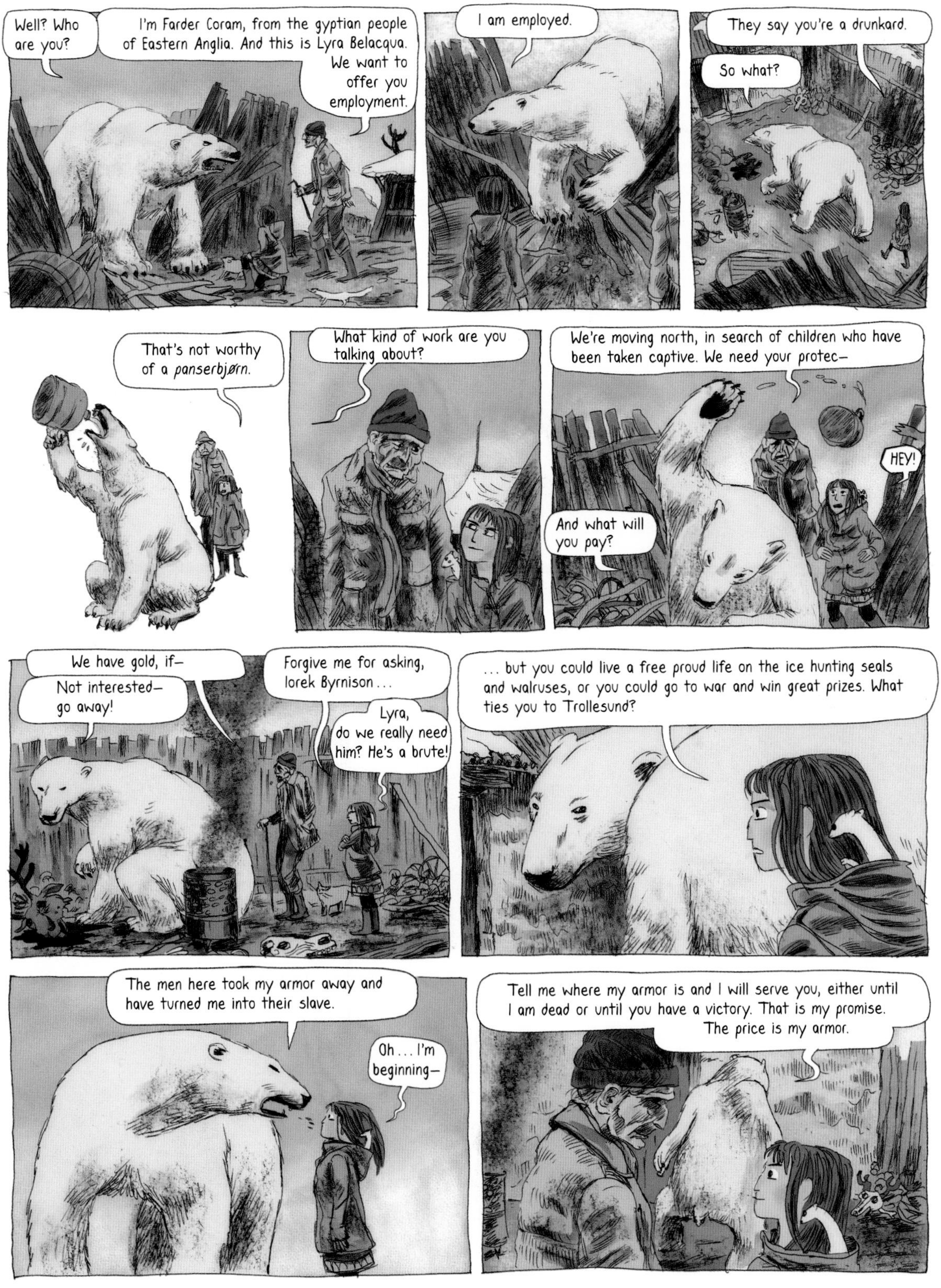

Well? Who are you?
I'm Farder Coram, from the gyptian people of Eastern Anglia. And this is Lyra Belacqua. We want to offer you employment.
I am employed.
They say you're a drunkard.
So what?
That's not worthy of a *panserbjørn*.
What kind of work are you talking about?
We're moving north, in search of children who have been taken captive. We need your protec—
HEY!
And what will you pay?
We have gold, if—
Not interested— go away!
Forgive me for asking, Iorek Byrnison . . .
Lyra, do we really need him? He's a brute!
. . . but you could live a free proud life on the ice hunting seals and walruses, or you could go to war and win great prizes. What ties you to Trollesund?
The men here took my armor away and have turned me into their slave.
Oh . . . I'm beginning—
Tell me where my armor is and I will serve you, either until I am dead or until you have a victory. That is my promise.
The price is my armor.

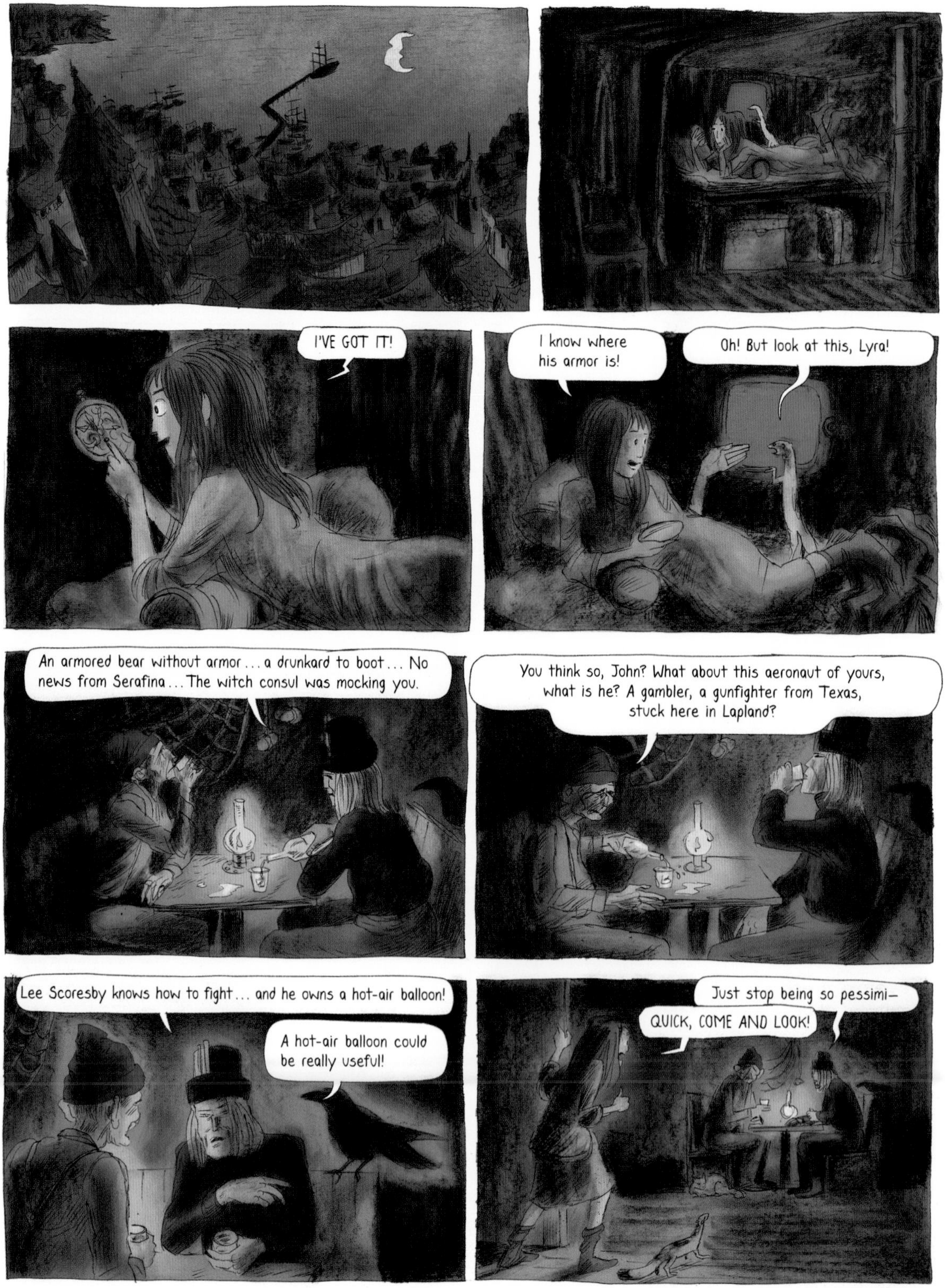
I'VE GOT IT!
I know where his armor is!
Oh! But look at this, Lyra!
An armored bear without armor... a drunkard to boot... No news from Serafina... The witch consul was mocking you.
You think so, John? What about this aeronaut of yours, what is he? A gambler, a gunfighter from Texas, stuck here in Lapland?
Lee Scoresby knows how to fight... and he owns a hot-air balloon!
A hot-air balloon could be really useful!
Just stop being so pessimi–
QUICK, COME AND LOOK!

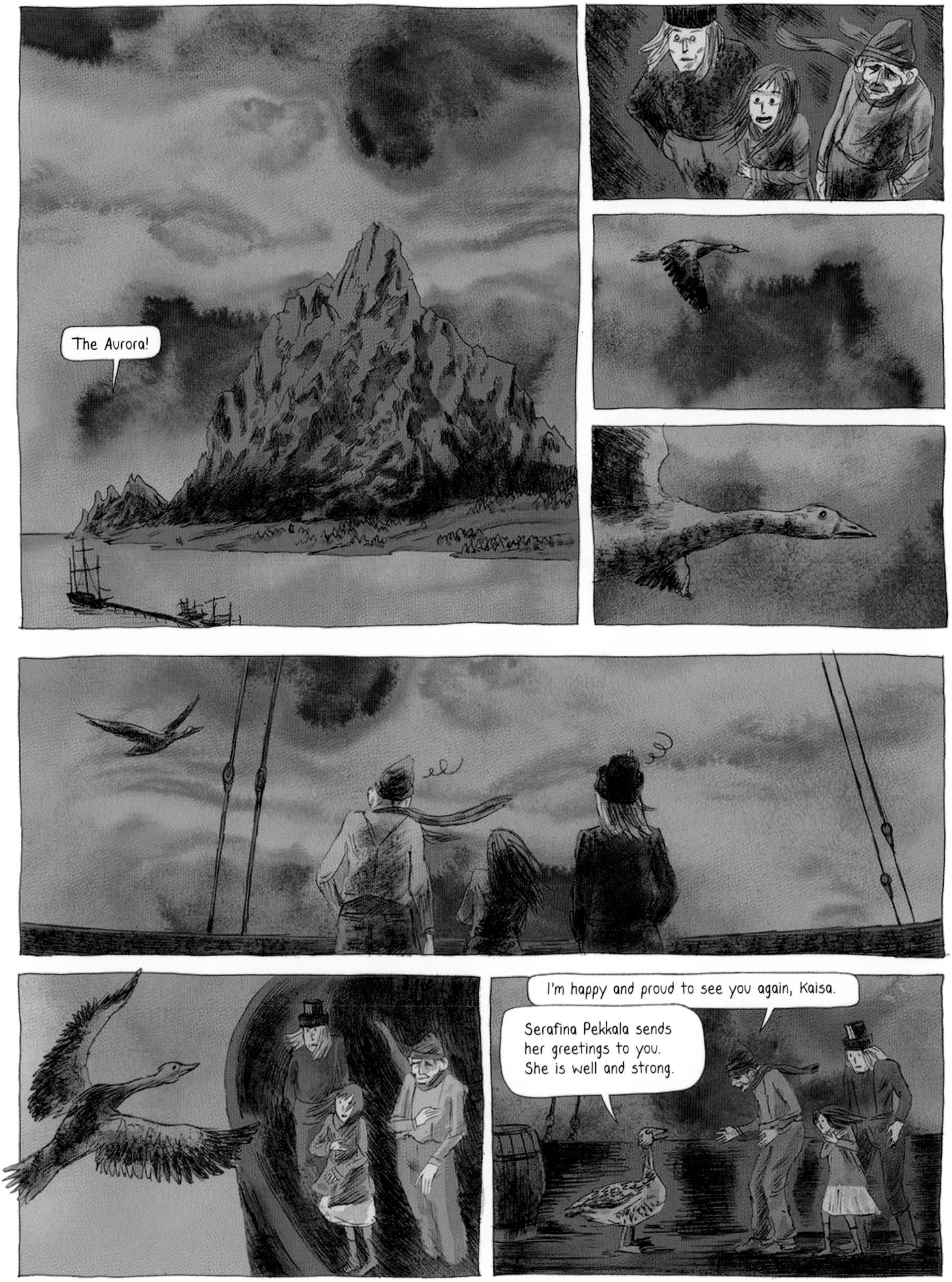
The Aurora!
I'm happy and proud to see you again, Kaisa.
Serafina Pekkala sends her greetings to you. She is well and strong.

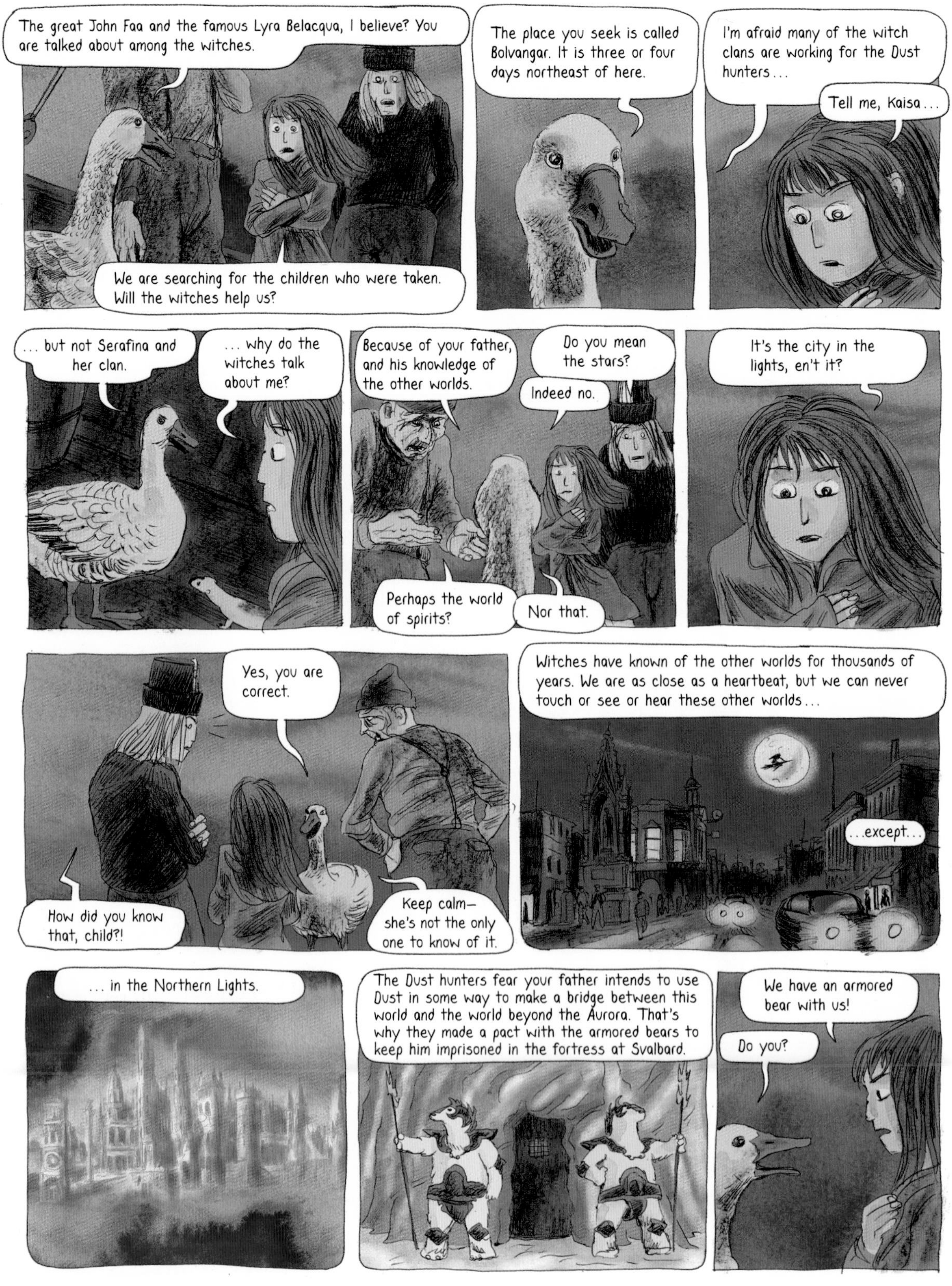
The great John Faa and the famous Lyra Belacqua, I believe? You are talked about among the witches.
We are searching for the children who were taken. Will the witches help us?
The place you seek is called Bolvangar. It is three or four days northeast of here.
I'm afraid many of the witch clans are working for the Dust hunters...
Tell me, Kaisa...
... but not Serafina and her clan.
... why do the witches talk about me?
Because of your father, and his knowledge of the other worlds.
Do you mean the stars?
Indeed no.
Perhaps the world of spirits?
Nor that.
It's the city in the lights, en't it?
Yes, you are correct.
How did you know that, child?!
Keep calm— she's not the only one to know of it.
Witches have known of the other worlds for thousands of years. We are as close as a heartbeat, but we can never touch or see or hear these other worlds...
...except...
... in the Northern Lights.
The Dust hunters fear your father intends to use Dust in some way to make a bridge between this world and the world beyond the Aurora. That's why they made a pact with the armored bears to keep him imprisoned in the fortress at Svalbard.
We have an armored bear with us!
Do you?

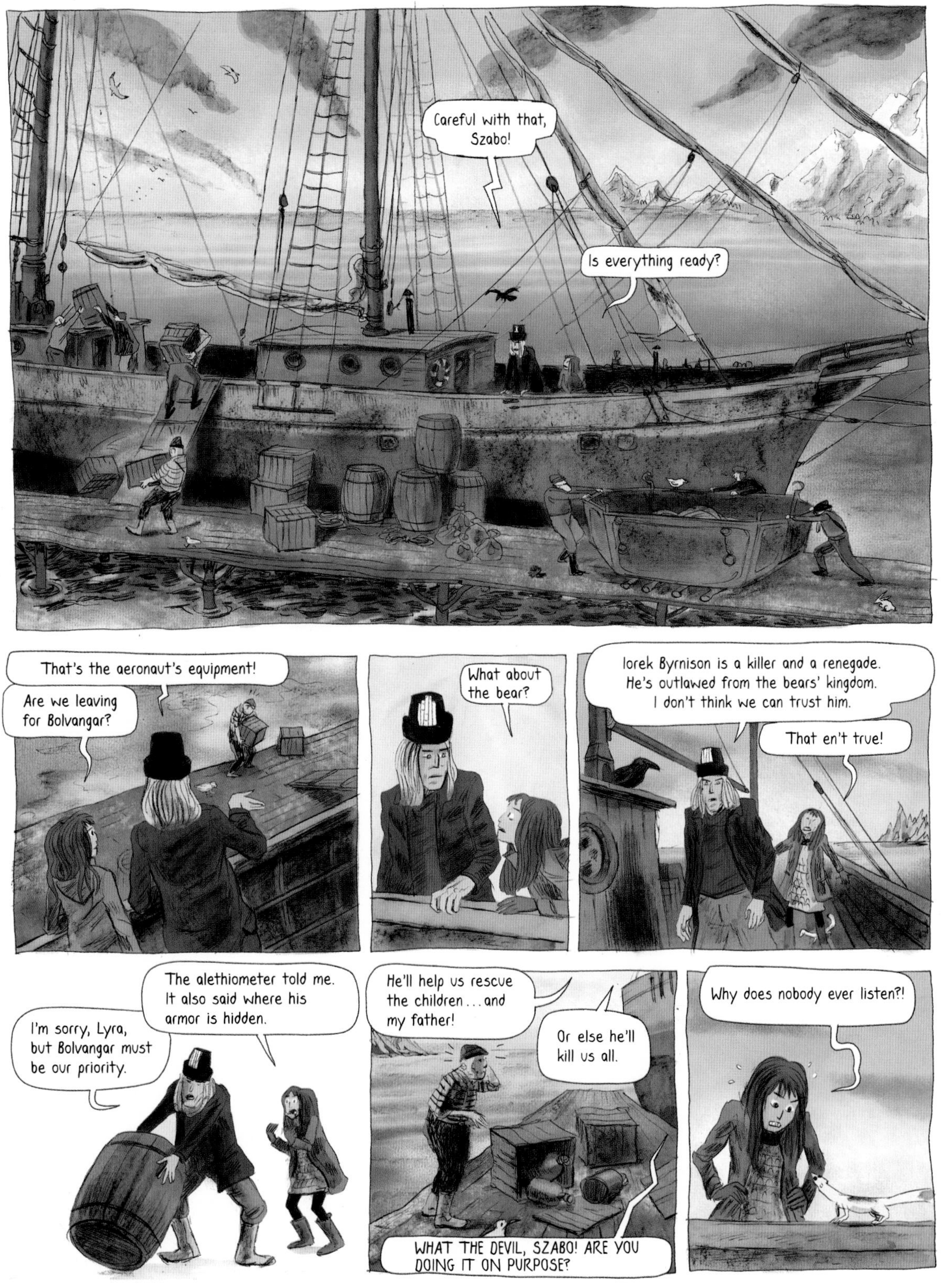
Careful with that, Szabo!
Is everything ready?
That's the aeronaut's equipment!
Are we leaving for Bolvangar?
What about the bear?
Iorek Byrnison is a killer and a renegade. He's outlawed from the bears' kingdom. I don't think we can trust him.
That en't true!
The alethiometer told me. It also said where his armor is hidden.
I'm sorry, Lyra, but Bolvangar must be our priority.
He'll help us rescue the children . . . and my father!
Or else he'll kill us all.
WHAT THE DEVIL, SZABO! ARE YOU DOING IT ON PURPOSE?
Why does nobody ever listen?!

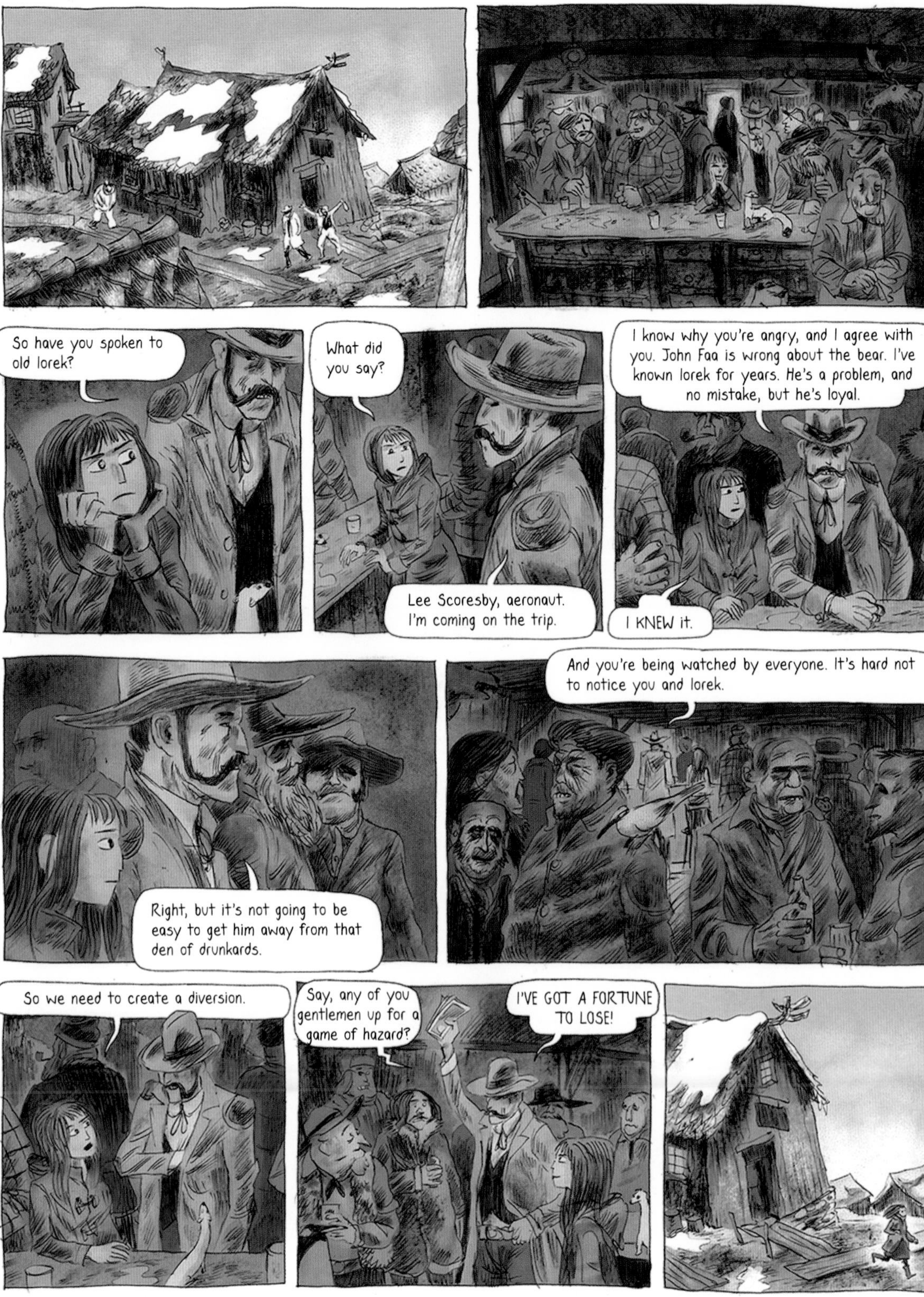
So have you spoken to old Iorek?
What did you say?
Lee Scoresby, aeronaut. I'm coming on the trip.
I know why you're angry, and I agree with you. John Faa is wrong about the bear. I've known Iorek for years. He's a problem, and no mistake, but he's loyal.
I KNEW it.
Right, but it's not going to be easy to get him away from that den of drunkards.
And you're being watched by everyone. It's hard not to notice you and Iorek.
So we need to create a diversion.
Say, any of you gentlemen up for a game of hazard?
I'VE GOT A FORTUNE TO LOSE!

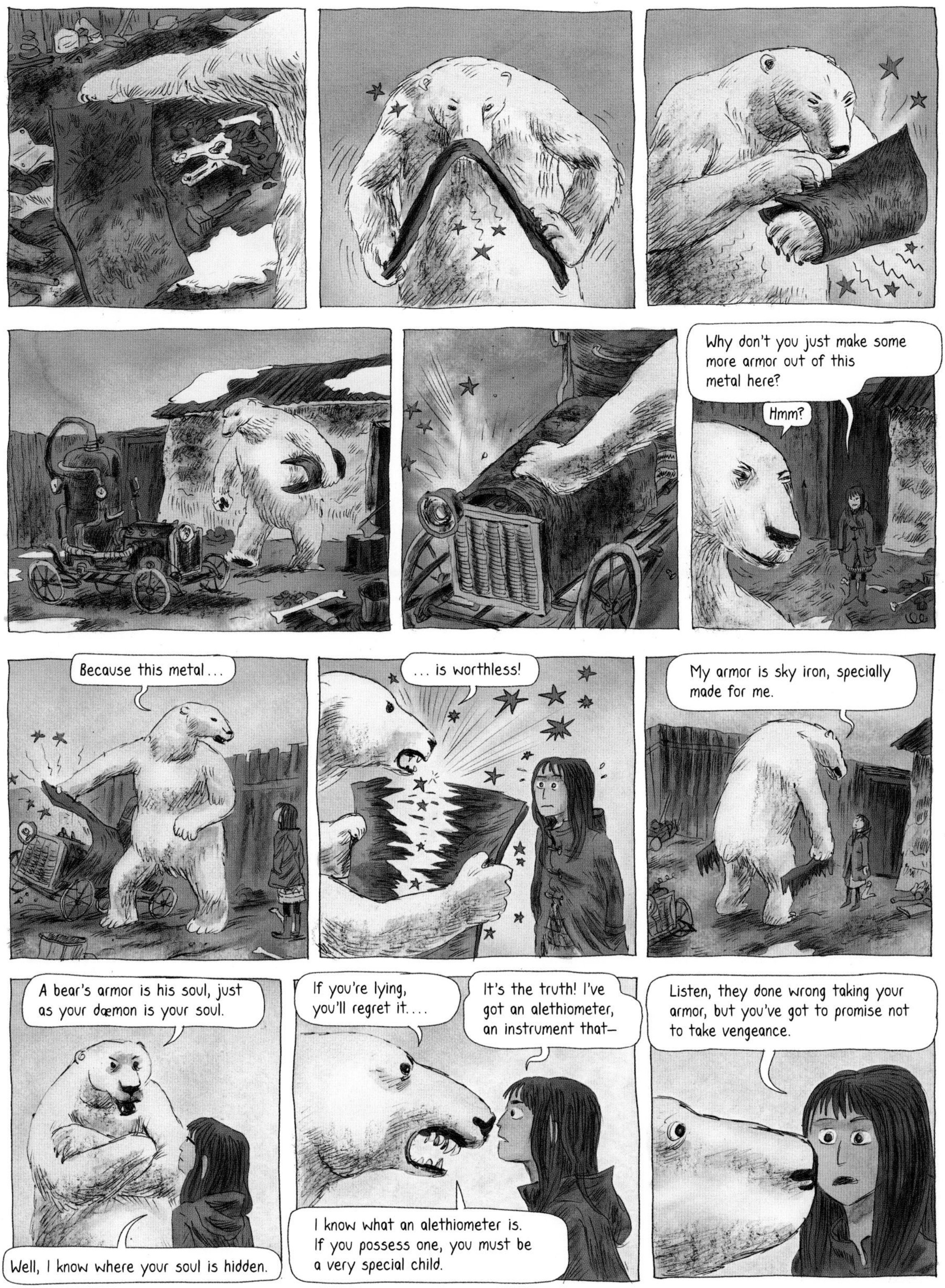
Why don't you just make some more armor out of this metal here?
Hmm?
Because this metal...
... is worthless!
My armor is sky iron, specially made for me.
A bear's armor is his soul, just as your dæmon is your soul.
Well, I know where your soul is hidden.
If you're lying, you'll regret it....
It's the truth! I've got an alethiometer, an instrument that—
I know what an alethiometer is. If you possess one, you must be a very special child.
Listen, they done wrong taking your armor, but you've got to promise not to take vengeance.

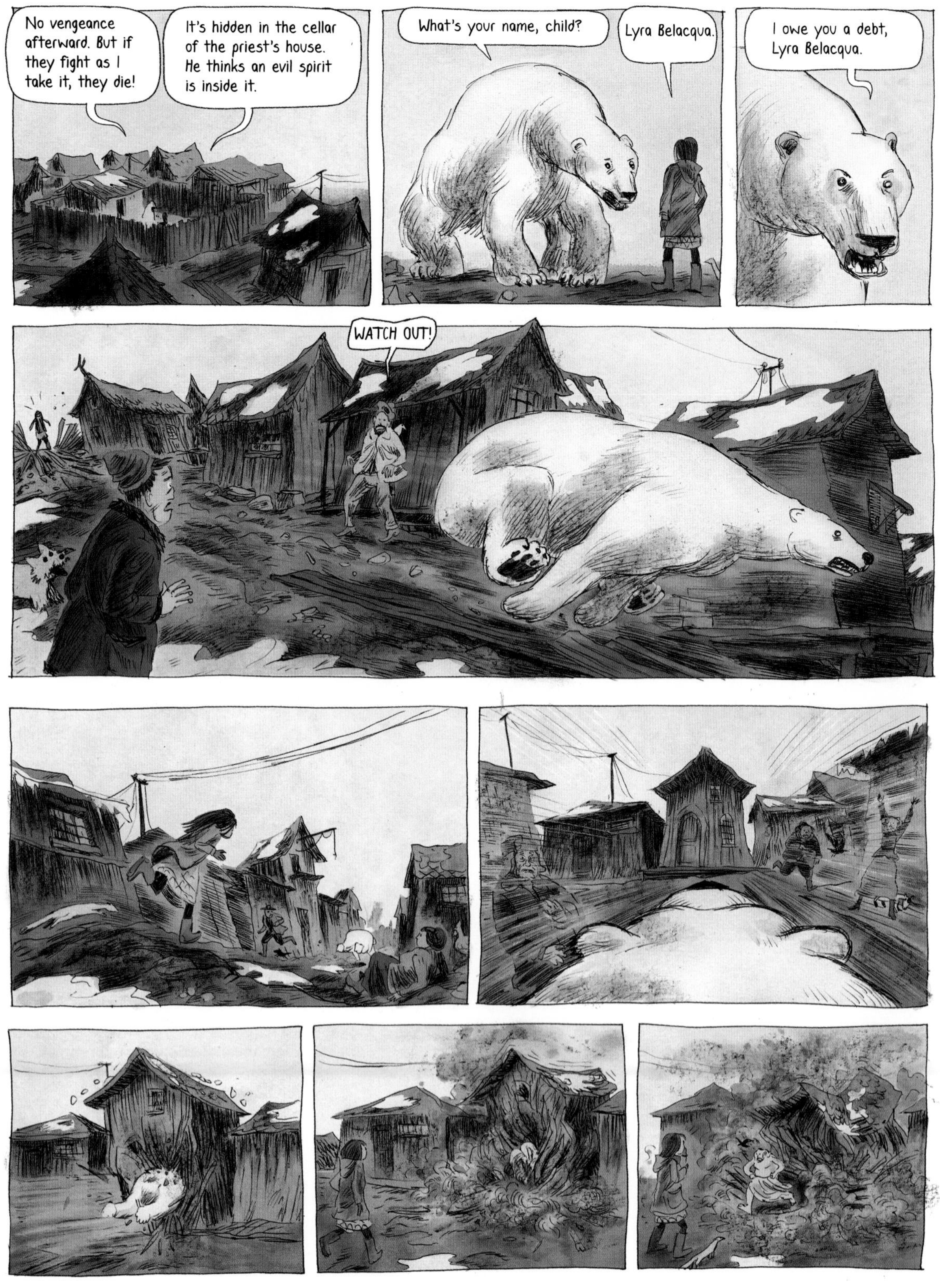
No vengeance afterward. But if they fight as I take it, they die!
It's hidden in the cellar of the priest's house. He thinks an evil spirit is inside it.
What's your name, child?
Lyra Belacqua.
I owe you a debt, Lyra Belacqua.
WATCH OUT!

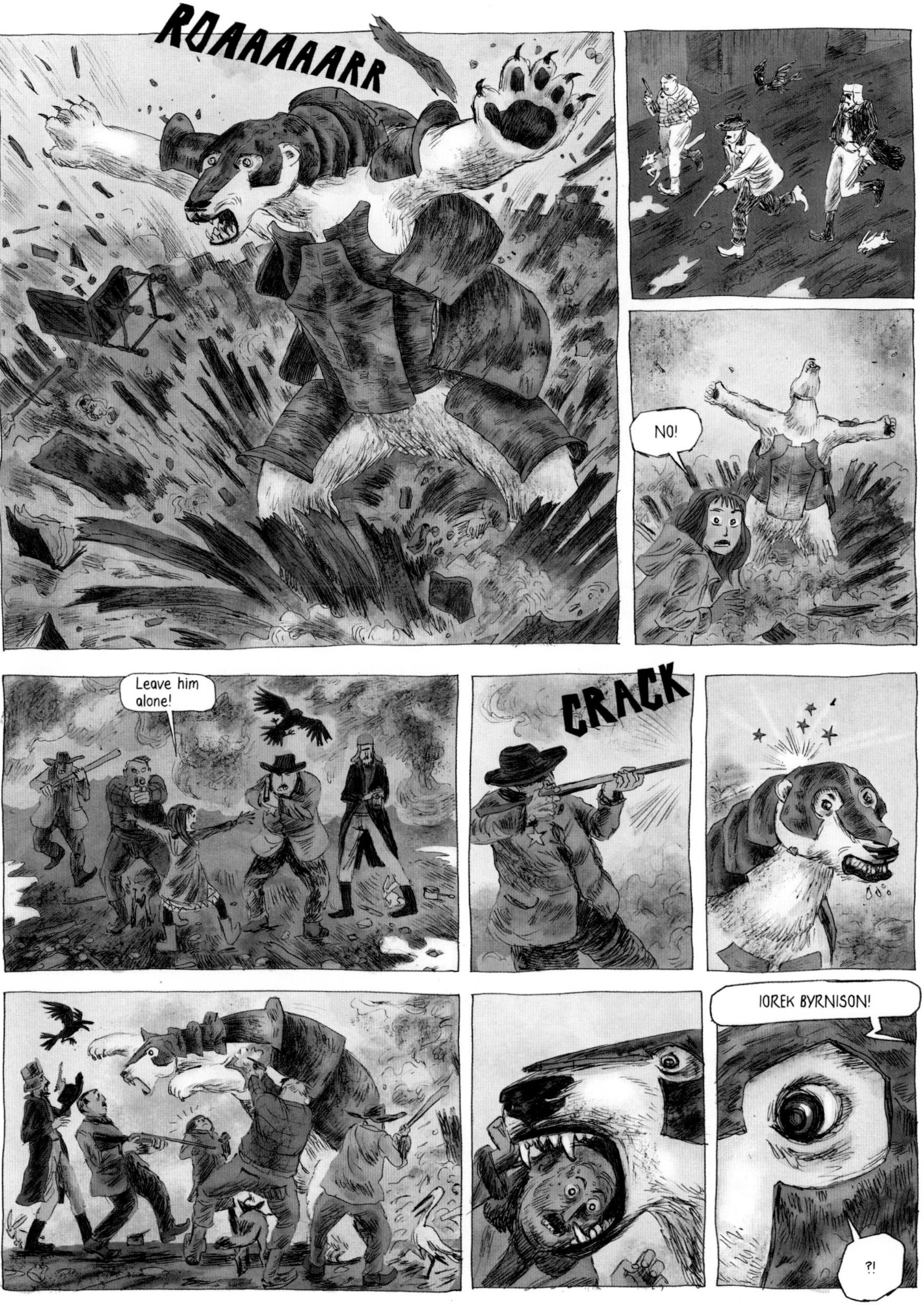
ROAAAAAARR
NO!
Leave him alone!
CRACK
IOREK BYRNISON!
?!

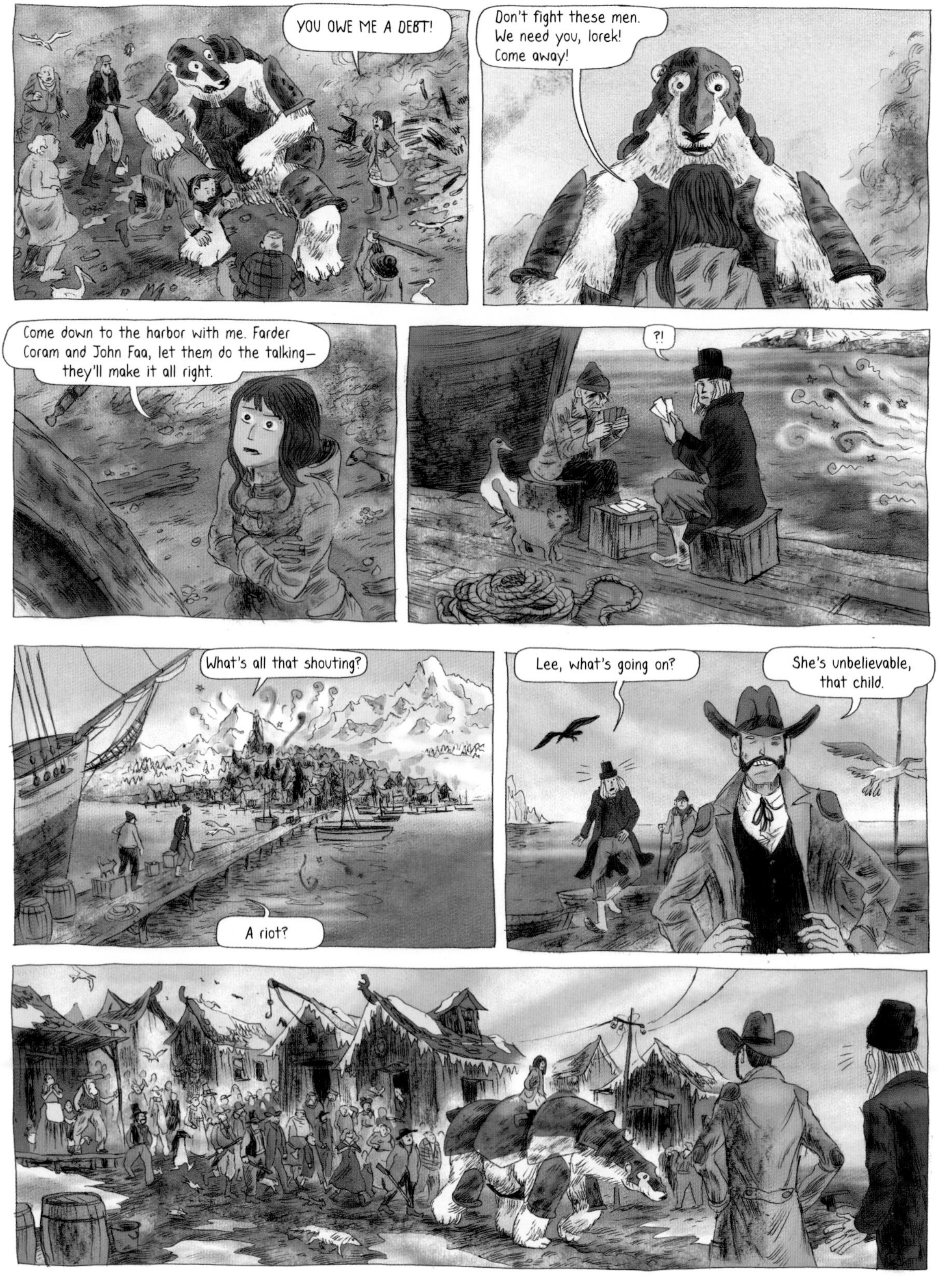
YOU OWE ME A DEBT!
Don't fight these men. We need you, Iorek! Come away!
Come down to the harbor with me. Farder Coram and John Faa, let them do the talking—they'll make it all right.
?!
What's all that shouting?
A riot?
Lee, what's going on?
She's unbelievable, that child.

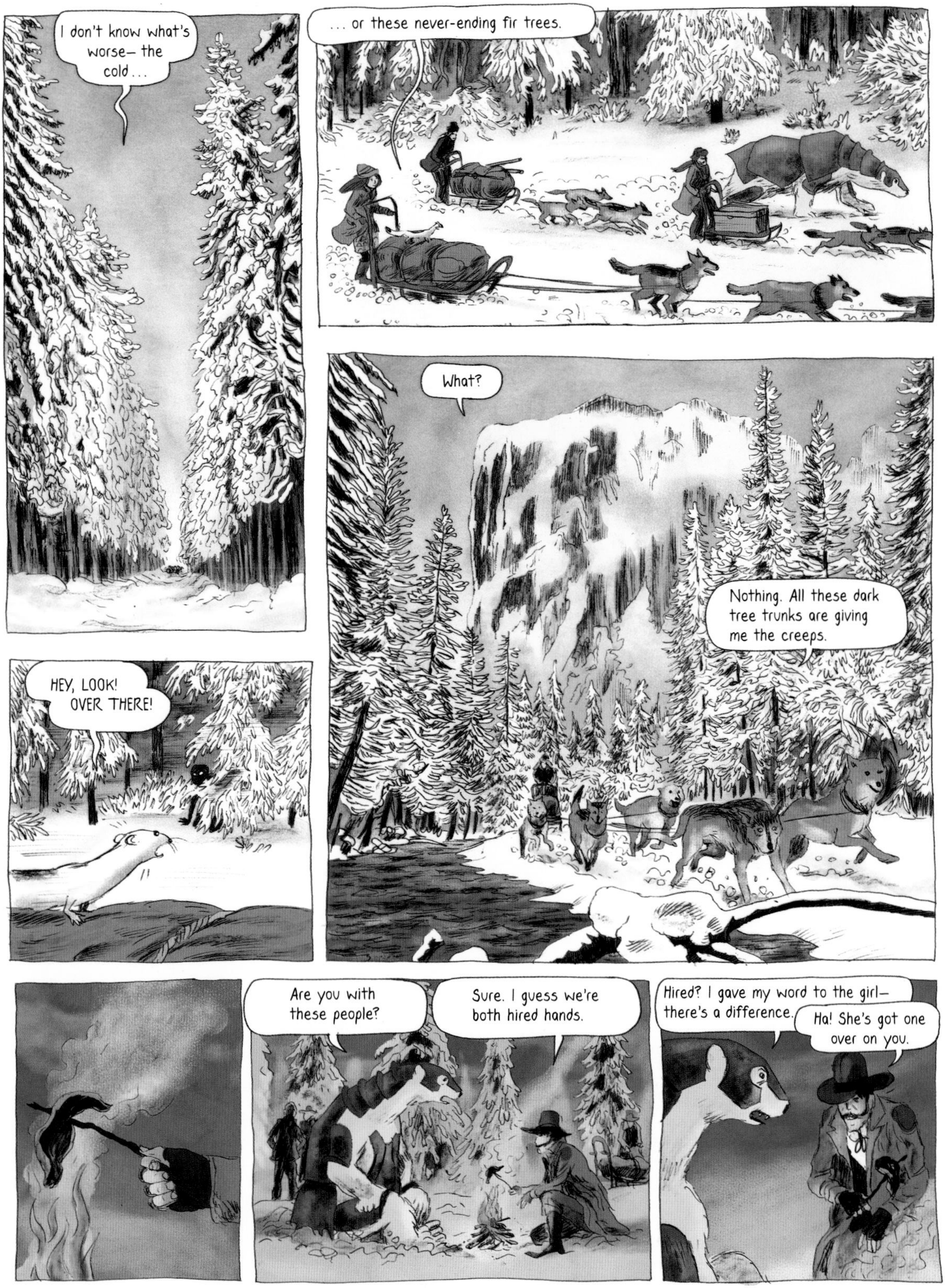
I don't know what's worse– the cold...
... or these never-ending fir trees.
What?
Nothing. All these dark tree trunks are giving me the creeps.
HEY, LOOK! OVER THERE!
Are you with these people?
Sure. I guess we're both hired hands.
Hired? I gave my word to the girl– there's a difference.
Ha! She's got one over on you.

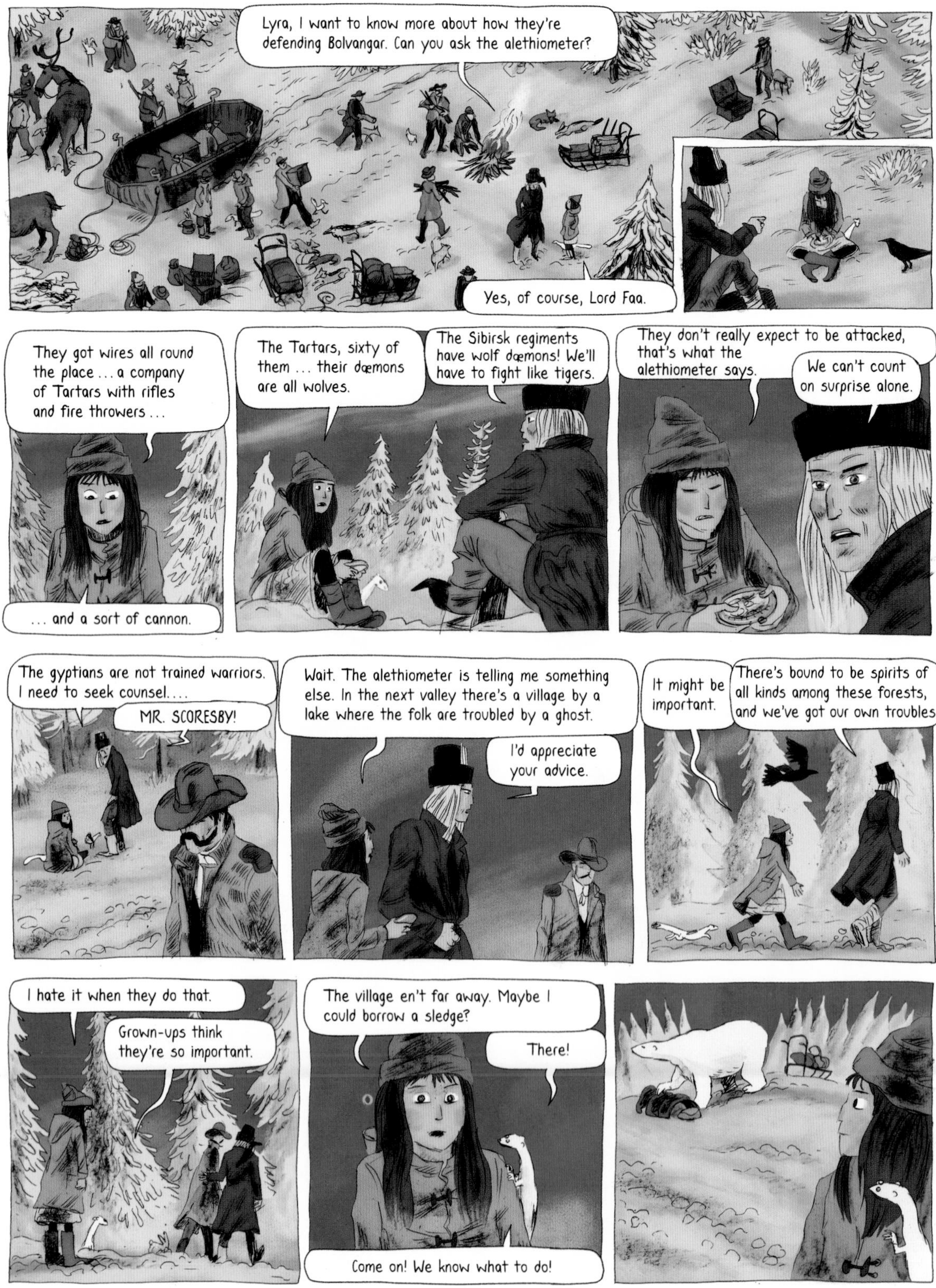
Lyra, I want to know more about how they're defending Bolvangar. Can you ask the alethiometer?
Yes, of course, Lord Faa.
They got wires all round the place . . . a company of Tartars with rifles and fire throwers . . .
. . . and a sort of cannon.
The Tartars, sixty of them . . . their dæmons are all wolves.
The Sibirsk regiments have wolf dæmons! We'll have to fight like tigers.
They don't really expect to be attacked, that's what the alethiometer says.
We can't count on surprise alone.
The gyptians are not trained warriors. I need to seek counsel. . . .
MR. SCORESBY!
Wait. The alethiometer is telling me something else. In the next valley there's a village by a lake where the folk are troubled by a ghost.
I'd appreciate your advice.
It might be important.
There's bound to be spirits of all kinds among these forests, and we've got our own troubles.
I hate it when they do that.
Grown-ups think they're so important.
The village en't far away. Maybe I could borrow a sledge?
There!
Come on! We know what to do!

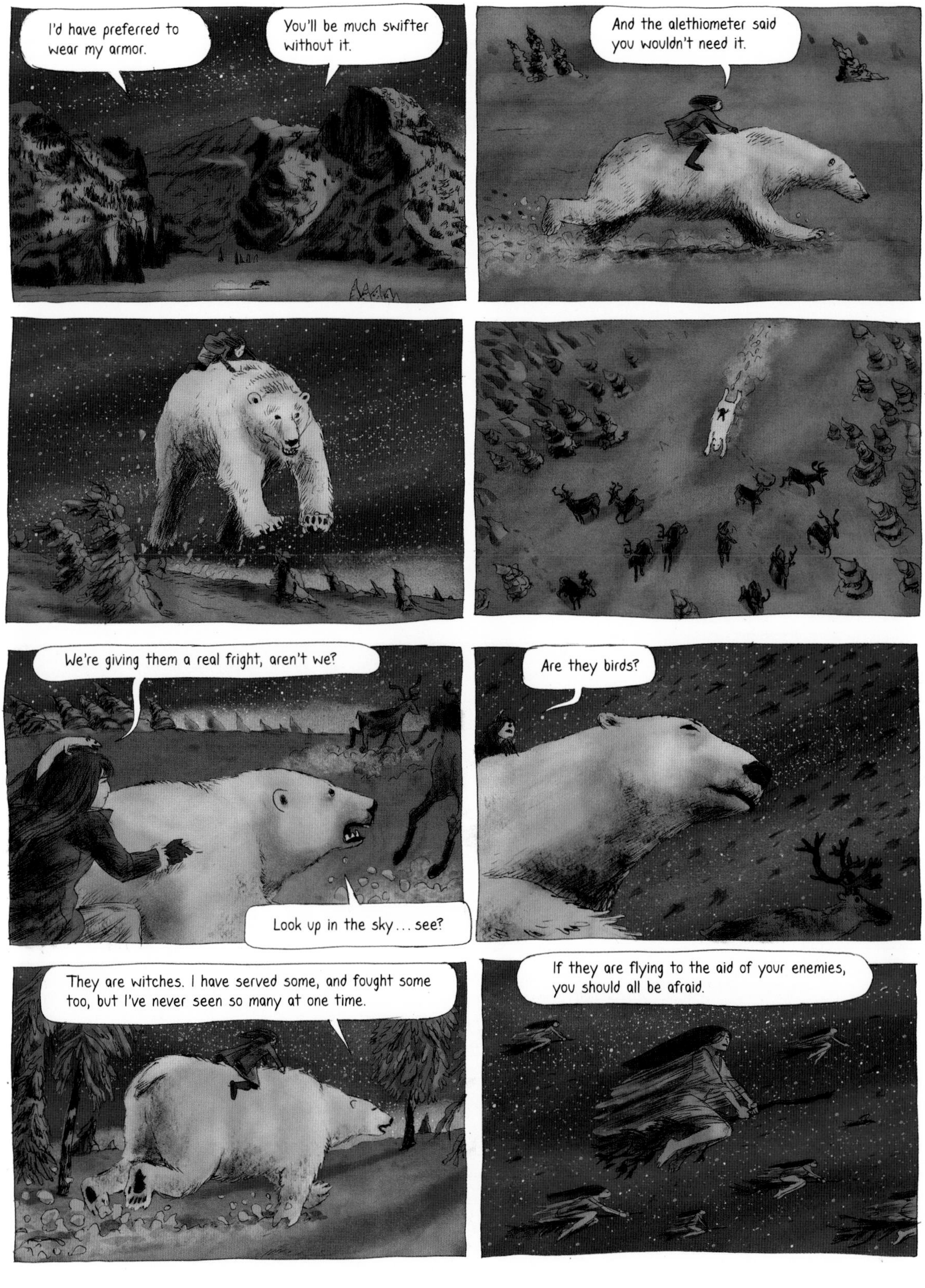

I'd have preferred to wear my armor.
You'll be much swifter without it.
And the alethiometer said you wouldn't need it.
We're giving them a real fright, aren't we?
Look up in the sky... see?
Are they birds?
They are witches. I have served some, and fought some too, but I've never seen so many at one time.
If they are flying to the aid of your enemies, you should all be afraid.

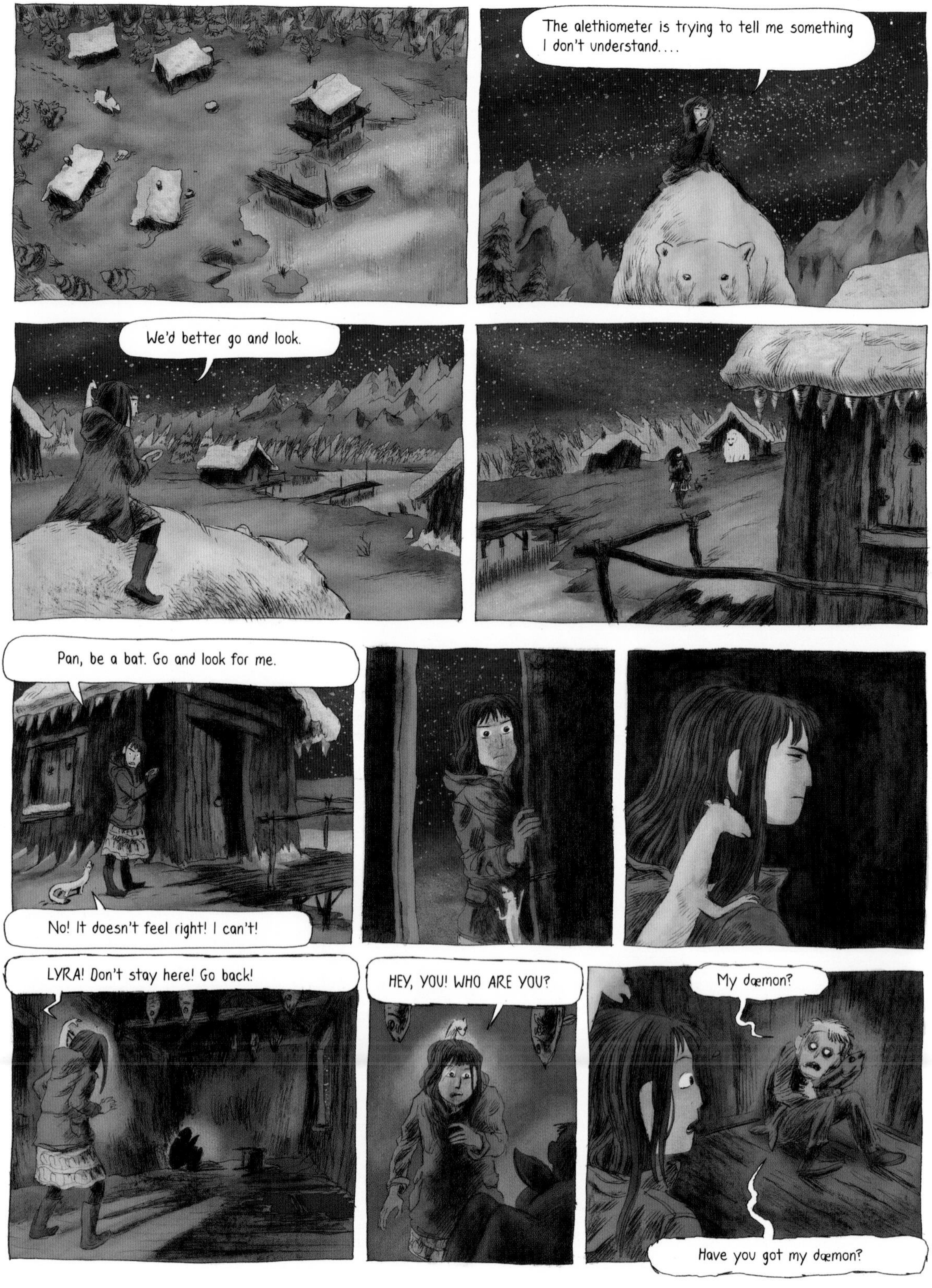
The alethiometer is trying to tell me something I don't understand. . . .
We'd better go and look.
Pan, be a bat. Go and look for me.
No! It doesn't feel right! I can't!
LYRA! Don't stay here! Go back!
HEY, YOU! WHO ARE YOU?
My dæmon?
Have you got my dæmon?

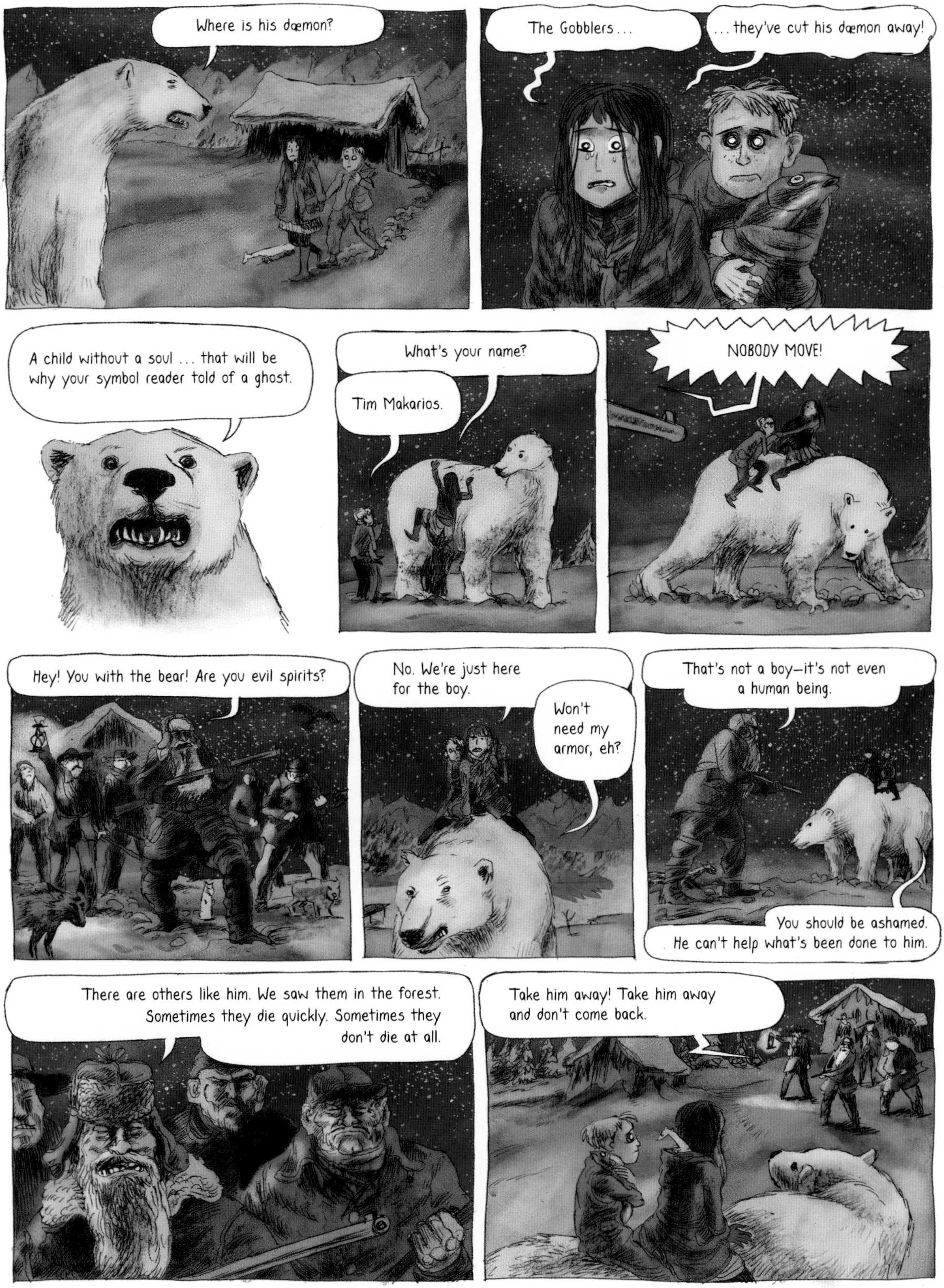

Where is his dæmon?
The Gobblers...
...they've cut his dæmon away!
A child without a soul ... that will be why your symbol reader told of a ghost.
What's your name?
Tim Makarios.
NOBODY MOVE!
Hey! You with the bear! Are you evil spirits?
No. We're just here for the boy.
Won't need my armor, eh?
That's not a boy—it's not even a human being.
You should be ashamed. He can't help what's been done to him.
There are others like him. We saw them in the forest. Sometimes they die quickly. Sometimes they don't die at all.
Take him away! Take him away and don't come back.

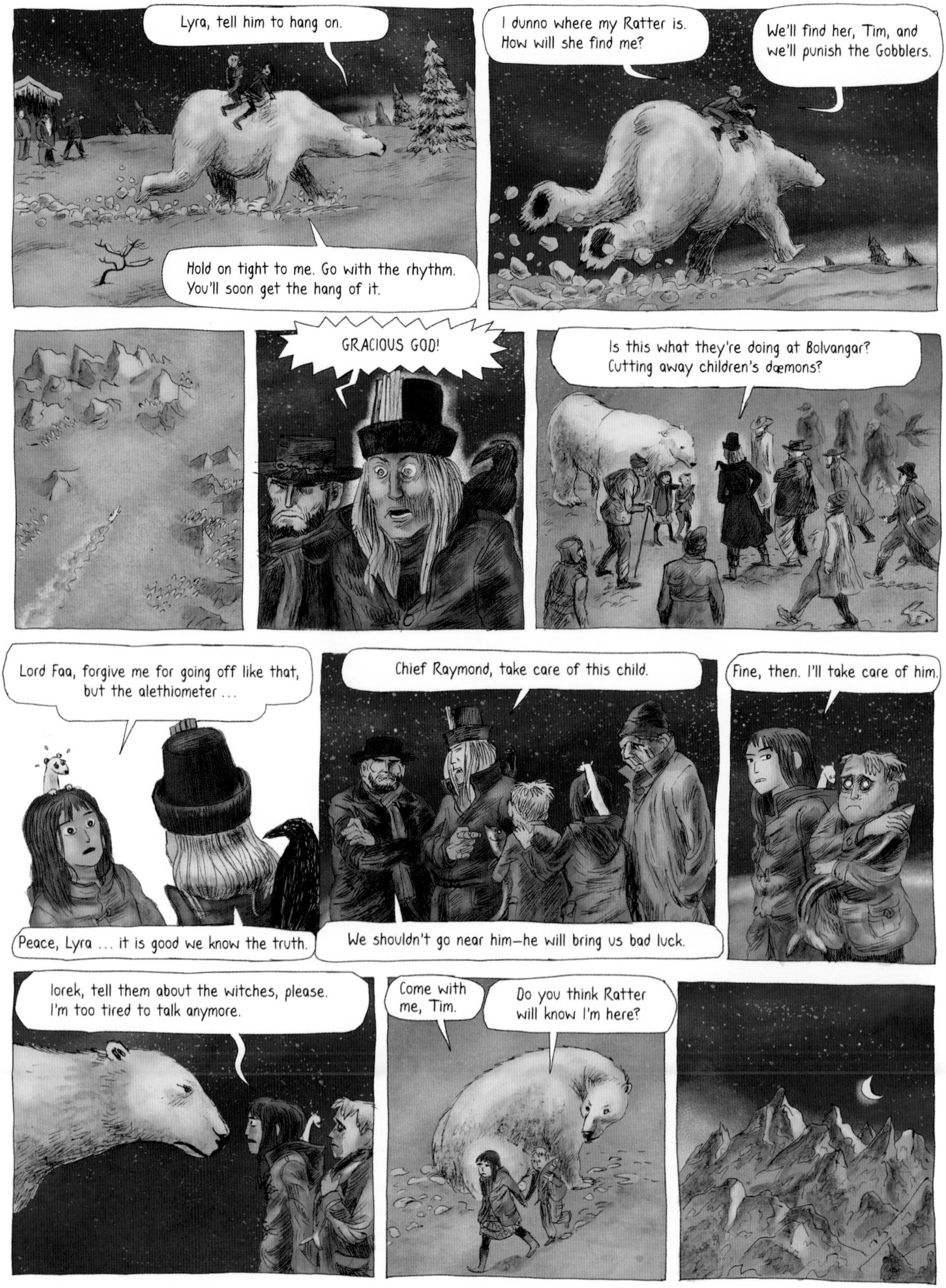

Lyra, tell him to hang on.
Hold on tight to me. Go with the rhythm. You'll soon get the hang of it.
I dunno where my Ratter is. How will she find me?
We'll find her, Tim, and we'll punish the Gobblers.
GRACIOUS GOD!
Is this what they're doing at Bolvangar? Cutting away children's dæmons?
Lord Faa, forgive me for going off like that, but the alethiometer . . .
Peace, Lyra . . . it is good we know the truth.
Chief Raymond, take care of this child.
We shouldn't go near him—he will bring us bad luck.
Fine, then. I'll take care of him.
Iorek, tell them about the witches, please. I'm too tired to talk anymore.
Come with me, Tim.
Do you think Ratter will know I'm here?

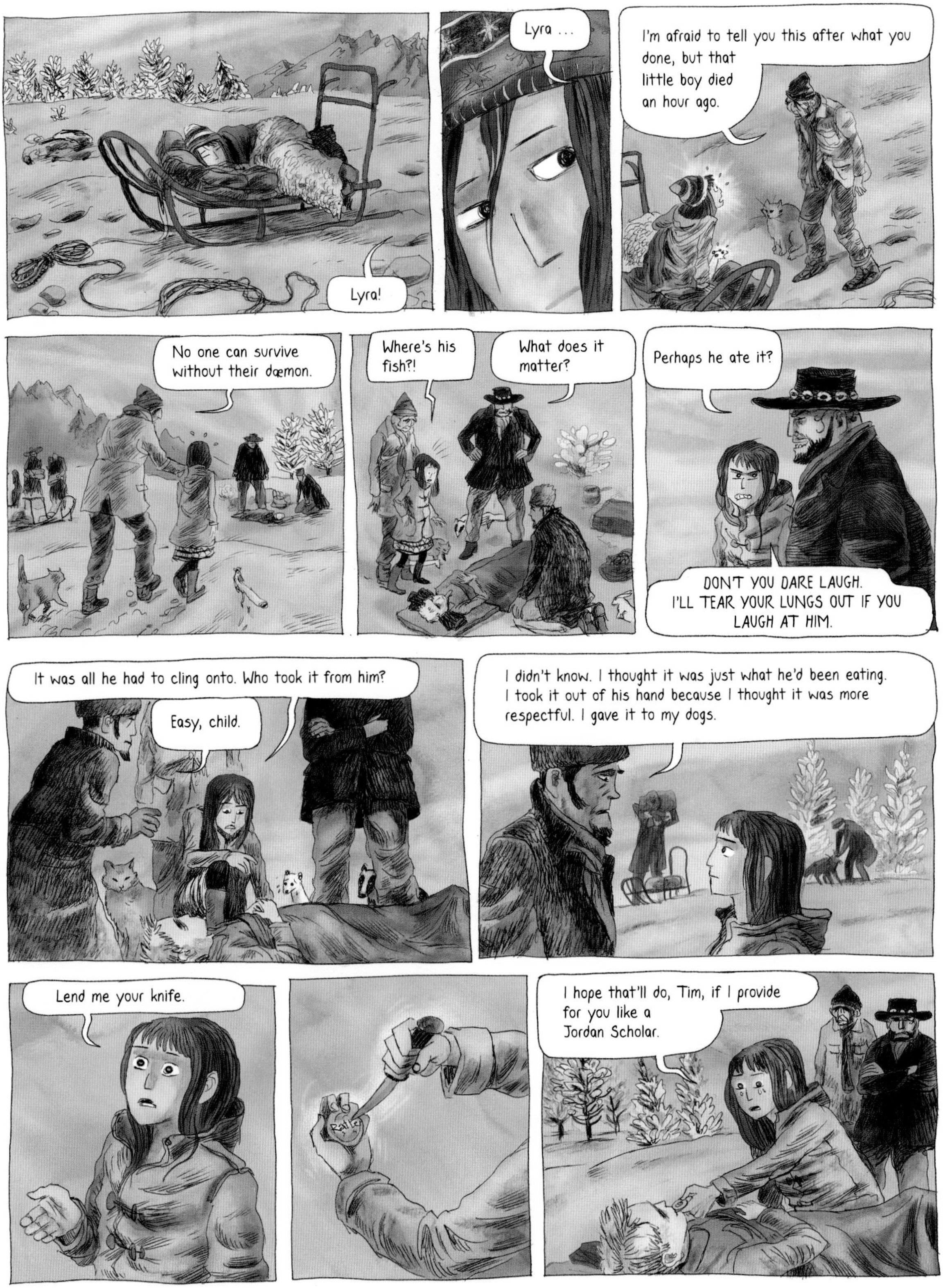
Lyra!
Lyra . . .
I'm afraid to tell you this after what you done, but that little boy died an hour ago.
No one can survive without their dæmon.
Where's his fish?!
What does it matter?
Perhaps he ate it?
DON'T YOU DARE LAUGH. I'LL TEAR YOUR LUNGS OUT IF YOU LAUGH AT HIM.
It was all he had to cling onto. Who took it from him?
Easy, child.
I didn't know. I thought it was just what he'd been eating. I took it out of his hand because I thought it was more respectful. I gave it to my dogs.
Lend me your knife.
I hope that'll do, Tim, if I provide for you like a Jordan Scholar.

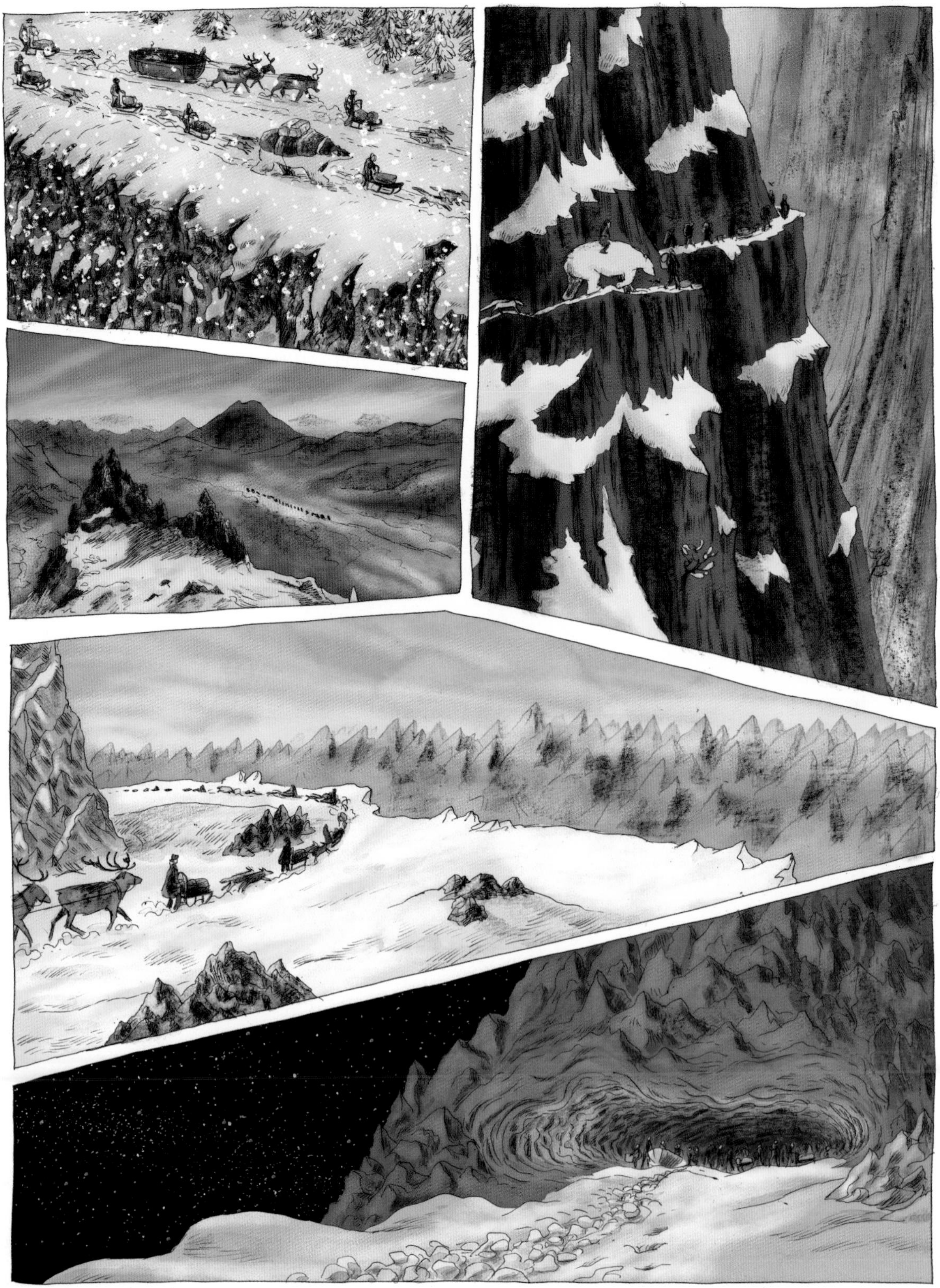

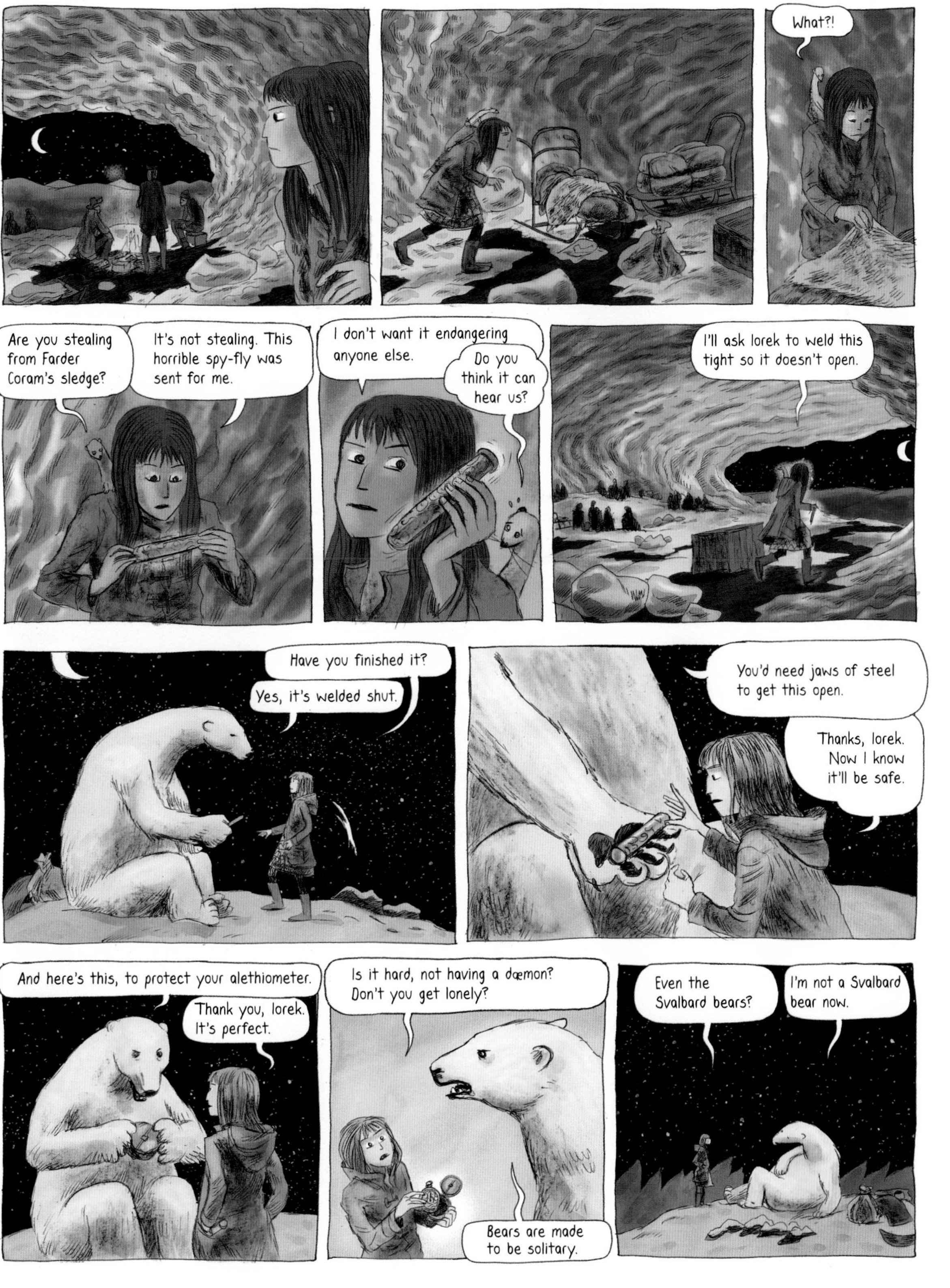
What?!
Are you stealing from Farder Coram's sledge?
It's not stealing. This horrible spy-fly was sent for me.
I don't want it endangering anyone else.
Do you think it can hear us?
I'll ask Iorek to weld this tight so it doesn't open.
Have you finished it?
Yes, it's welded shut.
You'd need jaws of steel to get this open.
Thanks, Iorek. Now I know it'll be safe.
And here's this, to protect your alethiometer.
Thank you, Iorek. It's perfect.
Is it hard, not having a dæmon? Don't you get lonely?
Bears are made to be solitary.
Even the Svalbard bears?
I'm not a Svalbard bear now.

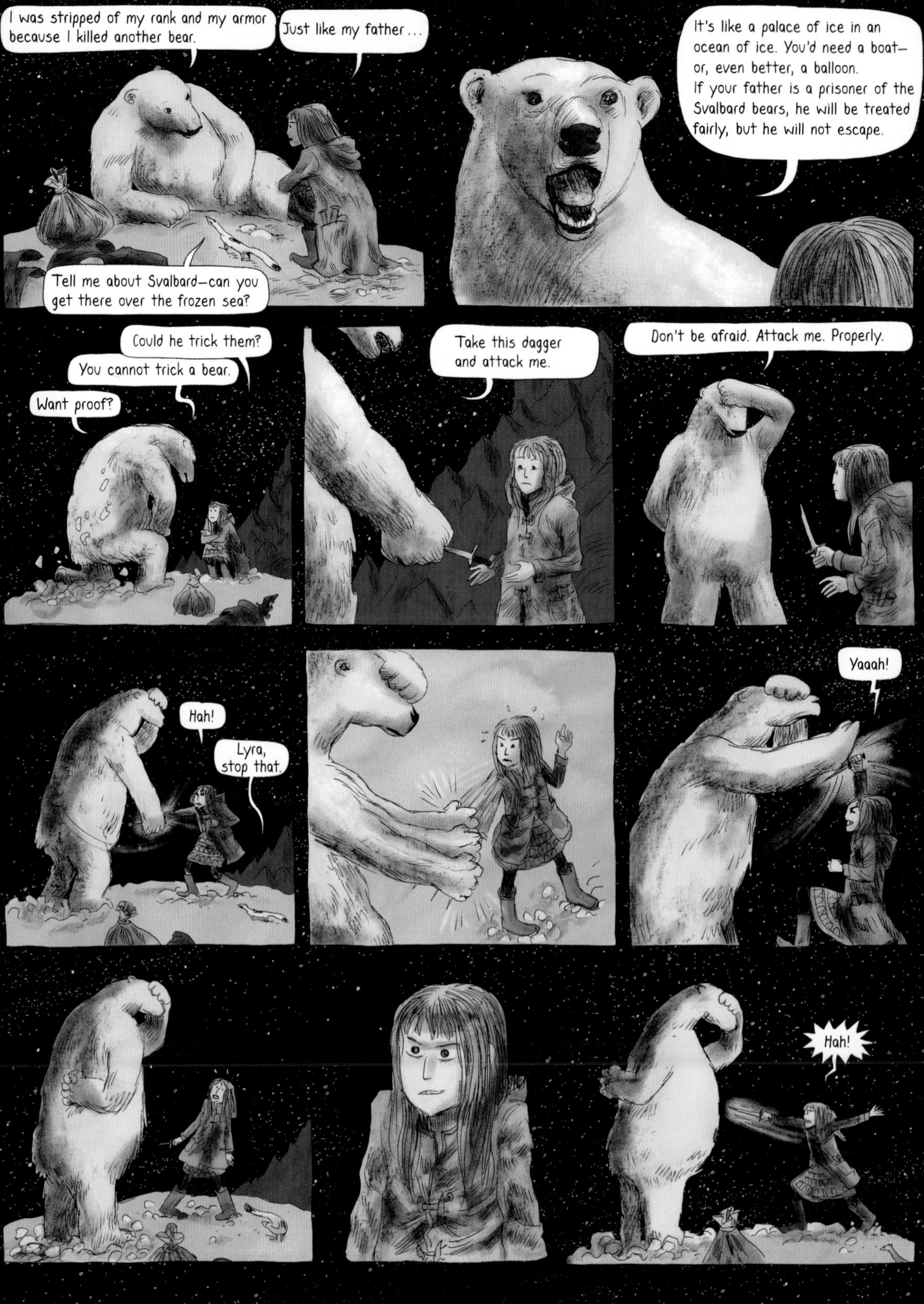
I was stripped of my rank and my armor because I killed another bear.
Just like my father . . .
Tell me about Svalbard—can you get there over the frozen sea?
It's like a palace of ice in an ocean of ice. You'd need a boat—or, even better, a balloon.
If your father is a prisoner of the Svalbard bears, he will be treated fairly, but he will not escape.
Could he trick them?
You cannot trick a bear.
Want proof?
Take this dagger and attack me.
Don't be afraid. Attack me. Properly.
Hah!
Lyra, stop that.
Yaaah!
Hah!

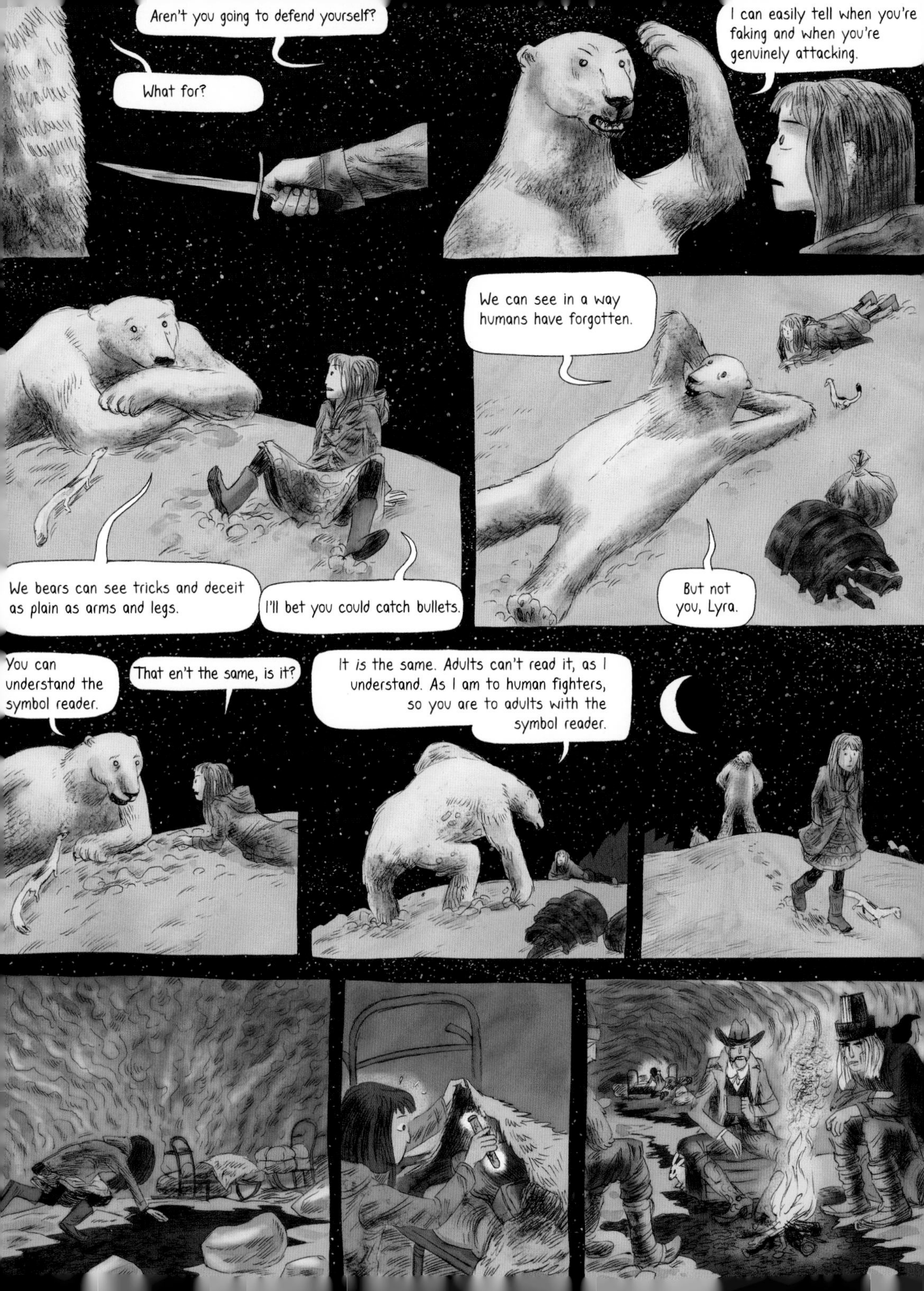
Aren't you going to defend yourself?
What for?
I can easily tell when you're faking and when you're genuinely attacking.
We bears can see tricks and deceit as plain as arms and legs.
I'll bet you could catch bullets.
We can see in a way humans have forgotten.
But not you, Lyra.
You can understand the symbol reader.
That en't the same, is it?
It *is* the same. Adults can't read it, as I understand. As I am to human fighters, so you are to adults with the symbol reader.

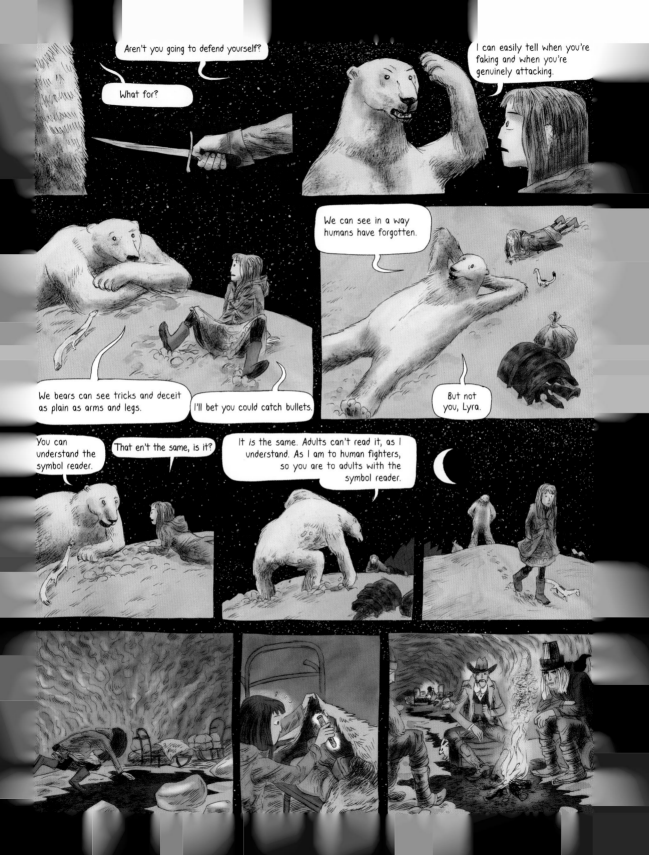

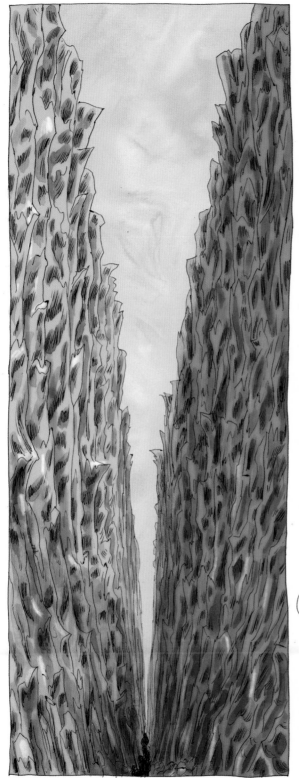

Lee...

Could you carry Iorek and his armor in your balloon?

I've done it before.

I rescued him one time from the Tartars—they had him trapped and were starving him out.

Bears aren't made to fly, but Lee saved me that day.

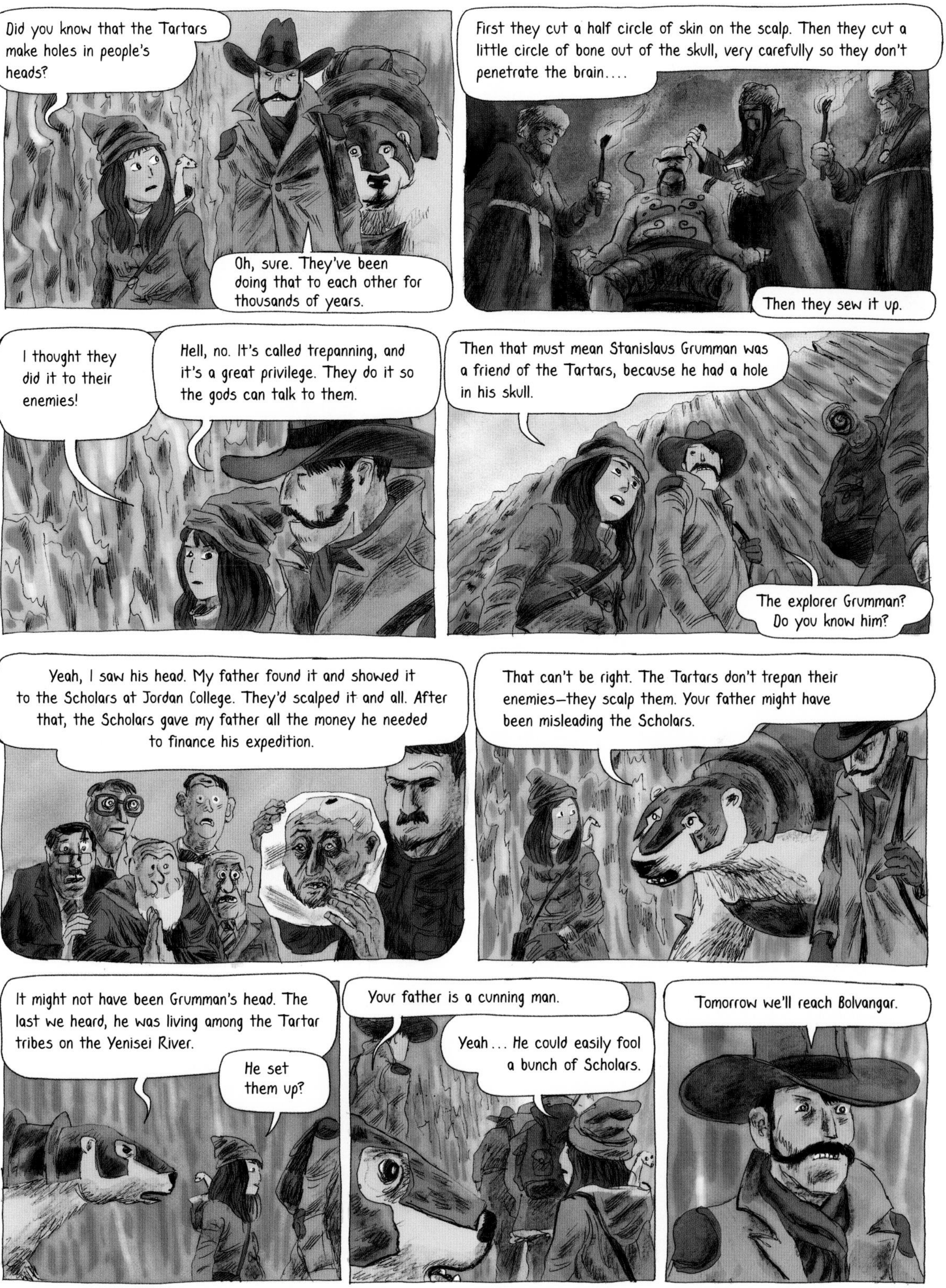
Did you know that the Tartars make holes in people's heads?
Oh, sure. They've been doing that to each other for thousands of years.
First they cut a half circle of skin on the scalp. Then they cut a little circle of bone out of the skull, very carefully so they don't penetrate the brain....
Then they sew it up.
I thought they did it to their enemies!
Hell, no. It's called trepanning, and it's a great privilege. They do it so the gods can talk to them.
Then that must mean Stanislaus Grumman was a friend of the Tartars, because he had a hole in his skull.
The explorer Grumman? Do you know him?
Yeah, I saw his head. My father found it and showed it to the Scholars at Jordan College. They'd scalped it and all. After that, the Scholars gave my father all the money he needed to finance his expedition.
That can't be right. The Tartars don't trepan their enemies—they scalp them. Your father might have been misleading the Scholars.
It might not have been Grumman's head. The last we heard, he was living among the Tartar tribes on the Yenisei River.
He set them up?
Your father is a cunning man.
Yeah... He could easily fool a bunch of Scholars.
Tomorrow we'll reach Bolvangar.

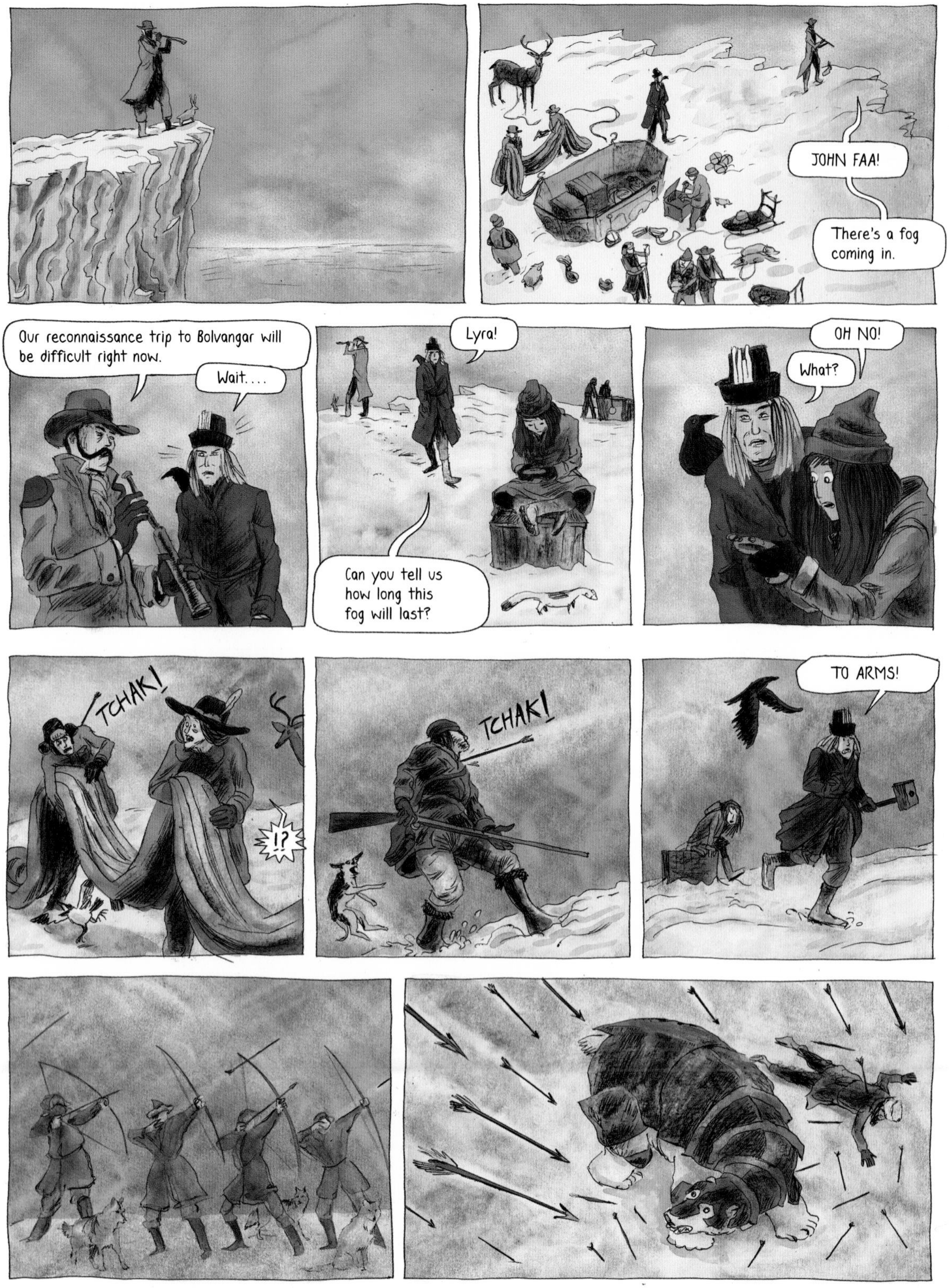
JOHN FAA!
There's a fog coming in.
Our reconnaissance trip to Bolvangar will be difficult right now.
Wait....
Lyra!
Can you tell us how long this fog will last?
OH NO!
What?
TCHAK!
!?
TCHAK!
TO ARMS!

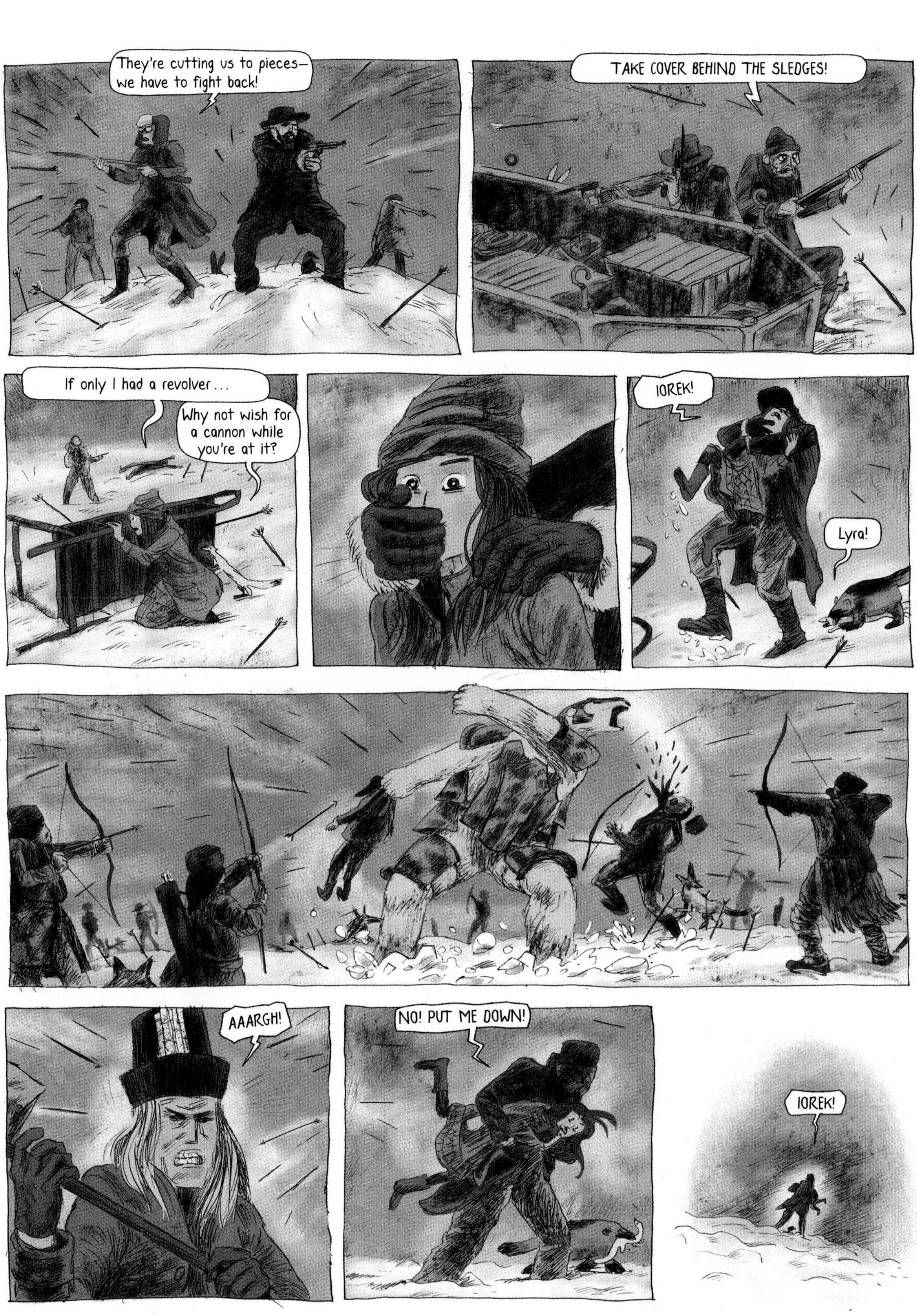
They're cutting us to pieces—we have to fight back!
TAKE COVER BEHIND THE SLEDGES!
If only I had a revolver...
Why not wish for a cannon while you're at it?
IOREK!
Lyra!
AAARGH!
NO! PUT ME DOWN!
IOREK!

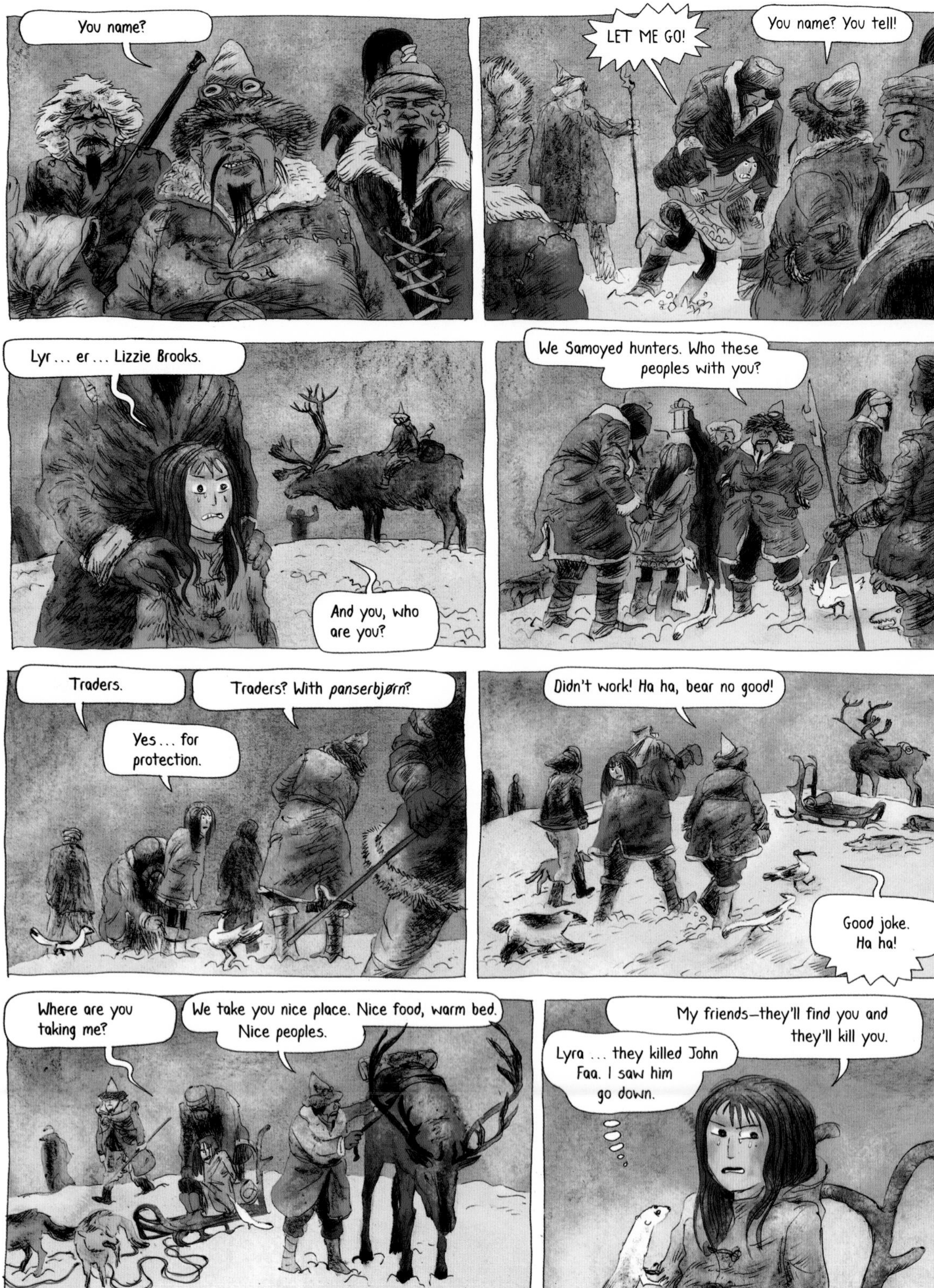
You name?
LET ME GO!
You name? You tell!
Lyr . . . er . . . Lizzie Brooks.
And you, who are you?
We Samoyed hunters. Who these peoples with you?
Traders.
Traders? With *panserbjørn*?
Yes . . . for protection.
Didn't work! Ha ha, bear no good!
Good joke. Ha ha!
Where are you taking me?
We take you nice place. Nice food, warm bed. Nice peoples.
My friends—they'll find you and they'll kill you.
Lyra . . . they killed John Faa. I saw him go down.

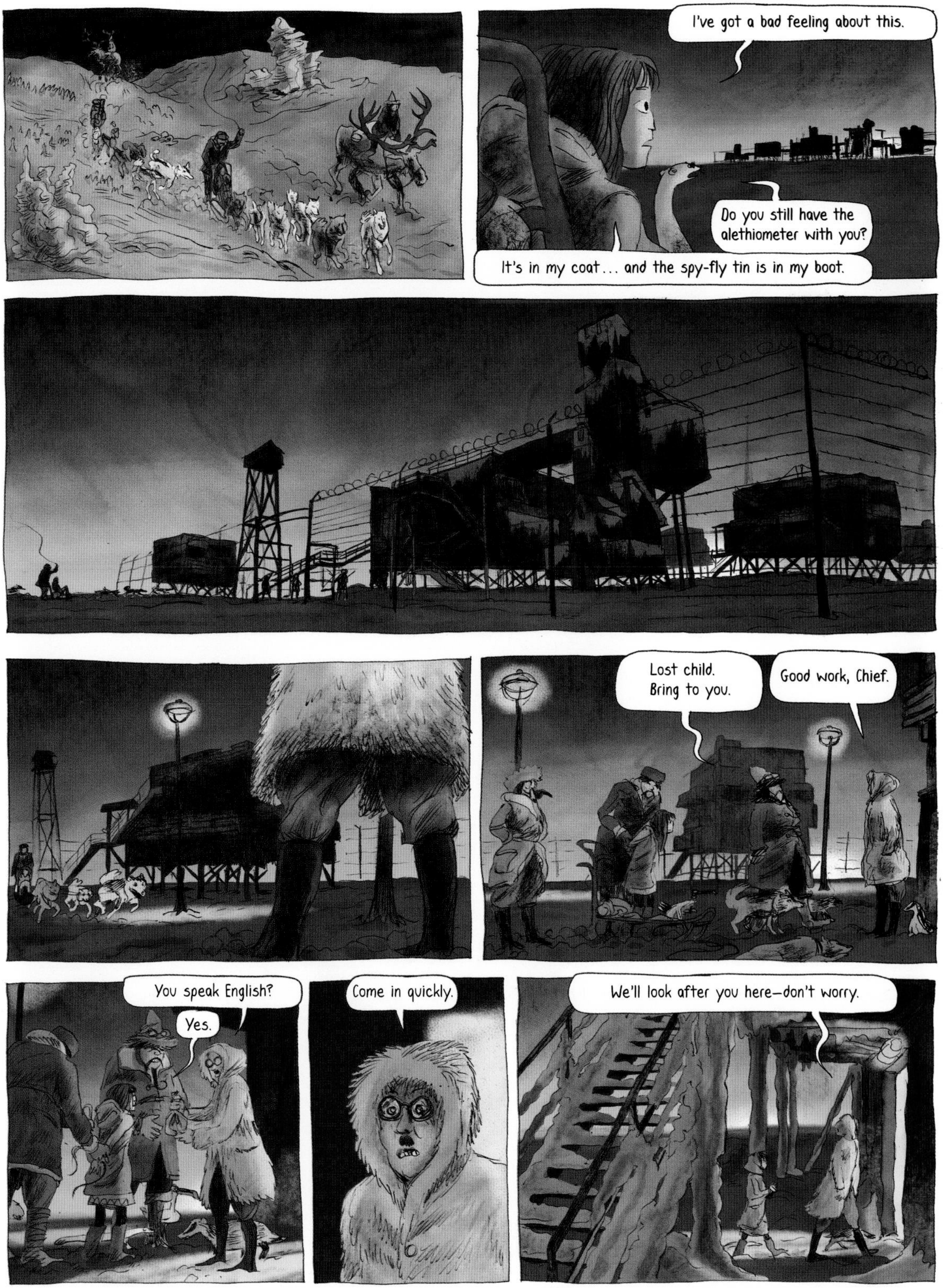

I've got a bad feeling about this.
Do you still have the alethiometer with you?
It's in my coat... and the spy-fly tin is in my boot.
Lost child. Bring to you.
Good work, Chief.
You speak English?
Yes.
Come in quickly.
We'll look after you here—don't worry.

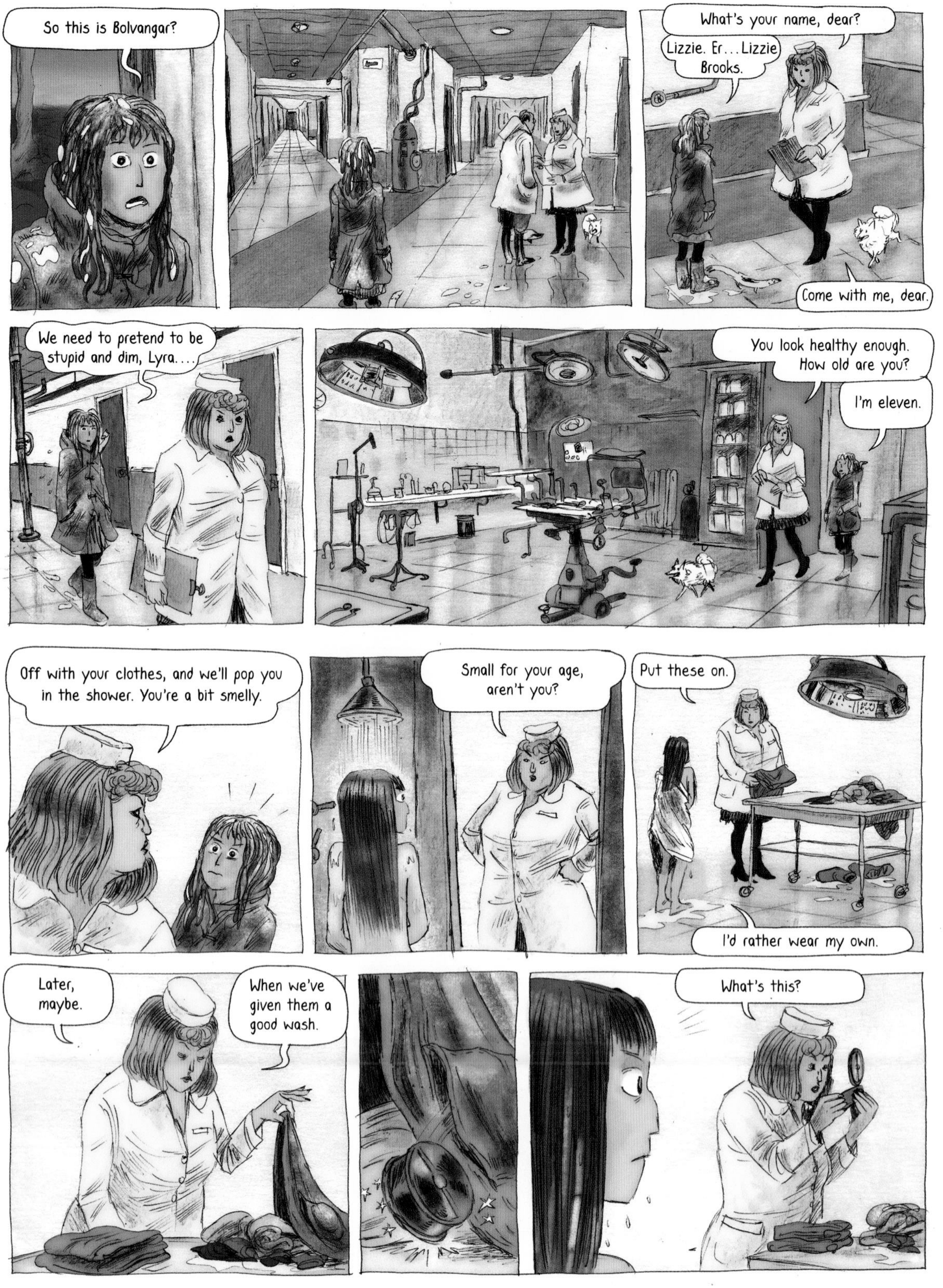
So this is Bolvangar?
What's your name, dear?
Lizzie. Er... Lizzie Brooks.
Come with me, dear.
We need to pretend to be stupid and dim, Lyra....
You look healthy enough. How old are you?
I'm eleven.
Off with your clothes, and we'll pop you in the shower. You're a bit smelly.
Small for your age, aren't you?
Put these on.
I'd rather wear my own.
Later, maybe.
When we've given them a good wash.
What's this?

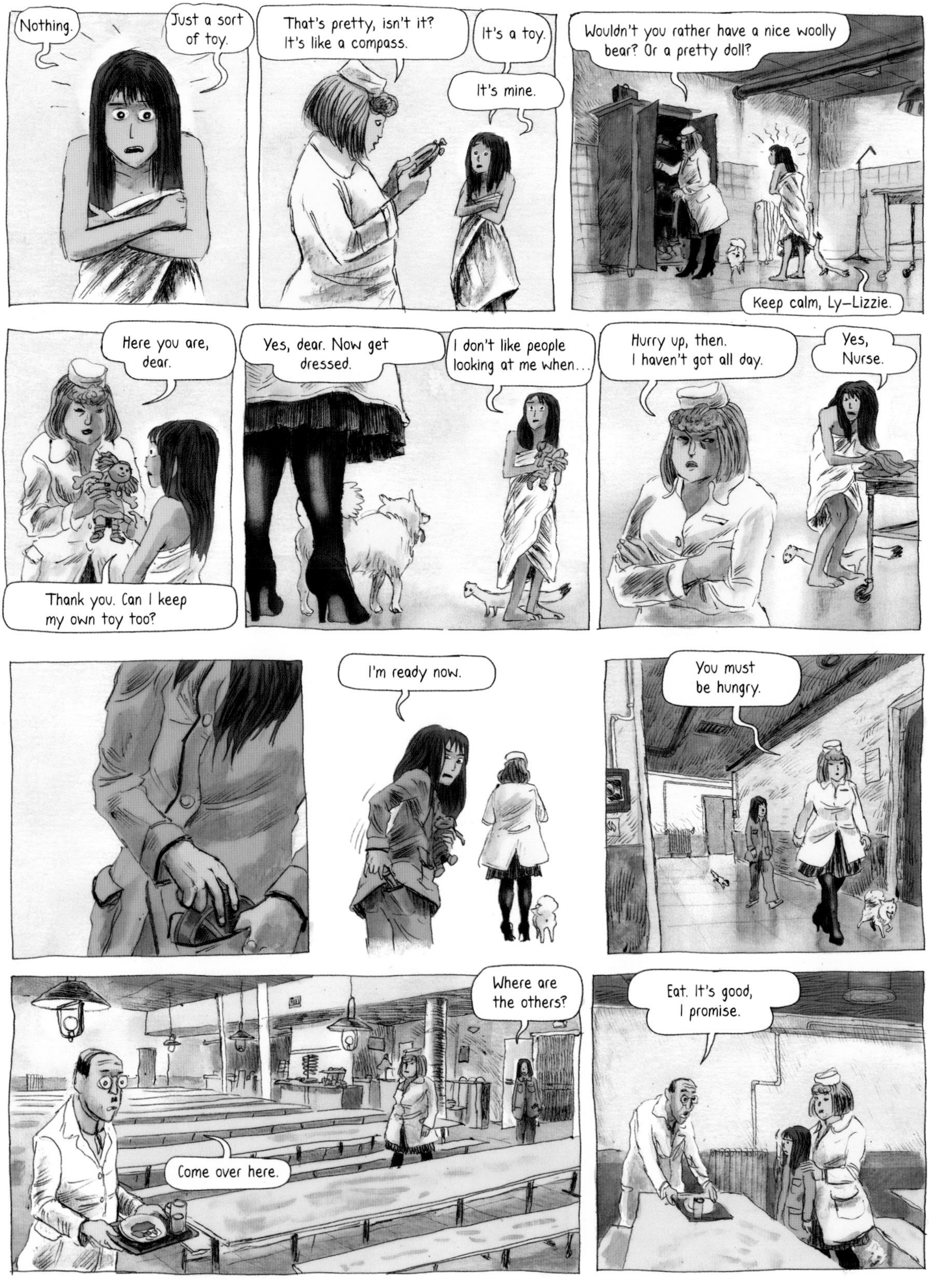
Nothing.
Just a sort of toy.
That's pretty, isn't it? It's like a compass.
It's a toy.
It's mine.
Wouldn't you rather have a nice woolly bear? Or a pretty doll?
Keep calm, Ly–Lizzie.
Here you are, dear.
Thank you. Can I keep my own toy too?
Yes, dear. Now get dressed.
I don't like people looking at me when...
Hurry up, then. I haven't got all day.
Yes, Nurse.
I'm ready now.
You must be hungry.
Where are the others?
Come over here.
Eat. It's good, I promise.

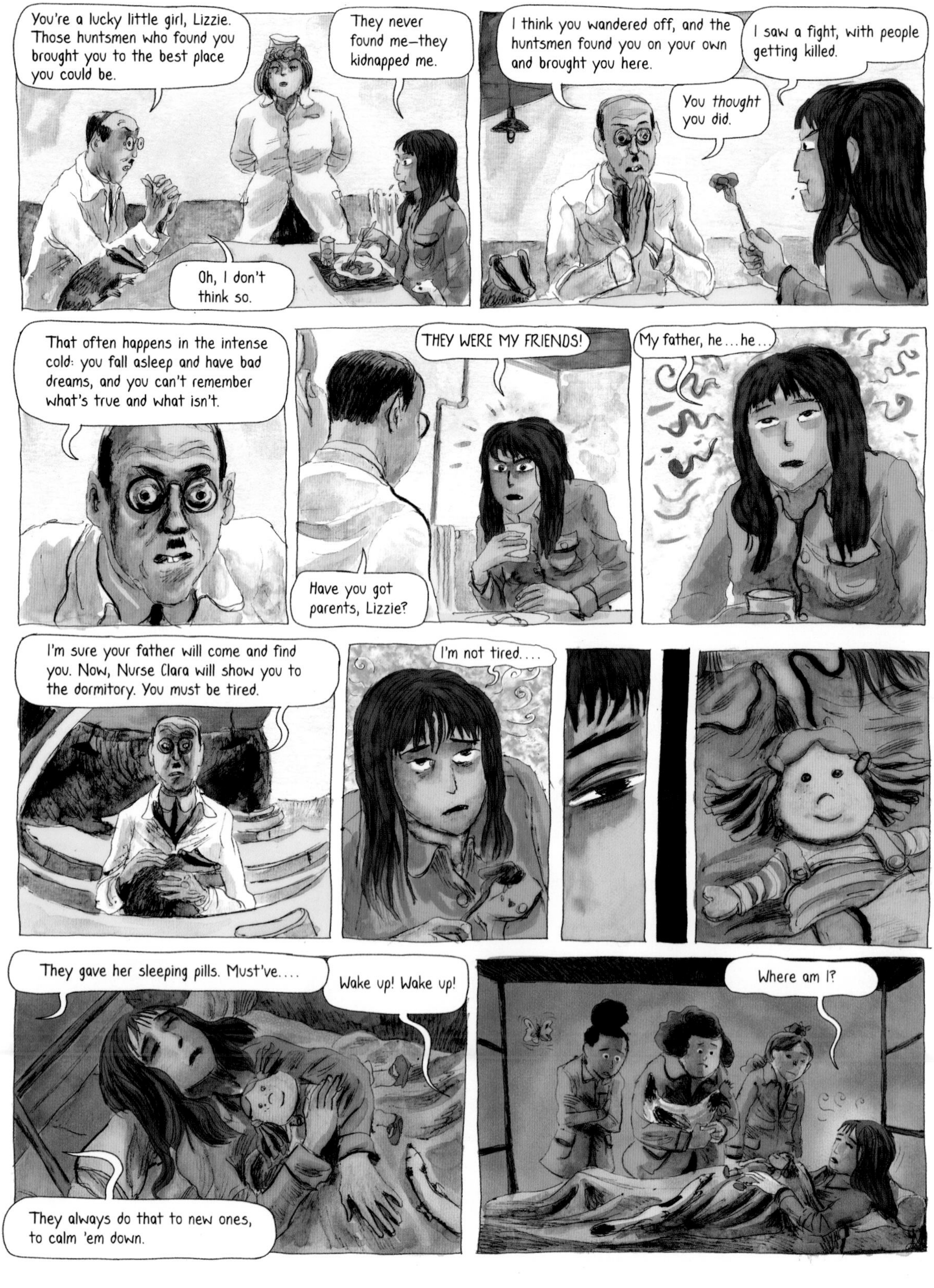
You're a lucky little girl, Lizzie. Those huntsmen who found you brought you to the best place you could be.
They never found me—they kidnapped me.
Oh, I don't think so.
I think you wandered off, and the huntsmen found you on your own and brought you here.
I saw a fight, with people getting killed.
You *thought* you did.
That often happens in the intense cold: you fall asleep and have bad dreams, and you can't remember what's true and what isn't.
THEY WERE MY FRIENDS!
Have you got parents, Lizzie?
My father, he...he...
I'm sure your father will come and find you. Now, Nurse Clara will show you to the dormitory. You must be tired.
I'm not tired....
They gave her sleeping pills. Must've....
Wake up! Wake up!
They always do that to new ones, to calm 'em down.
Where am I?

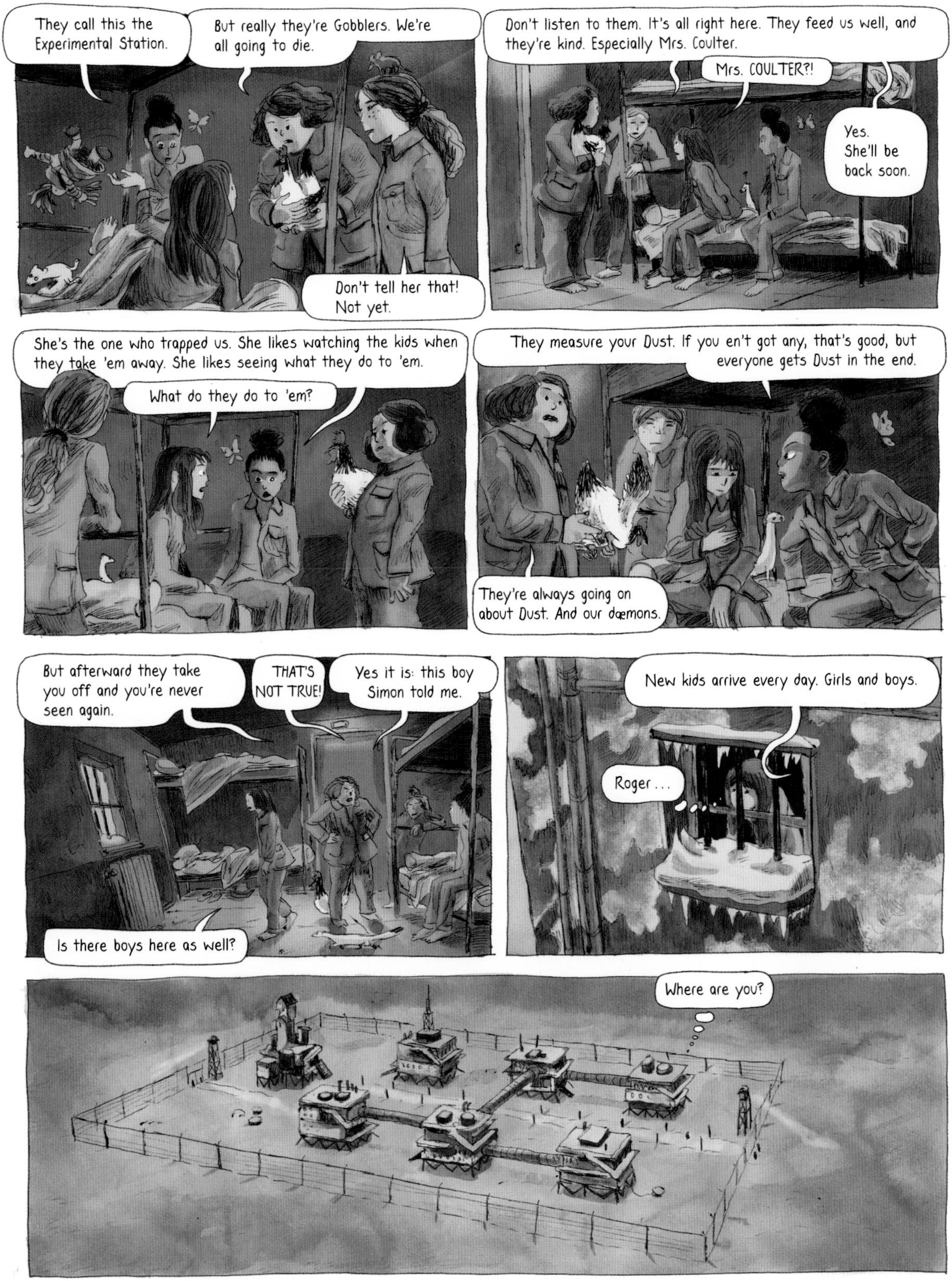
They call this the Experimental Station.
But really they're Gobblers. We're all going to die.
Don't tell her that! Not yet.
Don't listen to them. It's all right here. They feed us well, and they're kind. Especially Mrs. Coulter.
Mrs. COULTER?!
Yes. She'll be back soon.
She's the one who trapped us. She likes watching the kids when they take 'em away. She likes seeing what they do to 'em.
What do they do to 'em?
They measure your Dust. If you en't got any, that's good, but everyone gets Dust in the end.
They're always going on about Dust. And our dæmons.
But afterward they take you off and you're never seen again.
THAT'S NOT TRUE!
Yes it is: this boy Simon told me.
Is there boys here as well?
New kids arrive every day. Girls and boys.
Roger...
Where are you?

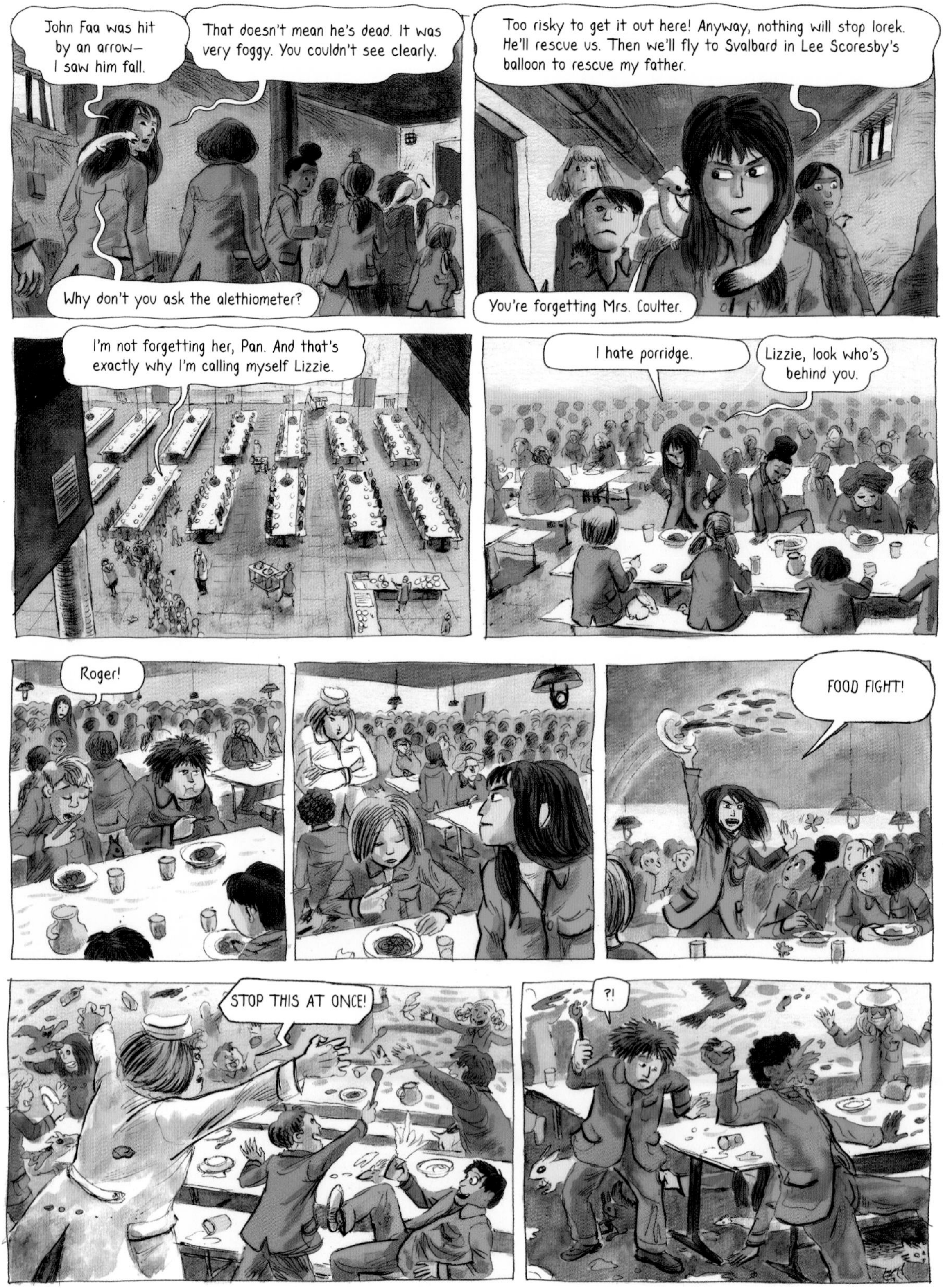
John Faa was hit by an arrow— I saw him fall.
That doesn't mean he's dead. It was very foggy. You couldn't see clearly.
Why don't you ask the alethiometer?
Too risky to get it out here! Anyway, nothing will stop Iorek. He'll rescue us. Then we'll fly to Svalbard in Lee Scoresby's balloon to rescue my father.
You're forgetting Mrs. Coulter.
I'm not forgetting her, Pan. And that's exactly why I'm calling myself Lizzie.
I hate porridge.
Lizzie, look who's behind you.
Roger!
FOOD FIGHT!
STOP THIS AT ONCE!
?!

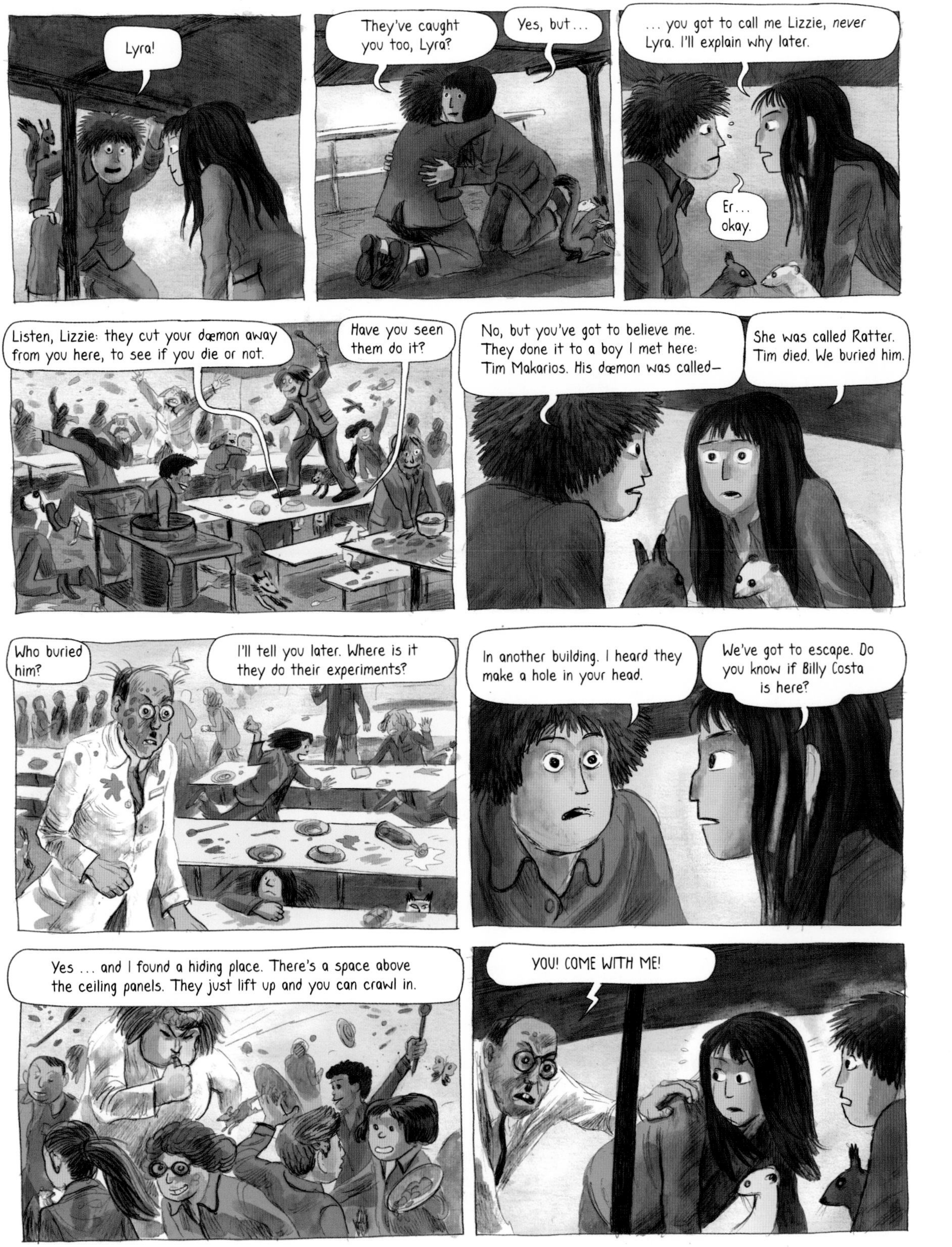

Lyra!
They've caught you too, Lyra?
Yes, but...
... you got to call me Lizzie, *never* Lyra. I'll explain why later.
Er... okay.
Listen, Lizzie: they cut your dæmon away from you here, to see if you die or not.
Have you seen them do it?
No, but you've got to believe me. They done it to a boy I met here: Tim Makarios. His dæmon was called—
She was called Ratter. Tim died. We buried him.
Who buried him?
I'll tell you later. Where is it they do their experiments?
In another building. I heard they make a hole in your head.
We've got to escape. Do you know if Billy Costa is here?
Yes ... and I found a hiding place. There's a space above the ceiling panels. They just lift up and you can crawl in.
YOU! COME WITH ME!

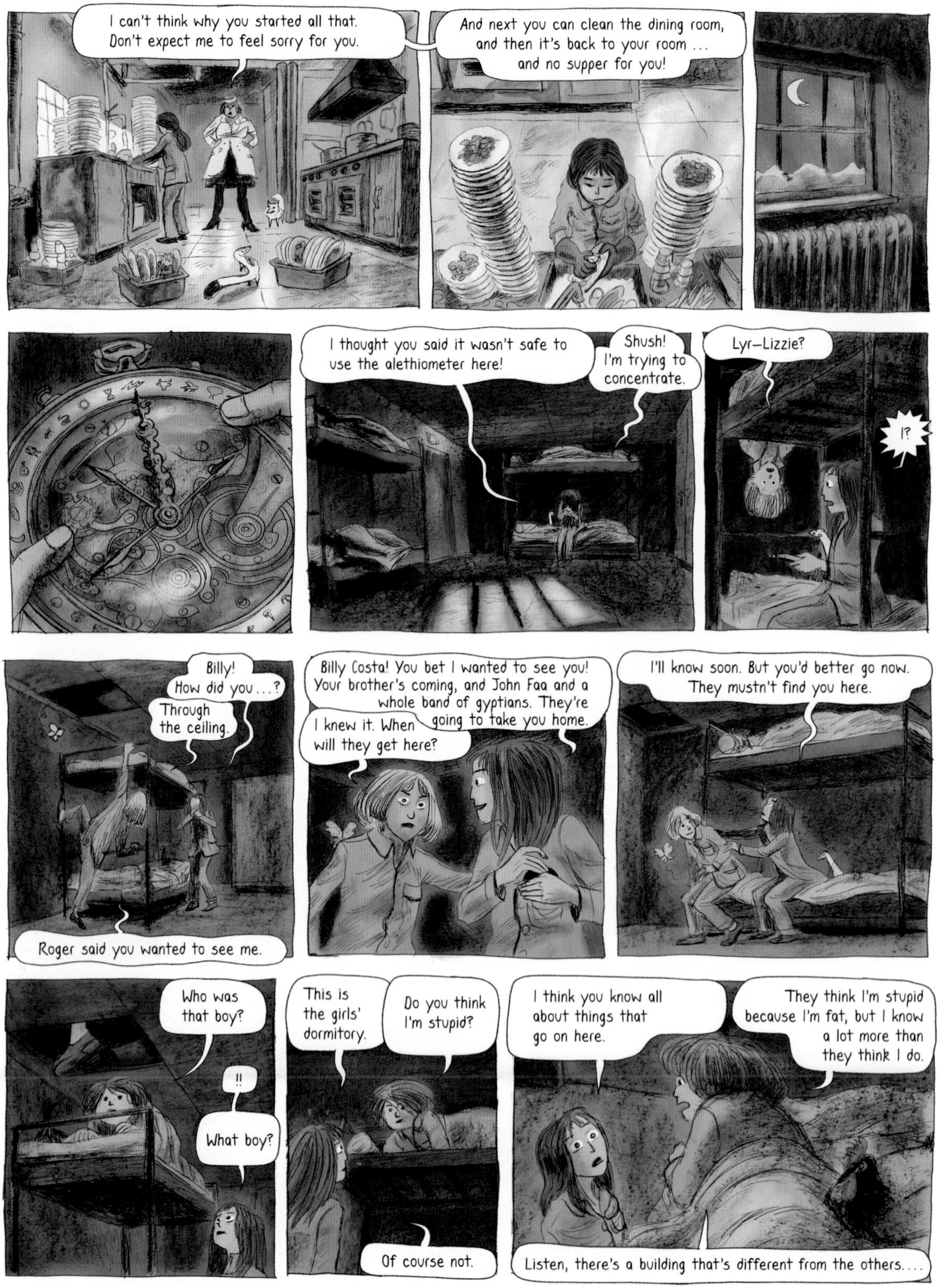
I can't think why you started all that. Don't expect me to feel sorry for you.
And next you can clean the dining room, and then it's back to your room . . . and no supper for you!
I thought you said it wasn't safe to use the alethiometer here!
Shush! I'm trying to concentrate.
Lyr—Lizzie?
!?
Billy! How did you . . . ?
Through the ceiling.
Roger said you wanted to see me.
Billy Costa! You bet I wanted to see you! Your brother's coming, and John Faa and a whole band of gyptians. They're going to take you home.
I knew it. When will they get here?
I'll know soon. But you'd better go now. They mustn't find you here.
Who was that boy?
!!
What boy?
This is the girls' dormitory.
Do you think I'm stupid?
Of course not.
I think you know all about things that go on here.
They think I'm stupid because I'm fat, but I know a lot more than they think I do.
Listen, there's a building that's different from the others. . . .

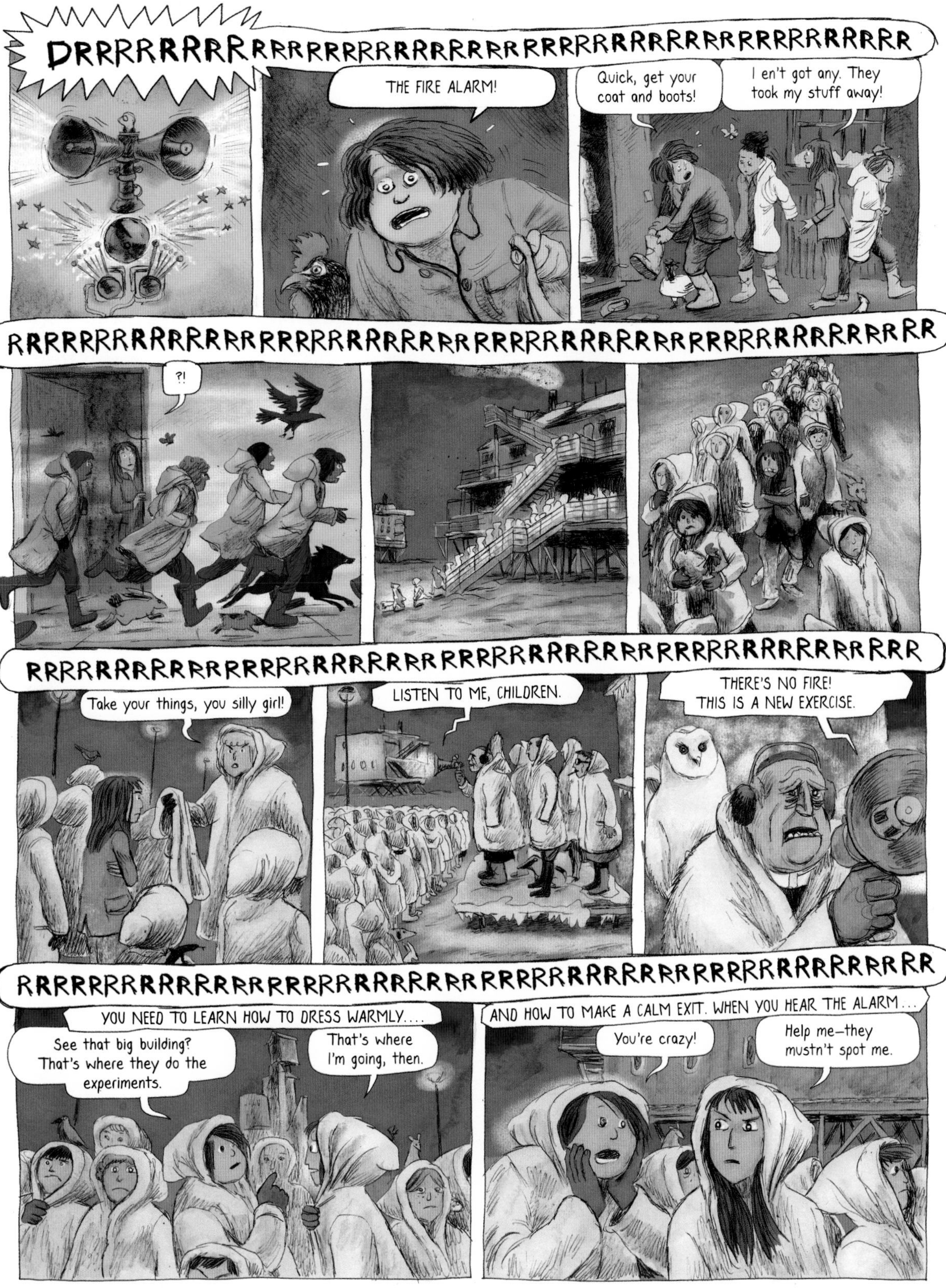
DRRRRRRRRRRRRRRRRRRRRRRRRRRRRRRRRRRRRRR
THE FIRE ALARM!
Quick, get your coat and boots!
I en't got any. They took my stuff away!
RRRRRRRRRRRRRRRRRRRRRRRRRRRRRRRRRRRRRRRRRRR
?!
RRRRRRRRRRRRRRRRRRRRRRRRRRRRRRRRRRRRRRRRRR
Take your things, you silly girl!
LISTEN TO ME, CHILDREN.
THERE'S NO FIRE! THIS IS A NEW EXERCISE.
RRRRRRRRRRRRRRRRRRRRRRRRRRRRRRRRRRRRRRRRRRR
YOU NEED TO LEARN HOW TO DRESS WARMLY....
See that big building? That's where they do the experiments.
That's where I'm going, then.
AND HOW TO MAKE A CALM EXIT. WHEN YOU HEAR THE ALARM...
You're crazy!
Help me—they mustn't spot me.

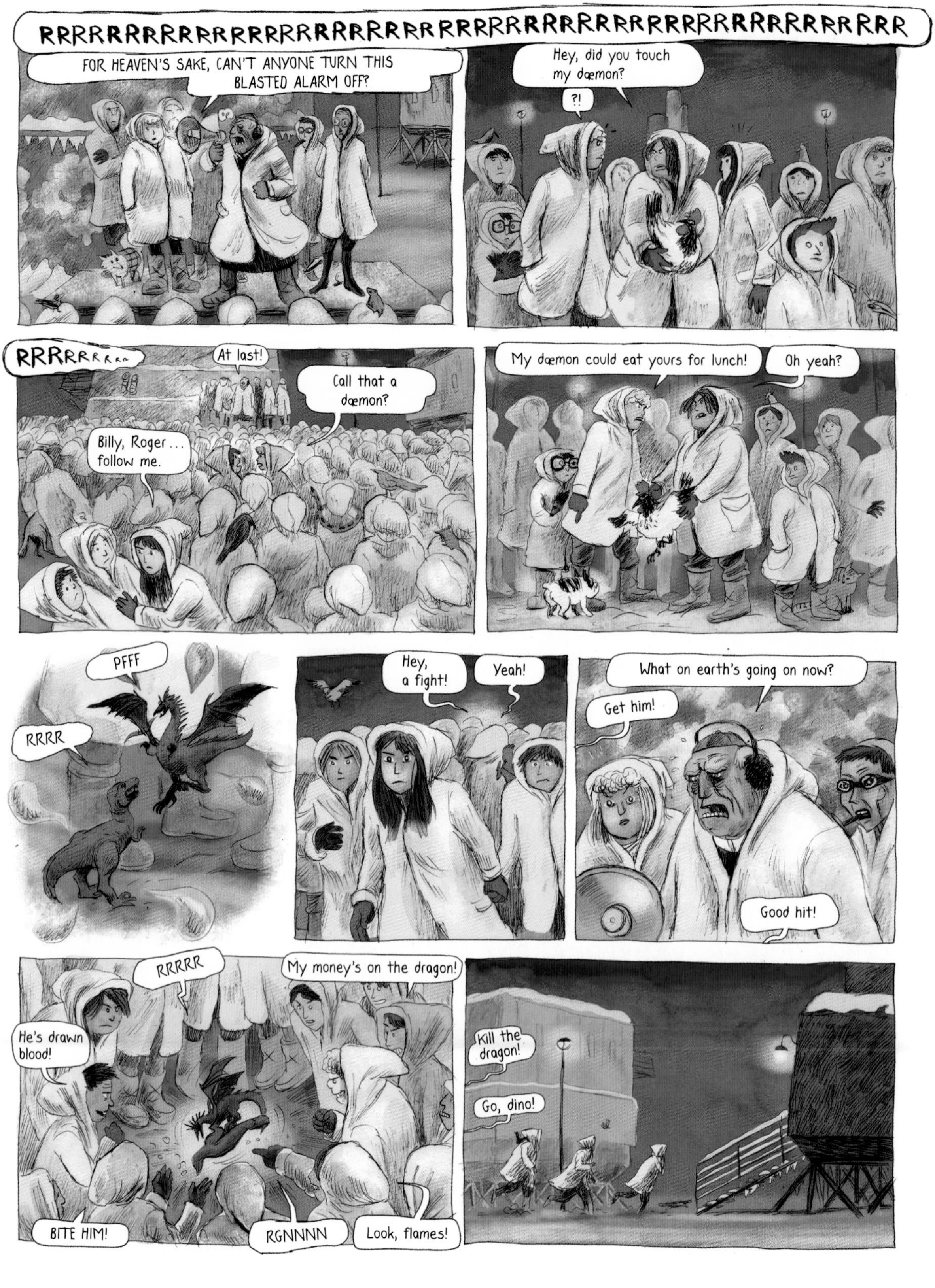

RRRRRRRRRRRRRRRRRRRRRRRRRRRRRRRRRRRRRRRRRRRRRRR
FOR HEAVEN'S SAKE, CAN'T ANYONE TURN THIS BLASTED ALARM OFF?
Hey, did you touch my dæmon?
?!
RRRRRRRRR
At last!
Call that a dæmon?
Billy, Roger... follow me.
My dæmon could eat yours for lunch!
Oh yeah?
PFFF
RRRR
Hey, a fight!
Yeah!
What on earth's going on now?
Get him!
Good hit!
RRRRR
My money's on the dragon!
He's drawn blood!
BITE HIM!
RGNNNN
Look, flames!
Kill the dragon!
Go, dino!

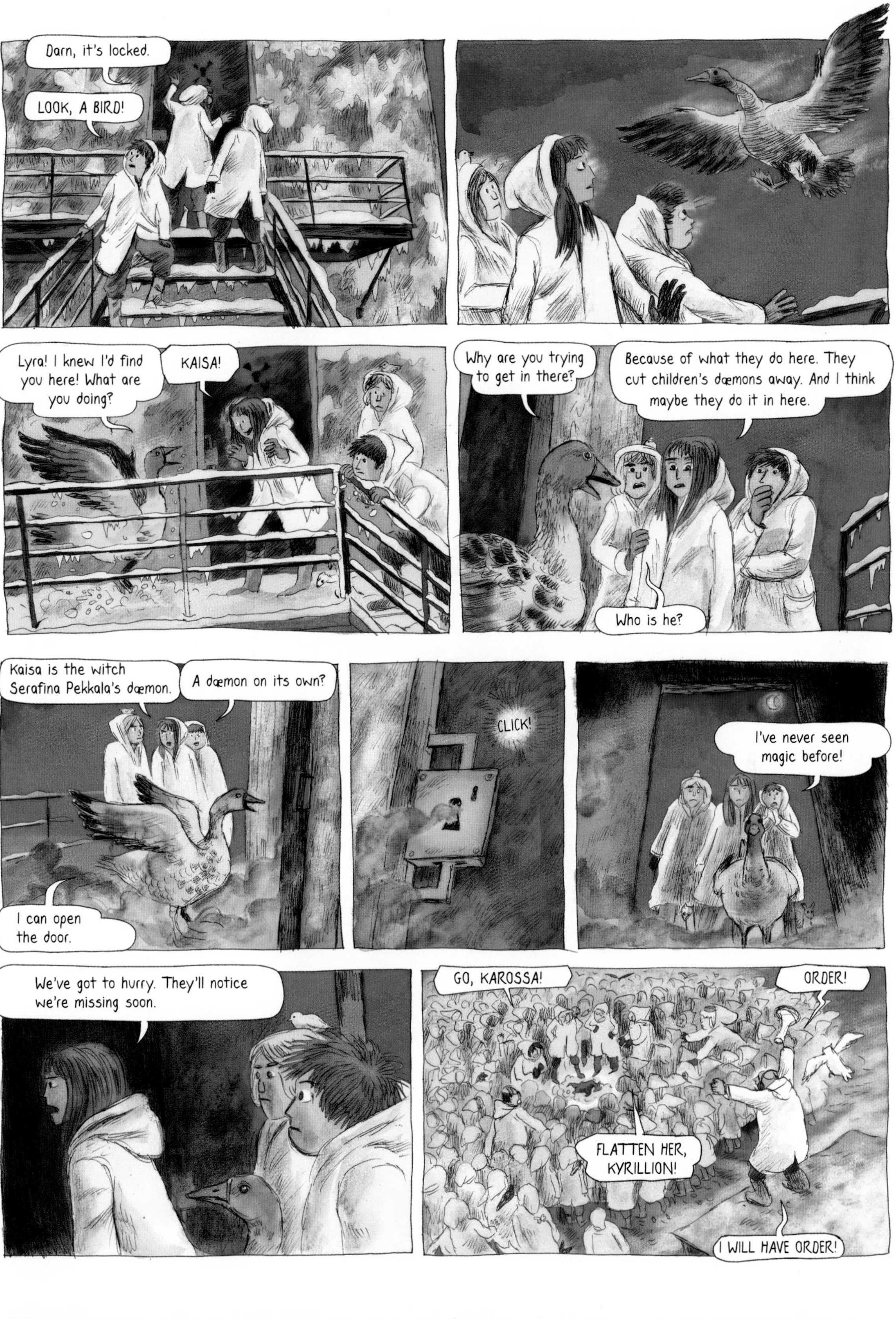
Darn, it's locked.
LOOK, A BIRD!
Lyra! I knew I'd find you here! What are you doing?
KAISA!
Why are you trying to get in there?
Because of what they do here. They cut children's dæmons away. And I think maybe they do it in here.
Who is he?
Kaisa is the witch Serafina Pekkala's dæmon.
A dæmon on its own?
I can open the door.
CLICK!
I've never seen magic before!
We've got to hurry. They'll notice we're missing soon.
GO, KAROSSA!
ORDER!
FLATTEN HER, KYRILLION!
I WILL HAVE ORDER!

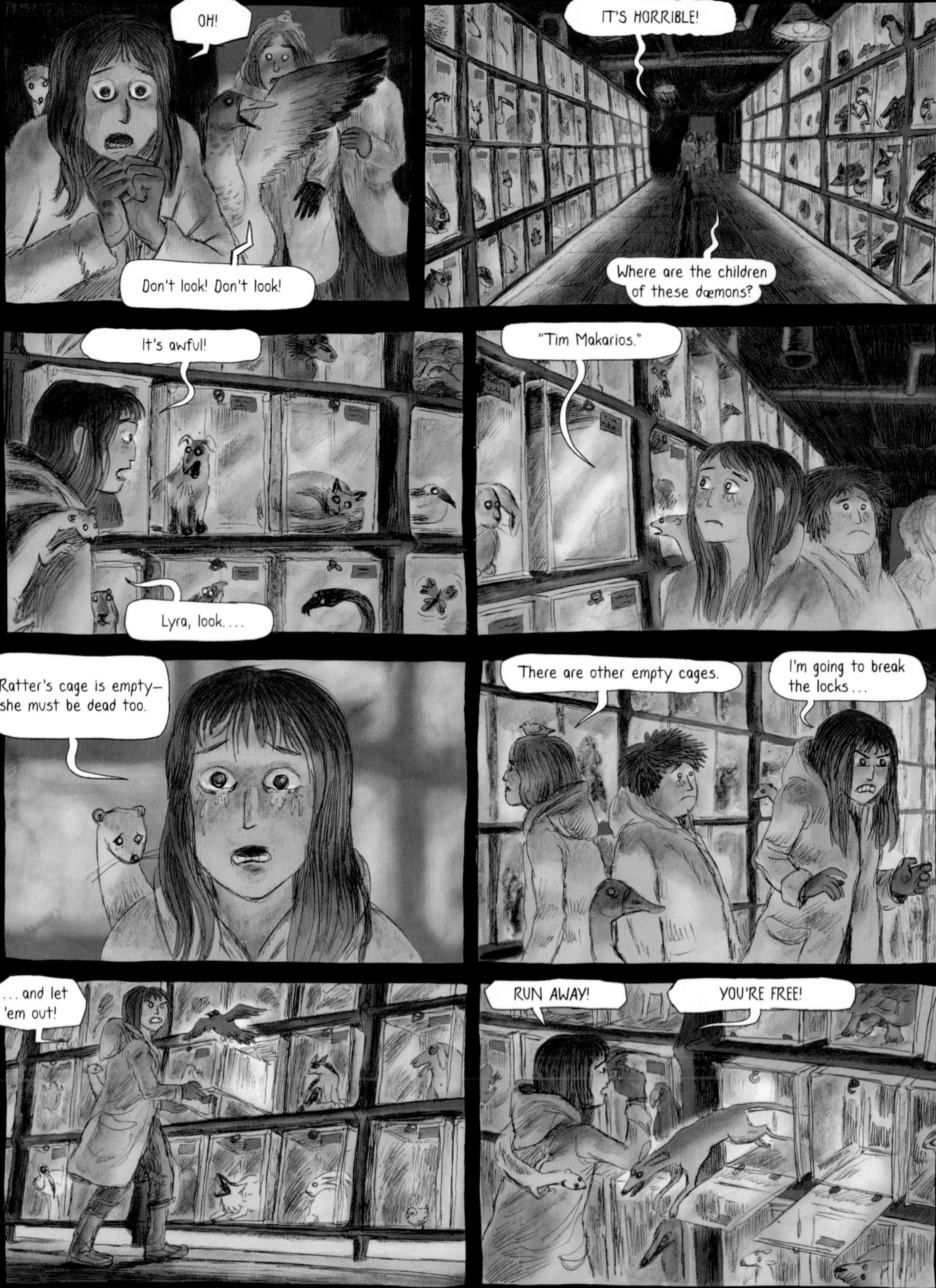
OH!
Don't look! Don't look!
IT'S HORRIBLE!
Where are the children of these dæmons?
It's awful!
Lyra, look. . . .
"Tim Makarios."
Ratter's cage is empty—she must be dead too.
There are other empty cages.
I'm going to break the locks . . .
. . . and let 'em out!
RUN AWAY!
YOU'RE FREE!

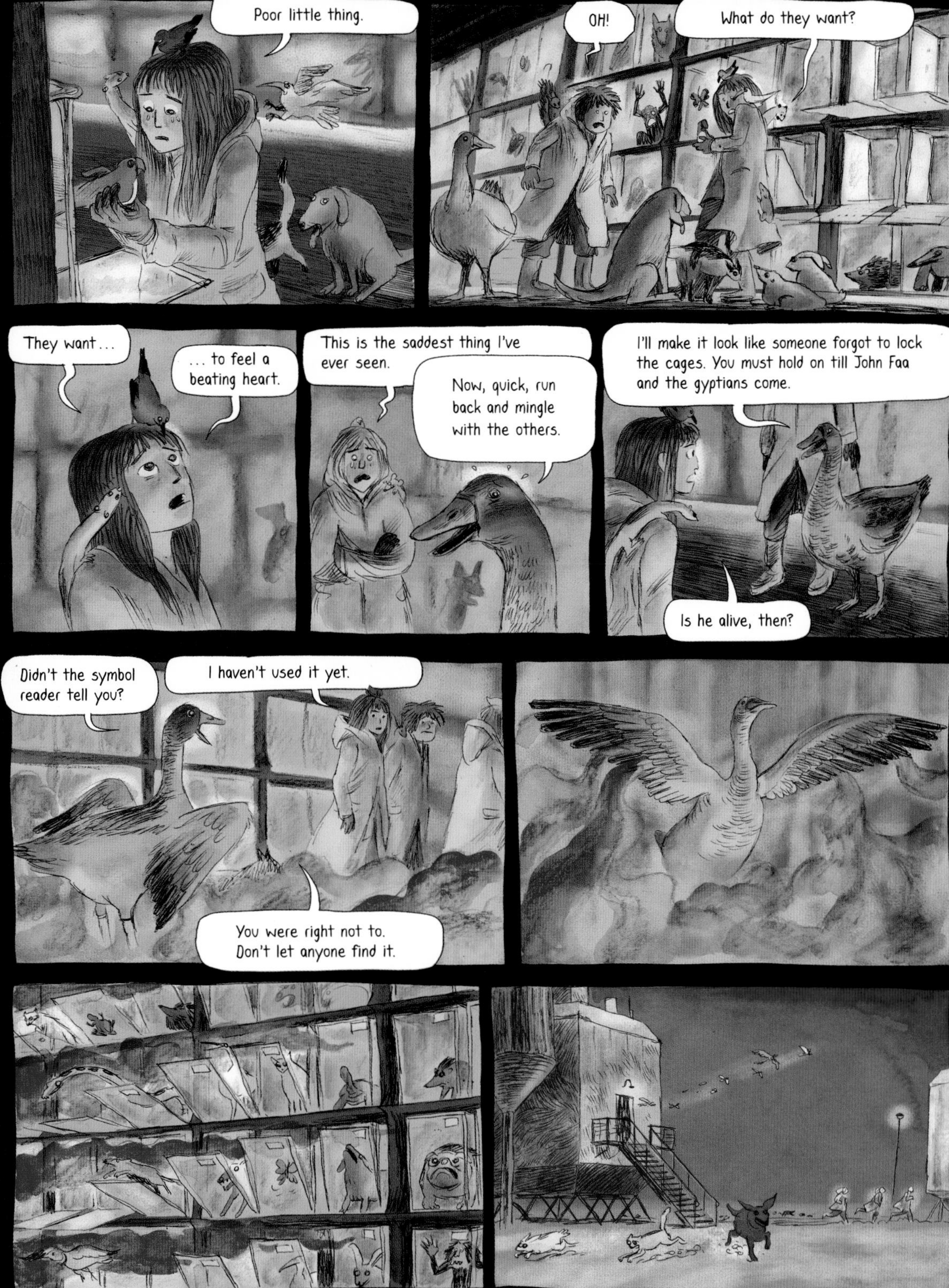
Poor little thing.
OH!
What do they want?
They want...
... to feel a beating heart.
This is the saddest thing I've ever seen.
Now, quick, run back and mingle with the others.
I'll make it look like someone forgot to lock the cages. You must hold on till John Faa and the gyptians come.
Is he alive, then?
Didn't the symbol reader tell you?
I haven't used it yet.
You were right not to. Don't let anyone find it.

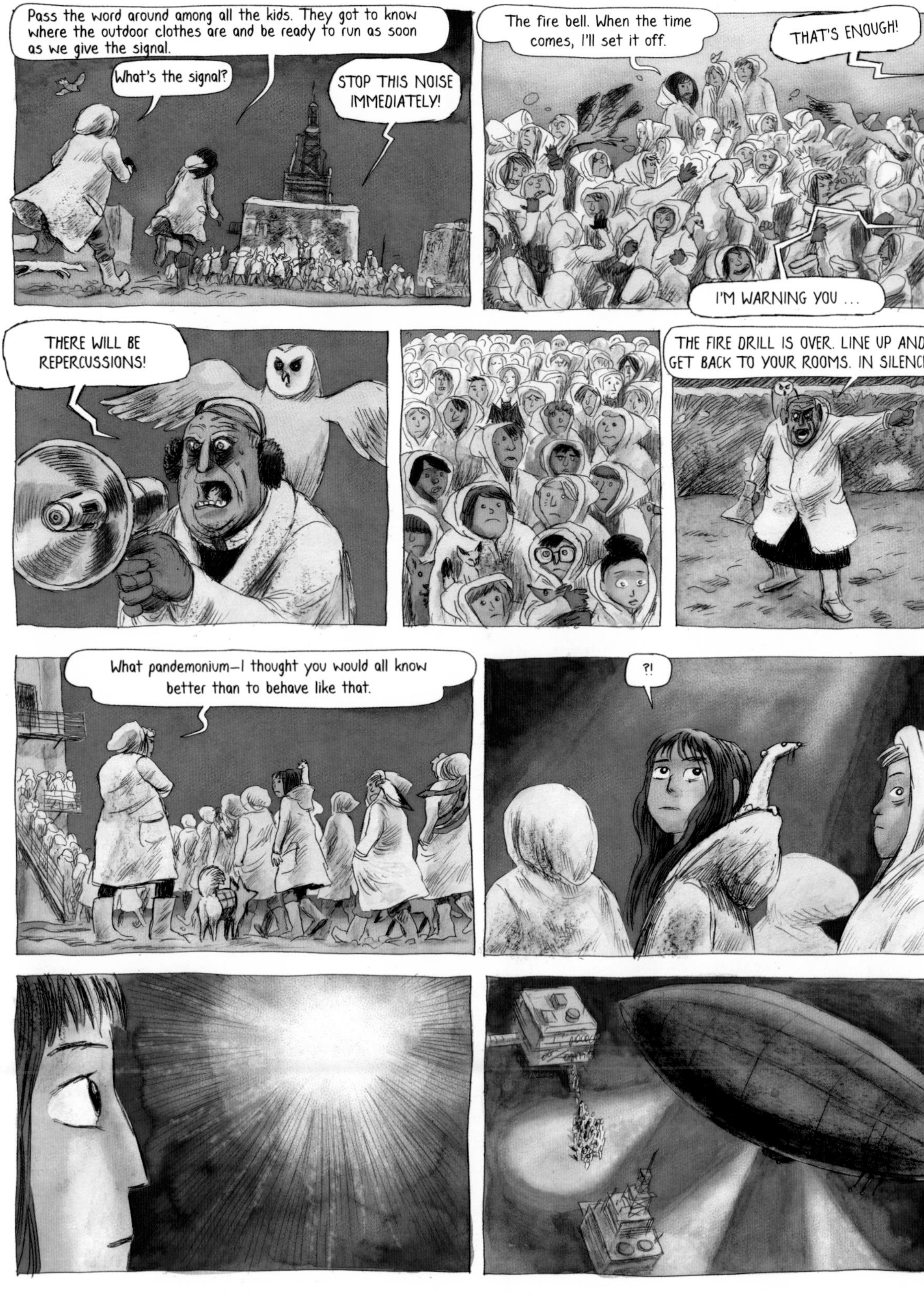
Pass the word around among all the kids. They got to know where the outdoor clothes are and be ready to run as soon as we give the signal.
What's the signal?
STOP THIS NOISE IMMEDIATELY!
The fire bell. When the time comes, I'll set it off.
THAT'S ENOUGH!
I'M WARNING YOU ...
THERE WILL BE REPERCUSSIONS!
THE FIRE DRILL IS OVER. LINE UP AND GET BACK TO YOUR ROOMS. IN SILENCE!
What pandemonium—I thought you would all know better than to behave like that.
?!

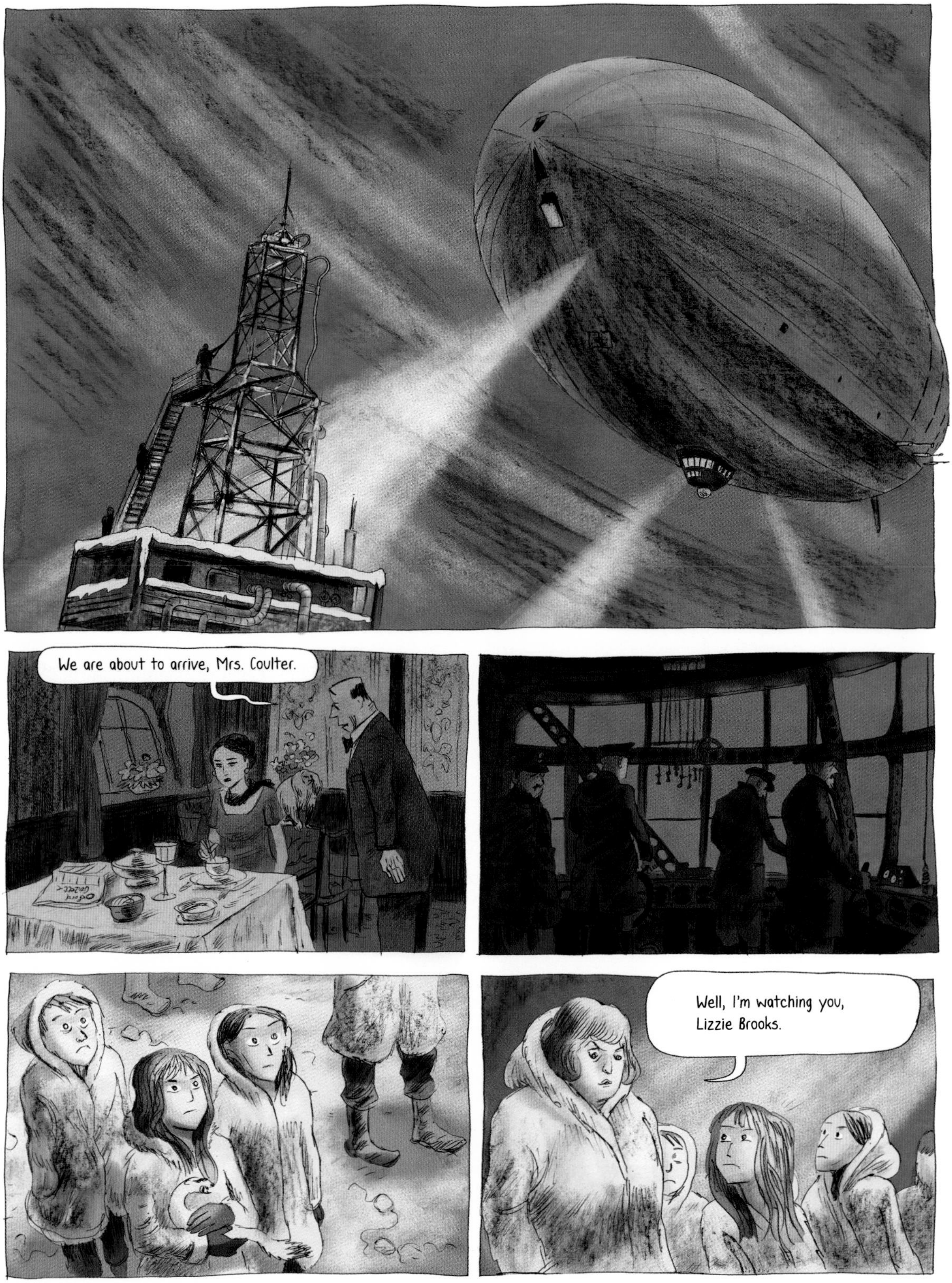
We are about to arrive, Mrs. Coulter.
Well, I'm watching you, Lizzie Brooks.

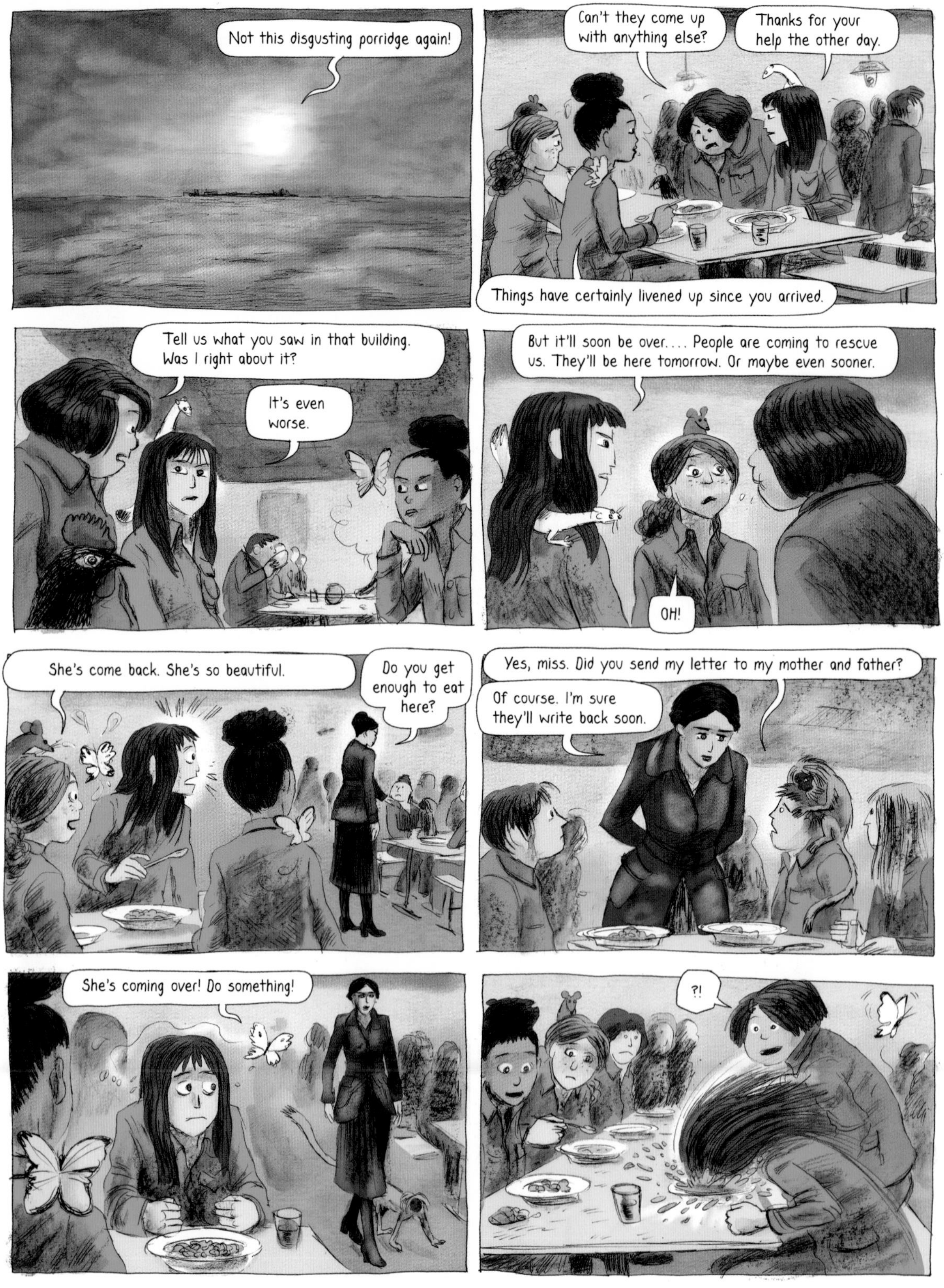
Not this disgusting porridge again!
Can't they come up with anything else?
Thanks for your help the other day.
Things have certainly livened up since you arrived.
Tell us what you saw in that building. Was I right about it?
It's even worse.
But it'll soon be over.... People are coming to rescue us. They'll be here tomorrow. Or maybe even sooner.
OH!
She's come back. She's so beautiful.
Do you get enough to eat here?
Yes, miss. Did you send my letter to my mother and father?
Of course. I'm sure they'll write back soon.
She's coming over! Do something!
?!

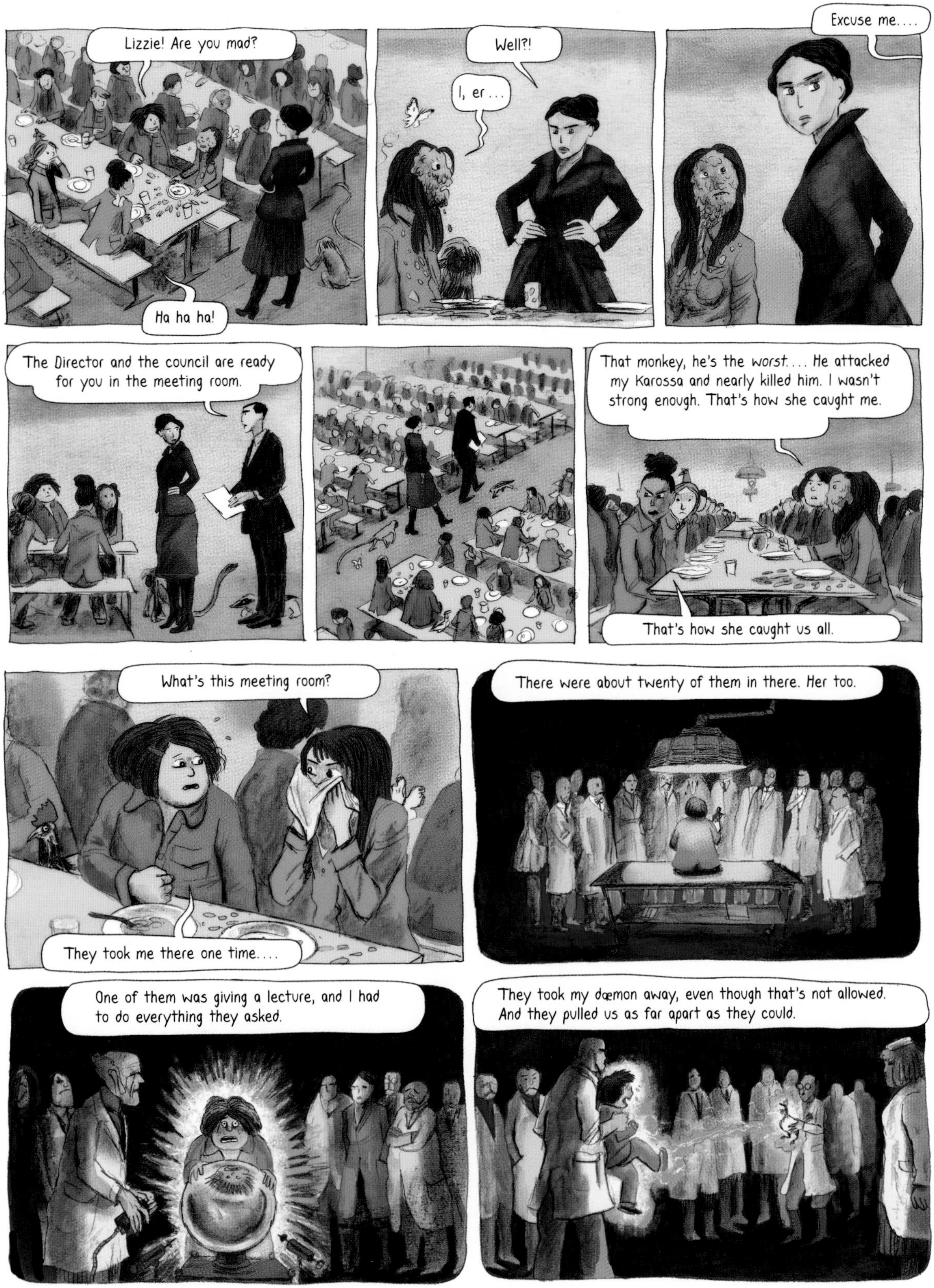
Lizzie! Are you mad?
Ha ha ha!
Well?!
I, er . . .
Excuse me. . . .
The Director and the council are ready for you in the meeting room.
That monkey, he's the *worst*. . . . He attacked my Karossa and nearly killed him. I wasn't strong enough. That's how she caught me.
That's how she caught us all.
What's this meeting room?
They took me there one time. . . .
There were about twenty of them in there. Her too.
One of them was giving a lecture, and I had to do everything they asked.
They took my dæmon away, even though that's not allowed. And they pulled us as far apart as they could.

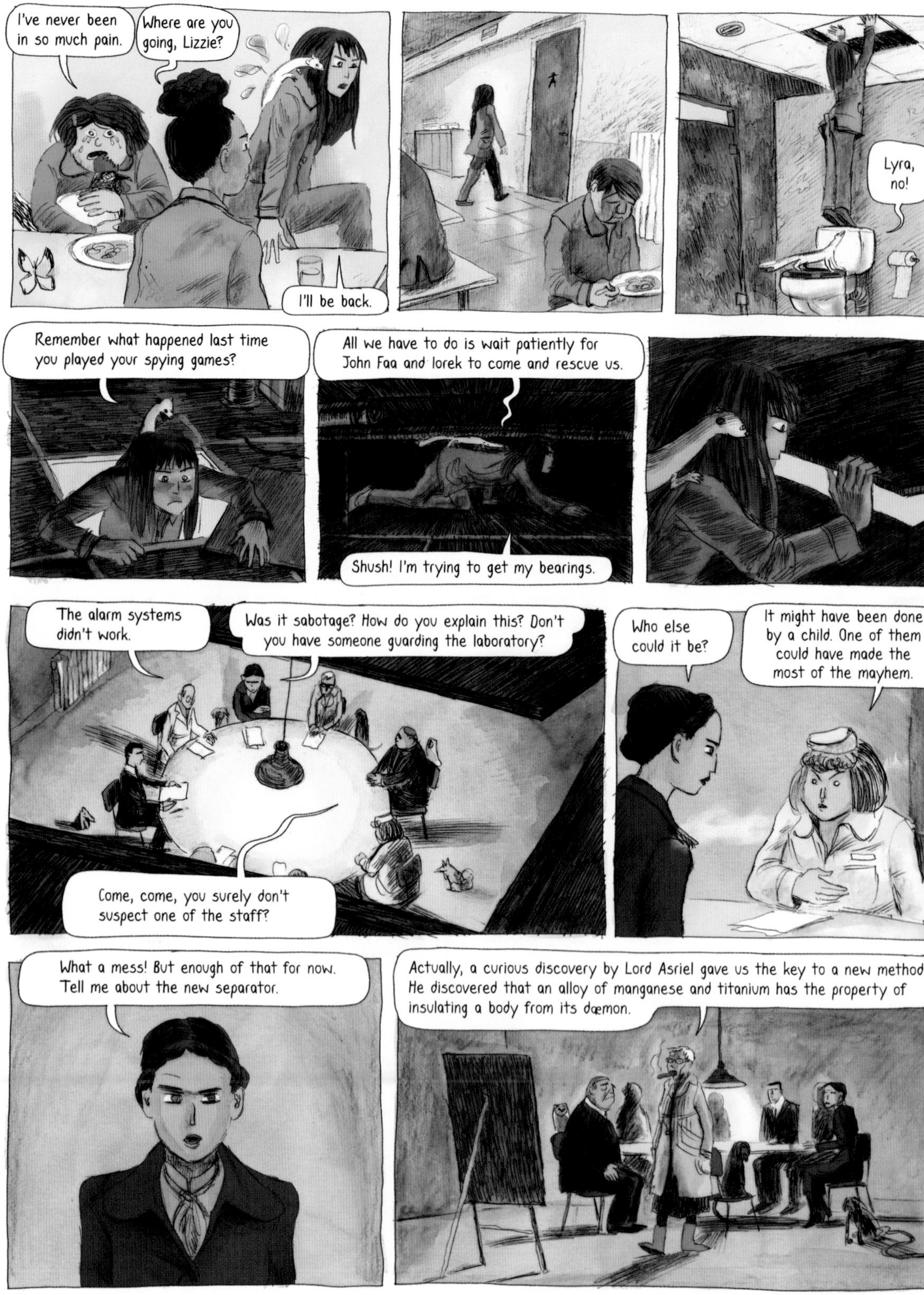
I've never been in so much pain.
Where are you going, Lizzie?
I'll be back.
Lyra, no!
Remember what happened last time you played your spying games?
All we have to do is wait patiently for John Faa and Iorek to come and rescue us.
Shush! I'm trying to get my bearings.
The alarm systems didn't work.
Was it sabotage? How do you explain this? Don't you have someone guarding the laboratory?
Come, come, you surely don't suspect one of the staff?
Who else could it be?
It might have been done by a child. One of them could have made the most of the mayhem.
What a mess! But enough of that for now. Tell me about the new separator.
Actually, a curious discovery by Lord Asriel gave us the key to a new method. He discovered that an alloy of manganese and titanium has the property of insulating a body from its dæmon.

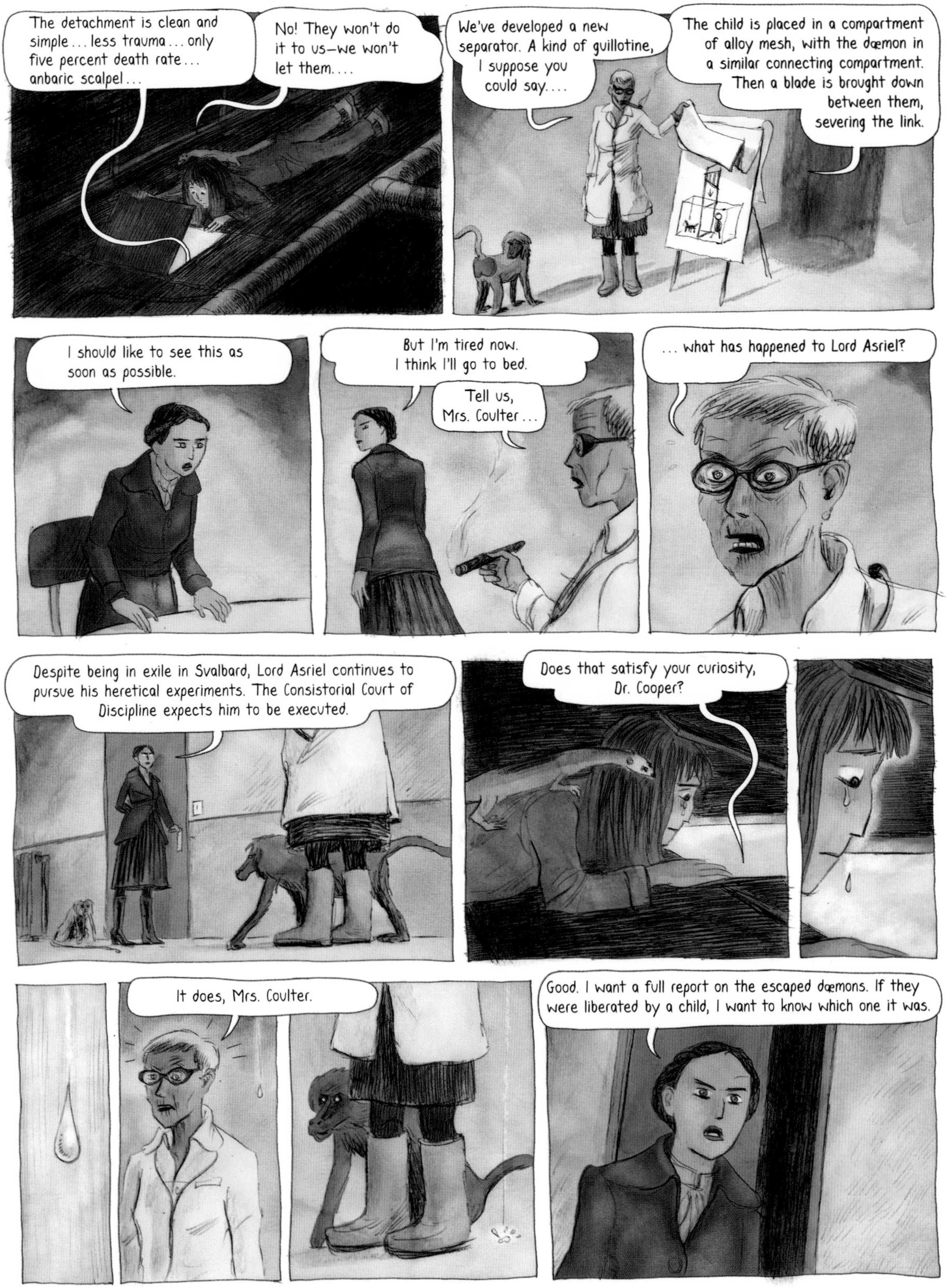
The detachment is clean and simple . . . less trauma . . . only five percent death rate . . . anbaric scalpel . . .
No! They won't do it to us—we won't let them. . . .
We've developed a new separator. A kind of guillotine, I suppose you could say. . . .
The child is placed in a compartment of alloy mesh, with the dæmon in a similar connecting compartment. Then a blade is brought down between them, severing the link.
I should like to see this as soon as possible.
But I'm tired now. I think I'll go to bed.
Tell us, Mrs. Coulter . . .
. . . what has happened to Lord Asriel?
Despite being in exile in Svalbard, Lord Asriel continues to pursue his heretical experiments. The Consistorial Court of Discipline expects him to be executed.
Does that satisfy your curiosity, Dr. Cooper?
It does, Mrs. Coulter.
Good. I want a full report on the escaped dæmons. If they were liberated by a child, I want to know which one it was.

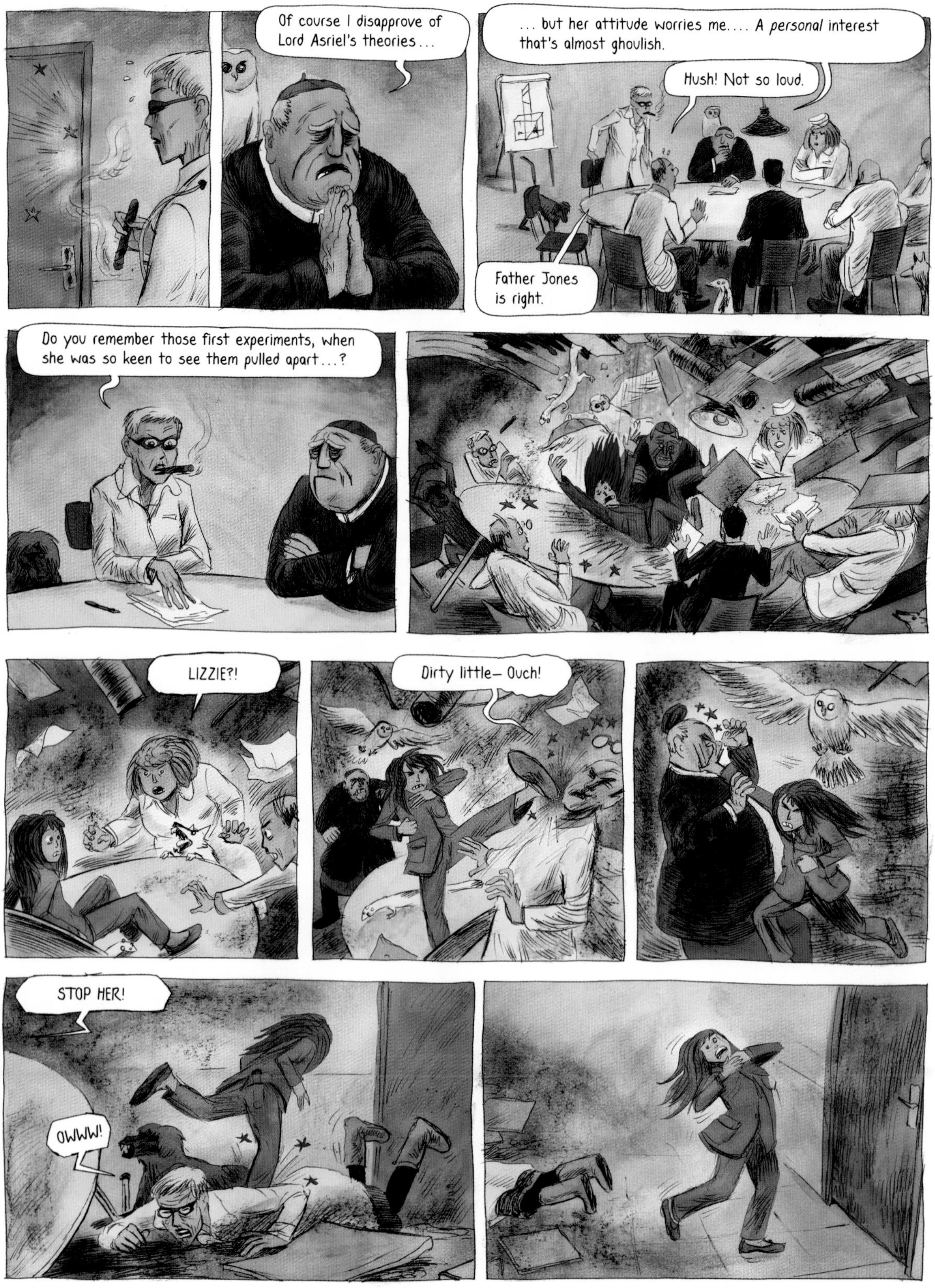
Of course I disapprove of Lord Asriel's theories...
... but her attitude worries me.... A *personal* interest that's almost ghoulish.
Hush! Not so loud.
Father Jones is right.
Do you remember those first experiments, when she was so keen to see them pulled apart...?
LIZZIE?!
Dirty little– Ouch!
STOP HER!
OWWW!

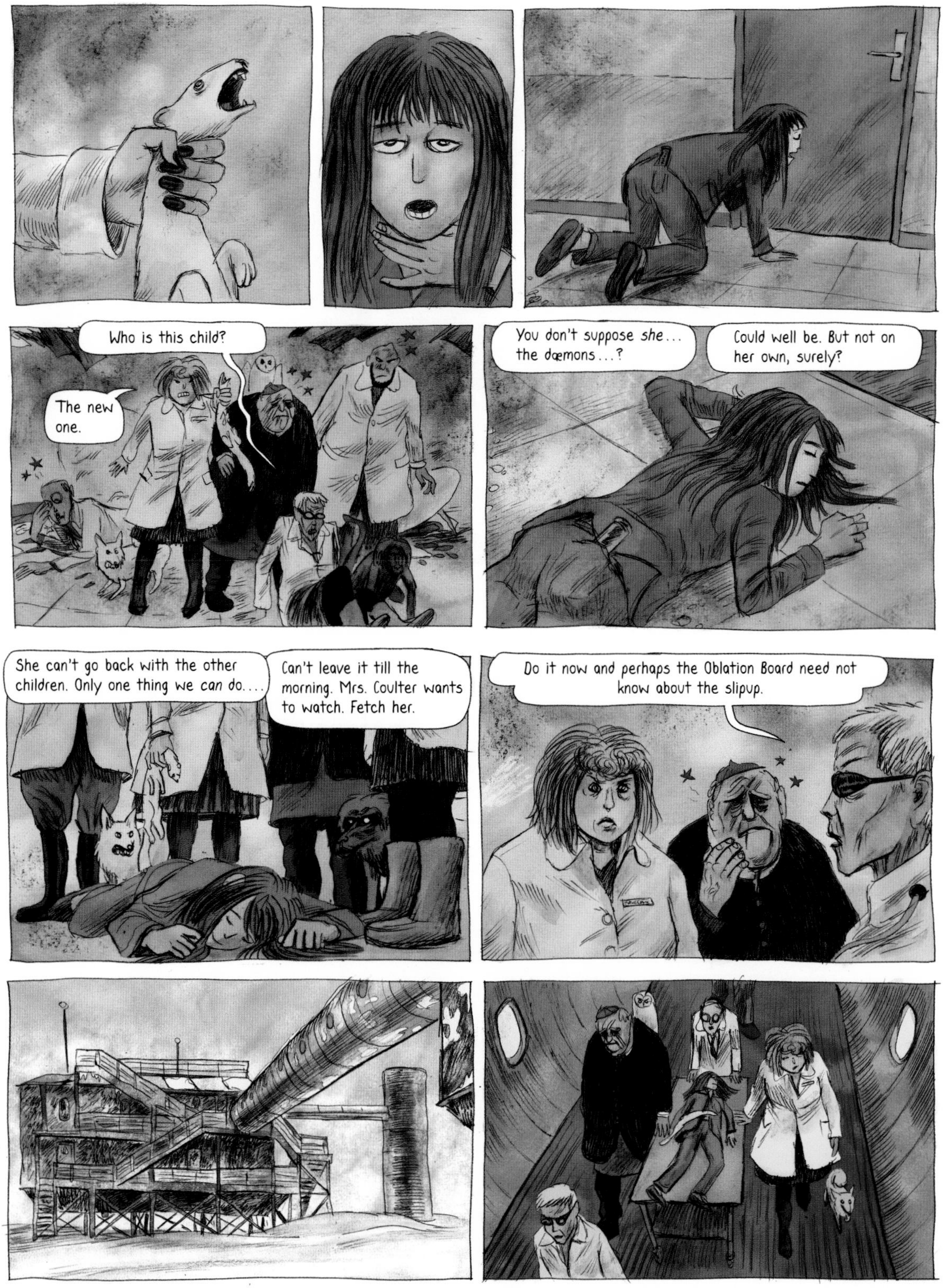

Who is this child?
The new one.
You don't suppose *she*... the dæmons...?
Could well be. But not on her own, surely?
She can't go back with the other children. Only one thing we *can* do....
Can't leave it till the morning. Mrs. Coulter wants to watch. Fetch her.
Do it now and perhaps the Oblation Board need not know about the slipup.

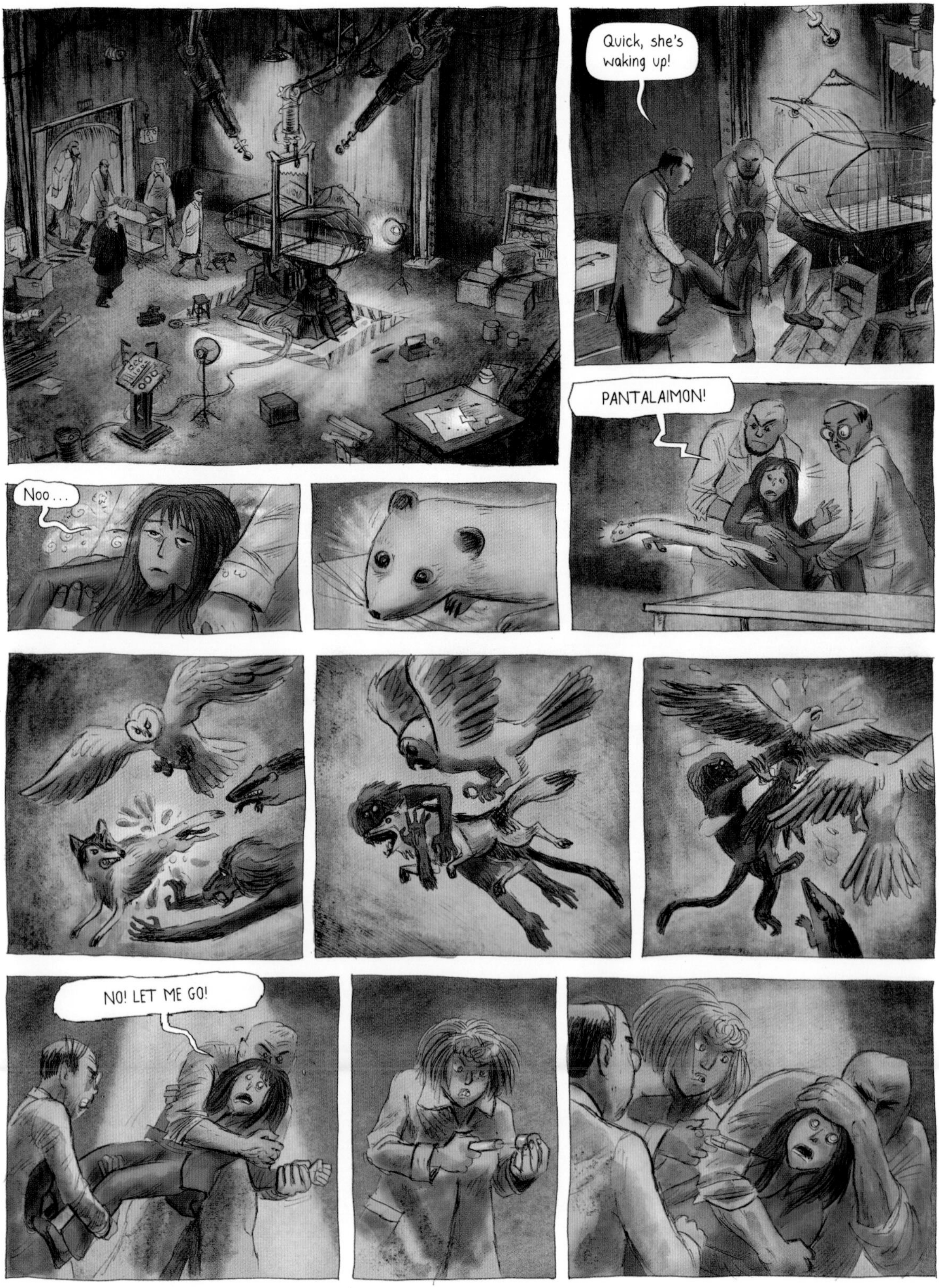
Quick, she's waking up!
PANTALAIMON!
Noo...
NO! LET ME GO!

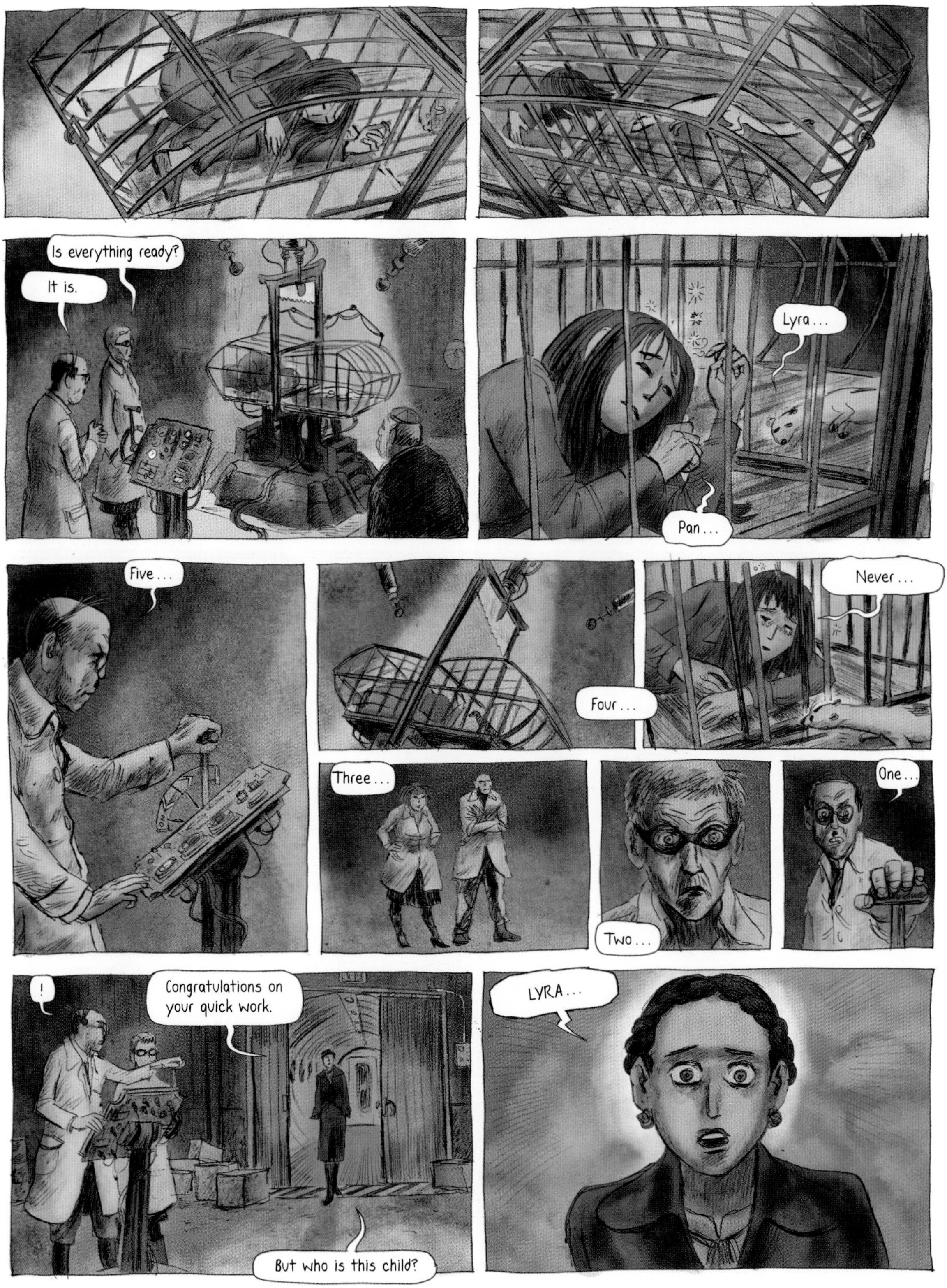
Is everything ready?
It is.
Lyra...
Pan...
Five...
Four...
Never...
Three...
Two...
One...
!
Congratulations on your quick work.
But who is this child?
LYRA...

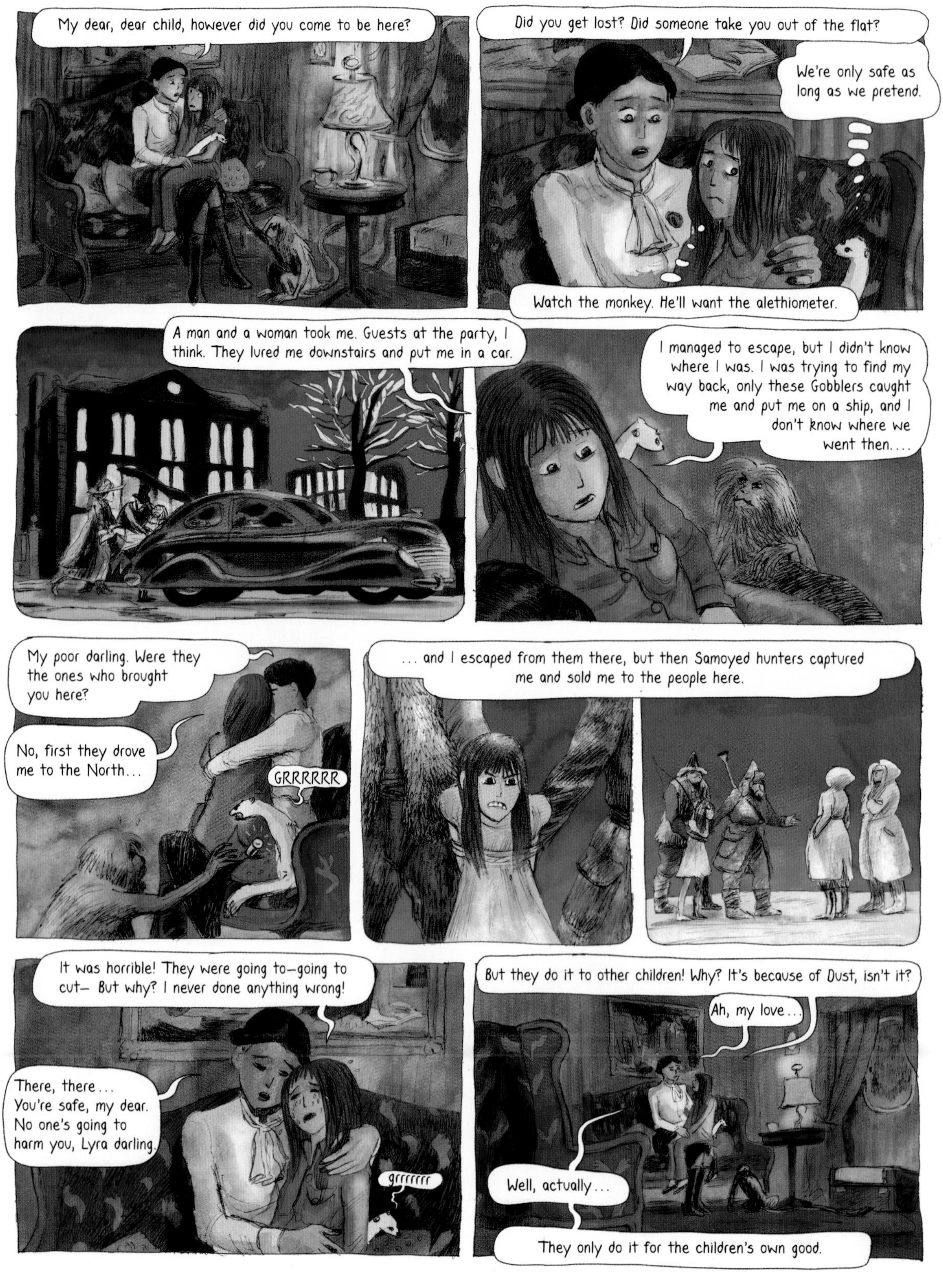

My dear, dear child, however did you come to be here?
Did you get lost? Did someone take you out of the flat?
We're only safe as long as we pretend.
Watch the monkey. He'll want the alethiometer.
A man and a woman took me. Guests at the party, I think. They lured me downstairs and put me in a car.
I managed to escape, but I didn't know where I was. I was trying to find my way back, only these Gobblers caught me and put me on a ship, and I don't know where we went then....
My poor darling. Were they the ones who brought you here?
No, first they drove me to the North...
GRRRRRR
... and I escaped from them there, but then Samoyed hunters captured me and sold me to the people here.
It was horrible! They were going to—going to cut— But why? I never done anything wrong!
There, there... You're safe, my dear. No one's going to harm you, Lyra darling.
grrrrrr
But they do it to other children! Why? It's because of Dust, isn't it?
Ah, my love...
Well, actually...
They only do it for the children's own good.

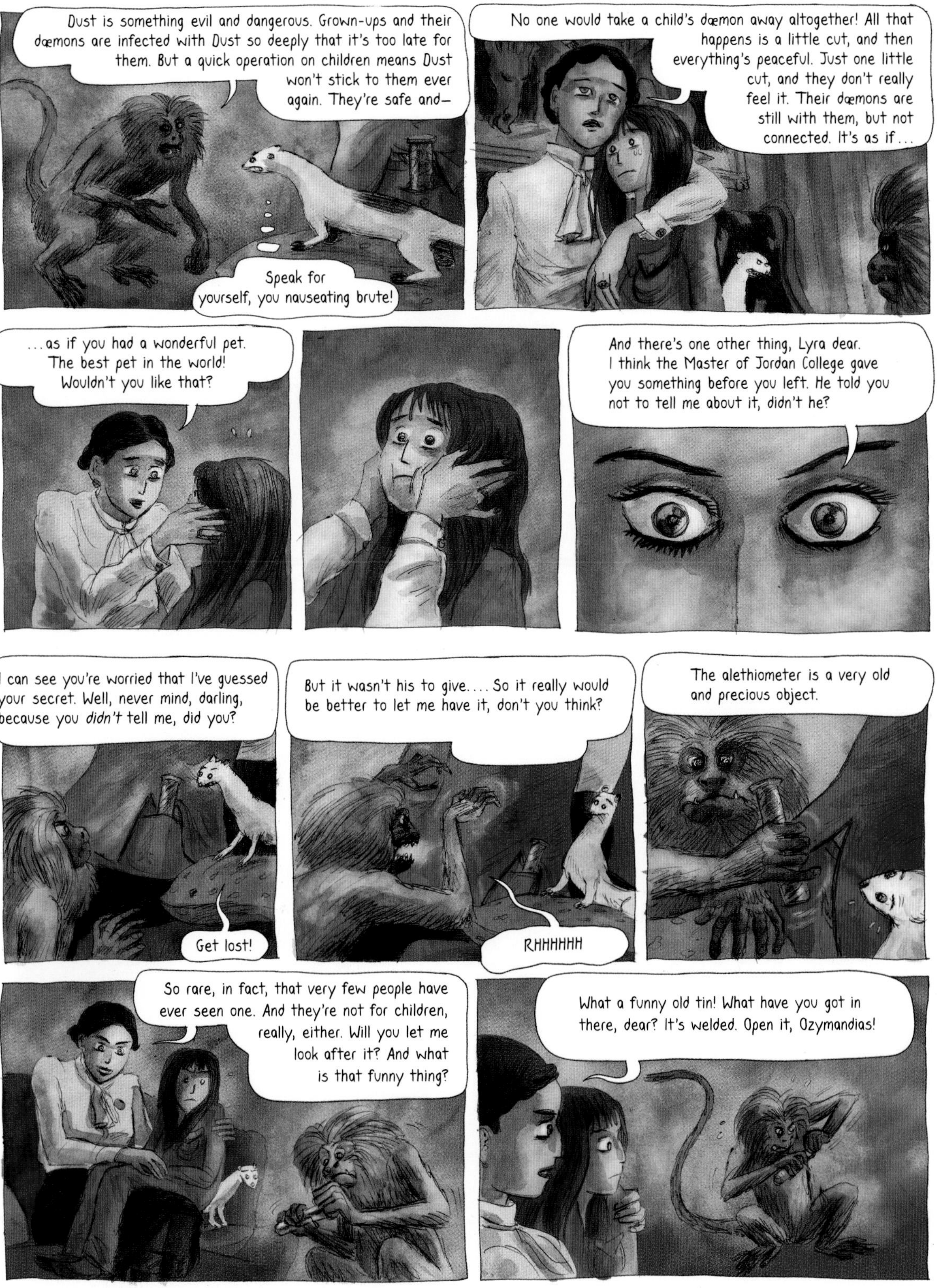

Dust is something evil and dangerous. Grown-ups and their dæmons are infected with Dust so deeply that it's too late for them. But a quick operation on children means Dust won't stick to them ever again. They're safe and—
Speak for yourself, you nauseating brute!
No one would take a child's dæmon away altogether! All that happens is a little cut, and then everything's peaceful. Just one little cut, and they don't really feel it. Their dæmons are still with them, but not connected. It's as if . . .
. . . as if you had a wonderful pet. The best pet in the world! Wouldn't you like that?
And there's one other thing, Lyra dear. I think the Master of Jordan College gave you something before you left. He told you not to tell me about it, didn't he?
I can see you're worried that I've guessed your secret. Well, never mind, darling, because you *didn't* tell me, did you?
Get lost!
But it wasn't his to give. . . . So it really would be better to let me have it, don't you think?
RHHHHHH
The alethiometer is a very old and precious object.
So rare, in fact, that very few people have ever seen one. And they're not for children, really, either. Will you let me look after it? And what is that funny thing?
What a funny old tin! What have you got in there, dear? It's welded. Open it, Ozymandias!

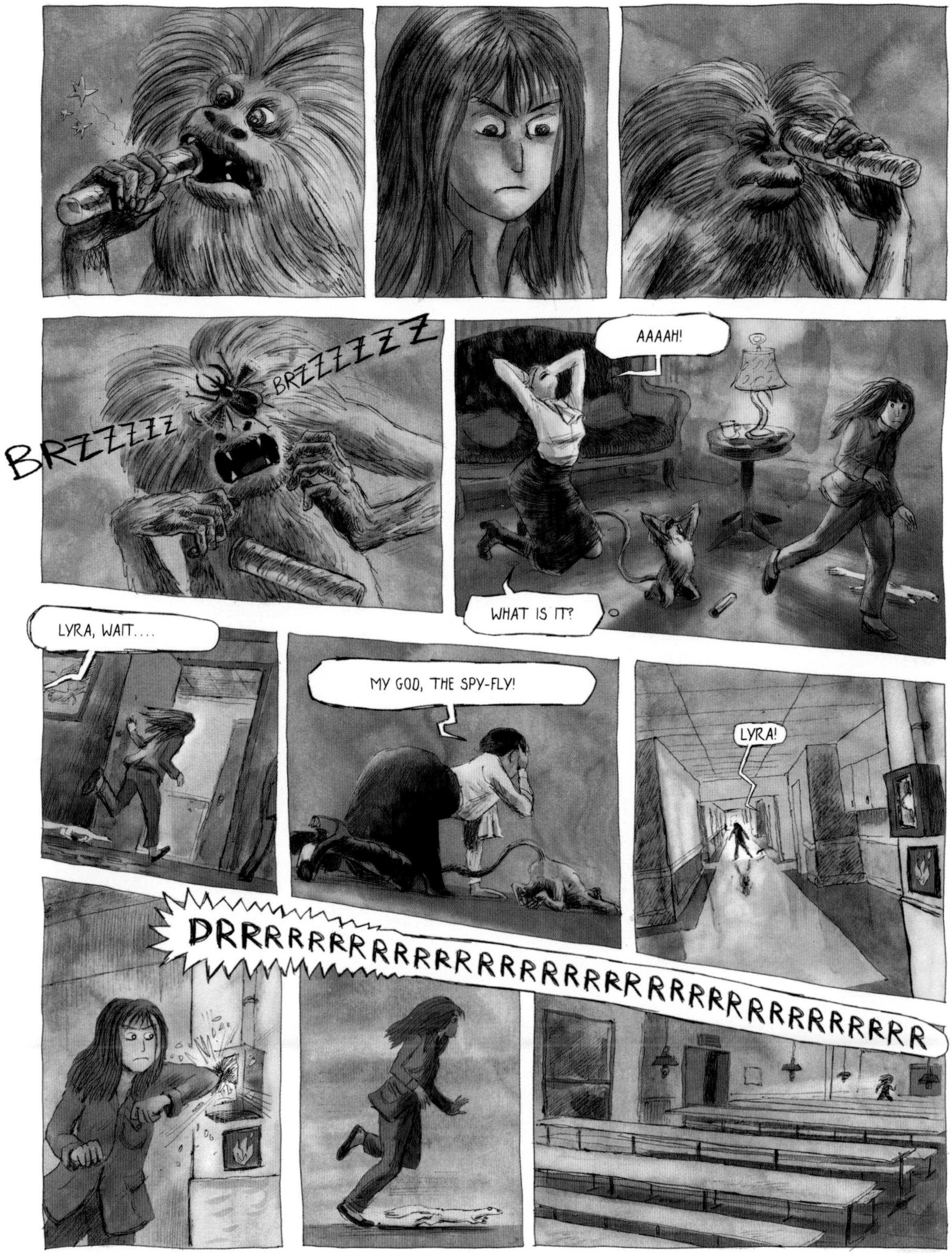
BRZZZZZZ
BRZZZZZZZ
AAAAH!
WHAT IS IT?
LYRA, WAIT....
MY GOD, THE SPY-FLY!
LYRA!
DRRRRRRRRRRRRRRRRRRRRRRRRRRRRRRRRRRRRRRR

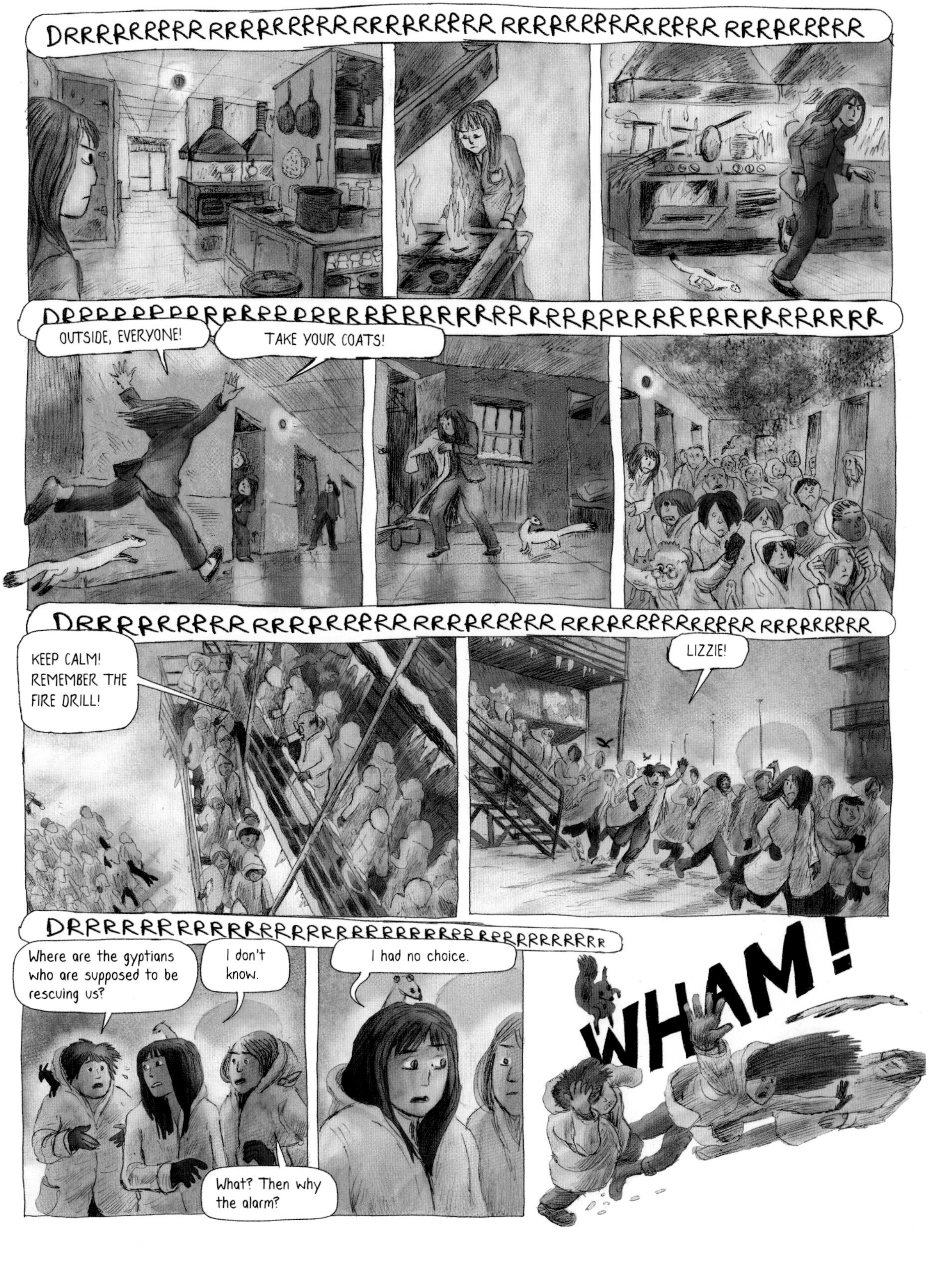
DRRRRRRRRR RRRRRRRRR RRRRRRRRR RRRRRRRRRRRRR RRRRRRRRR
DRRRRRRRRRRRRRRRRRRRRRRRRRRRRRRRRRRRRRRRRRRRRR
OUTSIDE, EVERYONE!
TAKE YOUR COATS!
DRRRRRRRRR RRRRRRRRR RRRRRRRRR RRRRRRRRRRRRR RRRRRRRRR
KEEP CALM! REMEMBER THE FIRE DRILL!
LIZZIE!
DRRRRRRRRRRRRRRRRRRRRRRRRRRRRRRRRRR
Where are the gyptians who are supposed to be rescuing us?
I don't know.
What? Then why the alarm?
I had no choice.
WHAM!

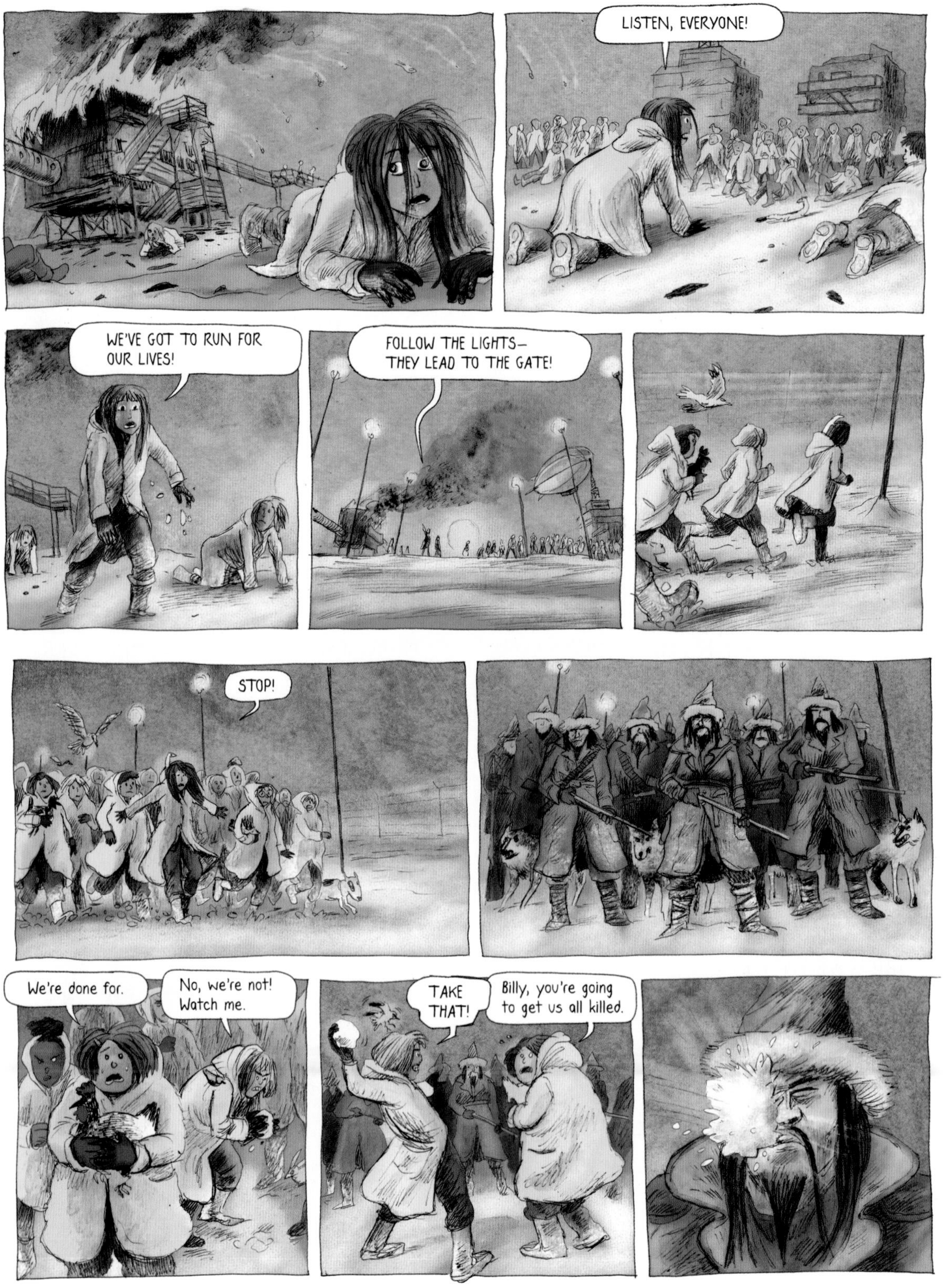
LISTEN, EVERYONE!
WE'VE GOT TO RUN FOR OUR LIVES!
FOLLOW THE LIGHTS— THEY LEAD TO THE GATE!
STOP!
We're done for.
No, we're not! Watch me.
TAKE THAT!
Billy, you're going to get us all killed.

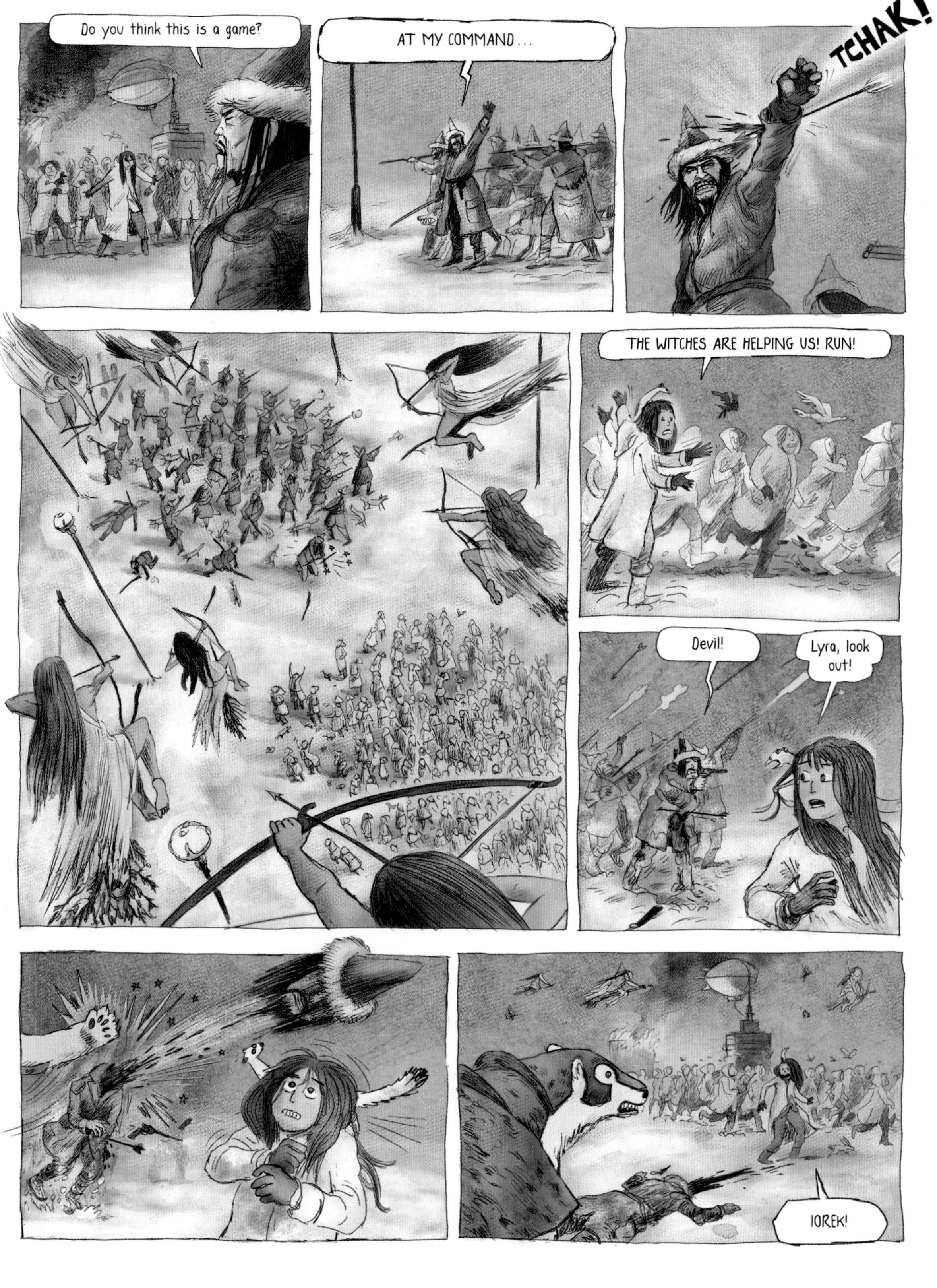
Do you think this is a game?
AT MY COMMAND...
TCHAK!
THE WITCHES ARE HELPING US! RUN!
Devil!
Lyra, look out!
IOREK!

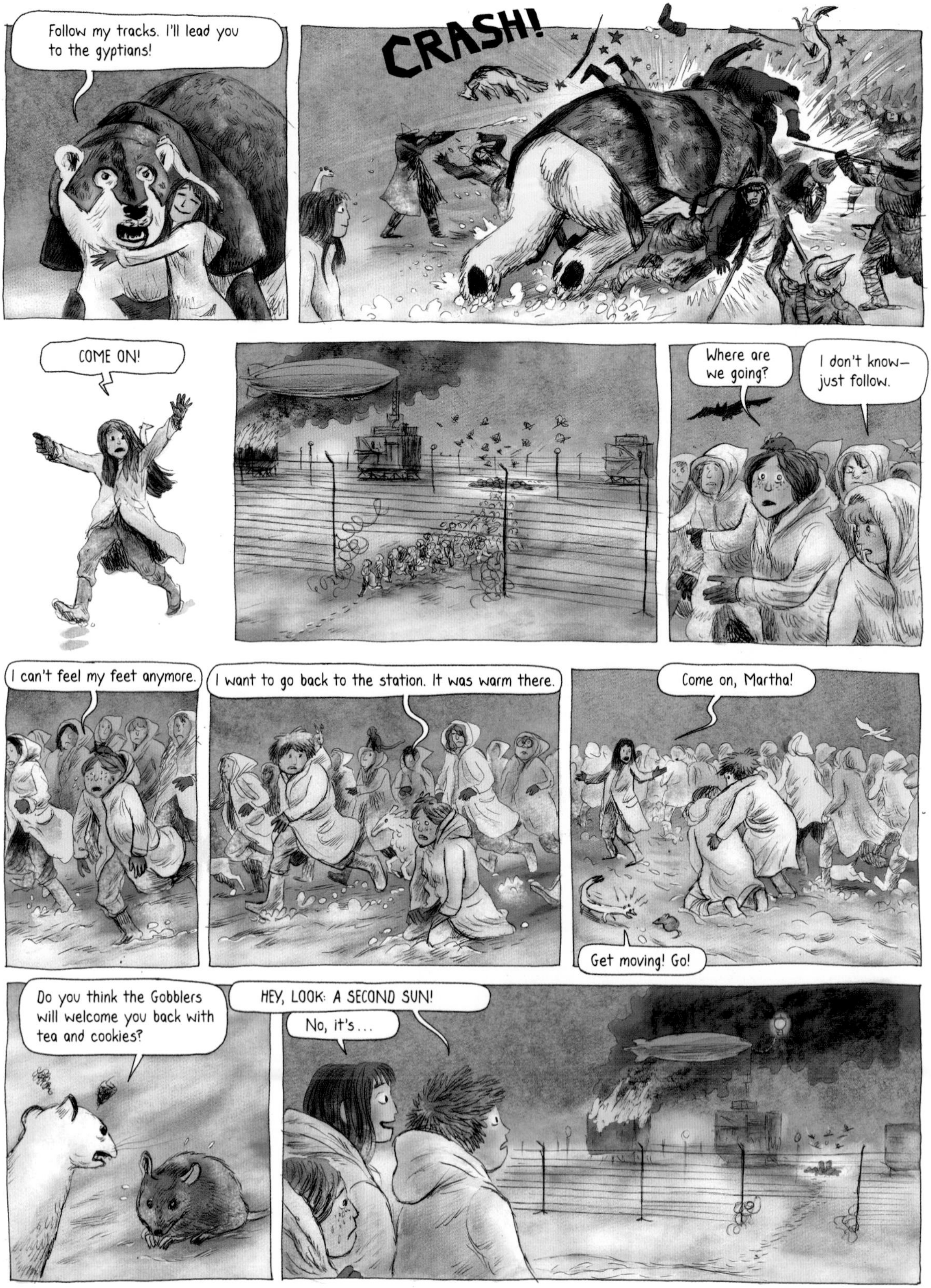
Follow my tracks. I'll lead you to the gyptians!
CRASH!
COME ON!
Where are we going?
I don't know—just follow.
I can't feel my feet anymore.
I want to go back to the station. It was warm there.
Come on, Martha!
Get moving! Go!
Do you think the Gobblers will welcome you back with tea and cookies?
HEY, LOOK: A SECOND SUN!
No, it's...

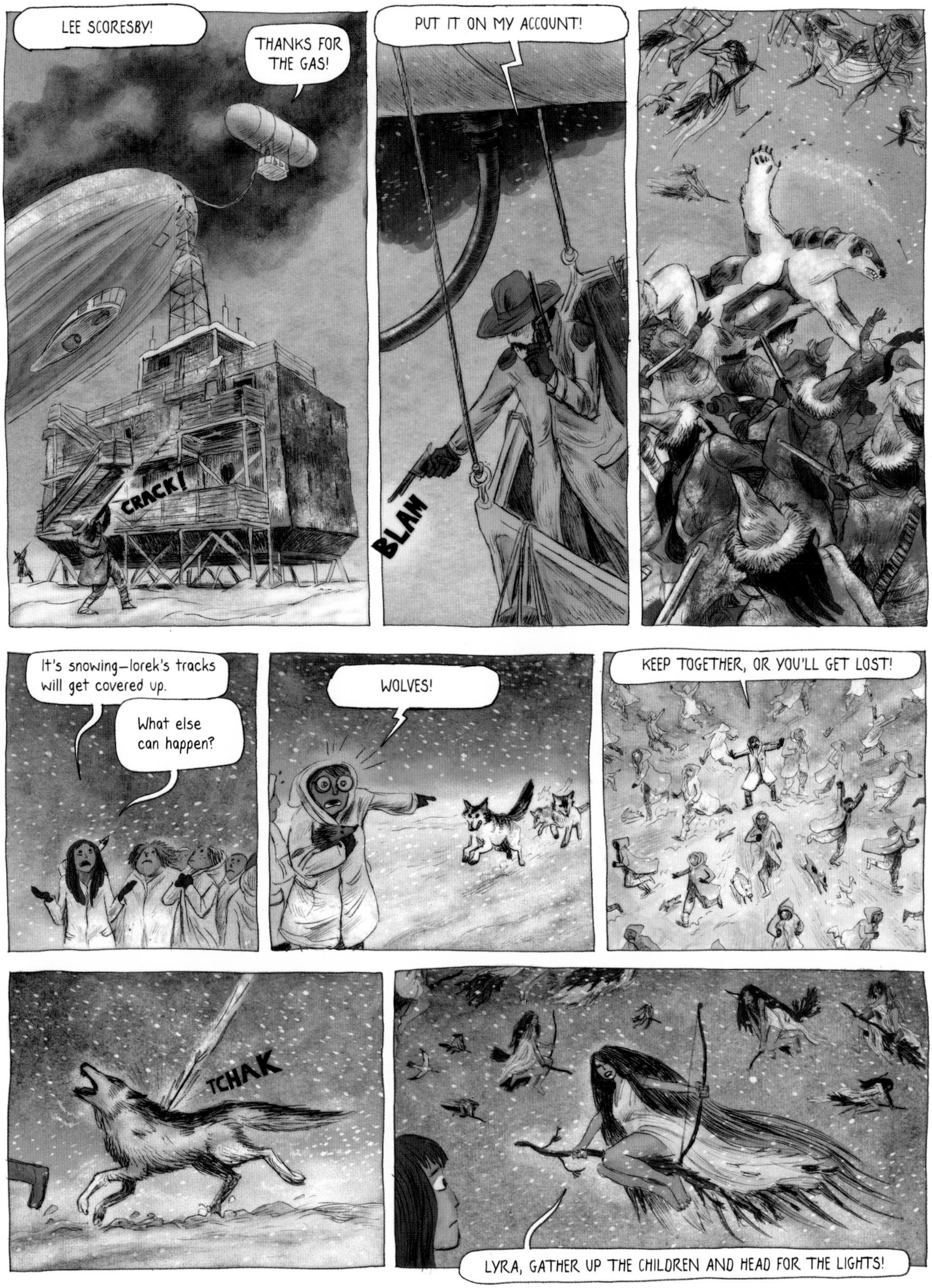
LEE SCORESBY!
THANKS FOR THE GAS!
CRACK!
PUT IT ON MY ACCOUNT!
BLAM
It's snowing—lorek's tracks will get covered up.
What else can happen?
WOLVES!
KEEP TOGETHER, OR YOU'LL GET LOST!
TCHAK
LYRA, GATHER UP THE CHILDREN AND HEAD FOR THE LIGHTS!

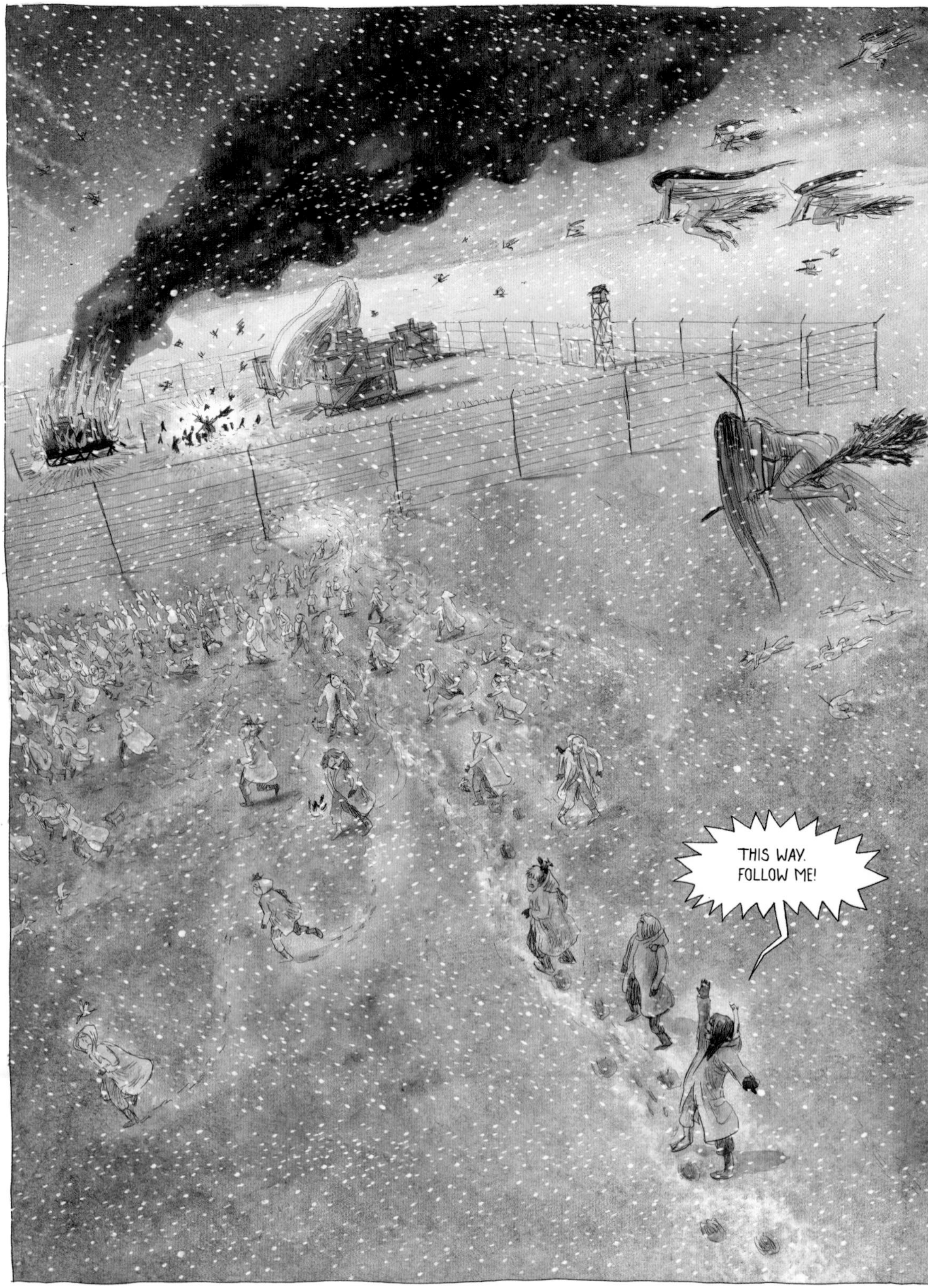
THIS WAY. FOLLOW ME!

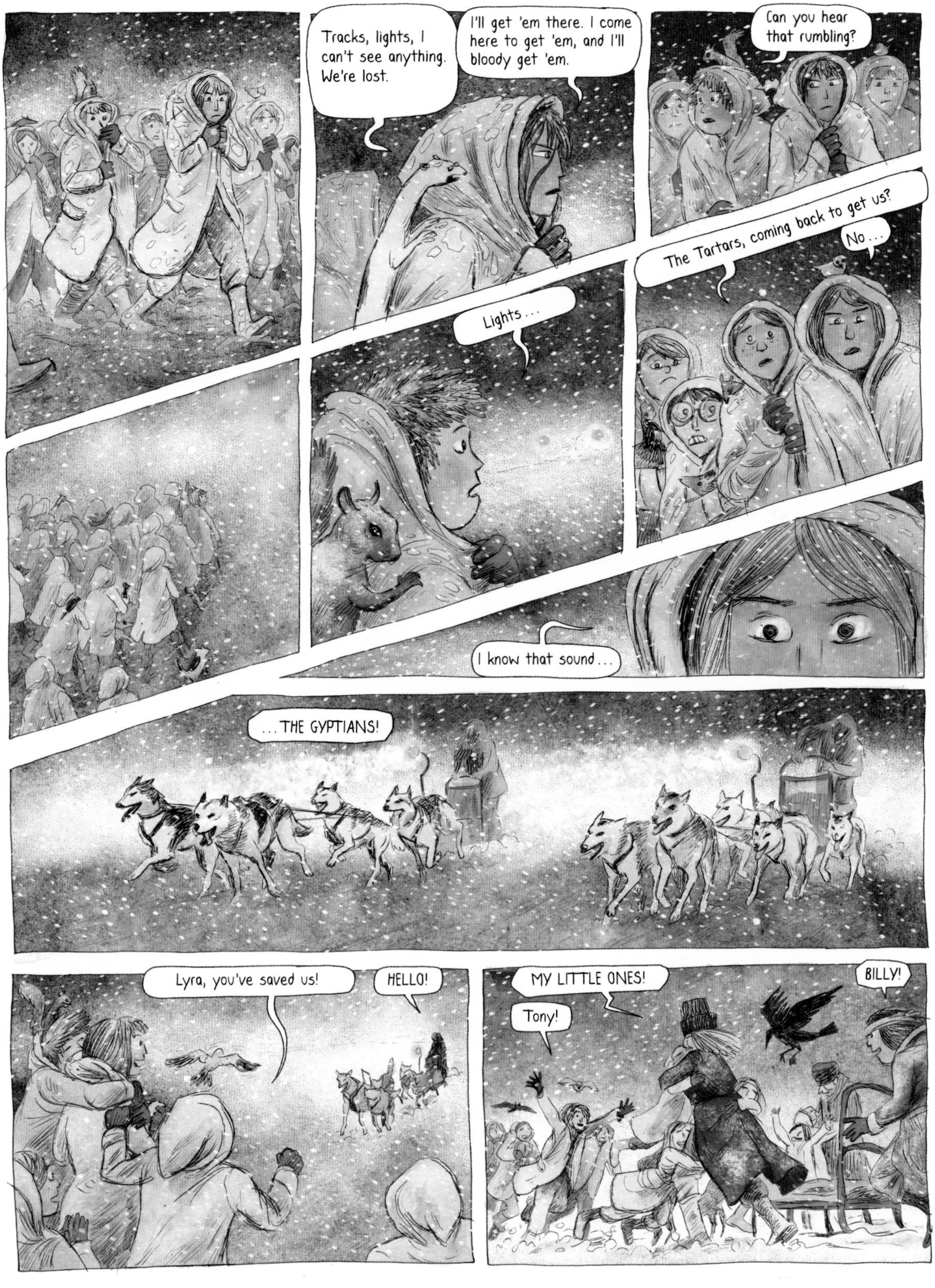
Tracks, lights, I can't see anything. We're lost.
I'll get 'em there. I come here to get 'em, and I'll bloody get 'em.
Can you hear that rumbling?
The Tartars, coming back to get us?
No...
Lights...
I know that sound...
...THE GYPTIANS!
Lyra, you've saved us!
HELLO!
MY LITTLE ONES!
Tony!
BILLY!

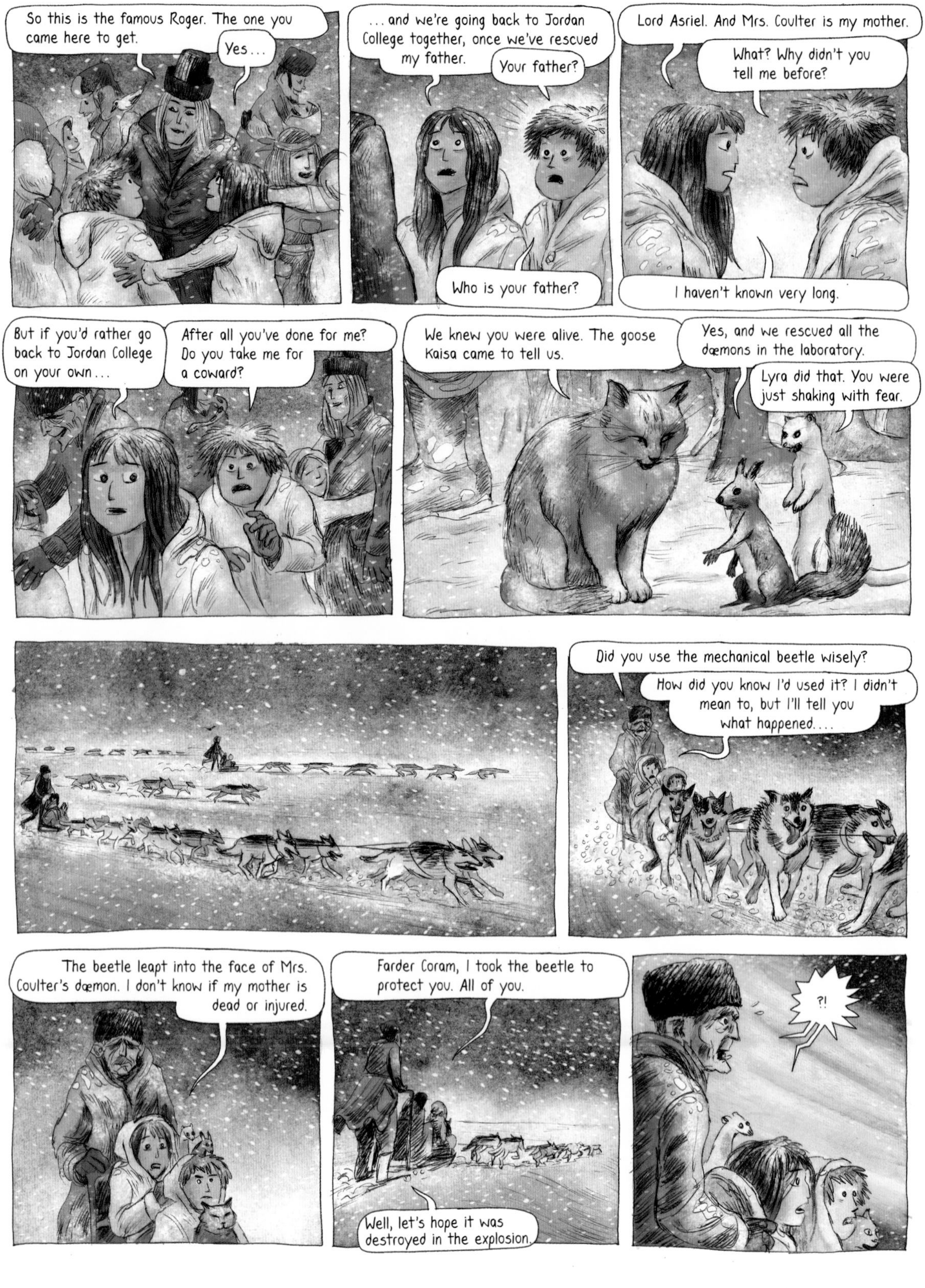
So this is the famous Roger. The one you came here to get.
Yes...
...and we're going back to Jordan College together, once we've rescued my father.
Your father?
Who is your father?
Lord Asriel. And Mrs. Coulter is my mother.
What? Why didn't you tell me before?
I haven't known very long.
But if you'd rather go back to Jordan College on your own...
After all you've done for me? Do you take me for a coward?
We knew you were alive. The goose Kaisa came to tell us.
Yes, and we rescued all the dæmons in the laboratory.
Lyra did that. You were just shaking with fear.
Did you use the mechanical beetle wisely?
How did you know I'd used it? I didn't mean to, but I'll tell you what happened....
The beetle leapt into the face of Mrs. Coulter's dæmon. I don't know if my mother is dead or injured.
Farder Coram, I took the beetle to protect you. All of you.
Well, let's hope it was destroyed in the explosion.
?!

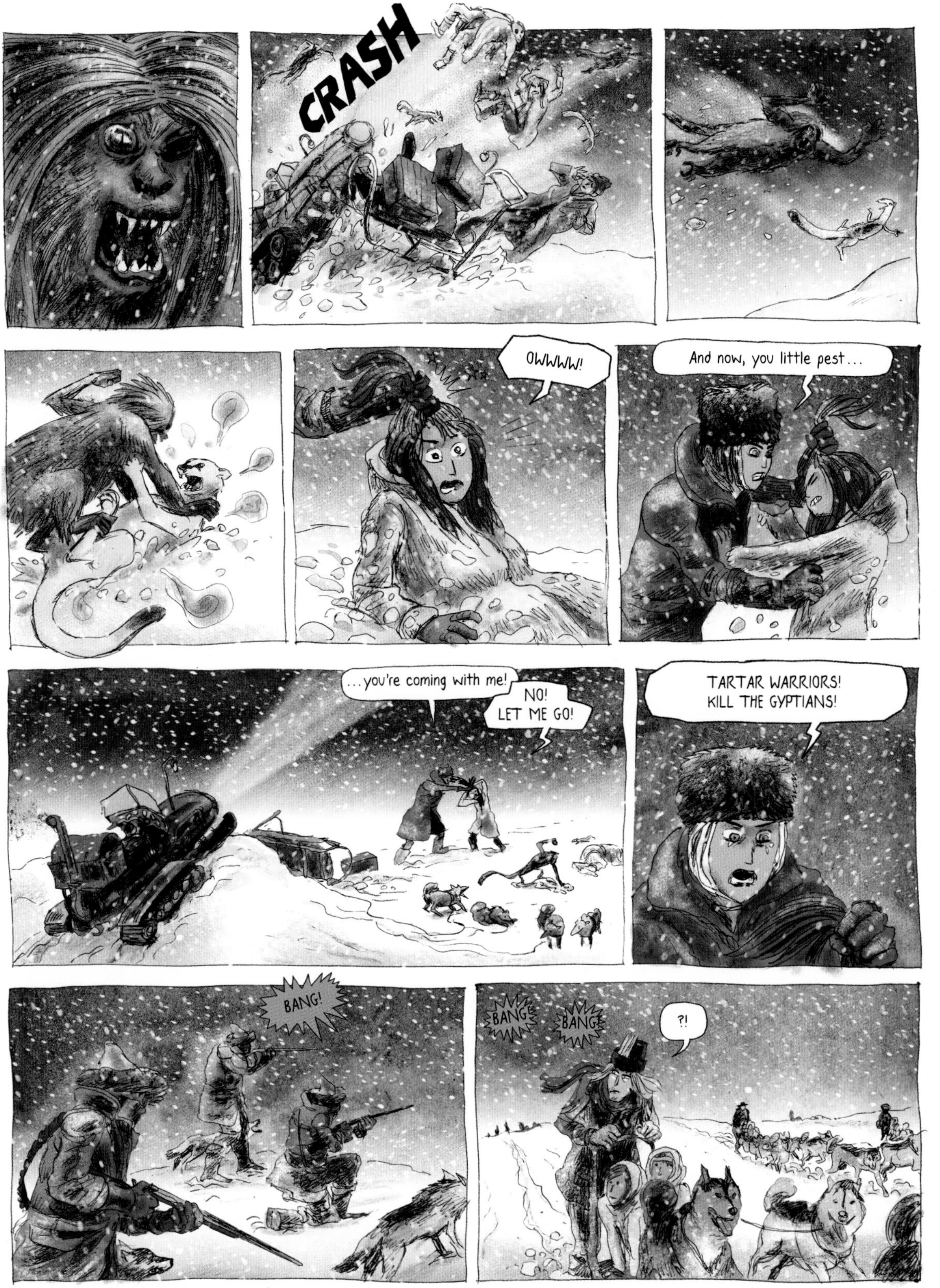
CRASH
OWWWW!
And now, you little pest...
...you're coming with me!
NO!
LET ME GO!
TARTAR WARRIORS!
KILL THE GYPTIANS!
BANG!
BANG
BANG
?!

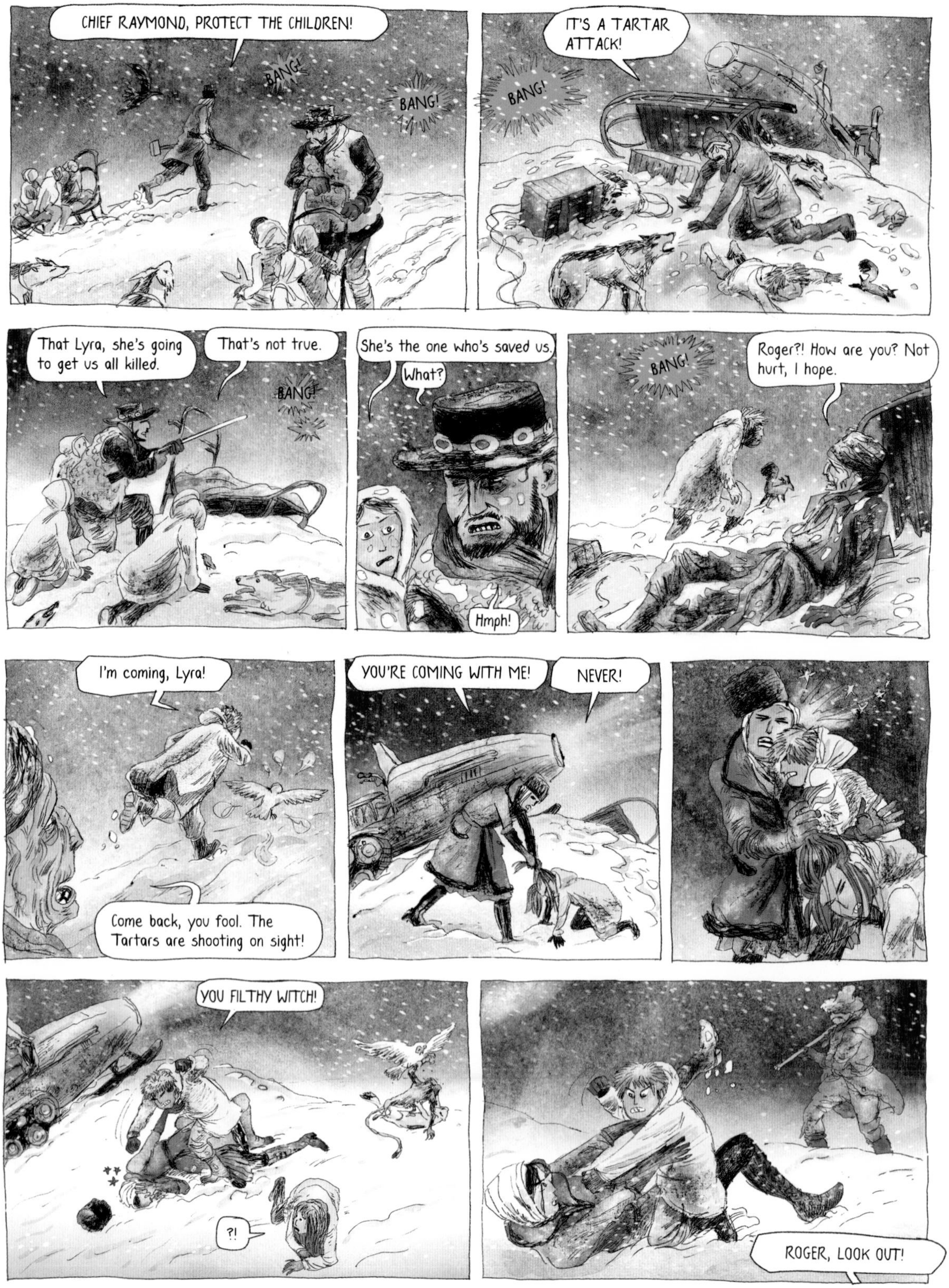

CHIEF RAYMOND, PROTECT THE CHILDREN!
BANG!
BANG!
IT'S A TARTAR ATTACK!
BANG!
That Lyra, she's going to get us all killed.
That's not true.
BANG!
She's the one who's saved us.
What?
Hmph!
BANG!
Roger?! How are you? Not hurt, I hope.
I'm coming, Lyra!
Come back, you fool. The Tartars are shooting on sight!
YOU'RE COMING WITH ME!
NEVER!
YOU FILTHY WITCH!
?!
ROGER, LOOK OUT!

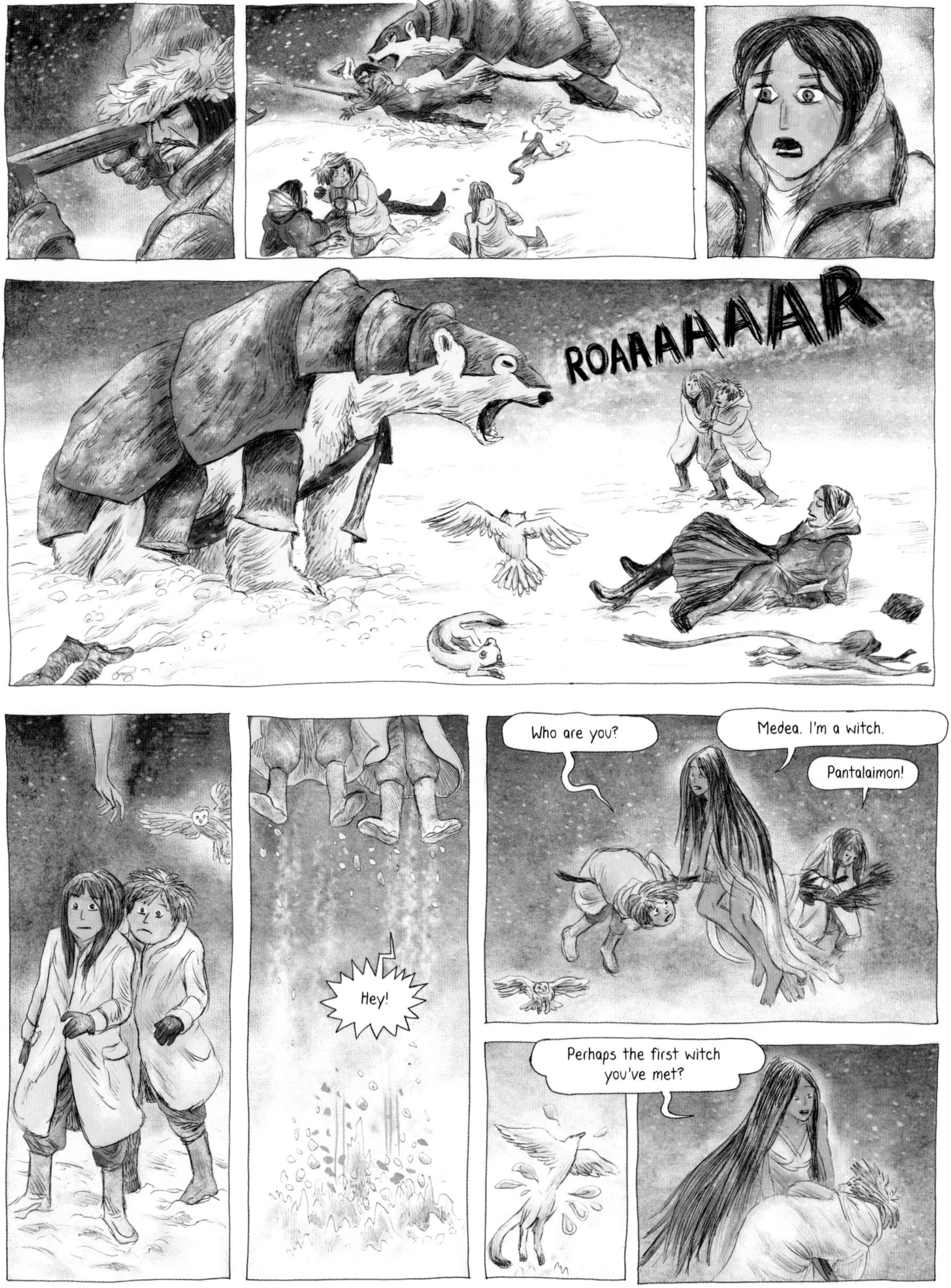
ROAAAAAAR
Who are you?
Medea. I'm a witch.
Pantalaimon!
Hey!
Perhaps the first witch you've met?

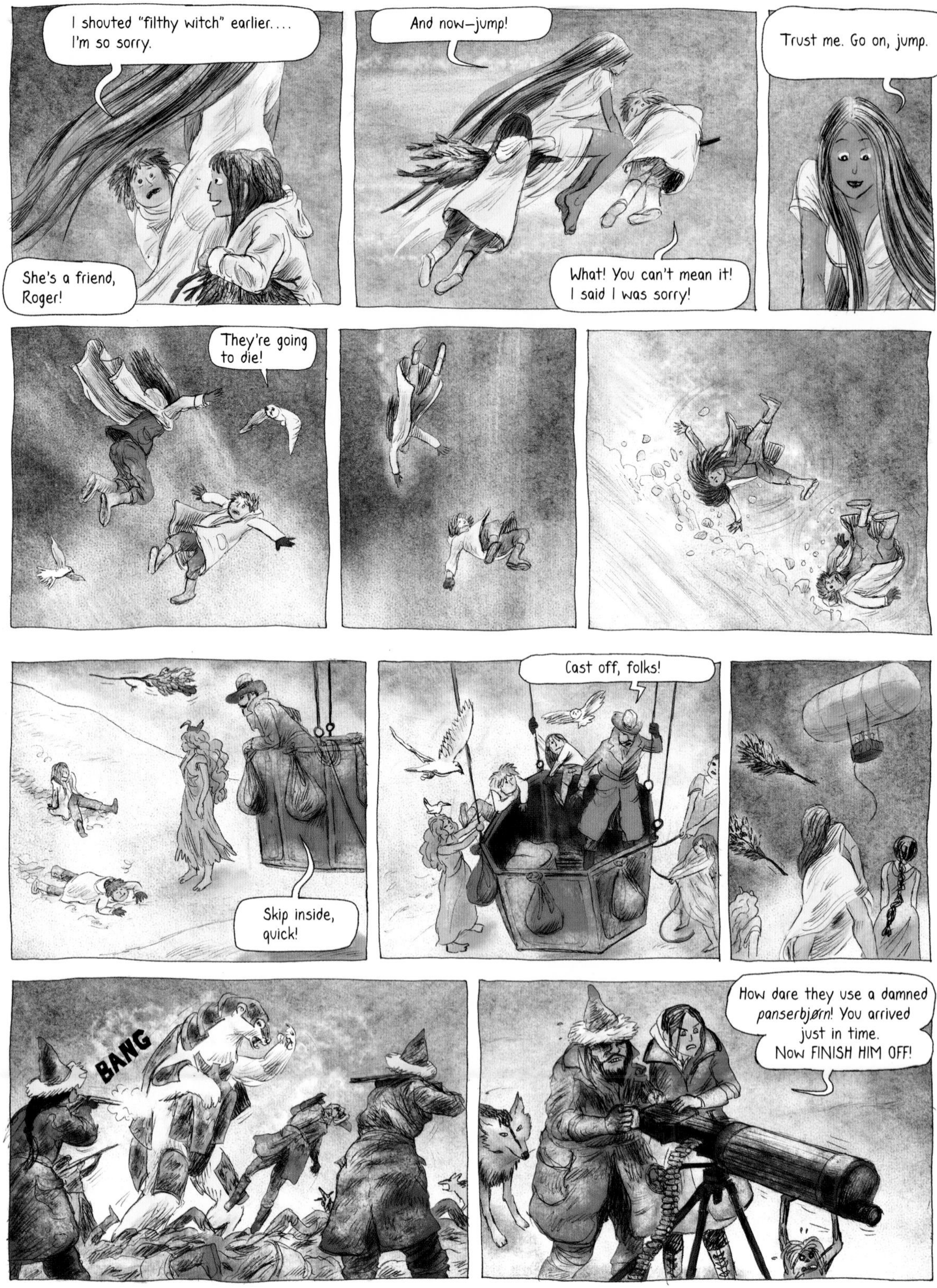

I shouted "filthy witch" earlier.... I'm so sorry.
She's a friend, Roger!
And now—jump!
What! You can't mean it! I said I was sorry!
Trust me. Go on, jump.
They're going to die!
Skip inside, quick!
Cast off, folks!
BANG
How dare they use a damned *panserbjørn*! You arrived just in time. Now FINISH HIM OFF!

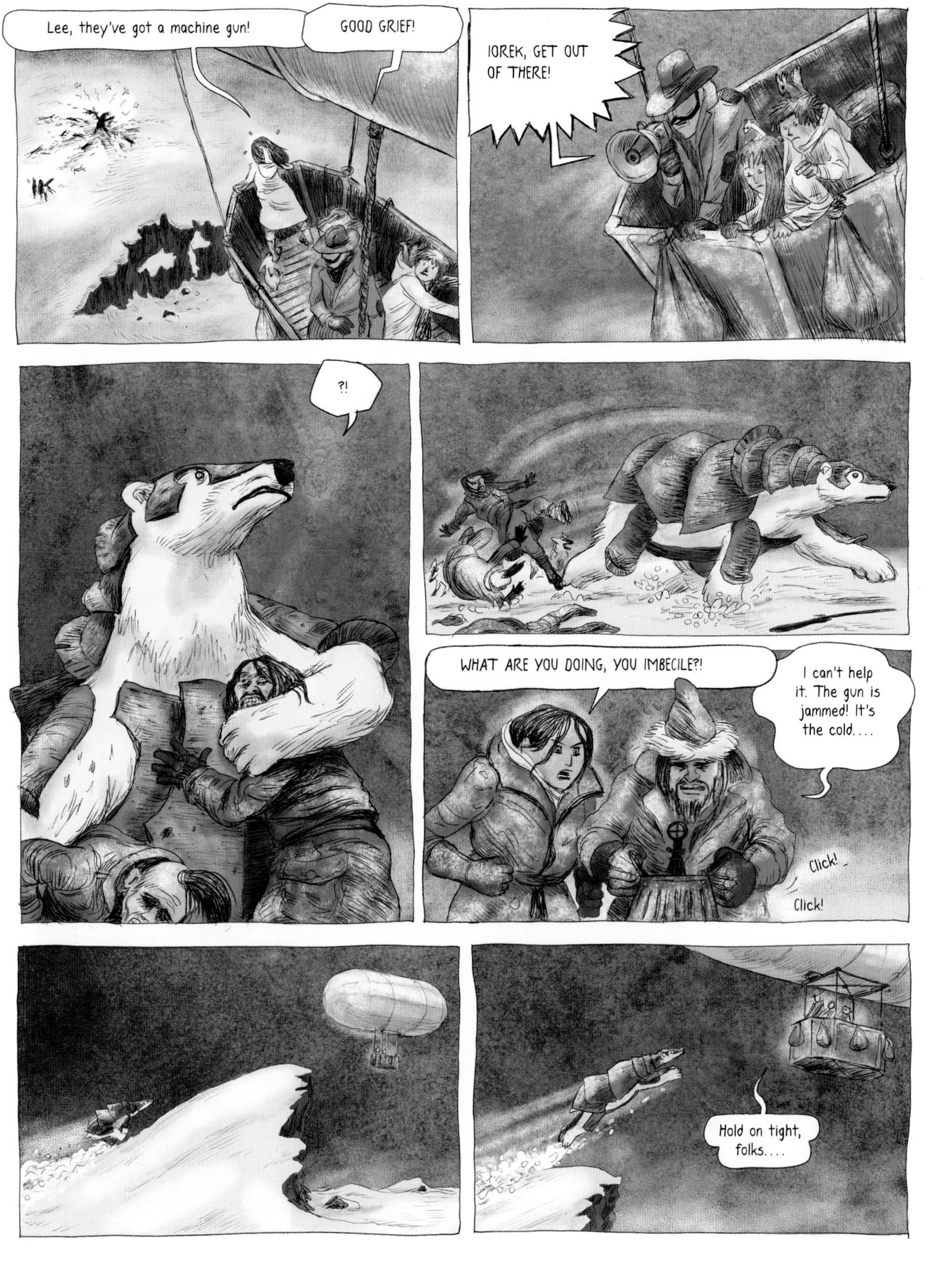

Lee, they've got a machine gun!
GOOD GRIEF!
IOREK, GET OUT OF THERE!
?!
WHAT ARE YOU DOING, YOU IMBECILE?!
I can't help it. The gun is jammed! It's the cold....
Click!
Click!
Hold on tight, folks....

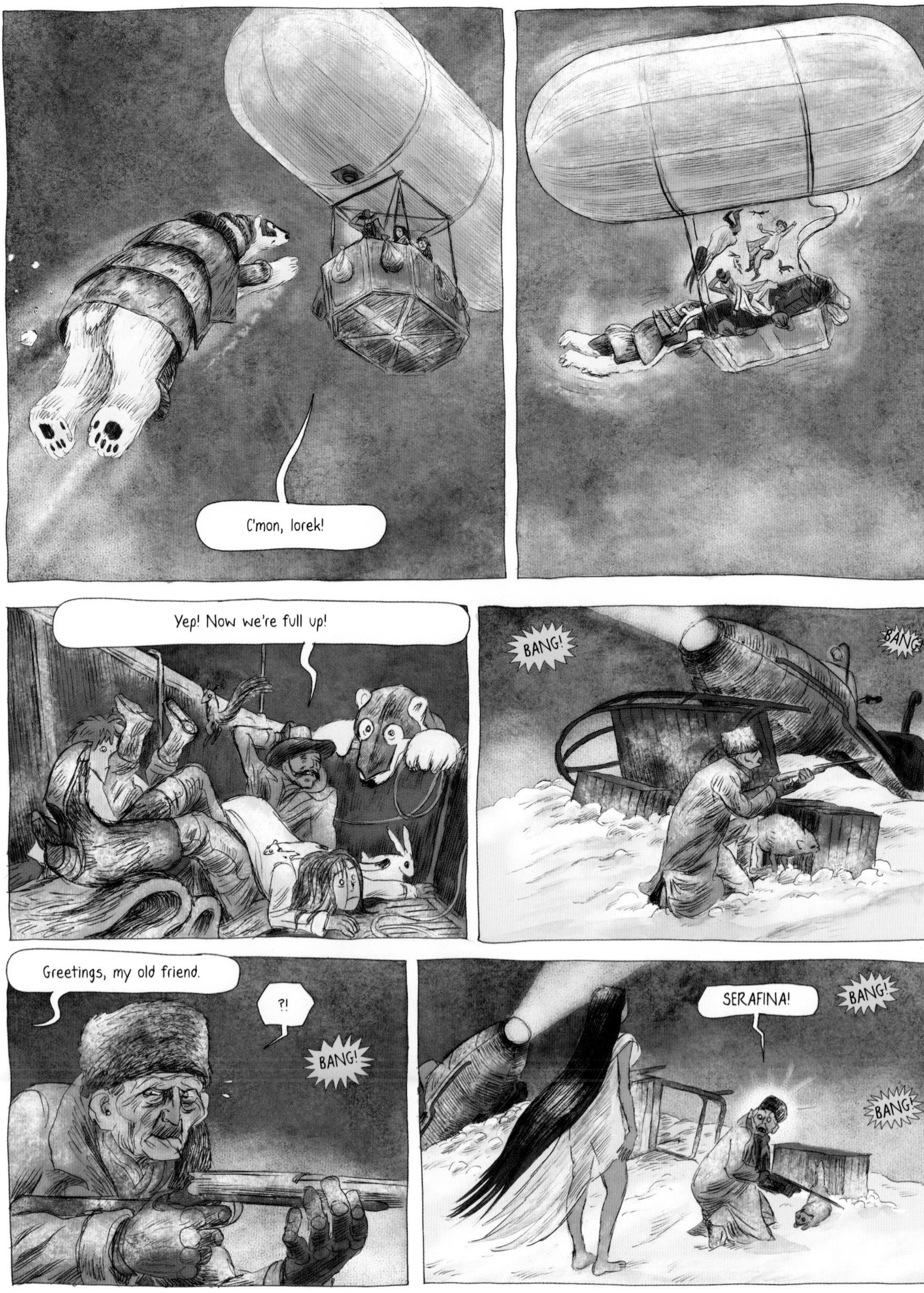
C'mon, Iorek!
Yep! Now we're full up!
BANG!
BANG!
Greetings, my old friend.
?!
BANG!
SERAFINA!
BANG!
BANG!

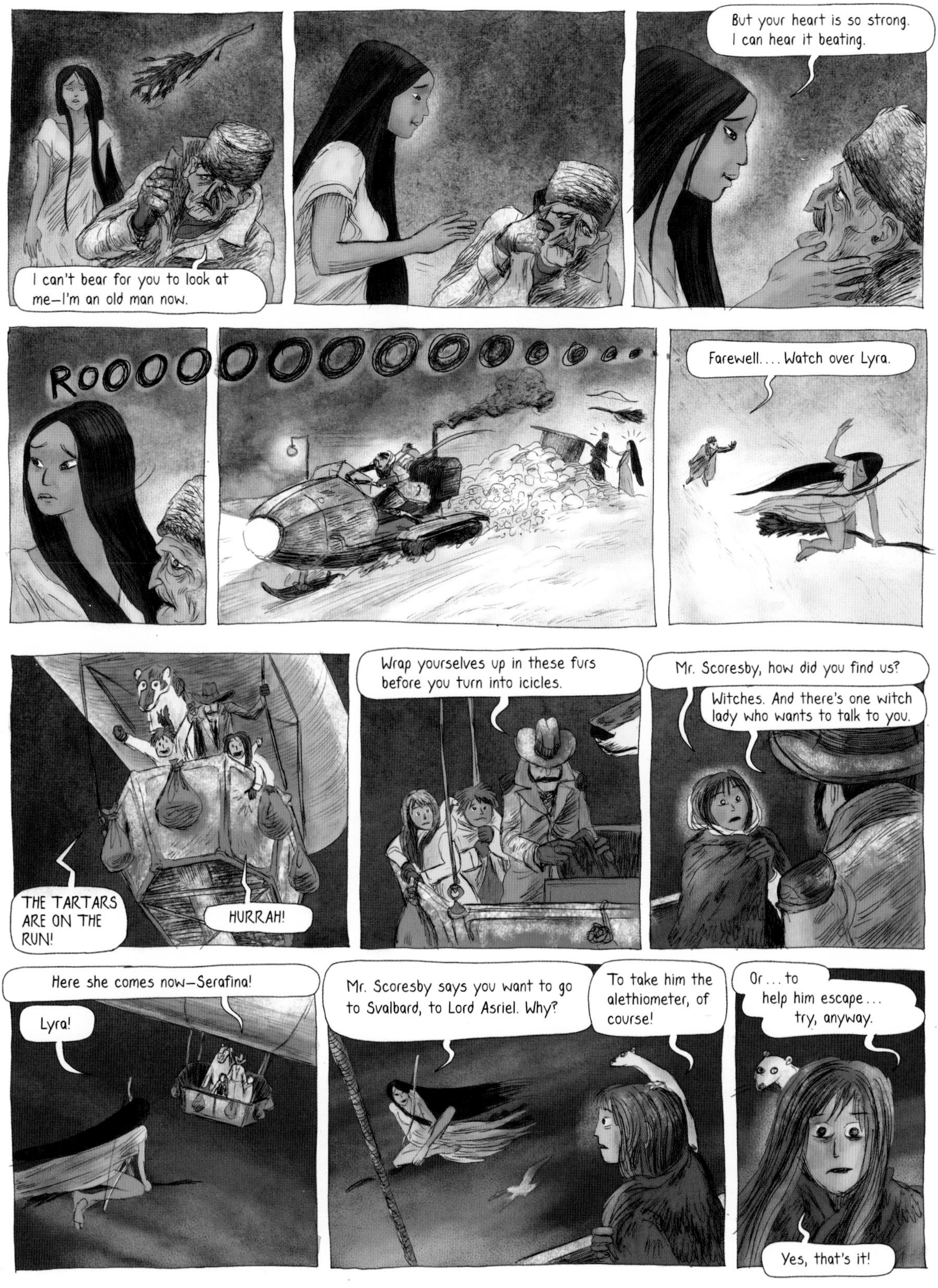
I can't bear for you to look at me—I'm an old man now.
But your heart is so strong. I can hear it beating.
ROOOOOOOOOOOOOO...
Farewell.... Watch over Lyra.
THE TARTARS ARE ON THE RUN!
HURRAH!
Wrap yourselves up in these furs before you turn into icicles.
Mr. Scoresby, how did you find us?
Witches. And there's one witch lady who wants to talk to you.
Here she comes now—Serafina!
Lyra!
Mr. Scoresby says you want to go to Svalbard, to Lord Asriel. Why?
To take him the alethiometer, of course!
Or... to help him escape... try, anyway.
Yes, that's it!

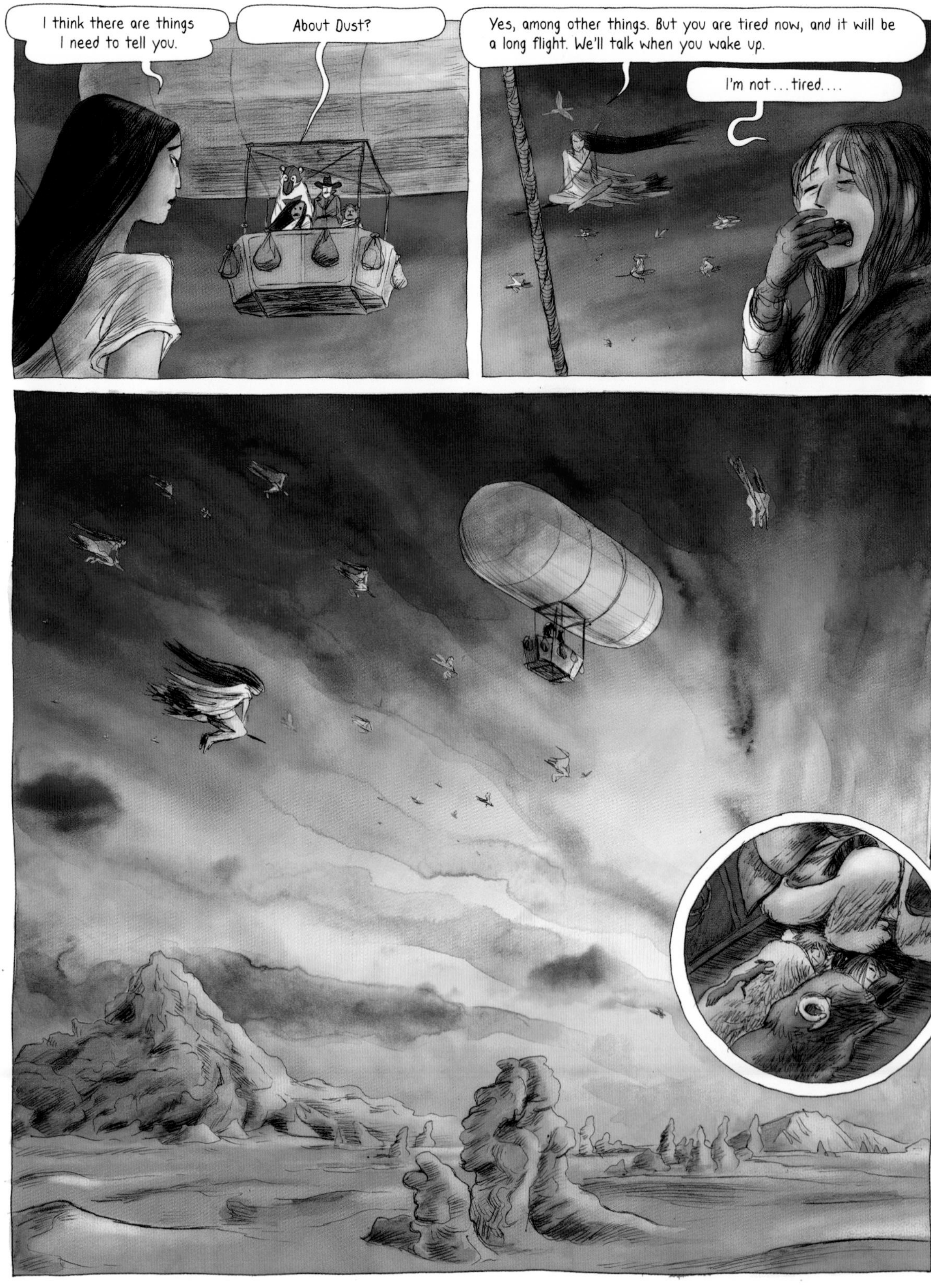
I think there are things I need to tell you.
About Dust?
Yes, among other things. But you are tired now, and it will be a long flight. We'll talk when you wake up.
I'm not . . . tired. . . .

PART III

SVALBARD

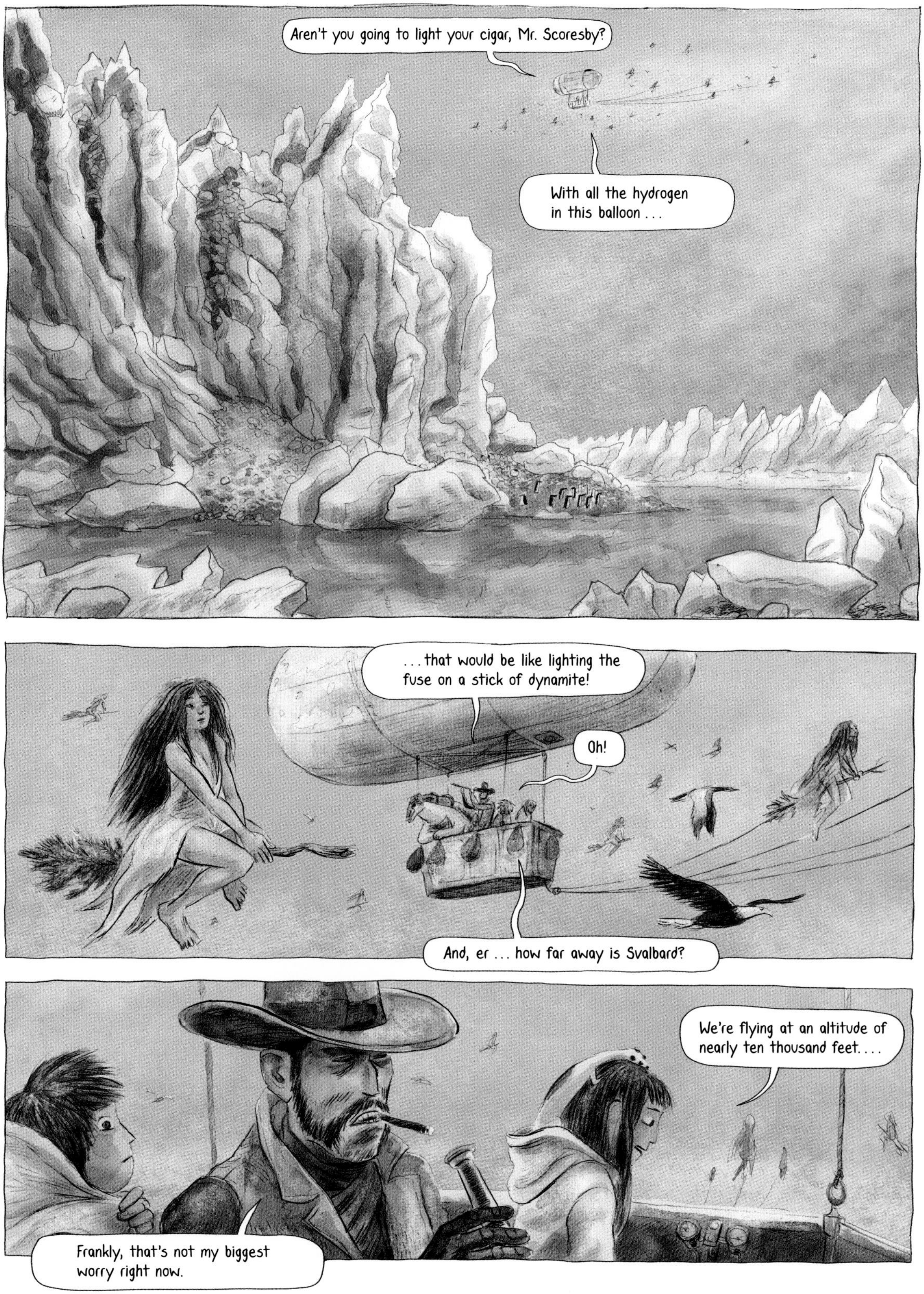
Aren't you going to light your cigar, Mr. Scoresby?
With all the hydrogen in this balloon . . .
. . . that would be like lighting the fuse on a stick of dynamite!
Oh!
And, er . . . how far away is Svalbard?
We're flying at an altitude of nearly ten thousand feet. . . .
Frankly, that's not my biggest worry right now.

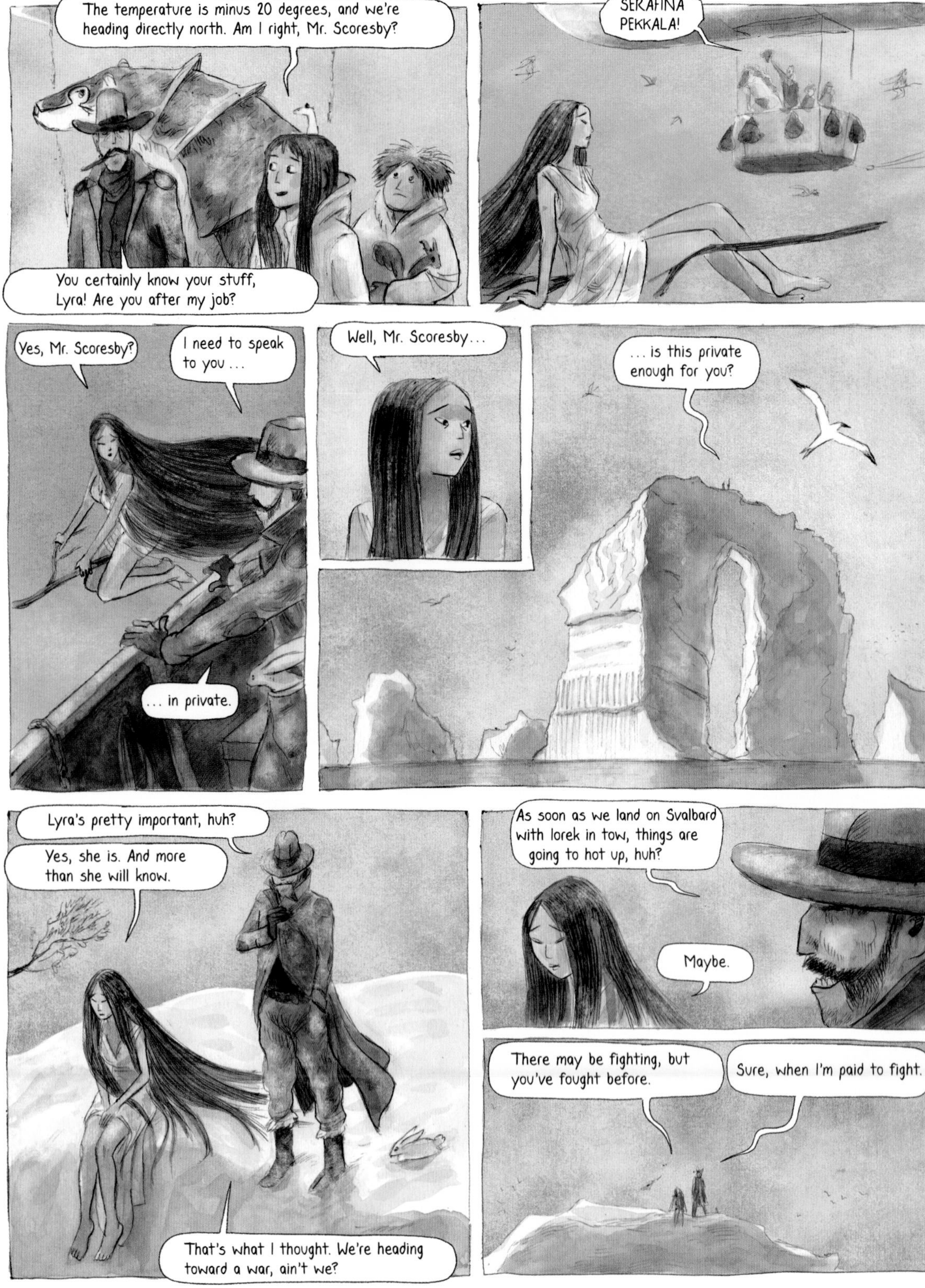

The temperature is minus 20 degrees, and we're heading directly north. Am I right, Mr. Scoresby?
You certainly know your stuff, Lyra! Are you after my job?
SERAFINA PEKKALA!
Yes, Mr. Scoresby?
I need to speak to you . . .
. . . in private.
Well, Mr. Scoresby . . .
. . . is this private enough for you?
Lyra's pretty important, huh?
Yes, she is. And more than she will know.
That's what I thought. We're heading toward a war, ain't we?
As soon as we land on Svalbard with Iorek in tow, things are going to hot up, huh?
Maybe.
There may be fighting, but you've fought before.
Sure, when I'm paid to fight.

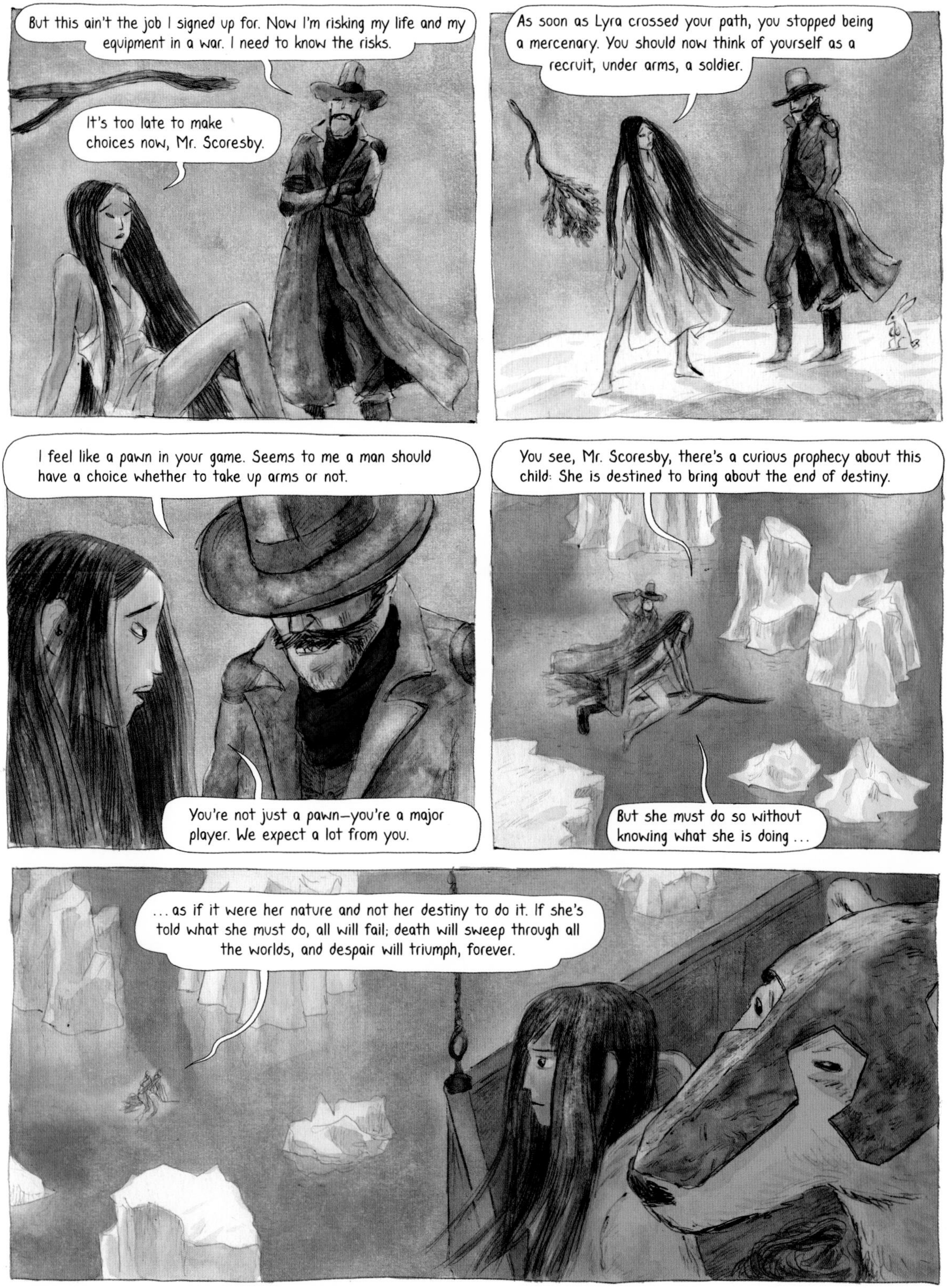
But this ain't the job I signed up for. Now I'm risking my life and my equipment in a war. I need to know the risks.
It's too late to make choices now, Mr. Scoresby.
As soon as Lyra crossed your path, you stopped being a mercenary. You should now think of yourself as a recruit, under arms, a soldier.
I feel like a pawn in your game. Seems to me a man should have a choice whether to take up arms or not.
You're not just a pawn—you're a major player. We expect a lot from you.
You see, Mr. Scoresby, there's a curious prophecy about this child: She is destined to bring about the end of destiny.
But she must do so without knowing what she is doing . . .
. . . as if it were her nature and not her destiny to do it. If she's told what she must do, all will fail; death will sweep through all the worlds, and despair will triumph, forever.

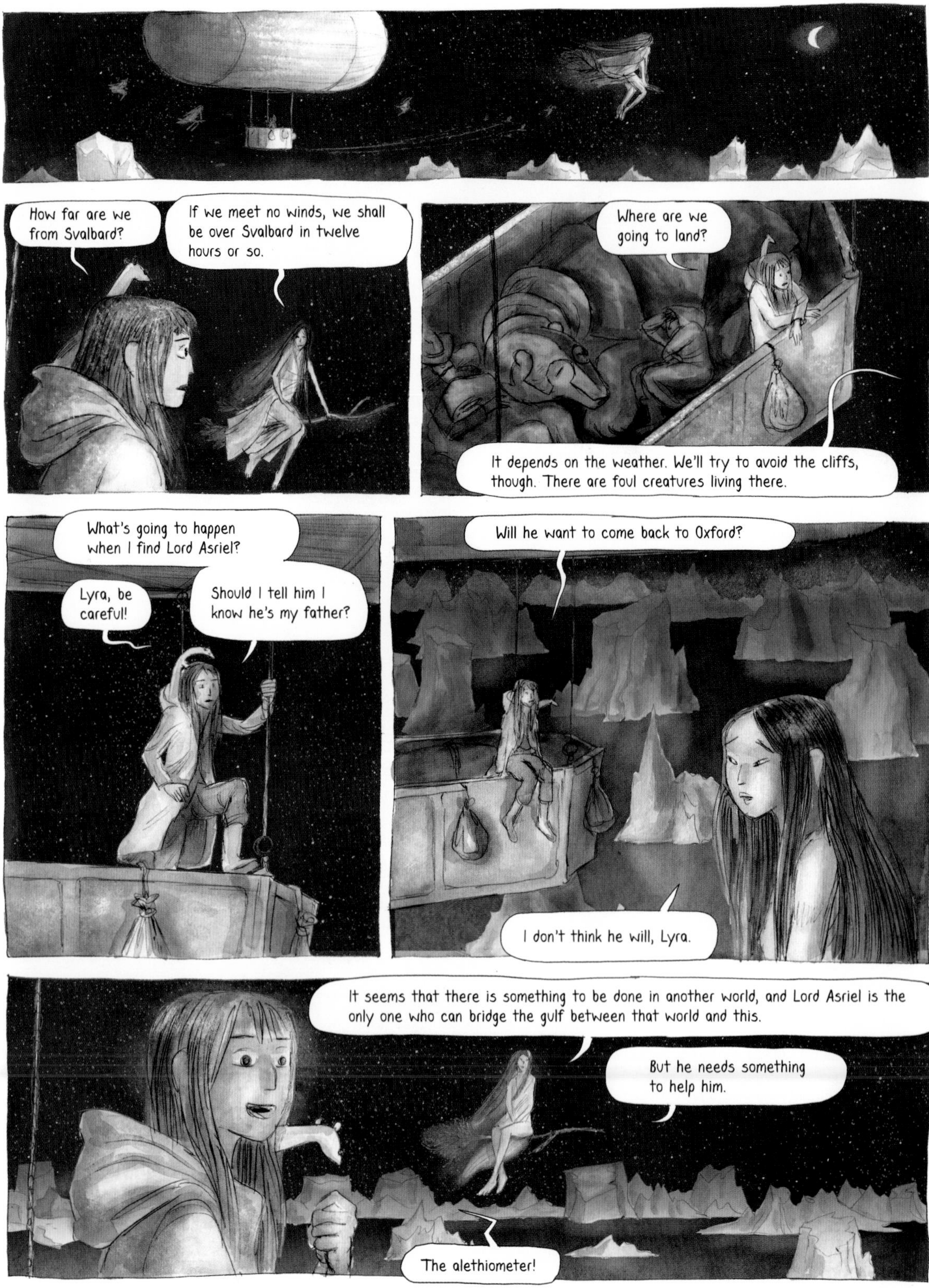
How far are we from Svalbard?
If we meet no winds, we shall be over Svalbard in twelve hours or so.
Where are we going to land?
It depends on the weather. We'll try to avoid the cliffs, though. There are foul creatures living there.
What's going to happen when I find Lord Asriel?
Lyra, be careful!
Should I tell him I know he's my father?
Will he want to come back to Oxford?
I don't think he will, Lyra.
It seems that there is something to be done in another world, and Lord Asriel is the only one who can bridge the gulf between that world and this.
But he needs something to help him.
The alethiometer!

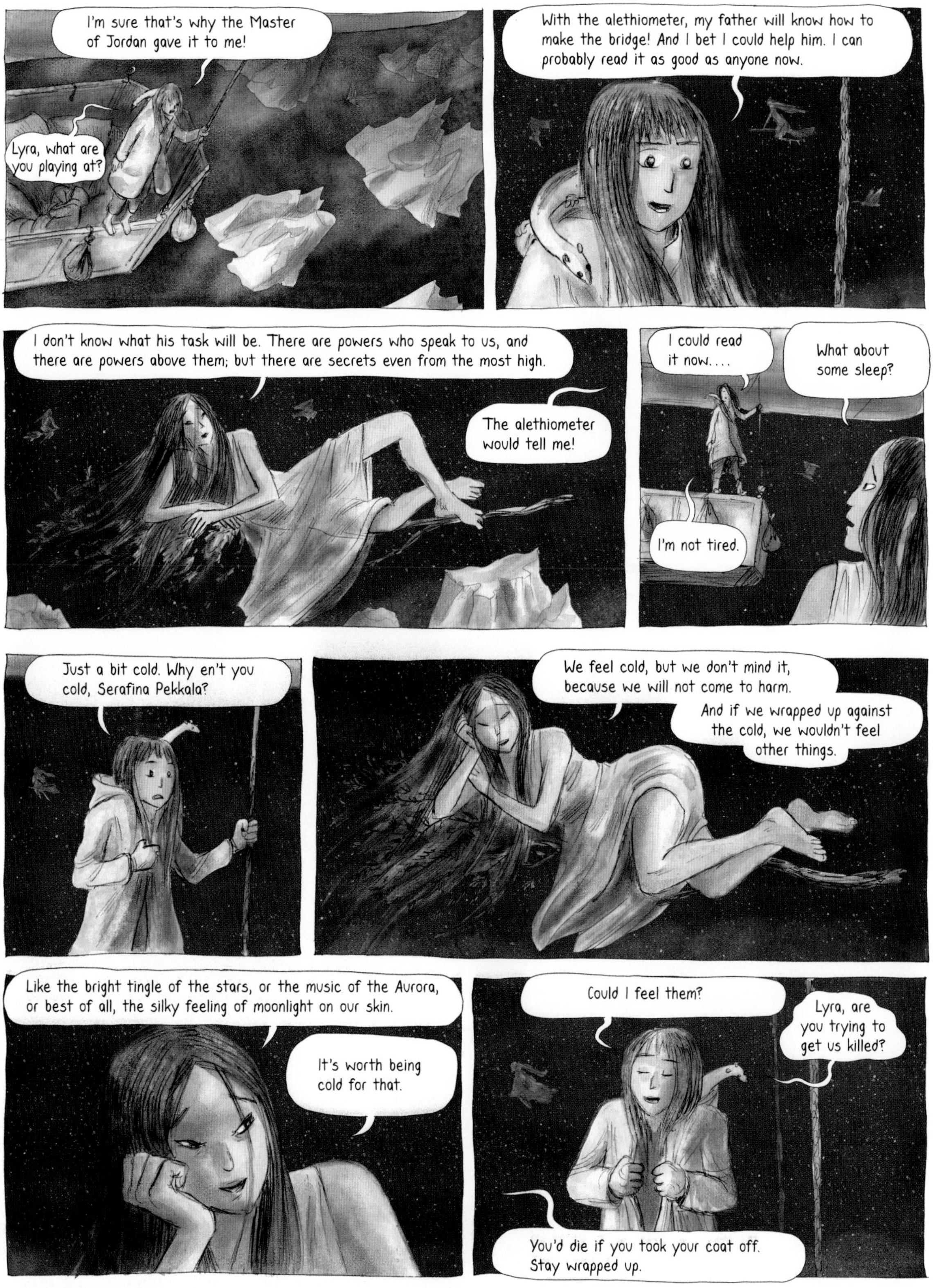
I'm sure that's why the Master of Jordan gave it to me!
Lyra, what are you playing at?
With the alethiometer, my father will know how to make the bridge! And I bet I could help him. I can probably read it as good as anyone now.
I don't know what his task will be. There are powers who speak to us, and there are powers above them; but there are secrets even from the most high.
The alethiometer would tell me!
I could read it now....
What about some sleep?
I'm not tired.
Just a bit cold. Why en't you cold, Serafina Pekkala?
We feel cold, but we don't mind it, because we will not come to harm.
And if we wrapped up against the cold, we wouldn't feel other things.
Like the bright tingle of the stars, or the music of the Aurora, or best of all, the silky feeling of moonlight on our skin.
It's worth being cold for that.
Could I feel them?
Lyra, are you trying to get us killed?
You'd die if you took your coat off. Stay wrapped up.

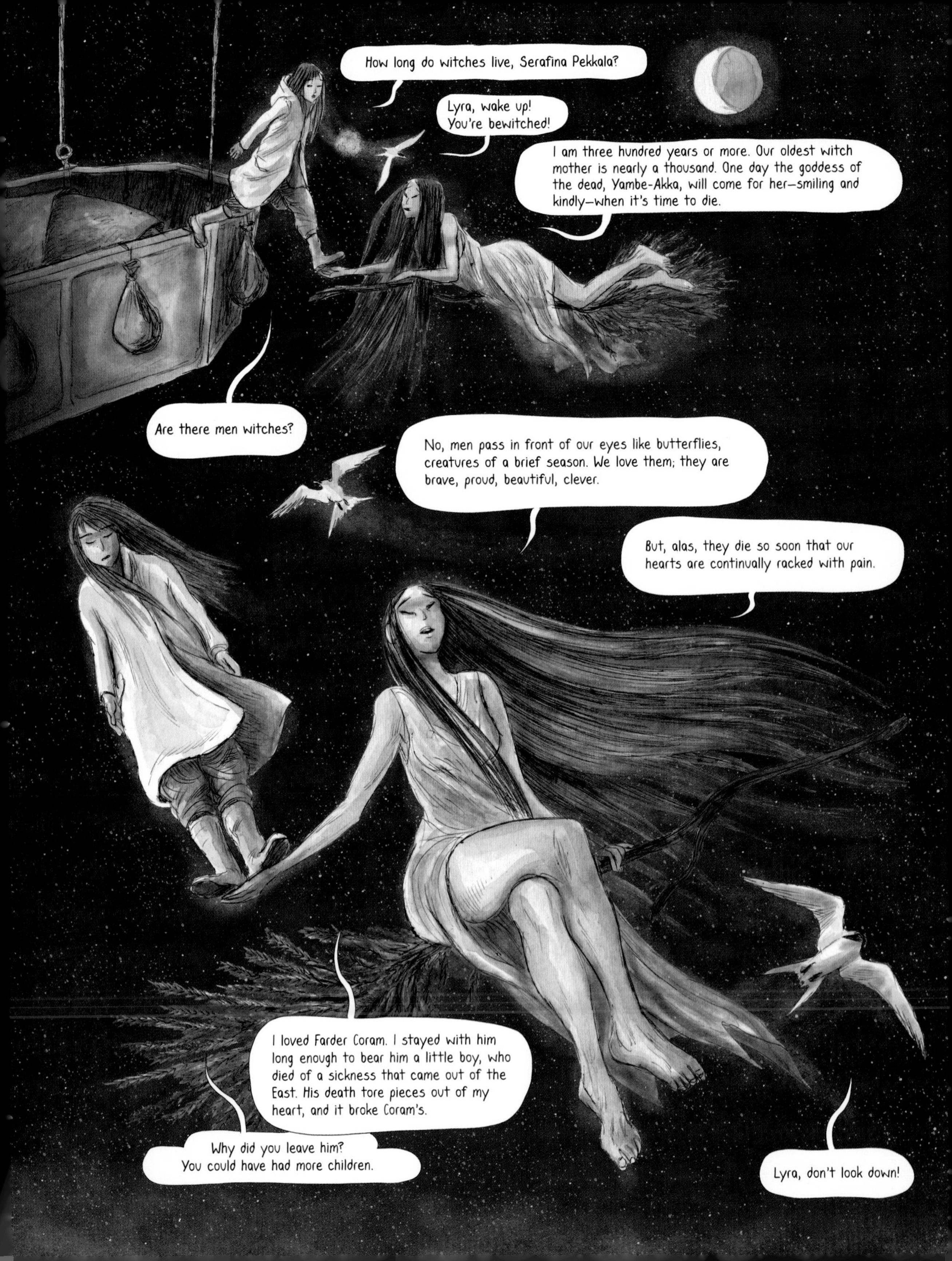
How long do witches live, Serafina Pekkala?
Lyra, wake up! You're bewitched!
I am three hundred years or more. Our oldest witch mother is nearly a thousand. One day the goddess of the dead, Yambe-Akka, will come for her—smiling and kindly—when it's time to die.
Are there men witches?
No, men pass in front of our eyes like butterflies, creatures of a brief season. We love them; they are brave, proud, beautiful, clever.
But, alas, they die so soon that our hearts are continually racked with pain.
I loved Farder Coram. I stayed with him long enough to bear him a little boy, who died of a sickness that came out of the East. His death tore pieces out of my heart, and it broke Coram's.
Why did you leave him? You could have had more children.
Lyra, don't look down!

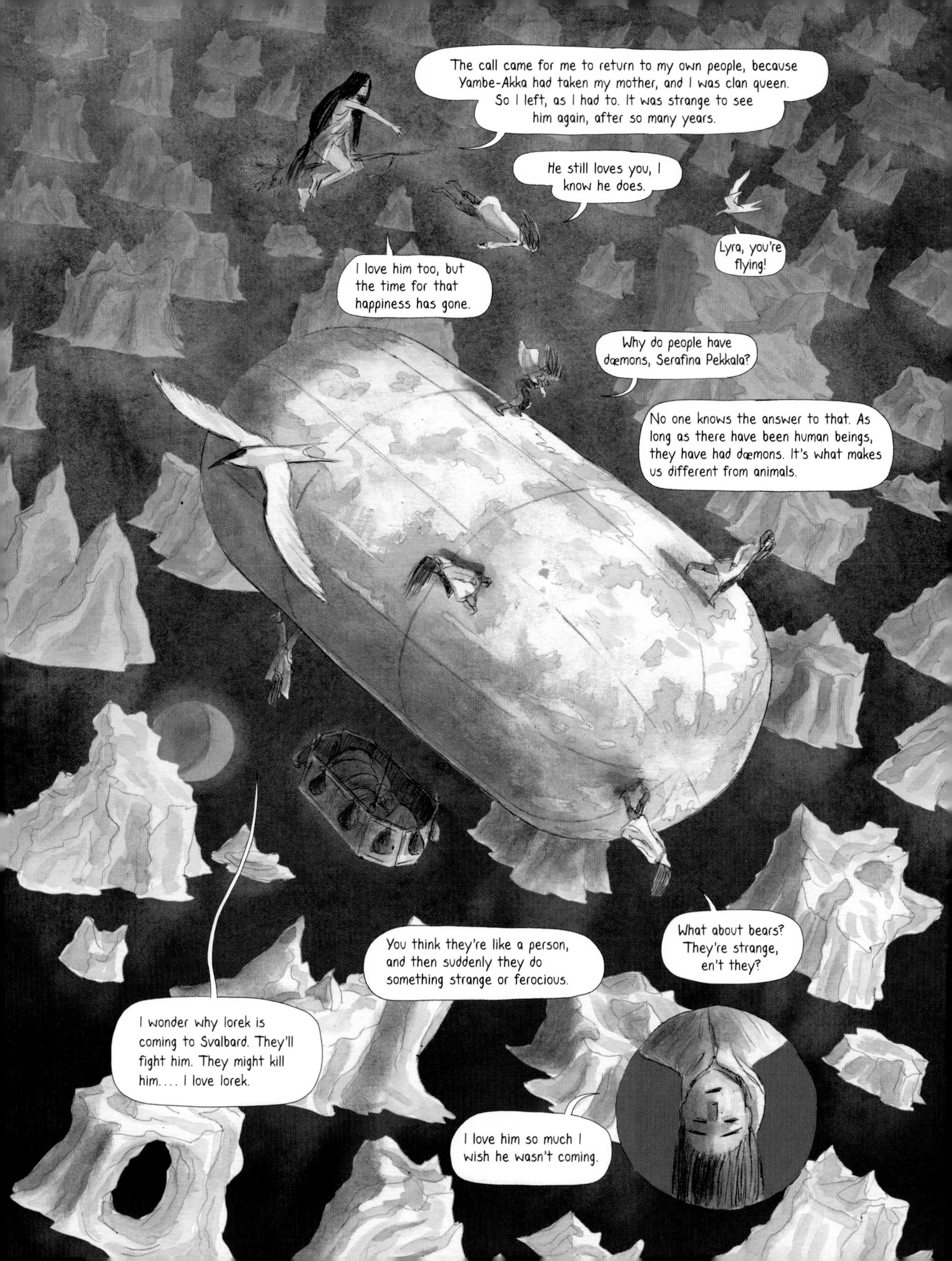
The call came for me to return to my own people, because Yambe-Akka had taken my mother, and I was clan queen. So I left, as I had to. It was strange to see him again, after so many years.
He still loves you, I know he does.
Lyra, you're flying!
I love him too, but the time for that happiness has gone.
Why do people have dæmons, Serafina Pekkala?
No one knows the answer to that. As long as there have been human beings, they have had dæmons. It's what makes us different from animals.
What about bears? They're strange, en't they?
You think they're like a person, and then suddenly they do something strange or ferocious.
I wonder why Iorek is coming to Svalbard. They'll fight him. They might kill him.... I love Iorek.
I love him so much I wish he wasn't coming.

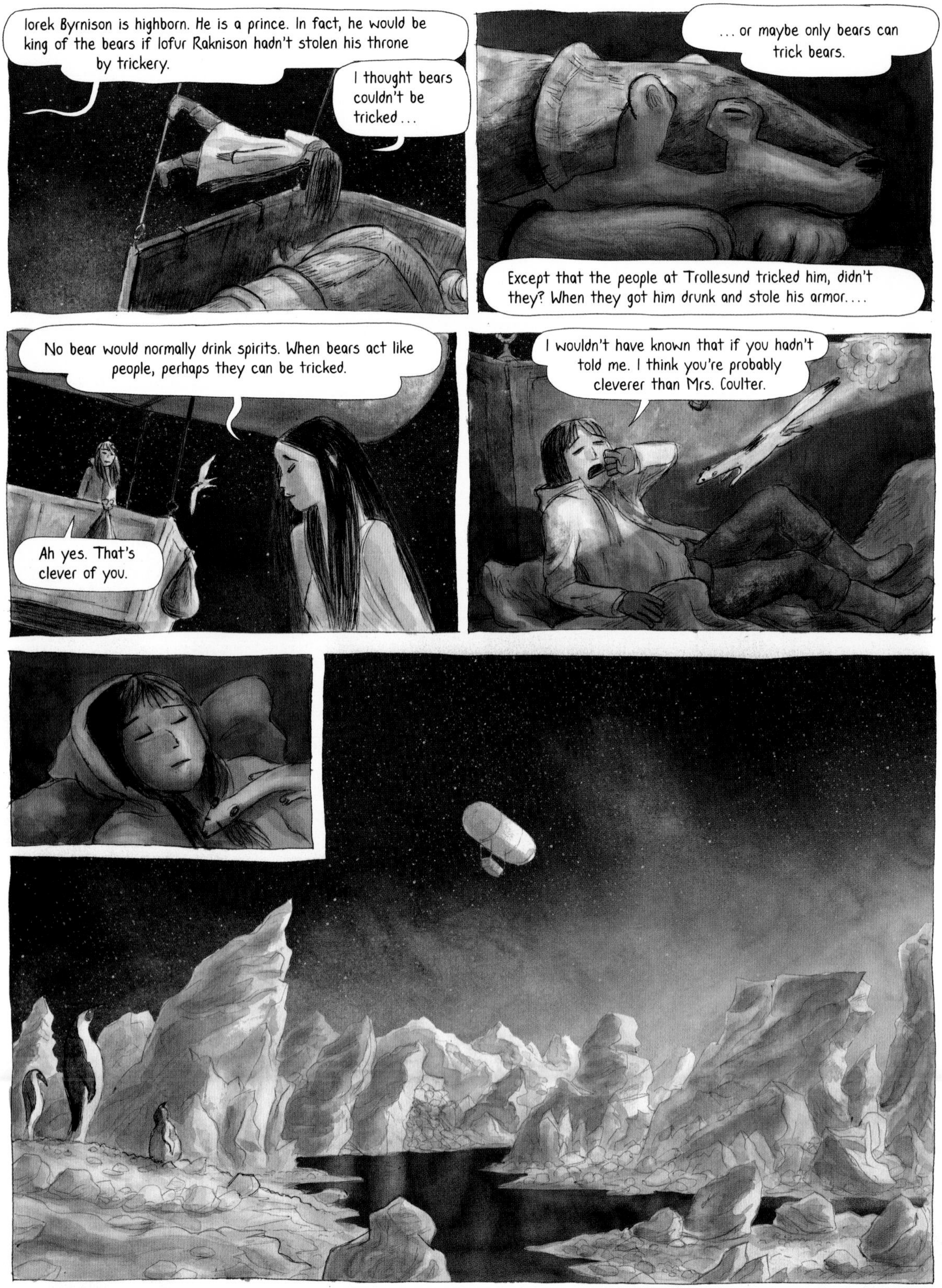
Iorek Byrnison is highborn. He is a prince. In fact, he would be king of the bears if Iofur Raknison hadn't stolen his throne by trickery.
I thought bears couldn't be tricked...
... or maybe only bears can trick bears.
Except that the people at Trollesund tricked him, didn't they? When they got him drunk and stole his armor....
No bear would normally drink spirits. When bears act like people, perhaps they can be tricked.
Ah yes. That's clever of you.
I wouldn't have known that if you hadn't told me. I think you're probably cleverer than Mrs. Coulter.

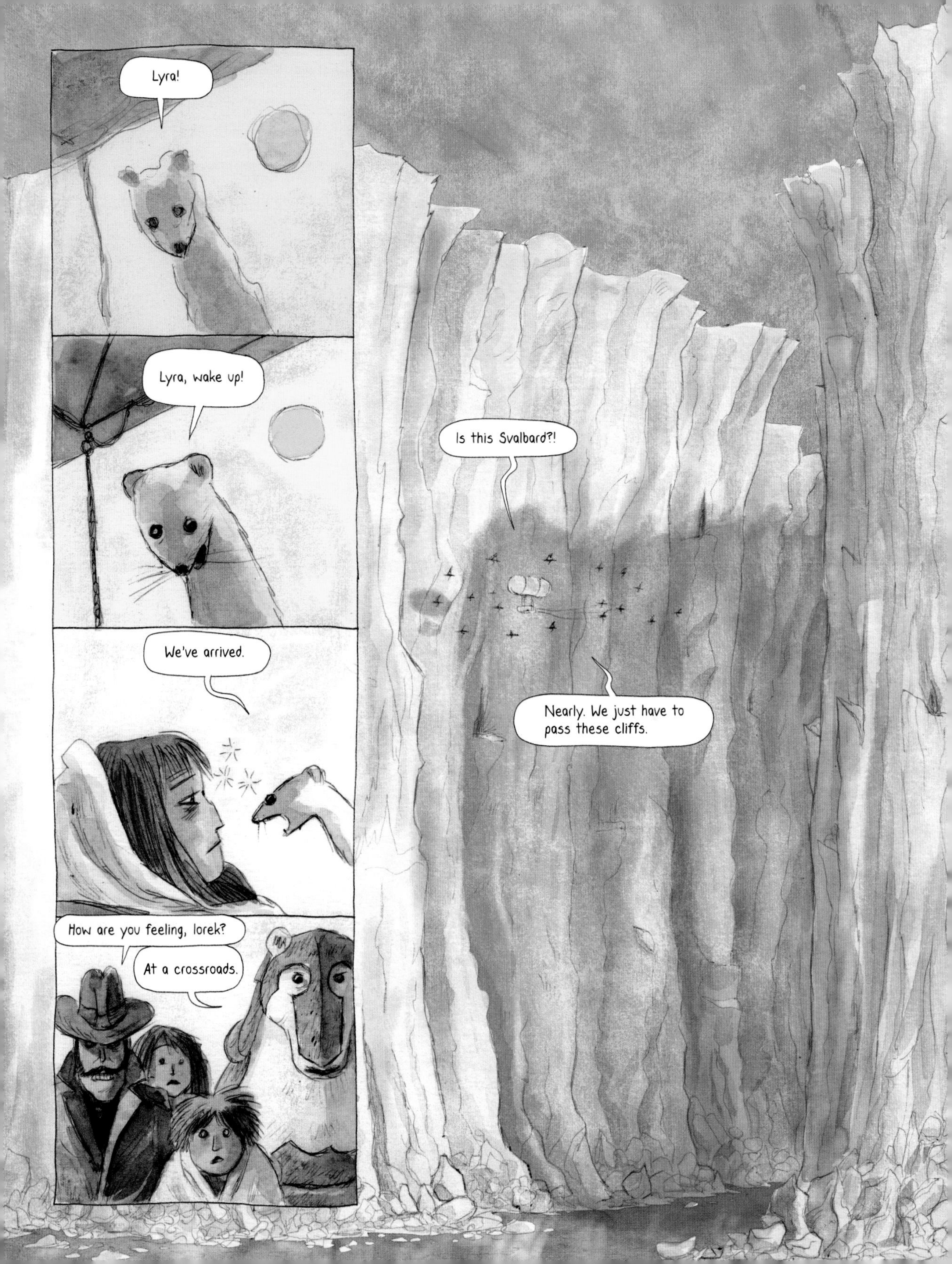
Lyra!
Lyra, wake up!
We've arrived.
How are you feeling, Iorek?
At a crossroads.
Is this Svalbard?!
Nearly. We just have to pass these cliffs.

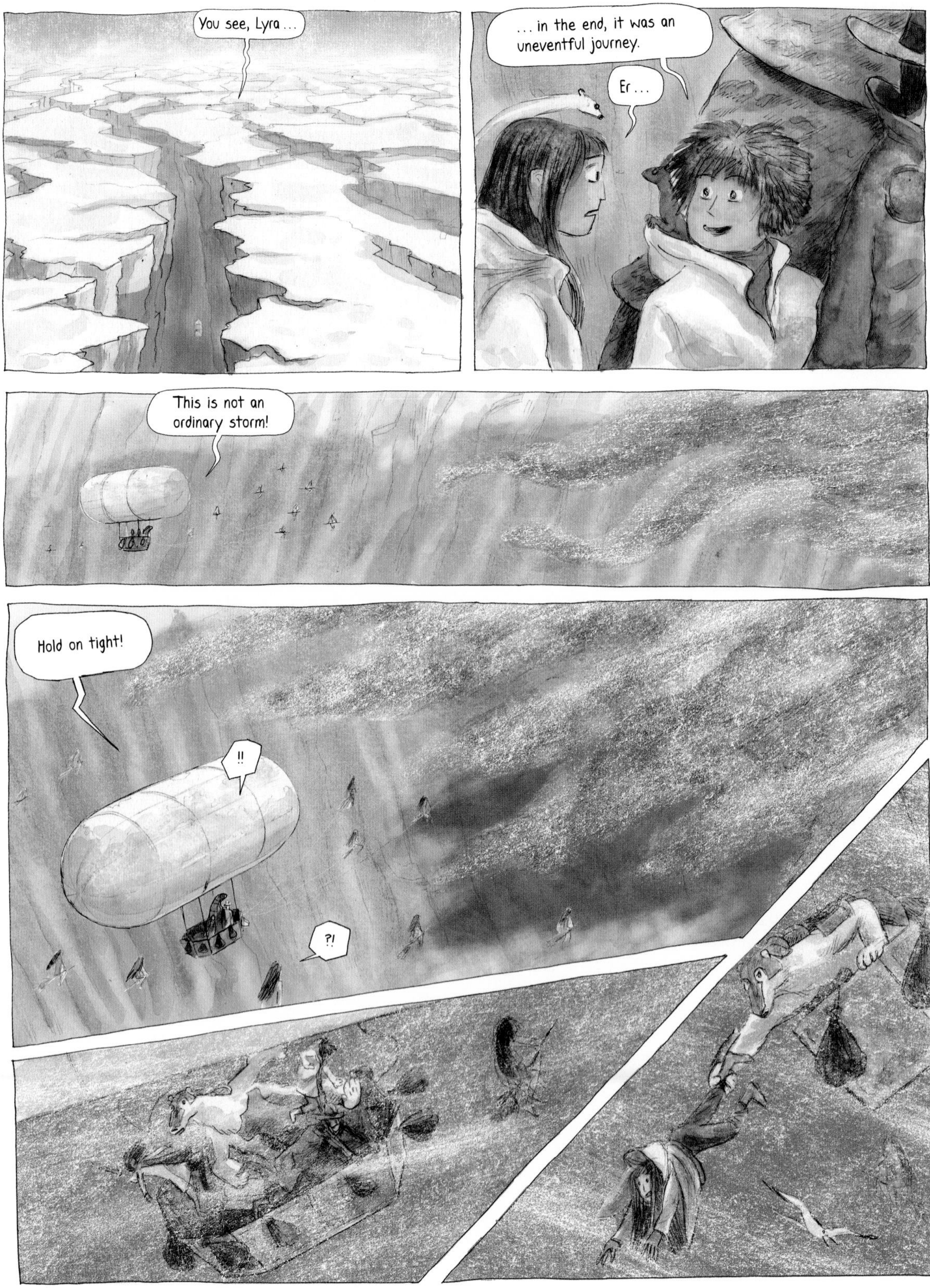
You see, Lyra . . .
. . . in the end, it was an uneventful journey.
Er . . .
This is not an ordinary storm!
Hold on tight!
!!
?!

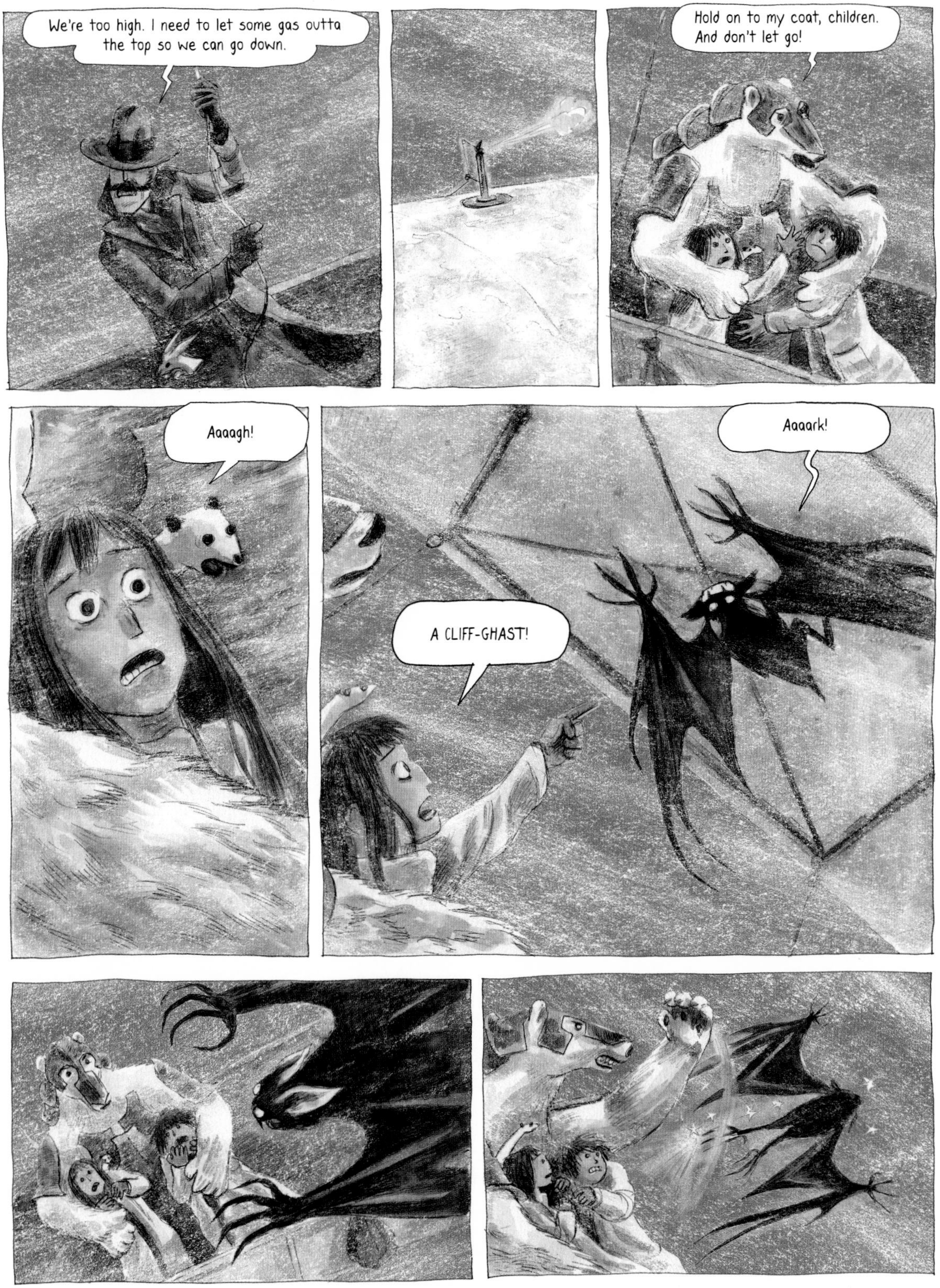
We're too high. I need to let some gas outta the top so we can go down.
Hold on to my coat, children. And don't let go!
Aaaagh!
Aaaark!
A CLIFF-GHAST!

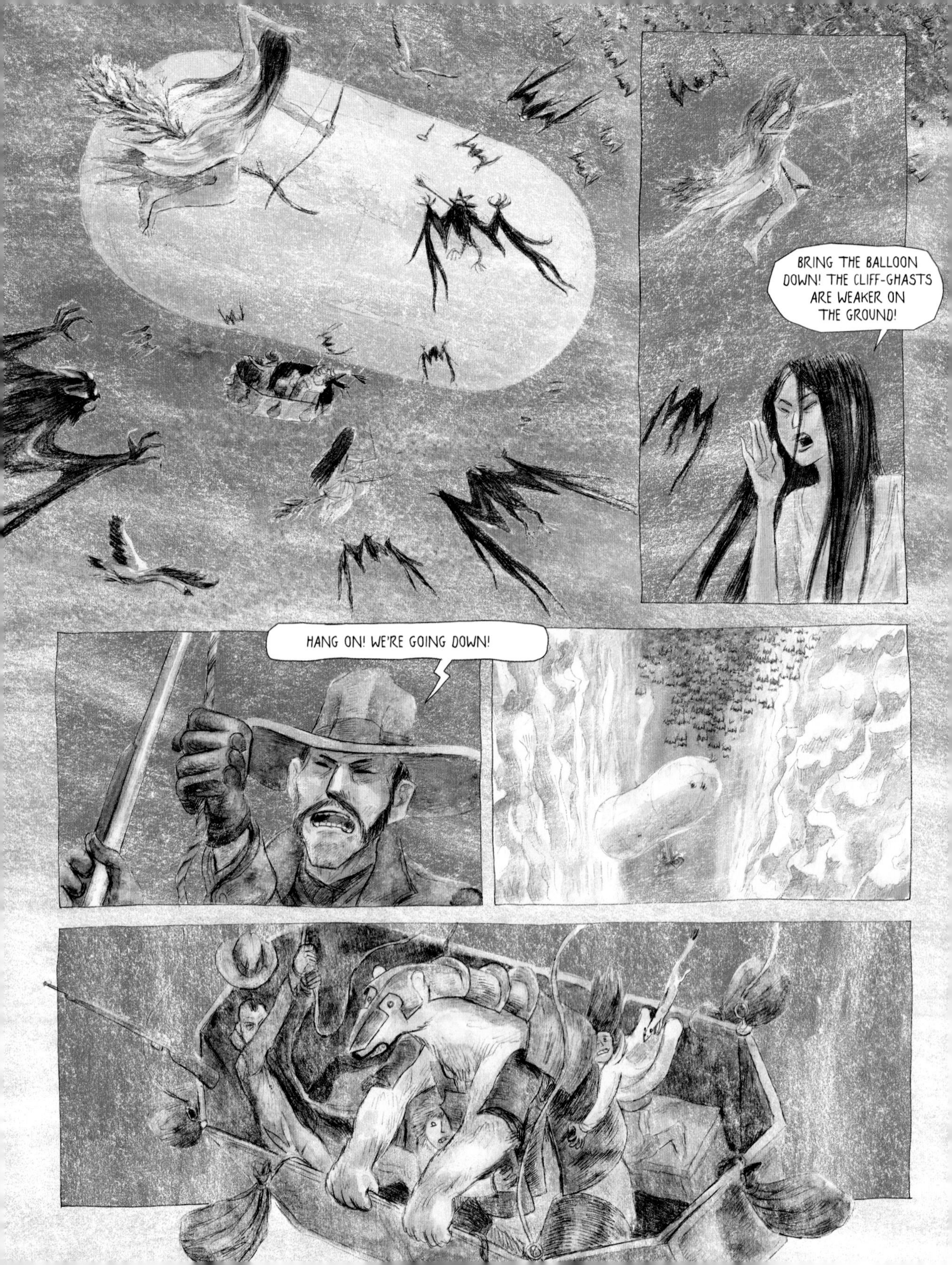
BRING THE BALLOON DOWN! THE CLIFF-GHASTS ARE WEAKER ON THE GROUND!
HANG ON! WE'RE GOING DOWN!

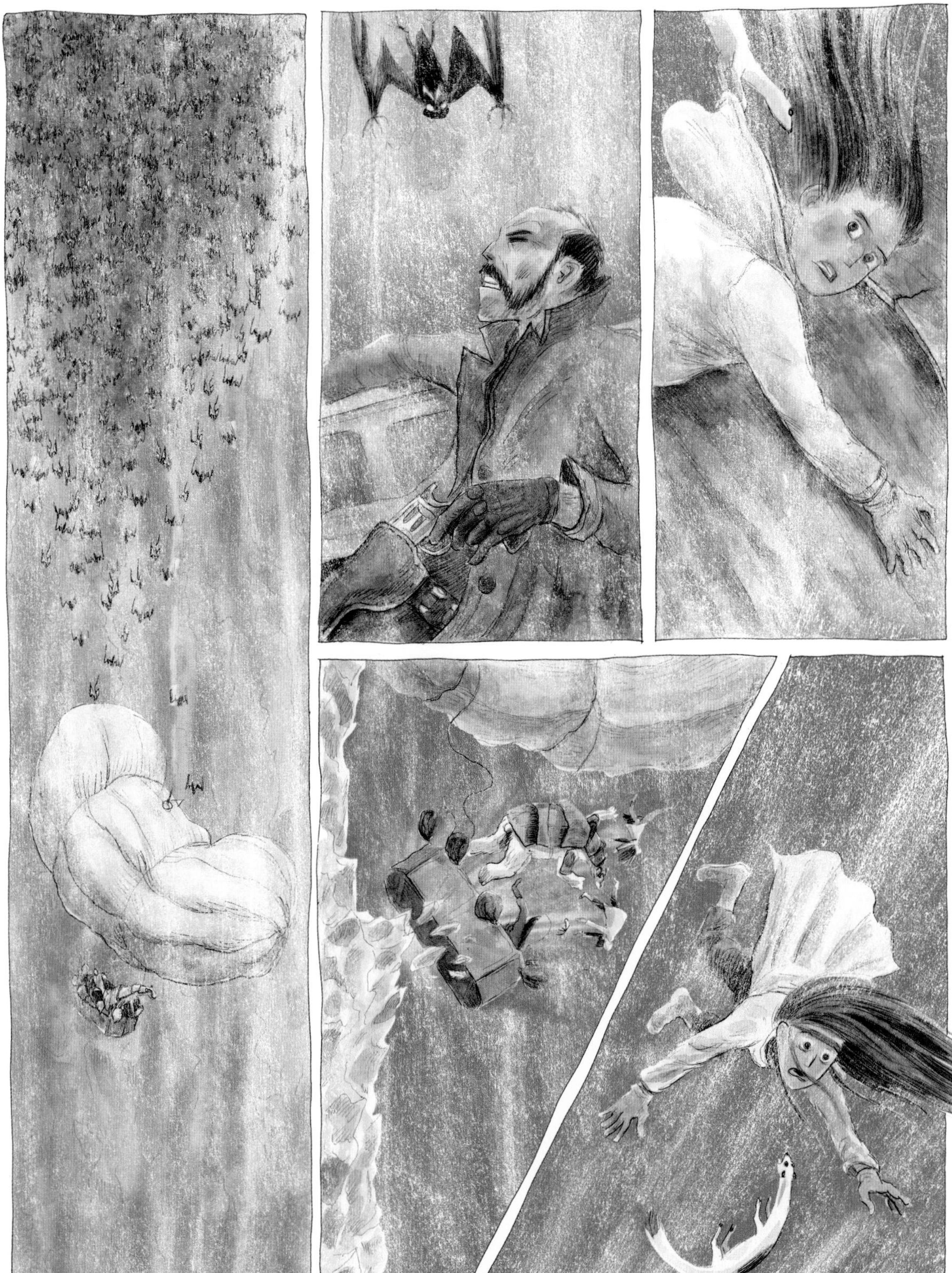

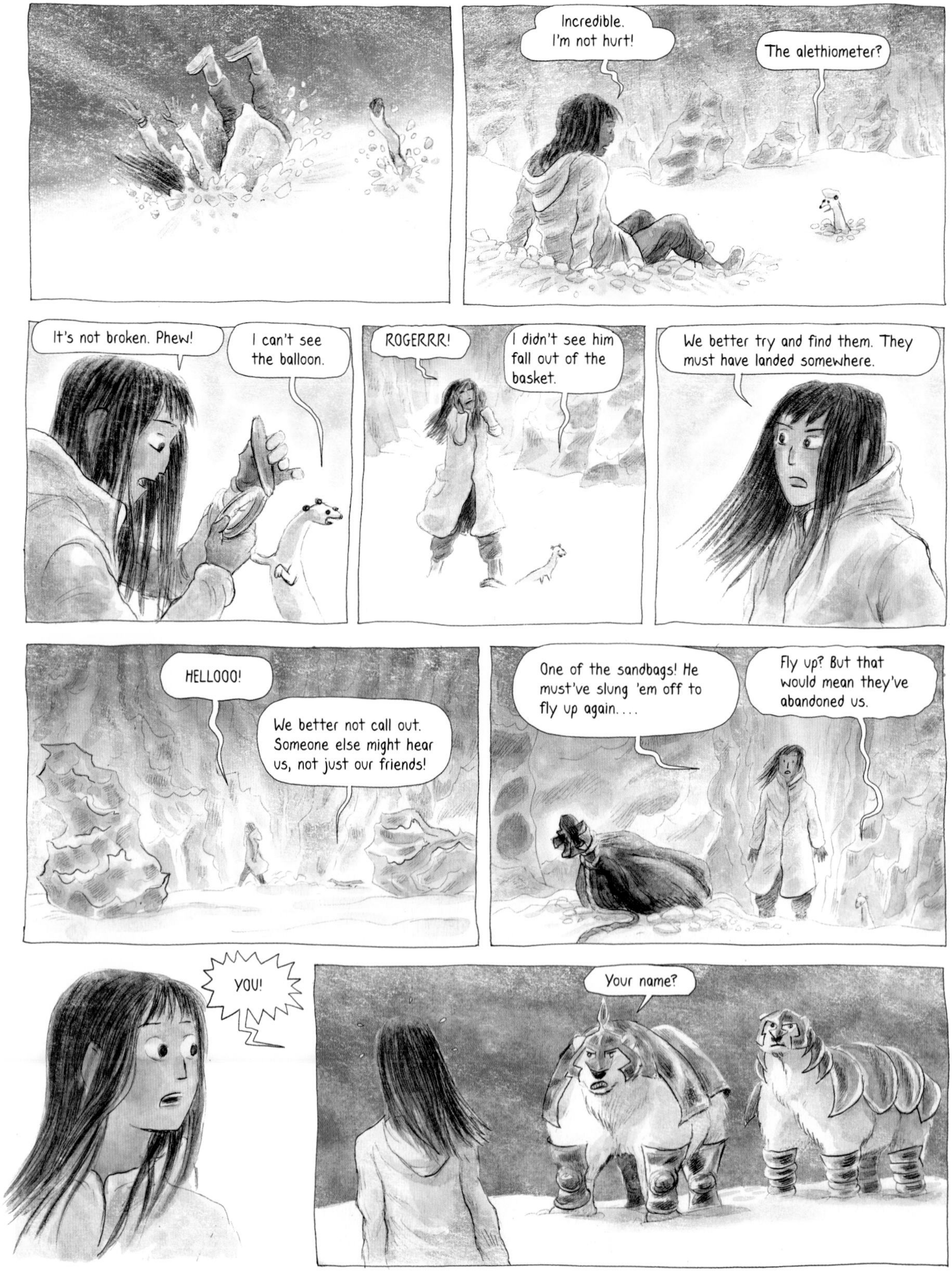

Incredible.
I'm not hurt!
The alethiometer?
It's not broken. Phew!
I can't see the balloon.
ROGERRR!
I didn't see him fall out of the basket.
We better try and find them. They must have landed somewhere.
HELLOOO!
We better not call out. Someone else might hear us, not just our friends!
One of the sandbags! He must've slung 'em off to fly up again....
Fly up? But that would mean they've abandoned us.
YOU!
Your name?

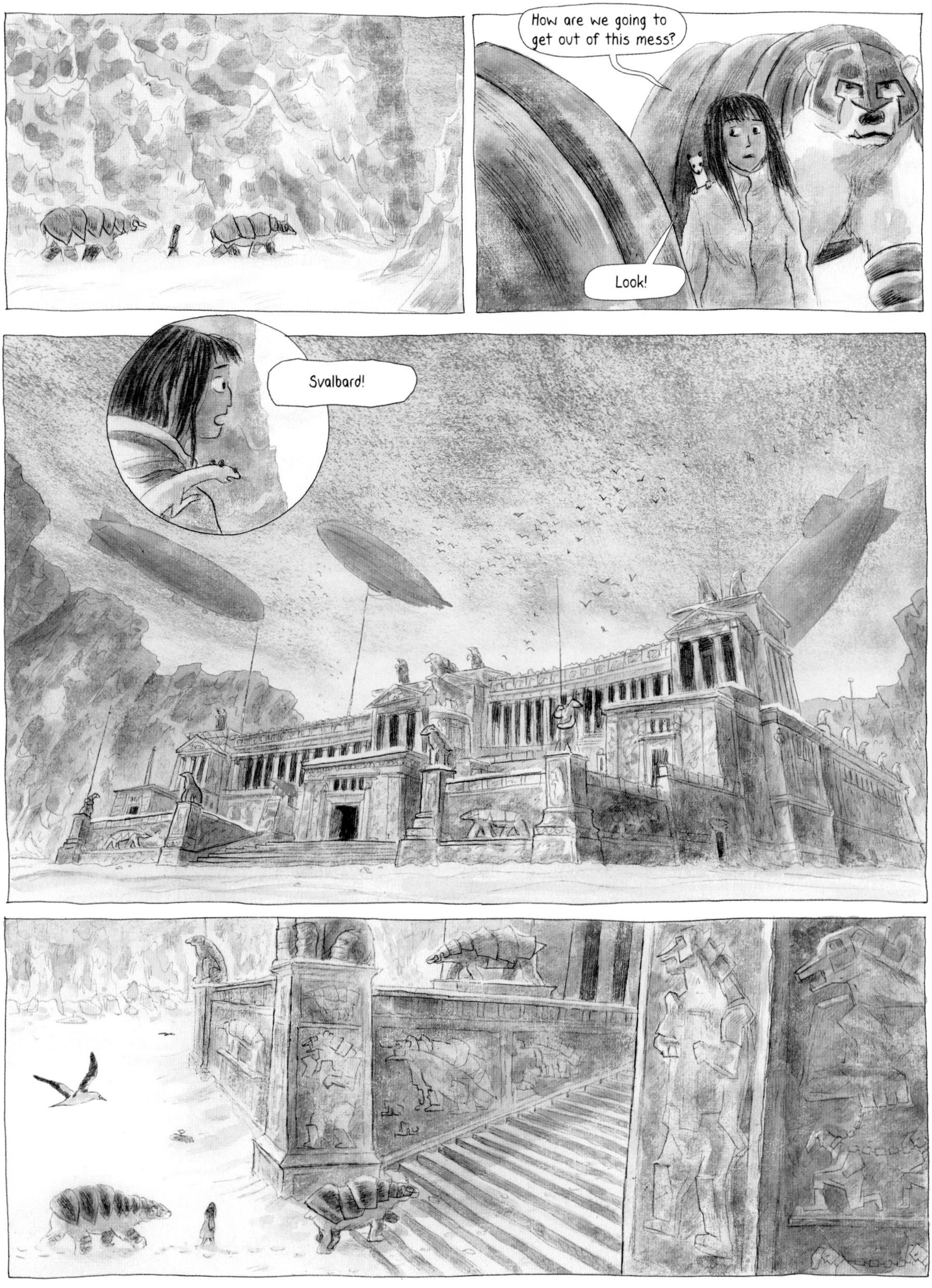
How are we going to get out of this mess?
Look!
Svalbard!

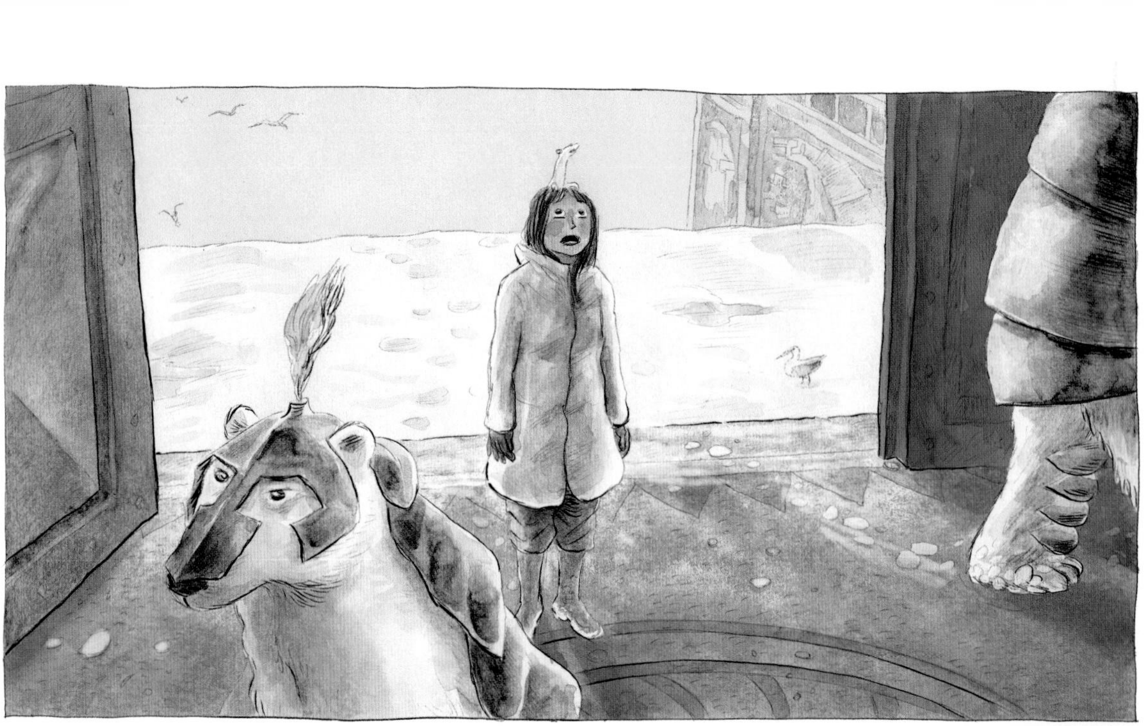

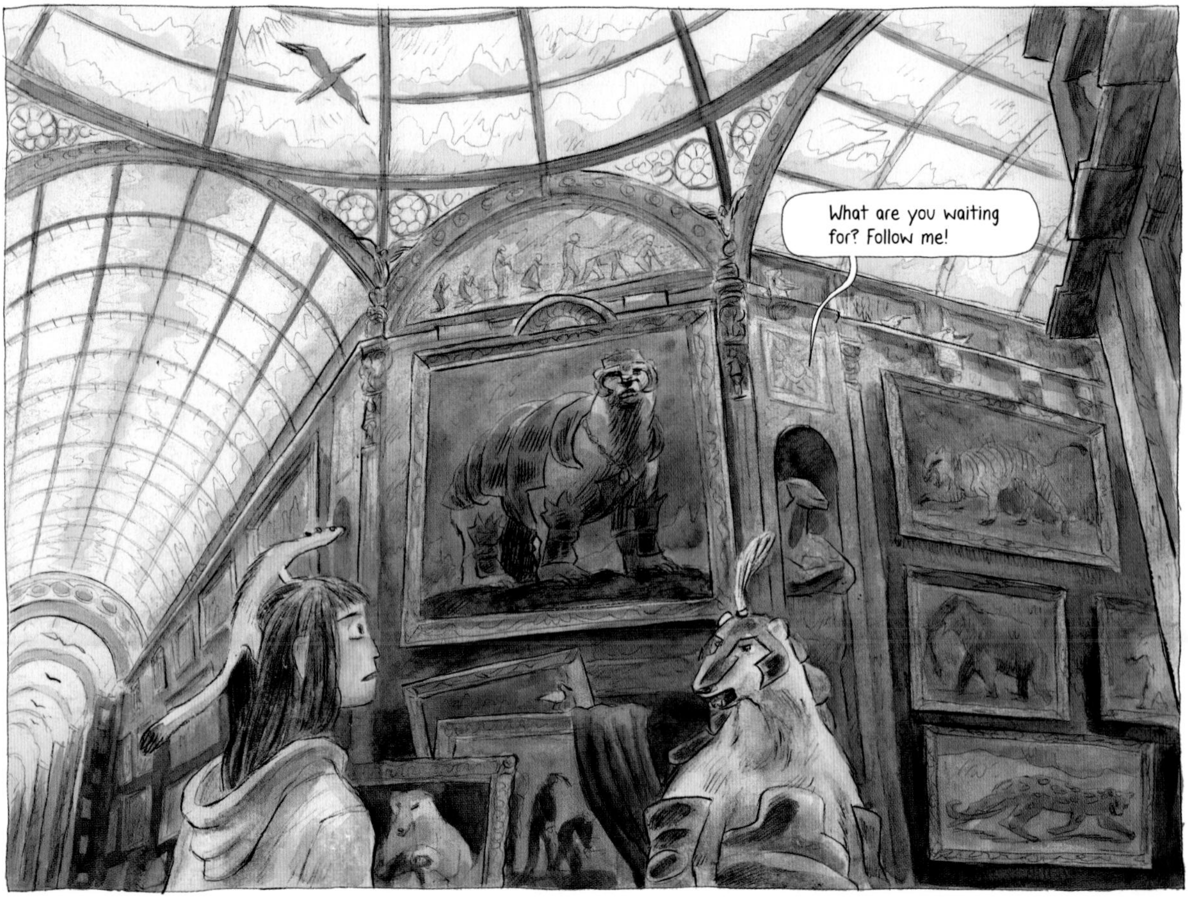
What are you waiting for? Follow me!

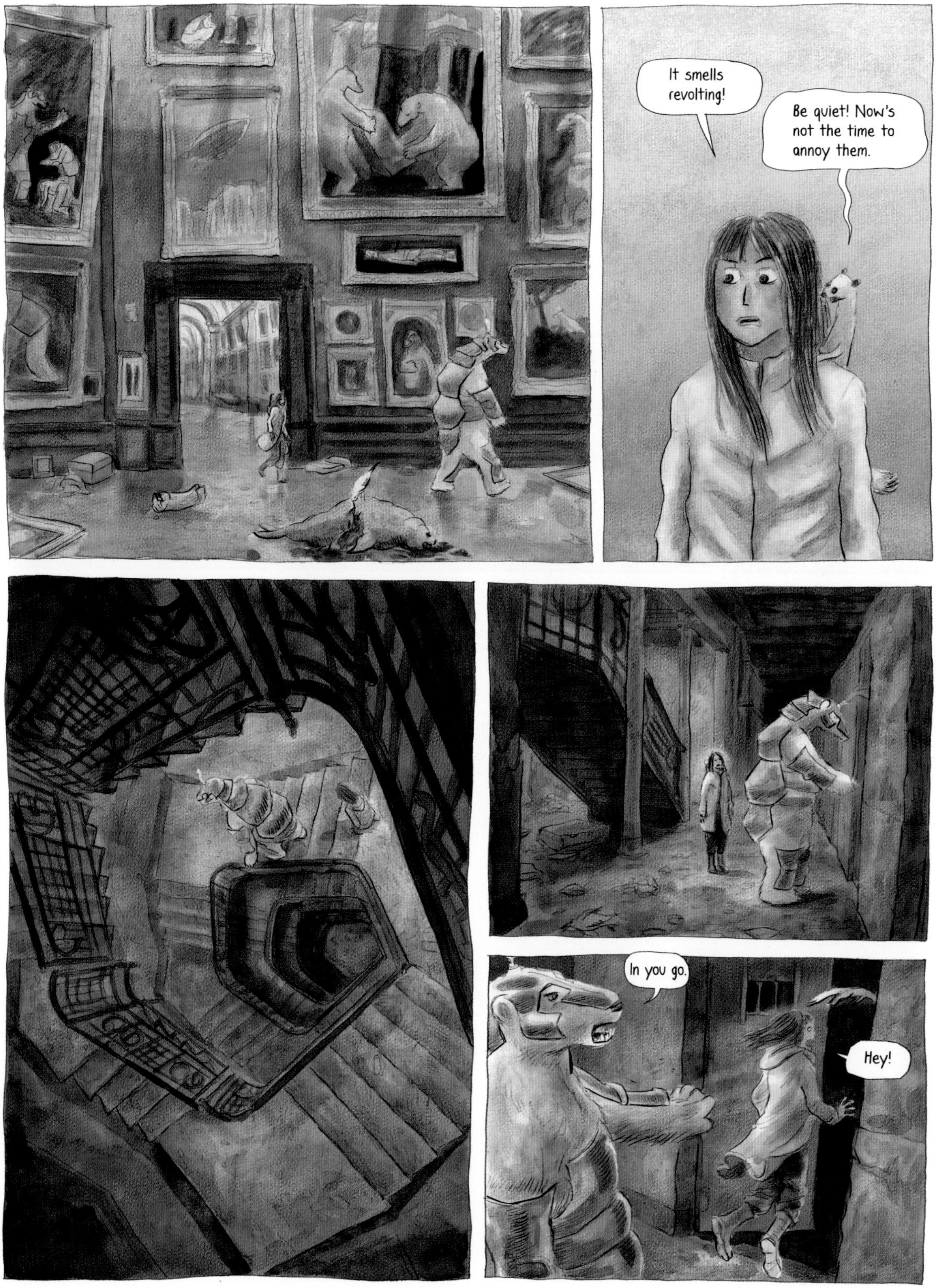
It smells revolting!
Be quiet! Now's not the time to annoy them.
In you go.
Hey!

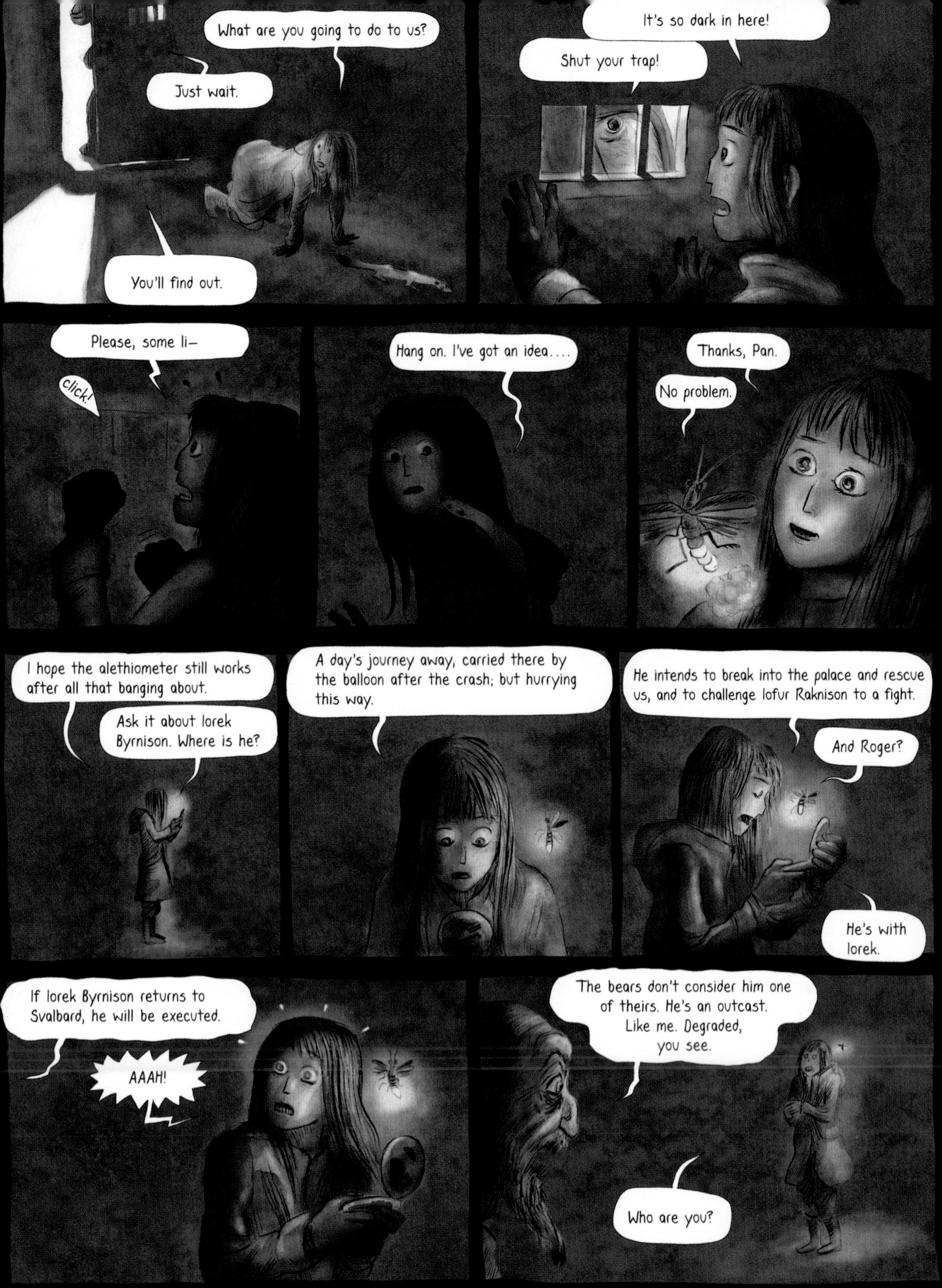
What are you going to do to us?
Just wait.
You'll find out.
It's so dark in here!
Shut your trap!
Please, some li–
click!
Hang on. I've got an idea. . . .
Thanks, Pan.
No problem.
I hope the alethiometer still works after all that banging about.
Ask it about Iorek Byrnison. Where is he?
A day's journey away, carried there by the balloon after the crash; but hurrying this way.
He intends to break into the palace and rescue us, and to challenge Iofur Raknison to a fight.
And Roger?
He's with Iorek.
If Iorek Byrnison returns to Svalbard, he will be executed.
AAAH!
The bears don't consider him one of theirs. He's an outcast. Like me. Degraded, you see.
Who are you?

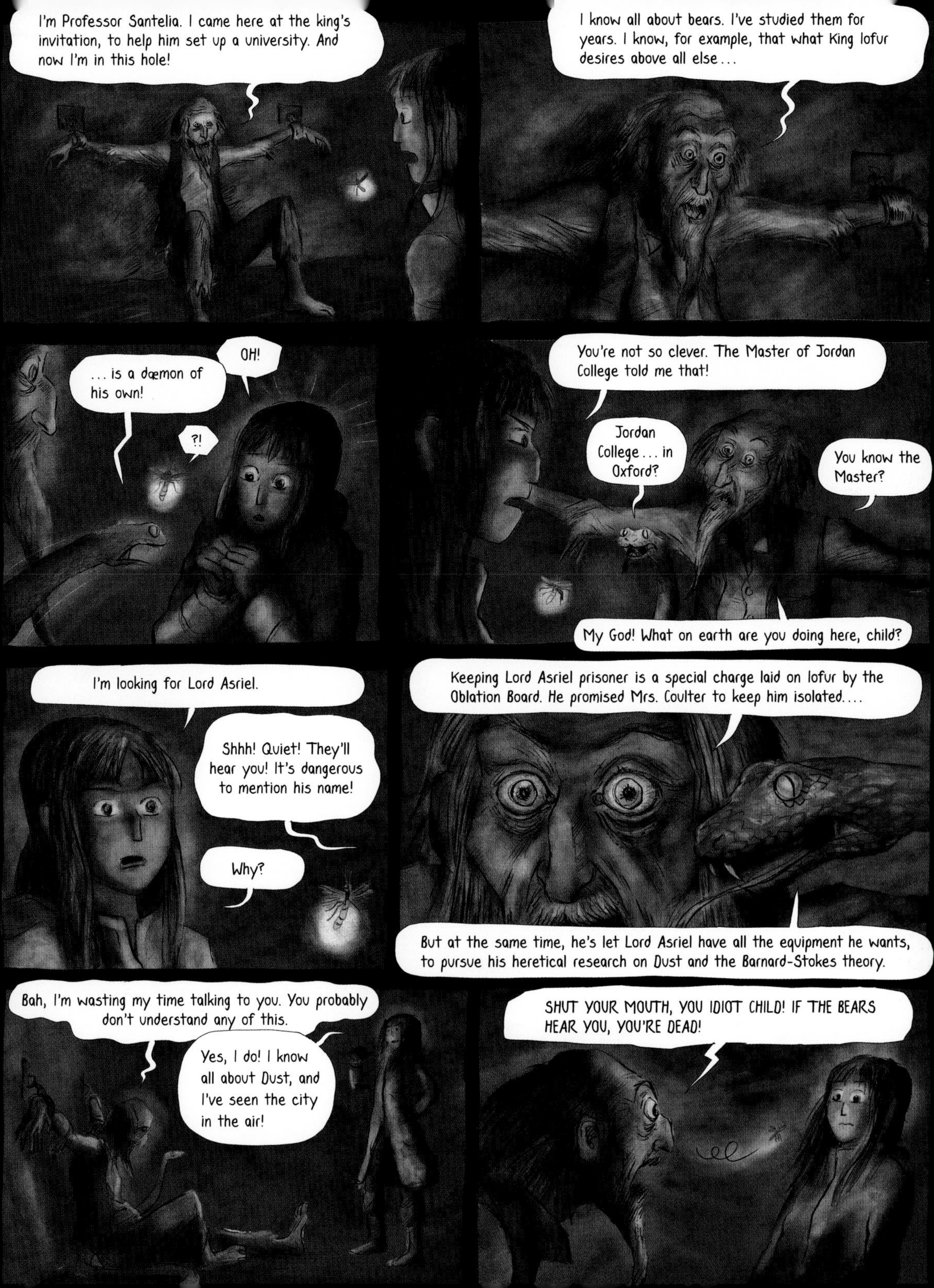
I'm Professor Santelia. I came here at the king's invitation, to help him set up a university. And now I'm in this hole!
I know all about bears. I've studied them for years. I know, for example, that what King Iofur desires above all else . . .
. . . is a dæmon of his own!
OH!
?!
You're not so clever. The Master of Jordan College told me that!
Jordan College . . . in Oxford?
You know the Master?
My God! What on earth are you doing here, child?
I'm looking for Lord Asriel.
Shhh! Quiet! They'll hear you! It's dangerous to mention his name!
Why?
Keeping Lord Asriel prisoner is a special charge laid on Iofur by the Oblation Board. He promised Mrs. Coulter to keep him isolated. . . .
But at the same time, he's let Lord Asriel have all the equipment he wants, to pursue his heretical research on Dust and the Barnard-Stokes theory.
Bah, I'm wasting my time talking to you. You probably don't understand any of this.
Yes, I do! I know all about Dust, and I've seen the city in the air!
SHUT YOUR MOUTH, YOU IDIOT CHILD! IF THE BEARS HEAR YOU, YOU'RE DEAD!

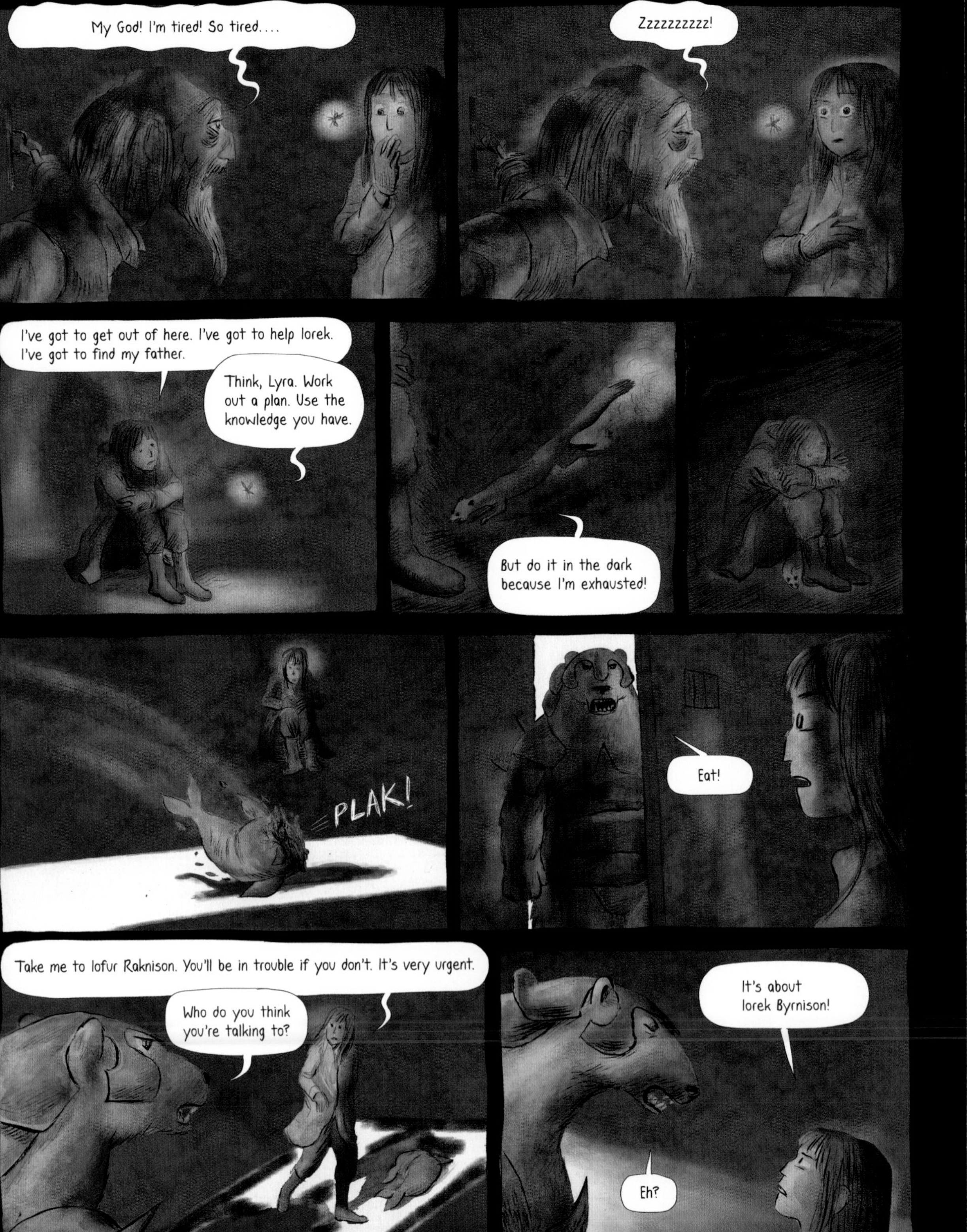
My God! I'm tired! So tired. . . .
Zzzzzzzzzz!
I've got to get out of here. I've got to help Iorek. I've got to find my father.
Think, Lyra. Work out a plan. Use the knowledge you have.
But do it in the dark because I'm exhausted!
PLAK!
Eat!
Take me to Iofur Raknison. You'll be in trouble if you don't. It's very urgent.
Who do you think you're talking to?
It's about Iorek Byrnison!
Eh?

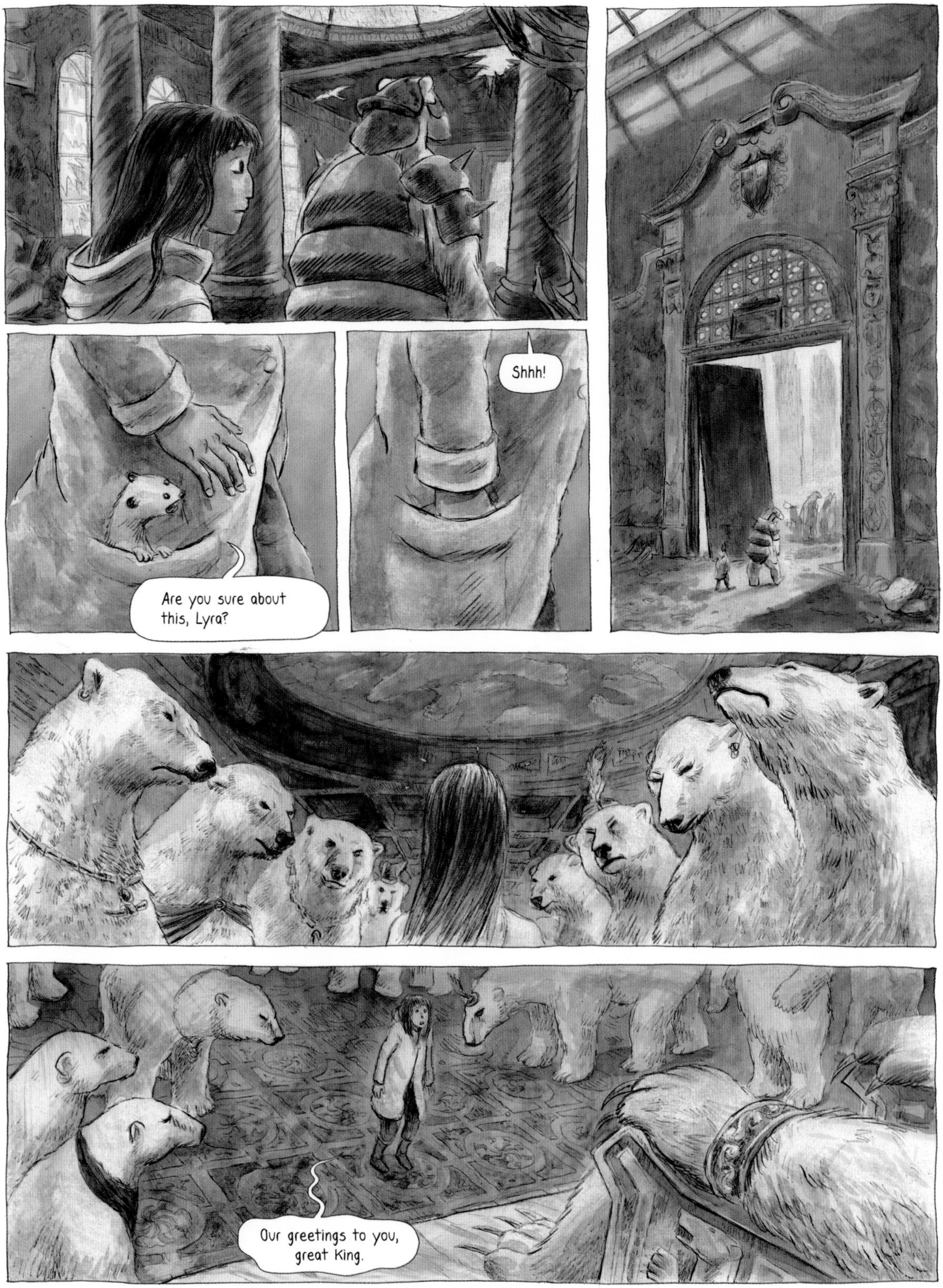
Are you sure about this, Lyra?
Shhh!
Our greetings to you, great King.

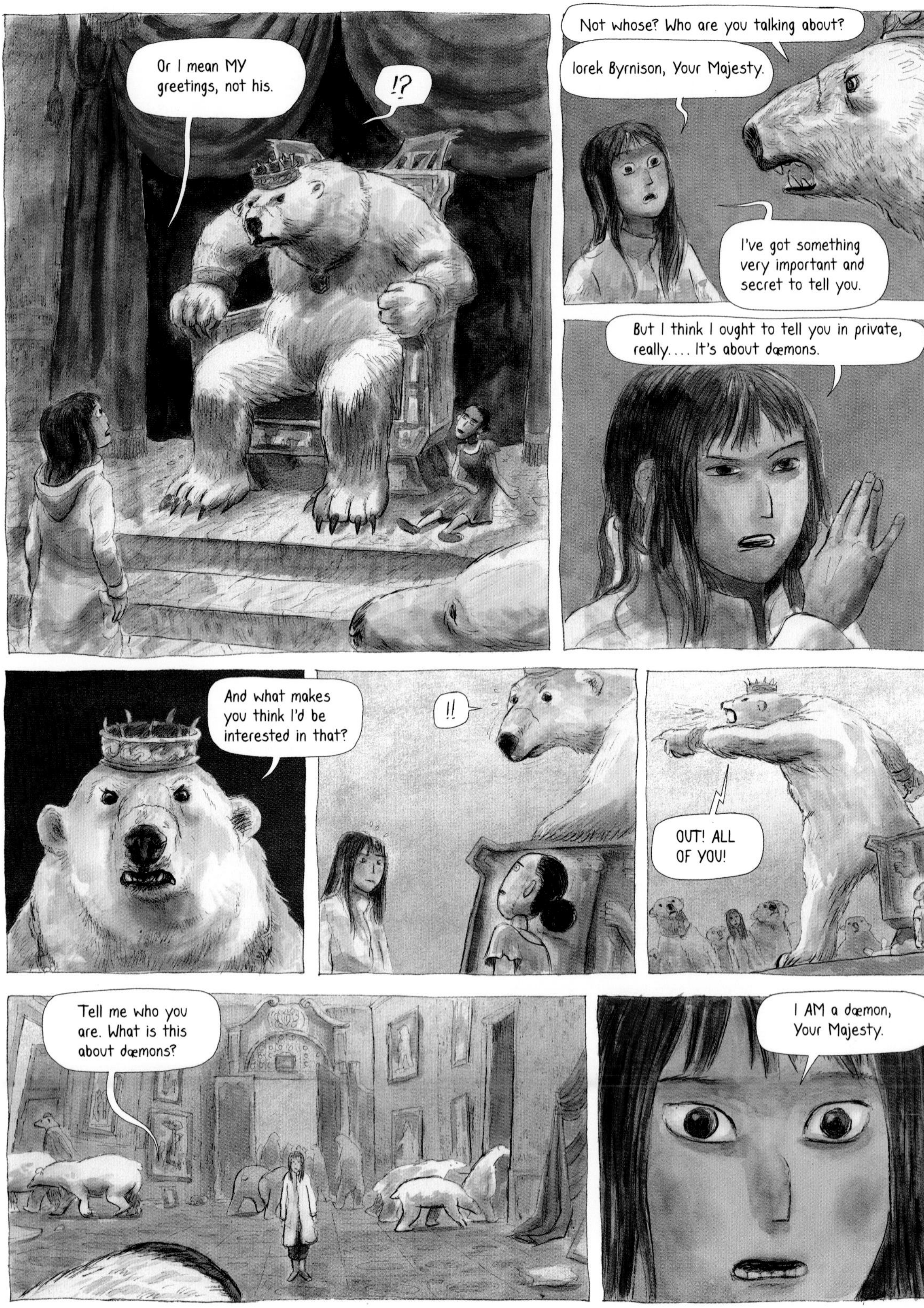

Or I mean MY greetings, not his.
!?
Not whose? Who are you talking about?
Iorek Byrnison, Your Majesty.
I've got something very important and secret to tell you.
But I think I ought to tell you in private, really.... It's about dæmons.
And what makes you think I'd be interested in that?
!!
OUT! ALL OF YOU!
Tell me who you are. What is this about dæmons?
I AM a dæmon, Your Majesty.

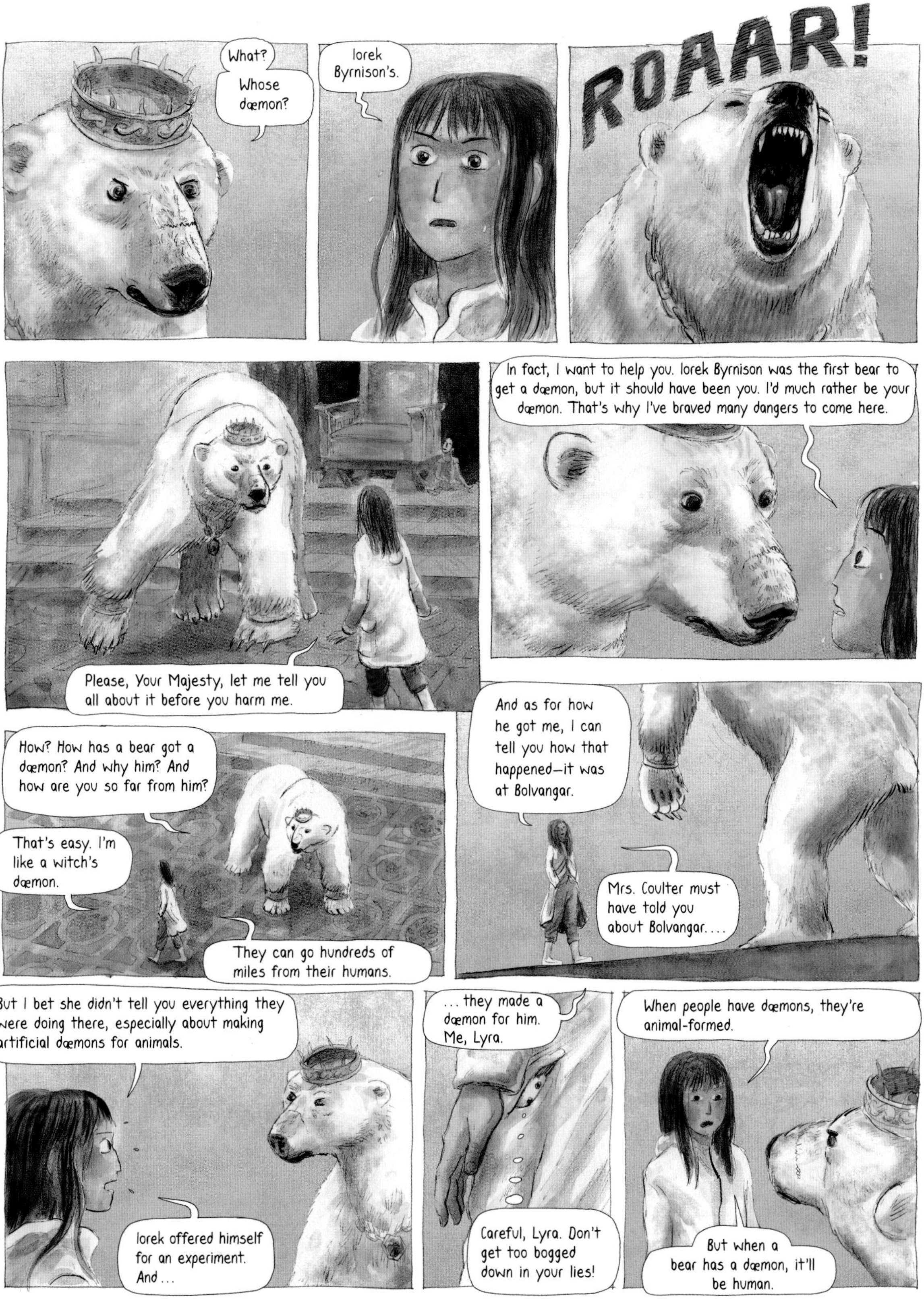
What?
Whose dæmon?
Iorek Byrnison's.
ROAAR!
Please, Your Majesty, let me tell you all about it before you harm me.
In fact, I want to help you. Iorek Byrnison was the first bear to get a dæmon, but it should have been you. I'd much rather be your dæmon. That's why I've braved many dangers to come here.
How? How has a bear got a dæmon? And why him? And how are you so far from him?
That's easy. I'm like a witch's dæmon.
They can go hundreds of miles from their humans.
And as for how he got me, I can tell you how that happened—it was at Bolvangar.
Mrs. Coulter must have told you about Bolvangar. . . .
But I bet she didn't tell you everything they were doing there, especially about making artificial dæmons for animals.
Iorek offered himself for an experiment. And . . .
. . . they made a dæmon for him. Me, Lyra.
Careful, Lyra. Don't get too bogged down in your lies!
When people have dæmons, they're animal-formed.
But when a bear has a dæmon, it'll be human.

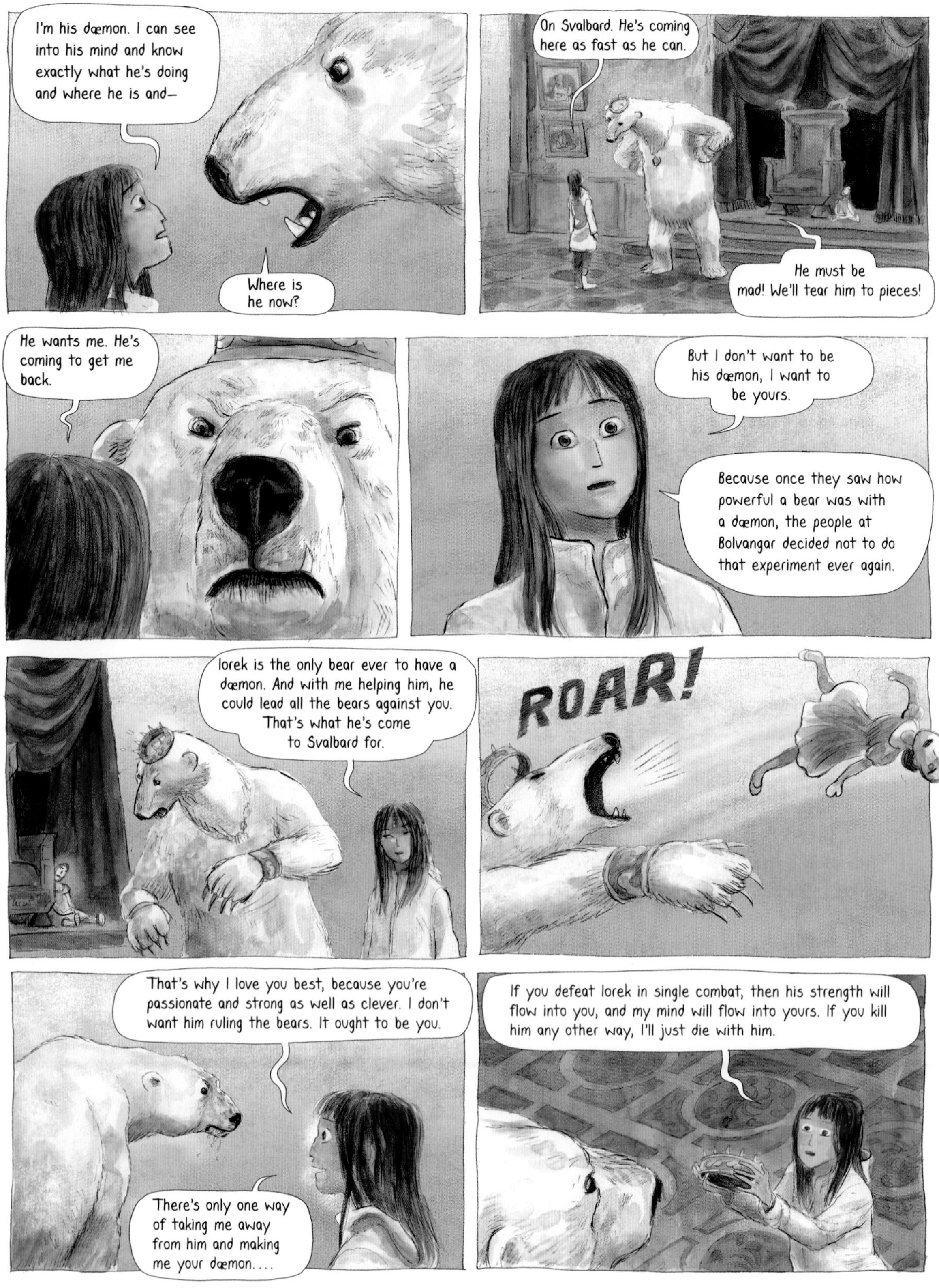
I'm his dæmon. I can see into his mind and know exactly what he's doing and where he is and—
Where is he now?
On Svalbard. He's coming here as fast as he can.
He must be mad! We'll tear him to pieces!
He wants me. He's coming to get me back.
But I don't want to be his dæmon, I want to be yours.
Because once they saw how powerful a bear was with a dæmon, the people at Bolvangar decided not to do that experiment ever again.
Iorek is the only bear ever to have a dæmon. And with me helping him, he could lead all the bears against you. That's what he's come to Svalbard for.
ROAR!
That's why I love you best, because you're passionate and strong as well as clever. I don't want him ruling the bears. It ought to be you.
There's only one way of taking me away from him and making me your dæmon. . . .
If you defeat Iorek in single combat, then his strength will flow into you, and my mind will flow into yours. If you kill him any other way, I'll just die with him.

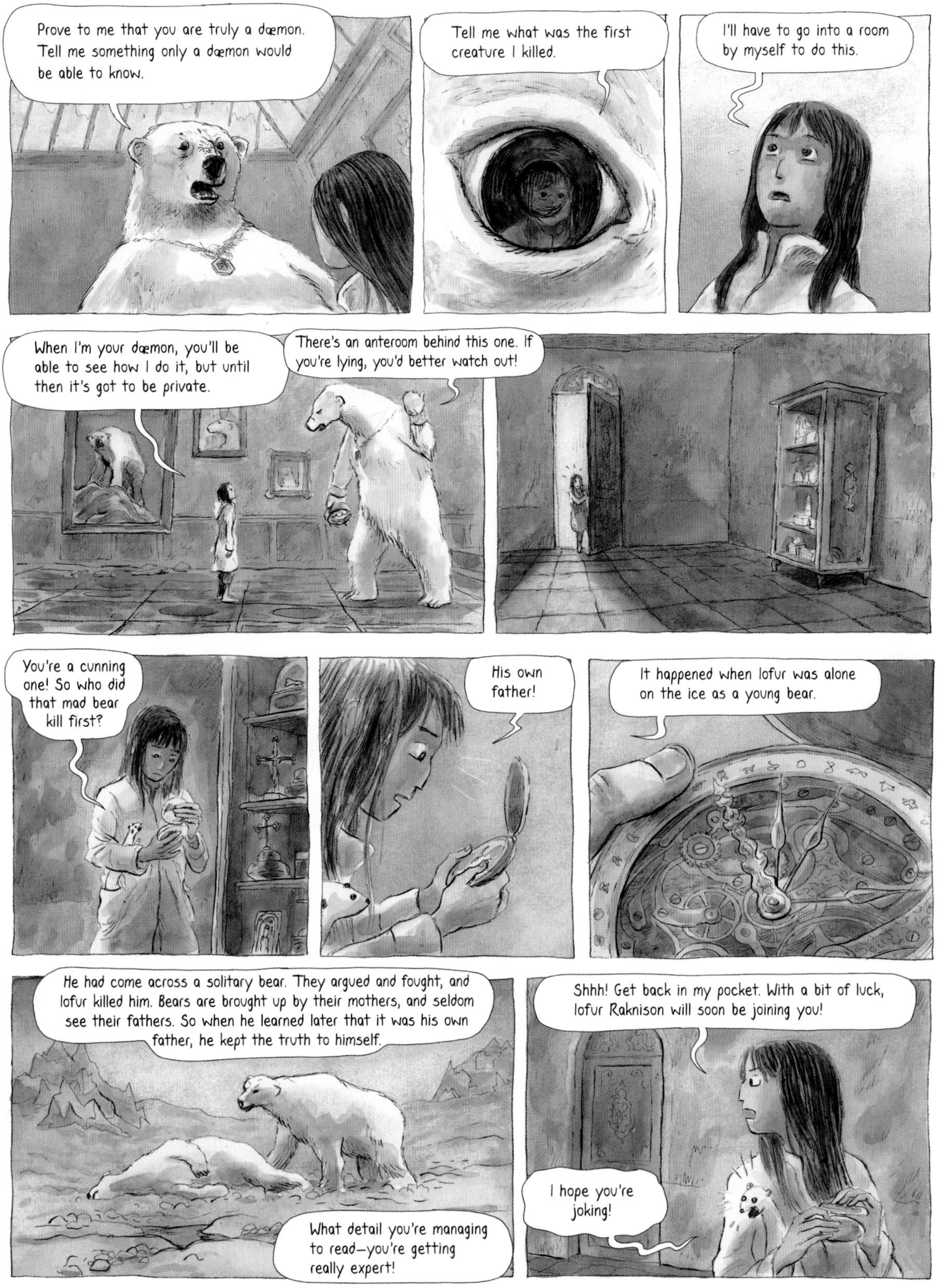
Prove to me that you are truly a dæmon. Tell me something only a dæmon would be able to know.
Tell me what was the first creature I killed.
I'll have to go into a room by myself to do this.
When I'm your dæmon, you'll be able to see how I do it, but until then it's got to be private.
There's an anteroom behind this one. If you're lying, you'd better watch out!
You're a cunning one! So who did that mad bear kill first?
His own father!
It happened when Iofur was alone on the ice as a young bear.
He had come across a solitary bear. They argued and fought, and Iofur killed him. Bears are brought up by their mothers, and seldom see their fathers. So when he learned later that it was his own father, he kept the truth to himself.
What detail you're managing to read—you're getting really expert!
Shhh! Get back in my pocket. With a bit of luck, Iofur Raknison will soon be joining you!
I hope you're joking!

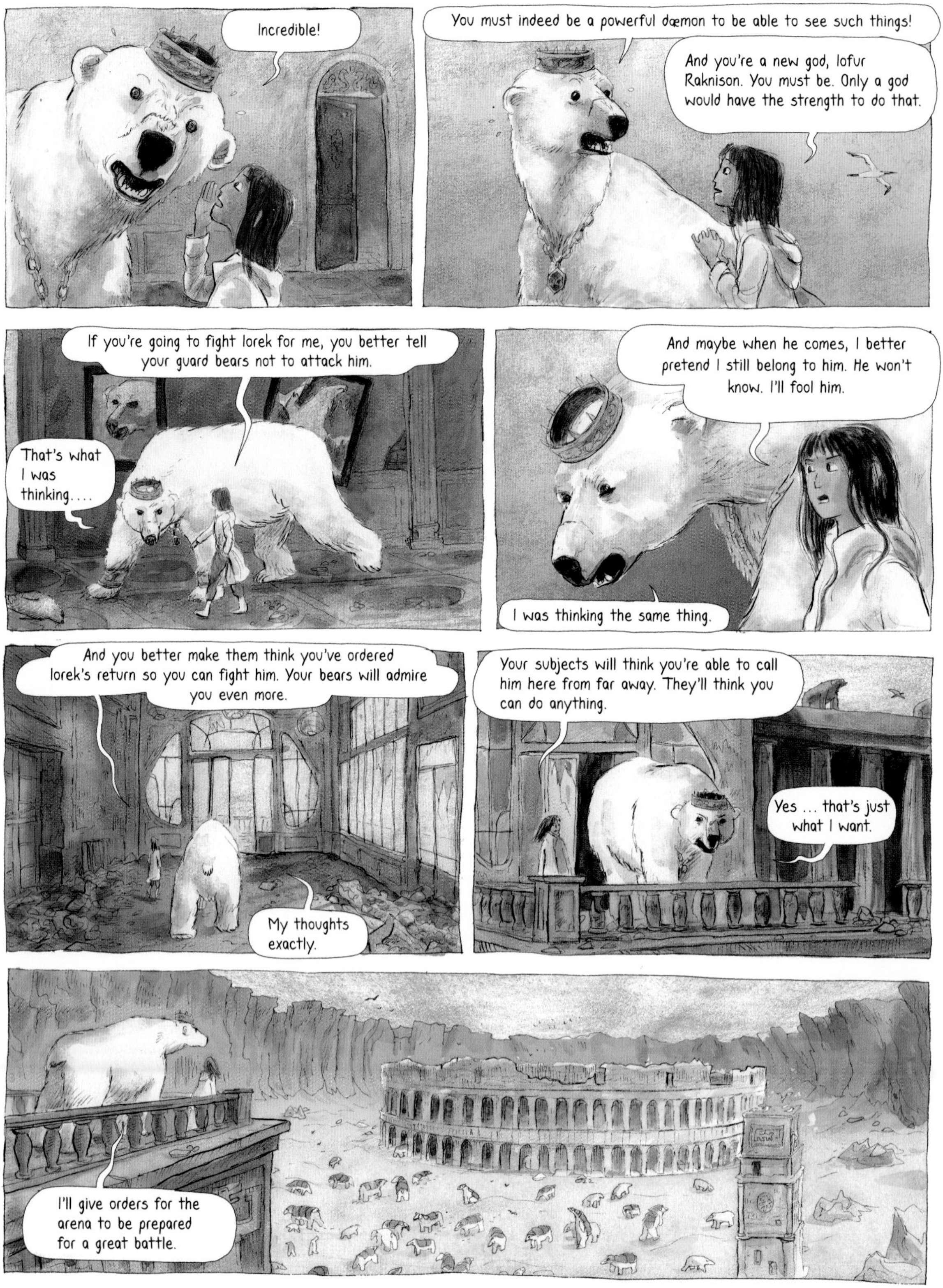
Incredible!
You must indeed be a powerful dæmon to be able to see such things!
And you're a new god, Iofur Raknison. You must be. Only a god would have the strength to do that.
If you're going to fight Iorek for me, you better tell your guard bears not to attack him.
That's what I was thinking. . . .
And maybe when he comes, I better pretend I still belong to him. He won't know. I'll fool him.
I was thinking the same thing.
And you better make them think you've ordered Iorek's return so you can fight him. Your bears will admire you even more.
My thoughts exactly.
Your subjects will think you're able to call him here from far away. They'll think you can do anything.
Yes ... that's just what I want.
I'll give orders for the arena to be prepared for a great battle.

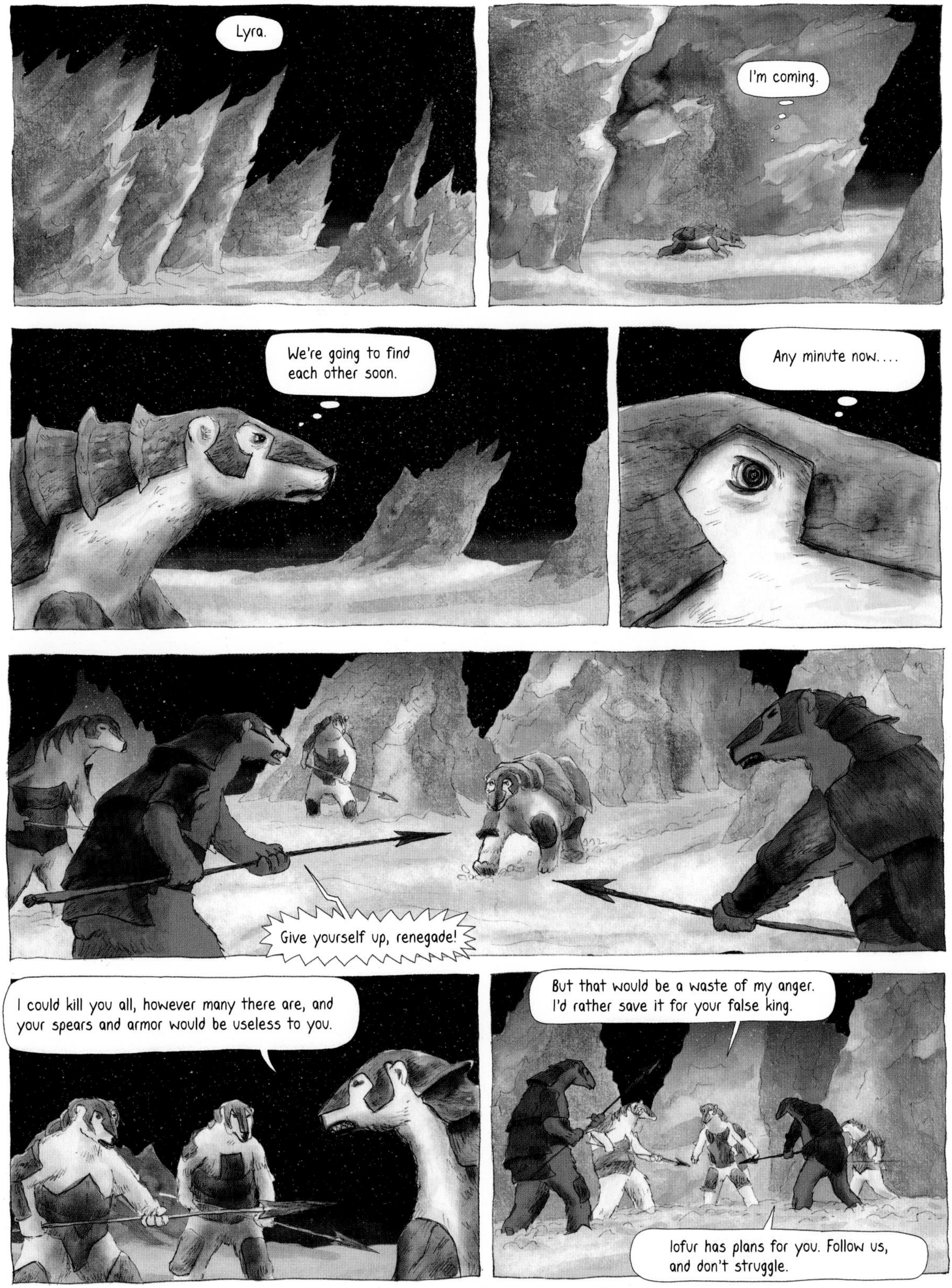
Lyra.
I'm coming.
We're going to find each other soon.
Any minute now....
Give yourself up, renegade!
I could kill you all, however many there are, and your spears and armor would be useless to you.
But that would be a waste of my anger. I'd rather save it for your false king.
Iofur has plans for you. Follow us, and don't struggle.

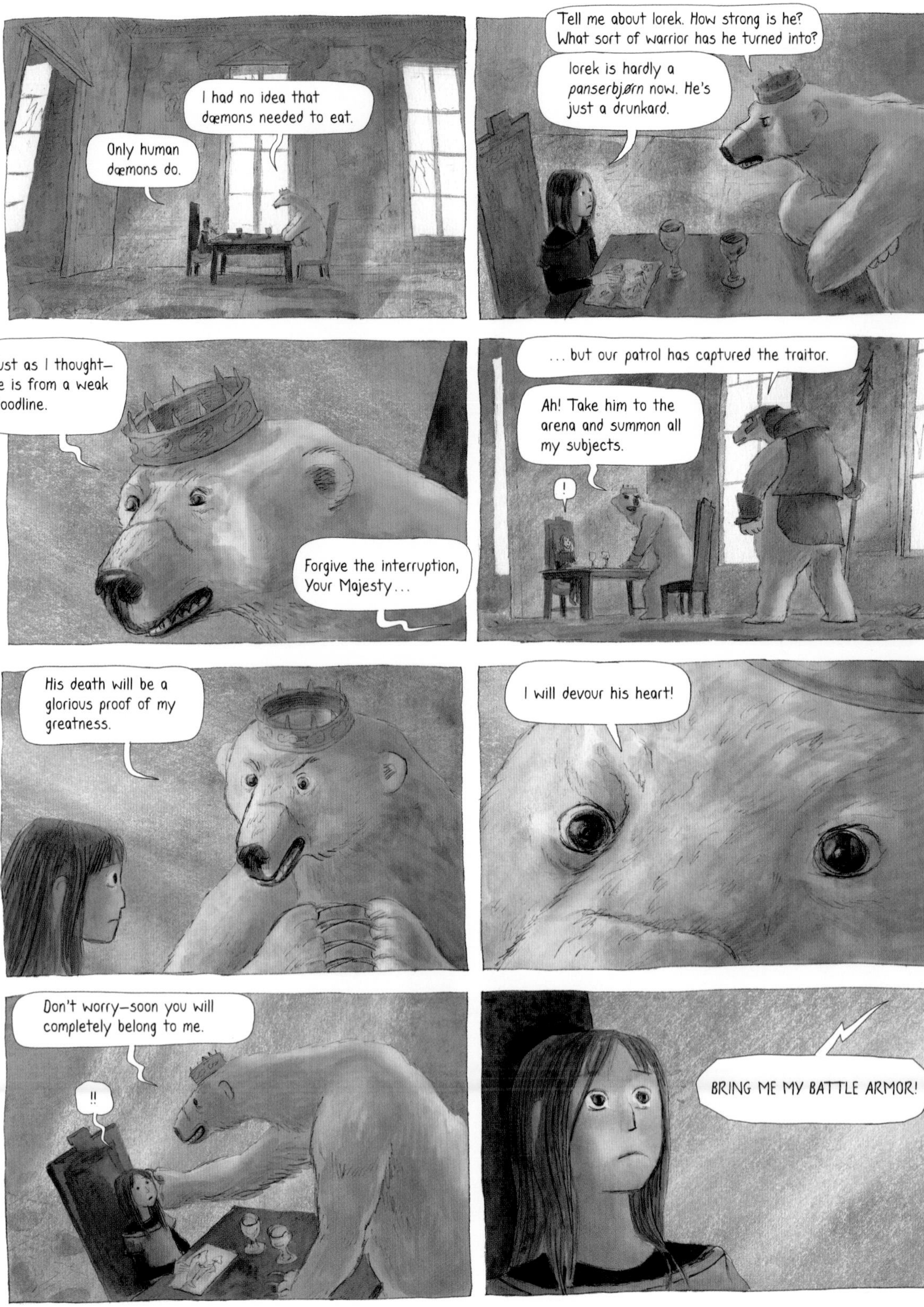
I had no idea that dæmons needed to eat.
Only human dæmons do.
Tell me about Iorek. How strong is he? What sort of warrior has he turned into?
Iorek is hardly a *panserbjørn* now. He's just a drunkard.
Just as I thought—he is from a weak bloodline.
Forgive the interruption, Your Majesty . . .
. . . but our patrol has captured the traitor.
Ah! Take him to the arena and summon all my subjects.
!
His death will be a glorious proof of my greatness.
I will devour his heart!
Don't worry—soon you will completely belong to me.
!!
BRING ME MY BATTLE ARMOR!

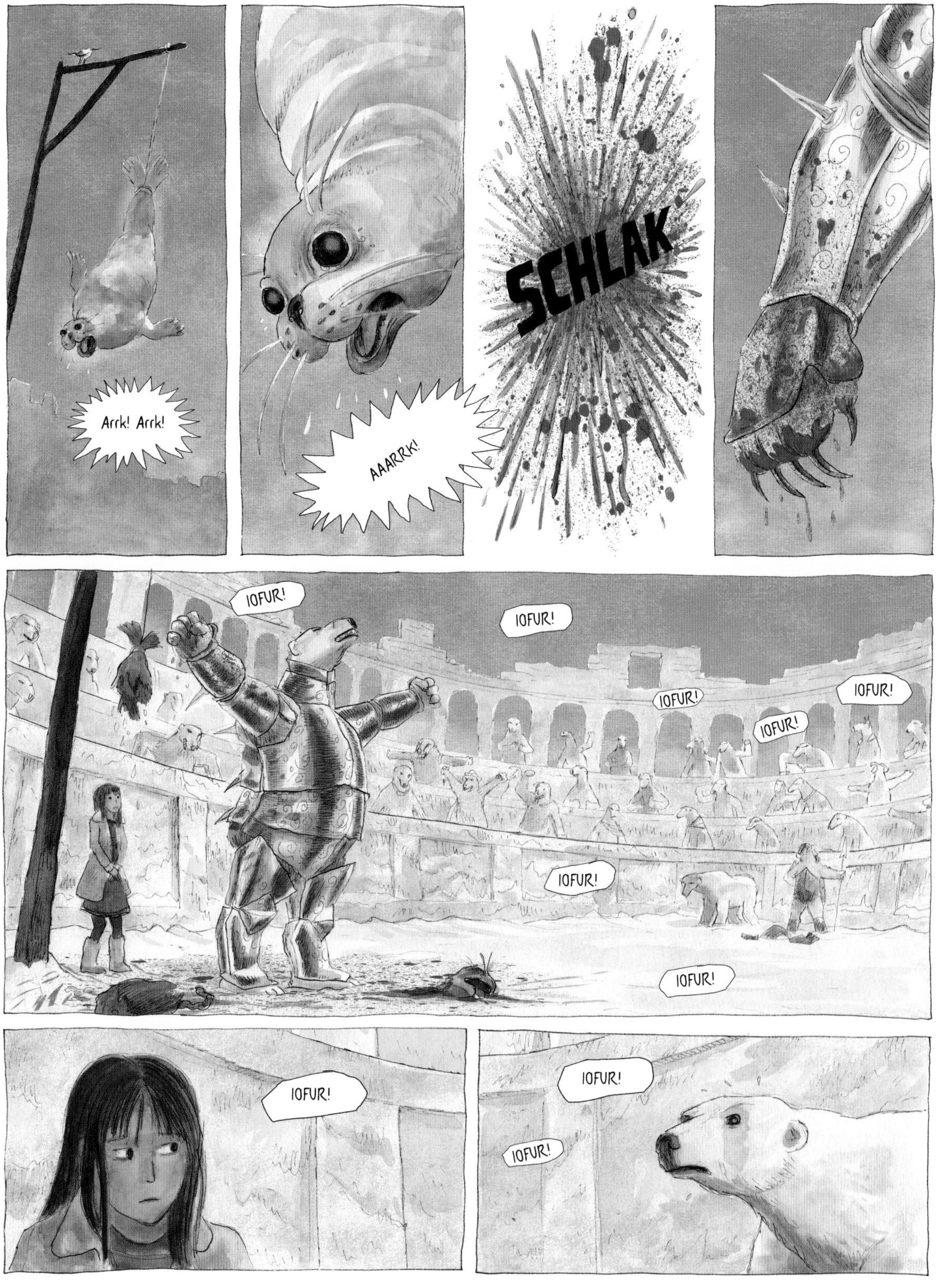
Arrk! Arrk!
AAARRK!
SCHLAK
IOFUR!
IOFUR!
IOFUR!
IOFUR!
IOFUR!
IOFUR!
IOFUR!
IOFUR!
IOFUR!
IOFUR!

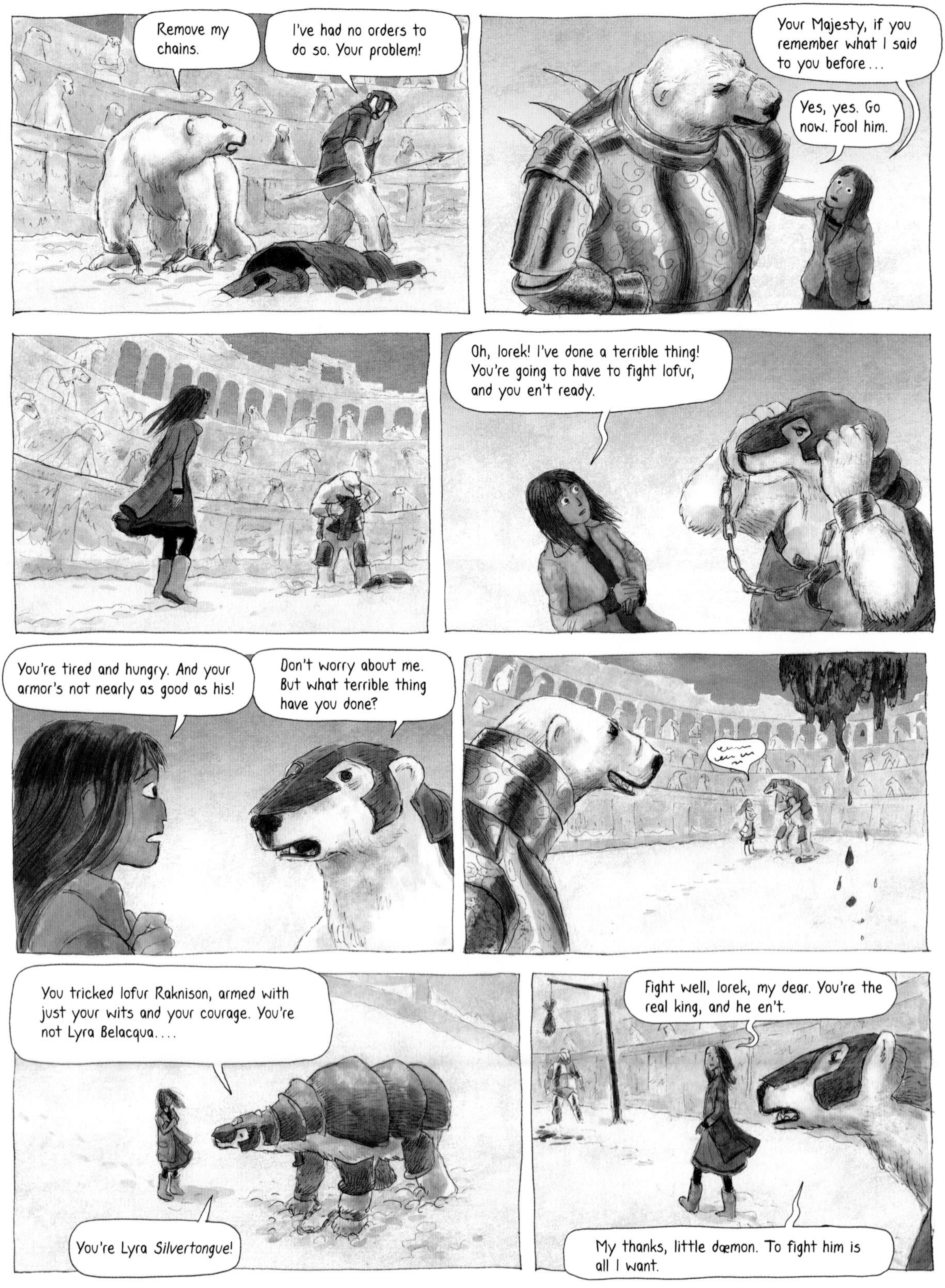
Remove my chains.
I've had no orders to do so. Your problem!
Your Majesty, if you remember what I said to you before…
Yes, yes. Go now. Fool him.
Oh, Iorek! I've done a terrible thing! You're going to have to fight Iofur, and you en't ready.
You're tired and hungry. And your armor's not nearly as good as his!
Don't worry about me. But what terrible thing have you done?
You tricked Iofur Raknison, armed with just your wits and your courage. You're not Lyra Belacqua….
You're Lyra *Silvertongue*!
Fight well, Iorek, my dear. You're the real king, and he en't.
My thanks, little dæmon. To fight him is all I want.

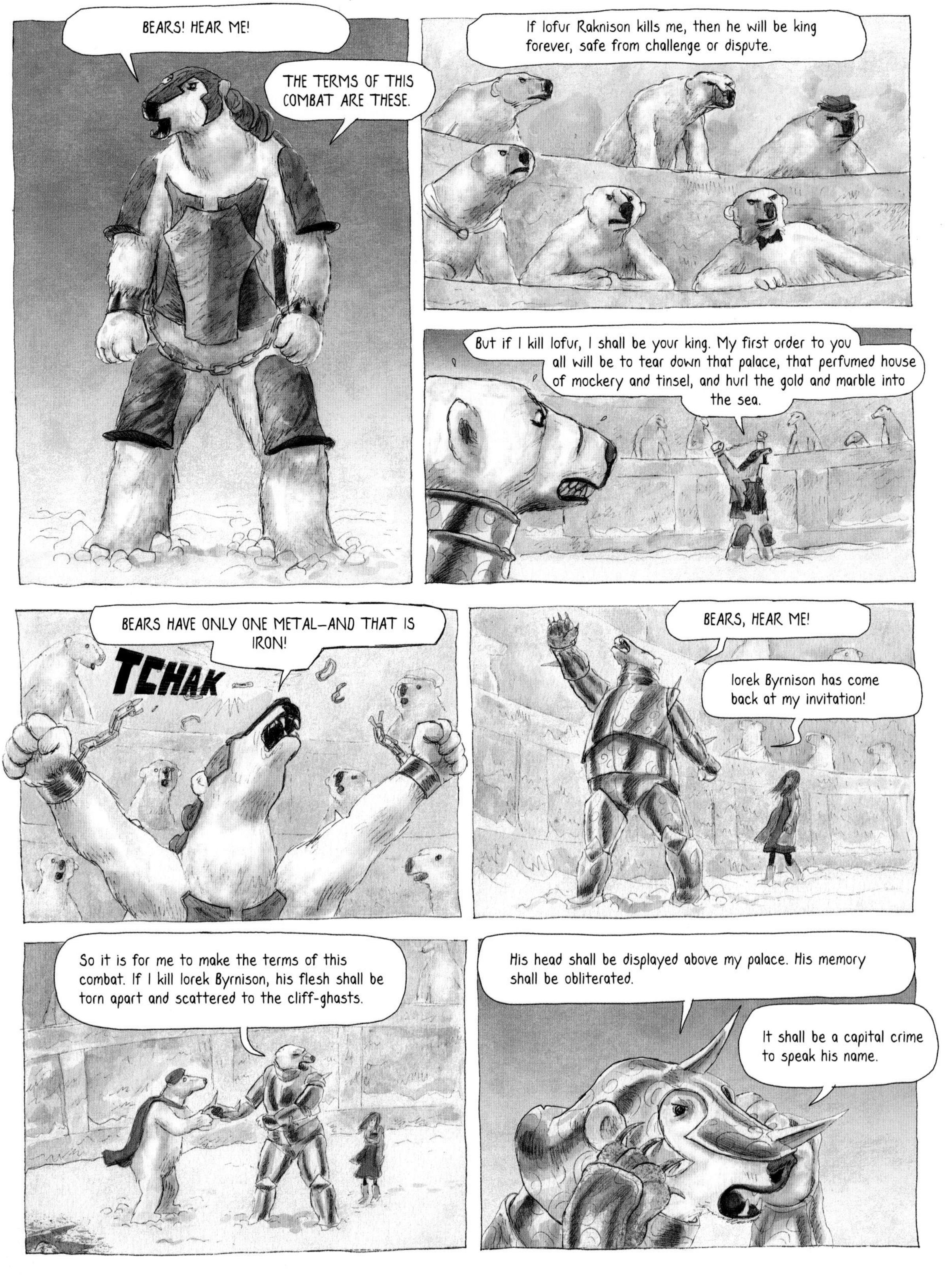
BEARS! HEAR ME!
THE TERMS OF THIS COMBAT ARE THESE.
If Iofur Raknison kills me, then he will be king forever, safe from challenge or dispute.
But if I kill Iofur, I shall be your king. My first order to you all will be to tear down that palace, that perfumed house of mockery and tinsel, and hurl the gold and marble into the sea.
BEARS HAVE ONLY ONE METAL—AND THAT IS IRON!
TCHAK
BEARS, HEAR ME!
Iorek Byrnison has come back at my invitation!
So it is for me to make the terms of this combat. If I kill Iorek Byrnison, his flesh shall be torn apart and scattered to the cliff-ghasts.
His head shall be displayed above my palace. His memory shall be obliterated.
It shall be a capital crime to speak his name.

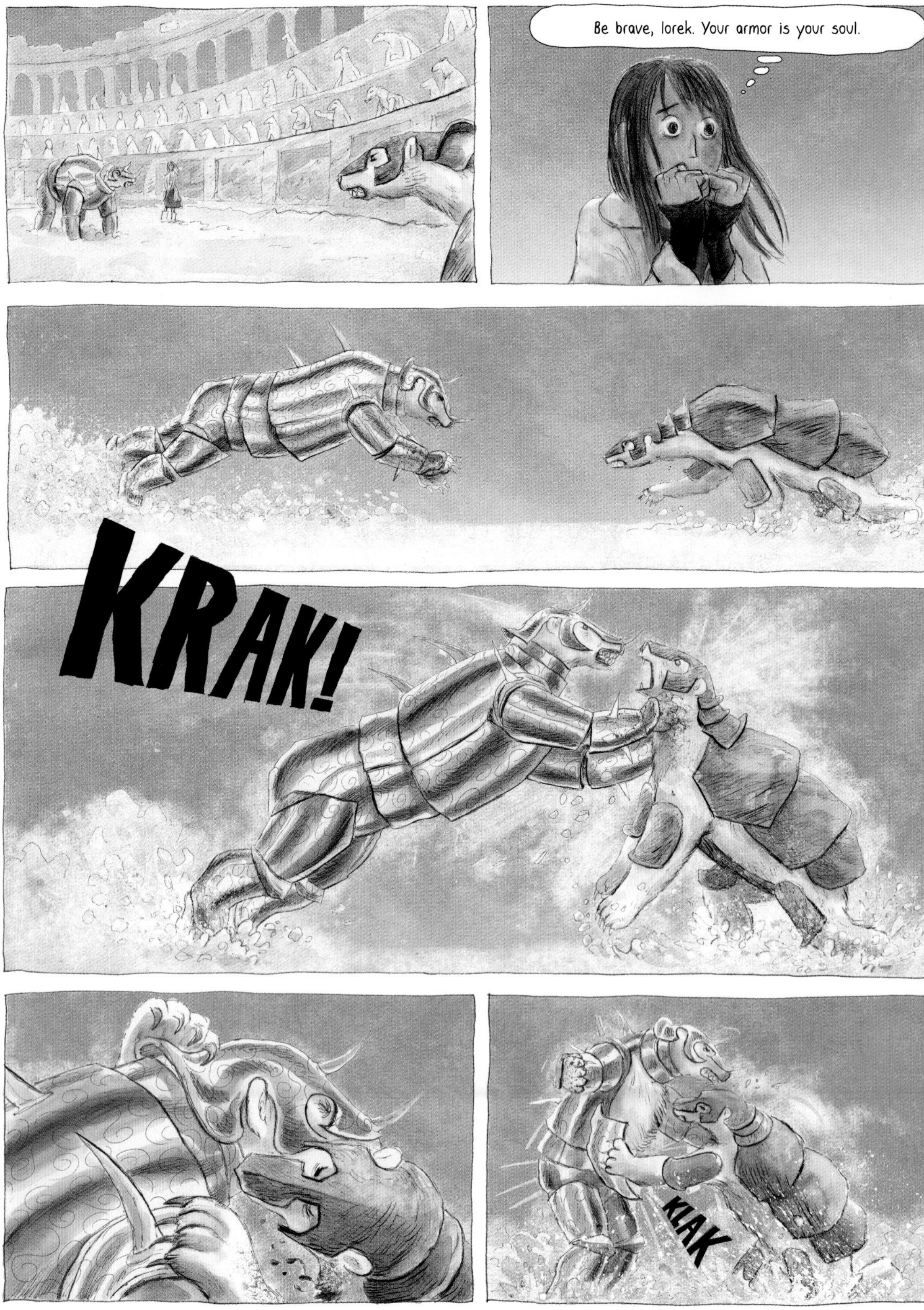
Be brave, Iorek. Your armor is your soul.
KRAK!
KLAK

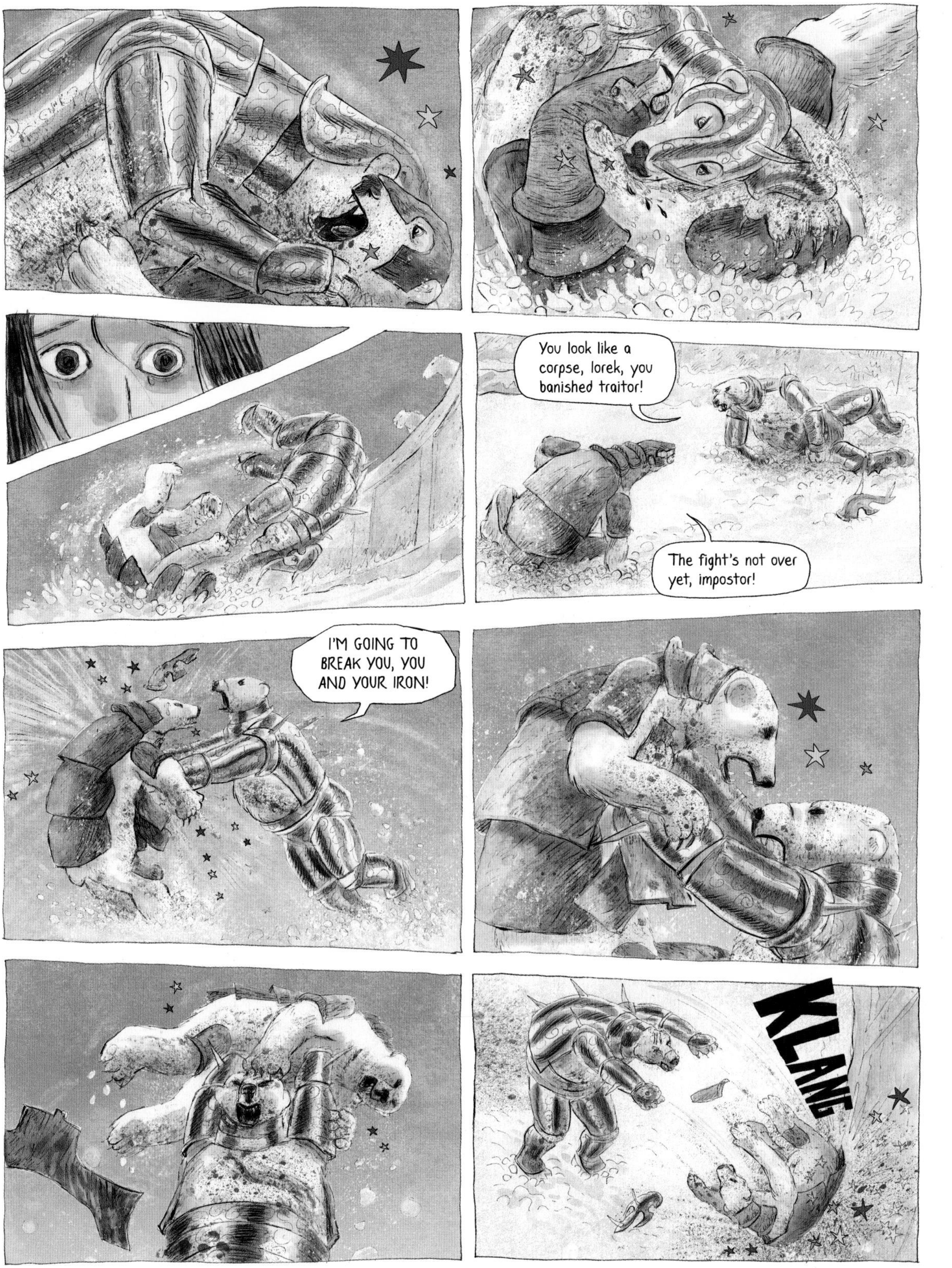
You look like a corpse, Iorek, you banished traitor!
The fight's not over yet, impostor!
I'M GOING TO BREAK YOU, YOU AND YOUR IRON!
KLANG

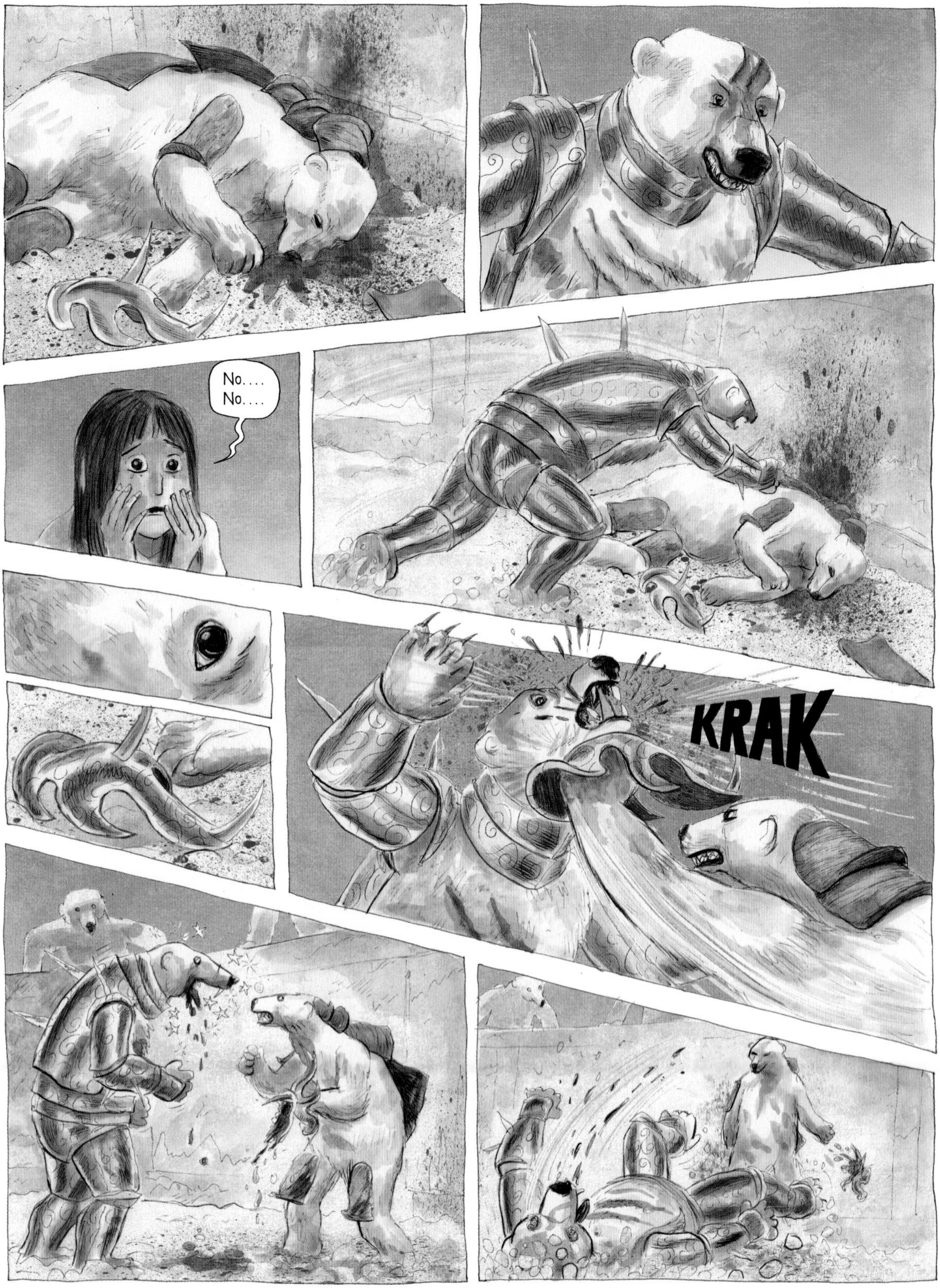
No....
No....
KRAK

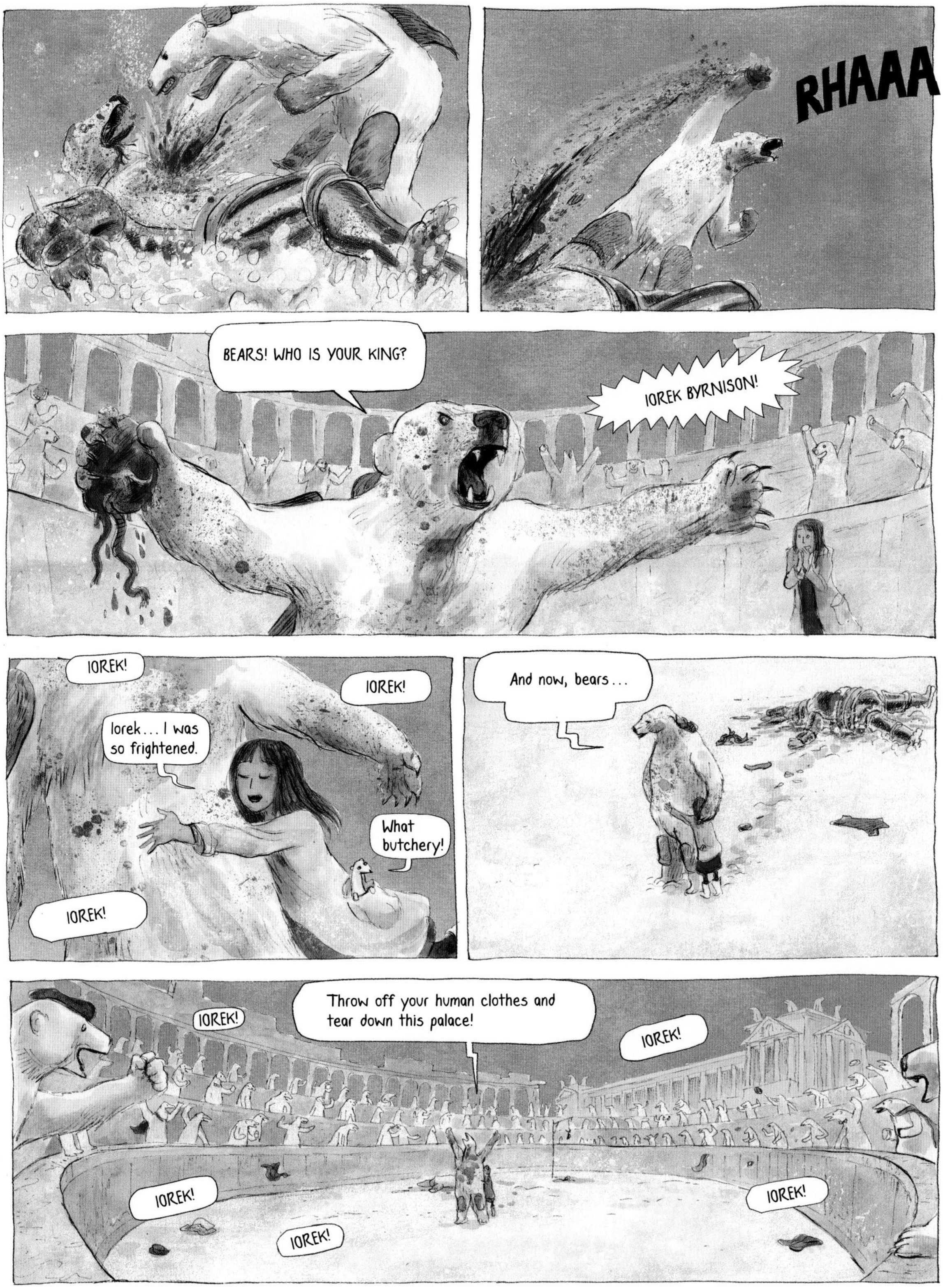
RHAAA
BEARS! WHO IS YOUR KING?
IOREK BYRNISON!
IOREK!
IOREK!
Iorek . . . I was so frightened.
What butchery!
IOREK!
And now, bears . . .
Throw off your human clothes and tear down this palace!
IOREK!
IOREK!
IOREK!
IOREK!
IOREK!

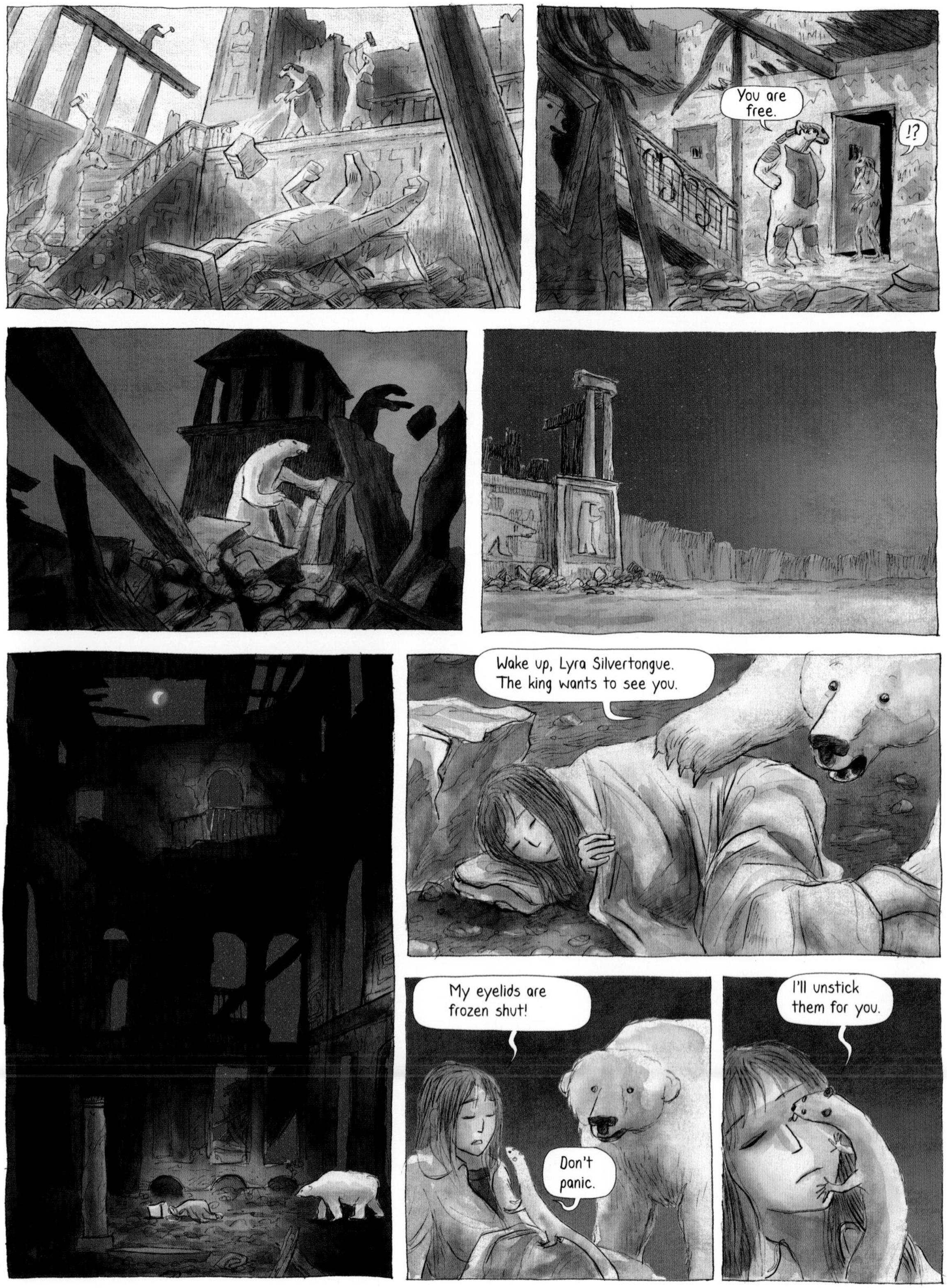
You are free.
!?
Wake up, Lyra Silvertongue. The king wants to see you.
My eyelids are frozen shut!
Don't panic.
I'll unstick them for you.

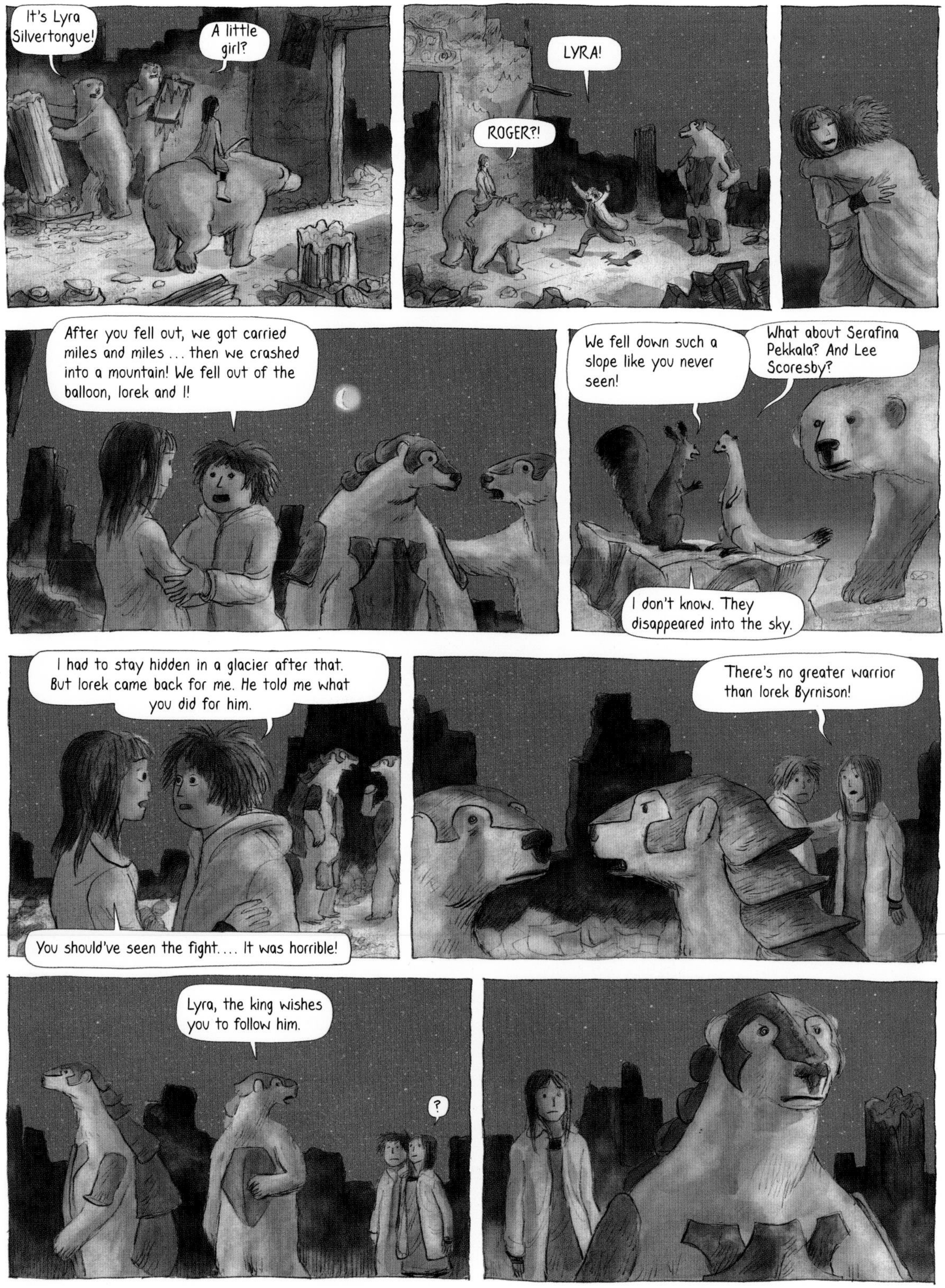
It's Lyra Silvertongue!
A little girl?
LYRA!
ROGER?!
After you fell out, we got carried miles and miles . . . then we crashed into a mountain! We fell out of the balloon, Iorek and I!
We fell down such a slope like you never seen!
What about Serafina Pekkala? And Lee Scoresby?
I don't know. They disappeared into the sky.
I had to stay hidden in a glacier after that. But Iorek came back for me. He told me what you did for him.
You should've seen the fight. . . . It was horrible!
There's no greater warrior than Iorek Byrnison!
Lyra, the king wishes you to follow him.
?

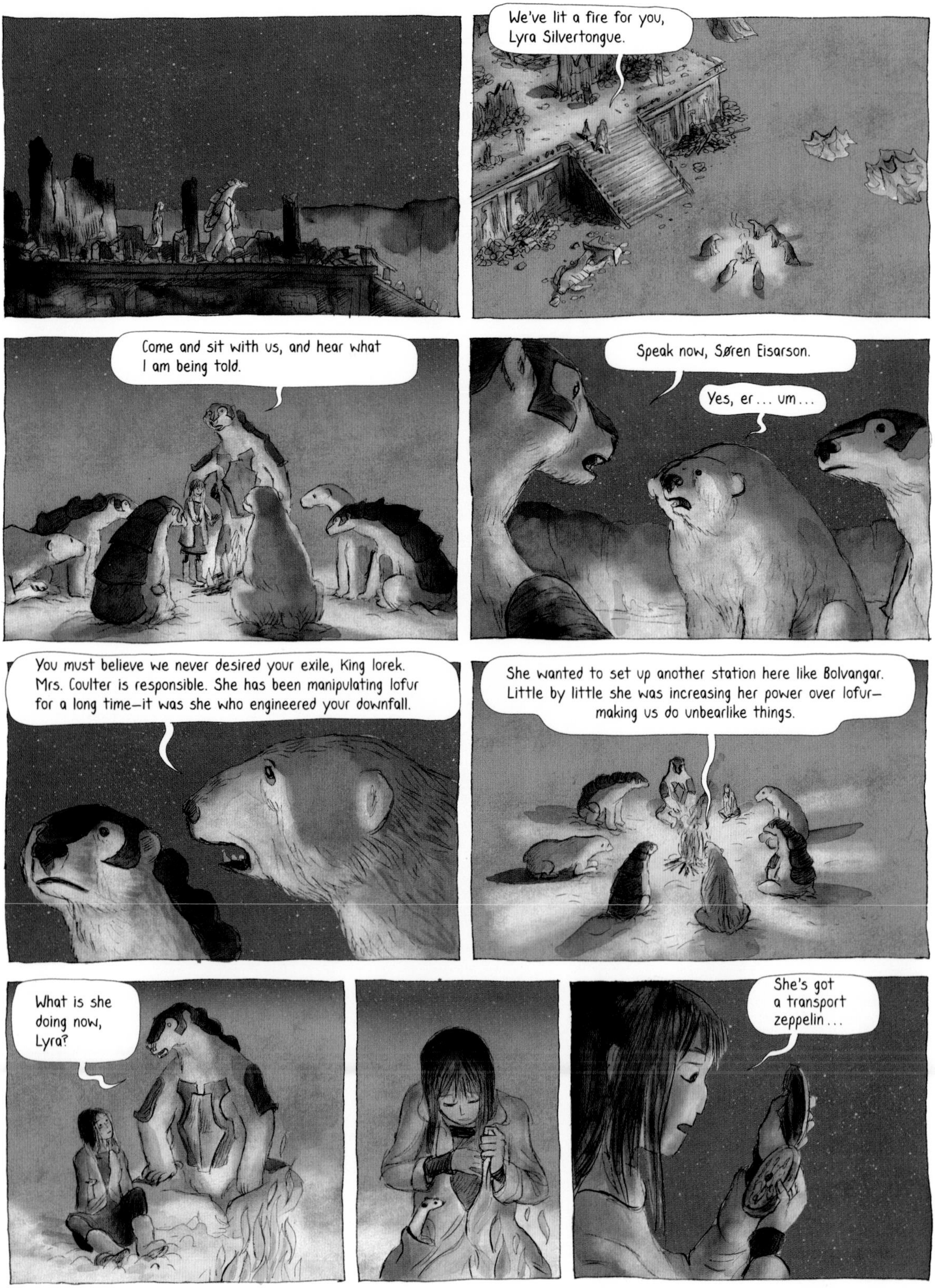
We've lit a fire for you, Lyra Silvertongue.
Come and sit with us, and hear what I am being told.
Speak now, Søren Eisarson.
Yes, er... um...
You must believe we never desired your exile, King Iorek. Mrs. Coulter is responsible. She has been manipulating Iofur for a long time—it was she who engineered your downfall.
She wanted to set up another station here like Bolvangar. Little by little she was increasing her power over Iofur—making us do unbearlike things.
What is she doing now, Lyra?
She's got a transport zeppelin...

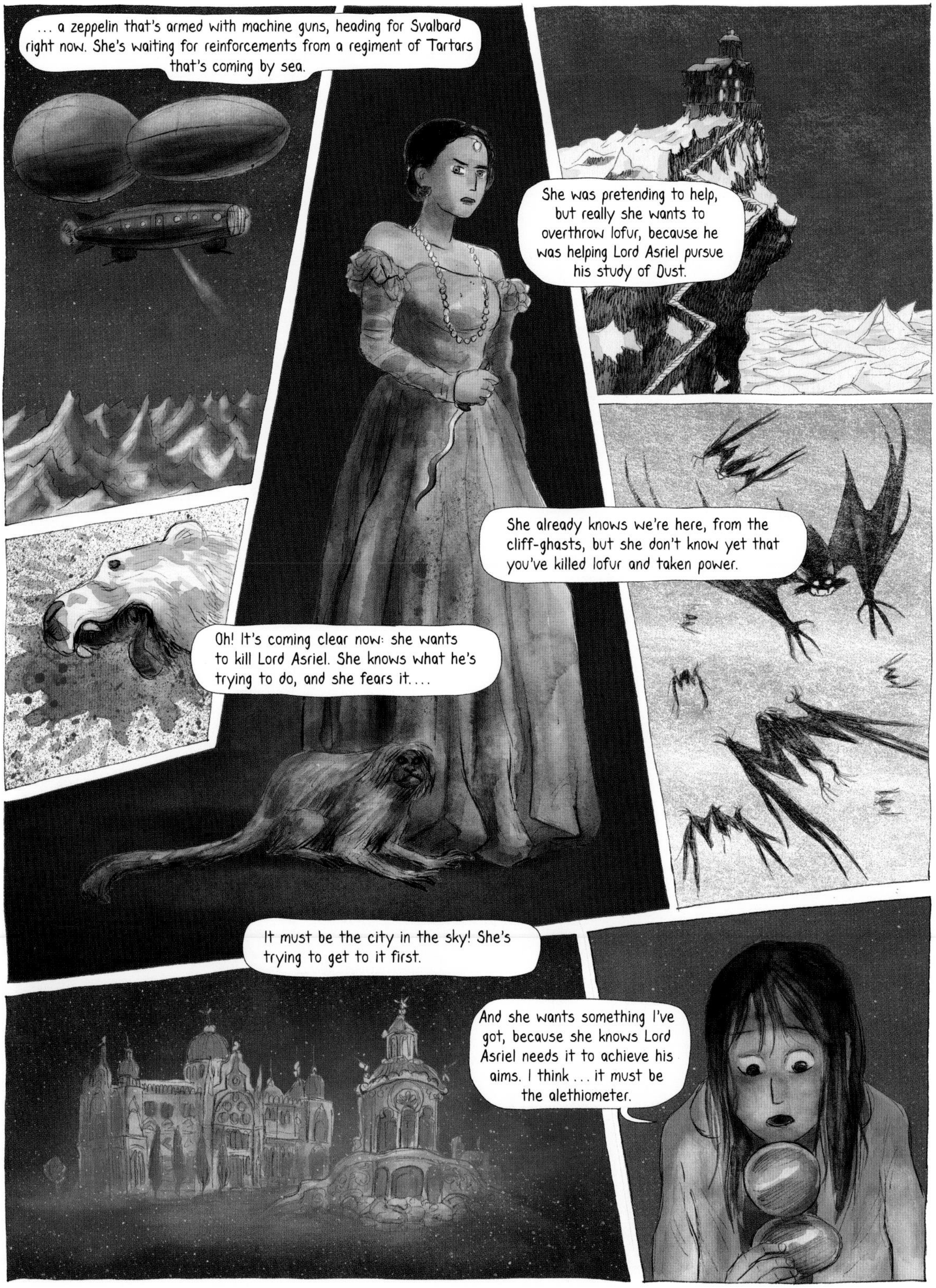
... a zeppelin that's armed with machine guns, heading for Svalbard right now. She's waiting for reinforcements from a regiment of Tartars that's coming by sea.
She was pretending to help, but really she wants to overthrow Iofur, because he was helping Lord Asriel pursue his study of Dust.
She already knows we're here, from the cliff-ghasts, but she don't know yet that you've killed Iofur and taken power.
Oh! It's coming clear now: she wants to kill Lord Asriel. She knows what he's trying to do, and she fears it....
It must be the city in the sky! She's trying to get to it first.
And she wants something I've got, because she knows Lord Asriel needs it to achieve his aims. I think... it must be the alethiometer.

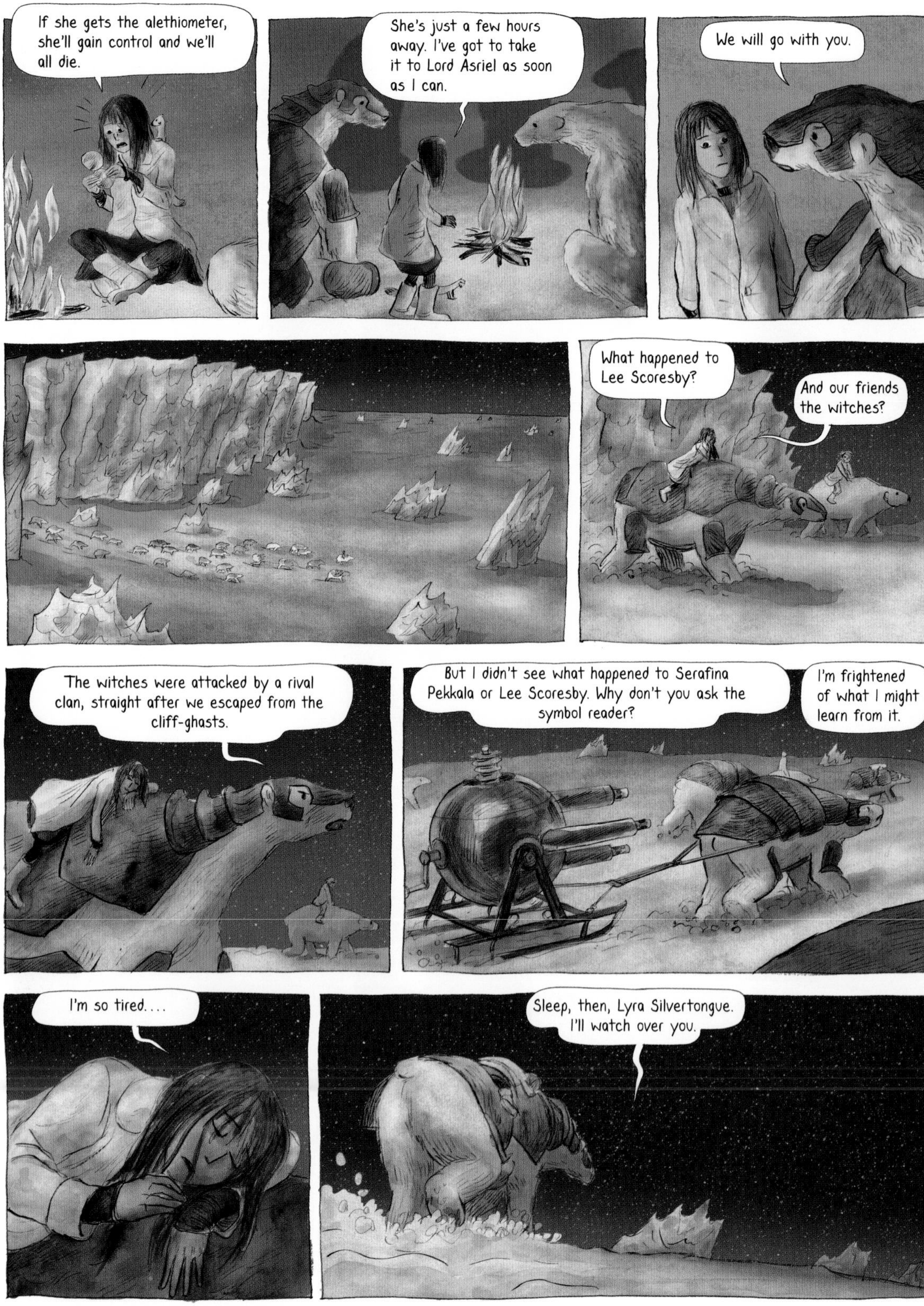
If she gets the alethiometer, she'll gain control and we'll all die.
She's just a few hours away. I've got to take it to Lord Asriel as soon as I can.
We will go with you.
What happened to Lee Scoresby?
And our friends the witches?
The witches were attacked by a rival clan, straight after we escaped from the cliff-ghasts.
But I didn't see what happened to Serafina Pekkala or Lee Scoresby. Why don't you ask the symbol reader?
I'm frightened of what I might learn from it.
I'm so tired....
Sleep, then, Lyra Silvertongue. I'll watch over you.

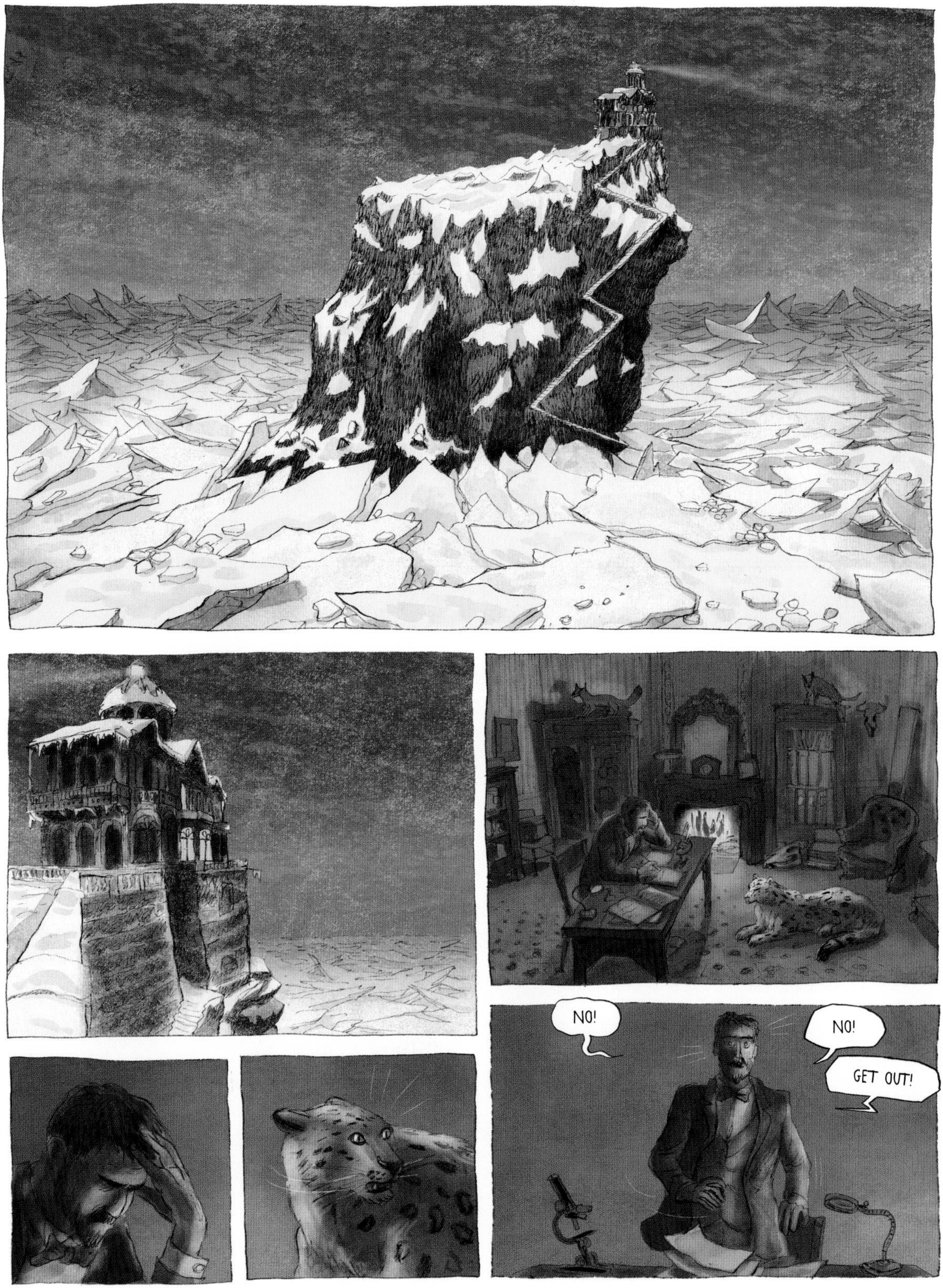
NO!
NO!
GET OUT!

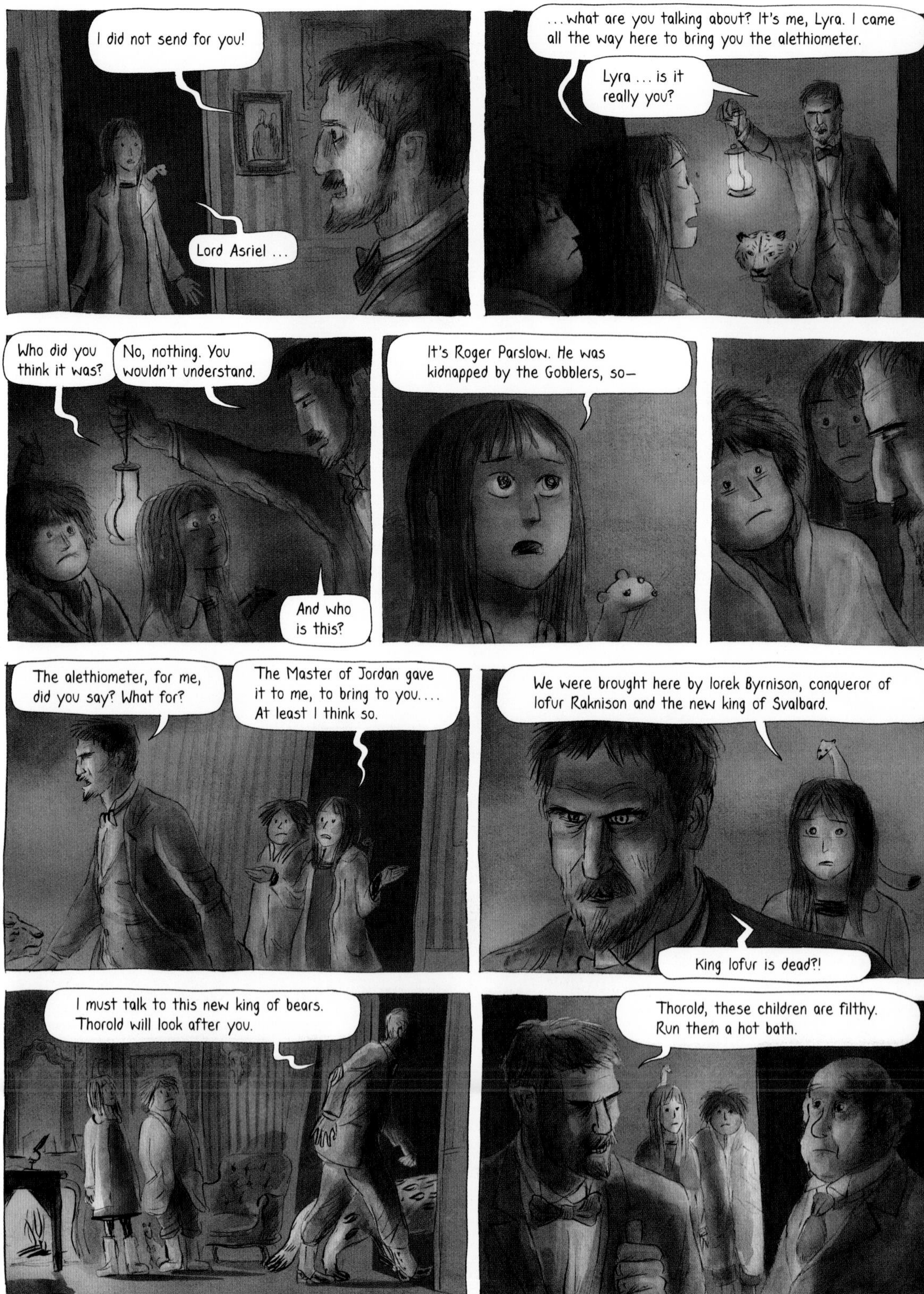
I did not send for you!
Lord Asriel . . .
. . . what are you talking about? It's me, Lyra. I came all the way here to bring you the alethiometer.
Lyra . . . is it really you?
Who did you think it was?
No, nothing. You wouldn't understand.
And who is this?
It's Roger Parslow. He was kidnapped by the Gobblers, so—
The alethiometer, for me, did you say? What for?
The Master of Jordan gave it to me, to bring to you. . . . At least I think so.
We were brought here by Iorek Byrnison, conqueror of Iofur Raknison and the new king of Svalbard.
King Iofur is dead?!
I must talk to this new king of bears. Thorold will look after you.
Thorold, these children are filthy. Run them a hot bath.

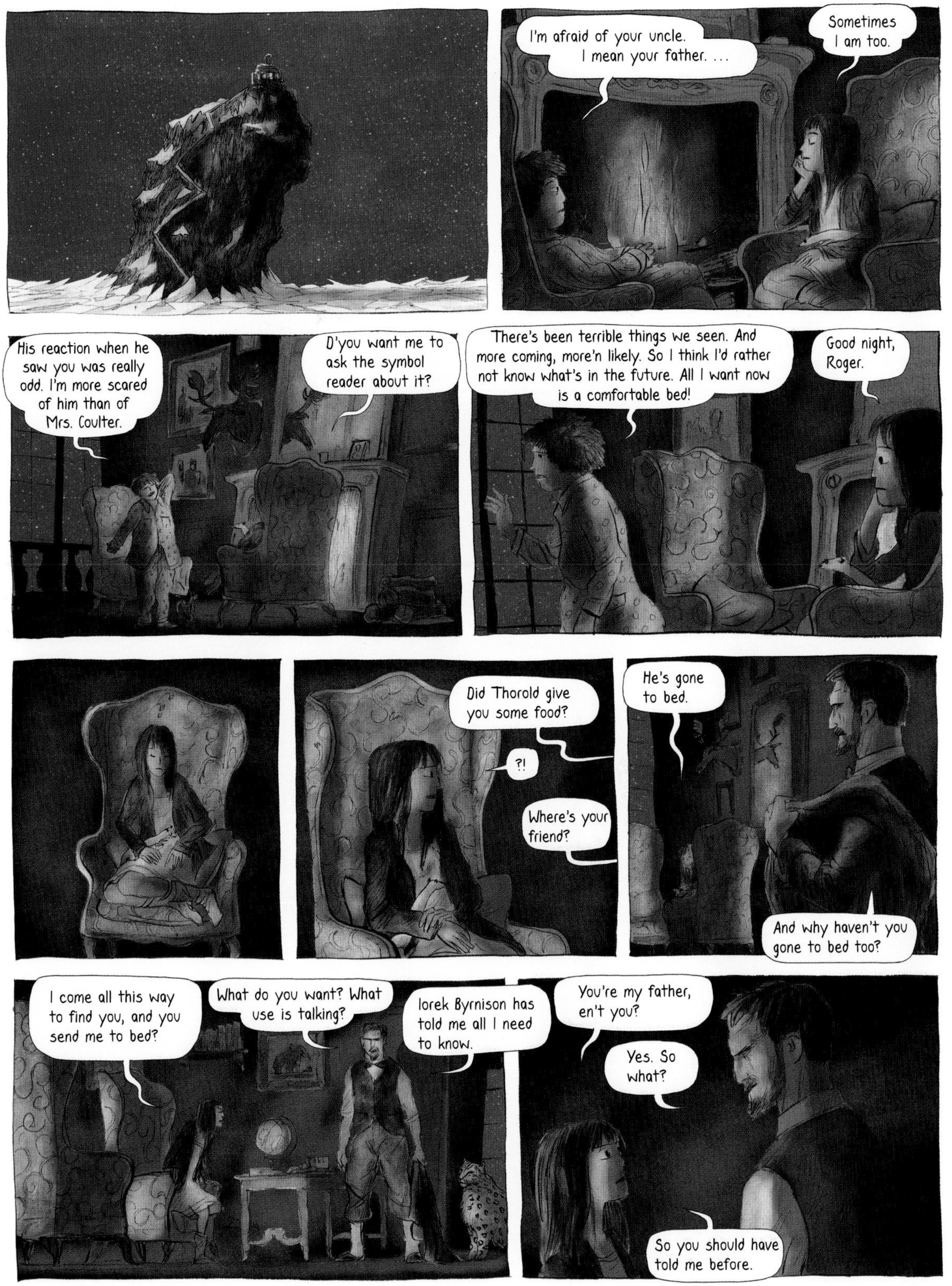
I'm afraid of your uncle. I mean your father. . . .
Sometimes I am too.
His reaction when he saw you was really odd. I'm more scared of him than of Mrs. Coulter.
D'you want me to ask the symbol reader about it?
There's been terrible things we seen. And more coming, more'n likely. So I think I'd rather not know what's in the future. All I want now is a comfortable bed!
Good night, Roger.
Did Thorold give you some food?
?!
Where's your friend?
He's gone to bed.
And why haven't you gone to bed too?
I come all this way to find you, and you send me to bed?
What do you want? What use is talking?
Iorek Byrnison has told me all I need to know.
You're my father, en't you?
Yes. So what?
So you should have told me before.

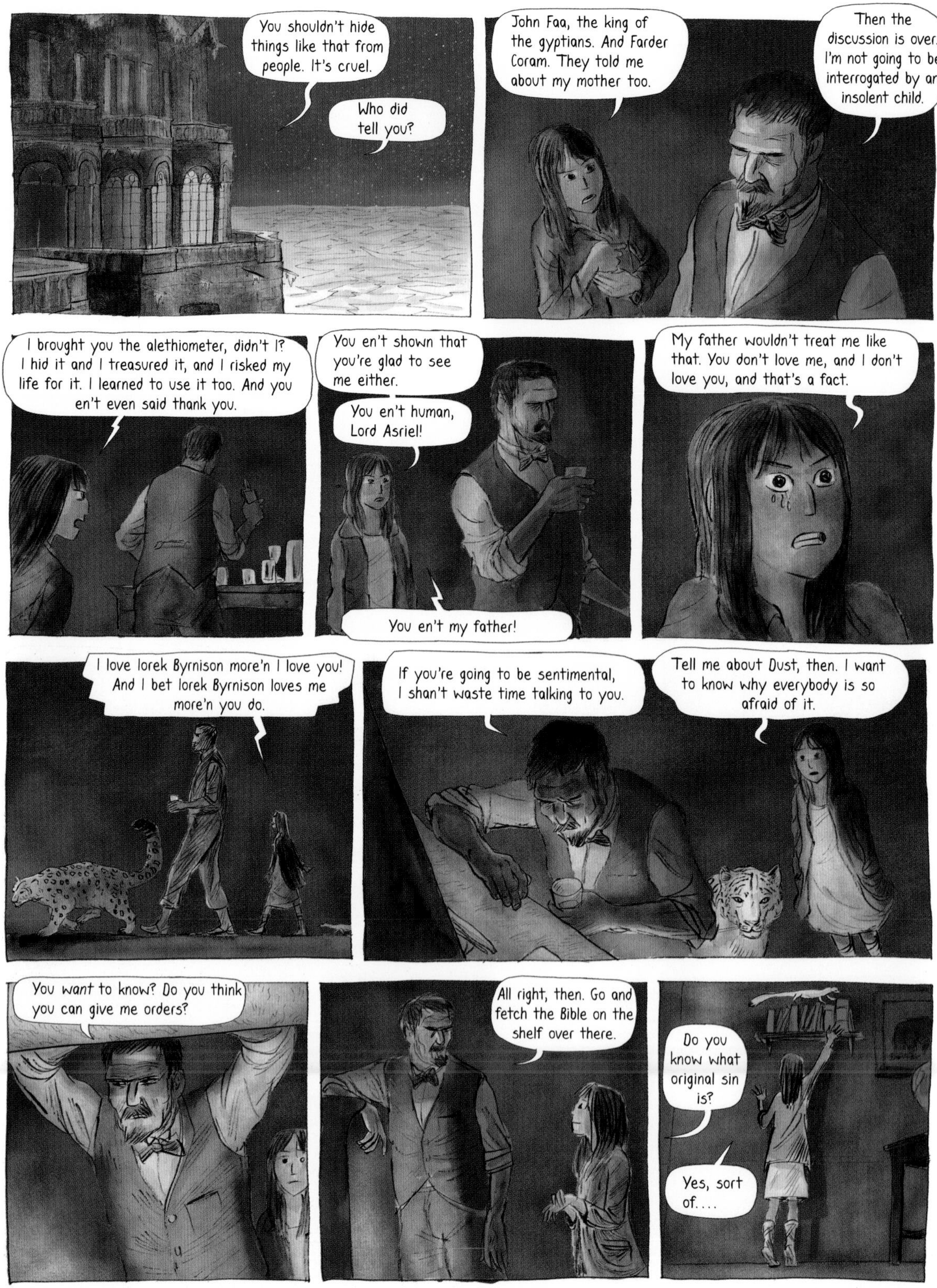
You shouldn't hide things like that from people. It's cruel.
Who did tell you?
John Faa, the king of the gyptians. And Farder Coram. They told me about my mother too.
Then the discussion is over. I'm not going to be interrogated by an insolent child.
I brought you the alethiometer, didn't I? I hid it and I treasured it, and I risked my life for it. I learned to use it too. And you en't even said thank you.
You en't shown that you're glad to see me either.
You en't human, Lord Asriel!
You en't my father!
My father wouldn't treat me like that. You don't love me, and I don't love you, and that's a fact.
I love Iorek Byrnison more'n I love you! And I bet Iorek Byrnison loves me more'n you do.
If you're going to be sentimental, I shan't waste time talking to you.
Tell me about Dust, then. I want to know why everybody is so afraid of it.
You want to know? Do you think you can give me orders?
All right, then. Go and fetch the Bible on the shelf over there.
Do you know what original sin is?
Yes, sort of....

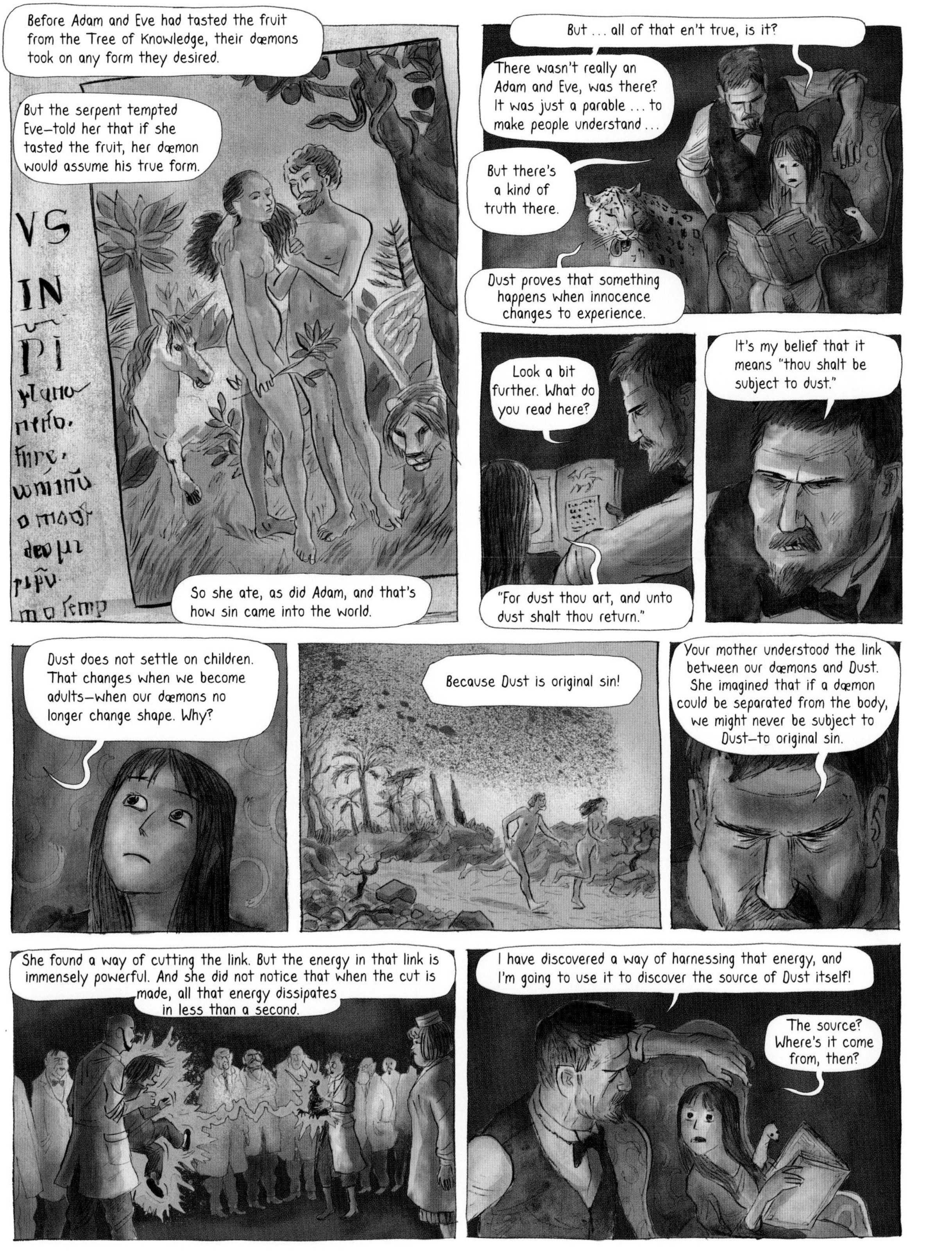

Before Adam and Eve had tasted the fruit from the Tree of Knowledge, their dæmons took on any form they desired.
But the serpent tempted Eve—told her that if she tasted the fruit, her dæmon would assume his true form.
So she ate, as did Adam, and that's how sin came into the world.
But . . . all of that en't true, is it?
There wasn't really an Adam and Eve, was there? It was just a parable . . . to make people understand . . .
But there's a kind of truth there.
Dust proves that something happens when innocence changes to experience.
Look a bit further. What do you read here?
"For dust thou art, and unto dust shalt thou return."
It's my belief that it means "thou shalt be subject to dust."
Dust does not settle on children. That changes when we become adults—when our dæmons no longer change shape. Why?
Because Dust is original sin!
Your mother understood the link between our dæmons and Dust. She imagined that if a dæmon could be separated from the body, we might never be subject to Dust—to original sin.
She found a way of cutting the link. But the energy in that link is immensely powerful. And she did not notice that when the cut is made, all that energy dissipates in less than a second.
I have discovered a way of harnessing that energy, and I'm going to use it to discover the source of Dust itself!
The source? Where's it come from, then?

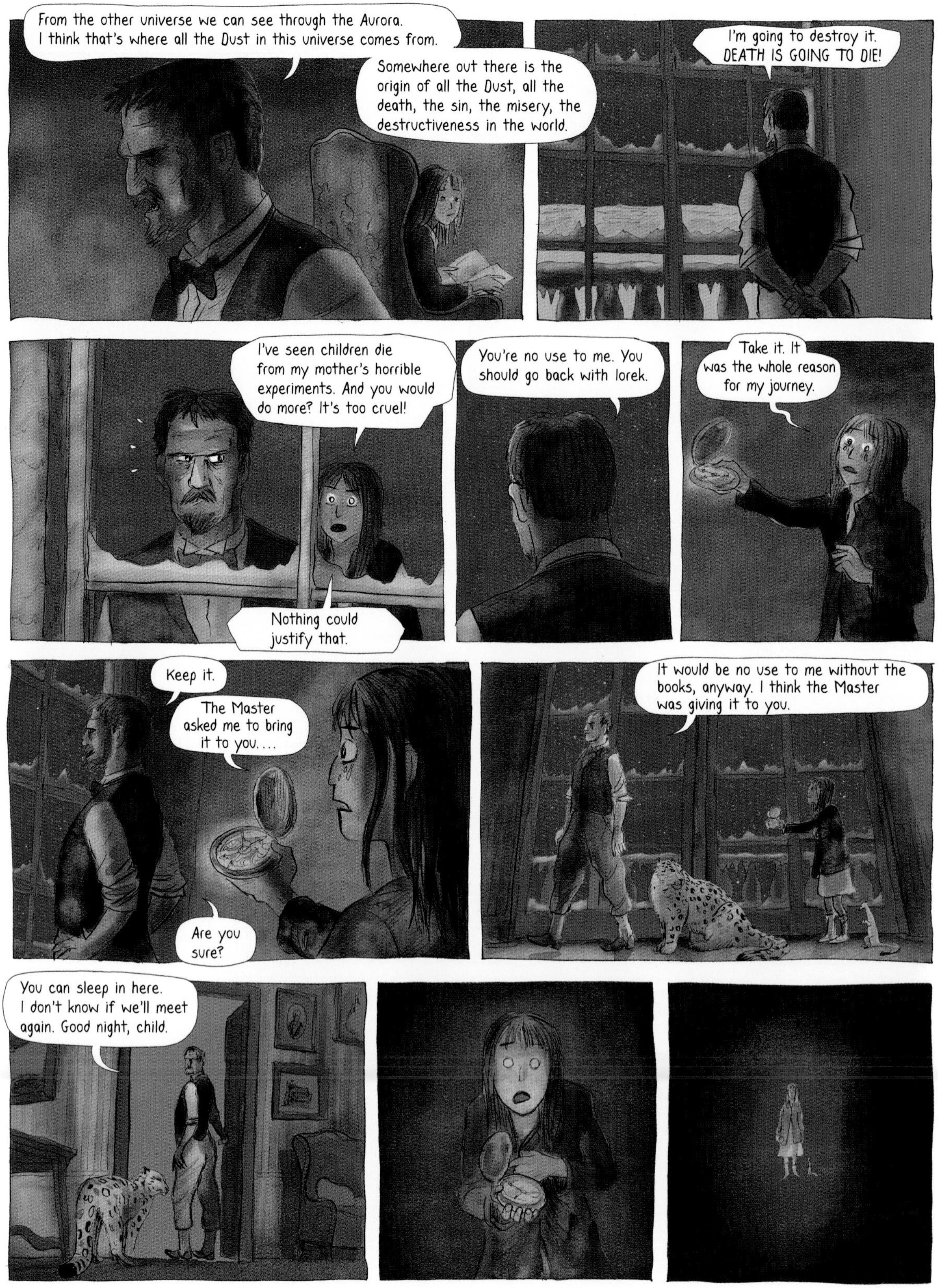
From the other universe we can see through the Aurora. I think that's where all the Dust in this universe comes from.
Somewhere out there is the origin of all the Dust, all the death, the sin, the misery, the destructiveness in the world.
I'm going to destroy it. DEATH IS GOING TO DIE!
I've seen children die from my mother's horrible experiments. And you would do more? It's too cruel!
Nothing could justify that.
You're no use to me. You should go back with Iorek.
Take it. It was the whole reason for my journey.
Keep it.
The Master asked me to bring it to you. . . .
Are you sure?
It would be no use to me without the books, anyway. I think the Master was giving it to you.
You can sleep in here. I don't know if we'll meet again. Good night, child.

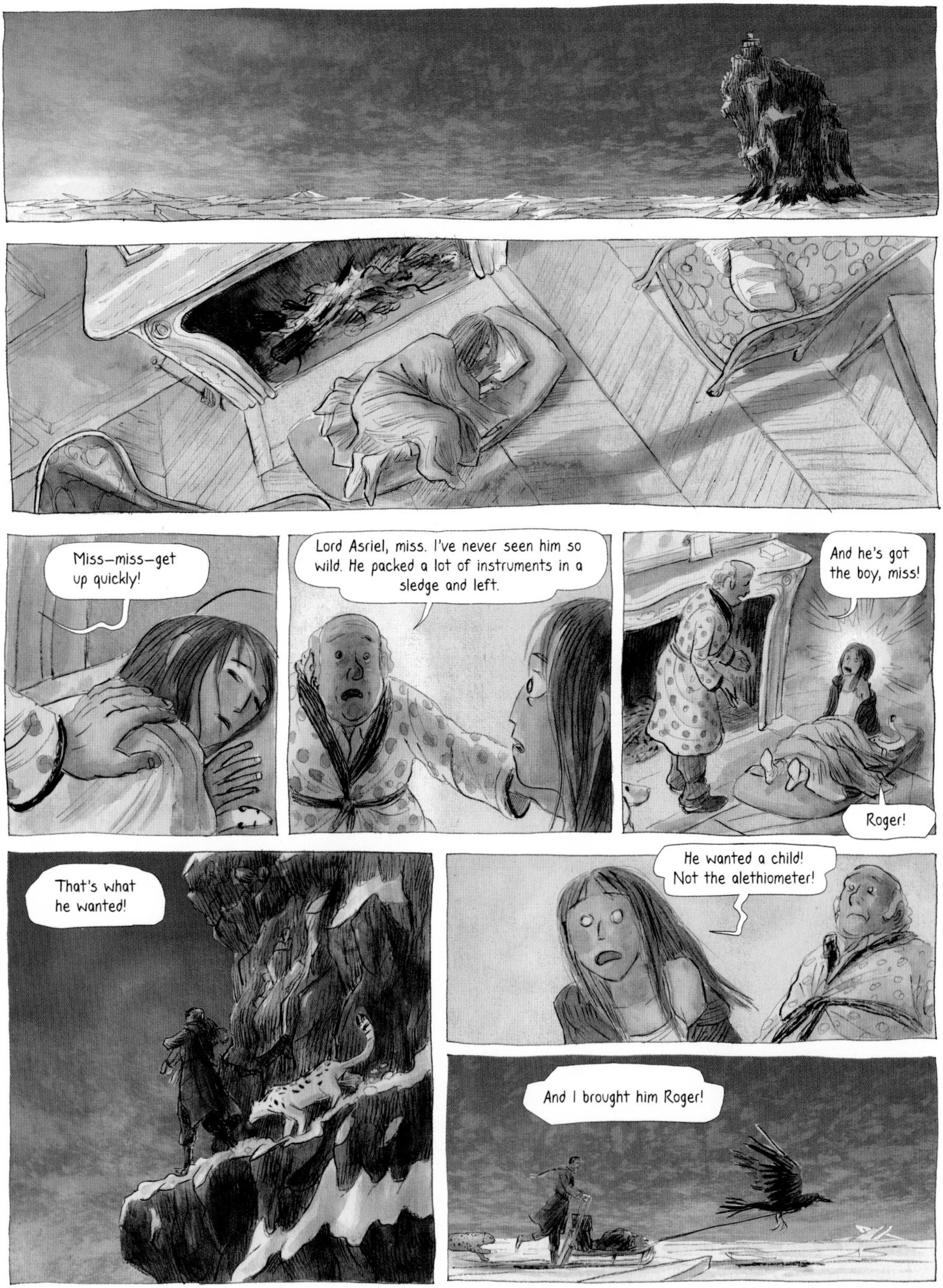
Miss—miss—get up quickly!
Lord Asriel, miss. I've never seen him so wild. He packed a lot of instruments in a sledge and left.
And he's got the boy, miss!
Roger!
That's what he wanted!
He wanted a child! Not the alethiometer!
And I brought him Roger!

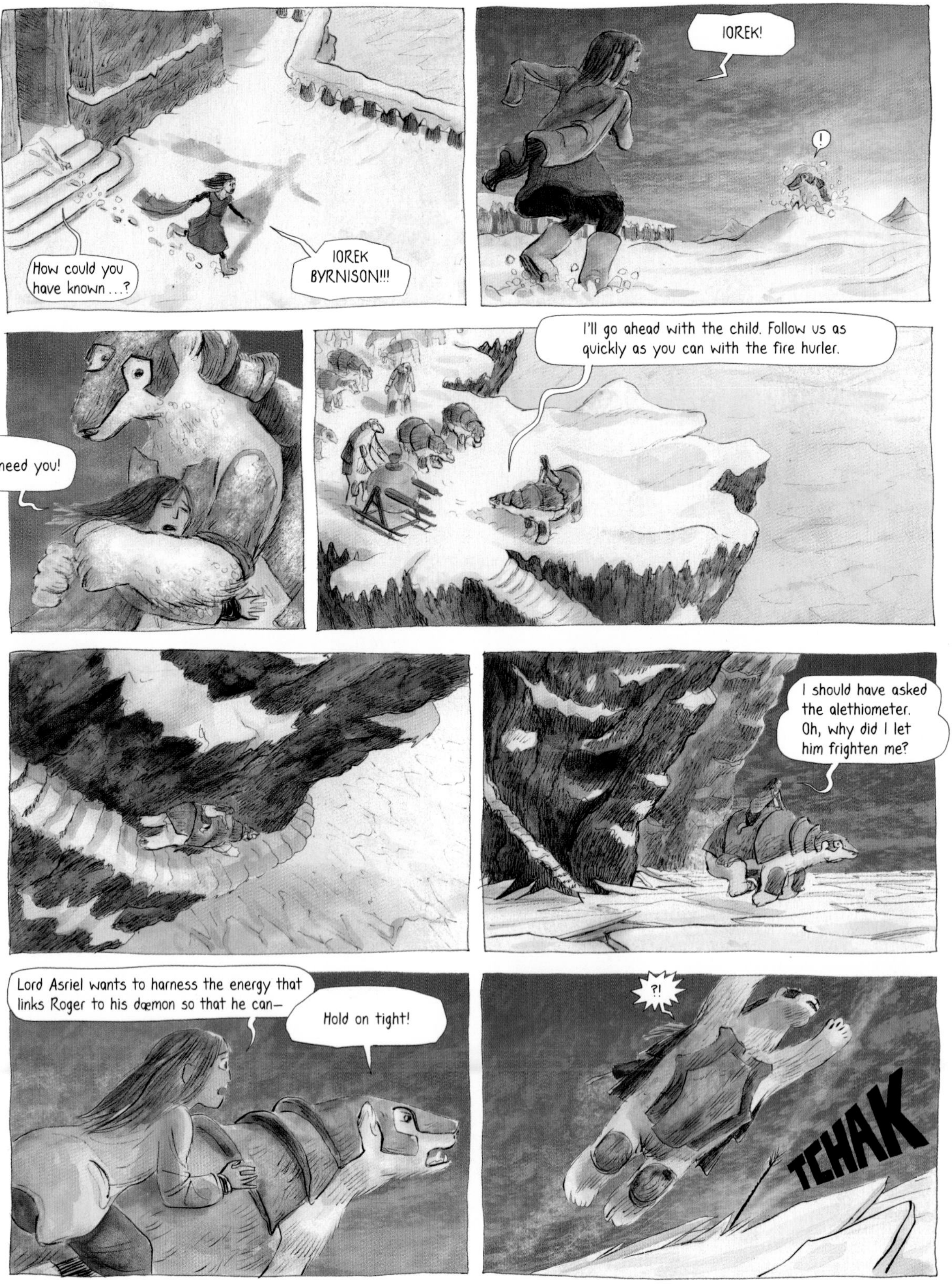
How could you have known . . . ?
IOREK BYRNISON!!!
IOREK!
!
I need you!
I'll go ahead with the child. Follow us as quickly as you can with the fire hurler.
I should have asked the alethiometer. Oh, why did I let him frighten me?
Lord Asriel wants to harness the energy that links Roger to his dæmon so that he can—
Hold on tight!
?!
TCHAK

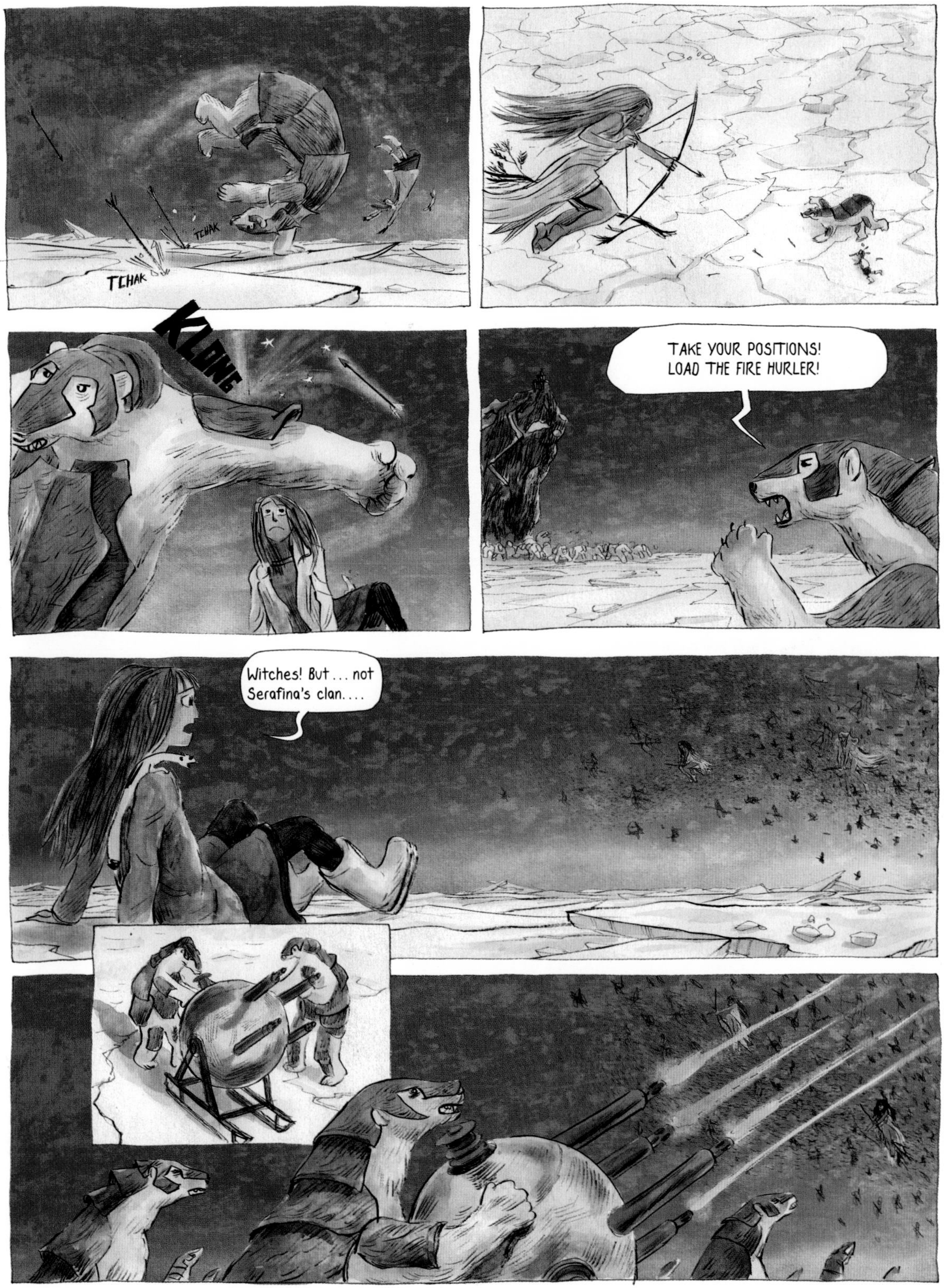
TCHAK
TCHAK
KLONG
TAKE YOUR POSITIONS! LOAD THE FIRE HURLER!
Witches! But . . . not Serafina's clan. . . .

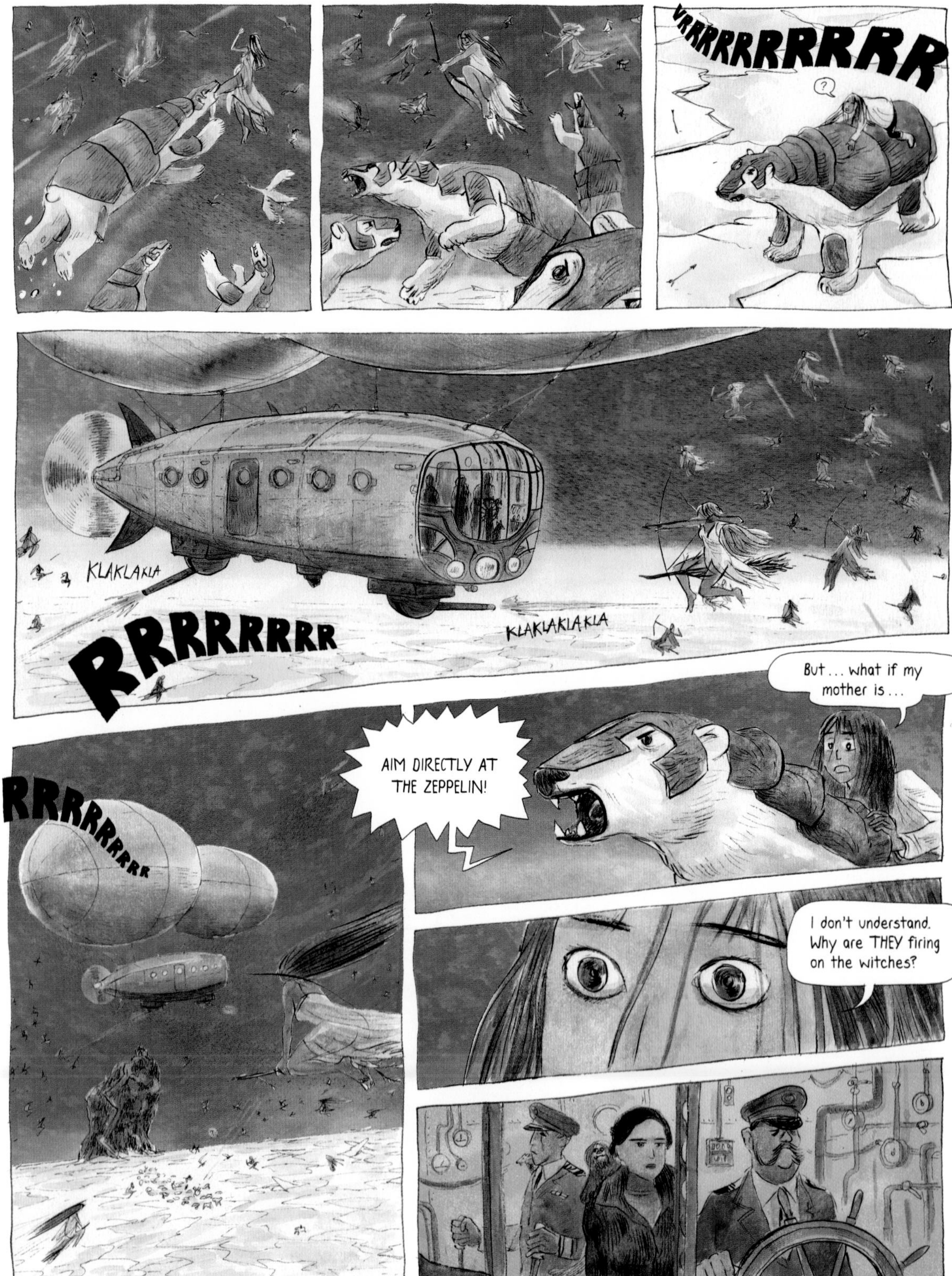
VRRRRRRRRRRR
?
KLAKLAKLA
RRRRRRRRR
KLAKLAKLAKLA
RRRRRRRRRRRRR
AIM DIRECTLY AT THE ZEPPELIN!
But... what if my mother is...
I don't understand. Why are THEY firing on the witches?

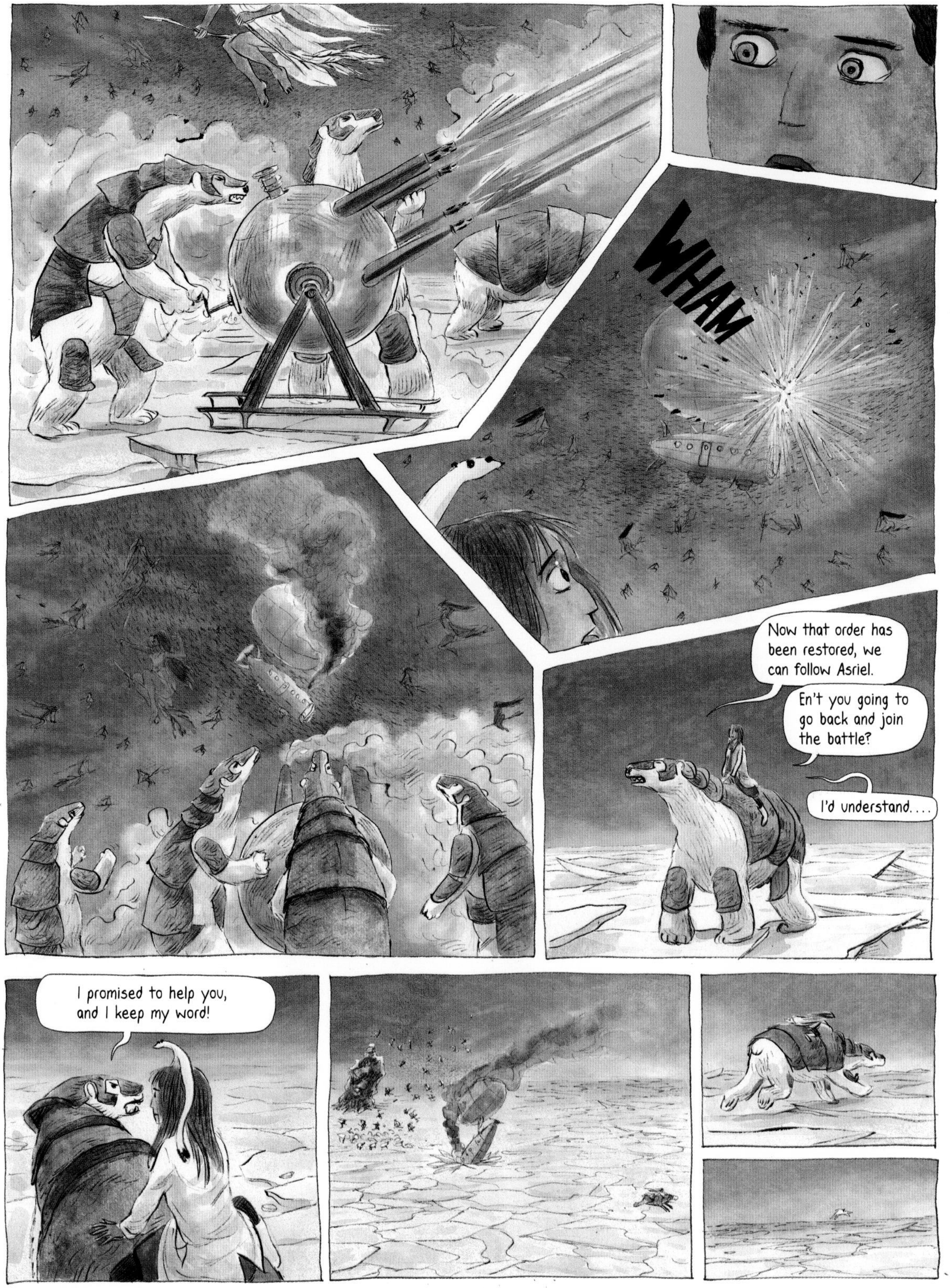
WHAM
Now that order has been restored, we can follow Asriel.
En't you going to go back and join the battle?
I'd understand. . . .
I promised to help you, and I keep my word!

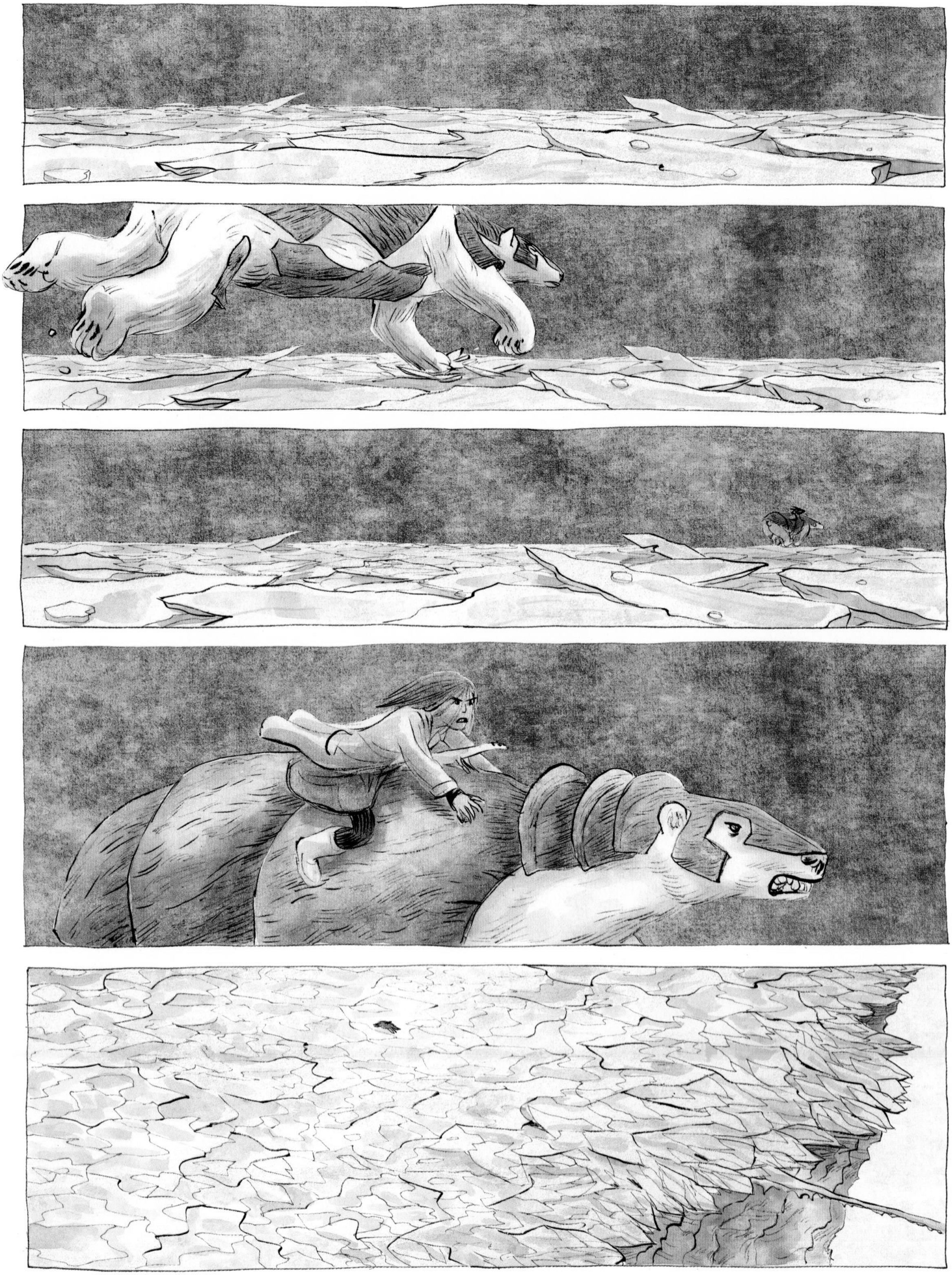

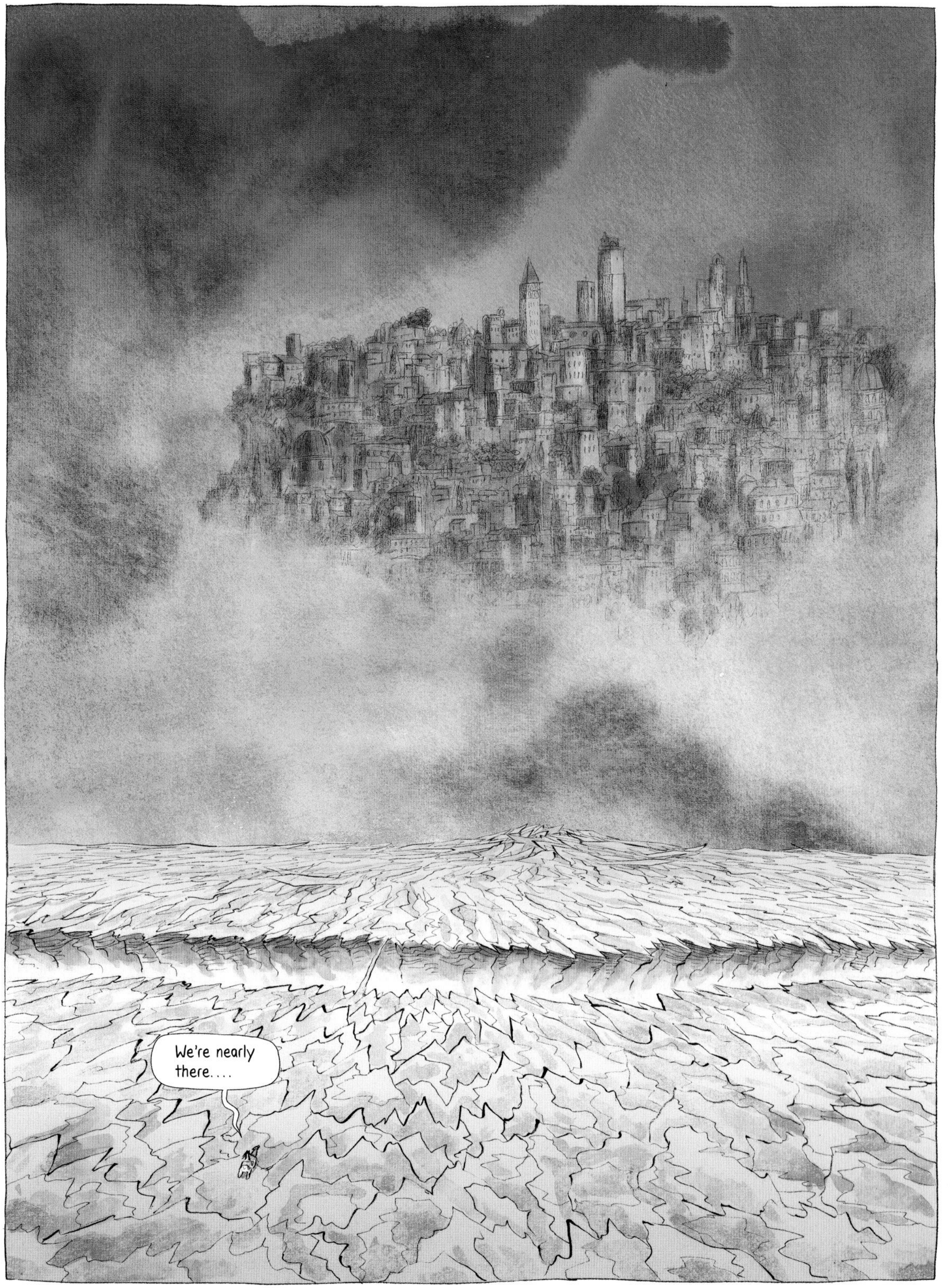
We're nearly there. . . .

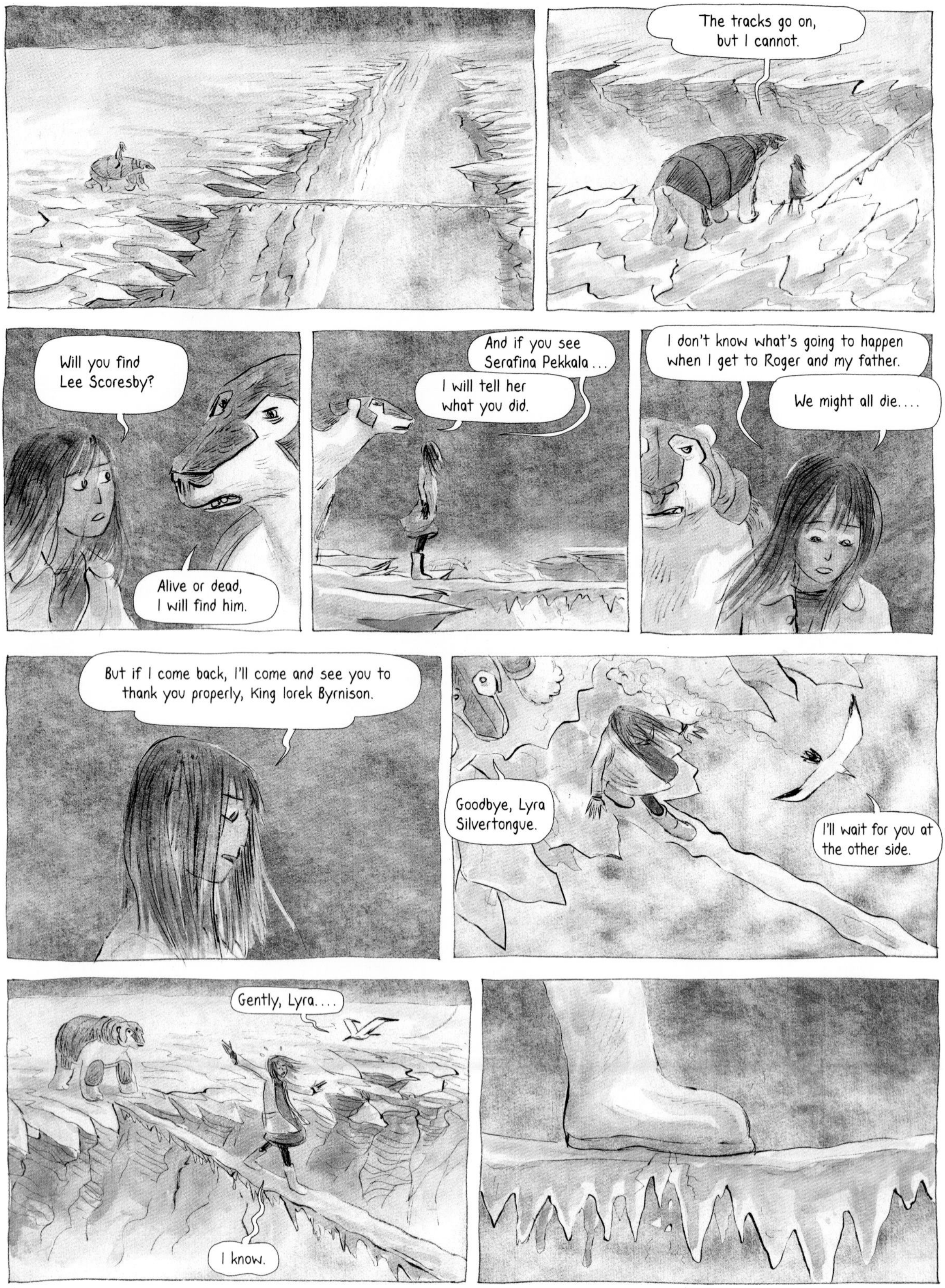
The tracks go on, but I cannot.
Will you find Lee Scoresby?
Alive or dead, I will find him.
And if you see Serafina Pekkala . . .
I will tell her what you did.
I don't know what's going to happen when I get to Roger and my father.
We might all die. . . .
But if I come back, I'll come and see you to thank you properly, King Iorek Byrnison.
Goodbye, Lyra Silvertongue.
I'll wait for you at the other side.
Gently, Lyra. . . .
I know.

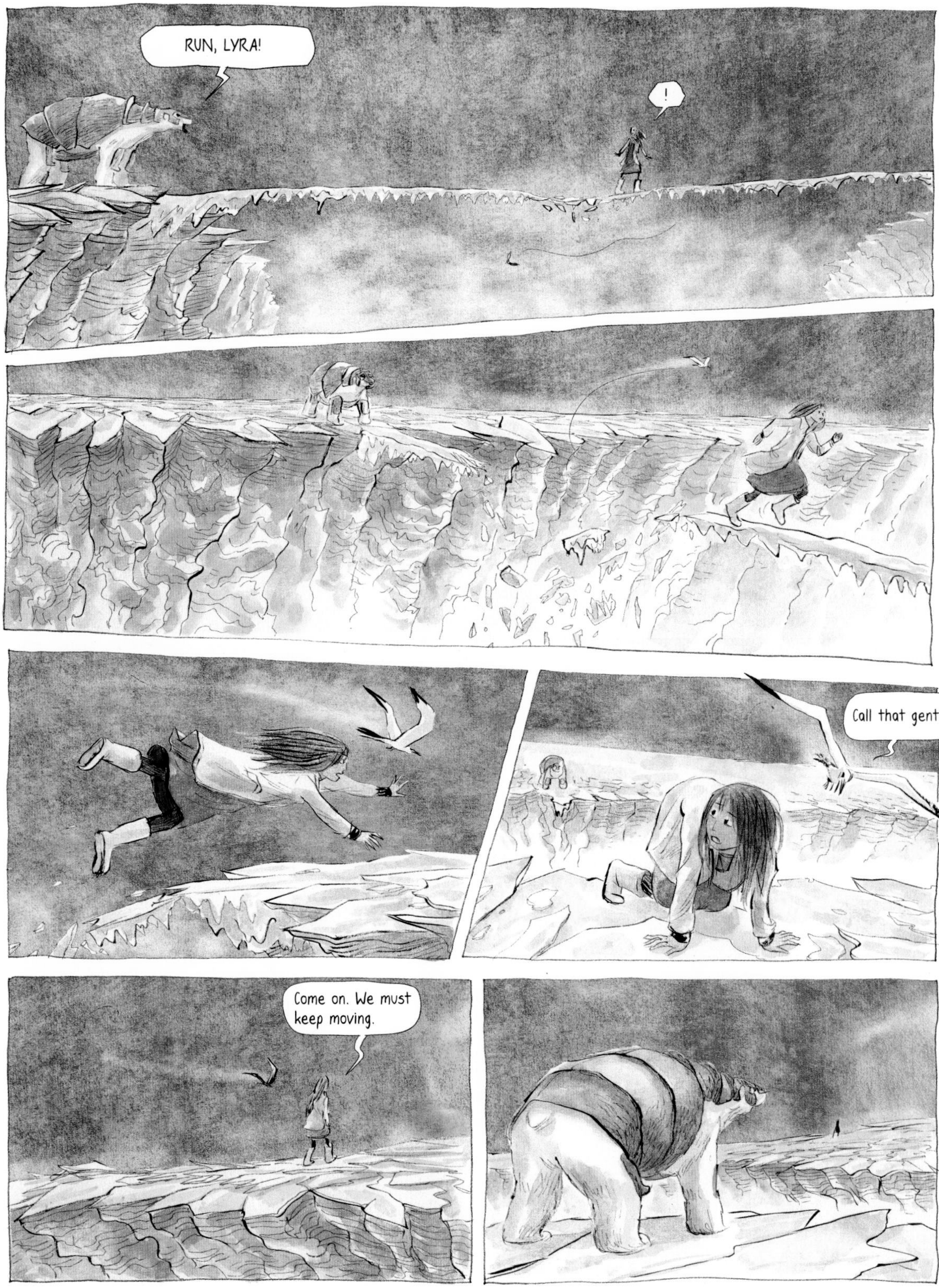
RUN, LYRA!
!
Call that gently?
Come on. We must keep moving.

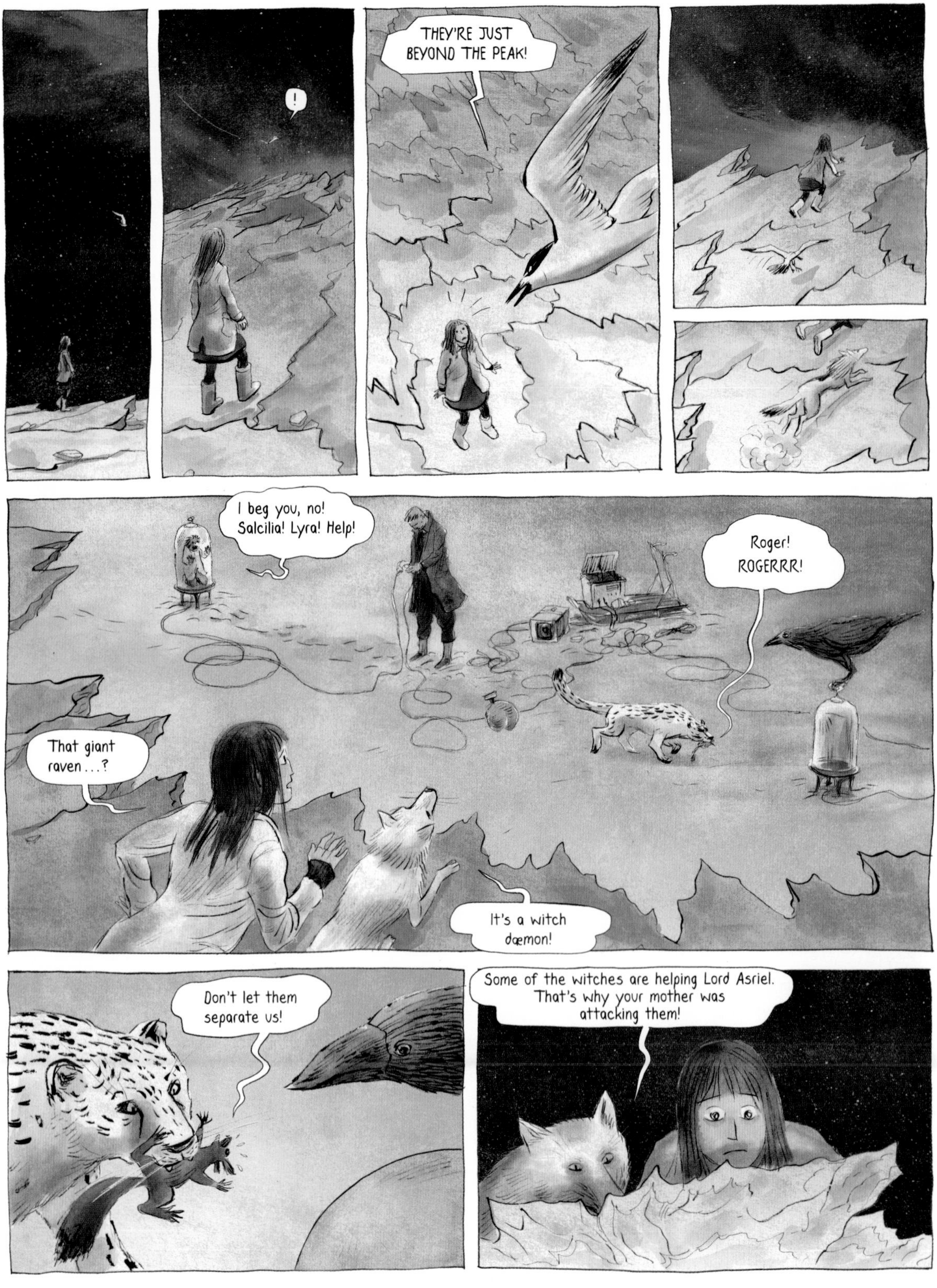
!
THEY'RE JUST BEYOND THE PEAK!
I beg you, no! Salcilia! Lyra! Help!
Roger! ROGERRR!
That giant raven...?
It's a witch dæmon!
Don't let them separate us!
Some of the witches are helping Lord Asriel. That's why your mother was attacking them!

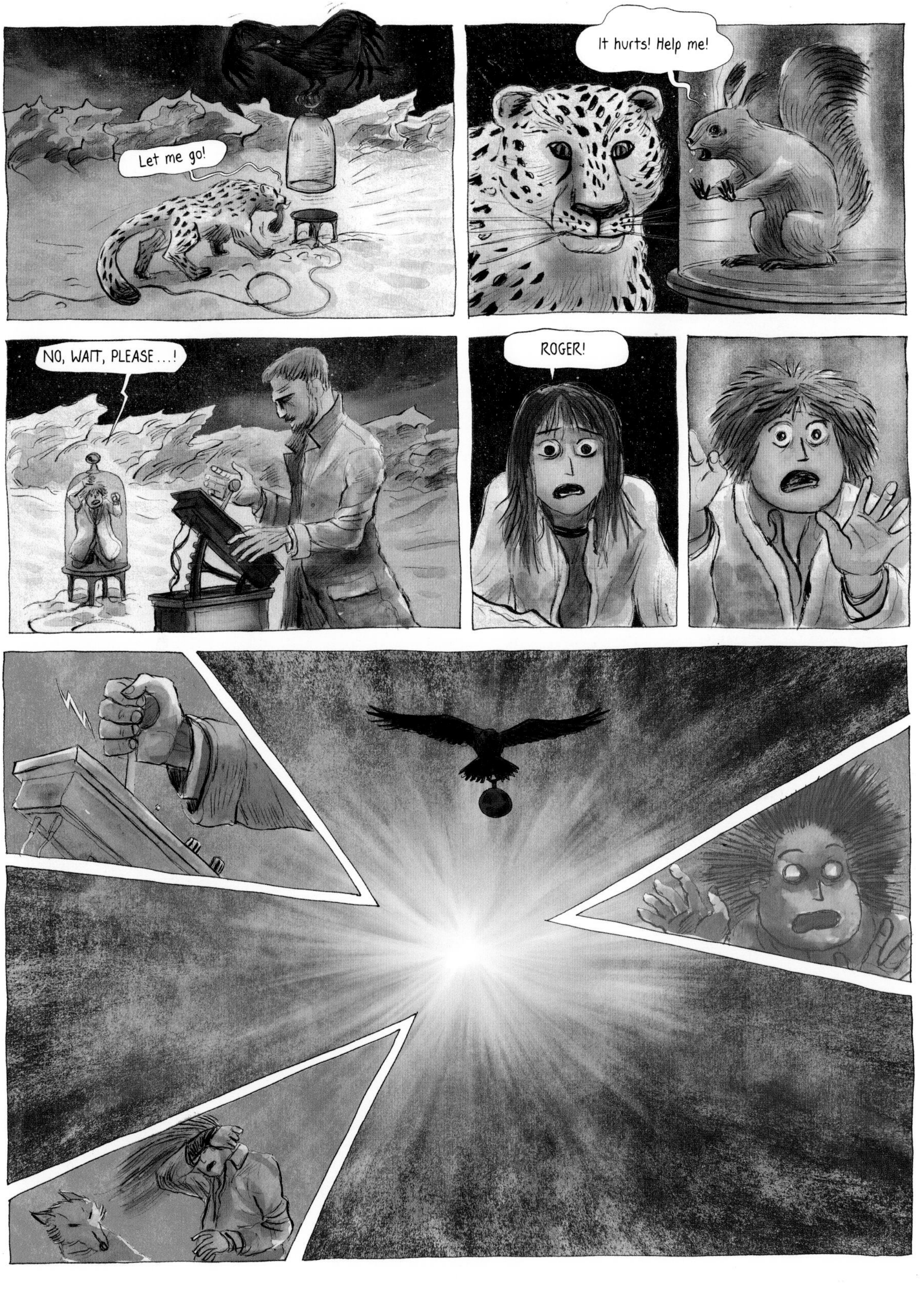
Let me go!
It hurts! Help me!
NO, WAIT, PLEASE . . . !
ROGER!

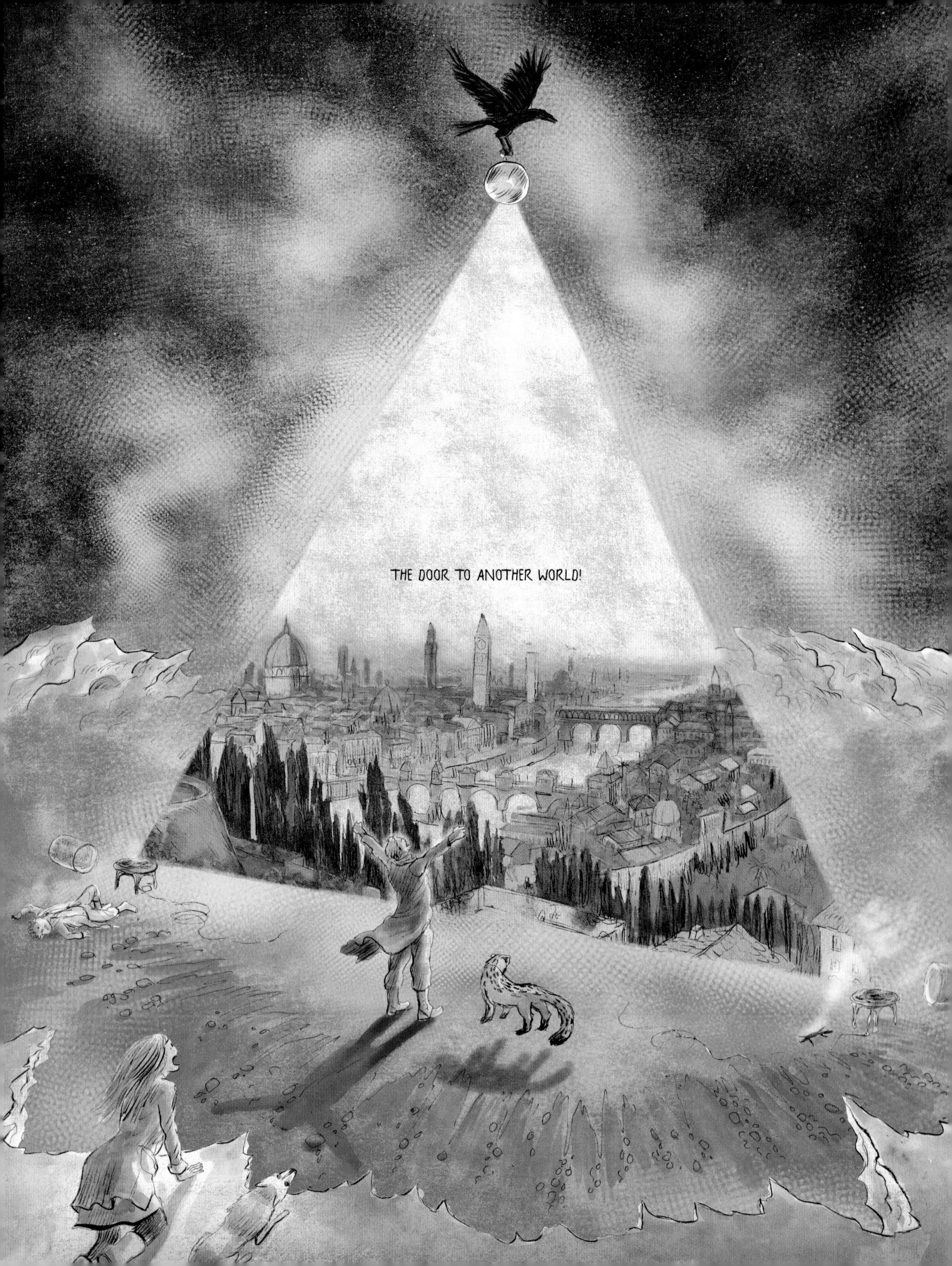
THE DOOR TO ANOTHER WORLD!

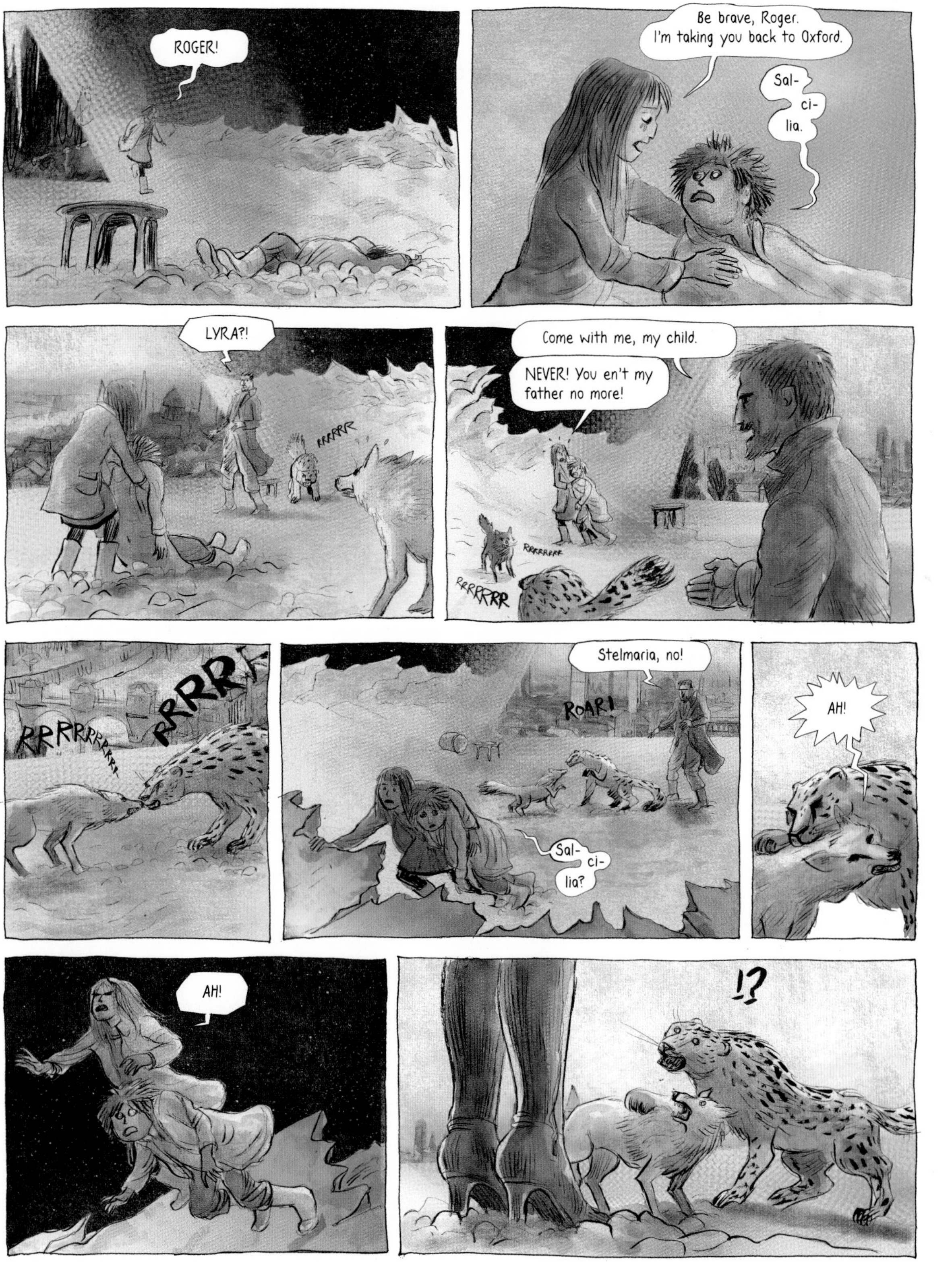
ROGER!
Be brave, Roger.
I'm taking you back to Oxford.
Sal-
ci-
lia.
LYRA?!
RRRRRR
Come with me, my child.
NEVER! You en't my father no more!
RRRRRRR
RRRRRRR
RRRRRRRRRRR
RRRRR
Stelmaria, no!
ROAR!
Sal-
ci-
lia?
AH!
AH!
!?

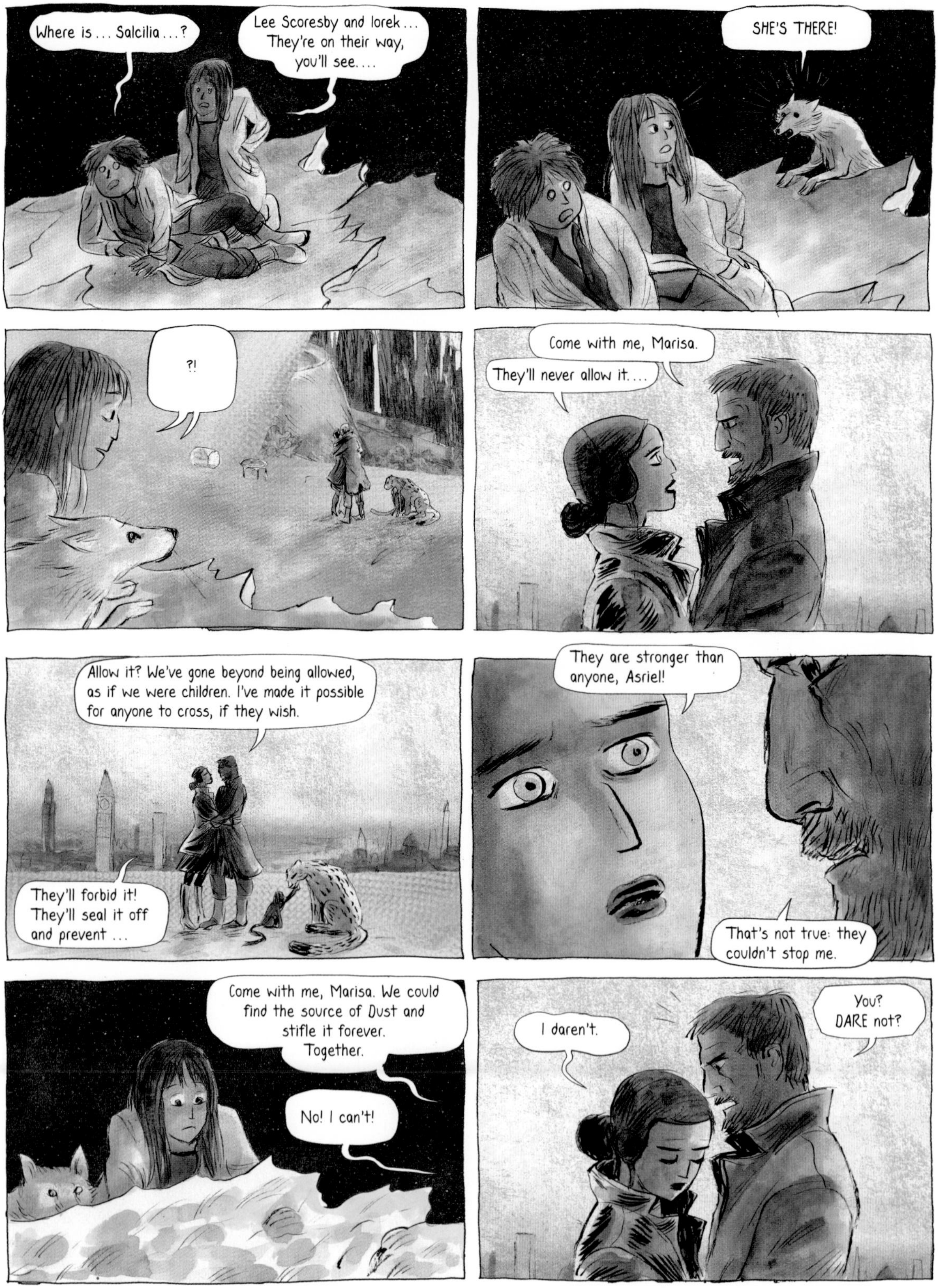
Where is . . . Salcilia . . . ?
Lee Scoresby and Iorek . . . They're on their way, you'll see. . . .
SHE'S THERE!
?!
Come with me, Marisa.
They'll never allow it. . . .
Allow it? We've gone beyond being allowed, as if we were children. I've made it possible for anyone to cross, if they wish.
They'll forbid it! They'll seal it off and prevent . . .
They are stronger than anyone, Asriel!
That's not true: they couldn't stop me.
Come with me, Marisa. We could find the source of Dust and stifle it forever. Together.
No! I can't!
I daren't.
You? DARE not?

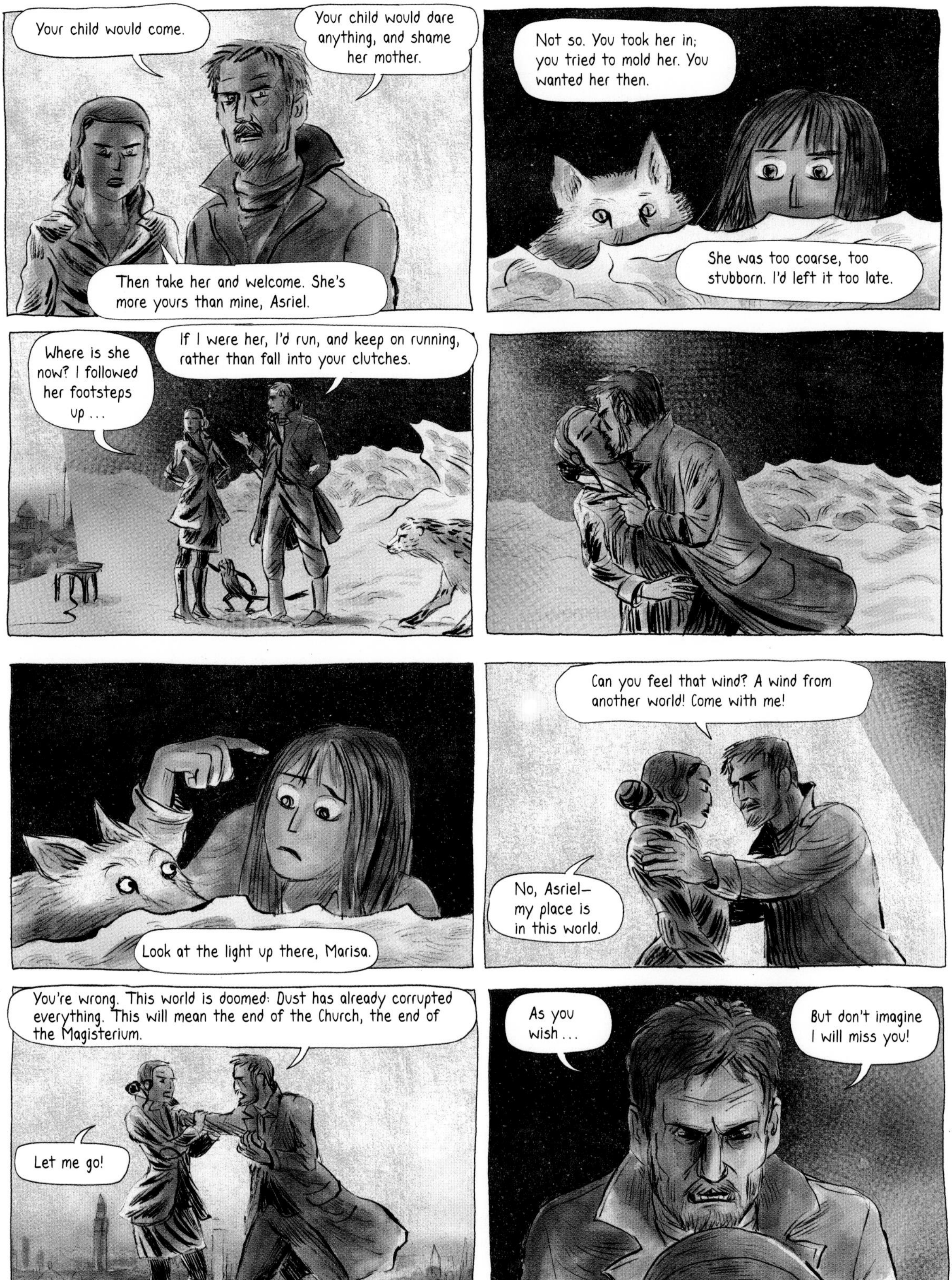
Your child would come.
Your child would dare anything, and shame her mother.
Then take her and welcome. She's more yours than mine, Asriel.
Not so. You took her in; you tried to mold her. You wanted her then.
She was too coarse, too stubborn. I'd left it too late.
Where is she now? I followed her footsteps up . . .
If I were her, I'd run, and keep on running, rather than fall into your clutches.
Look at the light up there, Marisa.
Can you feel that wind? A wind from another world! Come with me!
No, Asriel— my place is in this world.
You're wrong. This world is doomed: Dust has already corrupted everything. This will mean the end of the Church, the end of the Magisterium.
Let me go!
As you wish . . .
But don't imagine I will miss you!

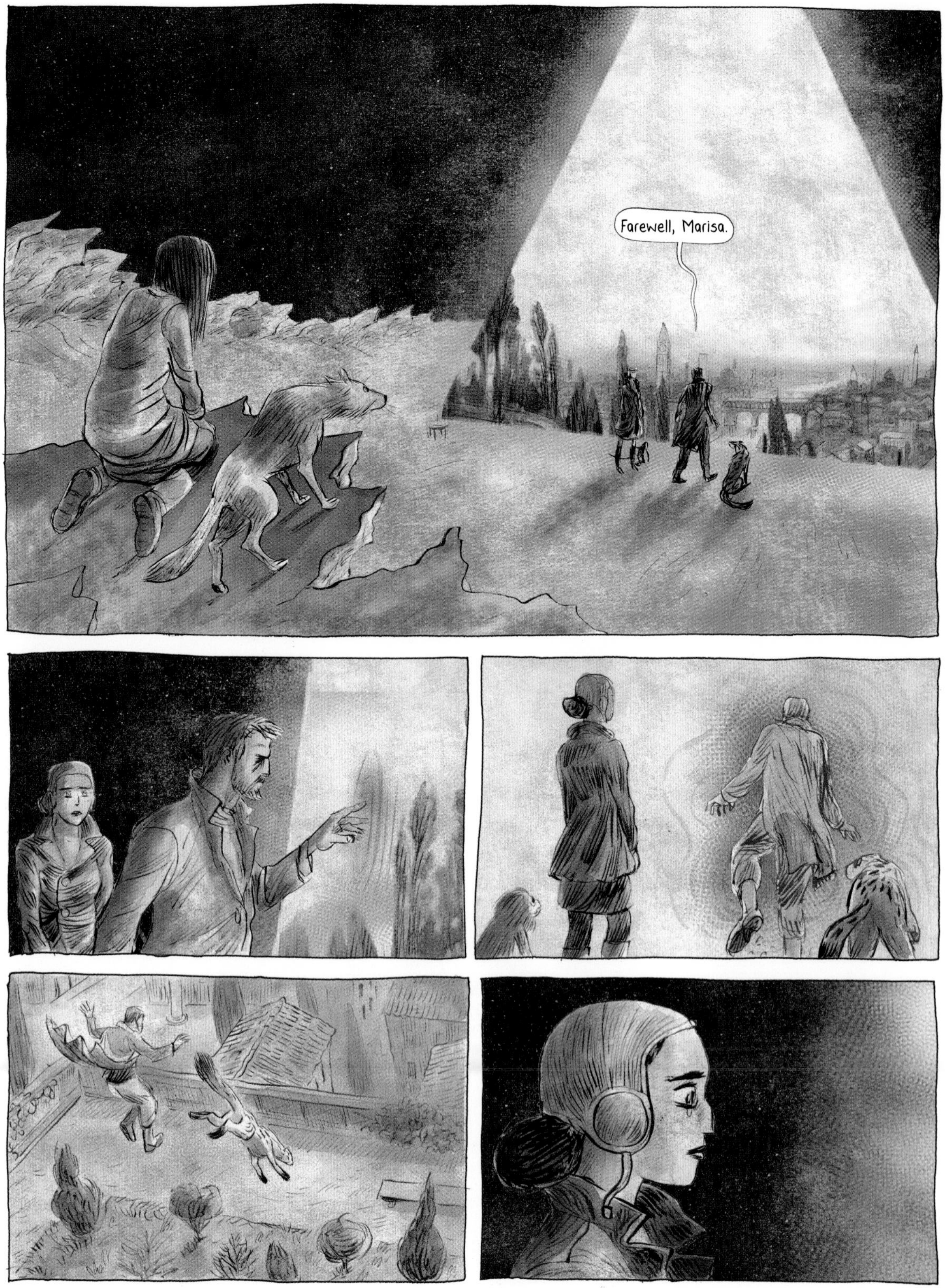
Farewell, Marisa.

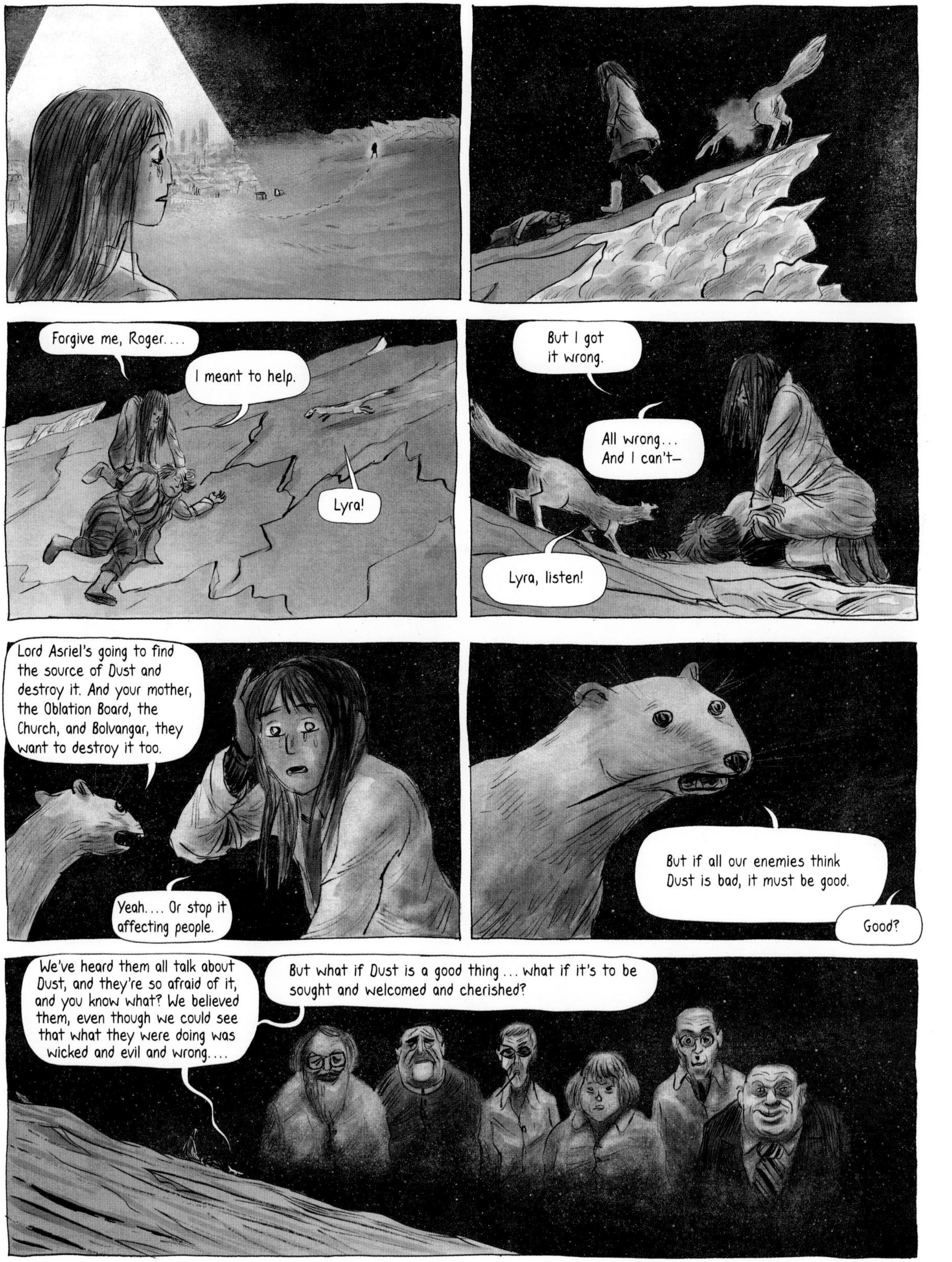
Forgive me, Roger....
I meant to help.
Lyra!
But I got it wrong.
All wrong... And I can't—
Lyra, listen!
Lord Asriel's going to find the source of Dust and destroy it. And your mother, the Oblation Board, the Church, and Bolvangar, they want to destroy it too.
Yeah.... Or stop it affecting people.
But if all our enemies think Dust is bad, it must be good.
Good?
We've heard them all talk about Dust, and they're so afraid of it, and you know what? We believed them, even though we could see that what they were doing was wicked and evil and wrong....
But what if Dust is a good thing... what if it's to be sought and welcomed and cherished?

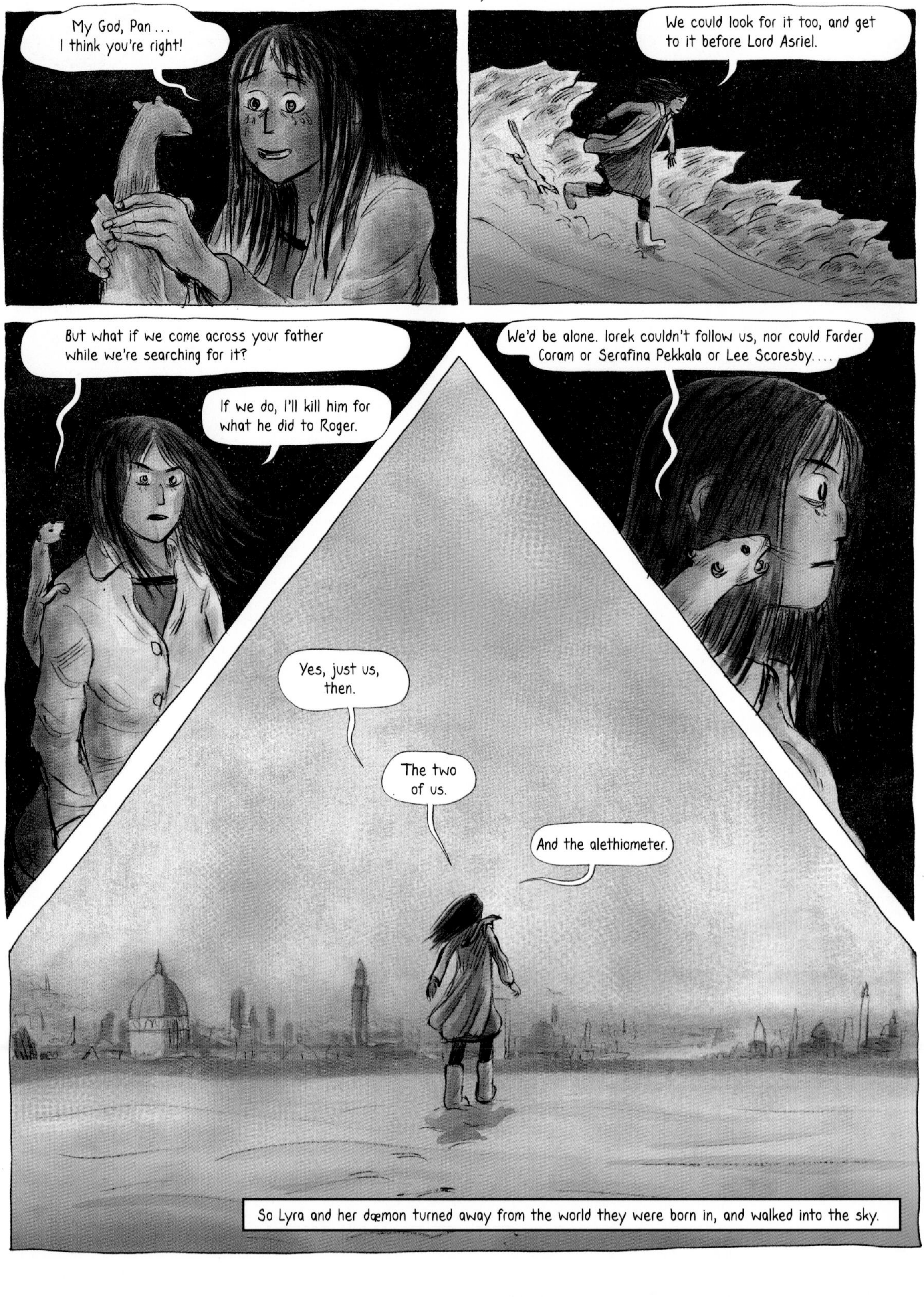

My God, Pan . . . I think you're right!
We could look for it too, and get to it before Lord Asriel.
But what if we come across your father while we're searching for it?
If we do, I'll kill him for what he did to Roger.
We'd be alone. Iorek couldn't follow us, nor could Farder Coram or Serafina Pekkala or Lee Scoresby. . . .
Yes, just us, then.
The two of us.
And the alethiometer.
So Lyra and her dæmon turned away from the world they were born in, and walked into the sky.